美国亚裔文学研究丛书

总主编　郭英剑

An Anthology of Asian American Literary Criticism

美国亚裔文学评论集

主编　郭英剑　赵明珠　冯元元

本研究受中国人民大学科学研究基金资助，系 2017 年度重大规划项目"美国亚裔文学研究"（编号：17XNLG10）的阶段性成果。

中国人民大学出版社
·北京·

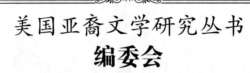

美国亚裔文学研究丛书
编委会

总 序

美国亚裔文学的历史、现状与未来

郭英剑

一、何为"美国亚裔文学"？

"美国亚裔文学"（Asian American Literature），简言之，是指由美国社会中的亚裔群体作家所创作的文学作品的总称。也有人称之为"亚裔美国文学"。在我国台湾学术界，更多地称为"亚美文学"。

然而，"美国亚裔文学"这个由两个核心词汇 ——"美国亚裔"和"文学"—— 所组成的术语，远没有她看上去那么简单。说她极其复杂，一点也不为过。因此，要想对"美国亚裔文学"有基本的了解，就需要从其中的两个关键词入手。

首先，"美国亚裔"中的"亚裔"，是指具有亚裔血统的美国人，但其所指并非一个单一的族裔，其组成包括了美国来自亚洲各国（或者与亚洲各国有关联）的人员群体及其后裔，比如美国华裔（Chinese Americans）、日裔（Japanese Americans）、菲律宾裔（Filipino Americans）、韩裔（Korean Americans）、越南裔（Vietnamese Americans）、印度裔（Indian Americans）、泰国裔（Thai Americans）等等。

根据联合国的统计，亚洲总计有 48 个国家。除此之外，还有我国的台湾地区，以及香港、澳门特别行政区。因此，所谓"美国亚裔"自然包括在美国的所有这 48 个亚洲国家以及我国台湾、香港、澳门社会群体的后裔，或者有其血统的人员。由此所涉及的各国（以及地区）迥异的语言、不同的文化、独特的人生体验，以及群体交叉所产生的多样性，包括亚洲各国由于战争交恶所带给后裔及其有关人员的深刻影响，就构成了"美国亚裔"这一群体具有的极端的复杂性。在美国统计局的定义中，美国亚裔细分为"东亚"（East

Asia)、"东南亚"（Southeast Asia）和南亚（South Asia）。[1] 当然，也正由于其复杂性，到现在为止有些亚洲国家在美国的后裔或者移民，尚未形成一个相对固定的族裔群体。

其次，文学主要由作家创作，由于"美国亚裔"群体的复杂性，自然导致"美国亚裔"的"作家"群体同样处于极其复杂的状态，但也因此使这一群体的概念具有相当大的包容性。凡是身在美国的亚裔后裔、具有亚洲血统或者后来移民美国的亚裔作家，都可以称之为"美国亚裔作家"。

由于亚裔群体的语言众多，加上一些移民作家的母语并非英语，因此，"美国亚裔文学"一般指的是美国亚裔作家使用英语所创作的文学作品。但由于历史的原因，学术界也把最早进入美国时，亚裔用本国语言所创作的文学作品，无论是口头还是文字作品——比如 19 世纪中期，华人进入美国时遭到拘禁时所创作的诗句，也都纳入"美国亚裔文学"的范畴之内。同时，随着全球化时代的到来，各国之间的文学与文化交流日益加强，加之移民日渐增加，因此，也将部分发表时为亚洲各国语言，但后来被翻译成英语的文学作品，也同样纳入"美国亚裔文学"的范畴。

最后，"美国亚裔"的划分，除了语言、历史、文化之外，还有一个地理因素需要考虑。随着时间的推移与学术界研究【特别是离散研究（Diaspora Studies）】的进一步深化，"美国亚裔"中的"美国"（America），也不单单指 the United States 了。我们知道，由于全球化时代所带来的人口流动性的极度增加，国与国之间的界限有时候变得模糊起来，人们的身份也变得日益具有多样性和流动性。比如，由于经济全球化的原因，美国已不单单是一个地理概念上的美国。经济与文化的构成，造就了可口可乐、麦当劳等商业品牌，它们都已经变成了流动的美国的概念。这样的美国不断在"侵入"其他国家，并对其不断产生巨大的影响。当然，一个作家的流动性，也无形中扩大了"美国"的概念。比如，一个亚洲作家可能移民到美国，一个美国亚裔作家也可能移民到其他国家。这样的流动性拓展了"美国亚裔"的定义与范畴。

为此，"美国亚裔文学"这一概念，有时候也包括一些身在美洲地区，但与美国有关联的作家用英语创作的作品，或者被翻译成英语的文学作品，也会被纳入这一范畴之内。

应该指出的是，由于"亚裔"群体进入美国的时间早晚不同，加上"亚裔"群体的复杂性，那么，每一个"亚裔"群体，都有其独有的美国族裔特征，比如华裔与日裔有所不同，印度裔与日裔也有所不同。如此一来，正如一些学者所认为的那样，各个族裔的特征最好应该分开来叙述和加以研究。[2]

1　参见：Karen R. Humes, Nicholas A. Jones, Roberto R. Ramirez (March 2011). "Overview of Race and Hispanic Origin: 2010" (PDF). United States Census Bureau. U.S. Department of Commerce.

2　参见：Chin, Frank, et al. "Preface" to *Aiiieeeee! An Anthology of Asian American Writers*. Edited by Frank Chin, Jeffery Paul Chan, Lawson Fusao Inada, and Shawn Wong. A Mentor Book. 1991. p.xi.

二、为何要研究"美国亚裔文学"?

虽然上文中提出,"美国亚裔"是个复杂而多元的群体,"美国亚裔文学"包含了极具多样化的亚裔群体作家,我们还是要把"美国亚裔文学"当做一个整体来进行研究。理由有三:

首先,"美国亚裔文学"与"美国亚裔作家"(Asian American Writers)最早出现时,即是作为一个统一的概念而提出。1974 年,赵健秀(Frank Chin)等学者出版了《哎咿!美国亚裔作家选集》。[1] 作为首部划时代"美国亚裔作家"的文学作品选集,该书通过发现和挖掘此前 50 年中被遗忘的华裔、日裔与菲律宾裔中的重要作家,选取其代表性作品,进而提出要建立作为独立的研究领域的"美国亚裔文学"(Asian American Literature)。[2]

其次,在亚裔崛起的过程中,无论是亚裔的无心之为,还是美国主流社会与其他族裔的有意为之,亚裔都是作为一个整体被安置在一起的。因此,亚裔文学也是作为一个整体而存在的。近年来,我国的"美国华裔文学"研究成为美国文学研究学界的一个热点。但在美国,虽然有"美国华裔文学"(Chinese American Literature)的说法,但真正作为学科存在的,则是"美国亚裔文学"(Asian American Literature),甚至更多的则是"美国亚裔研究"(Asian American Studies)。

再次,1970 年代之后,"美国亚裔文学"的发展在美国学术界逐渐成为研究的热点,引发了研究者的广泛关注。为此,旧金山州立大学、加州大学系统的伯克利分校、洛杉矶分校以及斯坦福大学率先设置了"美国亚裔研究系"(Department of Asian American Studies)或者"亚裔研究中心",成为早期美国亚裔研究的重镇。随后包括宾夕法尼亚大学、哥伦比亚大学、布朗大学、哈佛大学、耶鲁大学等常青藤盟校在内的众多美国高校也都陆续增添了"美国亚裔研究"(Asian American Studies)专业,开设了丰富多彩的亚裔文学与亚裔研究方面的课程,教学与研究成果丰富多彩。在我国台湾地区,包括台湾"中央研究院"、台湾师范大学等在内的研究机构与高校,大都开设有亚裔文学与亚裔研究方面的课程,召开过众多的国际会议,研究成果丰富。

那么,我们需要提出的一个问题是:在中国语境下,研究"美国亚裔文学"的意义与价值究竟何在? 我的看法如下:

第一,"美国亚裔文学"是"美国文学"的重要组成部分。不研究亚裔文学或者忽视甚至贬低亚裔文学,学术界对于美国文学的研究就是不完整的。如上文所说,亚裔文学的

1　Chin, Frank; Chan, Jeffery Paul; Inada, Lawson Fusao; Wong, Shawn. *Aiiieeeee! An Anthology of Asian-American Writers.* Howard University Press, 1974.

2　参见: Chin, Frank, et al. "Preface" to *Aiiieeeee! An Anthology of Asian American Writers.* Edited by Frank Chin, Jeffery Paul Chan, Lawson Fusao Inada, and Shawn Wong. A Mentor Book. 1991. pp.xi-xxii.

真正兴起是在 20 世纪六七十年代。美国六七十年代特殊的时代背景极大地促进了亚裔文学发展，自此，亚裔文学作品层出不穷，包括小说、戏剧、传记、短篇小说、诗歌等各种文学形式。在当下的美国，亚裔文学及其研究与亚裔的整体生存状态息息相关。种族、历史、人口以及政治诉求等因素促使被总称为"亚裔"的各个少数族裔联合发声，以期在美国政治领域和主流社会达到最大的影响力与辐射度。对此，学术界不能视而不见。

　　第二，我国现有的"美国华裔文学"研究，无法替代更不能取代"美国亚裔文学"研究。自从 1980 年代开始译介美国亚裔文学以来，我国国内的研究就主要集中在华裔文学领域，研究对象也仅为少数知名华裔作家及长篇小说创作领域。相较于当代国外亚裔文学研究的全面与广博，国内对于亚裔中其他族裔作家的作品关注太少。即使是那些亚裔文学的经典之作，如菲律宾裔作家卡洛斯·布洛桑（Carlos Bulosan）的《美国在我心中》（*America Is in the Heart*, 1946），日裔女作家山本久枝（Hisaye Yamamoto）的《第十七音节及其他故事》（*Seventeen Syllables and Other Stories*, 1949）、日裔约翰·冈田（John Okada）的《不一不仔》（*NO-NO Boy*, 1959），以及如今在美国文学界如日中天的青年印度裔作家裘帕·拉希莉（Jhumpa Lahiri）的作品，专题研究均十分少见。即便是像华裔作家任璧莲（Gish Jen）这样已经受到学者很大关注和研究的作家，其长篇小说之外体裁的作品同样没有得到足够的重视，更遑论国内学术界对亚裔文学在诗歌、戏剧方面的研究了。换句话说，我国学术界对于整个"美国亚裔文学"的研究来说还很匮乏，属于亟待开发的领域。实际上，在我看来，不研究"美国亚裔文学"，也无法真正理解"美国华裔文学"。

　　第三，在中国"一带一路"倡议与中国文化走出去的今天，作为美国文学研究的新型增长点，大力开展"美国亚裔文学"研究，特别是研究中国的亚洲周边国家如韩国、日本、印度等国在美国移民状况的文学表现，以及与华裔在美国的文学再现，使之与美国和世界其他国家以及我国台湾地区的"美国亚裔文学"保持同步发展，具有较大的理论意义与学术价值。

三、"美国亚裔文学"及其研究：历史与现状

　　从历史上看，来自亚洲国家的移民进入美国，可以追溯到 17 世纪。但真正开始较大规模的移民则是到了 19 世纪中后期。然而，亚裔一开始进入美国，就遭到了来自美国社会与官方的阻力与法律限制。从 1880 年代到 1940 年代这长达半个多世纪的岁月中，为了保护美国本土而出台的一系列移民法，都将亚洲各国人排除在外，禁止他们当中的大部分人进入美国大陆地区。直到 20 世纪 40 至 60 年代移民法有所改革时，这种状况才有所改观。其中的改革措施之一就是取消了国家配额。如此一来，亚洲移民人数才开始大规模上

升。根据 2010 年的美国国家统计局分析显示，亚裔是美国社会移民人数增长最快的少数族裔。[1]

"美国亚裔"实际是个新兴词汇。这个词汇的创立与诞生时间在 1960 年代后期。在此之前，亚洲人或者具有亚洲血统者通常被称为 Oriental（东方人）、Asiatic（亚洲人）和 Mongoloid（蒙古人、黄种人）。[2] 是美国历史学家市冈裕次（Yuji Ichioka）在 1960 年代末期，开创性地开始使用 Asian American 这个术语，[3] 从此，这一词汇开始被人们普遍接受和广泛使用。

与此同时，"美国亚裔文学"在随后的 1970 年代作为一个文学类别开始出现并逐步产生影响。1974 年，有两部著作几乎同时出版，都以美国亚裔命名。一部是《美国亚裔传统：散文与诗歌选集》，[4] 另外一部则是前面提到过的《哎咿！美国亚裔作家选集》。[5] 这两部著作，将过去长期被人遗忘的亚裔文学带到了聚光灯下，让人们仿佛看到了一种新的文学形式。其后，新的亚裔作家不断涌现，文学作品层出不穷。

最初亚裔文学的主要主题与主要内容为种族（race）、身份（identity）、亚洲文化传统、亚洲与美国或者西方国家之间的文化冲突，当然也少不了性别（sexuality）、社会性别（gender）、性别歧视、社会歧视等。后来，随着移民作家的大规模出现，离散文学的兴起，亚裔文学也开始关注移民、语言、家国、全球化、劳工、战争、帝国主义、殖民主义等问题。

如果说，上述 1974 年的两部著作代表着亚裔文学进入美国文学的世界版图之中，那么，1982 年著名美国亚裔研究专家金惠经（Elaine Kim）的《美国亚裔文学的创作及其社会语境》[6] 的出版，作为第一部学术著作，则代表着美国亚裔文学研究正式登上美国学术界的舞台。自此以后，不仅亚裔文学创作兴盛起来，亚裔文学研究也逐渐成为热点，成果不断推陈出新。

同时，人们对于如何界定"美国亚裔文学"等众多问题进行了深入的探讨，进一

1　参见：Wikipedia 依据 "U.S. Census Show Asians Are Fastest Growing Racial Group" (NPR.org) 所得出的数据统计。https://en.wikipedia.org/wiki/Asian_Americans。

2　Mio, Jeffrey Scott, ed. (1999). *Key Words in Multicultural Interventions: A Dictionary*. ABC-Clio ebook. Greenwood Publishing Group. p.20.

3　K. Connie Kang, "Yuji Ichioka, 66; Led Way in Studying Lives of Asian Americans," *Los Angeles Times*, September 7, 2002. Reproduced at ucla.edu by the Asian American Studies Center.

4　Wand, David Hsin-fu, ed. *Asian American Heritage: An Anthology of Prose and Poetry*. New York: Pocket Books, 1974.

5　Chin, Frank; Chan, Jeffery Paul; Inada, Lawson Fusao; Wong, Shawn. *Aiiieeeee! An Anthology of Asian-American Writers*. Howard University Press, 1974.

6　Kim, Elaine. *Asian American Literature: An Introduction to the Writings and Their Social Context*. Philadelphia: Temple University Press, 1982.

步推动了这一学科向前发展。相关问题包括：究竟谁可以说自己是美国亚裔（an Asian America）？这里的 America 是不是就是单指"美国"（the United States）？是否可以包括"美洲"（Americas）？如果亚裔作家所写的内容与亚裔无关，能否算是"亚裔文学"？如果不是亚裔作家，但所写内容与亚裔有关，能否算在"亚裔文学"之内？

总体上看，早期的亚裔文学研究专注于美国身份的建构，即界定亚裔文学的范畴，以及争取其在美国文化与美国文学中应得的席位，是 20 世纪七八十年代亚裔民权运动的前沿阵地。早期学者如赵健秀、徐忠雄（Shawn Wong）等为领军人物。随后出现的金惠经、张敬珏（King-Kok Cheung）、骆里山（Lisa Lowe）等人均成为了亚裔文学研究领域的权威学者，他／她们的著作影响并造就了第二代美国亚裔文学研究者。90 年代之后的亚裔文学研究逐渐淡化了早期研究中对于意识形态的侧重，开始向传统的学科分支、研究方法以及研究理论靠拢，研究视角多集中在学术马克思主义（academic Marxism）、后结构主义、后殖民、女权主义以及心理分析等。

进入 21 世纪以来，"美国亚裔文学"研究开始向多元化、全球化与跨学科方向发展。随着亚裔文学作品爆炸式的增长，来自阿富汗、印度、巴基斯坦、越南等族裔作家的作品开始受到关注，极大丰富与拓展了亚裔文学研究的领域。当代"美国亚裔文学"研究的视角与方法也不断创新，战争研究、帝国研究、跨国研究、视觉文化理论、空间理论、身体研究、环境理论等层出不穷。新的理论与常规性研究交叉进行，不但开创了新的研究领域，而且对于经典问题（例如身份建构）的研究提供了新的解读方式与方法。

四、作为课题的"美国亚裔文学"研究及其丛书

"美国亚裔文学"研究，是由我担任课题负责人的 2017 年度中国人民大学科学研究基金重大规划项目。"美国亚裔文学"研究丛书，即是该项课题的结题成果。这是国内第一套较为完整的"美国亚裔文学"方面的系列丛书，由文学史、文学作品选、文学评论集、学术论著等所组成，由我担任该丛书的总主编。

"美国亚裔文学"研究在 2017 年 4 月立项。随后，该丛书的论证计划，得到了国内外专家的一致认可。2017 年 5 月 27 日，中国人民大学科学研究基金重大规划项目"美国亚裔文学研究"开题报告会暨"美国亚裔文学研究高端论坛"在中国人民大学隆重召开。参加此次会议的专家学者全部为美国亚裔文学研究领域中的顶尖学者，包括美国加州大学洛杉矶分校的张敬珏教授、南京大学海外教育学院前院长程爱民教授、南京大学海外教育学院院长赵文书教授、北京语言大学应用外语学院院长陆薇教授、北京外国语大学潘志明教授、解放军外国语学院石平萍教授等。在此次会议上，我向与会专家介绍了该项目的基本

情况、未来研究方向与预计出版成果。与会专家对该项目的设立给予高度评价，强调在当今时代加强"美国亚裔文学"研究的必要性，针对该项目的预计研究及其成果，也提出了一些很好的建议。

根据计划，这套丛书将包括文学史 2 部：《美国亚裔文学史》和《美国华裔文学史》；文学选集 2 部：《美国亚裔文学作品选》和《美国华裔文学作品选》；批评文选 2 部：《美国亚裔文学评论集》和《美国华裔文学评论集》；访谈录 1 部：《美国亚裔作家访谈录》；美国学术论著 2 部（中译本）：*Articulate Silences* 和 *Chinese American Literature Without Borders*。同时，还计划出版若干学术专著和国际会议的论文集等。

根据我的基本设想，《美国亚裔文学史》和《美国华裔文学史》的撰写，将力图体现研究者对美国亚裔文学的研究进入到了较为深入的阶段。由于文学史是建立在研究者对该研究领域发展变化的总体认识上，涉及文学流派、创作方式、文学与社会变化关系、作家间的关联等各方面的问题，我们试图通过对亚裔义学发展进行总结和评价，旨在为当前亚裔文学和华裔文学的研究和推广做出一定贡献。

《美国亚裔文学作品选》和《美国华裔文学作品选》，除了记录、介绍等基本功能，还将在一定程度发挥形成民族认同、促进意识形态整合等功能。作品选编是民族共同体想象性构建的重要途径，也是作为文学经典得以确立和修正的最基本方式之一。因此，这样的作品选编，也会对美国亚裔文学的研究起到重要的促进作用。

《美国亚裔文学评论集》和《美国华裔文学评论集》，将主要选编美国、中国以及世界上最有学术价值的学术论文，虽然有些可能因为版权问题而不得不舍弃，但我们努力使之成为中国学术界研究"美国亚裔文学"和"美国华裔文学"的重要参考书目。

《美国亚裔作家访谈录》、美国学者的著作汉译、中国学者的美国亚裔文学学术专著等，我们将力图促使中美两国学者之间的学术对话，特别是希望中国的"美国亚裔文学"研究，既在中国的美国文学研究界，也在美国和世界上的美国文学研究界发出中国学者的声音。"一带一路"倡议的实施，使得文学研究的关注发生了转变，从过分关注西方话语，到逐步转向关注中国（亚洲）话语，我们的美国亚裔（华裔）文学研究，正是从全球化视角切入，思考美国亚裔（华裔）文学的世界性。

那么，我们为什么要对"美国亚裔文学"进行深入研究，并要编辑、撰写和翻译这套丛书呢？

首先，虽然"美国亚裔文学"在国外已有较大的影响，学术界也对此具有相当规模的研究，但在国内学术界，出于对"美国华裔文学"的偏爱与关注，"美国亚裔文学"相对还是一个较为陌生的领域。因此本课题首次以"亚裔"集体的形式标示亚裔文学的存在，旨在介绍"美国亚裔文学"，推介具有族裔特色和代表性的作家作品。

　　其次，选择"美国亚裔文学"为研究对象，其中也有对"美国华裔文学"的研究，希望能够体现我们对全球化视野中华裔文学的关注，也体现试图融合亚裔、深入亚裔文学研究的学术自觉。同时，在多元化多种族的美国社会语境中，我们力主打破国内长久以来专注"美国华裔文学"研究的固有模式，转而关注包括华裔作家在内的亚裔作家所具有的世界性眼光。

　　最后，顺应美国亚裔文学发展的趋势，对美国亚裔文学的研究不仅是文学研究界的关注热点，也是我国外语与文学教育的关注焦点。我们希望为高校未来"美国亚裔文学"的课程教学，提供一套高水平的参考丛书。

五、"美国亚裔文学"及其研究的未来

　　如前所述，"美国亚裔文学"在 20 世纪 70 年代逐渐崛起后，使得亚裔文学从沉默走向了发声。到 21 世纪，亚裔文学呈现出多元化的发展特征，更重要的是，许多新生代作家开始崭露头角。单就这些新的亚裔作家群体，就有许多值得我们关注的话题。

　　2018 年 6 月 23 日，"2018 美国亚裔文学高端论坛 —— 跨界：21 世纪的美国亚裔文学"在中国人民大学隆重召开。参加会议的专家学者将近 150 人。演讲嘉宾除了国内的美国亚裔文学研究领域中的著名专家学者外，还包括了我国台湾"中央研究院"的特聘教授、欧美研究所前所长李有成先生；我国台湾"中央研究院"特聘教授、欧美研究所前所长、华人世界著名的美国亚裔研究学者单德兴先生；我国台湾"中央研究院"副研究员、现在中央美术学院的访问教授王智明先生等。

　　在此次会议上，我提出来：今天，为什么要研究美国亚裔文学？我们要研究什么？

　　正如我们在会议通知上所说，美国亚裔文学在一百多年的风雨沧桑中历经"沉默"、"觉醒"、走向"发声"，见证了美国亚裔族群的沉浮兴衰。21 世纪以来，美国亚裔文学在全球冷战思维升温和战火硝烟不断的时空背景下，不囿于狭隘的种族主义藩篱，以"众声合奏"与"兼容并蓄"之势构筑出一道跨洋、跨国、跨种族、跨语言、跨文化、跨媒介、跨学科的文学景观，呈现出鲜明的世界主义意识。为此，我们拟定了一些主要议题。包括：1.美国亚裔文学中的跨洋书写；2.美国亚裔文学中的跨国书写；3.美国亚裔文学中的跨种族书写；4.美国亚裔文学中的跨语言书写；5.美国亚裔文学中的跨文化书写；6.美国亚裔文学的翻译跨界研究；7.美国亚裔文学的跨媒介研究；8.美国亚裔文学的跨学科研究等。

　　事实上，21 世纪以来，亚裔群体、亚裔所面临的问题、亚裔研究都发生了巨大的变化。从过去较为单纯的亚裔走向了跨越太平洋（transpacific）；从过去的彰显美国身份（claiming

America）到今天的批评美国身份（critiquing America）；过去单一的 America，现在变成了复数的 Americas，这些变化都值得引起我们的高度重视。由此所引发的诸多问题，也需要我们认真对待。比如：如何在"21 世纪"这个特殊的时间区间内去理解"美国亚裔文学"这一概念？有关"美国亚裔文学"的概念构建，是否本身就存在着作家的身份焦虑与书写的界限？如何把握"美国亚裔文学"的整体性与区域性？"亚裔"身份是否是作家在表达过程中去主动拥抱的归属之地？等等。

展望未来，随着新生代作家的迭出，"美国亚裔文学"将会呈现出更加生机勃勃的生命力，"美国亚裔文学"研究也将迎来更加光明的前途。

2018 年 8 月 28 日定稿于哈佛大学

专家推荐语

"美国亚裔文学研究丛书"包括美国亚裔文学史、美国亚裔文学作品选读、美国亚裔文学评论集、美国亚裔文学研究专著等，具有基础性、综合性、前沿性的特点。从研究范围看，将美国华裔文学研究拓展到美国亚裔文学，呈现出一幅更为完整的美国少数族裔文学版图。从研究深度看，论著作者均为美国亚裔文学研究领域著名专家，学术积累丰厚，研究水平一流。作为中国人民大学科学研究基金重大规划项目的研究成果，"美国亚裔文学研究丛书"为我们开展美国亚裔文学教学、研究、翻译提供了亟需的学术资源，有助于促进我们国家对美国文学全面深入的研究。

——王守仁，中国外国文学学会副会长、南京大学人文社会科学资深教授

This series is a groundbreaking work not just for the Asian American literary field, but for literature on the whole. As the first series of books about Asian American literature in China, it will undoubtedly inspire an unprecedented scholarly movement and bring greater and deserved awareness to issues including — but by no means limited to — gender, sexuality, and race as depicted through the lens and narratives of Asians and Asian Americans, perspectives too little seen and heard until now.

—Henry Louis Gates, Jr., Alphonse Fletcher University Professor and Director of the Hutchins Center for African and African American Research at Harvard University

Chinese American literature, for the past hundred years or so, has always straddled at least two cultures: the American and the Chinese. This ambitious and impressive series edited by Prof. Yingjian Guo brings the complex world of Chinese American writers to a broader Chinese-language readership. Such scholarship will help broaden, for Chinese scholars and students, the horizons of literary discourse and the range of appreciation for the Chinese American experience. Asian American literature, when read in a comparative light, reveals aspects of an American and Chinese American cultural terrain which spans politics, law, culture, and more. This collection will be useful for those in China, the Chinese diaspora, as well as the Americas to understand the rich linguistic, generational, political, and gendered diversity within Chinese American literature.

—Russell C. Leong, Editor of UCLA's *Amerasia Journal* (1977-2010); Author of *Phoenix Eyes and Other Stories* (The American Book Award), and; Current Editor of CUNY FORUM, for the City University of New York

美国亚裔文学研究的第一本专书 1982 年于美国出版，中文世界有关美国华裔文学的学术研究也始于 1980 年代，在接近"不惑之年"之际，实有必要盘点以往的研究成果，了解当前的学科生态，并策划未来的研究发展。郭英剑教授担任总主编的"美国亚裔文学研究丛书"，经过审慎规划，是中文世界有关此领域的第一套具规模、有系统的出版品，内容涵盖文学作品、文学评论、学术专书、文学史与访谈录等，多方位深度地提供有关美国亚裔文学与研究的代表作品，值得高度肯定。

——单德兴，台湾"中央研究院"欧美研究所前所长、特聘研究员

"美国亚裔文学研究丛书"涵盖面甚广，有文学创作，有文学史，有学术论著，有文学评论等，属单一领域的多元呈现，为近年来大陆出版界所少见，颇能反映大陆学术教育界在美国亚裔文学研究方面的具体成就。

——李有成，台湾"中央研究院"欧美研究所前所长、特聘研究员

"美国亚裔文学研究丛书"内容涵括文学史著作、文学作品选读、文学批评选集、学术论著，为国内第一套全面性介绍亚裔美国文学的丛书，中文学术著作之外亦有英文著作译本，具有推广文学以及搜集研究资料的双重功能，对于华语世界的亚裔美国文学研究极其重要。

——冯品佳，台湾交通大学前教务长、特聘教授

前　言

　　"美国亚裔文学"研究，是由中国人民大学"杰出学者"特聘教授郭英剑先生担任课题负责人的 2017 年度中国人民大学科学研究基金重大规划项目。"美国亚裔文学研究丛书"，是该项课题的结题成果，由郭英剑教授担任该套丛书的总主编。这是国内第一套较为完整的"美国亚裔文学"方面的系列丛书，由文学史、文学作品选、文学评论集、学术论著等组成。

　　《美国亚裔文学评论集》主要选编了美国与中国范围内在我们看来最有价值的有关美国亚裔文学研究的代表性学术论文。

　　本评论集共收录了英文评论文章十四篇、中文评论文章两篇。两个部分各按文章的发表时间排序，文章之前附有评论家简介与文章简介。其中，评论家简介主要是对学者的个人基本信息、研究领域以及代表成果的概述；文章简介则提供了所选文章的写作背景、主要观点及其学术贡献。希望这两个简介能够帮助读者尽快了解学者以及所选文章的中心思想与主要内容。

　　从整体上看，国内的"美国亚裔文学"研究处于刚刚起步阶段，呈现出诸如对内部各族裔的研究比重失衡、各体裁研究着力不均以及总体性研究匮乏等问题。为此，本评论集遵循历时性与共时性的双重选编原则，一方面向读者呈现带有创新性的理论范式研究成果，另一方面呈现对不同体裁作品的脉络性梳理以及最新研究成果，既有历史的纵切面，又体现当代美国亚裔文学创作与研究的丰富性。我们希望读者能够借助此评论集所提供的"点"，看到"美国亚裔文学"整个研究的"面"，也为国内的亚裔文学研究以及族裔文学研究开启新视角、注入新动力。

　　本评论集的英文文章，按照时间顺利序列，主题涉及美国亚裔的社会历史背景、美国亚裔概念的复杂性、赵（健秀）汤（亭亭）之争、性别与性、美国亚裔主体的形成与影响因素、美国亚裔文学理论范式的批判与创新、美国亚裔文学多种体裁的脉络化评述等。中国学者的评论文章选编了两篇：一为吴冰教授的《20 世纪兴起的美国亚裔文学》，另一篇为我国台湾学者单德兴教授的《绪论:〈他者与亚美文学〉及其脉络化意义》。这两篇中文文章代表着中国学者在美国亚裔文学研究中的高度和水平。

《美国亚裔文学评论集》的编选原则,是集总体性、历史性、经典性以及广泛性于一体。总体性是指所选文章并非针对单部作品或单一族裔文学的评论,而是针对美国亚裔文学研究理论范式与宏观问题的总体性评论;历史性是指所选文章涵盖了从 1982 年第一部美国亚裔文学研究专著问世到 2017 年的时间跨度;经典性在于所选文章是"美国亚裔文学"研究发展史上的经典之作,而评论家本人也为"美国亚裔文学"研究领域中的重要学者;广泛性则是指评论文章所涉体裁的丰富性,既有论述长篇小说、短篇小说者,也有探讨诗歌、戏剧、自传/回忆录、新媒体者,其中针对非小说体裁的评论均具有系统性梳理与权威性评价相结合的特征。

最后,需要说明的是,世界范围内的"美国亚裔文学"研究方兴未艾,代表性论著很多。对于编选者来说,除了上述的遴选原则之外,评论集成书的篇幅也是不得不考虑的一个因素,因此,我们不得不舍弃了不少好的论文。同时,有些很好的文章的版权问题得不到妥善解决,我们也只能忍痛割爱,这也令人感到遗憾。

无论如何,我们都希望《美国亚裔文学评论集》能够成为中国学术界研究"美国亚裔文学"的重要参考书目。

编者

2018 年 8 月 28 日

目 录

Table of Contents

Preface to *Asian American Literature: An Introduction to the Writings and Their Social Context*
《美国亚裔文学：作品及社会背景介绍》序言

Elaine H. Kim

评论家简介

金惠经（Elaine H. Kim），美国加利福尼亚大学伯克利分校博士，现为美国加利福尼亚大学伯克利分校族裔研究系荣休教授。研究领域包括：美国亚裔文学及文化、美国韩裔研究、亚洲和美国亚裔女性主义研究等。专著有《美国亚裔文学：写作及其社会背景介绍》（*Asian American Literature: An Introduction to the Writings and Their Social Context*, 1982）等。合著有《新鲜谈话 / 大胆凝视：美国亚裔艺术对谈》（*Fresh Talk/Daring Gazes: Conversations on Asian American Art*, 2003）、《回声阵阵：新韩裔美国人写作》（*Echoes Upon Echoes: New Korean American Writing*, 2003）等。合编有《危险女性：性别与朝鲜民族主义》（*Dangerous Women: Gender and Korean Nationalism*, 1998）、《激起更多浪潮：亚裔美国女性的新写作》（*Making More Waves: New Writing By Asian American Women*, 1997）、《东至美国：韩裔美国人生活故事》（*East To America: Korean American Life Stories*, 1996）等。

文章简介

金惠经（Elaine H. Kim）的《美国亚裔文学：作品及社会背景介绍》出版于 1982 年，

是首部系统评论美国亚裔文学的专著，已成为美国亚裔文学评论的经典之作。此书从美国亚裔社会历史的角度，按照年代为主、主题为辅的组织思路，追溯和探讨 19 世纪晚期至 20 世纪 80 年代期间美国亚裔文学作品中所反映的亚裔美国人的经历，重点讨论了作品中的亚裔美国意识与自我形象的演变过程。在本选集所收录的序言部分，金惠经介绍了本书的研究主旨、范围及方法；探讨了"美国亚裔"概念的含混性以及亚裔文学的文学形式与内容的张力等问题；概括了 19 世纪晚期至 20 世纪 80 年代期间美国亚裔文学的主要特色以及研究中应该注意的问题。

文章出处：Kim, Elaire H. *Asian American Literature: An Introduction to the Writings and Their Social Context.* Philadelphia: Temple UP, 1982, pp. xi-xix.

Preface to *Asian American Literature: An Introduction to the Writings and Their Social Context*

Elaine H. Kim

One of my students at Berkeley, a perceptive young man who had immigrated with his family from the People's Republic of China two years before, recently asked me why students form racial groups at schools and colleges in America. He was particularly puzzled that American-born Chinese who spoke little Chinese deliberately grouped themselves with immigrant Chinese, who spoke English haltingly. In Canton, he commented, a common language would have been a more important criterion for social compatibility than race. How could I have answered his question in a day? He had focused upon one contemporary manifestation of a fundamental problem, the roots of which are as deep as American history itself.

What I have attempted in this book is to trace the topography and rich textures of the Asian American experience as it is expressed in Asian American literature from the late nineteenth century to the present day. Although I have used my understanding of Asian American social history to interpret the literature, I have focused on the evolution of Asian American consciousness and self-image as expressed in the literature. For the purposes of this study, I have defined Asian American literature as published creative writings in English by Americans of Chinese, Japanese, Korean, and Filipino descent. This definition is problematical: it does not encompass writers in Asia or even writers expressing the American experience in Asian languages, although I have included some discussions of Japanese, Chinese, and Korean poetry about the Asian American experience that has been translated into English. This is not to say that writings in Asian languages are unimportant to a study of Asian American literature and experience: they are simply beyond the purview of this study, and I am confident that they will be presented elsewhere. Nor have I included in this book literature about Asia written by Asian Americans in English, except when it is revealing of the Asian American consciousness.

Calling this work a study of "Asian American" literature presents an enormous problem because, to begin with, the term Asian American is a controversial one. Like its predecessor, "Oriental," it was created in the West from the need to make racial categorizations in a racially divided or, at least, a racially diverse society. It has always been difficult for me to accept being called Oriental, since "Oriental" denotes east of somewhere, east of some other-defined center. Oriental is such an imprecise term: what is an Oriental flavor? an Oriental atmosphere or look? Asian American is a bit more precise. At least this term connotes an American identity for Asians, and it sounds more objective than Oriental. But Asian American and Asian Pacific American, while convenient for census count purposes, are also terms created and used to differentiate us from non-Asian and Pacific Americans. I would venture that the vast majority of persons of Chinese, Vietnamese, or Samoan ancestry would not, if asked, describe themselves as Asian and Pacific Americans but as Chinese, Vietnamese, or Samoan Americans, or indeed as Chinese, Vietnamese, and Samoans. To Asians all Orientals do not "look alike."[1] For instance, during the decades when Korea was colonized by Japan, enormous efforts were made by Korean Americans to clarify the distinctions between Koreans and Japanese, especially because the United States responded to that annexation by classifying Koreans in the United States with Japanese. No doubt many members of the Laotian, Cambodian, and Vietnamese communities in this country are confused when they are grouped together as Indochinese or as Southeast Asians. Distinctions among the various national groups sometimes do blur after a generation or two, when it is easier for us to see that we are bound together by the experiences we share as members of an American racial minority, but, when we do so, we are accepting an externally imposed label that is meant to define us by distinguishing us from other Americans primarily on the basis of race rather than culture.

That this book is about literature written in English by Asians from four different national groups means that I have accepted the externally imposed racial categorization of Asians in American society as an underlying assumption. Otherwise, I would have concentrated on a single ethnic group, such as Korean Americans, and I would have included literature written in Korean. Although I agree that the complexity of each group's American experience merits a separate study, I am myself interested in what Asians in America share and in how they can be compared within the context of their American experiences. I have noticed while studying this body of literature that, although it shares with most other literature thematic concerns such as love, desire for personal freedom and acceptance, and struggles against oppression and injustice, it is also shaped by other important particulars. American racism has been a critical factor in the Chinese, Japanese, Korean, and Filipino experience in the United States: it is no accident that literature by writers from those groups is often much concerned with this shared heritage. Racial policies and attitudes towards the different groups have often been quite similar, as have the responses to these policies and attitudes among them.

I believe that there is something to be gained from viewing the commonalities and differences among the four experiences as expressed in their literatures. I hope, for example, that my discussions of early Chinese, Japanese, Korean, and Filipino immigrant writers in Chapter 2 and of American-born and immigrant contemporary writers in Chapter 7 will vindicate my approach by demonstrating these commonalities and differences within the context of a shared American experience.

Whatever its origins, the racial classification of Asian Americans does in fact have its advantages for us. Our racial unity has been contributing to our strength, to our efforts to build community, and to the maintenance and development of a vital Asian American culture. This unity helps us function effectively in organizations and programs across the country: the Asian American Theatre Company in San Francisco, for example, showcases plays written, directed, and performed by persons of various Asian backgrounds and nativities and reflecting a wide range of perspectives and concerns; an Oakland Asian American language and employment training project offers programs for limited-English-speaking immigrants, who work closely with American-born and immigrant teachers of various national backgrounds; nearby bilingual Japanese, Filipino, Korean, and Chinese teachers provide childcare services for Korean, Chinese, Laotian, and Vietnamese pre-schoolers. Although most would agree that each nationality group should have its own identity and strengths, who would argue that pan-Asian American efforts should be cast aside?

While some readers may be bothered by the fact that this study focuses on four groups instead of one, others may criticize it for not encompassing all Asian Americans. I have included most of the literary figures from four or five generations of Asian Americans of Chinese, Japanese, Korean, and Filipino ancestry. But a reader of East Indian or Pakistani descent, for example, will search the book in vain for a discussion of his literature and culture in the United States. I can only beg the tolerance of my brothers and sisters from Southeast Asia and elsewhere by offering the argument that as yet there is relatively little literature in English expressing the sensibilities of very new population groups, such as Laotian, Cambodian, or Thai people, in the United States.

Some readers may fault me for including Korean American literature, which is hardly more plentiful than Vietnamese American writing at the moment, since the Korean American population is largely a new one too. Younghill Kang, however, emerged from among the handful of Koreans living in America long before the recent influx of immigrants and refugees from Asia began. Moreover, I could hardly resist including something about contemporary Korean immigrant writer Kichung Kim, whom I admire precisely because as a fellow Korean American I know he is poignantly expressing an experience shared by many people I know.

Since 1970, some Asian American literary history and criticism has been published, notably by Ronald Tanaka of Sacramento State University and Bruce Iwasaki of the Asian American Studies Center at UCLA.[2] Several anthologies of Asian American literature contain introductory essays of a general nature. The best known of these are in *Asian American Authors* (1972), edited by Kai-yu Hsu and Helen Palubinskas, and *Aiiieeeee! An Anthology of Asian-American Writers* (1974), edited by Frank Chin, Jeffery Paul Chan, Lawson Fusao Inada, and Shawn Hsu Wong.[3] As far as I know, however, mine is the first attempt to integrate the Asian American literary voice in one book-length study. I view this work as a beginning, a conversational gambit, and I trust that it will be complemented by many other studies that deal with issues I have not addressed.

Because the scope of this book is deliberately broad and detailed at the same time, it was difficult to decide how best to organize the materials contained here. I have been more concerned with breadth and variety than with classifications. I could have arranged the materials according to themes; I could have discussed writers of different nationalities separately instead of trying to weave them together; I could even have arranged the discussions around literary genre classifications, dealing first with poetry, then autobiographical writing, and finally with short stories and novels. What I did was to compromise: the arrangement is roughly chronological, beginning with early immigrant writings in English and ending with contemporary Asian American writers. The study is also organized — just as roughly — around themes, so I move from discussions of writing aimed at winning sympathy for Asian immigrants to writing that attempts to establish a self-defined cultural identity. Sometimes I group writers of different nationalities together, as in Chapters 2, 3, and 7, and at other times I discuss them separately, as in the chapters on Chinatown literature and on Japanese American family and community portrait literature, where I wanted to show how Chinese and Japanese American writers responded to the differences in their social experiences around the time of World War Ⅱ. The problem I faced was that the body of literature did not lend itself to a single type of arrangement. Although it might have been desirable, for example, to discuss Chinese, Japanese, Korean, and Filipino community portraiture together in one chapter, the result would have been unbalanced, since there are many more examples of Japanese American community portrait literature, undoubtedly because the Japanese American community experienced a longer history as a family society and there has always been a larger proportion of American-born, English-speaking Japanese American writers, for reasons discussed in the book. Moreover, the two Filipino writers who could have been classified as portrayers of the Filipino American community, Carlos Bulosan and Bienvenido

N. Santos, seemed more crucial to the chapters on early immigrant autobiography and on contemporary Asian American writing respectively. Since I found so few Filipino and Korean early immigrant writers, I decided to place them in Chapter 2 to show how early Asian immigrant autobiographical writing moves from Asia-orientation to expression of the immigrant's desire to find a place for himself in American life and culture. In order to organize the book in tidy thematic chapters, I would have had to resort to contrivance. I wanted the arrangement to be loose enough to reflect what I saw as the variety, diversity, and indeed the unevenness of the literature.

Traditionally, one of the problems facing Asian American and other racial minority writers in America has been that many readers insist on viewing their writing as sociological or anthropological statements about the group. Lately another view just as narrow has emerged that critical focus be concentrated on how minority writers express themselves instead of on what they say. Certainly both of these perspectives are limited and attention should be paid to both "literary" and "content" concerns. For the purposes of this study, however, I have deliberately chosen to emphasize how the literature elucidates the social history of Asians in the United States. The problem of understanding Asian American literature within its sociohistorical and cultural contexts is important to me because, when these contexts are unfamiliar, the literature is likely to be misunderstood and unappreciated. But the fact that this book is not an attempt to appreciate the formal literary merit of Asian American literature does not mean that I see no value in formal and stylistic interpretations; it only means that such interpretations were not my intention here. I feel certain that there are many more competent than I who will continue to address this question.

One of the fundamental barriers to understanding and appreciating Asian American literary self-expression has been the existence of race stereotypes about Asians in American popular culture. Probably more Americans know Fu Manchu and Charlie Chan than know Asian or Asian American human beings. Even the elite culture shares the popular stereotypes. Contemporary Chinese American playwright Frank Chin notes that New York critics of his play, "Chickencoop Chinaman," complained in the early 1970s that his characters did not speak, dress, or act "like Orientals."

Certainly reviews of Asian American literature by Anglo-American writers reveal that the criteria used to judge the literary merit of Asian American writing have not always been literary. Reviewers of Etsu Sugimoto's *A Daughter of the Samurai* (1925) praised the writer because she "pleads no causes, asks no vexing questions" at a time when the controversial issue of Japanese exclusion was still being spiritedly discussed. Critics of *East Goes West* (1937) lauded Younghill Kang for finding fault with Koreans and Korean society, but they were disturbed by his comments on America and Americans. Promoters of Pardee Lowe's *Father and Glorious Descendant* (1943) touted Lowe's enlistment in the U.S. Army during World War Ⅱ as evidence that he belonged to "one of America's loyal minorities" and that the book might therefore be worth reading. In more recent times, Daniel Okimoto's *American in Disguise* (1971) was appreciated by critics for having been written with "restraint" during a period of racial unrest, and Jeanne Wakatsuki Houston's *Farewell to Manzanar* (1973) was praised for its "lack of bitterness, self-pity, or solemnity" in portraying the internment of Japanese Americans during World War Ⅱ.[4]

Today, Maxine Hong Kingston complains that, although readers of various ethnic and racial backgrounds have responded to *The Woman Warrior* (1976) with profound understanding, she has also been very much misunderstood. In *Publisher's Weekly,* for example, one critic praised the book for its "myths rich and varied as Chinese brocade" and for prose "that often achieves the delicacy and precision of porcelain." According to this critic, "East meets West with ... charming results" in the book.[5] A closer look would have revealed that *The Woman Warrior* is deliberately anti-exotic and anti-nostalgic. There is nothing "charming" about the unexpected way Kingston satirically describes Chinese food, which Chinatown tourists think they know so well:

> "Eat! Eat!" my mother would shout at our heads bent over bowls, the blood pudding awobble in the middle of the table .... We'd have to face four- and five-day old leftovers until we ate it all. The squid eye would keep appearing at breakfast and dinner until eaten. Sometimes brown masses sat on every dish ... I would live on plastic.[6]

Some reviewers call upon other non-literary — and also non-sociological — aids to give them access to Kingston's writing. A *New York Times* critic, for example, notes with approval that Kingston's name indicates that she is married to an "American" (white), implying that she herself is not "American" and that her marriage has some significance to the book's approach to her Chinese American identity. In the *National Observer,* one reviewer defends his interpretations of *The Woman Warrior* by mentioning that his wife is Chinese Canadian.[7] Even the strengths of *The Woman Warrior,* such as its portrayal of ambiguity as central to the Chinese American experience, are misconstrued by some critics. Michael Malloy complains that "[i]t's hard to tell where her fantasies end and reality begins"; he is confused by her depiction of some Chinese women as aggressive and others as docile, as if there can only be one type of Chinese woman. These confusions are "especially hard for a non-Chinese," he concludes, "and that's the troubling aspect of the book."[8]

According to Kingston, the most gratifying responses to *The Woman Warrior* have come from Chinese American women, whose appreciation of the book is not interrupted by the sense that it contains the "mystery of a stubbornly, utterly foreign sensibility" that haunts some Anglo reviewers.[9]

In response to her realization that the reading public was generally ignorant about Chinese Americans, Kingston deliberately filled in the history lessons in *China Men* (1980), even listing historical facts, such as items of anti-Chinese legislation. Kingston contends that she felt compelled to do this, even at the risk of spoiling the dramatic moments in the narration, because sacrificing historical background for the sake of story in *The Woman Warrior* had not worked: "The reviews of my first book made it clear that people didn't know the history — or that they thought I didn't. While I was writing *China Men,* I just couldn't take that tension any more."[10] Kingston meant *China Men* almost as a continuation of William Carlos Williams' *In the American Grain,* which she feels is "the right way to write about American history, ... poetically and, it seems to me, truly." *China Men* picks up roughly where Williams' book left off, at about 1850. The problem is that, while American readers are familiar with Williams' characters, they do not necessarily know about Chinese Americans:

> The mainstream culture doesn't know the history of Chinese-Americans, which has been written and written well. The ignorance makes a tension for me, and in the new book I just couldn't take it anymore. So all of a sudden, right in the middle of the stories, plunk — there is an eight-page section of pure history. It starts with the Gold Rush and goes right through the various exclusion acts, year by year. There are no characters in it. It really affects the shape of the book and it might look quite clumsy.[11]

The challenge that Kingston and other Asian American writers face is how to preserve the artistic integrity of their writing and be understood at the same time by readers whose different cultural experiences might necessitate discourses and explanations that interfere with the art. According to Kingston, it may well be that, because of *China Men,* the road ahead will be easier, at least for some Chinese American fiction writers: "[M]aybe it will affect the shape of the novel in the future. Now maybe another Chinese-American writer won't have to write that history."[12]

In this book, as in *China Men,* there is movement between social history and literature — and for the same reason. The reader's familiarity with the sociohistorical context of Asian American literature cannot be assumed as it can in the case of Anglo-American literature. One is struck, for example, by the fact that even today most Asian American writing, whether in education, sociology, psychology, or literature, is usually prefaced by an explanatory overview of Asian American history. To those readers who are disconcerted by this book's movement between social history and literature and by my emphasis on sociohistorical rather than strictly formal concerns, I can only respond that I have found the knowledge of the social context of Asian American literature can mean the difference between understanding a work and completely misinterpreting it. In Louis Chu's *Eat a Bowl of Tea,* for example, the protagonist's sexual impotence must be viewed within the context of the Chinatown ghetto of aging bachelors, who are prevented by discriminatory laws and policies from establishing a tradition of normal family life. Without an understanding of this aspect of Chinese American history, one might conclude that the book is simply soft-core pornography and not a novel of manners. The bitterness and rage felt by John Okada's protagonist towards his mother in *No-No Boy* can be seen as an example of the generational conflicts that exist to some extent between all parents and children and also as an illustration of problems faced by the children of immigrant parents of many nationalities, but Ichiro's anguish cannot be fully understood apart from the context of the internment of Japanese Americans during World War II. The mother's attitudes towards Japan and the son's desire to be accepted as an American are key to understanding their relationship.

By studying Asian American literature, readers can learn about the Asian American experience from the point of view of those who have lived it. In this book, I trace Asian American self-images as they have evolved in response to changing social contexts. I also focus on ways in which individuals' self-images are related to attitudes towards Asia and America, to relationships within families, particularly between immigrant and American-born generations and between the sexes, and to the relationship between the individual and the ethnic community.

At the same time, it is important to remember that Asian Americans who write are not necessarily "typical" or "representative" of their nationality or racial group. No one expects John Steinbeck or Herman Melville to represent or typify all white Americans, or even all German Americans or Anglo-Americans, but because Asian Americans have been unfamiliar to most American readers, their visions and expressions are sometimes erroneously generalized. I recall the annoyance felt by a friend of mine when her non-Asian friends presented her with a copy of Maxine Hong Kingston's *The Woman Warrior*, saying, "Now I finally understand you." Maxine Hong Kingston is writing about *her* Chinese American experience and *the* Chinese American experience, but she has always stressed the need for many voices to speak out and express the diversity and variety of Chinese American life.

Notes

1. During World War II, when Japan was an enemy nation and China an ally, an article titled "How To Tell Your Friends from the Japs" appeared in *Time* magazine (Dec. 22, 1941), offering readers "a few rules of thumb" that were "not always reliable" since "there is no infallible way of telling them apart." According to the article, virtually all Japanese are short and thin, tending to "dry up ... as they age," while Chinese are tall and better built. Japanese can be distinguished by their hard-heeled, stiffly erect gait and their hesitancy and nervousness in conversation as well as by their loud laughter at inappropriate times. But the key difference between Chinese and Japanese, the writer contends, is in facial expression: the Chinese expression is "more placid, kindly, open," while the Japanese is "dogmatic, arrogant."

2. See, for example, Ronald Tanaka, "On the Metaphysical Foundations of Sansei Poetics," *Journal of Ethnic Studies* 7, no. 2 (summer 1979): 1—36; Bruce Iwasaki, "Response and Change for the Asian in America," *Roots: An Asian American Reader*, ed. Amy Tachiki *et al.* (Los Angeles: UCLA Asian American Studies Center, 1971), and "Introduction: Asian American Literature," *Counterpoint: Perspectives on Asian America,* ed. Emma Gee (Los Angeles: UCLA Asian American Studies Center, 1976).

3. Kai-yu Hsu and Helen Palubinskas, eds., *Asian American Authors.* Boston: Houghton Mifflin Co., 1972); Frank Chin, Jeffery Paul Chan, Lawson Fusao Inada, and Shawn Hsu Wong, eds., *Aiiieeeee! An Anthology of Asian-American Writers.* Washington, D.C.: Howard University Press, 1974).

4. On *A Daughter of the Samurai*, see New York *Tribune*, Nov. 22, 1925, p.10; on *East Goes West*, Ladie Hosie, "A Voice from Korea," *Saturday Review of Literature*, April 4, 1931, p. 707; on *Father and Glorious Descendant, Library Journal* 68, no. 7 (April 1, 1943): 287; on *American in Disguise*, Phoebe Adams, "Short Reviews: Books," *Atlantic Monthly* 227, no.4 (April 1971): 104; on *Farewell, to Manzanar, Saturday Review World*, Nov. 6, 1973, p.34, and *Library Journal*, Nov. 1, 1973, p.3257.

5. *Publisher's Weekly* 212 (Sept. 1976): 72.

6. Maxine Hong Kingston, *The Woman Warrior* (New York: Vintage Books, 1977), p. 108.

7. Jane Kramer, "On Being Chinese in China and America," *New York Times Book Review,* Nov. 7, 1976, p. 19; Michael T. Malloy, " 'The Woman Warrior': On Growing Up Chinese, Female, and Bitter," *National Observer,* Oct. 9, 1976, p. 25.

8. Malloy, " 'The Woman Warrior,' " p. 25.

9. Kramer, "On Being Chinese," p. 1.

10. Timothy Pfaff, "Talk with Mrs. Kingston," *New York Times Book Review,* June 18, 1980, p. 26.

11. *Ibid.*

12. *Ibid.*

The Woman Warrior versus the Chinaman Pacific: Must a Chinese American Critic Choose between Feminism and Heroism?
女勇士与中国佬的太平洋：美国华裔批评家一定要在女性主义和英雄主义之间做出选择吗？

King-Kok Cheung

评论家简介

　　张敬珏（King-Kok Cheung），美国加利福尼亚大学伯克利分校英语系博士，现为美国加利福尼亚大学洛杉矶分校英语系与美国亚裔研究中心教授。研究领域包括美国族裔文学、美国亚裔文学、华文及美国华裔文学、文艺复兴时期的英国文学（莎士比亚与弥尔顿）、世界文学、性别研究等。专著有《无界有文之华美文学：性别、文类、形式》（*Chinese American Literature without Borders: Gender，Genre，and Form, 2017*）、《无声胜有声：山本久惠、汤亭亭和小川乐》（*Articulate Silences: Hisaye Yamamoto，Maxine Hong Kingston，Joy Kogawa, 1993*）等。编著有《字词举足轻重：美国亚裔作家访谈》（*Words Matter: Conversations with Asian American Writers, 2000*）、《种族间美国亚裔文学指南》（*An Interethnic Companion to Asian American Literature, 1996*）、《十七音节》（*"Seventeen Syllables"：Hisaye Yamamoto, 1994*）、《美国亚裔文学：注释书目》（*Asian American Literature: An Annotated Bibliography, 1988*）等。合编有《希思美国文学选集》（*The Heath Anthology of American Literature, 2004*）等。

文章简介

　　1976 年，美国华裔作家汤亭亭的小说《女勇士》问世，作品中对中国文化经典的改写招致亚裔文化斗士赵健秀的激烈批判。两人之间以文本与批评文章的形式不断回应对方，分别以两人为代表的两派作家、学者，就华裔文学如何"真实再现"华裔在美生存状况等问题展开论争，从而形成旷日持久的美国亚裔文化界的所谓的"赵汤之争"大论战。文学评论家张敬珏 1990 年撰写的这篇文章是学界针对这一论战做出回应的代表性文章，也是亚裔女权主义研究的经典文献。文章在钩沉历史的基础上，剖析华裔创作中英雄主义与女权主义形成对抗的成因与表现。通过指出《女勇士》成为论战暴风眼的原因，通过详细分析以复原英雄主义传统矫正华裔男性刻板印象这一做法的实质与问题，文章揭示出当时文化界对《女勇士》的误读，论证汤亭亭的创作具有反对男权主义与反对种族主义的双重意义。

文章出处：Hirsch, Marianne., and Evelyn Fox Keller editors. *Conflicts in Feminism*. New York: Routledge, 1990, pp. 234-251.

The Woman Warrior versus the Chinaman Pacific: Must a Chinese American Critic Choose between Feminism and Heroism?

King-Kok Cheung

The title of the anthology notwithstanding, I will primarily be speaking not about topics that divide feminists but about conflicting politics of gender, as reflected in the literary arena, between Chinese American women and men.[1] There are several reasons for my choice. First, I share the frustrations of many women of color that while we wish to engage in a dialogue with "mainstream" scholars, most of our potential readers are still unfamiliar with the historical and cultural contexts of various ethnic "minorities." Furthermore, whenever I encounter words such as "conflicts," "common differences," or "divisive issues" in feminist studies, the authors more often than not are addressing the divergences either between French and Anglo-American theorists or, more recently, between white and nonwhite women. Both tendencies have the effect of re-centering white feminism. In some instances, women of color are invited to participate chiefly because they take issue with white feminists and not because what they have to say is of inherent interest to the audience. Finally, I believe that in order to understand conflicts among diverse groups of women, we must look at the relations between women and men, especially where the problems of race and gender are closely intertwined.

It is impossible, for example, to tackle the gender issues in the Chinese American cultural terrain without delving into the historically enforced "feminization" of Chinese American men, without confronting the dialectics of racial stereotypes and nationalist reactions or, above all, without wrestling with diehard notions of masculinity and femininity in both Asian and Western cultures. It is partly because these issues touch many sensitive nerves that the writings of Maxine Hong Kingston have generated such heated debates among Chinese American intellectuals. As a way into these intricate issues, I will structure my discussion around Kingston's work and the responses it has elicited from her Chinese American male critics, especially those who have themselves been influential in redefining both literary history and Asian American manhood.

Attempts at cultural reconstruction, whether in terms of "manhood" and "womanhood," or of "mainstream" versus "minority" heritage, are often inseparable from a wish for self-empowerment. Yet many writers and critics who have challenged the monolithic authority of white male literary historians remain in thrall to the norms and arguments of the dominant patriarchal culture, unwittingly upholding the criteria of those whom they assail. As a female immigrant of Cantonese descent, with the attendant sympathies and biases, I will survey and analyze what I construe to be the "feminist" and "heroic" impulses which have invigorated Chinese American literature but at the same time divided its authors and critics.

I

Sexual politics in Chinese America reflect complex cultural and historical legacies. The paramount importance of patrilineage in traditional Chinese culture predisposes many Chinese Americans of the older generations to favor male over female offspring (a preference even more overt than that which still underlies much of white America). At the same time Chinese American men, too, have been confronted with a history of inequality and of painful "emasculation." The fact that ninety percent of early Chinese immigrants were male, combined with anti-miscegenation laws and laws prohibiting Chinese laborers' wives from entering the U.S., forced these immigrants to congregate in the bachelor communities of various Chinatowns, unable to father a subsequent generation. While many built railroads, mined gold, and cultivated plantations, their strenuous activities and contributions in these areas were often overlooked by white historians. Chinamen were better known to the American public as restaurant cooks, laundry workers, and waiters, jobs traditionally considered "women's work."[2]

The same forms of social and economic oppression of Chinese American women and men, in conjunction with a longstanding Orientalist tradition that casts the Asian in the role of the silent and passive Other,[3] have in turn provided material for degrading sexual representations of the Chinese in American popular culture. Elaine H. Kim notes, for instance, that the stereotype of Asian women as submissive and dainty sex objects has given rise to an "enormous demand for X-rated films featuring Asian women and the emphasis on bondage in pornographic materials about Asian women," and that "the popular image of alluring and exotic 'dream girls of the mysterious East' has created a demand for 'Oriental' bath house workers in American cities as well as a booming business in mail order marriages."[4] No less insidious are the inscriptions of Chinese men in popular culture. Frank Chin, a well-known writer and one of the most outspoken revisionists of Asian American history, describes how the American silver screen casts doubts on Chinese American virility:

The movies were teachers. In no uncertain terms they taught America that we were lovable for being a race of sissies … living to accommodate the whitemen. Unlike the white stereotype of the evil black stud, Indian rapist, Mexican macho, the evil of the evil Dr. Fu Manchu was not sexual, but homosexual … Dr. Fu, a man wearing a long dress, batting his eyelashes, surrounded by muscular black servants in loin clothes, and with his bad habit of caressingly touching white men on the leg, wrist, and face with his long fingernails is not so much a threat as he is a frivolous offense to white manhood. [Charlie] Chan's gestures are the same, except that he doesn't touch, and instead of being graceful like Fu in flowing robes, he is awkward in a baggy suit and clumsy. His sexuality is the source of a joke running through all of the forty-seven Chan films. The large family of the bovine detective isn't the product of sex, but animal husbandry … *He never gets into violent things* [my emphasis].[5]

According to Chin and Jeffery Paul Chan, also a writer, "Each racial stereotype comes in two models, the acceptable model and the unacceptable model … The unacceptable model is unacceptable because he cannot be controlled by whites. The acceptable model is acceptable because he is tractable. There is racist hate and racist love."[6] Chin and Chan believe that while the "masculine" stereotypes of blacks, Indians, and Mexicans are generated by "racist hate," "racist love" has been lavished on Chinese Americans, targets of "effeminate" stereotypes:

The Chinese, in the parlance of the Bible, were raw material for the "flock," pathological sheep for the shepherd. The adjectives applied to the Chinese ring with scriptural imagery. We are meek, timid, passive, docile, industrious. We have the patience of Job. We are humble. A race without sinful manhood, born to mortify our flesh … The difference between [other minority groups] and the Chinese was that the Christians, taking Chinese hospitality for timidity and docility, weren't afraid of us as they were of other races. They loved us, protected us. Love conquered.[7]

If "racist love" denies "manhood" to Asian men, it endows Asian women with an excess of "womanhood." Elaine Kim argues that because "the characterization of Asian men is a reflection of a white male perspective that defines the white man's virility, it is possible for Asian men to be viewed as asexual and the Asian woman as only sexual, imbued with an innate understanding of how to please and serve." The putative gender difference among Asian Americans — exaggerated out of all proportion in the popular imagination — has, according to Kim, created "resentment and tensions" between the sexes within the ethnic community.[8]

Although both the Asian American and the feminist movements of the late sixties have attempted to counter extant stereotypes, the conflicts between Asian American men and women have been all the more pronounced in the wake of the two movements. In the last two decades many Chinese American men — especially such writers and editors as Chin and Chan —

have begun to correct the distorted images of Asian males projected by the dominant culture. Astute, eloquent, and incisive as they are in debunking racist myths, they are often blind to the biases resulting from their own acceptance of the datriarchal construct of masculinity. In Chin's discussion of Fu Manchu and Charlie Chan and in the perceptive contrast he draws between the stock images of Asian men and those of other men of color, one can detect not only homophobia but perhaps also a sexist preference for stereotypes that imply predatory violence against women to "effeminate" ones. Granted that the position taken by Chin may be little more than a polemicist stance designed to combat white patronage, it is disturbing that he should lend credence to the conventional association of physical aggression with manly valor. The hold of patriarchal conventions becomes even more evident in the following passage:

> The white stereotype of the Asian is unique in that it is the only racial stereotype completely devoid of manhood. Our nobility is that of an efficient housewife. At our worst we are contemptible because we are womanly, effeminate, devoid of all the traditionally masculine qualities of originality, daring, physical courage, creativity. We're neither straight talkin' or straight shootin'. The mere fact that four of the five American-born Chinese-American writers are women reinforces this aspect of the stereotype.[9]

In taking whites to task for demeaning Asians, these writers seem nevertheless to be buttressing patriarchy by invoking gender stereotypes, by disparaging domestic efficiency as "feminine," and by slotting desirable traits such as originality, daring, physical courage, and creativity under the rubric of masculinity.[10]

The impetus to reassert manhood also underlies the ongoing attempt by Chin, Chan, Lawson Inada, and Shawn Wong to reconstruct Asian American literary history. In their groundbreaking work *Aiiieeeee! An Anthology of Asian-American Writers*, these writers and co-editors deplored "the lack of a recognized style of Asian-American manhood." In a forthcoming sequel entitled *The Big Aiiieeeee! An Anthology of Asian American Writers,* they attempt to revive an Asian heroic tradition, celebrating Chinese and Japanese classics such as *The Art of War, Water Margin, Romance of the Three Kingdoms, Journey to the West,* and *Chushingura,* and honoring the renowned heroes and outlaws featured therein.[11]

The editors seem to be working in an opposite direction from that of an increasing number of feminists. While these Asian American spokesmen are recuperating a heroic tradition of their own, many women writers and scholars, building on existentialist and modernist insights, are reassessing the entire Western code of heroism. While feminists question such traditional values as competitive individualism and martial valor, the editors seize on selected maxims, purportedly derived from Chinese epics and war manuals, such as "I am the law," "life is war," "personal integrity and honor is the highest value," and affirm the "ethic of private revenge."[12]

The *Aiiieeeee!* editors and feminist critics also differ on the question of genre. According to Chin, the literary genre that is most antithetical to the heroic tradition is autobiography, which he categorically denounces as a form of Christian confession:

> The fighter writer uses literary forms as weapons of war, not the expression of ego alone, and does not [waste] time with dandyish expressions of feeling and psychological attitudinizing ... A Chinese Christian is like a Nazi Jew. Confession and autobiography celebrate the process of conversion from an object of contempt to an object of acceptance. You love the personal experience of it, the oozings of viscous putrescence and luminous radiant guilt ... It's the quality of submission, not assertion that counts, in the confession and the autobiography. The autobiography combines the thrills and guilt of masturbation and the porno movie.[13]

Feminist critics, many of whom are skeptical of either/or dichotomies (in this instance fighting vs. feeling) and are impatient with normative definitions of genre (not that Chin's criteria are normative), believe that women have always appropriated autobiography as a vehicle for *asserting,* however tentatively, their subjectivity. Celeste Schenck writes:

> The poetics of women's autobiography issues from its concern with constituting a female subject — a precarious operation, which ... requires working on two fronts at once, *both* occupying a kind of center, assuming a subjectivity long denied, *and* maintaining the vigilant, disruptive stance that speaking from the postmodern margin provides — the autobiographical genre may be paradigmatic of all women's writing.[14]

Given these divergent views, the stage is set for a confrontation between "heroism" and "feminism" in Chinese American letters.

II

The advent of feminism, far from checking Asian American chauvinism, has in a sense fueled gender antagonism, at least in the literary realm. Nowhere is this antagonism reflected more clearly than in the controversy that has erupted over Maxine Hong Kingston's *The Woman Warrior*. Classified as autobiography, the work describes the protagonist's struggle for self-definition amid Cantonese sayings such as "Girls are maggots in the rice," "It is more profitable to raise geese than daughters," "Feeding girls is feeding cowbirds" (51, 54). While the book has received popular acclaim, especially among feminist critics, it has been censured by several

Chinese American critics — mostly male but also some female — who tax Kingston for misrepresenting Chinese and Chinese American culture, and for passing fiction for autobiography. Chin (whose revulsion against autobiography we already know) wrote a satirical parody of *The Woman Warrior;* he casts aspersions on its historical status and places Kingston in the same company as the authors of Fu Manchu and Charlie Chan for confirming "the white fantasy that everything sick and sickening about the white self-image is really Chinese."[15] Jeffery Paul Chan castigates Knopf for publishing the book as "biography rather than fiction (which it obviously is)" and insinuates that a white female reviewer praises the book indiscriminately because it expresses "female anger."[16] Benjamin Tong openly calls it a "fashionably feminist work written with white acceptance in mind."[17] As Sau-ling Wong points out, "According to Kingston's critics, the most pernicious of the stereotypes which might be supported by *The Woman Warrior* is that of Chinese American men as sexist," and yet some Chinese American women "think highly of *The Woman Warrior* because it confirms their personal experiences with sexism."[18] In sum, Kingston is accused of falsifying culture and of reinforcing stereotype in the name of feminism.

At first glance the claim that Kingston should not have taken the liberty to infuse autobiography with fiction may seem to be merely a generic, genderneutral criticism, but as Susan Stanford Friedman has pointed out, genre is all too often gendered.[19] Feminist scholars of autobiography have suggested that women writers often shy away from "objective" autobiography and prefer to use the form to reflect a private world, a subjective vision, and the life of the imagination. *The Woman Warrior,* though it departs from most "public" self-representations by men, is quite in line with such an autobiographical tradition. Yet for a "minority" author to exercise such artistic freedom is perilous business because white critics and reviewers persist in seeing creative expressions by her as no more than cultural history.[20] Members from the ethnic community are in turn upset if they feel that they have been "misrepresented" by one of their own. Thus where Kingston insists on shuttling between the world of facts and the world of fantasy, on giving multiple versions of "truth" as subjectively perceived, her Chinese American detractors demand generic purity and historical accuracy. Perhaps precisely because this author is female, writing amid discouraging realities, she can only forge a viable and expansive identity by refashioning patriarchal myths and invoking imaginative possibilities,[21] Kingston's autobiographical act, far from betokening submission, as Chin believes, turns the self into a "heroine" and is in a sense an act of "revenge" (a word represented in Chinese by two ideographs which Kingston loosely translates as "report a crime") against both the Chinese and the white cultures that undermine her self-esteem. Discrediting her for taking poetic licence is reminiscent of those white reviewers who reduce works of art by ethnic authors to sociohistorical documentary.

The second charge concerning stereotype is more overtly gender-based. It is hardly coincidental that the most unrelenting critics (whose grievance is not only against Kingston but also against feminists in general) have also been the most ardent champions of Chinese American "manhood." Their response is understandable. Asian American men have suffered deeply from racial oppression. When Asian American women seek to expose anti-female prejudices in their own ethnic community, the men are likely to feel betrayed.[22] Yet it is also undeniable that sexism still lingers as part of the Asian legacy in Chinese America and that many American-born daughters still feel its sting. Chinese American women may be at once sympathetic and angry toward the men in their ethnic community: sensitive to the marginality of these men but resentful of their male privilege.

III

Kingston herself seems to be in the grips of these conflicting emotions. The opening legend of *China Men* captures through myth some of the baffling intersections of gender and ethnicity in Chinese America and reveals the author's own double allegiance. The legend is borrowed and adapted from an eighteenth-century Chinese novel entitled *Flowers in the Mirror*, itself a fascinating work and probably one of the first "feminist" novels written by a man.[23] The male protagonist of this novel is Tang Ao, who in Kingston's version is captured in the Land of Women, where he is forced to have his feet bound, his ears pierced, his facial hair plucked, his cheeks and lips painted red — in short, to be transformed into an Oriental courtesan.

Since Kingston explicitly points out at the end of her legend that the Land of Women was in North America, critics familiar with Chinese American history will readily see that the ignominy suffered by Tang Ao in a foreign land symbolizes the emasculation of Chinamen by the dominant culture. Men of Chinese descent have encountered racial violence in the U.S., both in the past and even recently.[24] Kingston's myth is indeed intimating that the physical torment in their peculiar case is often tied to an affront to their manhood.

But in making women the captors of Tang Ao and in deliberately reversing masculine and feminine roles, Kingston also foregrounds constructions of gender. I cannot but see this legend as double-edged, pointing not only to the mortification of Chinese men in the new world but also to the subjugation of women both in old China and in America. Although the tortures suffered by Tang Ao seem palpably cruel, many Chinese women had for centuries been obliged to undergo similar mutilation. By having a man go through these ordeals instead, Kingston, following the author of *Flowers in the Mirror,* disrupts the familiar and commonplace acceptance of Chinese women as sexual objects. Her myth deplores on the one hand the racist debasement of Chinese American men and on the other hand the sexist objectification of Chinese women. Although *China Men* mostly commemorates the founding fathers of Chinese America, this companion volume to *The Woman Warrior* is also suffused with "feminist anger." The opening myth suggests that the author objects as strenuously to the patriarchal practices of her ancestral culture as to the racist treatment of her forefathers in their adopted country.

Kingston reveals not only the similarities between Chinamen's and Chinese women's suffering but also the correlation between these men's umbrage at racism and their misogynist behavior. In one episode, the narrator's immigrant father, a laundryman who seldom opens his mouth except to utter obscenities about women, is cheated by a gypsy and harassed by a white policeman:

> When the gypsy baggage and the police pig left, we were careful not to be bad or noisy so that you [father] would not turn on us. We knew that it was to feed us you had to endure demons and physical labor. You screamed wordless male screams that jolted the house upright ...Worse than the swearing and the nightly screams were your silences when you punished us by not talking. You rendered us invisible, gone. (8)

Even as the daughter deplores the father's "male screams" and brooding silences, she attributes his bad temper to his sense of frustration and emasculation in a white society. As in analogous situations of Cholly Breedlove in Toni Morrison's *The Bluest Eye* and Grange Copeland in Alice Walker's *The Third Life of Grange Copeland,* what seems to be male tyranny must be viewed within the context of racial inequality. Men of color who have been abused in a white society are likely to attempt to restore their sense of masculinity by venting their anger at those who are even more powerless — the women and children in their families.

Kingston's attempt to write about the opposite sex in *China Men* is perhaps a tacit call for mutual empathy between Chinese American men and women. In an interview, the author likens herself to Tang Ao: just as Tang Ao enters the Land of Women and is made to feel what it means to be of the other gender, so Kingston, in writing *China Men*, enters the realm of men and, in her own words, becomes "the kind of woman who loves men and who can tell their stories." Perhaps, to extend the analogy further, she is trying to prompt her male readers to participate in and empathize with the experiences of women.[25] Where Tang Ao is made to feel what his female contemporaries felt, Chinese American men are urged to see parallels between their plight and that of Chinese American women. If Asian men have been emasculated in America, as the aforementioned male critics have themselves argued, they can best attest to the oppression of women who have long been denied male privilege.

IV

An ongoing effort to revamp Chinese American literary history will surely be more compelling if it is informed by mutual empathy between men and women. To return to an earlier point, I am of two minds about the ambitious attempt of the *Aiiieeeee!* editors to restore and espouse an Asian American heroic tradition. Born and raised in Hong Kong, I grew up reading many of the Chinese heroic epics — along with works of less heroic modes — and can appreciate the rigorous effort of the editors to introduce them to Asian American and non-Asian readers alike.[26] But the literary values they assign to the heroic canon also function as ideology. Having spoken out against the emasculation of Asian Americans in their introduction to *Aiiieeeee!,* they seem determined to show further that Chinese and Japanese Americans have a heroic — which is to say militant — heritage. Their propagation of the epic tradition appears inseparable from their earlier attempt to eradicate effeminate stereotypes and to emblazon Asian American manhood.[27] In this light, the special appeal held by the war heroes for the editors becomes rather obvious. Take, for example, Kwan Kung, in *Romance of the Three Kingdoms:*

> Loud, passionate, and vengeful, this "heroic embodiment of martial self-sufficiency" is antithetical in every way to the image of the quiet, passive, and subservient Oriental houseboy. Perhaps the editors hope that the icon of this imposing Chinese hero will dispel myths about Chinese American tractability.

While acquaintance with some of the Chinese folk heroes may induce the American public to acknowledge that Chinese culture too has its Robin Hood and John Wayne, I remain uneasy about the masculist orientation of the heroic tradition, especially as expounded by the editors who see loyalty, revenge, and individual honor as the overriding ethos which should be inculcated in (if not already absorbed by) Chinese Americans. If white media have chosen to highlight and applaud the submissive and nonthreatening characteristics of Asians, the Asian American editors are equally tendentious in underscoring the militant strain of their Asian literary heritage.[28] The refutation of effeminate stereotypes through the glorification of machismo merely perpetuates patriarchal terms and assumptions.

Is it not possible for Chinese American men to recover a cultural space without denigrating or erasing "the feminine"? Chin contends that "use of the heroic tradition in Chinese literature as the source of Chinese American moral, ethical and esthetic universals is not literary rhetoric and smartass cute tricks, not wishful thinking, not theory, not demagoguery and prescription, but simple history."[29] However, even history, which is also a form of social construct, is not exempt from critical scrutiny. The Asian heroic tradition, like its Western counterpart, must be re-evaluated so that both its strengths and limits can surface. The intellectual excitement and the emotional appeal of the tradition is indisputable: the strategic brilliance of characters such as Chou Yu and Chuko Liang in *Romance of the Three Kingdoms* rivals that of Odysseus, and the fraternal bond between the three sworn brothers — Liu Pei, Chang Fei, and Kuan Yu (Kwan Kung) — is no less moving than that between Achilles and Patrocles. But just as I no longer believe that Homer speaks for humanity (or even all mankind), I hesitate to subscribe wholeheartedly to the *Aiiieeeee!* editors' claim that the Asian heroic canon (composed entirely of work written by men though it contains a handful of heroines) encompasses "Asian universals."

Nor do I concur with the editors that a truculent mentality pervades the Chinese heroic tradition, which generally places a higher premium on benevolence than on force and stresses the primacy of kinship and friendship over personal power. By way of illustration I will turn to the prototype for Kingston's "woman warrior" — Fa Mu Lan (also known as Hua Mulan and Fa Muk Lan). According to the original "Ballad of Mulan" (which most Chinese children, including myself, had to learn by heart) the heroine in joining the army is prompted neither by revenge nor by personal honor but by filial piety. She enlists under male disguise to take the place of her aged father. Instead of celebrating the glory of war, the poem describes the bleakness of the battlefield and the loneliness of the daughter (who sorely misses her parents). The use of understatement in such lines as "the general was killed after hundreds of combats" and "the warriors returned in ten years" (my translation) connotes the cost and duration of battles. The "Ballad of Mulan," though it commits the filial and courageous daughter to public memory, also contains a pacifist subtext — much in the way that the *Iliad* conceals an antiwar message beneath its martial trappings. A re-examination of the Asian heroic tradition may actually reveal that it is richer and more sophisticated than the *Aiiieeeee!* editors, bent on finding belligerent models, would allow.[30]

Kingston's adaptation of the legend in *The Woman Warrior* is equally multivalent. Fa Mu Lan as re-created in the protagonist's fantasy does excel in martial arts, but her power is derived as much from the words carved on her back as from her military skills. And the transformed heroine still proves problematic as a model since she can only exercise her power when in male armor. As I have argued elsewhere, her military distinction, insofar as it valorizes the ability to be ruthless and violent — "to fight like a man" — affirms rather than subverts patriarchal mores.[31] In fact, Kingston discloses in an interview that the publisher is the one who entitled the book "The Woman Warrior" while she herself (who is a pacifist) resists complete identification with the war heroine:

> I don't really like warriors. I wish I had not had a metaphor of a warrior, a person who uses weapons and goes to war. I guess I always have in my style a doubt about wars as a way of solving things.[32]

Aside from the fantasy connected with Fa Mu Lan the book has little to do with actual fighting. The real battle that runs through the work is one against silence and invisibility. Forbidden by her mother to tell a secret, unable to read aloud in English while first attending American school, and later fired for protesting against racism, the protagonist eventually speaks with a vengeance through writing — through a heroic act of self-expression. At the end of the book her tutelary genius has changed from Fa Mu Lan to Ts'ai Yen — from warrior to poet.

Kingston's commitment to pacifism — through re-visioning and re-contextualizing ancient "heroic" material — is even more evident in her most recent book, *Tripmaster Monkey.* As though anticipating the editors of *The Big Aiiieeeee!,* the author alludes recurrently to the Chinese heroic tradition, but always with a feminist twist. The protagonist of this novel, Wittman Ah Sing, is a playwright who loves *Romance of the Three Kingdoms* (one of the aforementioned epics espoused by Chin). Kingston's novel culminates with Wittman directing a marathon show which he has written based on the *Romance.* At the end of the show he has a rather surprising illumination:

> He had made up his mind: he will not go to Viet Nam or to any war. He had staged the War of the Three Kingdoms as heroically as he could, which made him start to understand: The three brothers and Cho Cho were masters of the war; they had worked out strategies and justifications for war so brilliantly that their policies and their tactics are used today, even by governments with nuclear-powered weapons. And they *lost.* The clanging and banging fooled us, but now we know — they lost. Studying the mightiest war epic of all time, Wittman changed — beeen! — into a pacifist. Dear American monkey, don't be afraid. Here, let us tweak your ear, and kiss your other ear.[33]

The seemingly easy transformation of Wittman — who is curiously evocative of Chin in speech and manner — is achieved through the pacifist author's sleight of hand. Nevertheless, the novel does show that it is possible to celebrate the ingenious strategies of the ancient warriors without embracing, wholesale, the heroic code that motivates their behavior and without endorsing violence as a positive expression of masculinity.[34]

Unfortunately, the ability to perform violent acts implied in the concepts of warrior and epic hero is still all too often mistaken for manly courage; and men who have been historically subjugated are all the more tempted to adopt a militant stance to manifest their masculinity. In the notorious Moynihan report on the black family, "military service for Negroes" was recommended as a means to potency:

> Given the strains of the disorganized and matrifocal family life in which so many Negro youth come of age, the Armed Forces are a dramatic and desperately needed change: a world away from women, a world run by strong men of unquestioned authority.[35]

Moynihan believed that placing black men in an "utterly masculine world" will strengthen them. The black men in the sixties who worshipped figures that exploited and brutalized women likewise conflated might and masculinity. Toni Cade, who cautions against "equating black liberation with black men gaining access to male privilege," offers an alternative to patriarchal prescriptions for manhood:

> Perhaps we need to let go of all notions of manhood and femininity and concentrate on Blackhood ... It perhaps takes less heart to pick up the gun than to face the task of creating a new identity, a self, perhaps an androgynous self ... [36]

If Chinese American men use the Asian heroic dispensation to promote male aggression, they may risk remaking themselves in the image of their oppressors — albeit under the guise of Asian panoply. Precisely because the racist treatment of Asians has taken the peculiar form of sexism — insofar as the indignities suffered by men of Chinese descent are analogous to those traditionally suffered by women — we must refrain from seeking antifeminist solutions to racism. To do otherwise reinforces not only patriarchy but also white supremacy.

Well worth heeding is Althusser's caveat that when a dominant ideology is integrated as common sense into the consciousness of the dominated, the dominant class will continue to prevail.[37] Instead of tailoring ourselves to white ideals, Asian Americans may insist on alternative habits and ways of seeing. Instead of drumming up support for Asian American "manhood," we may consider demystifying popular stereotypes while reappropriating what Stanford Lyman calls the "kernels of truth" in them that are indeed part of our ethnic heritage. For instance, we need not accept the Western association of Asian self-restraint with passivity and femininity. I, for one, believe that the respectful demeanor of many an Asian and Asian American indicates, among other things, a willingness to listen to others and to resolve conflict rationally or tactfully.[38] Such a collaborative disposition — be it Asian or non-Asian, feminine or masculine — is surely no less valid and viable than one that is vociferous and confrontational.

V

Although I have thus far concentrated on the gender issues in the Chinese American cultural domina, they do have provocative implications for feminist theory and criticism. As Elizabeth Spelman points out, "It is not easy to think about gender, race, and class in ways that don't obscure or underplay their effects on one another."[39] Still, the task is to develop paradigms that can admit these crosscurrents and that can reach out to women of color and perhaps also to men.

Women who value familial and ethnic solidarity may find it especially difficult to rally to the feminist cause without feeling divided or without being accused of betrayal, especially when the men in their ethnic groups also face social iniquities. Kingston, for instance, has tried throughout her work to mediate between affirming her ethnic heritage and undermining patriarchy. But she feels that identification with Asian men at times inhibits an equally strong feminist impulse. Such split loyalties apparently prompted her to publish *The Woman Warrior* and *China Men* separately, though they were conceived and written together as an "interlocking story." Lest the men's stories "undercut the feminist viewpoint," she separated the female and the male stories into two books. She says, "I care about men ... as much as I care about women ... Given the present state of affairs, perhaps men's and women's experiences have to be dealt with separately for now, until more auspicious times are with us."[40]

Yet such separation has its dangers, particularly if it means that men and women will continue to work in opposing directions, as reflected in the divergences between the proponents of the Asian heroic tradition and Asian American feminists. Feminist ideas have made little inroad in the writing of the *Aiiieeeee!* editors, who continue to operate within patriarchal grids. White feminists, on the other hand, are often oblivious to the fact that there are other groups besides women who have been "feminized" and puzzled when women of color do not readily rally to their camp.

The recent shift from feminist studies to gender studies suggests that the time has come to look at women and men together. I hope that the shift will also entice both men and women to do the looking and, by so doing, strengthen the alliance between gender studies and ethnic studies. Lest feminist criticism remain in the wilderness, white scholars must reckon with race and class as integral experiences for both men and women, and acknowledge that not only female voices but the voices of many men of color have been historically silenced or dismissed. Expanding the feminist frame of reference will allow certain existing theories to be interrogated or reformulated.[41] Asian American men need to be wary of certain pitfalls in using what Foucault calls "reverse discourse," in demanding legitimacy "in the same vocabulary, using the same categories by which [they were] disqualified."[42] The ones who can be recruited into the field of gender studies may someday see feminists as allies rather than adversaries, and proceed to dismantle not just white but also male supremacy. Women of color should not have to undergo a self-division resulting from having to choose between female and ethnic identities. Chinese American women writers may find a way to negotiate the tangle of sexual and racial politics in all its intricacies, not just out of a desire for "revenge" but also out of a sense of "loyalty." If we ask them to write with a vigilant eye against possible misappropriation by white readers or against possible offense to "Asian American manhood," however, we will end up implicitly sustaining racial and sexual hierarchies. All of us need to be conscious of our "complicity with the gender ideologies" of patriarchy, whatever its origins, and to work toward notions of gender and ethnicity that are nonhierarchical, nonbinary, and nonprescriptive; that can embrace tensions rather than perpetuate divisions.[43] To reclaim cultural traditions without getting bogged down in the mire of traditional constraints, to attack stereotypes without falling prey to their binary opposites, to chart new topographies for manliness and womanliness, will surely demand genuine heroism.

Notes

1. Research for this essay is funded in part by an Academic Senate grant and a grant from the Institute of American Cultures and the Asian American Studies Center, UCLA. I wish to thank the many whose help, criticism, and encouragement have sustained me through the mentally embattled period of writing this essay: Kim Crenshaw, Donald Goellnicht, Marianne Hirsch, Evelyn Fox Keller, Elaine Kim, Elizabeth Kim, Ken Lincoln, Gerard Maré, Rosalind Melis, Jeff Spielberg, Sau-iing Wong, Richard Yarborough, and Stan Yogi.

   A version of this article was delivered at the 1989 MLA Convention in Washington, DC. My title alludes not only to Maxine Hong Kingston's *The Woman Warrior* and *China Men* but also Frank Chin's *The Chickencoop Chinaman* and *The Chinaman Pacific & Frisco R. Co.* The term "Chinamen" has acquired divers connotations through time: "In the early days of Chinese American history, men called themselves 'Chinamen' just as other newcomers called themselves 'Englishmen' or 'Frenchmen': the term distinguished them from the 'Chinese' who remained citizens of China, and also showed that they were not recognized as Americans.

Later, of course, it became an insult. Young Chinese Americans today are reclaiming the word because of its political and historical precision, and are demanding that it be said with dignity and not for name-calling" (Kingston, "San Francisco's Chinatown: A View from the Other Side of Arnold Genthe's Camera," *American Heritage* [Dec. 1978]: 37). In my article the term refers exclusively to men.

2. The devaluation of daughters is a theme explored in *The Woman Warrior* (1976; New York: Vintage, 1977); as this book suggests, this aspect of patriarchy is upheld no less by women than by men. The "emasculation" of Chinese American men is addressed in *China Men* (1980; New York: Ballantine, 1981), in which Kingston attempts to reclaim the founders of Chinese America. Subsequent page references to these two books will appear in the text. Detailed accounts of early Chinese immigrant history can be found in Victor G. Nee and Brett De Bary Nee, *Longtime Californ': A Documentary Study of an American Chinatown* (1973; New York: Pantheon, 1981); and Ronald Takaki, *Strangers from a Different Shore: A History of Asian Americans* (Boston: Little Brown, 1989), 79-131.

3. See Edward Said, *Orientalism* (New York: Vintage, 1979). Although Said focuses on French and British representations of the Middle East, many of his insights also apply to American perceptions of the Far East.

4. "Asian American Writers: A Bibliographical Review," *American Studies International* 22.2 (Oct. 1984): 64.

5. "Confessions of the Chinatown Cowboy," *Bulletin of Concerned Asian Scholars* 4.3 (1972): 66.

6. "Racist Love," *Seeing through Shuck,* ed. Richard Kostelanetz (New York: Ballantine, 1972), 65, 79. Although the cinematic image of Bruce Lee as a Kung-fu master might have somewhat countered the feminine representations of Chinese American men, his role in the only one Hollywood film in which he appeared before he died was, in Elaine Kim's words, "less a human being than a fighting machine" ("Asian Americans and American popular Culture," *Dictionary of Asian American History,* ed. Hyung-Chan Kim [New York: Greenwood Press, 1986], 107).

7. "Racist Love," 69.

8. "Asian American Writers: A Bibliographical Review," 64.

9. "Racist Love," 68. The five writers under discussion are Pardee Lowe, Jade Snow Wong, Virginia Lee, Betty Lee Sung, and Diana Chang.

10. Similar objections to the passage have been raised by Merle Woo in "Letter to Ma," *This*

Bridge Called my Back: Writings by Radical Women of Color, ed. Cherríe Moraga and Gloria Anzaldúa (1981; New York: Kitchen Table, 1983), 145; and Elaine Kim in *Asian American Literature: An Introduction to the Writings and Their Social Context* (Philadelphia: Temple UP, 1982), 189. Richard Yarborough delineates a somewhat parallel conundrum about manhood faced by African American writers in the nineteenth century and which, I believe, persists to some extent to this day; see "Race, Violence, and Manhood: The Masculine Ideal in Frederick Douglass's 'Heroic Slave,'" forthcoming in *Frederick Douglass: New Literary and Historical Essays,* ed. Eric J. Sundquist (Cambridge, MA: Cambridge UP). There is, however, an important difference between the dilemma faced by the African American men and that faced by Asian American men. While writers such as William Wells Brown and Frederick Douglass tried to reconcile the white inscription of the militant and sensual Negro and the white ideal of heroic manhood, several Chinese American male writers are trying to disprove the white stereotype of the passive and effeminate Asian by invoking its binary opposite.

11. *Aiiieeeee! An Anthology of Asian-American Writers* (1974; Washington: Howard UP, 1983), xxxviii; *The Big Aiiieeeee! An Anthology of Asian American Writers* (New York: New American Library, forthcoming). All the Asian classics cited are available in English translations: Sun Tzu, *The Art of War*, trans. Samuel B. Griffith (London: Oxford UP, 1963); Shi Nai'an and Luo Guanzhong, *Outlaws of the Marsh [The Water Margin],* trans. Sidney Shapiro (jointly published by Beijing: Foreign Language P and Bloomington: Indiana UP, 1981); Luo Guan-Zhong, *Romance of the Three Kingdoms,* trans. C. H. Brewitt-Taylor (Singapore: Graham Brash, 1986), 2 vols.; Wu Ch'eng-en, *Journey to the West,* trans. Anthony Yu (Chicago: U of Chicago P, 1980), 4 vols.; Takeda Izumo, Miyoshi Shoraku, and Namiki Senryu, *Chushingura (The Treasury of Loyal Retainers),* trans. Donald Keene (New York: Columbia UP, 1971). I would like to thank Frank Chin for allowing me to see an early draft of *The Big Aiiieeeee!.* For a foretaste of his exposition of the Chinese heroic tradition, see "This is Not an Autobiography," *Genre* 18 (1985): 109-30.

12. The feminist works that come to mind include Paula Gunn Allen, *The Sacred Hoop: Recovering the Feminine in American Indian Traditions* (Boston: Beacon: 1986); Nina Auerbach, *Communities of Women: An Idea in Fiction* (Cambridge: Harvard UP, 1978); Zillah R. Eisenstein, *The Radical Future of Liberal Feminism* (New York: Longman, 1981); Carol Gilligan, *In a Different Voice: Psychological Theory and Women's Development* (Cambridge: Harvard UP, 1982); Christa Wolf, *Cassandra: A Novel and Four Essays,* trans. Jan van Heurck (New York: Farrar, 1984). The Chinese maxims appear in the introduction to *The Big*

Aiiieeeee! (draft) and are quoted with the editors' permission. The same maxims are cited in Frank Chin, "This Is Not an Autobiography."

13. Chin, "This Is Not An Autobiography," 112, 122, 130.

14. "All of a Piece: Women's Poetry and Autobiography," *Life/Lines: Theorizing Women's Autobiography*, ed. Bella Brodzki and Celeste Schenck (Ithaca: Cornell UP, 1988), 286. See also Estelle Jelinek, ed., *Women's Autobiography: Essays in Criticism* (Bloomington: Indiana UP, 1980); Donna Stanton, *The Female Autograph* (New York: New York Literary Forum, 1984); Sidonie Smith, *Poetics of Women's Autobiography: Marginality and the Fictions of Self-Representation* (Bloomington: Indiana UP, 1987).

15. "The Most Popular Book in China," *Quilt* 4, ed. Ishmael Reed and Al Young (Berkeley: Quilt, 1984), 12. The essay is republished as the "Afterword" in *The Chinaman Pacific & Frisco R R. Co.* The literary duel between Chin, a self-styled "Chinatown Cowboy," and Kingston, an undisguised feminist, closely parallels the paper war between Ishmael Reed and Alice Walker.

16. "The Mysterious West," *New York Review of Books*, 28 April 1977: 41.

17. "Critic of Admirer Sees Dumb Racist," *San Francisco Journal*, 11 May 1977: 20.

18. "Autobiography as Guided Chinatown Tour?," *American Lives: Essays in Multicultural American Autobiography*, ed. James Robert Payne (Knoxville: U of Tennessee P, forthcoming). See also Deborah Woo, "The Ethnic Writer and the Burden of 'Dual Authenticity': The Dilemma of Maxine Hong Kingston," forthcoming in *Amerasia Journal*. Reviews by Chinese American women who identify strongly with Kingston's protagonist include Nellie Wong, "The Woman Warrior," *Bridge* (Winter 1978): 46-48; and Suzi Wong, review of *The Woman Warrior, Amerasia Journal* 4.1 (1977): 165-167.

19. "Gender and Genre Anxiety: Elizabeth Barrett Browning and H. D. as Epic Poets," *Tulsa Studies in Women's Literature* 5.2 (Fall 1986): 203-228.

20. Furthermore, a work highlighting sexism within an ethnic community is generally more palatable to the reading public than a work that condemns racism. *The Woman Warrior* addresses both forms of oppression, but critics have focused almost exclusively on its feminist themes.

21. Susanne Juhasz argues that because women have traditionally lived a "kind of private life, that of the imagination, which has special significance due to the outright conflict between societal possibility and imaginative possibility, [Kingston] makes autobiography from fiction, from fantasy, from forms that have conventionally belonged to the novel" ('Towards a Theory of Form in Feminist Autobiography.' *International Journal of Women's Studies* 2.1 [1979]: 62).

22. Cf, similar critical responses in the African American community provoked by Alice Walker's *The Color Purple* and Toni Morrison's *Beloved*.

    Although I limit my discussion to sexual politics in Chinese America, Asian American women are just as vulnerable to white sexism, as the denigrating stereotypes discussed by Kim earlier suggest.

23. Li Ju-Chen, *Flowers in the Mirror*, trans. and ed. Lin Tai-Yi (London: Peter Owen, 1965).

24. A recent case has been made into a powerful public television documentary: "Who Killed Vincent Chin?" (directed by Renee Tajima and Christine Choy, 1989). Chin, who punched a white auto-worker in Detroit in response to his racial slurs, was subsequently battered to death by the worker and his stepson with a baseball bat.

25. The interview was conducted by Kay Bonetti for the American Audio Prose Library (Columbia, MO, 1986).

    Jonathan Culler has discussed the various implications, for both sexes, of "Reading as a Woman" (*On Deconstruction: Theory and Criticism after Structuralism* [Ithaca: Cornell UP, 1982], 43-64); see also *Men in Feminism*, ed. Alice Jardine and Paul Smith (New York: Methuen, 1987).

26. The other modes are found in works as diverse as T'ao Ch'ien's poems (pastoral), Ch'u Yuan's *Li sao* (elegiac), selected writing by Lao Tzu and Chuang Tzu (metaphysical), and P'u Sung-Iing's *Liao-Chai Chih I* (Gothic). (My thanks to Shu-mei Shih and Adam Schorr for helping me with part of the romanization.) One must bear in mind, however, that Asian and Western generic terms often fail to correspond. For example, what the *Aiiieeeee!* editors call "epics" are loosely classified as "novels" in Chinese literature.

27. Epic heroes, according C. M. Bowra, are "the champions of man's ambitions" seeking to "win as far as possible a self-sufficient manhood" (*Heroic Poetry* [London: Macmillan, 1952], 14). Their Chinese counteiparts are no exception.

28. Benjamin R. Tong argues that the uneducated Cantonese peasants who comprised the majority of early Chinese immigrants were not docile but venturesome and rebellious, that putative Chinese traits such as meekness and obedience to authority were in fact "reactivated" in America in response to white racism ("The Ghetto of the Mind." *Amerasia Journal* 1.3 [1971]: 1-31). Chin, who basically agrees with Tong, also attributes the submissive and "unheroic" traits of Chinese Americans to Christianity ("This Is Not An Autobiography"). While Tong and Chin are right in distinguishing the Cantonese folk culture of the early immigrants from the classical tradition of the literati, they underestimate the extent to which mainstream

Chinese thought infiltrated Cantonese folk imagination, wherein the heroic ethos coexists with Buddhist beliefs and Confucian teachings (which do counsel self-restraint and obedience to parental and state authority). To attribute the "submissive" traits of Chinese Americans entirely to white racism or to Christianity is to discount the complexity and the rich contradictions of the Cantonese culture and the resourceful flexibility and adaptability of the early immigrants.

29. "This Is Not an Autobiography," 127.

30. Conflicting attitudes toward Homeric war heroes are discussed in Katherine Callen King, *Achilles: Paradigms of the War Hero from Homer to the Middle Ages* (Berkeley: U of California P, 1987). Pacifist or at least anti-killing sentiments can be found in the very works deemed "heroic" by Chin and the editors. *Romance of the Three Kingdoms* not only dramatizes the senseless deaths and the ravages of war but also betrays a wishful longing for peace and unity, impossible under the division of "three kingdoms." Even *The Art of War* sets benevolence above violence and discourages actual fighting and killing: "To subdue the enemy without fighting is the acme of skill" (77).

31. " 'Don't Tell': Imposed Silences in *The Color Purple* and *The Woman Warrior*." *PMLA* (March 1988): 166. I must add, however, that paradoxes about manhood inform Chinese as well as American cultures. The "contradictions inherent in the bourgeois male ideal" is pointed out by Yarborough: "the use of physical force is, at some levels, antithetical to the middle-class privileging of self-restraint and reason: yet an important component of conventional concepts of male courage is the willingness to use force" ("Race, Violence, and Manhood: The Masculine Ideal in Frederick Douglass's 'Heroic Slave' "). Similarly, two opposing ideals of manhood coexist in Chinese culture, that of a civil scholar who would never stoop to violence and that of a fearless warrior who would not brook insult or injustice. Popular Cantonese maxims such as "a superior man would only move his mouth but not his hands" (i.e. would never resort to physical combat) and "he who does not take revenge is not a superior man" exemplify the contradictions.

32. Interview conducted by Kay Bonetti.

33. *Tripmaster Monkey: His Fake Book* (New York: Knopf, 1989), 348.

34. I am aware that a forceful response to oppression is sometimes necessary, that it is much easier for those who have never encountered physical blows and gunshots to maintain faith in nonviolent resistance. My own faith was somewhat shaken while watching the tragedy of Tiananmen on television; on the other hand, the image of the lone Chinese man standing in front of army tanks reinforced my belief that there is another form of heroism that far excels

brute force.

35. Lee Rainwater and William L. Yancey, *The Moynikan Report and the Politics of Controversy* (Cambridge: M.I.T. Press, 1967), 88 (p. 42) in the original report by Daniel Patrick Moynihan).

36. "On the Issue of Roles," *The Black Woman: An Anthology,* ed. Toni Cade (York, ON: Mentor-NAL, 1970), 103; see also Bell Hooks, *Ain'f I a Woman: Black Women and Feminism* (Boston: South End Press, 1981), 87-117.

37. *Lenin and Philosophy and Other Essays* (New York: Monthly Review Press, 1971), 174—183.

38. Of course, Asians are not all alike, and most generalizations are ultimately misleading. Elaine Kim pointed out to me that "It's popularly thought that Japanese strive for peaceful resolution of conflict and achievement of consensus while Koreans — for material as much as metaphysical reasons — seem at times to encourage combativeness in one another" (personal correspondence, quoted with permission). Differences within each national group are no less pronounced.

39. *Inessential Woman: Problems of Exclusion in Feminist Thought* (Boston: Beacon, 1988), 115. I omitted class from my discussion only because it is not at the center of the literary debate.

40. Elaine Kim, *Asian American Literature: An Introduction to the Writings and Their Social Context* (Philadelphia: Temple UP, 1982), 209.

41. Donald Goellnicht, for instance, has argued that a girl from a racial minority "experiences not a single, but a double subject split; first, when she becomes aware of the gendered position constructed for her by the symbolic language of patriarchy; and second, when she recognizes that discursively and socially constructed positions of racial difference also obtain …[that] the 'fathers' of her racial and cultural group are silenced and degraded by the Laws of the Ruling Fathers" ("Father Land and/or Mother Tongue: The Divided Female Subject in *The Woman Warrior* and *Obasan*" paper delivered at the MLA Convention, 1988).

42. *The History of Sexuality,* vol. 1, trans. Robert Hurley (New York: Vintage, 1980), 101.

43. Teresa de Lauretis, *Technologies of Gender: Essays on Theory, Film, and Fiction* (Bloomington: Indiana UP, 1987), 11.

3

Heterogeneity, Hybridity, Multiplicity: Marking Asian American Differences
美国亚裔的内部差异：异质·杂糅·多元

Lisa Lowe

评论家简介

骆里山（Lisa Lowe），美国加利福尼亚大学圣克鲁斯分校文学博士，现为美国塔夫茨大学英语系教授。研究领域包括比较文学、大英帝国研究、美亚研究、跨国女权主义研究等。出版专著有《四大洲的亲密关系》（*The Intimacies of Four Continents*, 2015)、《移民法案：美国亚裔文化政治》(*Immigrant Acts: On Asian American Cultural Politics, 1996*)、《关键地形：法国和英国的东方主义》(*Critical Terrains: French and British Orientalisms*, 1991)。合著有《资本阴影下的文化政治》(*The Politics of Culture in the Shadow of Capital*, 1997)。除本书收录的论文，其他代表性论文有:《全球化》，收于《美国文化研究关键词》（第二版）一书（"Globalization," *Keywords for American Cultural Studies*, 2014);《推算国家和帝国》，收于《布莱克韦尔美国研究指南》一书（"Reckoning Nation and Empire," *Blackwell Companion to American Studies*, 2010);《全球化的隐喻》，收于《跨学科性和社会正义》一书（"Metaphors of Globalization," *Interdisciplinarity and Social Justice*, 2010）等。

文章简介

　　本文由文学评论家骆里山 1991 年发表于期刊《离散》，后被收入其专著《移民法案：美国亚裔文化政治》。这篇文章是美国亚裔文学研究界引用率最高的文献之一，也是被收录于相关评论集次数最多的文章之一，已成为族裔文学研究的经典文献。剖析与理解美国亚裔内部的差异性是研究美国亚裔主体性、美国亚裔文学与文化的首要问题。文章以"异质·杂糅·多元"三个关键词为纲，充分论证了族裔文学研究应该打破主流与边缘的对立，认识到身份政治的局限性，改变对亚裔政治身份的本质主义认知，以达到揭示亚裔主体复杂性的目的。文章为解释亚裔内部文化、社会与政治构成的差异性提出了一套全新的理论框架，不仅为阶级、性别、语言的研究拓展了空间，也为离散与跨国研究提供了理论支持。这一新的理论视角，将美国亚裔研究内部原先处于边缘地位的学术研究、将采用非主流形式与体裁创作的文学作品均置于与主流研究与创作平等的地位，从而为美国亚裔的研究与创作注入了开放、流动与多元的能量。

文章出处：*Diaspora:A Journal of Transnational Studies*, vol.l, no. l,1991; pp. 24-44.

Heterogeneity, Hybridity, Multiplicity: Marking Asian American Differences

Lisa Lowe

In a recent poem by Janice Mirikitani, a Japanese-American *nisei* woman describes her *sansei* daughter's rebellion.[1] The daughter's denial of Japanese-American culture and its particular notions of femininity reminds the *nisei* speaker that she, too, has denied her antecedents, rebelling against her own more traditional *issei* mother:

> I want to break tradition　　unlock this room
> 　　where women dress in the dark.
> 　　Discover the lies my mother told me.
> 　　The lies that we are small and powerless
> 　　that our possibilities must be compressed
> 　　to the size of pearls, displayed only as
> 　　passive chokers, charms around our neck.
>
> Break Tradition.
> 　　I want to tell my daughter of this room
> 　　of myself
> 　　filled with tears of shakuhatchi,
> 　　..............
> 　　poems about madness,
> 　　sounds shaken from barbed wire and
> 　　goodbyes and miracles of survival.
> 　　This room of open window where daring ones escape.
> My daughter denies she is like me ...
> 　　her pouting ruby lips, her skirts
> 　　swaying to salsa, teena marie and the stones,
> 　　her thighs displayed in carnivals of color.
> 　　I do not know the contents of her room.
> She mirrors my aging.
> She is breaking tradition. (9)

The *nisei* speaker repudiates the repressive confinements of her *issei* mother: the disciplining of the female body, the tedious practice of diminution, the silences of obedience. In turn, the crises that have shaped the *nisei* speaker — internment camps, sounds of threatening madness — are unknown to, and unheard by, her *sansei* teenage daughter. The three generations of Japanese immigrant women in this poem are separated by their different histories and by different conceptions of what it means to be female and Japanese. The poet who writes "I do not know the contents of her room" registers these separations as "breaking tradition."

In another poem, by Lydia Lowe, Chinese women workers are divided also by generation, but even more powerfully by class and language. The speaker is a young Chinese-American who supervises an older Chinese woman in a textile factory.

> The long bell blared,
> and then the *lo-ban*
> made me search all your bags
> before you could leave.
>
> Inside he sighed
> about slow work, fast hands,
> missing spools of thread —
> and I said nothing.
>
> I remember that day
> you came in to show me
> I added your tickets six zippers short.
> It was just a mistake.
>
> You squinted down
> at the check in your hands
> like an old village woman peers
> at some magician's trick.
>
> That afternoon
> when you thrust me your bags
> I couldn't look or raise my face.
> *Doi m-jyu.*
>
> Eyes on the ground,
> I could only see
> one shoe kicking against the other. (29)

This poem, too, invokes the breaking of tradition, although it thematizes another sort of stratification among Asian women: the structure of the factory places the English-speaking younger woman above the Cantonese-speaking older one. Economic relations in capitalist society force the young supervisor to discipline her elders, and she is acutely ashamed that her required behavior does not demonstrate the respect traditionally owed to parents and elders. Thus, both poems foreground commonly thematized *topoi* of diasporan cultures: the disruption and distortion of traditional cultural practices — like the practice of parental sacrifice and filial duty, or the practice of respecting hierarchies of age — not only as a consequence of immigration to the United States, but as a part of entering a society with different class stratifications and different constructions of gender roles. Some Asian American discussions cast the disruption of tradition as loss and represent the loss in terms of regret and shame, as in the latter poem. Alternatively, the traditional practices of family continuity and hierarchy may be figured as oppressively confining, as in Mirikitani's poem, in which the two generations of daughters contest the more restrictive female roles of the former generations. In either case, many Asian American discussions portray immigration and relocation to the United States in terms of a loss of the "original" culture in exchange for the new "American" culture.

In many Asian American novels, the question of the loss or transmission of the "original" culture is frequently represented in a family narrative, figured as generational conflict between the Chinese-born first generation and the American-born second generation.[2] Louis Chu's 1961 novel *Eat a Bowl of Tea,* for example, allegorizes in the conflicted relationship between father and son the differences between "native" Chinese values and the new "westernized" culture of Chinese-Americans. Other novels have taken up this generational theme; one way to read Maxine Hong Kingston's *The Woman Warrior* (1975) or Amy Tan's recent *The Joy Luck Club* (1989) is to understand them as versions of this generational model of culture, refigured in feminine terms, between mothers and daughters. However, I will argue that interpreting Asian American culture exclusively in terms of the master narratives of generational conflict and filial relation essentializes Asian American culture, obscuring the particularities and incommensurabilities of class, gender, and national diversities among Asians; the reduction of ethnic cultural politics to struggles between first and second generations displaces (and privatizes) inter-community differences into a familial opposition. To avoid this homogenizing of Asian Americans as exclusively hierarchical and familial, I would contextualize the "vertical" generational model of culture with the more "horizontal" relationship represented in Diana Chang's "The Oriental Contingent." In Chang's short story, two young women avoid the discussion of their Chinese backgrounds because each desperately fears that the other is "more Chinese," more "authentically" tied to the original culture. The narrator, Connie, is certain that her friend Lisa "never referred to her own background because it was more Chinese than Connie's, and therefore of a higher order. She was tact incarnate. All along, she had been going out of her way not to embarrass Connie. Yes, yes. Her assurance was definitely uppercrust (perhaps her father had been in the diplomatic service), and her offhand didacticness, her lack of self-doubt, was indeed characteristically Chinese-Chinese" (173). Connie feels ashamed because she assumes herself to be "a failed Chinese"; she fantasizes that Lisa was born in China, visits there frequently, and privately disdains Chinese-Americans. Her assumptions about Lisa prove to be quite wrong, however; Lisa is even more critical of herself for "not being genuine." For Lisa, as Connie eventually discovers, was born in Buffalo and was adopted by non-Chinese-American parents; lacking an immediate connection to Chinese culture, Lisa projects upon all Chinese the authority of being "more Chinese." Lisa confesses to Connie at the end of the story: "The only time I feel Chinese is when I'm embarrassed I'm not more Chinese — which is a totally Chinese reflex I'd give anything to be rid of!" (176). Chang's story portrays two women polarized by the degree to which they have each internalized a cultural definition of "Chineseness" as pure and fixed, in which any deviation is constructed as less, lower, and shameful. Rather than confirming the cultural model in which "ethnicity" is passed from generation to generation, Chang's story explores the "ethnic" relationship between women of the same generation. Lisa and Connie are ultimately able to reduce one another's guilt at not being "Chinese enough"; in one another they are able to find a common frame of reference. The story suggests that the making of Chinese-American culture — how ethnicity is imagined, practiced, continued — is worked out as much between ourselves and our communities as it is transmitted from one generation to another.

In this sense, Asian American discussions of ethnicity are far from uniform or consistent; rather, these discussions contain a wide spectrum of articulations that includes, at one end, the desire for an identity represented by a fixed profile of ethnic traits, and at another, challenges to the very notions of identity and singularity which celebrate ethnicity as a fluctuating composition of differences, intersections, and incommensurabilities. These latter efforts attempt to define ethnicity in a manner that accounts not only for cultural inheritance, but for active cultural construction, as well. In other words, they suggest that the making of Asian American culture may be a much "messier" process than unmediated vertical transmission from one generation to another, including practices that are partly inherited and partly modified, as well as partly invented.[3] As the narrator of *The Woman Warrior* suggests, perhaps one of the more important stories of Asian American experience is about the process of receiving, refiguring, and rewriting cultural traditions. She asks: "Chinese-Americans, when you try to understand what things in you are Chinese, how do you separate what is peculiar to childhood, to poverty, insanities, one family, your mother who marked your growing with stories, from what is Chinese? What is Chinese tradition and what is the movies?" (6). Or the dilemma of cultural syncretism might be posed in an interrogative version of the uncle's impromptu proverb in Wayne Wang's film *Dim Sum:* "You can take the girl out of Chinatown, but can you take the Chinatown out of the girl?" For rather than representing a fixed, discrete culture, "Chinatown" is itself the very emblem of fluctuating demographics, languages, and populations.[4]

I begin my article with these particular examples drawn from Asian American cultural texts in order to observe that what is referred to as "Asian America" is clearly a heterogeneous entity. From the perspective of the majority culture, Asian Americans may very well be constructed as different from, and other than, Euro-Americans. But from the perspectives of Asian Americans, we are perhaps even more different, more diverse, among ourselves: being men and women at different distances and generations from our "original" Asian cultures — cultures as different as Chinese, Japanese, Korean, Filipino, Indian, and Vietnamese — Asian Americans are born in the United States and born in Asia; of exclusively Asian parents and of mixed race; urban and rural; refugee and nonrefugee; communist-identified and anticommunist; fluent in English and non-English speaking, educated and working class. As with other diasporas in the United States, the Asian immigrant collectivity is unstable and changeable, with its cohesion complicated by intergenerationality, by various degrees of identification and relation to a "homeland," and by different extents of assimilation to and distinction from "majority culture" in the United States. Further, the historical contexts of particular waves of immigration within single groups contrast with one another; the Japanese-Americans who were interned during World War II encountered quite different social and economic barriers than those from Japan who arrive in southern California today. And the composition of different waves of immigrants differs in gender, class, and region. For example, the first groups of Chinese immigrants to the United States in 1850 were from four villages in Canton province, male by a ratio of 10 to 1, and largely of peasant backgrounds; the more recent Chinese immigrants are from Hong Kong, Taiwan, or Chinese mainland (themselves quite heterogeneous and of discontinuous "origins"), or from the Chinese diaspora in other parts of Asia, such as Malaysia, or Singapore, and they are more often educated and middle-class men and women.[5] Further, once arriving in the United States, very few Asian immigrant cultures remain discrete, inpenetrable communities. The more recent groups mix, in varying degrees, with segments of the existing groups; Asian Americans may intermarry with other ethnic groups, live in neighborhoods adjacent to them, or work in the same businesses and on the same factory assembly lines. The boundaries and definitions of Asian American culture are continually shifting and being contested from pressures both "inside" and "outside" the Asian origin community.

I stress heterogeneity, hybridity, and multiplicity in the characterization of Asian American culture as part of a twofold argument about cultural politics, the ultimate aim of that argument being to disrupt the current hegemonic relationship between "dominant" and "minority" positions. On the one hand, my observation that Asian Americans are heterogeneous is part of a strategy to destabilize the dominant discursive construction and determination of Asian Americans as a homogeneous group. Throughout the late nineteenth and early twentieth centuries, Asian immigration to the United States was managed by exclusion acts and quotas that relied upon racialist constructions of Asians as homogeneous;[6] the "model minority" myth and the informal quotas discriminating against Asians in university admissions policies are contemporary versions of this homogenization of Asians.[7] On the other hand, I underscore Asian American heterogeneities (particularly class, gender, and national differences among Asians) to contribute to a dialogue within Asian American discourse, to negotiate with those modes of argumentation that continue to uphold a politics based on ethnic "identity." In this sense, I argue for the Asian American necessity — politically, intellectually, and personally — to organize, resist, and theorize as Asian Americans, but at the same time I inscribe this necessity within a discussion of the risks of a cultural politics that relies upon the construction of sameness and the exclusion of differences.

1

The first reason to emphasize the dynamic fluctuation and heterogeneity of Asian American culture is to release our understandings of either the "dominant" or the emergent "minority" cultures as discrete, fixed, or homogeneous, and to arrive at a different conception of the general political terrain of culture in California, a useful focus for this examination since it has become commonplace to consider it an "ethnic state," embodying a new phenomenon of cultural adjacency and admixture.[8] For if minority immigrant cultures are perpetually changing — in their composition, configuration, and signifying practices, as well as in their relations to one another — it follows that the "majority" or dominant culture, with which minority cultures are in continual relation, is also unstable and unclosed. The suggestion that the general social terrain of culture is open, plural, and dynamic reorients our understanding of what "cultural hegemony" is and how it works in contemporary California. It permits us to theorize about the roles that ethnic immigrant groups play in the making and unmaking of culture — and how these minority discourses challenge the existing structure of power, the existing hegemony.[9] We should remember that Antonio Gramsci writes about *hegemony* as not simply political or economic forms of rule but as the entire process of dissent and compromise through which a particular group is able to determine the political, cultural, and ideological character of a state (*Selections*). Hegemony does not refer exclusively to the process by which a dominant formation exercises its influence but refers equally to the process through which minority groups organize and contest any specific hegemony.[10] The reality of any specific hegemony is that, while it may be for the moment dominant, it is never absolute or conclusive. Hegemony, in Gramsci's thought, is a concept that describes both the social processes through which a particular dominance is maintained and those through which that dominance is challenged and new forces are articulated. When a hegemony representing the interests of a dominant group exists, it is always within the context of resistances from emerging "subaltern" groups.[11] We might say that hegemony is not only the political process by which a particular group constitutes itself as "the one" or "the majority" in relation to which "minorities" are defined and know themselves to be "other," but it is equally the process by which positions of otherness may ally and constitute a new majority, a "counterhegemony."[12]

The subaltern classes are, in Gramsci's definition, prehegemonic, not unified groups, whose histories are fragmented, episodic and identifiable only from a point of historical hindsight. They may go through different phases when they are subject to the activity of ruling groups, may articulate their demands through existing parties, and then may themselves produce new parties; in *The Prison Notebooks*, Gramsci describes a final phase at which the "formations [of the subaltern classes] assert integral autonomy" (52). The definition of the subaltern groups includes some noteworthy observations for our understanding of the roles of racial and ethnic immigrant groups in the United States. The assertion that the significant practices of the subaltern groups may not be understood as hegemonic until they are viewed with historical hindsight is interesting, for it suggests that some of the most powerful practices may not always be the explicitly oppositional ones, may not be understood by contemporaries, and may be less overt and recognizable than others. Provocative, too, is the idea that the subaltern classes are by definition "not unified"; that is, the subaltern is not a fixed, unified force of a single character. Rather, the assertion of "integral autonomy" by not unified classes suggests a coordination of distinct, yet allied, positions, practices, and movements — class-identified and not class-identified, in parties and not, ethnic-based and gender-based — each in its own not necessarily equivalent manner transforming and disrupting the apparatuses of a specific hegemony. The independent forms and locations of cultural challenge — ideological, as well as economic and political — constitute what Gramsci calls a "new historical bloc," a new set of relationships that together embody a different hegemony and a different balance of power. In this sense, we have in the growing and shifting ethnic minority populations in California an active example of this new historical bloc described by Gramsci; and in the negotiations between these ethnic groups and the existing majority over what interests precisely constitute the "majority," we have an illustration of the concept of hegemony, not in the more commonly accepted sense of "hegemony-maintenance," but in the often ignored sense of "hegemony-creation."[13] The observation that the Asian American community and other ethnic immigrant communities are heterogeneous lays the foundation for several political operations: first, by shifting, multiplying, and reconceiving the construction of society as composed of two numerically overdetermined camps called the majority and the minority, cultural politics is recast so as to account for a multiplicity of various, nonequivalent groups, one of which is Asian Americans. Second, the conception of ethnicity as heterogeneous provides a position for Asian Americans that is both ethnically specific, yet simultaneously uneven and unclosed; Asian Americans can articulate distinct group demands based on our particular histories of exclusion, but the redefined lack of closure — which reveals rather than conceals differences — opens political lines of affiliation with other groups (labor unions, other racial and ethnic groups, and gay, lesbian, and feminist groups) in the challenge to specific forms of domination insofar as they share common features.

2

In regard to the practice of "identity politics" within Asian American discourse, the articulation of an "Asian American identity" as an organizing tool has provided a concept of political unity that enables diverse Asian groups to understand our unequal circumstances and histories as being related; likewise, the building of "Asian American culture" is crucial, for it articulates and empowers our multicultural, multilingual Asian origin community vis-à-vis the institutions and apparatuses that exclude and marginalize us. But I want to suggest that essentializing Asian American identity and suppressing our differences — of national origin, generation, gender, party, class — risks particular dangers: not only does it underestimate the differences and hybridities among Asians, but it also inadvertently supports the racist discourse that constructs

Asians as a homogeneous group, that implies we are "all alike" and conform to "types"; in this respect, a politics based exclusively on ethnic identity willingly accepts the terms of the dominant logic that organizes the heterogeneous picture of racial and ethnic diversity into a binary schema of "the one" and "the other." The essentializing of Asian American identity also reproduces oppositions that subsume other nondominant terms in the same way that Asians and other groups are disenfranchised by the dominant culture: to the degree that the discourse generalizes Asian American identity as male, women are rendered invisible; or to the extent that Chinese are presumed to be exemplary of all Asians, the importance of other Asian groups is ignored. In this sense, a politics based on ethnic identity facilitates the displacement of intercommunity differences — between men and women, or between workers and managers into a false opposition of "nationalism" and "assimilation." We have an example of this in recent debates where Asian American feminists who challenge Asian American sexism are cast as "assimilationist," as betraying Asian American "nationalism."

To the extent that Asian American discourse articulates an identity in reaction to the dominant culture's stereotype, even to refute it, I believe the discourse may remain bound to, and overdetermined by, the logic of the dominant culture. In accepting the binary terms ("white" and "non-white," or "majority" and "minority") that structure institutional policies about ethnicity, we forget that these binary schemas are not neutral descriptions. Binary constructions of difference use a logic that prioritizes the first term and subordinates the second; whether the pair "difference" and "sameness" is figured as a binary synthesis that considers "difference" as always contained within the "same," or that conceives of the pair as an opposition in which "difference" structurally implies "sameness" as its complement, it is important to see each of these figurations as versions of the same binary logic. My argument for heterogeneity seeks to challenge the conception of difference as exclusively structured by a binary opposition between two terms by proposing instead another notion of difference that takes seriously the conditions of heterogeneity, multiplicity, and nonequivalence. I submit that the most exclusive construction of Asian American identity — which presumes masculinity, American birth, and speaking English — is at odds with the formation of important political alliances and affiliations with other groups across racial and ethnic, gender, sexuality, and class lines. An essentialized identity is an obstacle to Asian American women allying with other women of color, for example, and it can discourage laboring Asian Americans from joining unions with workers of other colors. It can short-circuit potential alliances against the dominant structures of power in the name of subordinating "divisive" issues to *the* national question.

Some of the limits of identity politics are discussed most pointedly by Frantz Fanon in his books about the Algerian resistance to French colonialism. Before ultimately turning to some Asian American cultural texts in order to trace the ways in which the dialogues about identity and difference are represented within the discourse, I would like to briefly consider one of Fanon's most important texts, *The Wretched of the Earth (Les damnés de la terre,* 1961). Although Fanon's treatise was cited in the 1960s as the manifesto for a nationalist politics of identity, rereading it now in the 1990s we find his text, ironically, to be the source of a serious critique of nationalism. Fanon argues that the challenge facing any movement dismantling colonialism (or a system in which one culture dominates another) is to provide for a new order that does not reproduce the social structure of the old system. This new order, he argues, must avoid the simple assimilation to the dominant culture's roles and positions by the emergent group, which would merely caricature the old colonialism, and it should be equally suspicious of an uncritical nativism, or racialism, appealing to essentialized notions of precolonial identity. Fanon suggests that another alternative is necessary, a new order, neither an assimilationist nor a nativist inversion, which breaks with the structures and practices of cultural domination and which continually and collectively criticizes the institutions of rule. One of the more remarkable turns in Fanon's argument occurs when he identifies both bourgeois assimilation and bourgeois nationalism as conforming to the same logic, as responses to colonialism that reproduce the same structure of cultural domination. It is in this sense that Fanon warns against the nationalism practiced by bourgeois neocolonial governments. Their nationalism, he argues, can be distorted easily into racism, territorialism, separatism, or ethnic dictatorships of one tribe or regional group over others; the national bourgeoisie replaces the colonizer, yet the social and economic structure remains the same.[14] Ironically, he points out, these separatisms, or "micro-nationalisms" (Mamadou Dia, qtd. in Fanon 158), are themselves legacies of colonialism. He writes: "By its very structure, colonialism is regionalist and separatist. Colonialism does not simply state the existence of tribes; it also reinforces and separates them" (94). That is, a politics of ethnic separatism is congruent with the divide-and-conquer logic of colonial domination. Fanon links the practices of the national bourgeoisie that has assimilated colonialist thought and practice with nativist practices that privilege one tribe or ethnicity over others; nativism and assimilationism are not opposites but similar logics both enunciating the old order.

Fanon's analysis implies that an essentialized bourgeois construction of "nation" is a classification that excludes other subaltern groups that could bring about substantive change in the social and economic relations, particularly those whose social marginalities are due to class:

peasants, workers, transient populations. We can add to Fanon's criticism that the category of nation often erases a consideration of women and the fact of difference between men and women and the conditions under which they live and work in situations of cultural domination. This is why the concentration of women of color in domestic service or reproductive labor (childcare, homecare, nursing) in the contemporary United States is not adequately explained by a nation-based model of analysis (see Glenn). In light of feminist theory, which has gone the furthest in theorizing multiple inscription and the importance of positionalities, we can argue that it may be less meaningful to act exclusively in terms of a single valence or political interest — such as ethnicity or nation — than to acknowledge that social subjects are the sites of a variety of differences.[15] An Asian American subject is never purely and exclusively ethnic, for that subject is always of a particular class, gender, and sexual preference, and may therefore feel responsible to movements that are organized around these other designations. This is not to argue against the strategic importance of Asian American identity, nor against the building of Asian American culture. Rather, I am suggesting that acknowledging class and gender differences among Asian Americans does not weaken us as a group; to the contrary, these differences represent greater political opportunity to affiliate with other groups whose cohesions may be based on other valences of oppression.

3

As I have already suggested, within Asian American discourse there is a varied spectrum of discussion about the concepts of ethnic identity and culture. At one end, there are discussions in which ethnic identity is essentialized as the cornerstone of a nationalist liberation politics. In these discussions, the cultural positions of nationalism (or ethnicism, or nativism) and of assimilation are represented in polar opposition: nationalism affirming the separate purity of its ethnic culture is opposed to assimilation of the standards of dominant society. Stories about the loss of the "native" Asian culture tend to express some form of this opposition. At the same time, there are criticisms of this essentializing position, most often articulated by feminists who charge that Asian American nationalism prioritizes masculinity and does not account for women. At the other end, there are interventions that refuse static or binary conceptions of ethnicity, replacing notions of identity with multiplicity and shifting the emphasis for ethnic "essence" to cultural hybridity. Settling for neither nativism nor assimilation, these cultural texts expose the apparent opposition between the two as a constructed figure (as Fanon does when he observes that bourgeois assimilation and bourgeois nationalism often conform to the same colonialist logic). In tracing these different discussions about identity and ethnicity through Asian American cultural debates, literature, and film, I choose particular texts because they are accessible and commonly held. But I do not intend to limit *discourse* to only these particular textual forms; by *discourse,* I intend a rather extended meaning — a network that includes not only texts and cultural documents, but social practices, formal and informal laws, policies of inclusion and exclusion, and institutional forms of organization, for example, all of which constitute and regulate knowledge about the object of that discourse, Asian America.

The terms of the debate about nationalism and assimilation become clearer if we look first at the discussion of ethnic identity in certain debates about the representation of culture. Readers of Asian American literature are familiar with attacks by Frank Chin, Ben Tong, and others on Maxine Hong Kingston, attacks which have been cast as nationalist criticisms of Kingston's "assimilationist" works. Her novel/autobiography *The Woman Warrior* is the primary target of such criticism, since it is virtually the only "canonized" piece of Asian American literature; its status can be measured by the fact that the Modern Language Association is currently publishing *A Guide to Teaching 'The Woman Warrior* in its series that includes guides to Cervantes's *Don Quixote* and Dante's *Inferno.* A critique of how and why this text has become fetishized as the exemplary representation of Asian American culture is necessary and important. However, Chin's critique reveals other kinds of tensions in Asian American culture that are worth noting. He does more than accuse Kingston of having exoticized Chinese-American culture; he argues that she has "feminized" Asian American literature and undermined the power of Asian American men to combat the racist stereotypes of the dominant white culture. Kingston and other women novelists such as Amy Tan, he says, misrepresent Chinese history in order to exaggerate its patriarchal structure; as a result, Chinese society is portrayed as being even more misogynistic than European society. While Chin and others have cast this conflict in terms of nationalism and assimilationism, I think it may be more productive to see this debate, as Elaine Kim does in a recent essay ("'Such Opposite'"), as a symptom of the tensions between nationalist and feminist concerns in Asian American discourse. I would add to Kim's analysis that the dialogue between nationalist and feminist concerns animates precisely a debate about identity and difference, or identity and heterogeneity, rather than a debate between nationalism and assimilationism; it is a debate in which Chin and others stand at one end insisting upon a fixed masculinist identity, while Kingston, Tan, or feminist literary critics like Shirley Lim and Amy Ling, with their representations of female differences and their critiques of sexism in Chinese culture, repeatedly cast this notion of identity into question. Just as Fanon points out that some forms of nationalism can obscure class, Asian American feminists point out that Asian American nationalism — or the construction of an essentialized, native Asian American subject — obscures gender. In other words, the struggle that is framed as a conflict between the apparent opposites of nativism and assimilation can mask what is more properly characterized as a struggle between the desire to essentialize ethnic identity and the fundamental condition of heterogeneous differences against which such a desire is spoken. The trope that opposes nativism and assimilationism can be itself a colonialist figure used to displace the challenges of heterogeneity, or subalternity, by casting them as assimilationist or anti-ethnic.

The trope that opposes nativism and assimilation not only organizes the cultural debates of Asian American discourse but figures *in* Asian American literature, as well. More often than not, however, this symbolic conflict between nativism and assimilation is figured in the *topos* with which I began, that of generational conflict. Although there are many versions of this *topos,* I will mention only a few in order to elucidate some of the most relevant cultural tensions. In one model, a conflict between generations is cast in strictly masculinist terms, between father and son; in this model, mothers are absent or unimportant, and female figures exist only as peripheral objects to the side of the central drama of male conflict. Louis Chu's *Eat a Bowl of Tea* (1961) exemplifies this masculinist generational symbolism, in which a conflict between nativism and assimilation is allegorized in the relationship between the father Wah Gay and the son Ben Loy, in the period when the predominantly Cantonese New York Chinatown community changes from a "bachelor society" to a "family society."[16] Wah Gay wishes Ben Loy to follow Chinese tradition, and to submit to the father's authority, while the son balks at his father's "old ways" and wants to make his own choices. When Wah Gay arranges a marriage for Ben Loy, the son is forced to obey. Although the son had had no trouble leading an active sexual life before his marriage, once married, he finds himself to be impotent. In other words, Chu's novel figures the conflict of nativism and assimilation in terms of Ben Loy's sexuality: submitting to the father's authority, marrying the "nice Chinese girl" Mei Oi and having sons, is the so-called traditional Chinese male behavior. This path represents the nativist option, whereas Ben Loy's former behavior — carrying on with American prostitutes, gambling, etc. — represents the alleged path of assimilation. At the nativist Chinese extreme, Ben Loy is impotent and is denied access to erotic pleasure, and at the assimilationist American extreme, he has great access and sexual freedom. Allegorizing the choice between cultural options in the register of Ben Loy's sexuality, Chu's novel suggests that resolution lies at neither pole, but in a third "Chinese-American" alternative, in which Ben Loy is able to experience erotic pleasure with his Chinese wife. This occurs only when the couple moves away to another state, away from the father; Ben Loy's relocation to San Francisco's Chinatown and the priority of pleasure with Mei Oi over the begetting of a son (which, incidentally, they ultimately do have) both represent important breaks from his father's authority and from Chinese tradition. Following Fanon's observations about the affinities between nativism and assimilation, we can understand Chu's novel as an early masculinist rendering of culture as conflict between the apparent opposites of nativism and assimilation, with its oedipal resolution in a Chinese-American male identity; perhaps only with hindsight can we propose that the opposition itself may be a construction that allegorizes the dialectic between an articulation of essentialized ethnic identity and the context of heterogeneous differences.

Amy Tan's much more recent *The Joy Luck Club* (1989) refigures this *topos* of generational conflict in a different social context, among first- and second-generation Mandarin Chinese in San Francisco, and more importantly, between women. Tan's *Joy Luck* displaces *Eat a Bowl* not only because it deviates from the figuration of Asian American identity in a masculine oedipal dilemma by refiguring it in terms of mothers and daughters, but also because *Joy Luck* multiplies the sites of cultural conflict, positing a number of struggles — familial and extrafamilial — as well as resolutions, without privileging the singularity or centrality of one. In this way, *Joy Luck* ultimately thematizes and demystifies the central role of the mother-daughter relationship in Asian American culture.

Joy Luck represents the first-person narratives of four sets of Chinese-born mothers and their American-born daughters. The daughters attempt to come to terms with their mothers' demands, while the mothers simultaneously try to interpret their daughters' deeds, expressing a tension between the "Chinese" expectation of filial respect and the "American" inability to fulfill that expectation. By multiplying and subverting the model of generational discord with examples of generational concord, the novel calls attention to the heterogeneity of Chinese-American family relations. On the one hand, mothers like Ying-ying St. Clair complain about their daughters' Americanization:

> For all these years I kept my mouth closed so selfish desires would not fall out. And because I remained quiet for so long now my daughter does not hear me. She sits by her fancy swimming pool and hears only her Sony Walkman, her cordless phone, her big, important husband asking her why they have charcoal and no lighter fluid.
>
> ... because I moved so secretly now my daughter does not see me. She sees a list of things to buy, her checkbook out of balance, her ashtray sitting crooked on a straight table.
>
> And I want to tell her this: We are lost, she and I, unseen and not seeing, unheard and not hearing,

unknown by others. (67)

The mother presents herself as having sacrificed everything for a daughter who has ignored these sacrifices. She sees her daughter as preoccupied with portable, mobile high tech commodities which, characteristically, have no cords, no ties, emblematizing the mother's condemnation of a daughter who does not respect family bonds. The mother implies that the daughter recognizes that something is skewed and attempts to correct it — balancing her checkbook, straightening her house — but in the mother's eyes, she has no access to the real problems; being in America has taken this understanding away. Her daughter, Lena, however, tends to view her mother as unreasonably superstitious and domineering. Lena considers her mother's concern about her failing marriage as meddlesome; the daughter's interpretation of their antagonism emphasizes a cultural gap between the mother who considers her daughter's troubles her own, and the daughter who sees her mother's actions as intrusive, possessive, and worst of all, denying the daughter's own separate individuality.

On the other hand, in contrast to this and other examples of disjunction between the Chinese mothers and the Chinese-American daughters, *Joy Luck* also includes a relationship between mother and daughter in which there is an apparent coincidence of perspective; tellingly, in this example the mother has died, and it is left to the daughter to "eulogize" the mother by telling the mother's story. Jing-mei Woo makes a trip to China, to reunite with her recently deceased mother's two daughters by an earlier marriage, whom her mother had been forced to abandon almost 40 years before when fleeing China during the Japanese invasion. Jing-mei wants to fulfill her mother's last wish to see the long-lost daughters; she wishes to inscribe herself in her mother's place. Her narration of the reunion conveys her utopian belief in the possibility of recovering the past, of rendering herself coincident with her mother, narrating her desire to become again "Chinese."

> My sisters and I stand, arms around each other, laughing and wiping the tears from each other's eyes. The flash of the Polaroid goes off and my father hands me the snapshot. My sisters and I watch quietly together, eager to see what develops.
>
> The gray-green surface changes to the bright colors of our three images, sharpening and deepening all at once. And although we don't speak, I know we all see it: Together we look like our mother. Her same eyes, her same mouth, open in surprise to see, at last, her long-cherished wish. (288)

Unlike Lena St. Clair, Jing-mei does not seek greater autonomy from her mother; she desires a lessening of the disparity between their positions that is accomplished through the narrative evocation of her mother after she has died. By contrasting different examples of mother-daughter discord and concord, *Joy Luck* allegorizes the heterogeneous culture in which the desire for identity and sameness (represented by Jing-mei's story) is inscribed within the context of Asian American differences and disjunctions (exemplified by the other three pairs of mothers and daughters). The novel formally illustrates that the articulation of one, the desire for identity, depends upon the existence of the others, or the fundamental horizon of differences.

Further, although *Joy Luck* has been heralded and marketed as a novel about mother-daughter relations in the Chinese-American family (one cover review characterizes it as a "story that shows us China, Chinese-American women and their families, and the mystery of the mother-daughter bond in ways that we have not experienced before"), I would suggest that the novel also represents antagonisms that are not exclusively generational but are due to different conceptions of class and gender among Chinese-Americans. Towards the end of the novel, Lindo and Waverly Jong reach a climax of misunderstanding, in a scene that takes place in a central site of American femininity: the beauty parlor. After telling the stylist to give her mother a "soft wave," Waverly asks her mother, Lindo, if she is in agreement. The mother narrates:

> I smile. I use my American face. That's the face Americans think is Chinese, the one they cannot understand. But inside I am becoming ashamed. I am ashamed she is ashamed. Because she is my daughter and I am proud of her, and I am her mother but she is not proud of me. (255)

The American-born daughter believes she is treating her mother, rather magnanimously, to a day of pampering at a chic salon; the Chinese-born mother receives this gesture as an insult, clear evidence of a daughter ashamed of her mother's looks. The scene not only marks the separation of mother and daughter by generation but, perhaps less obviously, their separation by class and cultural differences that lead to different interpretations of how female identity is signified. On the one hand, the Chinese-born Lindo and American-born Waverly have different class values and opportunities; the daughter's belief in the pleasure of a visit to an expensive San Francisco beauty parlor seems senselessly extravagant to the mother whose rural family had escaped poverty only by marrying her to the son of a less humble family in their village. On the other hand, the mother and daughter also conflict over definitions of proper female behavior. Lindo assumes female identity is constituted in the practice of a daughter's deference to her elders, while for Waverly, it is determined by a woman's financial independence from her parents and her financial equality with men and by her ability to speak her desires, and it is cultivated and signified in the styles and shapes that represent middle-class feminine beauty. In this sense, I ultimately read *Joy*

Luck not as a novel which exclusively depicts generational conflict among Chinese-American women, but rather as a text that thematizes the trope of the mother-daughter relationship in Asian American culture; that is, the novel comments upon the idealized construction of mother-daughter relationships (both in the majority culture's discourse about Asian Americans and in the Asian American discourse about ourselves), as well as upon the kinds of differences — of class and culturally specific definitions of gender — that are rendered invisible by the privileging of this trope.[17]

Before concluding, I want to turn to a final cultural text which not only restates the Asian American narrative that opposes nativism and assimilation but articulates a critique of that narrative, calling the nativist/assimilationist dyad into question. If *Joy Luck* poses an alternative to the dichotomy of nativism and assimilation by multiplying the generational conflict and demystifying the centrality of the mother-daughter relationship, then Peter Wang's film A *Great Wall* (1985) — both in its emplotment and in its very medium of representation — offers yet another version of this alternative. Wang's film unsettles both poles in the antinomy of nativist essentialism and assimilation by performing a continual geographical juxtaposition and exchange between a variety of cultural spaces. *A Great Wall* portrays the visit of Leo Fang's Chinese-American family to the People's Republic of China and their month-long stay with Leo's sister's family, the Chao family, in Beijing. The film concentrates on the primary contrast between the habits, customs, and assumptions of the Chinese in China and the Chinese-Americans in California by going back and forth between shots of Beijing and Northern California, in a type of continual filmic "migration" between the two, as if to thematize in its very form the travel between cultural spaces. From the first scene, however, the film foregrounds the idea that in the opposition between native and assimilated spaces, neither begins as a pure, uncontaminated site or origin; and as the camera eye shuttles back and forth between, both poles of the constructed opposition shift and change. (Indeed, the Great Wall of China, from which the film takes its title, is a monument to the historical condition that not even ancient China was "pure," but co-existed with "foreign barbarians" against which the Middle Kingdom erected such barriers.) In this regard, the film contains a number of emblematic images that call attention to the syncretic, composite quality of all cultural spaces: when the young Chinese Liu finishes the university entrance exam his scholar-father gives him a Coca-Cola; children crowd around the single village television to watch a Chinese opera singer imitate Pavarotti singing Italian opera; the Chinese student learning English recites the Gettysburg Address. Although the film concentrates on both illustrating and dissolving the apparent opposition between Chinese Chinese and American

Chinese, a number of other contrasts are likewise explored: the differences between generations both within the Chao and the Fang families (daughter Lili noisily drops her bike while her father practices tai chi; Paul kisses his Caucasian girlfriend and later tells his father that he believes all Chinese are racists when Leo suggests that he might date some nice Chinese girls); differences between men and women (accentuated by two scenes, one in which Grace Fang and Mrs. Chao talk about their husbands and children, the other in which Chao and Leo get drunk together); and, finally, the differences between capitalist and communist societies (highlighted in a scene in which the Chaos and Fangs talk about their different attitudes toward "work"). The representations of these other contrasts complicate and diversify the ostensible focus on cultural differences between Chinese and Chinese-Americans, as if to testify to the condition that there is never only one exclusive valence of difference, but rather cultural difference is always simultaneously bound up with gender, economics, age, and other distinctions. In other words, when Leo says to his wife that the Great Wall makes the city "just as difficult to leave as to get in," the wall at once signifies the construction of a variety of barriers — not only between Chinese and Americans, but between generations, men and women, capitalism and communism — as well as the impossibility of ever remaining bounded and inpenetrable, of resisting change, recomposition, and reinvention. We are reminded of this impossibility throughout the film, but it is perhaps best illustrated in the scene in which the Fang and Chao families play a rousing game of touch football on the ancient immovable Great Wall.

The film continues with a series of wonderful contrasts: the differences in the bodily comportments of the Chinese-American Paul and the Chinese Liu playing ping pong, between Leo's jogging and Mr. Chao's tai chi, between Grace Fang's and Mrs. Chao's ideas of what is fitting and fashionable for the female body. The two families have different senses of space and of the relation between family members. In one subplot, the Chinese-American cousin Paul is outraged to learn that Mrs. Chao reads her daughter Lili's mail; he asks Lili if she has ever heard of "privacy." This later results in a fight between Mrs. Chao and Lili in which Lili says she has learned from their American cousins that "it's not right to read other people's mail." Mrs. Chao retorts: "You're not 'other people,' you're my daughter. What is this thing, 'privacy'?" Lili explains to her that "privacy" can't be translated into Chinese. "Oh, so you're trying to hide things from your mother and use western words to trick her!" exclaims Mrs. Chao. Ultimately, just as the members of the Chao family are marked by the visit from their American relatives, the Fangs are altered by the time they return to California, each bringing back a memento or practice from their Chinese trip. In other words, rather than privileging either a nativist or assimilationist view, or even espousing a "Chinese-American" resolution of differences, *A Great Wall* performs a filmic "migration" by shuttling between the various cultural spaces; we are left, by the end of the film, with a sense of culture as dynamic and open, the result of a continual process of visiting and revisiting a plurality of cultural sites.

In keeping with the example of *A Great Wall,* we might consider as a possible model for the ongoing construction of ethnic identity the migratory process suggested by Wang's filming technique and emplotment: we might conceive of the making and practice of Asian American culture as nomadic, unsettled, taking place in the travel between cultural sites and in the multivocality of heterogeneous and conflicting positions. Taking seriously the heterogeneities among Asian Americans in California, we must conclude that the grouping "Asian American" is not a natural or static category; it is a socially constructed unity, a situationally specific position that we assume for political reasons. It is "strategic" in Gayatri Spivak's sense of a "strategic use of a positive essentialism in a scrupulously visible political interest" (205). The concept of "strategic essentialism" suggests that it is possible to utilize specific signifiers of ethnic identity, such as Asian American, for the purpose of contesting and disrupting the discourses that exclude Asian Americans, while simultaneously revealing the internal contradictions and slippages of Asian American so as to insure that such essentialisms will not be reproduced and proliferated by the very apparatuses we seek to disempower. I am not suggesting that we can or should do away with the notion of Asian American identity, for to stress only our differences would jeopardize the hard-earned unity that has been achieved in the last two decades of Asian American politics, the unity that is necessary if Asian Americans are to play a role in the new historical bloc of ethnic Californians. In fact, I would submit that the very freedom, in the 1990s, to explore the hybridities concealed beneath the desire of identity is permitted by the context of a strongly articulated essentialist politics. Just as the articulation of the desire for identity depends upon the existence of a fundamental horizon of differences, the articulation of differences dialectically depends upon a socially constructed and practiced notion of identity. I want simply to remark that in the 1990s, we can afford to rethink the notion of ethnic identity in terms of cultural, class, and gender differences, rather than presuming similarities and making the erasure of particularity the basis of unity. In the 1990s, we can diversify our political practices to include a more heterogeneous group and to enable crucial alliances with other groups — ethnicity-based, class-based, gender-based, and sexuality-based — in the ongoing work of transforming hegemony.

Notes

Many thanks to Elaine Kim for her thought-provoking questions, and for asking me to deliver portions of this essay as papers at the 1990 meetings of the Association of Asian American Studies and of the American Literature Association; to James Clifford, who also gave me the opportunity to deliver a version of this essay at a conference sponsored by the Center for Cultural Studies at UC Santa Cruz; to the audience participants at all three conferences who asked stimulating questions which have helped me to rethink my original notions; and to Page duBois, Barbara Harlow, Susan Kirkpatrick, George Mariscal, Ellen Rooney, and Kathryn Shevelow, who read drafts and offered important comments and criticism.

1. *Nisei* refers to a second-generation Japanese-American, born to immigrant parents in the US; *Sansei,* a third-generation Japanese-American, *Issei* refers to a first-generation immigrant.

2. See Kim, *Asian,* for the most important book-length study of the literary representations of multi-generational Asian America,

3. Recent anthropological discussions of ethnic cultures as fluid and syncretic systems echo these concerns of Asian American writers, See, for example, Fischer; Clifford. For an anthropological study of Japanese-American culture that troubles the paradigmatic construction of kinship and filial relations as the central figure in culture, see Yanagisako.

4. We might think, for example, of the shifting of the Los Angeles "Chinatown" from its downtown location to the suburban community of Monterey Park. Since the 1970s, the former "Chinatown" has been superceded demographically and economically by Monterey Park, the home of many Chinese-Americans as well as newly arrived Chinese from Hong Kong and Taiwan. The Monterey Park community of 63,000 residents is currently over 50% Asian. On the social and political consequences of these changing demographics, see Fong.

5. Chan's history of the Chinese immigrant populations in California, *Bittersweet,* and her history of Asian Americans are extremely important in this regard. Numerous lectures by Ling-chi Wang at UC San Diego in 1987 and at UC Berkeley in 1988 have been very important to my understanding of the heterogeneity of waves of immigration across different Asian-origin groups.

6. The Chinese Exclusion Act of 1882 barred Chinese from entering the U.S., the National Origins Act prohibited the entry of Japanese in 1924, and the Tydings-McDuffie Act of 1934 limited Filipino immigrants to 50 people per year. Finally, the most tragic consequence of anti-Asian racism occurred during World War II when 120,000 Japanese-Americans (two-thirds

of whom were American citizens by birth) were interned in camps. For a study of the anti-Japanese movement culminating in the immigration act of 1924, see Daniels. Takaki offers a general history of Asian origin immigrant groups in the United States.

7. The model minority myth constructs Asians as aggressively driven overachievers; it is a homogenizing fiction which relies upon two strategies common in the subordinating construction of racial or ethnic otherness — the racial other as knowable, familiar ("like us"), and as incomprehensible, threatening ("unlike us"); the model minority myth suggests both that Asians are overachievers and "unlike us" and that they assimilate well, and are thus "like us." Asian Americans are continually pointing out that the model minority myth distorts the real gains, as well as the impediments, of Asian immigrants; by leveling and homogenizing all Asian groups, it erases the different rates of assimilation and the variety of class identities among various Asian immigrant groups. Claiming that Asians are "overrepresented" on college campuses, the model minority myth is one of the justifications for the establishment of informal quotas in university admissions policies, similar to the university admission policies which discriminated against Jewish students from the 1930s to the 1950s.

8. In the last two decades, greatly diverse new groups have settled in California; demographers project that by the end of the century, the "majority" of the state will be comprised of ethnic "minority" groups. Due to recent immigrants, this influx of minorities is characterized also by greater diversity within individual groups: the group we call Asian Americans no longer denotes only Japanese, Chinese, Koreans, and Filipinos, but now includes Indian, Thai, Vietnamese, Cambodian, and Laotian groups; Latino communities in California are made up not only of Chicanos, but include Guatemalans, Salvadorans, and Colombians. It is not difficult to find Pakistani, Armenian, Lebanese, and Iranian enclaves in San Francisco, Los Angeles, or even San Diego. While California's "multi-culturalism" is often employed to support a notion of the "melting pot," to further an ideological assertion of equal opportunity for California's different immigrant groups, I am, in contrast, pursuing the ignored implications of this characterization of California as an ethnic state: that is, despite the increasing numbers of ethnic immigrants apparently racing to enjoy California's opportunities, for racial and ethnic immigrants there is no equality, but uneven development, nonequivalence, and cultural heterogeneities, not only between, but within, groups.

9. For an important elaboration of the concept of "minority discourse," see JanMohamed and Lloyd.

10. This notion of "the dominant" — defined by Williams in a chapter discussing the "Dominant,

Residual, and Emergent" as "a cultural process ... seized as a cultural system, with determinate dominant features: feudal culture or bourgeois culture or a transition from one to the other" — is often conflated in recent cultural theory with Gramsci's concept of hegemony. Indeed, Williams writes: "We have certainly still to speak of the 'dominant' and the 'effective,' and in these senses of the hegemonic" (121), as if the dominant and the hegemonic are synonymous.

11. See Gramsci, "History." Gramsci describes "subaltern" groups as by definition not unified, emergent, and always in relation to the dominant groups:

> The history of subaltern social groups is necessarily fragmented and episodic. There undoubtedly does exist a tendency to (at least provisional stages of) unification in the historical activity of these groups, but this tendency is continually interrupted by the activity of the ruling groups; it therefore can only be demonstrated when an historical cycle is completed and this cycle culminates in a success. Subaltern groups are always subject to the activity of ruling groups, even when they rebel and rise up: only 'permanent' victory breaks their subordination, and that not immediately. In reality, even when they appear triumphant, the subaltern groups are merely anxious to defend themselves (a truth which can be demonstrated by the history of the French Revolution at least up to 1830). Every trace of independent initiative on the part of subaltern groups should therefore be of incalculable value for the integral historian. (54-55)

12. "Hegemony" remains a suggestive construct in Gramsci, however, rather than an explicitly interpreted set of relations. Contemporary readers are left with the more specific task of distinguishing which particular forms of challenge to an existing hegemony are significantly transformative, and which forms may be neutralized or appropriated by the hegemony. Some cultural critics contend that counterhegemonic forms and practices are tied by definition to the dominant culture and that the dominant culture simultaneously produces and limits its own forms of counter-culture. I am thinking here of some of the "new historicist" studies that use a particular notion of Foucault's discourse to confer authority to the "dominant," interpreting all forms of "subversion" as being ultimately "contained" by dominant ideology and institutions. Other cultural historians, such as Williams, suggest that because there is both identifiable variation in the social order over time, as well as variations in the forms of the counter-culture in different historical periods, we must conclude that some aspects of the oppositional forms are not reducible to the terms of the original hegemony. Still other theorists, such as Ernesto Laclau and Chantal Mouffe, have expanded Gramsci's notion of hegemony to argue that in advanced capitalist society, the social field is not a totality consisting exclusively of the

dominant and the counterdominant, but rather that "the social" is an open and uneven terrain of contesting articulations and signifying practices. Some of these articulations and practices are neutralized, while others can be linked to build important pressures against an existing hegemony. See Laclau and Mouffe, especially pp. 134-145. They argue persuasively that no hegemonic logic can account for the totality of "the social" and that the open and incomplete character of the social field is the precondition of every hegemonic practice. For if the field of hegemony were conceived according to a "zero-sum" vision of possible positions and practices, then the very concept of hegemony, as plural and mutable formations and relations, would be rendered impossible. Elsewhere, in "Hegemony and New Political Subjects," Mouffe goes even further to elaborate the practical dimensions of the hegemonic principle in terms of contemporary social movements.

13. Adamson reads *The Prison Notebooks* as the postulation of Gramsci's activist and educationalist politics; in chapter 6, he discusses Gramsci's two concepts of hegemony: hegemony as the consensual basis of an existing political system in civil society, as opposed to violent oppression or domination, and hegemony as a historical phase of bourgeois development in which class is understood not only economically but also in terms of a common intellectual and moral awareness, an overcoming of the "economic-corporative" phase. Adamson associates the former (hegemony in its contrast to domination) with "hegemony-maintenance," and the latter (hegemony as a stage in the political moment) as "hegemony-creation." Sassoon provides an excellent discussion of Gramsci's key concepts; she both historicizes the concept of hegemony and discusses the implications of some of the ways in which hegemony has been interpreted. Sassoon emphasizes the degree to which hegemony is opposed to domination to evoke the way in which one social group influences other groups, making certain compromises with them in order to gain their consent for its leadership in society as a whole.

14. Amilcar Cabral, the Cape Verdean African nationalist leader and theorist, echoes some fundamental observations made by Fanon: that the national bourgeoisie will collaborate with the colonizers and that tribal fundamentalism must be overcome or it will defeat any efforts at unity. In 1969, Cabral wrote ironically in "Party Principles and Political Practice" of the dangers of tribalism and nativism: "No one should think that he is more African than another, even than some white man who defends the interests of Africa, merely because he is today more adept at eating with his hand, rolling rice into a ball and putting it into his mouth" (57).

15. I am thinking here especially of de Lauretis; Spivak; and Minh-ha. The latter explains the multiple inscription of women of color:

[M] any women of color feel obliged [to choose] between ethnicity and womanhood: how can they? You never have/are one without the other. The idea of two illusorily separated identities, one ethnic, the other woman (or more precisely female), partakes in the Euro-American system of dualistic reasoning and its age-old divide-and-conquer tactics ... The pitting of anti-racist and anti-sexist struggles against one another allows some vocal fighters to dismiss blatantly the existence of either racism or sexism within their lines of action, as if oppression only comes in separate, monolithic forms. (105)

16. For a more extensive analysis of generational conflict in Chu's novel, see Gong. Gong asserts that "The father/son relationship represents the most critical juncture in the erosion of a traditional Chinese value system and the emergence of a Chinese American character. Change from Chinese to Chinese American begins here" (74-75).

17. There are many scenes that resonate with my suggestion that generational conflicts cannot be isolated from either class or the historicity of gender. In the third section of the novel, it is class difference in addition to generational strife that founds the antagonism between mother and daughter: Ying-ying St. Clair cannot understand why Lena and her husband, Harold, have spent an enormous amount of money to live in a barn in the posh neighborhood of Woodside. Lena says: "My mother knows, underneath all the fancy details that cost so much, this house is still a barn"(151). In the early relationship between Suyuan Woo and her daughter, Jing-mei, the mother pushes her daughter to become a success, to perform on the piano; we can see that such desires are the reflection of the mother's former poverty, her lack of opportunity as both a poor refugee and a woman, but the daughter, trapped within a familial framework of explanation, sees her mother as punishing and invasive. Finally, the mother and daughter pair An-mei and Rose Hsu dramatize a conflict between the mother's belief that it is more honorable to keep personal problems within the Chinese family and the daughter's faith in western psychotherapy: the mother cannot understand why her daughter would pay a psychiatrist, a stranger, to talk about her divorce, instead of talking to her mother: the mother who was raised believing one must not show suffering to others because they, like magpies, would feed on your tears says of the daughter's psychiatrist, "really, he is just another bird drinking from your misery" (241).

Works Cited

Adamson, Walter. *Hegemony and Revolution: A Study of Antonio Gramsci's Political and Cultural Theory.* Berkeley: U of California P. 1980.

Cabrai, Amilcar. *Unity and Struggle: Speeches and Writings of Amilcar Cabral.* Trans. Michael Wolfers. New York: Monthly Review, 1979.

Chan, Sucheng. *Asian Americans: An Interpretive History.* Boston: Twayne, 1991,

——. *This Bittersweet Soil: The Chinese in California Agriculture, 1860–1910.* Berkeley: U of California P, 1986.

Chang, Diana. "The Oriental Contingent." *The Forbidden Stitch.* Ed. Shirley Geok-Lin Lim, Mayumi Tsutakawa, and Margarita Donnelly. Corvallis: Calyx, 1989, 171-177.

Chu, Louis. *Eat a Bowl of Tea.* Seattle: U of Washington P, 1961.

Clifford, James. *The Predicament of Culture: Twentieth Century Ethnography, Literature, and Art.* Cambridge: Harvard UP, 1988.

Daniels, Roger. *The Politics of Prejudice.* Berkeley. U of California P, 1962.

Fanon, Frantz. *The Wretched of the Earth.* Trans. Constance Farrington. New York: Grove, 1961.

Fischer, Michael M. J. "Ethnicity and the Post-modern Arts of Memory" *Writing Culture.* Ed. James Clifford and George Marcus. Berkeley: U of California P, 1986.

Fong, Timothy. "A Community Study of Monterey Park, California." Diss. U of California, Berkeley.

Glenn, Evelyn Nakano. "Occupational Ghettoization: Japanese-American Women and Domestic Service, 1905–1970." *Ethnicity* 8 (1981): 352-386.

Gong, Ted. "Approaching Cultural Change Through Literature: From Chinese to Chinese-American." *Amerasia* 7 (1980): 73-86.

Gramsci, Antonio. "History of the Subaltern Classes: Methodological Criteria." *Selections* 52-60.

——. *Selections from the Prison Notebooks.* Ed. and trans. Quinton Hoare and Geoffrey Nowell Smith. New York: International, 1971.

A Great Wall. Dir. Peter Wang. New Yorker Films, 1985,

JanMohamed, Abdul, and David Lloyd, eds. *The Nature and Context of Minority Discourse.* New York: Oxford UP, 1990.

Kim, Elaine. *Asian American Literature: An Introduction to the Writings and Their Social Context.* Philadelphia: Temple UP, 1982.

——. "'Such Opposite Creatures': Men and Women in Asian American Literature." *Michigan Quarterly Review* (1990): 68-93.

Kingston, Maxine Hong. *The Woman Warrior.* New York: Random, 1975.

Laclau, Ernesto, and Chantal Moufle. *Hegemony and Socialist Strategy.* London: Verso, 1985. Lauretis, Teresa de. *Technologies of Gender.* Bloomington: Indiana UR, 1987.

Lowet Lydia. "Quitting Time." *Ikon 9, Without Ceremony: A Special Issue by Asian Women United.* Spec, issue of *Ikon* 9 (1988): 29.

Minh-ha, Trinh T. *Woman, Native, Other: Writing Postcoloniality and Feminism.* Bloomington: Indiana UP, 1989.

Mirikitani, Janice. "Breaking Tradition." *Without Ceremony.* 9.

Mouffe, Chantal. "Hegemony and New Political Subjects: Toward a New Concept of Democracy." *Marxism and the Interpretation of Culture.* Ed. Cary Nelson and Lawrence Grossberg. Urbana: U of Illinois, 1988. 89-104.

Sassoon, Anne Showstack. "Hegemony, War of Position and Political Intervention." *Approaches to Gramsci.* Ed.

Anne Showstack Sassoon. London: Writers and Readers, 1982.

Spivak, Gayatri. *In Other Worlds*. London: Routledge, 1987.

Takaki, Ronald. *Strangers From a Different Shore: A History of Asian Americans*. Boston: Little, 1989.

Tan, Amy. *The Joy Luck Club*. New York: Putnam's, 1989.

Williams, Raymond. *Marxism and Literature*. Oxford: Oxford UP, 1977.

Yanagisako, Sylvia. *Transforming the Past: Kinship and Tradition among Japanese Americans*. Stanford: Stanford UP, 1985.

4

The Fiction of Asian American Literature
美国亚裔文学的虚构

Susan Koshy

评论家简介

　　苏珊·柯西（Susan Koshy），美国加州大学洛杉矶分校英语系博士，现为美国伊利诺伊大学美亚研究和英语系副教授。研究领域包括：美亚研究、美国研究、后殖民主义研究等。出版专著有《性归化：亚裔美国人和混血》（*Sexual Naturalization: Asian Americans and Miscegenation*, 2005）。合编有《跨国南亚人：一个新离散社群的形成》（*Transnational South Asians: The Making of a Neo-Diaspora*, 2008）。除本书收录的论文，其他代表性论文有《美国亚裔小说的兴起》，收于《剑桥美国小说史》（"The Rise of the Asian American Novel" *The Cambridge History of the American Novel*, 2011）一书；《国外公平审判运动：远距离民族主义和后帝国的焦虑》，收于《正义的倡导：人权、跨国女性主义和代表政治》（"The Campaign for Fair Trials Abroad: Long-Distance Nationalism and Post-Imperial Anxiety" *Just Advocacy: Human Rights, Transnational Feminism, and the Politics of Representation*, 2005）一书；以及《后现代底层：全球化理论与族裔、地区和后殖民研究的主题》，收于《次要的跨国主义》（"The Postmodern Subaltern: Globalization Theory and the Subject of Ethnic, Area, and Postcolonial Studies" *Minor Transnationalism*, 2005）一书等。

文章简介

　　自 1965 年美国移民和国籍法案颁布以来至 20 世纪末，美国亚裔人口分布发生质变；与此同时，随着全球化的扩张与深入，文学创作的全球化与在地化交错深入，这导致美国亚裔文学的创作性质和场域发生巨变，其构成亦日益凸显层级性、杂糅性与异质性。苏珊·柯西教授 1996 年撰写的这篇文章即在这样的背景下对世纪之交的美国亚裔文学研究的现状与问题给予犀利的剖析与批判，至今对美国亚裔文学研究产生着重要影响。文章通过分析三项讨论美国亚裔文学研究范式的研究成果，揭示不同历史阶段对美国亚裔文学不同界定的局限性，指出这些研究在阐释方法上的弊端。而针对 20 世纪末的理论研究现状，文章明确指出美国亚裔文学研究在新的时代背景下，单纯地将族裔性向泛族裔性扩张、盲目紧跟与囊括其他理论思潮的做法是错误的。理论界应该对"美国亚裔"本身的指涉性与其存在前提等重大理论问题做出深刻研究，而不应该采取"策略性推延"的态度。理论界应该理性面对与深刻反思美国亚裔文学理论的弱点与滞后性。

文章出处：*The Yale Journal of Criticism*, vol. 9, no. 2, 1996, pp. 315-342.

The Fiction of Asian American Literature

Susan Koshy

Epistemology is true as long as it accounts for the impossibility of its own beginning and lets itself be driven at every stage by its inadequacy to the things themselves. It is, however, untrue in the pretension that success is at hand and that states of affairs would ever simply correspond to its constructions and aporetic concepts.

——Theodor W. Adorno

Asian American Literature: Institutional Legacies

The boundaries of what constitutes Asian American literature have been periodically interrogated and revised, but its validity as an ordering rubric has survived these debates and repeatedly been salvaged by pointing to some existing or imminent stage of ethnogenesis, in which its representational logic would be manifest. Inherent in more recent definitions of the term has been the practice of a strategic deferral — an invocation of the work of culture-building that the debates themselves perform, and through which Asian American identity and its concomitant literature would come into being. Unlike African American, Native American or Chicano literature, Asian American literature inhabits the highly unstable temporality of the "about-to-be," its meanings continuously reinvented after the arrival of new groups of immigrants and the enactment of legislative changes. However, the tactic of deferral in the interests of institutional consolidation has had its costs, and it is these costs that this essay will consider.

The affirmation of ethnic identity as a means of political and institutional space-claiming, and the very newness of the field which originated in the late sixties, have deferred questions about its founding premises. But it is precisely this question, "How are we to conceptualize Asian American literature taking into account the radical disjunctions in the emergence of the field?" that it has now become historically and politically most urgent to ask, because of pressures both inside and outside the community. The radical demographic shifts produced within the Asian American community by the 1965 immigration laws have transformed the nature and locus of literary production, creating a highly stratified, uneven and heterogeneous formation, that cannot easily be contained within the models of essentialized or pluralized ethnic identity suggested by the rubric Asian American literature, or its updated post-modern avatar

Asian American literatures. [1] Moreover, we have entered a transnational era where ethnicity is increasingly produced at multiple local and global sites rather than, as before, within the parameters of the nation-state. This dispersal of ethnic identity has been intensified, in the case of Americans of Asian origin, by dramatic geopolitical realignments under way in the Pacific, that have reshaped the political imaginaries of "Asia" and "America" and the conjunctions between these two entities. Asian American literary production takes place within and participates in this transformed political and cultural landscape. Asian American Studies is, however, only just beginning to undertake a theoretical investigation of these changes, rendering itself peripheral to the developments inside its constituent group. Instead of an engagement with the new critical forces shaping its interdisciplinary project, much of the scholarship in the field has either continued to rely on paradigms of ethnicity produced in the inaugural moment of the field, or has sought to incorporate the changes through the fashionable but derivative vocabulary of post-modernism, post-colonialism or post-structuralism; formulaic invocations of "multiculturalism" "hybridity" "plural identities" or "border-crossing" are used promiscuously without any effort to link them to the material, cultural or historical specificities of the various Asian American experiences. Although substantial historical scholarship has been produced, the field has been weak in theoretical work, especially when compared to Chicano, Native American and African American Studies. The lack of significant theoretical work has affected its development and its capacity to address the stratifications and differences that constitute its distinctness within ethnic studies.

I will substantiate these arguments by reviewing the interpretive methods adopted thus far in delineating the boundaries of Asian American literature. I will do this by examining three paradigmatic attempts to discuss what constitutes Asian American literature, and analyzing the methodological problems and impasses revealed in these critical works: Frank Chin's Preface and Introduction to *Aiiieeeee! An Anthology of Asian-American Writers* (1974); Elaine Kim's full-length study *Asian American Literature: An Introduction to the Writings and Their Social Context* (1982), and her shorter essay on the subject, "Defining Asian American Realities Through Literature" (1987); and two essays by Shirley Geok-lin Lim, "Twelve Asian American Writers: In Search of Self-Definition" (1990), and "Assaying the Gold: Or, Contesting the Ground of Asian American Literature" (1993). [2] The methodological problems in these essays partake of larger historical/political and institutional legacies: the inadequacy of the pluralistic idiom of inclusion to confront the contradictions and heterogeneities within the field; the tensions between the formulation of a political identity and the critical task of situating the heterogeneity of ethnic literary production; the risks of archival recovery of ethnic texts without adequate theoretical and comparative work on the various literatures that constitute the field; and finally, the failure to come to terms with the scope and transformative impact of transnationalism on Asian American ethnicity. As an Asian American and a scholar in the field, I feel our most urgent task is to theoretically engage these problems and generate new conceptual frames that work in the interests of social change.

One of the major preoccupations in the field of Asian American literature has thus far been in documenting and compiling a rapidly expanding corpus, both through the recovery of older, neglected writers,[3] and the incorporation of new writers from the established and from the less-known immigrant groups from Korea, Southeast and South Asia. Since the official categorization of some of these groups under the designation "Asian American" is as recent as 1980 when, for instance, Asian Indians classified since 1950 as "other white" lobbied for and won reclassification in the census, the work of compilation is obviously one of urgency within the field. Moreover, the recognition ethnicity has recently accrued within an academy anxiously reconstituting its American canon has led to an increase in courses, job openings, and student interest in this emergent field. Hence, the proliferation of anthologies and bibliographies within the field bringing together the range of primary source material in order to meet this recent surge in demand.[4] But if the expansion of the field proceeds at this pace, without a more substantial theoretical investigation of the premises and assumptions underlying our constructions of commonalty and difference, we run the risk of unwittingly annexing the newer literary productions within older paradigms, overlooking radical disjunctions within more established formations like Chinese and Japanese American literature, and perpetuating hierarchies within the field.

The pluralism of inclusion, while appropriate for the task of building what Alastair Fowler has defined as the "potential canon" or "the entire written corpus, together with all surviving oral literature," can only fulfill a short-term, though crucial purpose.[5] I share with John Guillory a suspicion of a "liberal consensus whose name is 'pluralism' and whose pedagogic agenda has been exhausted in the gesture of 'opening the canon.'"[6] Pluralism offers us a means of expanding the potential canon, certainly, but as Werner Sollors has noted, this expansion is undertaken in the name of the very categories through which exclusion formerly operated; the pluralist method thus always carries the danger of reifying the categories that canonical change should work to transform.[7] Sollors offers some necessary cautions about the "mosaic procedure" that organizes many anthologies of ethnic literature: "The published results of this 'mosaic' procedure are the readers and compendiums made up of diverse essays on groups of ethnic writers who may have little in common except so-called ethnic roots while, at the same time, obvious and important literary and cultural connections are obfuscated." The latest Asian American anthologies (even more so than the earlier ones) cannot even assume the existence of common ethnic roots, since they work to include the writings of as many of their different constituent groups as possible. Moreover, since the category Asian American is itself so novel, and has undergone such radical changes of meaning in a very short while, its value as an organizing framework for literary production is much more problematic than even Sollors's generalized critique would suggest. If the theoretical challenge posed by the nomenclature is met with the assertion of an outmoded identity politics, or the more recent trend towards the postulation of a nebulous pan-Asian American consciousness, we risk repressing important connections between Asian and Asian American literature and misconceiving the dynamic, nomadic and dispersed nature of ethnogenesis in a transnational era, in the interests of recuperating a fictional notion of unity.

Although Shirley Lim has confidently asserted that "the pluralizing 's' which does not appear in discussions of Asian American literature is everywhere today assumed when critics discuss the emerging shape of Asian American literary studies" ("CGA," 162), I would argue, firstly, that such tacit acknowledgements do not relieve us of responsibility for theoretical articulations of the multiple, conflicted and emergent formations that constitute Asian American literature and, secondly, that critical work which proceeds in the absence of such theoretical delineations avoids what is one of the major challenges facing the field today, namely, to examine the impact of the recent demographic and geopolitical changes on the reconstitution of ethnicity among all the Asian American groups. The pluralism that Lim invokes merely offers an "additive approach," when what we need is a transformation of the paradigms ("CP," 276). Elaine Kim's *Asian American Literature: An Introduction to the Writings and Their Social Context*, which focuses on the writings of Chinese, Japanese, Filipino and Korean Americans, an invaluable contribution to the field in its time, offers now an obsolete mapping of the field. It remains, to date, the only book-length study that attempts to treat Asian American literature as a whole. Most other critical work offers thematic, sociohistorical, or rhetorical analyses of individual texts, authors or ethnic groups focusing on generational narratives, assimilation, motifs of resistance or feminist emergence, or the challenge to stereotypes or cliches.

Shifting Boundaries of Asian American Ethnicity

What makes the category "Asian American" so complex is that it has undergone reconfiguration more rapidly and to an extent that none of the other ethnic categories have. A brief summary will help elucidate this. The following account provides merely an overview: it is not intended to delineate exhaustively the many shifts, nuances and disjunctures in the historical constitution of Asian Americans. There are legitimate differences of interpretation over the content and significance of each pattern; however, such differences and debates are beyond the scope of my concerns here. Broadly speaking, then, one can chart five different historical patterns of ethnicity formation.

1) From the mid-nineteenth century to World War Ⅱ, ethnicity was shaped by policies of containment and exclusion that the various Asian national groups encountered on their arrival in the U.S.[8] Economic competition and racist ideologies triggered the hostility of the white working class, particularly on the West Coast, leading to the passage of exclusionary immigration laws that were enacted first against the Chinese, then against the Japanese, Indians and Filipinos, barring their entry into the country.[9] Between the late nineteenth and early twentieth century, over 600 pieces of anti-Asian legislation were passed limiting or excluding Asians from access to housing, education, intermarriage, employment and land ownership.[10] Immigration laws limiting the entry of women, laws against miscegenation, and harsh, nomadic working conditions produced bachelor communities with such a skewed gender ratio among Chinese, Indians and Filipinos that communities were unable to reproduce themselves.[11]

The status of the various Asian national groups within the U.S. fluctuated historically, since it depended in part on the relations between the U.S. and their home governments. However, all the Asian groups posed the threat of economic competition domestically, and thus, as employers recruited new groups of Asians to fill the vacuum created by the exclusion of others, the hostility of nativist workers was redirected against the newcomers.

Legislative policies of exclusion and containment shaped the contours of the early Asian immigrant communities, as did the loyalties and allegiances of the various immigrant groups. Each of the groups identified itself by regional or national origin, and often occupied ethnic enclaves that reinforced these associations. Frequently, patterns of labor recruitment created narrow and cohesive sub-national identities: most of the earliest Chinese immigrants were from Guangdong province, the Japanese laborers were primarily from four prefectures in Japan, and the Indian workers from three districts in Punjab. Although the earliest Korean immigrants were more heterogeneous in origin, religious affinities did exist among them: 40% were Christian. Among Filipinos, 90% were Catholic (*SFD*, 31-62). Language barriers and the existence of strong national rivalries in their home-countries often led the different Asian ethnic groups to actively dissociate from each other. Despite their sense of cultural distinctiveness, however, in the popular imagination, Asians were commonly identified as "Orientals" or "Asiatics" and were seen as sharing physical and psychological attributes.

2) The next historical shift in ethnic formation took place between World War II and the beginning of the protest movements of the sixties.[12] This period produced significant changes in the composition, status and boundaries of Asian American communities. The alignments of the War redefined the relationships of the various Asian national groups to each other and to the U.S. With World War II, Chinese and Filipino Americans found themselves viewed as favored allies; the enmity Korean Americans had long felt towards their colonizers, the Japanese, suddenly coincided with public sentiment; Asian Indians gained public consideration because of their country's strategic importance to Allied plans to block the Japanese advancement westward.[13] For Japanese Americans, however, Pearl Harbor was a wrenching, isolating and harrowing experience: they were classified as "enemy aliens," interned, and their communities on the West Coast destroyed.

The war against Nazism overseas and the need to combat Japanese propaganda calling for a pan-Asian alliance to fight Euro-American racism, made impossible the continuance of discriminatory practices and immigration laws. Consequently, the conditions of Asian Americans improved significantly. Restrictions on housing, employment, land ownership, naturalization, and miscegenation were gradually lifted. Furthermore, changes in immigration law allowed for the revitalization and augmentation of declining ethnic communities. Immigration from the Philippines, China and India was reopened, although severely restricted. However, loopholes in the law and the passage of the 1948 Displaced Persons Act and the 1953 Refugee Relief Act increased the number of immigrants. Most importantly, the War Brides Act, which allowed Asian wives and children of U.S. servicemen to enter on a non-quota basis, substantially increased the size of ethnic communities and created a more balanced gender ratio. Most immigrants entering at this time were women. The Chinese American community tripled in size between 1940 and 1960; for other groups the changes were less dramatic, but important. The Korean War also prompted a new wave of immigration from that country. Illegal immigration was prevalent among all groups, but most significant among Chinese Americans; in fact, the Border Patrol, now associated in the public consciousness with Mexican Americans, was established to combat illegal Chinese entries (*MRA*, 74).

While the 1940s focused public antagonism on Japanese Americans, the anti-Communist witch-hunts of the 1950s shifted attention to Chinese Americans. Raids, deportations, surveillance and the implementation of a Confession Program (involving information gathering and loyalty tests) fractured and terrorized the Chinese American community. In Ronald Takaki's succinct formulation: "The new peril was seen as yellow in race and red in ideology" (*SFD*, 415).

3) The identity-category "Asian American" was a product of the struggles of the 1960s but has been used to organize and interpret this set of immigrant experiences retrospectively and prospectively. The struggles of the 1960s also led to the establishment of the academic discipline of Asian American Studies. The term "Asian American" emerged in the context of civil rights, Third World and anti-Vietnam war movements and was self-consciously adopted (in preference to "Oriental" or "Yellow") primarily on university campuses where the Asian American Movement enjoyed the broadest support.[14] The opening up of higher education and the demographic changes of the post-War years made possible, for the first time, the presence of Japanese, Filipino and Chinese American students in significant numbers on some university campuses. From these beginnings, the term "Asian American" has passed into academic and bureaucratic, and thence into popular usage.

The Asian American Movement was pivotal in creating a pan-Asian identity politics that represented their "unequal circumstances and histories as being related."[15] Asian American was a political subject position formulated to make visible a history of exclusion and discrimination against immigrants of Asian origin. This identity was then extended to represent the interests and circumstances of a very different group of Asian newcomers, who were entering the country with the change in immigration laws in 1965, and were destined to alter radically the demographic make-up of the constituency into which they were incorporated.

4) The next pattern of ethnic formation emerged with the change in immigration laws in 1965 and extended to the end of the next decade. During the Cold War, the U.S. claim to world leadership in the name of democracy and justice created pressure for changes in immigration policies that would place Asians on an equal footing with Europeans. Simultaneously, the Civil Rights Movement intensified domestic and international awareness of and opposition to racial discrimination. The passage of the 1965 immigration laws was a result of these combined internal and external pressures. The new laws allowed for an annual quota of 20,000 from each Asian country and the reunification of immediate family members on a non-quota basis. As a result, Asian Americans, who were under 1% of the U.S. population in 1965, increased to 2.8% in 1990, and are projected at 10.1% by 2050, making them the fastest growing minority group in the country. Japanese Americans, who comprised the largest group in 1960 representing 47% of the Asian American population, have declined rapidly to third position in the 1990 Census (11.7%),

barely ahead of Asian Indians (11.2%) and Korean Americans (10.9%). Chinese Americans make up the largest group in the 1990 Census (23%), closely followed by Filipino Americans (19%).[16] The influx of newer groups has further diversified the identity of Asian Americans. After 1975, large numbers of Vietnamese, Lao, Hmong, Mien and Cambodians entered the United States as refugees. In the 1980 Census, immigrants from India lobbied for and won reclassification from the "other white" category to Asian Indian.

The arrival of new immigrants after 1965 has transformed the group from a predominantly American-born constituency to a group which is 65% foreign-born.[17] The new immigrants carry strong homeland identifications, speak many different languages, practice various religions and have a multiplicity of political affiliations. Some of the recent immigrants, especially Chinese and Indians, are part of "second phase migrations" arriving in the U.S. not from their countries of origin, but from Chinese diasporas in Singapore, Malaysia, and Cambodia or Indian diasporas in Uganda, Surinam, Fiji or Trinidad. Even when joining older groups, the newer immigrants add layers of class difference: whereas many of the earlier Chinese, Filipino and Indian immigrants were nonliterate laborers, the new arrivals from these groups include large numbers of middle-class professionals. The incorporation of such diverse groups within the notion of an Asian American identity has proved very difficult since their arrival has profoundly de-stabilized the formation. High-lighting the ironies of the new immigration, B.O. Hing, an Asian American leader, observes: "The success of one thing that we have fought for, namely, fair and equal immigration policies, has institutionalized a system which keeps us in constant flux" (Quoted in *AAP*, 95). Hing's comments overlook a further stratification in the constituency produced by the substantial number of Asians who are entering the country illegally, and are subsequently trapped within the most exploitative conditions of existence as workers in sweatshops, restaurant and brothels. This destabilization of the Asian American constituency has been engaged within the discipline primarily through the rhetoric of pluralism. Once we include the experiences of all the constituent groups, it is reasoned, the representational logic of the rubric will become apparent. Furthermore, the conventional wisdom goes, the dissemination of a pan-Asian consciousness will eventually unify the various Asian groups.

5) Finally, the fifth and latest historical pattern of ethnic identity formation has emerged in the last decade or so, and the scripts it has produced have further transformed the constituency we refer to as Asian America. This shift has been initiated by the reconfiguration of aspects of ethnicity within a transnational context. During this period, relations between the U.S. and Asia have undergone dramatic change and we have entered a transnational era that is remaking

economic, political, and cultural relations in the Pacific. As a result, ethnicity, can no longer be solely contextualized within the problematic of whether and how Asian Americans will be incorporated into the American body politic, but must also be read through the deterritorialization of ethnic identity. This transformation has begun to be engaged within the discipline, but is generally treated as a product or added feature of the fourth pattern, and addressed, if at all, through the overstrained and inadequate vocabulary of pluralism. The remaking of aspects of Asian American ethnicity during this period will be the subject of the last section of my essay. In historicizing these developments, I do not mean to imply that they are linear or progressive in their emergence; older formations often nest inside newer identity formations, or are unevenly developed across and within generations or ethnic groups. Certain patterns may be more significant in the experience of some groups than others. It is precisely because of the discontinuities and stratifications produced during these different periods that the concept of Asian American identity becomes such a complex one. The rhetoric and tropes that have been generated within the discipline to address or contain these differentiations, including the founding rubric of the discipline, are breaking under the strain of representing such heterogeneity. In the face of the staggering diversity of these emergent formations, interpellated by the transition from ethnicity to panethnicity, occupying differential positions in the vast imaginaries called "Asia," "America" and "Asian America," we face the theoretical challenge of constructing and examining our literatures and histories, without erasing our differences and conflicts.

Defining the Literature: The Arithmetic of Inclusion

In this section I will examine three paradigmatic discussions of Asian American literature. Each of them attempts to map the field of Asian American literary production, and the boundaries they draw reveal the political temper of their historical moment, as well as the defining forces within the field of Asian American Studies. It is, therefore, critical to examine these attempts as definitive moments in the development of the field. Despite the progressively greater "inclusiveness" that marks the efforts of these different critics, the practice of an additive approach leaves unresolved, and even obscures, fundamental theoretical questions about the rubric as an enunciatory and interpretive category. For Chin and Kim, Chinese American and Japanese American literature forms the core of the field, the source of the tropes, themes and paradigms of ethnicity that constitute the literature. For all three critics, "other" Asian American literatures (Filipino, Korean, South Asian, Southeast Asian) are added on as auxiliary formations in deference to numerical ratios, the changing Census classifications, or the critic's own ethnic affiliation; or incorporated through the free-floating idioms of postmodernism (multiplicity, hybridity) that lack any historical specificity or cultural thickness. To use numbers as a gauge of our ability to integrate various literary traditions is fundamentally fallacious; it offers the palliative of inclusion without requiring any serious theoretical engagement with analyzing the grounds of our commonalty/differences. The certainty and precision of numbers assume the power within critical discourse of signifying integration and coverage: note the rhetorical echoes in Shirley Lim's title "Twelve Asian American Writers: In Search of Self-Definition," or Jessica Hagedorn's insistence in her recent anthology, *Charlie Chan Is Dead*, that her inclusion of forty-eight different writers is an index of her commitment to the meanings of contemporary Asian American fiction.

In choosing these particular critical texts for analysis, I am attempting to investigate the modalities of primary definition. As a result, the concern of the essay is not to provide a comprehensive survey of all the participants in these debates, but to examine some of the influential ones. Furthermore, I am not suggesting that all these efforts were part of either a self-conscious, individual or collaborative effort to shape and authorize an Asian American literary canon. Canon-formation does not take place through a single referendum but is rather the product, as Barbara Herrnstein Smith's deft summary indicates, "of a series of continuous interactions among a variably constituted object, emergent conditions, and the mechanisms of cultural selection and transmission."[18] Within a new field like Asian American literary studies, certain emergent conditions and mechanisms of cultural transmission have exercised a critical influence over the definition of Asian American literature. Firstly, the pace of production of critical and theoretical statements about the writings has lagged well behind the prolific production of anthologies of Asian American literature. This is, in part, because significant scholarly energy has been directed towards editing and introducing the works of individual or groups of Asian American authors. This practice of what Wendell Harris has called "fortunate sponsorship" has almost become a cottage industry in the field (112). Certainly, some degree of effort in sponsoring the work of newer or unfamiliar writers is constructive in an emergent field, but it cannot assume a disproportionate importance, nor can the task be discharged through biographical summary or thematic observations on the texts, the favored modes in many introductions. One of the consequences of this prioritization of scholarly activity has been a theoretical weakness within the field.[19] When this problem is compounded by other conditions like the status of Asian American literature as an emergent field, and the enormous demand among readers and teachers of American literature for guidance in interpreting this literature, it becomes clearer why the influence of the few critical texts to undertake an analysis of the entire field has been so great. Thus, often inadvertently, these evaluations have assumed a canon-forming power. Moreover, it has become commonplace in the discipline for even leading scholars to refer to Chinese and Japanese American texts as the "canonical" Asian American texts and to refer to other Asian American texts as "marginal" "peripheral" or "emergent" Asian American literatures. It is thus not so much a canon, but a phantom canon that the analysis of the following works will reveal.

The category "Asian American literature" gained recognition with the publication of several anthologies in the 1970s among which Frank Chin's offers the most polemical and influential elaboration of Asian American literature. Chin's anthology was published in the aftermath of the Asian American Movement of the 1960s and works from many of its ideological premises: that the separate circumstances of Asian ethnic groups are linked by a common history of exclusion and racism, that the myth of assimilation has been used to neutralize ethnic resistance and deny racial stratification, and that an assertive identity politics can be the basis of challenging Anglo hegemony. Chin's anthology works aggressively to enunciate and promote an Asian American identity that is independent of the determinations of white supremacy, and the search for autonomy leads him to formulate such authenticity in purist and separatist terms. He distinguishes between "real" Asian Americans who are "American born and raised, who got their China and Japan from the radio, off the silver screen, from television, out of comic books, from the pushers of white American culture" and "Americanized Asians," first-generation immigrants who maintain strong cultural ties to their countries of origin while fulfilling the subservient stereotype of the humble and passive Oriental (*AA*, vii). The authentic Asian American is here defined as a prototypical No-No Boy[20]: a political subject who says no to Asia, no to America and is decidedly male.[21] Paradoxically, in order to claim an Asian American identity in defiance of hegemonic codifications, Chin is led to disclaim connections with Asia. He focuses on the domestic context of ethnic identity formation and on generational distance from Asia. Clearly, Chin's rejection of the Asian part of his identity is an effort to repudiate the prevailing stereotype of Asians as perpetual foreigners in America, and to affirm the experiences of the many Asians in America at *this time*, who are several generations removed from the homeland experience. But this formulation is vitiated by its obsession with the white gaze.

Chin's Introduction also put in place the idea of an essential Asian American identity derived from the experiences and narratives of American-born Chinese and Japanese Americans which he names "the Asian American sensibility" (*AA*, ix). This notion has long survived Chin's anthology and often functions as a founding assumption in other discussions in Asian American Studies, often despite critics' heated disagreement with Chin's other views. Recent discussions of Asian American Literature (including Kim's and Lim's), have taken issue with Chin's anti-feminist and anti-immigrant postulations of Asian American literature; however, in their privileging of Chinese and Japanese American texts, and their inability to theorize the relationship between the newer and older formations, they inadvertently reproduce the framework employed by him. Even the current shift to the use of the plural *literatures* usually functions as a semantic cover for the continued reliance on essentialist paradigms through a token acknowledgement of the need for change. But the theorizing of this change is deferred — described as being beyond the scope of the current project, or reassuringly projected as being likely to be undertaken by others in the field. When such practices of deferral are accompanied by a tendency to group-specific research undertaken by "insiders" that eschews any comparative or theoretical work, the cumulative effect is a theoretical weakness in our conceptualization of the field as a whole.

Elaine Kim's discussion of Asian American literature increases the number of groups covered, by adding Korean American literature to Chin's list of Chinese, Japanese and Filipino American texts, but this expansion of the field seems arbitrarily based on the accident of ethnic affiliation rather than on any critical or literary criteria. As Kim admits in a later retrospective evaluation of her exclusion of South and Southeast Asian literatures from her study:

> I admitted at the time that this definition was arbitrary, prompted by my own inability to read Asian languages and my own lack of access to South and Southeast Asian communities. But for these shortcomings, I wrote, I would have included in my introductory study works written in Asian languages and works written by writers from Vietnamese American, Indian American, and other communities. Nonetheless, it is true that I wanted to delineate and draw boundaries around whatever I thought of as Asian American identity and literature [italics mine]. (*CC*, viii)

The carte-blanche Kim accorded her own decisions on defining Asian American literature is evidence of the degree of cultural authority that sometimes attaches to insiderism, and which, unchecked by vigilant scrutiny and challenge, can operate in powerfully exclusionary forms.[22]

The focus in Kim's analysis, as in Chin's, is on positing a literature that is expressive of the Asian American experience understood as sociologically distinct, separate from the mainstream, and shaped by settlement in the United States and the effects of American racism. But since Kim rejects Chin's central distinction between "real" and "fake" Asian American sensibilities — the crucial idea of authenticity that demarcates the boundaries of the Chin tradition — her definition of the literature incorporates the writings of first-generation immigrants and sojourners, which

Chin had dismissed as the ventriloquist production of white racism. Instead of the notion of authenticity or "cultural integrity," Kim opts for an organizing framework that is chronological. Projecting the idea of a linear evolutionary pattern onto the emergence of Asian American identity allows her to claim a constitutive logic to the rubric "Asian American literature." Her projections of such a development are tentative but hopeful: "Distinctions among the various national groups sometimes do blur after a generation or two, when it is easier for us to see what we share as members of an American racial minority ... " (*AIW*, xii). Focusing on chronological emergence allows her to shift the emphasis from the internal stratifications and differences within Asian American literature to a unity-in-the-making. Moreover, such a formulation not only fails to recognize the differential and uneven insertion of the various national groups into America by locating them in the same progressive march toward greater unity, it also fails to account for the fact that the increasing racial diversity of Asian Americans disallows any easy assumption of a unifying racial identity.

In her later essay, Kim also argues that a broad thematic concern "claiming America" characterizes the writing ("DA," 88). Methodologically, the study seems to be straining to construct a notion of commonalty. The purported commonalty is so broad as to be inclusive of other ethnic literatures, even though it is described as unique to Asian American literature. Another effect of the thematic criteria she introduces is to suture the quite disparate productions of Filipino and Korean Americans to Asian American literature by repressing the historical contexts of colonization, exile and post-colonial modernization that render their representation as local, American-based literatures much more problematic than in the case of earlier Chinese or Japanese American literature. The unique specificities of the colonial relationship between the U.S. and the Philippines, the topos of return that haunts Filipino American writing, and the continuities between Filipino and Filipino American writing create a distinctive literary formation that does not conform to prescriptions about Asian American writing derived from Japanese American and Chinese American literature.[23] Finally, much of the more recent writing, as I will show, is situated in a transnational context where America is not the exclusive locus of identification. While, on the one hand, Kim's delineation of Asian American literature is more inclusive than Chin's, her defining criteria work to reproduce the hegemony of the forms of Japanese and Chinese American literature by failing to reconfigure the field through the specificities of Korean and Filipino American writing.

Similarly, when Kim seeks to include Burmese American Wendy Law-Yone's *The Coffin Tree* within the same schema, she fails to distinguish between the refugee experience of forced dislocation, radical discontinuity and political uncertainty, and the voluntary experience of migration, except by treating the former as a more extreme expression of the drive to "claim America" common to both. Kim's methods of incorporation are symptomatic of a larger problem. With a new self-consciousness in the field about the hegemony of Japanese and Chinese American literatures, essayists and anthologists seeking to include underrepresented Asian American groups often use one particular group to stand in for the rest. References to Filipino and Vietnamese American literature, in particular, have come to operate in this fashion in the field. While the task of creating new conceptual models is avoided, such annexing of newer formations has acquired the persuasive force of comprehensiveness now. What it institutionalizes is a perception of the transposability of the newer literatures and the foundational status of the established ones. One generic outcome of such scholarly procedures is that the critical essay breaks down into lists of thematic similarities that invoke a "tradition" through sheer numerical force and the power of proxies. Another result of the rush to incorporate the newer groups is that with the quantity of available materials quite low in many cases, an industry is emerging to produce materials to fill this demand. While on the one hand, the effort to encourage writers from less-known groups is commendable, publishing numerous hastily-compiled, weakly-conceived anthologies is, finally, counter-productive. Availability of texts cannot be an end in itself. Furthermore, since the newer material is frequently being made available through collaborative autobiographies and student writing, where the extent of mediation is very high (especially where translation complicates the process of transmission), we need to interrogate the structures that determine literary production. In the case of collaborative autobiographies, where the reconstitution of the absent figure of the underrepresented is caught up in the epistemic violence of a disciplinary emphasis on concrete experience and sovereign subjectivity, and where the place of the collaborator is marked by a singular transparency, we cannot proceed without a historical critique of the collaborating/ editorial subject. Autobiographical voicing is a fraught project in this context. An uncritical recourse to productivity in order to facilitate inclusion might only create a disciplinary formation where some of the groups stand in quasi-ethnographical relation to others.

In Lim's earlier essay "Twelve Asian American Writers: In Search of Self-Definition," the number stands in for breadth of coverage although all the writers discussed as "Asian American" are either Japanese or Chinese American. What is most troubling about this kind of slippage is its institutional reproduction over several decades in the field, as we have seen in the criticism of Chin and Kim. Lim notes that Asian American writing is part of the macrocosm of American writing but also reveals "certain inextricably Asian psychological and philosophical perspectives.

A strong Confucian patriarchal orientation is a dominant element and with that the corollary of female inferiority ..." (237). Not only is this statement incredibly reductive, but the collapsing of the distinctions between Asian and Confucian reveals what Gayatri Spivak has called a "sanctioned ignorance" about the cultural diversity of Asia that, interestingly enough, has its antecedents in American Orientalist writings, which have long centralized East Asian cultures because of a history of trade, military and missionary contacts between these areas and the U.S.[24]

This problem is compounded by the publication of Lim's essay in the MLA anthology *Redefining American Literary History* that undertakes as its project precisely what the essay most neglects to perform within the context of its own field. Moreover, the two other essays on Asian American literature included in the anthology focus on the work of Maxine Hong Kingston. The narrowness in the scope of what is covered as Asian American writing, and the complete absence of reference to this as an issue, suggest a kind of axiomatic force such an equivalence has gathered within the discipline, from which it is being disseminated amongst general readers of ethnic and American literature.

What is heartening are the significant critical shifts in the theoretical assumptions about Asian American literature between Lim's two essays. Shirley Lim's recent essay "Assaying the Gold" shows itself to be more aware of the dangers of an uncritical acceptance of the rubric Asian American literature, although the analytic methods and lexicon employed within the essay often finesse rather than confront the problems raised. Although she acknowledges, on the one hand, that "the rubric 'Asian American literature'... is both exceedingly contemporary, a newly invented epistemological tool, and already collapsing under the weight of its own contradictions," Lim avoids the implications of her own insight by settling for the nostalgic prediction that the increasing heterogeneity of the field will produce a greater pan-Asian consciousness among writers and readers. The evidence Lim summons to support this hope is rather slender and shifts between literary and sociological arenas. According to Lim, there are more signs of "biculturalism" "multiculturalism" and "borderland" negotiations in recent Asian American literary texts. By way of sociological support for her position, Lim argues that a greater solidarity has emerged among Asian Americans in response to mainstream American discrimination and as a result of coalition building among Asian Americans. And these factors, we are told, augur well for the emergence of a new phase in Asian American writing: "The stage is set for the transformation of Asian American literature into Pan-Asian American readings, from the old singular ethnic body into a multiethnic body ... and we are already reading the scripts" (164-165).

The major problem with Lim's critical assertions is that they make predictions about the growth of a socio-historical, political, economic and cultural phenomenon like pan-Asian consciousness by using evidence drawn from a limited arena. In this respect, Lim repeats an error often made by cultural critics who read in the changes effected in the academy seismic socio-cultural transformations. Pan-Asian consciousness has enjoyed its greatest success on college campuses, as researchers of the Asian American movement have pointed out, but its political effectivity and acceptance in the Asian American constituency as a whole has been much more uneven. Contrary to Lim's neat predictions, sociological research on the future of Asian American panethnicity is more mixed in its findings, indicating simultaneously the growth of pan-Asian organizations and increased conflicts among them.[25] Yen Le Espiritu has identified the ethnic and class inequality within the pan-Asian structure, the influx of post-65 immigrants, and the reduction of public funding sources as causes of potential conflict among the various Asian ethnic groups (51). Moreover, contrary to the early hopes of activists, the institutionalization of Asian American Studies has had little effect on the various communities and, over time, the gulf between the community and the academy has only widened. I will also argue in greater detail later that changes in the political distribution system are likely to further interrupt the growth of pan-Asian consciousness. The projection of a pan-Asian framework as encompassing the future direction of the literature is premature, unsubstantiated and seeks to effect an emotional resolution to the problems of political identity raised by the very use of the term "Asian American." As in the work of Kim, the legitimacy of the rubric is finally salvaged as a signifier by pointing to a future in which it shall come to be. In the case of Kim and Lim, pluralism offers the avenue for that deferral: once everyone has been included, the representational truth of the rubric will be made manifest: "the next stage is for Asian Americans to become reflective of the multiple ethnicities that already compose their identity" ("CGA," 164).

Lim uses the terms "biculturalism" "multiculturalism" and "borderland" consciousness to represent some of the shifts discernible in the coding of ethnicity in contemporary Asian American literature, and then lists the work of writers who exemplify these new paradigms like Jessica Hagedorn, Bharati Mukherjee and David Henry Hwang. Multiculturalism is a term so capacious that recognition of it as a textual feature signals a critic's self-positioning as progressive and up-to-date, rather than illuminating in any specific way the dynamics of the text. If it is a reference to an official policy that shapes the terms of social interaction and literary production, then a term like "multiculturalism" would mean something very different in the case of a Mukherjee novel like *Jasmine* than, say, in the case of a Hagedorn novel like *Dogeaters*.[26] But Lim makes no effort to differentiate between the usages — consequently, the terminology functions as a loose and free-floating signifier of Asian Americanness that lacks any cultural density. *Jasmine* begins in a Punjab enmeshed in religious conflict between Sikhs and Hindus — the post-colonial sequel to the fostering of ethno-religious separatism, in the interests of political control, by the British colonial regime in India — an official multicultural policy that in colonialist and nationalist forms has had murderous consequences. Once she arrives in the U.S., Jasmine enters into a different version of a multicultural imaginary, where her cultural difference as an Indian female (which lacks referential density in the U.S.), is reinscribed as exotic sexual power. In Hagedorn's text, the legacy of Spanish and American colonialism have created a society obsessed with colonial genealogies and infatuated with Hollywood films, caught in a modernity marked by political corruption and poverty, where sexual desire becomes the site for the inscription of the incoherence, exploitation and violence that signify its experience of "multiculturalism." It could be argued that multiculturalism operates in so many different registers in these two texts that it differentiates them from each other rather than unifies them as *Asian American texts*. Finally, the use of multiculturalism as a unifying feature of contemporary Asian American texts leaves so many questions unanswered. Do Asian American texts operate the category of multiculturalism any differently from other ethnic texts? Do they share more in common with each other in this respect than they do with "mainstream" texts? Since multiculturalism in its broadest sense has become a feature of most modern societies and texts, surely we need some more finely honed criteria if we are to argue for its common existence in these two and other Asian American texts. Critics of Asian American literature need to be particularly vigilant that their institutional location as interpreters of "Asian American literature" does not predispose them to recycle and accommodate disparate cultural products into the existing categories of their discipline, or into the convenient catch-all terms generated by pluralism. Instead, the expansion of the literature must be accompanied by the generation of new criteria on the basis of which our selections are made. Cultural production is a much messier process than the available categories of ethnicity allow for. It is therefore imperative, as Werner Sollors points out, "that the categorization of writers — and literary critics — as 'members' of ethnic groups is understood to be a very partial, temporary and insufficient categorization at best" (256). In the case of Asian Americans, who are categorized within the most novel and artificial of ethnic formations, the mutability and fictionality of membership is a much more intense experience, one that needs to be foregrounded and not dispelled in our theorizations of Asian American literature.

Before I turn to the last part of my argument, I would like to briefly analyze a recent heated exchange between Jessica Hagedorn, the editor of one of the latest anthologies of Asian American fiction, *Charlie Chan Is Dead*, and Sven Birkerts, who reviewed the anthology for *The New York Times Book Review*.[28] The exchange serves as a critical parable for the arguments I have made thus far about the axiomatic status of Asian American literature within the discipline, the theoretical weakness within the field, and the recourse to the affirmation of ethnic identity to defer addressing the challenges of its heterogeneity. My comments on the following exchange also prepare the way for the last part of my essay in which I will discuss the effects of transnational forces on Asian American ethnicity, the failure of the discipline to take up this challenge in a significant way, and the incoherence that attaches to the term as a result of this failure.

The conflict between Hagedorn and Birkerts takes place over the ordering rubric for her collection — "Asian American fiction." For Birkerts, the problem with the anthology is its insufficiently formulated inclusiveness:

To begin with, there are just too many different kinds of inclusions, everything from Indian-born Meena Alexander's aggressively hip "Manhattan Music" to "1 Would Remember," a simple and powerful story by Carlos Bulosan, a Filipino born in 1913. "Asian American" has here become a term so hospitable that half the world's population can squeeze in under its banner. Generous and catholic, yes — but the mix is also jarring and too eclectic. The chaos is compounded — if chaos can be — by Ms. Hagedorn's reliance on an alphabetical ordering (effectively eliminating any impression of generational change) and by the unevenness of the contributions. First-rate work by authors like Joy Kogawa, David Wong Louie, Jose Garcia Villa, John Yau and Jocelyn Lieu must sit side by side with a number of less than distinguished stories from the post-modernist grab bag.

Hagedorn's acid retort to the reviewer directs his attention once again to the inclusiveness of the collection as its defining feature. But she neither explains the need for, or grounds of, such inclusiveness within the contemporary context of Asian American fiction:

Rather than dealing with the literature presented in "Charlie Chan Is Dead: An Anthology of Contemporary Asian American Fiction" (Dec. 19), Sven Birkerts spends more than half of his review obsessing over the writers' bloodlines, and complaining that my inclusion of 48 writers as "Asian American" may have been too "hospitable." What exactly are his criteria for categorizing someone as Asian American? Since this is the first anthology of its kind, is this really the time to be narrow? ...

Is Mr. Birkerts an immigration official or a literary critic? Should we all send in our passports and green cards for verification? ... What I hope from any reviewer of "Charlie Chan Is Dead" is that he or she treat seriously the form and substance of our literature.[28]

Birkerts's perplexity in confronting the staggering range of writings in the anthology is hardly surprising given the lack of an adequate theoretical or historical framework, a clear articulation of the criteria of selection, or in the absence of either, an explanation about the inability to provide such statements given the exceeding novelty of the field, the artificial conjunctions it effects, and the enormous transformations it has undergone within the last decades. Instead, both Elaine Kim, who has written a brief Preface, and Jessica Hagedorn, who provides an Introduction, invoke the celebration of differences, and the "international," as heady auguries of the new and liberating future that belongs to Asian American literature, and a sign of its break from the narrow cultural nationalism of its founding moment in the sixties. Hagedorn's page-length catalog that characterizes the "hipness" of her selections as "funky" "sassy" "sexy" substitutes affirmation for analysis. All too often the critical responsibilities that attend the task of introducing an inaugural volume ("the first anthology of Asian American fiction by a commercial publisher in this country ") to a largely unfamiliar public are discharged by citing difference within a dizzying post-modern schema of montage and juxtaposition: "Some of these writers were originally poets, some still are. Others only write fiction. Some were born in the Philippines, some in Seattle. A few in Hawaii. Others in Toronto or London … Seoul. Greeley, Colorado. India. Penang. Moscow, Idaho" (xxix-xxx). This technique has the effect of positing the arbitrariness of the category at the level of haphazard global positionings that emerge as signifies of the unpredictable and the provocative, rather than as the product of specific historical conditions. The only gloss Hagedorn provides on the relationship between her category and the global list of place names is the following summation: "Asian American literature? Too confining a term, maybe. World literature? Absolutely" (xxx). Why, then, has the editor retained the first label when a clearly better one is at hand? Or, to quote the Michael Jackson song, what does it mean for Asian Americans to say "We are the World"? Both the Introduction and the Preface list (but do not explain or theorize) the dizzying array of differences but then move on to achieve closure by sounding the note of "celebration." The overwhelming need seems to be to reconstitute wholeness at the level of mood, so that identity can emerge at the level of emotion, when it cannot be created through theoretical or critical interpretation.

For his part, the conflation of the ethnic with the local/domestic is the grounding assumption in Birkerts's understanding of ethnic literature. His primary difficulty in reading the anthology and locating its rationale derives from his understanding of how "difference" operates as a signifier in literary production — as a category or categories of intelligibility that narrow the focus, producing a kind of "special interest subjectivity."[29] Contrary to his expectations, the Chan anthology "turns the funnel upside down" on the trend among anthologists to "narrow the focus, screening down by race, sex, ethnicity, sexual orientation, geography, age or topical criteria." In this anthology, the locus of the ethnic shifts to the global. The term "minority" which is popularly taken to signify the fractional, peripheral, tangential seems to counter its own logic in assuming another aspect as overwhelming, or engulfing: "half the world's population can squeeze in under its banner." His consternation with the range of writings is imaged through the very geography that assumes the burden of imposing coherence on the notion of identity. The distance between the two perspectives that emerges in this encounter — between the Asian American writer-anthologist and the general reader — operating as it does as a site of charged accusations and defences, points to the necessary theoretical work that needs to be undertaken in elucidating the fictionality of the rubric.

We have now entered an era in which the dispersion and re-configuration of ethnic identity among Asian Americans will only accelerate, and it is to these new forces, which will recast aspects of ethnic formation, that I will now turn, in order to make some suggestions for the reorientation of theoretical investigations within the field.

Rethinking American Literature and Theory

The emergence of pan-Asian ethnicity has been a vexed, conflicted and incomplete process, especially in the recent past, and is further complicated by the fact that no readily available symbols or grounds of cultural commonalty exist within such a heterogeneous formation. But Yen Le Espiritu argues that the problem of a lack of cultural commonalties, far from being unique to Asian Americans, is in fact typical, in various degrees, of the process of panethnicization in the U.S.: "culture has followed panethnic boundaries rather than defined them" because "panethnic groups in the United States are products of political and social processes, rather than of cultural bonds" (13). While Espiritu's statement has certainly been true of the historical experiences of African Americans and Native Americans, for groups like Latin Americans and Asian Americans who have a shorter, more internally uneven history of being shaped by American location, and whose panethnic formation is being continuously destabilized and transformed by fresh waves of immigration, the presumption of a progressive development of panethnicity is much less predictable.

Two structural factors will significantly interrupt the formation of panethnicity in patterns that were conceivable in the past: a more conservative political climate that is increasingly hostile to structuring access along ethnic lines, and changes in the global economy that will significantly impact ethnic formation. I will analyze the transformative potential of both definitive shifts.

The 1994 elections have produced a transformed political landscape in which a more conservative agenda has defined discussions of welfare, affirmative action, and immigration. In addition, the recent recession, the temporization of the workforce, the numerous layoffs and decline in real wages, and the reduction in federal spending have created an embattled public that, mobilized by conservative rhetoric, has shown support for the curtailment of affirmative action and welfare programs and restrictions on immigration. The recent Supreme Court rulings that have mandated standards of "compelling federal interest" and "strict scrutiny" for affirmative action programs in education and federal contracts have reinforced this trend. What we see as a result of these changes that are already under way (and only likely to intensify) is that a polity which structured access along ethnic lines since the civil rights era is slowly curtailing these policies. As social scientists have pointed out, the ascriptive force of the state is crucial to the production and consolidation of ethnicity. Joane Nagel notes that ethnic resurgences are strongest when the state uses the ethnic category as a unit in economic allocations and political representations (Quoted in *AAP*, 10). When these identifications are reinforced over a period of time through the coincidence of political and economic interests, the emergence of panethnicity is encouraged despite lack of common cultural bonds. In other words, "shifts in ethnic boundaries are often a direct response to changes in the political distribution system" (*AAP*, 11). The recent structural changes in the political distribution system would seem to suggest that the state's increasing unwillingness to legitimize ethnic labels as determinants of access may lead to a weakening of panethnicity, especially among predominantly foreign-born Asian American populations.

To suggest that the panethnic rubric may not be as effective in producing the more stable formations of the past is not to argue that the alternative narrative of assimilation will define the orientation and identifications of Asians in the U.S. Contrary to a long-standing tradition amongst critics that sets ethnicization in opposition to assimilation, I would argue that ethnicization will be influenced by a transnational context through polyethnic contacts across and within ethnic groups both inside and outside the country. It is here that I differ from Werner Sollors, who also challenges the ethnic identity versus assimilation opposition; however, Sollors undoes the opposition only to recuperate the transethnic within a narrowly domestic conception of American national identity.[30] For this reason, Sollors's formulations about ethnic literature are more successful in the analysis of aspects of the African American tradition or second- and third-generation writers from other groups, but are inadequate to addressing the patterns found in more recent immigrant writing. Americanization/assimilation which was earlier associated with "Anglo conformity" will probably give way to a process of Americanization where most groups can, as Arjun Appadurai puts it, "renegotiate their links to their diasporic identities from their American vantage points."[31] It is precisely because the assimilationary process is losing its former power that presidential candidate Patrick Buchanan and conservative critic Peter Brimelow (author of *Alien Nation*) have issued alarmist calls for a "pause" in immigration similar to the one between 1924 and 1965; or, for a restriction to European-only immigration to reinvigorate the absorptive process.[32] At present, entry into the U.S. entails an adjustment to American codes and practices (what we have called assimilation), but it also enables investments/remittances that reestablish links to the home-country, return visits under a new status, and the entry of family members into the U.S. Within this context, becoming American does not necessarily involve a loss of the home culture, or a choice between ethnicity or mainstreaming as in earlier patterns of immigration to this country.

The globalization of capital, the transnationalization of production, the migrations of diverse peoples, the varying trajectories of arrival, departure and return (immigrants, exiles, refugees, temporary workers, intellectual exchange visitors), the creation of global information superhighways, and the electronic transfer of images and capital, have seen an exponential increase in the sites, frequency and variety of cross-cultural exchange. The shift from multinational corporations to transnational corporations with a global strategy has proliferated the points of exchange, transfer and contact. The world-wide move away from socialist policies following the collapse of the Soviet Union, accompanied by the lowering of trade barriers and the spread of consumer culture, has encouraged this shift. Whereas multinationals maintained autonomous subsidiaries with separate strategies in various countries, transnational companies support a global strategy that is conceived and implemented in a world-wide setting. As a result, they create circuits of capital, personnel and information that have multiple nodes, each more closely linked and dependent on the others, than within the older multinational system.

The rapid economic growth of parts of Asia (Japan, Singapore, China, Vietnam, Malaysia, Philippines, Indonesia and India) over the last few decades has led to the proliferation of such transnational networks linking America and Asia, and as we move into what is being called the Pacific Century, these processes will only accelerate and proliferate. The emergence of the "borderless economy" has intensified linkages that defy containment within the nation state. Plans are under way to establish a free trade zone between the U.S. and Pacific Rim countries modelled on NAFTA; Chinese government officials are establishing a Special Economic Zone linking the Yunan region to Laos and Vietnam; trade links within ASEAN and SAARC countries have increased and strengthened.[33] The effect of these changes on Asian Americans will be substantial. Asian Americans, who have historically disavowed their connections to Asia in order to challenge racist stereotypes as perpetual foreigners, will be able to renegotiate their links to Asia; mainstream Americans will reencounter Asia within changed geopolitical alignments, which will not allow easy assumptions of patronage and wardship that stemmed from privileges of extraterritoriality and conquest in the nineteenth and early twentieth century.[34]

What we see appearing are global networks that do not conform to earlier models of departure from Asia and settlement in America that occurred within a vastly different geopolitical economy. For instance, patterns of reverse migration are beginning to emerge among Chinese Americans and Korean Americans due to strengthened economic conditions and the increase in living standards in their homecountry, and a decline in living standards in the U.S. Over the last four years, the number of people who received immigration visas from South Korea to the U.S. has fallen by more than half, from 25, 500 in 1990 to 10, 800 in 1994, simultaneously, in each of these four years between 5,000 and 6,500 people have returned to Korea, compared to 800 in 1980.[35] Such reverse migrations may also take place amongst the other Asian American groups if the economic and political situations in their home countries improve.

Nor is migration exclusively a sign of "cosmopolitan" class privilege. Poverty and gender do not impede migration but inflect the forms it takes. Garment sweatshops in some of the major U.S. cities draw on immigrant female workers, most of whom are Asian and Latin American.[37] Owners of ethnic grocery stores, restaurants, or the ubiquitous 7-11 convenience stores employ impoverished workers from their home countries for low wages, sometimes using the prospective green card as a lure. Tony Chan's film *Combination Platter* provides a sympathetic view of the predicament of the restaurant owner of The Szechuan Inn, Mr. Lee, and the undocumented workers whom he employs, both of whom are under siege by the INS, while they purvey to oblivious New Yorkers one of the staples of their ethnic experience — Chinese take-out at cheap rates. The film cuts between the hectic, hot and crowded male world of the kitchen workers and the leisurely, loquacious and self-absorbed world of the dining-room clientele, connected by commerce and separated from contact. Asian Americans inhabit both sides of the divide in this film, highlighting class differentiations within the group. The film follows Robert, who works as a waiter in the restaurant while he pursues, during his off-hours, his elusive quest for a green card, always under threat of exposure and deportation to Hong Kong.

Gender further defines the forms and trajectories of migration and the production of ethnicity in a transnational context. The international sex-trade has connected Thailand and the Philippines to America, Japan and Europe through package flesh tours, prostitution smuggling rings and mail-order bride catalogs (representations of these global networks appear in Jessica Hagedorn's *Dogeaters* and Wanwadee Larsen's *Confessions of a Mail Order Bride*) .[37] The debtcrisis in countries like Sri Lanka and the Philippines has created an enormous outflow of female migrant workers to the Middle East, Japan, Singapore, the U.S. and Europe, just as the entry of large numbers of middle-class women into the workforce in the West, and the increased prosperity of some Middle Eastern and Asian countries, has led to an enormous demand for such labor.[38] By March 1988, approximately 175, 000 Filipinas were working overseas (about 81,000 as domestic workers) and sending home between $60-$100 million in foreign exchange (*BBB*, 187-188). The recent protests in the Philippines against governmental indifference to the plight of its foreign workers — following the execution by the Singapore government of Flor Contemplacion, an overseas Filipina maid — highlight the growing symbolic importance of the migrant worker in the Filipino national consciousness.[39] The short story "Jasmine" from Bharati Mukherjee's collection *The Middleman and Other Stories* explores the layered ironies in the relationship between Lara, a white feminist who is a performance artist, and Jasmine, the young Indian woman from Trinidad, whom she employs as a nanny or "day-mommy."[40] Lara's professionalism and feminism are enabled and subsidized by Jasmine's illegal status in the country, the underside to the successes of a liberal women's movement that argued from a platform of access, individual rights and emancipation from domesticity.

The sites for the production of heterogeneous Asian ethnicities, therefore, defy easy containment within national boundaries. Ethnicity metamorphoses at multiple sites of transit, return, and arrival in the movement between and within nations; it can no longer be solely defined through the negotiation between origin and destination. It is imperative that Asian American Studies move beyond comforting affirmations of pluralism and the celebration of differences as the terms of their engagement with these transformative processes taking place.

The disjunctions and multiple migrations that deterritorialize ethnicity are the subject of many of the newer stories produced by Asian Americans. When ethnic identity is produced through multiple location, ethnic categories become destabilized and, consequently, open to misrecognition and reinscription. Once the narrator leaves Pakistan in Sara Suleri's *Meatless Days*, her family experience of the trauma of Partition and the genocidal divisiveness of the Bangladesh War render her loath to attach identity to place. The luminous and elliptical prose of the narrative refuses to name in the language of belonging the spaces through which she moves after her arrival in the U.S.[41] Her discourse discreedy skirts the available American categories of identity, "ethnic" "minority" or "Asian American," locating itself instead in the transmogrifications to which identity is subject in the spaces opened up by death and displacement in her stories. The potential for reinscription of ethnic codings is taken up in a comic mode in Mira Nair's *Mississippi Masala*. Her story revises prototypical narratives of ethnic formation, and the rubric "Asian American" strains to contain the displacements through which ethnicity travels. The film moves between Africa and America but the result is not a narrative of African America as we have come to think about it. Instead, the story is the unfamiliar one of displaced Indians moving across two continents. India as the space of "origin" never materializes as locale in the film; instead, India emerges in the Ugandan context as the boundary produced by British colonialism in the insertion of a middleman minority into an African colonial state, and then redrawn in post-Independence Idi Amin's Uganda, to reassert black nationhood through the expulsion of "foreign" elements. Within the racialized imagination of Mississippi, Ugandan "Indians" are an unfamiliar category misrecognized through older categories (Indian? American Indian — African? African American?). If the film unsettles our ideas about the category Asian American, it also ironizes the confidence with which we read the category African American by offering us another African American story set in Mississippi. The fictions of the putatively more stable Asian ethnic formations, like Chinese Americans and Japanese Americans, also show the effects of the diasporic renegotiation of identities as in Peter Wang's film *The Great Wall* or in David Mura's *Turning Japanese*, both stories of return to the country of origin.[42] The topos of return, which had appeared in earlier Asian American narratives as an imagined or actual end-point to the action allowing for resolution to the dilemmas of identification, appears as one more nodal point in an ongoing action that highlights the perplexities and paradoxes of belonging. Many of these stories deliberately avoid closure, ending with their characters beginning a new journey, in transit, or on the road.

However, travel possesses a different valence in each story because of important political and material differences. Suleri enters the U.S. as a student, a voluntary migration enabled by her class status, although her decision to leave seems to be precipitated by the political crises that follow the Bangladesh War. In *Mississippi Masala*, once again, political turmoil prompts the journey but this journey is a forced migration. Turned into political refugees, the Ugandan Indian extended family arrives in the U.S. with sufficient capital (that circulates through a diasporic ethnic network) to enter into a niche market at an opportune moment when the motel business was being abandoned by other Americans. The Chinese American family in *The Great Wall* is financially stable enough to afford an extended visit to China which, like Mura's, is a journey of cultural recovery. Mura himself is the beneficiary of a cultural exchange program that funds his one-year visit to Japan, and the cultural links that are sponsored by the two countries are underwritten by economic and political interests. The journeys undertaken from America are visits supported by a "strong" passport and a "hard" currency and involve an eventual return to a comfortable existence.

The earlier patterns of Asian immigrant experiences created more bounded immigrant communities where differentiations were experienced most keenly in separation from the dominant culture, from the home country, or across gender and generational divisions. The distance between Asia and America was more formidable at that time, the passages more dangerous, and the communications more tenuous, as the stories of Maxine Hong Kingston's *China Men* suggest.[43] The temporality of immigration as it emerges through the tropes of amnesia, exhaustion, and deferral mythifies the experience of Chinese laborers who made the journey to America fired by the ambition to make money and return, but were forced by harsh working conditions, poor salaries or new attachments to delay or abandon the idea of return. But some of the newer fictions of Asian American writers show the emergence of different "chronotopes" of immigration that represent the production of ethnicity in passage through a smaller world where national borders are more porous.[44] Arjun Appadurai delineates the challenges that the transnational poses for theorizations of American ethnicity:

> The formula of hyphenation (as in Italian-Americans, Asian-Americans, and African-Americans) is reaching the point of saturation, and the right-hand side of the hyphen can barely contain the unruliness of the left-hand side ... The politics of ethnic identity in the United States is inseparably linked to the global spread of originally local national identities. For every nation-state that has exported significant numbers of its populations to the United States as refugees, tourists, or students, there is now a delocalized *transnation*, which retains a special ideological link to a putative place of origin but is otherwise a thoroughly diasporic collectivity. No existing conception of Americanness can contain this large variety of transnations. (424)

Recently, critic Sau-ling Wong has coined a new term, "denationalization," to refer to some of the changes that I have discussed in this essay.[45] It is necessary to address her criticisms in some detail since they have appeared at a crucial moment in the development of the field. While Wong acknowledges the significance of transnational influences on Asian American ethnicity, she cautions against a "trend" she sees as potentially depoliticizing: the loss of focus on "domestic" issues in a preoccupation with the "diasporic." However, the term "denationalization," which, according to the OED, means "to make (an institution, etc.) no longer national; to divest of its character as belonging to the whole nation, or to a particular nation" distorts the complexity, range and effects of transnational perspectives on the field. It is important to recognize that the transnational is not antithetical to the national; it both reconstitutes the national, and exceeds it in crucial ways. Hence, Wong's conceptualization of these phenomena through the term denationalization is tendentious and fundamentally flawed. Moreover, the usage is vitiated by the associations of the term. The term "denationalized" is widely used in neoimperialist theory where it refers to the indigenous elites who collaborate with transnational corporate interests, setting them in an exploitative relationship to, and severed from the interests of, the people at large. Is Wong implying a parallel between transnational cultural critics and such elites? Since she does not indicate the source of her terminology, the prior associations of the term make her usage highly problematic. I would also argue that, in the politically contentious nineties, where the rhetoric against immigrants is so highly charged, a term like "denationalization" can be easily appropriated into right-wing arguments about the difficulty of incorporating Asians into American nationhood.

Many of the problems in her essay can be traced to the framing of false oppositions (between what she calls "domestic" and "diasporic" perspectives, and between politics and theory) from which conclusions are derived. In fact, a striking feature of the essay is the manner in which it attempts to resolve complex interrelated affiliations into neat sets of priorities in the name of *praxis*. The whole reason for employing perspectives for Asian American Studies that go beyond location in America is that it is often impossible fully to understand and respond to the local without a comprehension of global forces and institutions. Furthermore, diasporic loyalties do not necessarily prevent Asian Americans from mobilizing as Asian Americans: for example, Asian Americans organized in record numbers to oppose the recent proposed restrictions in immigration along with many Latin Americans. It is likely that the politics of Asian Americans will be more and more defined by issue-based strategic alliances with other groups as a way of responding to the political complexities of the nineties.

A further problem is the confusion at the descriptive and conceptual level of key terms like "transnational" "international" and "borderless economy" through which she advances her argument. For instance, Wong argues that the Third World linkages influencing the founding of Asian American Studies were "inherently transnational in outlook" (3). This is part of a defensive move to assert that the founding moment of the field was not far removed from current theoretical concerns. However, the "transnational" influences on the field today have few precedents in the "international" linkages and connections that shaped the originary moment of the field. It is patronizing, on the one hand, to seek to rehabilitate historically specific ethnic identifications by representing them in contemporary vocabulary, and misleading, on the other hand, to dismiss current concerns as a "trend."

Most disturbing are the conclusions which the argument (that at times proceeds by implication, inferences from conversations, and speculations about interlocutors) draws. Wong asserts that the focus of the field must remain the originary one of "claiming the Americas" and "commitment to the place where one resides" (19). These, she claims, are the founding principles of Asian American Studies. It is baffling that such a simplistic formula is held to be adequate for dealing with the vastly changed and complex political realities of the nineties. When such formulas are then aligned with the issue of "commitment" we are on perilous ground, indeed. After all, one usually hears the rhetoric of commitment in relation to Asian Americans from quite different sources. Moreover, the issue of "commitment" holds a particularly painful history for Asian Americans whose loyalty to America has been historically impugned by racist allegations (coded as "alienness" or "unassimilability"), most notably in the instance of the internment of Japanese Americans and the administering of a loyalty questionnaire. Certainly, doubts about the "commitment to the place one resides" have not been raised with respect to the politics of other diasporic groups like Irish Americans or Jewish Americans. If this is the route we are to take, how will we measure commitment, and who will serve as arbiter of these proceedings? The study of the influence of transnationalism in the field is not a "trend" that conforms to white expectations of theoretical sophistication, or the matter of a referendum among Asian American critics about the future development of the field. Wong's essay is problematic for the conservative tendency of its conclusions, the weakness of the evidence offered, the frequently distorting representation of the positions it challenges, and the preemptive nature of the intervention it makes to the development of the field in new directions.

It is clear from the foregoing analysis that the boundary marking of the field is caught up in a perception of competing needs: the tension between the need for political identity and the need to represent the conflicted and heterogeneous formation we call "Asian American." These needs are antagonistic to each other only if we work from the assumption that there is a "real" Asian American identity to which our vocabulary and procedures can be adequate. Hence, the pluralist computation that the sum of the parts will give us the whole. I would contend that "Asian American" offers us a rubric that we cannot not use. But our usage of the term should rehearse the catachrestic status of the formation. I use the term "catachresis" to indicate that there is no literal referent for the rubric "Asian American," and, as such, the name is marke by the limits of its signifying power. It then becomes our responsibility to articulate the inner contradictions of the term and to enunciate its representational inconsistencies and dilemmas. For, as Adorno notes, "criticizing epistemology also means ... retaining it."[46] Asian American Studies is uniquely positioned to intervene in current theoretical discussions on ethnicity, representation and writing not despite of, but because of, the contested and contestatory nature of its formation.

Notes

1. The first critical anthology that deals exclusively with Asian American literary studies was published under the title *Reading the Literatures of Asian America*, ed. Shirley Geok-lin Lim and Amy Ling (Philadelphia: Temple University Press, 1992).

2. *Aiiieeeee! An Anthology of Asian-American Writers*, ed. Chin et al. (Washington, D.C.: Howard University Press, 1974), hereafter abbreviated *AA*; Kim, *Asian American Literature: An Introduction to the Writings and Their Social Context* (Philadelphia: Temple University Press, 1982), hereafter abbreviated *AIW*; Kim, "Defining Asian American Realities Through Literature," *Cultural Critique* 6/7 (1987): 87-111, hereafter abbreviated "DA"; Lim, "Twelve Asian American Writers: In Search of Self-Definition," in *Redefining American Literary History*, ed. A. LaVonne Brown Ruoff and Jerry W. Ward Jr. (New York: Modern Language Association of America, 1990), 237-250; and Lim, "Assaying the Gold: Or, Contesting the Ground of Asian American Literature," *New Literary History* 24 (1993): 147-169, hereafter abbreviated "CGA."

3. See *Island*: *Poetry and History of Chinese Americans on Angel Island*, 1910-1940, ed. Him Mark Lai et al. (San Francisco, 1980); *Songs of Cold Mountain*: *Cantonese Rhymes from San Francisco's Chinatown*, ed. and trans. Marlon K. Hom (Berkeley: University of California Press, 1987); Amy Ling, *Between Worlds: Women Writers of Chinese Ancestry* (New York: Pergamon Press, 1990); *Ayumi: A Japanese American Anthology*, ed. Janice Mirikitani (San Francisco, 1980). The University of Washington Press has played a very important role in reprinting the work of older writers like John Okada, Carlos Bulosan, Monica Sone and many others.

4. Some of the important anthologies and bibliographies include *Asian-American Authors*, ed. Kai-yu Hsu and Helen Palubinskas (Boston, 1972); *Asian American Heritage: An Anthology of Prose and Poetry*, ed. David Hsin-Fu Wand (New York, 1974); *Breaking*

Silence: An Anthology of Contemporary Asian American Poets, ed. Joseph Bruchac (New York, 1983); *Asian American Literature: An Annotated Bibliography*, ed. King-Kok Cheung and Stan Yogi (New York: Modern Language Association of America, 1988); *The Forbidden Stitch: An Asian American Women's Anthology*, ed. Shirley Geok-lin Lim and Mayumi Tsutakawa (Corvallis, Or.: Calyx Books, 1989); *Making Waves*, ed. Asian Women United of California (Boston: Beacon Press, 1989); *Charlie Chan Is Dead*: *An Anthology of Contemporary Asian American Fiction*, ed. Jessica Hagedorn (New York: Penguin Books, 1993), hereafter abbreviated CC.

5. Quoted in Wendell V. Harris, "Canonicity," *PMLA* 106.1 (1991): 112.

6. John Guillory, "Canon, Syllabus, List: A Note on the Pedagogic Imaginary," *Transition* 52 (1991):39.

7. Werner Sollors, "A Critique of Pure Pluralism," in *Reconstructing American Literary History*, ed. Sacvan Bercovitch (Cambridge, Mass.: Harvard University Press, 1986), 255, hereafter abbreviated "CP."

8. For comprehensive accounts of Asian American history see Sucheng Chan, *Asian Americans*: *An Interpretive History* (Boston: Twayne, 1991), hereafter abbreviated *AAIH*; Ronald Takaki, *Strangers From a Different Shore* (Boston: Little, Brown, 1989), hereafter abbreviated *SFD*; and *Dictionary of Asian American History*, ed. Hyung-Chan Kim (New York: Greenwood Press, 1986).

9. See *Labor Immigration Under Capitalism: Asian Workers in the United States Before World War II*, ed. Lucie Cheng and Edna Bonacich (Berkeley: University of California Press, 1984); Joan M. Jensen, *Passage From India: Asian Indian Immigrants in North America* (New Haven: Yale University Press, 1988); H. Brett Melendy, *Asians in America: Filipinos, Koreans, and East Indians* (Boston: Twayne, 1977); Alexander Saxton, *The Indispensable Enemy: Labor and the Anti-Chinese Movement in California* (Berkeley: University of California Press, 1971); and Roger Daniels, *The Politics of Prejudice*: *The Anti-Japanese Movement in California and the Struggle forJapanese Exclusion* (New York: Atheneum, 1968).

10. Yen Le Espiritu, *Asian American Panethnicity: Bridging Institutions and Identities* (Philadelphia: Temple University Press, 1992), 135, hereafter abbreviated *AAP*.

11. The Japanese government encouraged the emigration of women to create more stable immigrant communities, and retained a loophole in the 1907 Gentlemen's Agreement that restricted the emigration of laborers, but allowed the parents, wives and children of

laborers already in America to enter (*SFD*, 46-47). As a result, 46% of Japanese in Hawaii and 34.5% on the mainland by 1920 were women. Korean immigrant communities also had a higher ratio of women (21% by 1920). The women were drawn by the more attractive conditions for family life in Hawaii; and many entered the Unites States as picture brides with Japanese passports issued to them as Japanese colonial subjects under the Gentlemen's Agreement (56). Numbers of Indian and Filipino men married Mexican women.

12. See Bill Ong Hing, *Making and Remaking Asian America Through Immigration Policy, 1850-1990* (Stanford: Stanford University Press, 1993), especially 43-78, hereafter abbreviated as *MR4*; *SFD*, 357-420; *AAIH*, 121-144.

13. The War which "began" for other Americans with Pearl Harbor had long roused the passions and anxieties of Asian Americans whose home-countries had been pulled into it much earlier. The time-lag in perception carried no small irony, since the entry of the U.S. into the war brought abrupt shifts in status for Asian Americans as well as opportunities long denied. These ironies are skilfully explored by the young Korean American narrator, Faye, in Kim Ronyoung's *Clay Walls* (Seattle: University of Washington Press, 1987).

14. For a detailed history of the Movement see William Wei, *The Asian American Movement* (Philadelphia: Temple University Press, 1993).

15. Lisa Lowe, "Heterogeneity, Hybridity, Multiplicity: Marking Asian American Differences," *Diaspora* 1.1 (1991): 30, hereafter abbreviated "HH."

16. See *Statistical Record of Asian Americans*, ed. Susan B. Gall and Timothy L. Gall (Detroit: Gale Research, Inc., 1993): 569-693, hereafter abbreviated *SRAA*.

17. Among many of the groups, the percentage of foreign-born is even higher, 81.9% for Koreans, 90.4% for Vietnamese, and 93.9% for Laotians (*SRAA*, 572).

18. Barbara Herrnstein Smith, "Contingencies of Value," in *Canons*, ed. Robert von Hallberg (Chicago: University of Chicago Press, 1984), 30.

19. The work of scholars like E. San Juan Jr., Lisa Lowe, David Palumbo-Liu, Sau-ling C. Wong represents an important exception to this general trend.

20. The term "no-no boy" was used to describe Nisei (American-born, second generation Japanese American) men who refused to answer affirmatively the two "loyalty" questions on the Selective Service questionnaire issued by the War Department in 1943. The questions addressed their willingness to serve in the army and swear unqualified allegiance to the United States, and their willingness to forswear all allegiance to Japan.

This political stance defines the main character Ichiro in John Okadas novel *No-No Boy* (Seatde, 1979), the double negative signifying the complete dislocation of Ichiro, who is no longer Japanese and can never be American within the discursive construction of Americanness produced through the questionnaire.

21. For feminist critiques of Chin's formulations of an Asian American tradition see King-Kok Cheung, "The Woman Warrior versus the Chinaman Pacific: Must a Chinese American Critic Choose Between Feminism and Heroism?" in *Conflicts in Feminism*, ed. Marianne Hirsch and Evelyn Fox Keller (New York: Routledge, 1990), 234-251; Elaine Kim, "'Such Opposite Creatures': Men and Women in Asian American Literature," *Michigan Quarterly Review* (1990): 68-93; "CGA," 154-155; "HH," 33-34.

22. Even as late as Kim's essay on Asian American literature for the *Columbia Literary History of the United States* (1988), she continues to exclude writings by South Asians. "Asian American Literature," in *Columbia Literary History of the United States*, ed. Emory Elliott (New York: Columbia University Press, 1988), 811-821.

23. Oscar Campomanes, "Filipinos in the United States and Their Literature of Exile" in *Reading the Literatures of Asian America*, 49-78.

24. The problems with the use of the term are numerous. Fredric Wakeman and Peter Bol have indicated that the term "Confucian" is a modern coinage without an equivalent in premodern Chinese, and Lionel Jensen has traced its origins to the Jesuits in China. After "Confucianism" had waned, the Western term was picked up by Chinese intellectuals and used as a way to identify the Chinese elite. This narrow sense of the term was extended by others to include traditional Chinese culture as a whole, and subsequently to refer to the entire East Asian region in ways that are homogenizing and ahistorical. Qtd. in Arif Dirlik, "Confucius in the Borderlands," *Boundary 2* 22 (Fall 1995): 261. According to Dirlik, the eighties have witnessed a revival of "Confucianism" as an explanatory framework that links the economic miracle of newly industrialized Asian countries with their cultural ethos: "The Confucian revival of the eighties is best understood as the articulation of two discourses — a discourse on Confucianism as a functional component of an emergent Global Capitalism, and a discourse on Confucianism (predating the former) as a problem in Chinese intellectuals' identity" (265). The circulation of the term within these discourses and its Orientalist genealogy reveal that its use as a descriptive is highly problematic.

25. See *AAP*, esp. ch. 3 and ch. 6.

26. Bharati Mukherjee, *Jasmine* (New York: Grove Weidenfeld, 1989); Jessica Hagedorn, *Dogeaters* (New York: Pantheon Books, 1990).

27. Sven Birkerts, "In Our House There Were No Chinese Things," *The New York Times Book Review*, December 19, 1993, 17.

28. Jessica Hagedorn, The *New York Times Book Review*, January 23, 1994, 27.

29. I am speaking specifically of the way the ethnic and mainstream are constructed as oppositions in popular perception, and am calling this assumption into question. The burden of referentiality is quite different in mainstream writing that assumes a "common knowledge" of its cultural matrices among readers, and are less pressed to establish such knowledge or to dismantle and reconstruct it. The historical and cultural contexts that ethnic texts activate as they anticipate their multiple audiences has often led to the misperception that they are narrower or less "universal" than mainstream literature.

30. Werner Sollors, *Beyond Ethnicity: Consent and Descent in American Culture* (New York: Oxford University Press, 1986).

31. Aijun Appadurai, "Patriotism and Its Futures," *Public Culture* 5.3 (1993): 424.

32. Peter Brimelow, *Alien Nation: Common Sense About America's Immigration Disaster* (New York: Random House, 1995).

33. Kenichi Ohmae, "Putting Global Logic First," *Harvard Business Review* (Jan-Feb 1995): 122.

34. For an account of changing American attitudes to China and India over the last two centuries, see Harold R. Isaacs, *Scratches on Our Minds: American Views of China and India* (White Plains, N.Y., 1958).

35. Pam Belluck, "Healthy Korean Economy Draws Immigrants Home," *New York Times*, August 22, 1995, A1, A12.

36. The illegal status of many of these women makes them even more vulnerable to exploitation in an industry caught in relentless global competition with companies that have located overseas where labor costs are 1/4 of U.S. costs. Moreover, as Gary Gereffi points out, technological innovations are making possible the performance of technology-intensive and high-value-added stages of apparel production within the U.S., ensuring the increasing growth and resilience of the industry domestically and its continuing need for cheap labor. "Global Sourcing and Regional Divisions of Labor in the Pacific Rim," in Arif Dirlik, ed., *What's in a Rim? Critical Perspectives on the Pacific Region Idea* (Boulder, CO: Westview Press, 1993), 51-68.

37. Wanwadee Larsen, *Confessions of a Mail Order Bride: American Life Through Thai Eyes* (Far Hills, N.J., 1989).

38. Cynthia Enloe, *Bananas, Beaches & Bases: Making Feminist Sense of International Politics* (Berkeley, 1989), esp. 35-41 on sex-tourism, and 177-194 on domestic servants; hereafter abbreviated *BBB*.

39. This conflict between the Philippines and Singapore also exposes the economic contradictions within the myth of "Asian values" long propagated by the Lee Kuan Yew government as the sign of its successful assimilation of Western capitalism and its successful resistance to Western cultural influence. The invocation of a pan-Asian framework in Asia is frequently state-sponsored and covers over uneven development between and within various Asian nations.

40. Bharati Mukherjee, "Jasmine," *The Middleman and Other Stories* (New York: Grove Press, 1988), 123-135.

41. Sara Suleri, *Meatless Days* (Chicago: University of Chicago Press, 1989).

42. David Mura, *Turning Japanese*: *Memoirs of a Sansei* (New York: Atlantic Monthly Press, 1991).

43. Maxine Hong Kingston, *China Men* (New York: Knopf, 1980).

44. M.M. Bakhtin, *The Dialogic Imagination*, ed. Michael Holquist and trans. Caryl Emerson and Michael Holquist (Austin, TX: University of Texas Press, 1981). Bakhtin defines chronotope as "the intrinsic connectedness of temporal and spatial relationships that are artistically expressed in literature" (84).

45. Sau-ling C. Wong, "Denationalization Reconsidered: Asian American Cultural Criticism at a Theoretical Crossroads," *Amerasia Journal* 21.1/2 (1995): 1-27.

46. Theodor W. Adorno, *Against Epistemology — A Metacritique: Studies in Husserl and the Phenomenological Antinomie*, trans. Willis Domingo (Oxford: Basil Blackwell, 1982), 27.

5

Gender and Sexuality
in Asian American Literature
总论美国亚裔文学中的性别与性

Sau-ling Cynthia Wong, and Jeffrey Santa Ana

评论家简介

黄秀玲（Sau-ling Cynthia Wong），美国斯坦福大学英美文学博士，现任美国加利福尼亚大学伯克利分校族裔研究系荣休教授。研究领域包括：美国华裔的华文与英文文学、华人离散、移民写作和电影、跨国接受研究、美国亚裔文学：跨国性，全球化与人口流动性、性别与性、经典形成等。专著有《阅读美国亚裔文学：从必要到奢华》（*Reading Asian American Literature: From Necessity to Extravagance*, 1993）。编著有《汤亭亭之〈女勇士〉专题研究》（*Maxine Hong Kingston's The Woman Warrior: A Casebook*, 1999）。合编有《美亚网：族裔、国家主义与网际空间》（*Asian America.net: Ethnicity, Nationalism, and Cyberspace*, 2003）、《美国亚裔文学指南》（*A Resource Guide to Asian American Literature*, 2001）、《美国新移民：第二语言教育者必读》（*New Immigrants in the United States: Readings for Second Language Educators*, 2000）等。除本书所收录的论文，其他代表性论文有《重思去国家化：处于理论十字路口的美亚文化批评》，发表于《美亚学刊》（"Denationalization Reconsidered: Asian American Cultural Criticism at a Theoretical Crossroads" *Amerasia Journal*, 1995）等。

杰弗里·圣·安那（Jeffrey Santa Ana），美国加利福尼亚大学伯克利分校英语博士，现任石溪大学英语系副教授。研究领域包括：20 世纪和 21 世纪的美国文学与文化、迁徙与离散、后殖民主义与全球化、性别、人文环境、记忆、美国亚裔等。专著有《种族感情：亚洲美国在资本主义文化中的情感》(*Racial Feelings: Asian America in a Capitalist Culture of Emotion*, 2015)。

文章简介

　　文章系统梳理了 19 世纪 50 年代至 20 世纪末美国亚裔文学中的性别与性方面的书写，呈现出在美国亚裔文化批评框架下，学界对性别与性问题的研究历程，充分揭示出性别与性的问题研究与族裔历史、族裔身份的研究是紧密联系的。文章首先概述了此领域的"综述性"研究成果，接下来按照划分的三个历史时期评析了美国亚裔文学中性别与性的文学呈现特征。为了体现性别与性本身的社会文化建构性，文章在前两个时期的论述中采取了将男女作家分述的方式深入剖析各自的书写主题和创作特色，进而总结同一历史阶段男女作家创作的相似特征。而文章对第三个历史时期的介绍则跨越了男女作家的界限，从异质性、性别主题的重复与差异、跨界书写与酷儿书写等方面展开述评，为我们从性别角度揭示出美国亚裔身份的复杂性。

文章出处：*Signs: Journal of Women in Culture and Society*，25 Jan. 1999, pp. 171-226.

Gender and Sexuality in Asian American Literature

Sau-Ling Cynthia Wong and Jeffrey Santa Ana

This essay aims to provide an overview of representations of gender and sexuality in Asian American literature and of the developments in Asian American cultural criticism that have made the study of such representations possible. The difficulties of the task are manifold, for there is no satisfactory theoretical vocabulary for the interconnectedness, mutual constitution, and operational simultaneity of race/ethnicity, gender, and sexuality. In academic investigations each of these has a history of serving as a discrete analytic category, but it is in fact impossible to separate their workings, and Asian American cultural critics have long struggled to characterize their complex interrelationships and to resist their separation. Mitsuye Yamada deplores the notion that "ethnicity" and "womanhood" are "at war with each other" and resents the pressure on women of color to choose between the two (1981, 73); Elaine Kim speaks of the "American tangle of race and gender hierarchies" and describes Asian American political and sexual objectification as having been "tightly plaited" (1990b, 69); and Sau-ling Wong considers gender and ethnicity "fused": "Ethnicity is, in some sense, always already gendered, and gender always already ethnicized" (1992,126). Analyzing Asian women in global capital, Lisa Lowe asserts in that "throughout lived social relations, it is apparent that labor is gendered, sexuality is racialized, and race is class-associated" (1996, 164), and King-Kok Cheung states that "from the beginning, race and gender have been intertwined in Asian American history and literature" (1997b, 10). David Eng and Alice Hom express their interest in "the intersection of racial and (homo) sexual difference" and their "unwilling [ness] to bifurcate [their] identities into the racial and the sexual" (1998a, 1, 4). Similar statements abound throughout the literature.

[*Signs:Journal of Women in Culture and Society* 1999,vol.25 no.1]

Spatial, scientific, and kinship metaphors; the use of process verbs instead of nouns; and definition by negation all indicate critics' attempts to articulate the notion that "Asian

*We thank the editors of *Signs* for the opportunity to write this review essay; David Eng for his invaluable feedback on queer writing; King-Kok Cheung for suggesting, and Wen-Ching Ho for helping us secure, Chi's work from Taiwan; and Marie Lo for her research assistance and input on Asian Canadian literature. Special appreciation is also due die wonderful students in our Spring 1998 course on gender and sexuality in Asian American literature, on whom we tried out some of the ideas in this article.

Americanness," gender, and sexuality cannot be considered *independent* of one another, nor can they be regarded as merely additive isolates. Among such terms, intersectionality is perhaps the most widely used today, but, as with other spatial metaphors, it still assumes preexisting, disparate "tracks" and thus does not suggest a more integrated kind of relationality. In this essay, we use ad hoc language to render our vision of this relationality, but a comprehensive theoretical solution to the problem cannot be undertaken here.

A second difficulty of our project concerns its scope. Hardly any aspect of human existence is untouched by race/ethnicity, gender, and sexuality, broadly conceived, which means that virtually all of Asian American literature could fall within the purview of this essay. Furthermore, as scholars' collective understanding of these concepts deepens, literary texts that previously appeared to be irrelevant may take on new significance: a story purportedly about "universal" human experiences now may be specified as "Asian American," or a text previously known mainly for its "ethnic content" may now be read for its insights on gender construction. We concentrate on primary sources that have emerged in the evolving critical tradition as of special interest to scholars of gender and sexuality, although not all of these deal explicitly with gender and sexuality. Our understanding of gender and sexuality in Asian American literature, however, is necessarily shaped by studies of the same topics in larger cultural contexts, especially with regard to film and television.[1] Moreover, with, the increasing popularity of cultural studies approaches, many Asian American critics interested in gender and sexuality analyze not only print literature but also theater, film, video, photography and other visual art, performance art, popular culture, and even fashion and cosmetic surgery, often within the same study.[2] We recognize, then, that our focus on print literature of a belletristic character is, to some extent, arbitrary, dictated more by practical constraints on scope and by our own backgrounds than by theoretical justifications.[3] We hope that the unavoidable gaps in our coverage will be partly compensated for by the delineation of a serviceable "big picture."

An overview of overviews

A number of secondary sources already provide cross-ethnic and cross-gender "big pictures"

---

1   Sec, e.g.Engelhardt 1976; E. Wong 1978; Tajima 1989; Fung 1991a, 1991b; Mar-chetti 1993; and Hamamoto 1994.
2   See, e.g., Moy 1993; S. C Wong 1993b; E. Kim 1996; L. Lowe 1996; Kondo 1997; R. Lee 1999; and Palumbo-Liu 1999.
3   We consider ourselves primarily literary scholars, and we are more informed about and attuned to prose narratives than to drama and poetry; to East Asian American more than to South and Southeast Asian American literature, and to older, "canonized" titles more than to recent works. Furthermore, while the categories in our framework may show a materialist bias, we do not subscribe to a mechanistic-reflective model of literature; we prefer to emphasize the performative power of language, of naming and narrating.

of various aspects of gender and sexuality in Asian American literature. Elaine Kim's *Asian American Literature: An Introduction to the Writings and Their Social Context* (1982), although a broad general study, is so saturated with observations on gender and sexuality that it is still the most useful introduction to the subject for a newcomer to Asian American literature. Kim identifies Asian American gender and sexuality stereotypes from the late nineteenth and early twentieth centuries that are, with variations, still operative in American society today (3-22), and she introduces the debates about Asian American manhood and womanhood that centered on Frank Chin and Maxine Hong Kingston beginning in the so-called cultural nationalist period (173-213). Many of the sociohistorical phenomena that Kim links to representations of gender and sexuality — male labor immigration and bachelorhood, family separation, Exclusion and antimiscegenation laws, prostitution, internment, and other acts of institutional racism. Orientalist exoticization of Asian sexuality, emasculation of men, and hyperfeminization of women — came to be revisited by other scholars. Although these concerns were shared by many during the Asian American movement (Ting 1998), Kim's book focuses them for literary scholars in particular.

Kim also offers a briefer and more focused overview of gender and sexuality in her survey essay "'Such Opposite Creatures': Men and Women in Asian American Literature" (1990b). She addresses the stereotypical desexualization of Asian American men and hypersexualization of Asian American women: "Asian women are only sexual for the same reason that Asian men are asexual: both exist to define the white man's virility and the white race's superiority" (70). In separate sections on male and female images, she reviews key texts published between 1937 (when Younghill Kang's *East Goes West* appeared) and 1989 (when Amy Tan's *The Joy Luck Club* and Kingston's *Tripmaster Monkey* both came out), noting recurrent themes such as Asian American men's preoccupation with white women as a symbol of American promise, their metaphoric association of the Asian woman with the homeland, the weak(ened) or absent man of the family, women's heroization of strong mothers, and the vitality of mother-daughter bonds. Kim argues that when "Asian patriarchy was pushed aside or subsumed by an American patriarchy that did not, because of racism, extend its promise to Asian American men," the men responded by "attempting to reassert male authority over the cultural domain and over women by subordinating feminism to nationalist concerns" (1990b, 75). However, the same conditions empowered some women (73), allowing them to "claim America" as well as a female self and subjectivity for themselves (81). As in all of her work, Kim insists here on the importance of historical understanding to issues such as gender roles.

Russell Leong's foreword (1995a) to Geraldine Kudaka's *On a Bed of Rice: An Asian*

American Erotic Feast (1995) offers a historical account of how Asian Americans' "lives, including our sexuality, were tested by our experience of race and racism in the United States" (xiv). In addition to discriminatory legislation and damaging stereotypes, Leong stresses global colonial encounters as a source of distorted racial/sexual images of Asians. He discusses libidinal inhibitions caused by immigrant families' urgent struggles for survival and the "model minority" pressure to conform (sexually and otherwise), especially for American-born generations. His essay also provides glimpses of significant cultural moments in Asian American writing on gender and sexuality, from Cantonese folk rhymes in the Exclusion period to texts of the 1990s.

The mid-1990s saw the publication of several useful overviews of Asian American gay and lesbian writing as well. Karin Aguilar-San Juan's "Landmarks in Literature by Asian American Lesbians" (1993) is the product of a search for pioneers in an emerging tradition. Alice Hom and Ming-Yuen Ma (1993) offer an extensive list of published and forthcoming literary projects (1993, 26-30), and David Eng and Candace Fujikane (1995) introduce issues such as coming out, empowerment, and coalitional politics; the revision of dominant history; the "rice queen" and "sticky rice" phenomena; class disparities, exploitation, and violence within homosexual relationships; and HIV/AIDS. Russell Leong's introduction (1996b) to *Asian American Sexualities: Dimensions of the Gay and Lesbian Experience* (1996a) explores "linkages between race and same-sex sexuality" (2), and his extensive footnotes are a rich source of information on literature by lesbian, gay, and bisexual Asian American writers; early Asian American publications and courses on gender and sexuality; and community activism, including HIV/AIDS activism.

Cheung's *Interethnic Companion to Asian American Literature* (1997a) contains a thumbnail review of stereotypical representations of Asian American men and women; androcentric cultural nationalism; feminist interventions (both U.S.-oriented and in conjunction with "third world" critiques of imperialism and white liberal feminism); and the recent surge in lesbian and gay writing and theorizing (1997b, 10-13). In the same volume, Jinqi Ling explores the "'emasculation' of the Asian American man; the politics of simultaneous articulations of gendered subjectivities; and gender transgression as a representational strategy for disrupting hierarchical assumptions about heterosexual relationships" (1997, 312). Although the stated topic of his essay is masculinity, Ling is in fact interested in the general "broadening of discourse on gender" in recent times and its potential for effecting social change (331-32). He sees the mid-1970s as a turning point in Asian American literary practice, after which "the issue of gender has become a consciously employed identity politics in Asian American literature" (313).

Yen Le Espiritu's *Asian American Women and Men: Labor, Lams, and Love,* also published in 1997, analyzes the "intersections of race, class, and gender" for a general readership to show how the "historical oppression of Asian American men and women, along both material and cultural lines ... (re)structures the rules of gender in the Asian American community" (7). Written by a social scientist, this interdisciplinary book makes extensive reference to works of literature whose portrayals of Asian American women and men illustrate the author's gender analysis. The chapter most useful to the newcomer is "Ideological Racism and Cultural Resistance, Constructing Our Own Images" (86-107); however, Espiritu's approach discourages isolating this chapter from material on immigration laws, labor market forces, income statistics, and other nonliterary phenomena. Espiritu emphasizes the seeming duality of racialized gender: "Asian men have been cast as both hypersexual and asexual, and Asian women have been rendered both superfeminine and masculine" (106), depending on the ideological need of the dominant society in any given historical situation.

Gender, sexuality, and history

A view shared by most if not all of the above critics is that gender and sexuality in Asian American literature cannot be understood apart from Asian American history. The emergence, transformation, or persistence of specific gender and sexuality themes is always tied to historical conditions. Heeding our predecessors' concern with adequate historical contextualization, we have organized this review essay chronologically into periods (which we refer to simply as the first, second, and third periods), with thematic sections under each. Primary sources mostly follow a chronological presentation (which foreshortens the first century of Asian presence in the United States but gives more detailed attention to publications since the Asian American movement of the late 1960s and early 1970s). Secondary sources, however, are not necessarily treated chronologically; if a "late" critical study radically revises our view of an "early" literary work, it may be discussed in conjunction with the latter.

The "history" to which we allude, of course, is itself historically produced. The narrativization of "Asian American history," a recently invented category, is a complex subject (S. Chan 1996), and feminist challenges to Asian American historiography have cast doubt on the notion of a unanimously accepted account of the past (see, e.g., E. Kim 1990a; Okihiro 1994). Even though documented events, such as the passage of the Chinese Exclusion Act, the internment of Japanese Americans, and the anti-Filipino riot in Watsonville, clearly have an "objective" existence, their meaning for Asian Americans is a contested matter. There is no universal Asian American subject who is ethnic first, before being gender-or sexuality-identified, just as there is no such thing as a gender-or sexuality-transcending, genetically ethnic history. Eithne Luibheid (1998) has studied the ways immigration legislation was used to regulate Asian Americans' and other groups' sexualities (both hetero-and homo-), and Jennifer Ting (1995, 1998) has persuasively demonstrated that certain Asian American historical narratives widely circulated since the Asian American movement of the late 1960s and early 1970s are shot through with implicit assumptions about gender and sexuality. For example, standard descriptions of Exclusion's grievous "distortions" of Chinese American life — the "bachelor society," the shortage of women, abnormal female-male ratios, male sexual deprivation, enforced childlessness, "paper sons," etc. — are pervaded by heteronormativity, which allows for "only two categories of thinking sex — conjugal heterosexuality and nonconjugal heterosexuality" (Ting 1995, 274) and construes same-sex bonds as abnormal. Furthermore, heteronormativity often has a naturalized racial dimension, such that certain desires (e.g., an Asian American man's attraction to white women) become culturally unintelligible or unacceptable. Thus racial formation cannot be conceptualized as prior or superordinate to gender and sexuality formations, and care must be taken to acknowledge the real historical injuries inflicted on Asian Americans without replicating gender and sexuality "default assumptions," such as the "normality" (and implied universal desirability) of the patriarchal family.

We treat men's and women's writings in separate subsections in the first and second periods in order to historically contextualize Asian American gender and sexuality as sociocultural constructs. If racial formations of the Asian American subject cannot be adequately understood apart from gender and sexuality, it is also important to recognize the ways racist laws and discriminatory practices affect first and second period writers' understandings of themselves as gendered and sexual beings. That first period male writers, for instance, implicitly understand racially motivated acts of violence as distortions and disruptions of their own manhood and patriarchal claims to power, and that they routinely express concerns about a (patriarchal) masculinity crisis, calls for an examination of their work in a gender-specific category of "men's writing." By the same token, women writers of the first and second periods faced androcentric and Orientalist manipulations of their gender and sexuality and racially gendered violence-psychological and physical — that repressed their sexuality. For these reasons, it is helpful to recognize gender-specific thematic concerns in these periods in separate categories on men's and women's writing.[1]

Finally, while issues from the first and second periods persist in the third, more recent writings by counternormative or transgressive (e.g., queer) Asian Americans problematize previous understandings of many of these issues as gender-specific. Transgendered Asian American writers, for example, may be less concerned with delineating and claiming a masculine or feminine identity than with criticizing the violence of a heteronormative American culture that considers people with ambiguous or multiple genders to be aberrant or sick. Likewise, contemporary literary and critical collaborations between Asian American women and men elide or at the very least resist notions of "natural" gender difference in writing. Collaborations such as Eng and Hom's recent queer studies anthology (1998b) and this review essay underscore the need for diverse methodologies that argue against an essentializing difference between women's and men's writings in the third period.

The first period: Violence and "deviance" (1850s–1950s)

The first period is marked on the material level by predominantly male immigration, a relatively small population of women, few conjugal families and American-born offspring, the overt use of racial categories to oppress Asians, and strong assimilationist pressures from the dominant society.[2] On the whole, literary treatment of gender and sexuality tends to be more implicit and less theoretically driven than in later periods, although tremendous variations exist. Works by male writers often depict an Asian American male subjectivity produced through violence. Asian American women experience violence too, but typically in different forms, and women writers have had to battle both racism and patriarchy from the start. Yet, even during this early period, writers of both sexes modify the archetypal patriarchal Asian family in various ways.

During the first period, Asian American gender and sexuality were understood, first (by the dominant society), as so at odds with white norms as to be at best exotic, at worst freakish, and, later (by Asian Americanists), as oppression-induced departures from "normal" gender and sexual roles in a "natural" family formation. From the beginning, discriminatory racial practices

---

1 The role of violence in the construction of Asian American gender and sexuality is addressed in J. Chang 1995 (esp. for women poets) and Nguyen 1997.

2 Within this period, World War II, of course, is a watershed event that precipitated drastic changes in gender roles for Asian Americans; nevertheless, we decided not to further subdivide the first period so as to stress its contrasts with the changes wrought by the 1960s social movements and the 1965 immigration reform, which transformed the Asian American population on an immense scale.

have presented Asian American men's gender and sexuality as deviant. "America's capitalist economy," Espiritu explains, "wanted Asian male workers but not their families. To ensure greater profitability from immigrants' labor and to decrease the costs of reproduction — the expenses of housing, feeding, clothing, and educating the workers' dependents — employers often excluded 'nonproductive' family members such as women and children" (1997, 17). A whole series of Exclusion laws, including legislation that revoked a U.S. woman's citizenship upon marriage to an "alien ineligible to citizenship," ensured a long-term lack of women in early Asian immigrant communities. Such laws led to a conspicuous absence of wives and traditional families in Chinese immigrant communities and resulted in "bachelor societies" of single Asian men who performed "'feminized' forms of work — such as laundry, restaurant, and other service-sector jobs" (L. Lowe 1996, 11).

Policies restricting Asian immigration to male laborers have been responsible for many of the stereotypes that distort the gender and sexuality of Asian American men. Disfiguring images of them as sexual predators, "emasculated Fu Manchus," "asexual Charlie Chans," and moral degenerates (Eng and Fujikane 1995,60) emerged from a set of norms that upheld a patriarchal Euro-American nuclear family as the model for citizenship and national identity.[1] The stereotype of the emasculated Asian American male, Jinqi Ling maintains, "evokes a scenario in which being a woman necessarily implies an inferior social existence, to be both feared and repudiated" (1997, 313).[2] Exclusionary immigration and labor policies, racially gendered definitions of American citizenship, and, as Lowe argues, racialized definitions of citizenship also "ascribed 'gender' to the Asian American subject. Up until 1870, American citizenship was granted exclusively to white male persons; in 1870, men of African descent could become naturalized, but the bar to citizenship remained for Asian men until the repeal acts of 1943-1952. Whereas the 'masculinity' of the citizen was first inseparable from his 'whiteness,' as the state extended citizenship to nonwhite male persons, it formally designated these subjects as 'male' as well" (1996,11). Lowe's analysis reveals a sex/gender system in U.S. immigration and labor practices that, in barring Asian immigrant laborers from "normative conceptions of the masculinity legally defined as white" (Eng and Hom 1998a, 5), effectively naturalized ideas of Asian males as "emasculated" and "feminized"

---

1 Interestingly, over the decades the image of Asian men as sexual predators has largely faded from the public imagination, at least for East Asian groups, leaving the desexualized image more firmly in place.

2 But also see J. Ling's caution that the terms *emasculation* and *feminization,* though related, are not synonymous. The former more fully suggests the overall social consequence of the displacement of Asian men's subject position, while the latter refers to one specific form of Asian men's racial gendering in the United States (1997, 314). Also useful is Ling's reminder about the true interventionary value of "emasculation" as a trope (1997, 317).

in their work, in their communities, and even in relation to their own cultural norms. Moreover, in prohibiting Asian immigrant men from forming nuclear families, exclusionary naturalization policies employed a 'technology' of racialization and gendering" (L. Lowe 1996, 11) that rendered them abnormal and transgressive.

Men's writing

Despite laws that sought to regulate Asian Americans' sexual behavior and restrict normative gender and sexuality to Euro-Americans, early Asian immigrant men did, of course, have sexual and procreative relationships. Asian American male writers from this era express the hardships, the pleasures, and the disappointments of attempting to forge sexual, platonic, and familial relations with Asian and non-Asian women alike, but because of legal prohibitions on Asian women's immigration to North America and the consequent high male-to-female ratio in Asian "bachelor societies," early male immigrants often sought relationships with American-born, usually white, women, even though they were legally barred from marrying whites.[1] Portrayals of such relationships and expressions of desire for white women are salient features in the writings of early Asian immigrant men and significantly affect their representations of Asian masculinity and relations among Asian American males.

Women in these narratives are often agents of masculine subject formation, frequently serving as fetishized objects of male appropriation and bonding and as figures of both U.S. and various Asian national identifications. The poems in *Songs of Gold Mountain* (M. Hom 1987), a compilation of Chinese folk rhymes composed by a small number of literate, most likely merchant-class, men in San Francisco's Chinatown and published in the 1910s, abound in expressions of heterosexual yearning — sometimes barely veiled in laments on family separation written in female personae, as allowed by classical Chinese poetic conventions, and at other times explicitly pornographic, in the anonymous male poets' fantasies about dalliances with prostitutes. The figure of the white woman hardly appears in these poems; nevertheless, she has a proxy presence in the depictions of second-generation, American-born Chinese women — a rare commodity whose Westernized ways and air of sexual freedom both tantalize the immigrant men and provoke in them intense cultural anxieties (S. C. Wong 1991).

The fetishization of women also takes other forms. If the "culturally pure" Asian woman, especially in her role as mother, wife, and lover, signifies the Asian homeland, white women

---

1 For an examination of the "racialization of Asian manhood and womanhood" in representations of interracial sexuality (white males and Asian females) in Hollywood film and television, see Espiritu 1997, especially chap. 5.

often represent American ideals of "freedom" "Western culture" and "civilization." White women may embody immigrant men's dreams of assimilation to an American society that offers acceptance, well-being, and the securities and comforts of a new home. Often in these narratives, the possibility of relationships and ultimately marriage between Asian men and white women suggests a cultural bridging of Eastern ("Oriental") and Western (American) nationalities. In his autobiographical novel *East Goes West* ([1937] 1997), for example, Younghill Kang portrays the life of Korean immigrants Chungpa Han and two of his friends. The three men struggle to adapt to New York life during the 1920s and 1930s, and romantic relations with white women are central to their quest to gain acceptance and identify themselves as Americans (even though none of the relationships results in a satisfying, permanent union). As Elaine Kim observes, Han believes that romantic love for a white woman will make him "that much more a part of Western civilization" (1982, 41). Yet this dream of interracial romance also carries great potential for violence. Han relates a nightmare in which he and "some frightened-looking Negroes" are trapped inside a cellar set on fire by a mob of white men holding torches (Y. Kang [1937] 1997, 369). Han's nightmare graphically portrays the violence with which discriminatory racial policies were often implemented and through which early Asian immigrant men understood themselves as excluded from the rights and privileges of patriarchal white America.

In the stories of Carlos Bulosan and Bienvenido N. Santos, two Filipino American writers of the "pioneering generation" (Campomanes 1992,55), America of the 1930s and 1940s is a place of labor abuse, racism, and sexual exploitation for Filipino men. At the same time, it is the site of bonds of compassion, empathy, and love in enduring male friendships. During this time, the United States was home to hundreds of thousands of Filipinos, most of them single men looking for jobs harvesting crops, canning meat, and performing other sorts of menial labor. In Bulosan's and Santos's stories, violence is a persistent tact of life for Pinoys (early Filipino immigrant men) who, due to the scarcity of fellow countrywomen in the United States, pursue relationships with white women.[1] Bulosan's "The Romance of Magno Rubio" (1979a) is a tragicomic portrayal of the kinds of hardships Pinoys faced in these romantic relations: Magno, a poor migrant field laborer, puts himself into debt buying gifts to court a white woman, only to find that she is already married and has cheated him out of his money. In many of Bulosan's other stories, too, white women signify an America that is prohibited to Pinoys, with the prohibition sometimes enforced

---

1 Studies of U.S. imperialism in the Philippines underscore the presence of white women there as agents of colonial domination. A more comprehensive examination of white women in early Filipino American narratives should thus take into account the roles they have played in Philippine culture as icons of Euro-American ideals and identity (see Rafael 1993, 1995).

by physical violence.[1] The function of women — both Filipino and white — in Bulosan's predominantly male world receives incisive feminist analysis by Rachel Lee (1995a), who argues that Bulosan's idealized vision of brotherhood (Filipino, American, or world-labor) in *America Is in the Heart* depends on brutal containment of the figure of the erotic woman, an aspect of gender and sexuality underexplored in Asian American scholarship on Bulosan, which usually discusses him in terms of migration and labor history.

Like Bulosan's betrayed and forlorn Filipino exiles, the Pinoys in Santos's short stories endure both physical and mental violence in relationships with white women. In "The Door," the perpetrators of violence are themselves Pinoys who have internalized racist oppression ([1955] 1979, 86-97). Delfin, a Filipino man, is cuckolded by his "blonde American wife," and, in the eyes of other Pinoys, his knowledge of her adultery and his inability to do anything about it disgraces all Filipino men. Their internalization of America's racialized violence provokes in them a desire for vengeance and justice that is equally violent, resulting in narrative rehearsals of grisly female mutilation and murder (89). Despite this portrayal of a brutal, vengeful wrath, however, Pinoys in Santos's stories more often than not show compassion for one another. Indeed, "The Door" begins with a brief prologue in which the narrator tenderly reaches out to an old friend at the funeral of another much-loved Filipino friend. The two men share a bond of trust and empathy that counters the self-loathing violence of Pinoys hurting other Pinoys. In both Bulosan's and Santos's writings, bonds of devotion and endurance between Pinoys are an implicit resistance to the patriarchal labor abuses and racism of dominant white America, and, despite moments of "emasculating" humiliation and shame in their stories, both writers suggest that there are ways for men to express their masculinity other than through dehumanizing acts of violence and exploitation.

In their attempt to depict cross-cultural relations among other American ethnic groups, Japanese American male writers such as Toshio Mori build bridges between the United States and Japan and portray a growing concern about international tensions (Yogi 1997, 128). Mori has written poignantly about the lives of the Issei (first-generation Japanese immigrants) and the Nisei (second-generation, American-born Japanese). In his postwar stories in *Yokohama, California* ([1949] 1985), for instance, "Mori is careful to infuse his characters, even the most self-deluded, with dignity and respect" (Yogi 1997, 131), and the "proud and aging Issei" in his story "Operator,

---

1 See, e.g., Bulosan 1979, 1983a. For more portrayals of white women as betrayers, maternal providers of solace, and benefactors of Western learning and culture, see Bulosan's autobiography (1973), as well as the essays, poems and stories in Bulosan 1983b and the special issue of *Amerasia Journal* on Bulosan (R. Leong 1979).

Operator!" ([1938] 1979) is, according to Hisaye Yamamoto, "kin to the Filipino expatriates in Bienvenido Santos's 'The Day the Dancers Came'" (1979, 11). Mori's tender portrayal of Issei men who express the fullest range of complex human emotions is further evidence of first period male writing that challenges dehumanizing racist practices and regulations in North America.

As Stan Yogi contends, Nisei writing during and after the internment of over 110,000 Nikkei (people of Japanese ancestry in North and South America) poses serious questions about nationalism and Japanese American identity: "For some [the internment] resulted in fierce embracing of a thoroughly 'American' identity. For others, it led to bitter disillusionment over what were perceived to be the empty rhetorical promises of American equality and justice. Others fell between these two extremes, as Japanese Americans attempted to cope with the traumas of forced removal from their homes and internment in desolate camps scattered throughout the United States" (1997, 132). John Okada's *No-No Boy* (1957), one of the most significant fictional accounts of Japanese Americans during and after their internment in relocation camps, brings together issues of nationalism, manhood, and sexuality in its account of Japanese American men's wartime suffering. It tells the story of a young Nisei man, Ichiro Yamada, who answers "no" to questions regarding his allegiance and faithfulness to serve in the U.S. army. The identity crisis that Ichiro faces in the conflict between assimilation to America and loyalty to the Japanese homeland is, in many respects, a gendered one. To acquire some semblance of a normative American male identity, Ichiro believes he must "sever his ties" to his immigrant mother, a pro-Japan zealot who is largely influential in Ichiro's double-negative response to questions about his American patriotism. While his mother makes impossible his dream of patriarchal authority and familial normalcy, it is through the love and forgiveness of another Japanese woman, Emi, his Nisei lover, that Ichiro "comes to understand his American identity." Thus she represents a "regenerative force" in the novel (E. Kim 1990b, 72). In a perceptive analysis of the novel's critique of a "false dichotomy in Japanese American identity," Jinqi Ling contends that Ichiro's "burden is his history as a no-no boy, one rendered illegitimate by the official definition of the only acceptable past for young Japanese American men: a record of service in the U.S. military" (1995, 366-67). Both Kim's and Ling's analyses expose the gendered implications of Ichiro's identity crisis, that is, his castratory affiliation with a maternalized Japanese homeland and his conflict with the normative masculinity that service in the American armed forces would bestow. In fact, a closer look at the various male characters' female companions reveals traces of a racial/gender system in which the white war heroes, the normative males, are "awarded" trophy blondes (whom Japanese American war heroes can look at but not touch), while "losers" deserve only the women considered less desirable.

The gendered representations of assimilation to Euro-American culture in the writing of first period Chinese American men are often set against a backdrop of Asian-specific traditions. One of the earliest writers to do this was Lin Yutang, whom Elaine Kim includes on her list of Asian "ambassadors of good will" (1982,27). Lin's simplistic and dichotomous gendering of Asians and Americans as respectively feminine and masculine speaks to white readers who buy into Western stereotypes of the "Orient." For example, Lin's best-known book in English, *My Country and My People* (1937), has a chapter titled "The Chinese Mind," in which the author claims that the "Chinese head, like the feminine head, is full of common sense" (1937, 80).

Chin-Yang Lee is another Chinese American male writer of the first period who relies on stereotypes of Asians for white readers accustomed to depictions of exotic and fey "Orientals." His novel *The Flower Drum Song* (1957) concerns Chinese families who face cultural problems of adjustment and assimilation in San Francisco's Chinatown. Central to the book's theme of generational conflict between "old" Chinese ways and "new" American norms are problems of patriarchal authority, filial piety, and marriage outside of one's class and ethnicity. Lee treats these problems comically, showing Chinese Americans as "unreasonable" and "unmanly" people (E. Kim 1982, 107). Similarly, in his autobiography, *Father and Glorious Descendant* (1943), Pardee Lowe attempts to resolve the filial problem of an Americanized Chinese son marrying a white woman against his father's wishes, presenting his own marriage and the subsequent birth of his mixed-race son as a metaphor for bridging the cultural divide between Asia and North America. Implicitly, however, Lowe's objective is to claim an American patriarchal authority by recognizing his father as "truly an American" by virtue of Lowe's marriage.

Lin's, Lee's, and Lowe's writings have all been the targets of biting and even hostile criticism from Asian American studies scholars. Most notable among these critics are masculinist writers Frank Chin, Jeffery Paul Chan, and Shawn Hsu Wong. Along with Lawson Fusao Inada, they have attacked Lee and Lin in particular as Asians who, in their alleged desire to be like white Americans, perpetuate emasculating stereotypes about Asian men: "They consciously set out to become American, in the white sense of the word, and succeeded in becoming 'Chinese American' in the stereotypical sense of the good, loyal, obedient, passive, law-abiding, cultural sense of the word" (F. Chin et al. 1974, xiv). Chin especially has railed against the "effeminacy" of Asian American literature, arguing that Lowe's autobiography, in conjunction with some popular works by Asian American women, confirms "white male supremacist stereotype [s]" about Asian Americans (1972, 67).

However, other scholars point out works, such as H. T. Tsiang's *And China Has Hands* (1937), that portray the lives of early Asian immigrant men sensitively and realistically (see E. Kim 1982, 109; Palumbo-Liu 1999, 49-58). Tsiang's book is a fictional account of a New York laundry-man's disappointment and frustration with the tedium of menial labor, an uiifulfilling sexual and romantic life, and incessant encounters with racism and crime; eventually, he dies when a labor strike in which he is picketing erupts into violence. Tsiang's sympathetic portrayal of early Asian immigrant men places him in the company of such compassionate male writers of the first period as Kang, Bulosan, Santos, and Mori.

Women's writing

During the earliest period of labor immigration, a number of factors made it difficult for Asian American women to create literature: patriarchal values in the Asian countries that militated against women's literacy and self-expression; the harsh lives of Asian American women as prostitutes, wives, mothers, and/or co-laborers with the men, which made the time and energy needed to write a luxury; and dominant society's lack of interest in Asian women except in ethnographic, missionary, or philanthropic contexts. Only glimpses of early Chinese American women's lives can be caught in the male-authored texts of the period.

In an event highly emblematic of later cultural developments, a "Chinese Lady," Afong Moy, was put on display in native costume in museums and novelty/freak shows between 1834 and 1837 (Yung 1986, 17; Moy 1993, 12). American reactions ranged from admiration of her exotic beauty and fetishistic fascination with her bound feet to disgust over her alien features (Yung 1986, 17). Many early Asian American women came (or were brought) to the United States as prostitutes or "picture brides." As Luibheid points out, U.S. immigration laws played an active part in constructing the sexualities of Asian prostitutes and wives (1998, 118-156, 157-188). For Anglo-Americans, images of Asian American women as exotic, alluring sex objects, depraved prostitutes, or victims of Asian patriarchy in need of rescue were not only a rationale for legislative discrimination (S. Chan 1991) but also a means of cultural management of otherness. Stereotypes derived from this period, such as the meek "lotus blossom" or the manipulative "dragon lady," have exerted a long-lasting effect on the American popular imagination and hindered the ability of Asian American women to represent themselves and make their voices heard (see, e.g., Tajima 1989).

In an inhospitable sociohistorical context, the very existence of Sui Sin Far (pseudonym for Edith Maude Eaton, 1865-1914), claimed by some to be the first Asian American fictionist in

English, is a cause for wonderment. A mixed-race (British-Chinese) woman who lived at various times in Canada, Jamaica, and the United States, Sui led a life that discouraged essentialist notions of Asian American identity and made her a fittingly complex foremother of Asian American literature. Her work anticipates many gender and sexuality themes of interest today, and she has been especially admired by Asian American feminists both for her independence as an outspoken, self-supporting single woman and for her antiracist, antisexist stories in *Mrs. Spring Fragrance* (Sui 1912) and in journalistic pieces.[1]

Sui worked in the Western tradition of sentimental fiction, producing short stories for women's and other magazines. Many focus on women and children, most are set in Chinatown, and several are about miscegenation. Although they may seem stylistically conventional, the stories are vehicles for destabilizing gender and racial categories through what Annette White-Parks identifies as their "tr0icksterism." Whereas histories of early Chinese Americans all too frequently see women only "in ratios" (of their population relative to men's) and in a family context (White-Parks 1995, 119), Sui delineates women individually and explicitly questions patriarchal familial authority and traditional gender roles. Moreover, in defiance of the colonial, ethnographic discourse of the time, she debunks white culture's universalism by revealing its racist underpinnings (e.g., in Exclusion laws and hypocritical Christian practices). The motif of cross-dressing in a cross-cultural setting (in "'The Smuggling of Tie Co" and "A Chinese Boy-Girl") provides an especially effective device for expressing her understanding of race and gender as inextricably linked. Min Song (1998) examines the class and homosexual dimensions in "The Smuggling of Tie Co," which he describes as a category-subverting "tale of gendered Orientalism" (308).

The period between the 1910s and World War II appears to have been a relatively quiet one for Asian American women writers, at least according to the surveys of nationality-specific literatures in Cheung 1997a. This might be a cultural toll exacted by anti-immigration policies. Between the 1920s and early 1940s, some Nisei women, however, did publish in small literary magazines and literary sections of Japanese American newspapers (Yogi 1997, 128-30); one of the best known is Hisaye Yamamoto. Another group of Asian American women publishing in English are those Elaine Kim calls "ambassadors of goodwill" (1982, 27) and Amy Ling "'unofficial diplomats and bridges between East and West" (1990a, 59): highly educated Japanese and Chinese women from elite. Westernized backgrounds who wrote about their native cultures for an Anglo-American

---

1 Sui's works were recently republished (Sui 1995), strengthening an already strong scholarly interest in them by critics such as Amy Ling (1990a, 1990b) and Annette White-Parks (1995).

audience. Etsu Sugimoto's autobiographical novel *A Daughter of the Samurai* (1925) fits the description, as do the works of Helena Kuo, Adet Lin, Lin Tai-yi (Anor Lin), Mai-mai Sze, and Han Suyin (see A. Ling 1990a, 56-103), who became active in the wake of the Japanese invasion of China in the 1930s, the subsequent formal outbreak of World War Ⅱ, and U.S. entry into the fray, hoping, in part, to win Western friends for China's war effort.

The prominence of the autobiographical mode among the "ambassador" writers raises questions about gender and genre and about women as ethnographic Others and cultural translators (L. Kang 1995; Su 1998; see also S. Lim 1994). It was a traumatic colonial/imperialist encounter that brought the Chinese writers to the West and inspired their writing (a pattern that also applies to some third period works). Among the benefits of Westernization for such women was the opportunity to acquire literacy and receive a formal education, which was traditionally denied to women. Add the fact that acquisition of English was typically through missionary schooling, and the ambiguous, troubled positioning of women between Asian patriarchy (whose influence continues into "modern" nationalism) and Western colonialism becomes evident, an issue that will be hotly debated during the second period. The works of the "ambassador" writers have received scant critical attention from Asian Americanists thus far (perhaps because their direct effectiveness as ethnic/minority cultural nationalist project is not obvious), although recent scholarship more attentive to subtle negotiations of gender and national and transnational identity is exposing previously obscured aspects of Asian American gender and sexuality.

Internment experiences during World War Ⅱ profoundly altered the power relationships between Issei parents and Nisei children and between men and women, generally to the benefit of those previously subordinated, and they resulted as well in increased output by Japanese American women writers. Some published in internment camp magazines (Yogi 1997, 132–134), and, immediately following the war, several published narratives set before and during internment. These include Mine Okubo's brief illustrated memoir of camp life, *Citizen 13660* ([1946] 1983); Monica Sone's autobiography, *Nisei Daughter* ([1953] 1979); and Hisaye Yamamoto's short stories collected in *Seventeen Syllables and, Other Stories* (1988). (Wa-kako Yamauchi also began writing in camp, but her first book of fiction was not published until 1994.) Sone's autobiography traces the formation of a racialized, gendered subjectivity from before World War Ⅱ through postinternment family dispersal. Her depictions of the exotic Japaneseness of her mother, ostensibly for comic relief, are, in critic Traise Yamamoto's (1999) view, a sign of "masking" a strategy of simultaneous disclosure and concealment that she finds characteristic of a number of Japanese American women's works, including two later autobiographies about internment by Jeanne Wakatsuki Houston and James Houston (1973) and Yoshiko Uchida (1982). In these texts, race-based historical violence receives more subdued treatment than in John Okada's *No-No Boy*, and its workings are also seen in such "feminine" domains as quotidian domestic arrangements, food choices, and social rituals.

Among women writers of the first period, Hisaye Yamamoto stands out for her subtle realizations of gender and sexual relationships. Her best-known stories were published immediately after the war: "Seventeen Syllables" and "Yoneko's Earthquake" are set in prewar rural California and "The Legend of Miss Sasagawara" in camp. Yamamoto's stories "often explore tensions between issei men and issei women, and also the relationships between nisei and issei, especially the bonds between mothers and daughters" (Yogi 1997, 135). They situate women's sexual repression and awakening in a complex context where cultural differences, class disparities, interethnic tension, and collective trauma all come into play Yogi (1989) and Cheung (1993) see Yamamoto as engaging in peculiarly "feminine" narrative strategies—"buried plots" and "double voicing." Yamamoto's "The High-Heeled Shoes, a Memoir" "may be the earliest Asian American work, that deals with transgender and transvestite issues," according to R. Leong (1995a, xxiv), and, according to Cheung, the first to address sexual harassment (1993, 58).

Because the Chinese were the "good Asians" during World War Ⅱ, postwar Chinese American women's writing has a distinctly different cast from its Japanese American counterpart. Jade Snow Wong's controversial *Fifth Chinese Daughter* ([1945] 1989) is a case in point. Its account of growing up female in a sexist, authoritarian Chinese immigrant family and of liberation through Americanization fits well into the hegemonic immigrant success story, which made it an official U.S. propaganda vehicle in the 1950s and still ideologically useful in today's educational institutions (Su 1994). Wong's narrative links her to the female "ambassadors," but within a domestic U.S. setting, for she too raises the question of women's positioning vis-à-vis patriarchy and colonialism ("external" or "internal"). While early critics take issue with Wong's "model minority" stance (e.g., F. Chin er al. 1991, xxix-xxx; E. Kim 1982, 69-72), recent critics tend to be interested in feminist recuperations (e.g., Cobb 1988; Goldman 1992), in interrogating differential critical deployments of racial and sexual difference (J. Ling 1998, 140-146), and in Wong's narrativization of the racialized, gendered working body in political economy and discourse (Palumbo-Liu 1999, 138-146).

The second period: Self-definition and self-representation (1960s–1980s)

The second period begins with the Civil Rights and other liberation movements, including the Asian American movement and the feminist movement. The liberalization of immigration policy in 1965, which lifted restrictions on immigration from Asia, also radically altered the demographic composition and cultural processes of the Asian American population. This period saw the first widespread use of the coalitional term "Asian American" as a self-conscious political act and the first explicit definitions of Asian American ethnic identity as inseparable from gender and sexuality. Both male and female writers were galvanized by the cultural project of antiracist, anti-Orientalist self-representation. Openly gay Asian American writers began publishing in this period, but the cultural landscape was dominated by a debate between heterosexual men and women, encapsulated by Elaine Kim in her phrase "Chinatown cowboys and warrior women" (1982) and by King-Kok Cheung in her "The Chinaman Pacific versus the Woman Warrior" (1990).

The late 1960s and early 1970s are often labeled the "cultural nationalist period." However, to ensure the understanding that cultural nationalism has not been and should not be monopolized by masculinists, who were highly vocal at the time, we refer to it as the "androcentric cultural nationalist period," whose waning can be marked with the publication of Kingston's *The Woman Warrior* in 1976, with its attendant controversies. Feminist interventions in representational politics are a hallmark of the late 1970s and the 1980s.

Men's writing

The anti-Vietnam War protests and the Civil Rights era had an immediate and irrevocable effect on the writing of Asian American men from the 1960s through the 1980s. In fact, much of their writing today expresses revolutionary cultural changes from the liberation and antiwar movements of the past thirty years. By the early 1970s, many Asian American writers, men in particular, were angrily denouncing more than a century's racist caricatures and stereotypes. These writers — largely second-and third-generation — articulated a platform for an Asian American cultural nationalist project that, in addition to asserting solidarity with other racially oppressed minorities, called for vociferous indictment of past and present injustices against Asian Americans. Writers from this second period strove to achieve a new self-image based on Asian Americans' demands for self-representation and self-definition in all aspects of American culture (E. Kim 1982, 173).

Many male writers of this period are concerned with overcoming emasculating distortions of Asian men's gender and sexuality, an endeavor that was to be achieved through tactics reminiscent of the male-dominated Black Power movement of the 1960s. Ting notes that "writing throughout the period represents Asian American sexuality as repressed, shaped, and channeled by systems of race and capitalism … There is substantial evidence that even individuals who were not convinced of systemic Asian American oppression agreed that the distortion of sexuality kept Asian Americans from realizing their full humanity" (1998, 77). The concerns of Asian American male writers of the second period are inextricable from matters of gender and sexuality — matters that intersect with the issues of family and patriarchy taken up by male writers in the first period. Thus, while the formation of a counterhegemonic Asian American male subjectivity is a major concern in much of the men's writing of this period, its construction was deeply affected by white patriarchal norms and regulations. At the same time that they denounce oppressive American practices that "emasculate" Asian men, though, these writers also uphold a system of racial gendering as a paradigm for claiming their own manhood — a paradigm that, in addition to reinstating paternal authority and the nuclear family as cultural norms, reinforces racist stereotypes that link violence and aggression with the sexuality and gender of other ethnic minority men. For example, Frank Chin, perhaps the best known of the androcentric cultural nationalist writers, relies on misogyny and homophobia in his attempt to delineate and construct a (hetero)normative Asian American manhood. In his critique of racist Hollywood caricatures of Asian men, for example, Chin glorifies stereotypes of aggression in black, Latino, and Native American men: "Unlike the white stereotype of the evil black stud, Indian rapist, Mexican macho, the evil of the evil Dr. Fu Manchu was not sexual, but homosexual" (1972, 66).

Although Louis Chu wrote *Eat a Bowl of Tea* ([1961] 1979) approximately ten years before the androcentric agenda of the second period was established, he is perhaps the first male writer to articulate the struggle for a new (masculine) Asian American identity. Like Tsiang in *And China Has Hands* (1937), Chu does not euphemize his account of the daily lives of the mostly aging immigrant men in New York's Chinatown. The novel's portrayal of two generations of Chinese American immigrants — old-timers and the families they eventually bring over from China or initiate in the United States — pivots on "the uneasy truce between American-born children and their patriarchal elders" (Hsiao 1992,152). In focusing the novel on lonely old bachelors, old-timer fathers who can only pass on to their children lives of poverty and hard work, a married couple whose only child is produced by the wife's infidelity, and the inability of elderly immigrant men to maintain familial traditions through paternal authority, Chu depicts a crisis in patriarchy and emphasizes the need for a new breed of Chinese Americans. In many respects, he expresses the agenda for much of the second period's androcentric cultural nationalism. Women in his novel, as in much second period men's writing, propel the patriarchal crisis in male-dominated Asian American communities by helping to institute the replacement of traditional patriarchy with a new set of Americanized paternal norms. Men's writing of the 1970s continues to portray rejections of old-world family ways in favor of a new Asian American selfhood. For example, Milton Murayama's *All I Asking for Is My Body* ([1975] 1988) tells the story of two Nisei brodiers living in Hawaii during World War II who desire lives of self-determination away from repressive family strictures.

In the tradition of *Eat a Bowl of Tea,* the works of Chinese American writers Frank Chin and Jeffery Paul Chan help set the agenda for the masculinist literary endeavors of the second period. A central and enormously controversial feature of their writing is the quest for an authentic Asian American masculinity. Cultural nationalist writers seek an original Asian American manhood that is U.S.-centric and thus derived from a historical and mythological context of early Asian immigrant laborers; they see these laborers as an integral part of a masculinized Western American landscape. In their attempt to associate with and recover lost and "extinct" Asian American male forefathers, the cultural nationalists seek an authentic Asian male identity that is premised on conventional ideals of Western manhood: the admirable hypervirile qualities of'rebelliousness, resilience, and aggression in such romantic popular American figures as the invulnerable and adventurous cowboy (E. Kim 1982, 177), the fearless and indomitable pioneer, and the brawny working-class laborer laying the railroads of the great American West. The cultural nationalists' struggle to construct an authentic male subjectivity for themselves through the recuperation and mimesis of "lost" father figures underscores the centrality of white American norms of family and patriarchy in their work. Such norms, moreover, are not only targets of their antiracist criticism but also standards for an American way of life that they want to appropriate for Asian American culture.[1]

To rescue Asian American men from a history of castratory white racist oppression, cultural nationalist writers of the second period argue for an Asian American sensibility that counters gender-distorted stereotypes of Asians. In "Racist Love" (1972), Frank Chin and Jeffery Paul Chan proclaim literature and art as intrinsic components to the production of an original Asian American cultural sensibility. The language of art and literature, they maintain, is especially relevant to cultural experiences that produce masculine integrity and self-determination: "On the simplest level, a man, in any culture, speaks for himself. Without a language of his own, he no longer is a man but a ventriloquist's dummy at worst and at best a parrot ... The tyranny of

---

1 But note, too, F. Chin's increasing turn to specifically Asian ideals of manhood, esp. in *Donald Duk* (1991).

language has been used by white culture to suppress Chinese-American and Japanese-American culture and exclude the Asian-American sensibility from operating in the mainstream of American consciousness" (1972, 77).

Scholars have noted the motif of sickly Asian women in Chin's work. In the aptly titled story "A Chinese Lady Dies" (1988b), a diseased Asian mother signifies a Chinatown that is "a stagnating enclave of dying men and women, locked up in cramped quarters" (S. C. Wong 1993a, 146). For Chin, the masculinizing project of recovering lost paternal origins of early Asian American forefathers is futile within the pathological confines of urban Chinese American communities. Relationships with Asian women often thematize the containment of Asian men in stereotypical roles of emasculated fathers and effeminate sons. Further, in Chin's fiction, dysfunctional relations between Asian men and women mirror the reality of Asian American male artists who, according to Chin, are outnumbered and therefore emasculated by Asian American women writers. His oft-repeated contention that Asian American writing is dominated by women (and a gay man, David Henry Hwang) explains his association of Asian females with death, decay, and futility as symbols of Asian male castration.

As in the first period, white women also figure prominently in second period men's writing. As wives, girlfriends, and adulterous lovers, they are fetishized objects for the construction of a heteronormative Asian American masculine subject. In Jeffery Paul Chan's "The Chinese in Haifa" (1974a), an Asian American man's adulterous relations with a white woman suggest his liberating transition from asexual Chinese family strictures to an eroticized American independence and freedom. In Shawn Hsu Wong's *Homebase* ([1979] 1991), the Chinese American narrator, Rainsford Chan, has an imaginary Caucasian girlfriend who represents a dominant white culture that excludes Asians from Americanness. Rainsford's eventual rejection of his white girlfriend's "love" helps him to connect with ancestral Asian fathers who allow him to claim America as his own. In contrast to this soul-searching denial of interracial love, Daniel Okimoto, in his autobiography, *American in Disguise,* avers that intermarriage is the "key to assimilation" (1971, 156). Okimoto divulges his attempts at overcoming feelings of self-negation and racial inferiority through courting and marrying a "beautiful, blue-eyed blonde," the "crowning evidence of having made it" as a man in mainstream America (201).

Tracing patrilineal descent to a past of Asian male forebears is also a central feature in men's writing of the second period. In many of these works, ineffectual fathers — like ailing mothers — serve as further reason for the Asian male's need to find an identificatory sense of purpose in the manly terrain of the West. Frank Chin's play *The Chickencoop Chinaman* (1981) and his short stories from *The Chinaman Pacific and Frisco R.R. Co.* (1988a) focus on an Asian American man's move from stagnating urban confines to the emancipatory male-homosocial world of the Old West, where the masculinity-fortifying potential of reviving a lost patriarchal heritage counters images of embarrassing, "unmanly" Chinatown fathers (S. C. Wong 1993a, 146-147).

If many of these second period writers depict barren and decaying Chinatowns, they also seek to replace them with a vital, U.S.-centric Asian patriarchy. In showing the death of Asian American urban centers, masculinist second period writers romanticize their own demise as part of the "extinction" of folkloric American men. Frank Chin, for instance, imagines his own death as a brave, manly act of self-sacrifice that transcends the cowardice and pathology of his Chinatown characters. Like Natty Bumppo in James Fenimore Cooper's *The Pioneers,* who traces the contours of his name on his own tombstone before disappearing in the western wilderness to die alone, Chin figures his own death as the stuff of heroic folklore, linking him to the vanished cultures of cowboys, Indian warriors, and frontiersmen. As Daniel Kim observes, the fantasized male-homosocial world of American heroes in which Chin envisions himself is largely a product of self-loathing. Chin's example suggests "that the moral violence we inflict on our assimilated identities is perhaps intended for the 'white man' we glimpse within the shape of our 'Americanized' selves, the 'white man' we wish to beat out of ourselves but cannot" (D. Kim 1998, 294). This psychoanalytic reading of Chin's work exposes a "masochistic" self-hatred, which is at the heart of much androcentric cultural nationalist writing.

During the second period, despite the dominance of heterosexism in Asian American men's writing, gay writers were already creating works that anticipate many of the queer themes that become more explicit in the third period. Notable among them is Paul Stephen Lim, whose plays (1977, 1985a, 1985b, 1989) address issues such as the so-called rice queen phenomenon and the relationship between language and sexual as well as racial/ethnic identity.

Women's writing

Contemporaneous with these writers' efforts at masculine self-definition and self-representation, Asian American women writers were engaged in a similar project, which some saw as especially challenging given their need to contend with Eastern and Western patriarchy as well as racism. Even during the androcentric cultural nationalist period, Asian American women's voices were loud and assertive, fueled by the Civil Rights, anti-Vietnam War, Asian American, and feminist movements and the sexual revolution. Their "searc [h] for a new self-image" (E. Kim 1982, 173) took many forms. For example, a number of feminist poets associated with the Asian American Movement, such as Jessica Hagedorn, Geraldine Kudaka, Genny Lim, Janice Mirikitani, Barbara Noda, Nellie Wong, Kitty Tsui, Merle Woo, and Mitsuye Yamada, critiqued the oppression of Asian American women, expressed solidarity with Third World women in Asia and elsewhere, discerned connections between sexism and colonialism, challenged Orientalist stereotypes, reconstructed female ancestors' forgotten lives, claimed a matrilineal heritage on American soil, explored family dynamics, celebrated love between women, reclaimed female sexuality, and declared a new image; tough, powerful, resourceful, independent, and courageous, neither "lotus blossom" nor "dragon lady." Among these, Noda, Tsui, and Woo are considered pioneer lesbian writers as well. In some ways, compared to the difficult emergence of gay subjectivity from Asian American masculinist cultural projects, it seems that the struggles, discourse, and consciousness of Asian American lesbians were eased somewhat by their connections with feminism; the strong woman is a model and goal for both heterosexual and lesbian feminists.

The title of Kingston's 1976 bestseller *The Woman Warrior* captures this spirit. The book's publication catalyzed an acrimonious and long-running debate on Asian American gender and sexuality (among other issues) that effectively marked the end of androcentric cultural nationalism's dominance.[1] *The Woman Warrior*; variously labeled nonfiction, autobiography, autoethnography, and fiction, narrates a second-generation Chinese American girl's coming of age in the 1950s and 1960s in the shadow of a domineering mother, caught between a patriarchal Chinese culture and a racist American society. The book's phenomenal popularity with white feminist readers again raises the issues of Asian American women writers' possible complicity with racism, Orientalism, and the ethnographic gaze and their role in efforts to rehabilitate Asian American manhood. The tensions between feminism and cultural nationalism have been examined in many studies (see Cheung 1990; Bow 1993), and *The Woman Warrior* has generated a veritable industry of critical analysis outside Asian American studies as well. Its affinities with poststructuralist and deconstructionist theories have made it a favorite in academia and attracted numerous applications of feminist theory but have also raised questions about misreading and cooptation, the dynamics of institutionalization and canonization, and the limits of "universal sisterhood" (R. Lee 1995b; Hattori 1998b). The appearance of *The Woman Warrior* may be said to have inaugurated a "multiculturalist" phase in the reception of Asian American literature, whose contradictions have persisted, erupting again with Amy Tan's *The Joy Luck Club* (1989),

---

1　The literature on this controversy is so vast that its contours can only be sketched here; for further details and references, see S. Lim 1991 and S. C. Wong 1998, another crossover hit featuring mother-daughter relationships and Chinese sexism (among other subjects) and attracting considerable mainstream feminist attention.

It is not unusual to find readers who consider the two books practically synonymous with Asian American women's literature (or even Asian American literature), unbeholden to any context. It is much more productive, not to mention intellectually defensible, however, to understand them within the framework of Asian American women's writing, and their focus on mother-daughter relationships as part of a feminist agenda to preserve memory and establish a matrilineal tradition.[1]

In addition to autobiography and fiction thematizing matrilineage, women writers have used historical fiction to imaginatively reconstruct the lives of strong women who could be claimed as foremothers (see, e.g., Mc Cunn 1981; Uchida 1987). Scholars have contributed to this primary literature by facilitating the writing of autobiographies by immigrant women (e.g., anthropologist Akemi Kikumura has recorded her mother's oral history in *Through Harsh Winters* [1981] and Sucheng Chan has edited Mary Paik Lee's *Quiet Odyssey* [1990] and by producing, often in collaboration with the community, feminist anthologies such as Asian Women United of California's *Making Waves* (1989) and Lim and Tsutakawa's *The Forbidden Stitch* (1989).

There are obvious similarities between the masculinist and feminist projects within the second period. The male writers establish a patriline, the female ones, a matriline, and both turn to the construction of heroic ancestors and the invention of new images to rehabilitate Asian American manhood or womanhood. Both must also deal with modifications to the concept of family as biologically based. From Chu (1961) 1979C in which an "illegitimate" son from an affair is adopted into the Wong family in post-World War II New York Chinatown and M. Leong 1975 (in which a sonless — but not daughterless — restaurant worker wants to adopt a disabled young gambler) to Kogawa 1982 (in which an aunt and uncle become surrogate parents after the protagonist's mother is killed by the atom bomb in Japan) and Kadohata 1989 (which focuses on an itinerant Japanese American stepfamily in post-internment America), we see a pattern of Asian American families adapting to collective injuries of exclusion, racism, internment, and war by replacing, to use Edward Said's terms, "filiation" with "affiliation" (see also Li 1992).

---

1 *Depictions* of mother-daughter (and grandmother-granddaughter) relationships (surveyed in S. C. Wong 1995b [176-180] and Ghymn 1995 [11-36]) are frequently found in women's writing from almost .all Asian American subgroups and in Asian Canadian literature. Among the works that address the theme of matrilineage in general — nor just in the figure of the mother but also in grandmothers/matriarchs, aunts/surrogare mothers, and a multigen-erational female line — are the following: in the first period, H. Yamamoto 1988; Wong and Cressy 1952; and, in the second period, Chuang (1968) 1986; Cha 1982; Kogawa 1982; Law-Yone 1983; R, Kim 1987; Kadohata 1989; Hayslip 1989; Sasaki 1991. For a radical lesbian perspective on matri-lineage, see also the short fiction cited in S. C. Wong 1995b; Woo 1981; and Tsui 1983.

However, there are also striking differences between the male and female projects. Vivian Chin (personal communication) notes that the masculinist project is fraught with anxiety about proper genealogy, authenticity, "traceability" and fixity of identity, whereas the feminist project appears more comfortable with fluidity, multiplicity, and indeterminacy of both origin and identity. Chinese American literature is filled with anxious, heirless patriarchs; in addition to the titles mentioned above, there are Chin-Yang Lee's *The Flower Drum Song* (1957), Jeffery Paul Chan's "Jack-rabbit" (1974b), and Frank Chin's *The Tear of the Dragon* (1981) and "The Only Real Day" (1976). A similar concern is found in Japanese and Filipino American literature: in Okada's *No No Boy*, young Japanese American men either die or, like Ichiro, are unable to form a family; in Santos's stories, such as "The Day the Dancers Came" aging Filipino men die heirless ([1955] 1979, 113-128). Where miscegenation occurs, the non-Asian often has to be culturally redefined as comparable to the "genuine article" to be acceptable: in Lin Yutang's *Chinatown Family* (Lin 1948), the Italian daughter-in-law must be redefined as Chinese, and in Santos's "Scent of Apples" ([1955] 1979, 21-29), the white wife has to "become" Filipino, in spite of the existence of a fine son.

Anxiety over miscegenation is not entirely absent in Asian American women's literature (e.g., Cliuang Hua's *Crossings* [(Chuang 1968) 1986] and, in the third period, Gish Jen's *Mona in the Promised Land* [1996]), but the mother figure is less likely to be a "border patrol" than a survivor whose important legacy is her personal strength rather than her genetic and cultural legitimacy. Daughters in women's writing are not immune from paternal authority — the patriarchs in *Crossings* and in Wendy Law-Yone's *The Coffin Tree* (1983) are as powerful and violent as those in the men's stories — but pedigree is much less of an obsession in the women's writing than in the men's.

The third period: Multiple selves, sites, transgressions (late 1980s to the present)

Asian American literature in the third period is marked by queer activism and theoretical projects, continued demographic change in the U.S. and Asian American populations, multiculturalism (and its backlash) in U.S. cultural politics, and the growing impact of globalization and other forces of postmodernity. Within Asian American literary and cultural studies, many have argued that a paradigm shift of sorts has taken place (E. Kim 1992; Omi and Takagi 1995; S. Lim 1997). The publication of Lisa Lowe's influential essay "Heterogeneity, Hybridity, Multiplicity: Marking

Asian American Differences" in 1991 is one indicator of the shift, which Cheung summarizes in a recent review essay on Asian American literary studies: "Whereas identity politics — with its stress on cultural nationalism and American nativity — governed earlier theoretical and critical formulations, the stress is now on heterogeneity and diaspora. The shift has been from seeking to 'claim America' to forging a connection between Asia and Asian America; from centering on race and on masculinity to revolving around the multiple axes of ethnicity, gender, class, and sexuality; from being concerned primarily with social history and communal responsibility to being caught in the quandaries and possibilities of postmodernism and multiculturalism" (1997b, 1).

Third period literature treats issues of gender and sexuality in the contexts of poststructuralism-inflected treatments of subjectivities; increasingly visible male writers who self-consciously explore earlier periods' concerns about masculinity in new frameworks (e.g., socioeconomically privileged men with transnational mobility); feminist writers who articulate a growing "postcolonial" awareness of historical violence against women in Asia and the United States; a flowering of writing and theorizing about and by lesbians and gay men; open affirmations of sexual gratification, experimentation, and transgressions; and a greater willingness to confront sensitive topics such as family dysfunction and incest.

Heterogeneity

The third period, barely a decade old, is an exciting period for students of gender and sexuality in Asian American literature. Having gained a certain security from the labors of the second period, from a modest but distinctly friendlier commercial interest, and from a cultural climate in which multiculturalism and global cultural flows are recognized (if not always accepted) ideas, Asian American writers have been engaging in bold explorations of gender and sexuality — some continuations of earlier concerns, and some new and particular to their era.

Internal ethnic diversity among Asian Americans has been increasing since the immigration reforms of 1965, but the cumulative effects of recent family-based immigration and the influx of Asian migrants as a result of historical events such as the end of the Vietnam War have noticeably increased heterogeneity in the Asian American population during the 1990s. The strong presence of Filipino, Korean, various South Asian, and Vietnamese and other Southeast Asian writers has eroded tine dominance of the Chinese and Japanese in earlier periods. With this diversity comes a new range of perspectives on gender and sexuality that necessitates attention to subgroup-specific variations of "Asian American gender and sexuality." As Richard Fung (1991b) maintains in the context of gay porn, not all Asian American sexuality is constructed the same. Russell Leong, too, writes, "Within the 'Asian' or 'Pacific' category itself are subcategories of gendered sexual and racialized traits ascribed to different groups by white Americans, e.g., Hawaiians, Chinese, Filipino, Thai, and Japanese" (1996b, 3). Moreover, the specific cultural norms of a given Asian culture must be taken into account, as Cheung (1993) points out in connection with the differing Chinese and Japanese meanings of "silence" for men and women and Santa Ana (1998) with regard to the Filipino "Maria Clara" feminine ideal. At least one subgroup-specific (South Asian [Ratti 1993]) anthology on sexuality has appeared, and we expect to see continued efforts at finer differentiations in understandings of Asian American gender and sexuality in the future.

The production of anthologies, a crucial aspect of second period self-definition and self-representation, continues in the 1990s but moves beyond implicitly heterosexual feminist or masculinist projects. *On a Bed of Rice* (Kudaka 1995) is a collection of Asian American erotica intended to break taboos and celebrate Asian American sexuality. While a balanced representation of women from various ethnic communities was a central concern in the 1989 volume *Making Waves,* its sequel, *Making More Waves,* is governed by other principles of selection, including "sexuality and sexual orientation" (Kim, Villanueva, and Asian Women United of California 1997, xii). Gay and lesbian writers are well represented in *Charlie Chan Is Dead* (Hagedorn 1993). *Between the Lines* (Chung, Kim, and Lemeshewsky 1987), *The Very Inside* (Lim-Hing 1994b), *Asian American Sexualities* (R. Leong 1996a), *Q&A: Queer in Asian America* (Eng and Horn 1998b), and *Rice: Explorations into Gay Asian Culture and Politics* (Cho 1998) are all dedicated to explorations of homosexuality and related issues.

Gender-specific issues: Repetition and difference

The 1990s have seen a veritable explosion of publishing activity by male Asian American writers. Some continue the theme of constructing a tradition of heroic male ancestors (e.g., stories in Bacho 1997; Pak 1998), while others are explicitly devoted to exploring male subjectivity in relation to gender and sexuality.[1] Correspondingly, the study of masculinity has been gaining momentum.[2] Viet Thanh Nguyen's (1997) study of "remasculation," for example, theorizes the role of the state in the construction of a violent Chinese American masculinity in second and third period writings.

In many works of the third period as well, violence is no less central to subject formation than

---

1 See, e.g., G. Lee 1991, Mura 1991, 1996; Chang-Rae Lee 1995.
2 See, e.g., Jachison Chan 1993; S. C. Wong 1993b, 1995a; Eng 1995; Cheung 1998; Hattori 1998a.

in the works of a Carlos Builosan or a Frank Chin. Forms of violence ranging from boxing and street fights to torture, crucifixion, and rioting are found, for example, in Gus Lee's retrospective account of post-World War Ⅱ coming of age in a rough San Francisco neighborhood (1991); in Peter Racho's story of an American-born priest confronting violence in religion and war on his visit to the Philippines (1991) and in his short stories about boxing, martial arts training, and working-class street life in *Dark Blue Suit* (1997) (many first published in the second period); in Heinz Insu Fenkl's novel about an Amerasian boy growing up in the brutal streets of Pupyong, Korea, between the Korean and Vietnam Wars (1996); in Murayama's exploration of World War II and postwar Hawaiian manhood in the masculine arenas of boxing, war, work, and politics (1998);[1] and in the explosions of interethnic (Black-Korean and other) urban violence in Chang-Rae Lee's *Native Speaker* (1995) and Leonard Chang's *The Fruit'n Food* (1996). Despite the variety of settings in these works — the United States, Asia, or both — collectively and intertextually, they highlight the continuities between the U.S.'s colonial, military, and economic presence in Asia, past and present, and the predicament of Asian American males in America's racially heterogeneous cities.

Compared to the first period or even the second, the well-being of the Asian American male, superficially defined by socioeconomic status, education level, or some such statistical measure, has clearly improved. Blatant legislative impediments to "normal" heterosexual male attainments — sexual liaisons, marriage, having children, holding a job, and so on — have been lifted in the post-Civil Rights era. Nevertheless, male anxiety over emasculation and failed paternity lingers in Asian American men's writing in the form of fear of cultural extinction resulting from excessive assimilation. Sau-ling Wong (1995a) has analyzed this in David Wong Louie's short stories in *Pangs of Love* (1991), in which the lack of heirs is a recurrent theme. Louie's educated and affluent male characters court and sometimes attract white women but typically fail to keep them. In Chang-Rae Lee's *Native Speaker* (1995) as well, the U.S.-born Korean protagonist marries a white woman, but their mixed-race son dies and his wife leaves. Perfect English, middle-class status, residential integration, mainstream "cultural literacy," even a white wife — in short, all the accoutrements of a "model minority" — are insufficient to insure the Asian American man against identity loss.

David Mura's autobiographical *Turning Japanese* (1991) and *Where the Body Meets Memory* (1996) appear to be exceptions to this pattern, despite sharing a poststructuralist, postmodernist

---

1 Murayama's *Five Years on a Rock* (1994), which is set between these two works in time, is also part of the Oyama family saga but is told from the mother's point of view.

sensibility with Louie and Chang-Rae Lee. Mura's narrator is able to "buy" a certain amount of masculinity with affluence and American cultural fluency. Furthermore, he claims self-healing through reconnection with Japanese American internment history. Nevertheless, the recovery of his masculinity can be attributed as much to his cultural pilgrimage to 1980s Japan, then masculinized by its wealth, power, and technological know-how in what might be considered a new form of Orientalism.

As the Mura example shows, the study of constructions of gender and sexuality in terms of nationalism, transnationalism, and diaspora can be fruitful, and it has indeed been gaining momentum in Asian American studies in the past few years. In addition to nation-specific studies, such as Elaine Kim and Chungmoo Choi's *Dangerous Women: Gender and Korean Nationalism* (1998), many recent works theorize, and/or read individual literary or filmic texts in terms of, gender and sexuality as they relate to constructions of nationality and citizenship; transnational exchanges of bodies, goods, and cultures; diasporic consciousness; and related issues.[1] David Henry Hwang's play *M. Butteijty* (1986) often appears in these discussions because of its popular success as a border-crossing cultural product and its complex treatment of gender-bending (including cross-dressing) in transnational, racialized contexts.

Linking women to nationalism, transnationalism, and diaspora already has a long history in postcolonial studies. In the case of Asian American women's writing, such approaches reveal patterns in the literature of matrilineage that the notion of self-definition/self-representation (with its primarily domestic U.S. context) cannot by itself illuminate. Certainly, Asian American women writers' interest in matrilineage has continued in the third period;[2] however, there is also a cluster of texts that depict women's violent, involuntary involvement with colonialism and imperialism, which not only accounts for their (or their families') diasporic relocation to the West but often becomes a bitter yet potentially empowering part of a maternal heritage. In contrast to men's texts, where actual physical violence or psychological encounters with violence are sometimes ascribed redemptive value, in the women's works violence tends to be grotesque and obscene.[3] In the latter, protagonists are often represented as singular individuals whose

---

1 These include Koshy 1994; R. Lee 1995a; Lye 1995; L. Lowe 1996; Thoma 1996; E. Kim and L. Lowe 1997; Kondo 1997; So 1997; Chiang 1998a; Li 1998; Palumbo-Liu 1999; T. Yamamoto 1999; and S. C. Wong, in press.

2 For examples of third period literature of matrilineage, see Cheong 1991; Mara 1991; A. Tan 1991; F. Ng 1993; Chong 1994; stories in Yamauchi 1994; stories in Divakaruni 1995; Nunez 1995; Shigekuni 1995; Badami 1996; Jen 1996; M. Ng 1998; among others.

3 Falling within this pattern arc Nieh (1981) 1998 (published in book form in Chinese in 1976 and first translated into English in 1981; S. C. Wong [in press] details its complex publication history, which reflects the violences of the modern Chinese diaspora); Cha (1982) 1994; R. Kim 1987; Mukherjee 1989; Mara 1991; Law-Yone 1993; Can 1997; Keller 1997.

particular vicissitudes are nevertheless open to allegorical readings or are placed in the context of transgenerational networks of women. Often a shocking maternal secret is revealed to the North-American-born daughter, forever altering her preoccupations with assimilation, her view of the Asian ancestral land, and her definition of womanhood. In these works, female sexuality creates a unique vulnerability to colonial or anticolonial, nationalist violence, but it is also a source of strength and the basis of bonds among women. Sara Suieri's *Meatless Days* (1989) and many of Meena Alexander's works (esp. *Nantpally Road* [1991] and *The Shock of Arrival* [1996]), though not conforming entirely to the above pattern, are also key texts on the topic of the violent postcolonial, diasporic dislocation of women. Amy Tan's popular *The Joy Luck Club* and *The Kitchen God's Wife* may be considered versions of the pattern that have been sanitized for popular consumption. Bharati Mukherjee's *Jasmine* (1989) also shares many features with the texts in this group, but it has been highly controversial because Western colonial and hegemonic U.S. national narratives can readily be recuperated in the figure of the title character.

In comparison to mother-daughter relationships, which can be traced to the first period, father-daughter relationships as a significant theme in Asian American literature appears to be a fairly recent phenomenon.[1] The 1980s saw the publication of Kingston's *China Men* (1981), a tribute to male ancestors by a Chinese American woman, and Kadohata's *The Floating World* (1989), about an itinerant Japanese American family in the rural South after World War Ⅱ. In the 1990s, there are Amy Tin's *The Kitchen God's Wife* (1991); Fae Myenne Ng's *Bone* (1993); Sigrid Nunez's *A Feather on the Breath of God* (1995); Lois-Ann Yamanaka's *Wild Meat and the Bully Burgers* (1996) and *Biu's Hanging* (1997); and Patti Kim's *A Cab Called Reliable* (1997). Interestingly, Kadohata, Tan, and Ng all portray "make-do families" in which the father of the household is biologically unrelated to the young female protagonist, a pattern noted in Kafka 1997 (63-64) and, in a way, a continuation of the "affiliative" modifications to the Asian patriarchal family begun in the first period.

Varieties of transgressiveness

Gender and sexual transgressiveness of various kinds is another important characteristic of the third period. (The most noteworthy of these, the rise of queer writing, is discussed in a separate section below.) Shawn Wong's *American Knees* (1995) exemplifies the trend toward overt expressions of sexuality, and it is one of the few erotic works in Asian American literature

---

1 We are indebted to Stephen Lee for alerting us to the importance of this theme.

devoted to delineation of adult (hetero)sexuality. Its interweaving of the erotic with both sincere and parodic renditions of Asian American discourse suggests a link between the political and the personal, between an ethnic category often associated with the social sciences and activities typically viewed as intensely private. In *American Knees* — as in Evelyn Lau's *Runaway* (1989), R. Zamora Linmark's *Rolling the R's* (1995), Mura's *Where the Body Meets Memory* (1996), Catherine Liu's *Oriental Girls Desire Romance* (1997), and Mei Ng's *Eating Chinese Food Naked* (1998) — sexuality is deployed, whether inarticulately, deliberately, defiantly, or in celebration, to counteract images of Asian American men and women as the asexual model minority.

An interesting aspect of this phenomenon is the proliferation of titles in recent Asian American women's writing (literary and otherwise) related to wildness. This trend contrasts markedly with the prevalence of titles featuring "daughter" in the first period, and it signals a resistance to defining female subjectivity only or primarily in terms of familial and cultural roles. The title of Ginu Kamani's *Junglee Girl* (1995), which is filled with tales of sexual awakening and transgressions, uses an Indian word meaning "from the jungle, wild" to describe "a wild and uncontrollable woman." Evelina Galang's *Her Wild American Self* (1996) is about Filipina American female subjectivity, and Anita Rau Badami's *Tamarind Mem* (1996) depicts a woman "as sour as tamarind" who rebels against the confining life of a proper memsahib. Elaine Kim (1996) analyzes the figure of the "bad woman" in several Asian American visual artists, and Kim and Choi's anthology on gender and Korean nationalism is titled *Dangerous Women* (1998). Another recent anthology uses the title *Dragon Ladies: Asian American Feminists Breathe Fire* (Shah 1997), reclaiming for feminist purposes one of the most damaging stereotypes of Asian American women.[1]

The "madwoman in the attic" figure was important in the development of Anglo-American feminist literary criticism, and Asian American women's writing has its share of madwomen, whose insanity may be read as a product of society's repressions. Examples include the title character in Hisaye Yamamoto's "Miss Sasagawara" (in H. Yamamoto 1988); the split-personality protagonist in Hualing Nieh's *Mulberry and Peach* ([1981] 1998); Moon Orchid in Kingston's *The Woman Warrior* (1976); Mrs. Oka in Wakako Yamauchi's *And the Soul Shall Dance* (1990); the speaker in Law-Yone's *The Coffin Tree* (1983); the crazy, addicted, often suicidal characters in Evelyn Lau's *Fresh Girls* (1993); the temporarily incapacitated protagonist in Holly Uyemoto's

---

1 Of course, the "wild woman" type does not have to be advertised in the title; see, e.g. Adhikary 1993; stories in S. Lee 1994; S.Lim 1966; Yamanaka 1996.

Go (1995); the notoriously insane Mala, who is suspected of murder, in Shani Mootoo's *Cereus Blooms at Night* (1996); the incest victim in Patricia Chao's *Monkey King* (1997); and the shamanisric mother in Nora Okja Keller's *Comfort Woman* (1997), whose "divine madness" gives a spiritual dimension to madness.[1]

While the representation of madwomen is long-standing in Asian American literature, a greater readiness to tackle sensitive or even taboo areas of gender and sexuality has been noticeable in recent years. Incest, for example, is openly represented in Sky Lee's *Disappearing Moon Cafe*(1990) and in Chao's *Monkey King* (1997) (although less explicit incestuous overtones have been present in Asian American writing at least as far back as Frank Chin and Law-Yone). Sexual activity among, or sexual victimization of, children and young adolescents appears in Lois-Ann Yamanaka's *Saturday Night at the Pahala Theater* (1993), *Wild Meat and the Bully Burgers* (1996), and *Blu's Hanging* (1997); Kamani's *Junglee Girl* (1995); R. Zamora Linmark's *Rolling the R's* (1995); and Patti Kim's *A Cab Called Reliable* (1997).

Queer writing (1990s)

The word queer, in a sociopolitical context, denotes "a political practice based on transgressions of the normal and normativity rather than a straight/gay binary of the heterosexual/homosexual identity" (Eng and Hom 1998a, 1). Queer writing, then, resists and frequently subverts a white patriarchal political economy that regulates gender, sexual, and racial identities. Emerging from gay and lesbian organizations in the 1980s and from the feminist writings of Asian American lesbians in the 1970s and 1980s (Eng and Horn 1998a, 2-3), Asian American queer writing largely expresses the transgressive cultural practices of lesbian, gay, bisexual, and transgender Asian Americans. Such writings allow Asian Americans to organize and theorize with the goals of resisting a generalized heteronormative Asian American identity and challenging an Asian American cultural politics that "relies on the construction of sameness and the exclusion of differences" (L. Lowe 1996, 68).

In Asian American queer writing, critics and fiction writers speak directly to one another. Indeed, many of the fiction writers are critics and scholars as well, challenging the heterosexual androcentrism of the cultural nationalists and articulating possibilities for conceptualizing multiplicitous and heterogeneous Asian American identities in both their art and criticism. Richard Fung, for example, is a filmmaker and critic whose work interrogates paradigmatic

---

1   Studies of madness in Asian Amerian women's literature include Ghymn 1995 and Chiu 1996, among others.

aesthetics of white masculinity. Most "images of men and male beauty," he writes, "are still of white men and white male beauty. These are standards against which we compare both ourselves and often our brothers — Asian, black, native, and Latino" (1991b, 149). Russell Leong offers a similar critique of a dominant white male culture that ascribes model minority "virtues" of socioeconomic advancement to Asian Americans while denying them sexual and gender diversity (1996b). As Fung and Leong suggest, Asian American queer writings are largely invested in contesting white racist stereotypes of Asian American gender and sexuality. In "Chamwe at the Club," for example, Margaret Mihee Choe rages against oppressive ideals of white femininity and berates Caucasian women who have a sexual fetish for Asian females: "I want my sisters / but so does WASP Woman ... / My sisters / are all with white girls. / Look at me! I shout inside" (1993, 2). L, Vannareth (1993) and Maurice L. Hoo (1993) also offer poignant critiques of gay white male standards of beauty and the self-loathing that such standards inflict in young Asian men who desire sexual relations with white males only. In *Bite Hard* (1997), Justin Chin takes his criticism of white male beauty to a comical extreme, lampooning urban gay men who worship hypervirile, gym-toned bodies. His prose poem, "Buffed Fag," satirizes the desire for the smooth muscular physique and derisive arrogance that are conventionally attributes of privileged gay white men, and, in his most recent work, Chin aims his acerbic wit at the Mr. Asian of Northern California pageant, which he regards as nothing more than a "pageantry of staged machismo" for Asian American men insecure with their masculinity (1999, 139). These men, Chin explains, want to prove that they are heterosexual and "normal" to controvert emasculating stereotypes that render Asian men effeminate and queer. What is wrong, though, Chin asks, with being considered passive, sexless, nerdy, evil, a Fu Manchu or a computer technician "if that is really what one is?" (134).

In criticizing white standards of beauty and desire that negate or limit Asian men's gender and sexuality, queer writers call into question white men's sexual power. Martin F. Manalansan disrupts the stereotypical "rice queen" role of the white male "top" having sex with a submissive Asian male "bottom." In his poem "Your Cio-Cio San," Manalansan tops his white male lover, warning him to "wait till morning, when my mask is in order / and I crack the whip for real" (1993, 12). In their contributions to *On a Bed of Rice,* Timothy Liu (1995b) and L. T. Goto (1995) demystify phallocentric ideals of male power that associate masculine self-worth with penis size; their writings contest stereotypes of the emasculating, diminutive Asian penis. "Smaller penises!" Goto wryly exclaims. "Doesn't the world know that we have enough to worry about other than the size of our 'wee-wees'?" (177).

The artists and scholars in *The Very Inside* (Lim-Hing 1994b) debunk the Orientalist notion of a white civilization that is superior to and dominant over Asian "primitives" and "savages," Anu, a South Asian lesbian poet, denounces the white civilizer's sexual exoticization of her "Indian" physical features and boldly affirms her lesbian sexuality as an identifying feature that is equally important to her South Asian ethnicity (1994), and Peou Lakhana's "Who Am I?" is a counterpart to Anu's poem that depicts her struggle against "an ex-lover / who sees me as the 'exotic oriental'" (1994, 41). Dwight Okira's (1993) poetry embraces his "wholeness" as an Asian American and rejects those who view him as a foreigner living in the United States with a clichéd split identity. In drama, Chay Yew criticizes the West's otherization of Asians as foreign, mythical creatures, deconstructing a racial and sexual dichotomy of Western "civilization" and a uniform, exotic "Orient." In *Porcelain* (1997), he provides a harrowing account of a young gay Chinese man accused of murdering his white English lover in a London public toilet. In jail, the gay Chinese man challenges a straight white psychologist's racist and homophobic questions: "Are you afraid of finding out that we're just the same as you? Have the same feelings and the same fears as you? How we are so much alike? You and I?" (1997, 33).

If queer writings express a boisterous resistance to white racist stereotypes of Asian Americans, they simultaneously articulate colorful and provocative depictions of same-sex love and desire between Asians of various American-born and immigrant ethnicities. Here, erotic visibility counters the disempowering metaphor of silence in Asian American history. Sexually charged images of Asians joyously and audaciously asserting their passions undermine disfiguring fabrications of Asian Americans as desexualized racial subjects. Further, celebratory depictions of same-sex love and desire in Asian American queer writing contest notions of homosexuality as culturally unintelligible in Asian American communities. As Dana Y. Takagi contends, the very presence of gay and lesbian Asian Americans problematizcs "the silences surrounding homosexuality in Asian America" (1996, 27). In Shani Mootoo's "Out on Main Street" (1993), for example, lesbians loudly and freely show their affection for each other in their own South Asian Canadian neighborhood. Horn and Ma have written perceptively on the way sexual stereotypes of effeminate Oriental men and submissive Asian women render gay males hypervisible and lesbians virtually unrecognizable in Asian American history (1993, 43).

Queer Asian American narratives abound with loud declarations of homoerotic desire that crash against regulatory norms of gender and sexuality. In Tsui's poem "Gloriously," the speaker "stroke[s]" "tongue [s]" and "finger[s]" her female lover to orgasm (1995, 172); and the narrator of Hsu Tzi Wong's story "Mangoes" describes reaching the point of climax as her Asian female lover exclaims: "Yes ... I want you to come. I want you to sing in all your glory" (1995, 152). The Asian American gangster lesbians in Chea Villanueva's stories (1995, 1997) aggressively assert "butch dyke" identities and brag of their ability to satisfy women more than any man can (1997, 12-13). In his poem "We Pass Each One," Chi-Wai Au yearns for the passionate, breathy embraces of other Asian men. The poem's concluding lines, "What will you answer, / my beautiful Asian brother, / when I say come / make love to me" (1993, 21), contradicts stereotypes of Asian men as "bottoms" who are incapable of dating one another.[1] Queer writings that celebrate same-sex erotic unions between Asians and Pacific Islanders have "created a dialogue around the problems of cross-racial dating between gays from different Asian/Pacific ethnic groups as well as dating between immigrant and American-born Asian/Pacific gays" (Eng and Fujikane 1995, 61). Many lesbian and gay Asian American writers refute asexual images by eroticizing Asian culture and expressing sexually charged longings for connection and reciprocity with other Asians. Indigo Chih-Lien Som's poem "Just Once before I Die I Want Someone to Make Love to Me in Cantonese" (1993) eroticizes the language itself; and Anu's "Silence of Home" (1993) dispels notions of silence as asexuality by expressing sensual yearning for her native India.

Bisexuality is an important topic in the project of problematizing the limitations of the homosexual/heterosexual binary. Jeeyeun Lee's "Chickenshit" (1993) is a coming-out narrative that interrogates the refusal of both gay and straight cultures to accept bisexuals. Her criticism of biphobia is especially cogent in her portrayal of lesbians who negate her same-sex desire because she has not yet had physical sexual relations with another woman. The bisexual Chinese American narrator in Russell Leong's "A Yin and Her Man" (1995b) reveals his erotic fascination with his Asian girlfriend's new boyfriend, a recent immigrant from China. Here too, Asianness itself is eroticized in the narrator's double fascination with the boyfriend and with ethnic commodities such as bronze Buddha figurines and Cantonese food.

Individually and as a body, queer writings emphasize the sexual diversity of Asian American culture: "Yes! there really are left-handed, Asian Dykes in New Mexico! Tze-Hei Yong exclaims in "New Mexico APL" (1994, 7). As Yong's poem makes clear, loudly articulating the presence of lesbians and gays is a major concern for queer writers who claim membership in a variety of heterogeneous sociocultural settings throughout Asian America. Even outright erotica aims not only to sexually arouse readers of their fiction but also to portray the diversity and humanity of

---

1 On internalized racism and repressive "sexual object choice" in Asian American gay men, see Ma's analysis in Hom and Ma 1993 (38).

queer Asian American cultures. In his introduction to *Quter PAPI Porn,* a recent anthology of gay Pilipino, Asian, and Pacific Islander erotica, Joel B.Tan explains that the stories in his book stretch the boundaries of race, sex, and desire: "If you are wanting vanilla with a dash of the orient," Tan warns, "this ain't it ... Like a rich bubbling pot of menudo, this book is mouthwatering — but potentially dangerous" (1998, 9). Asian American queer writings are "dangerous" because they are inherently political in their attention and challenge to issues and concerns of cross-cultural identity politics. They call for the "unfixing" of identity categories in favor of a concept of self that emerges from the fusion of race, class, gender, sexuality, and ethnicity. As Ma argues, it is a political advantage for queer Asian Americans to advocate antiessentialist definitions of sexual identity. If "API gay men," for instance, were to claim and define identity as "a political act," Ma contends, they would be able to negotiate constantly their "various positions both within and outside of dominant culture" (Horn and Ma 1993, 39). Empowered by antiessentialist identity politics, queer writers have also been able to engage in provocative discussions about the inclusion and marginalization of certain ethnic groups under the immense racial category of Asian and Pacific Islanders.[1]

Many queer narratives link same-sex love and desire with political activism in addition to identity politics. In the case of Asian American lesbian writing, the eroticization of radical politics helps counter notions of invisibility while depicting queer political activism as itself sexy. In her story "I Was Looking for You, I Was Looking Good" (1993, 51-58), Sharon Lim-Hing alternately describes the erotic thrill of picking up a beautiful woman at a night club and the sexually charged tension permeating an anti-Gulf War demonstration. Justin Chin's "Chinese Restaurant" brings together queerness and Asian Americanness, linking queer activist politics with the plight of Chinese immigrants laboring under exploitive conditions (1997). Much Asian American gay men's writing takes up the particular politics of AIDS activism and awareness as well. That they often eroticize this theme demonstrates a resistance to a mainstream homophobic culture that tries to censure and deprive gay men of their sexuality by regarding AIDS as just punishment tor their "aberrant" sexual behavior. In Joel Tan's "Night Sweats," the narrator makes love to his Puerto Rican boyfriend who is dying of AIDS in a sterile hospital room. "That night, with one orgasmic thrust, I bade Lazarus farewell" (1995, 411). Other Asian American writers, both gay and straight, narrate the ways HIV and AIDS affect their relationships with their families, lovers, and with themselves. Siong-Huat Chua's "Traditional Medicine" is a moving portrayal of a young

---

1 See Lim-Hing 1994b (v) and Eng and Hom 1998a (9) for persuasive arguments about the problems with the API category as an umbrella term that ignores or obscures the reality of underrepresented Pacific Islanders.

Chinese American gay man's pain and frustration as he attempts to divulge to his conservative father that he has AIDS (1993); and Dan Kwong, in his play *The Dodo Vaccine,* admits that he's a "heterosexual Asian-American male" trying to overcome "the denial that HIV is an issue for me as a straight man" (1995, 432).

Asian American queer writings attest to an array of complex familial issues that range from incisive criticism of patriarchal family values to loving validation of parent/child bonds. Writers who are critical of traditional nuclear families bring into focus problems of male violence against family members and often present the family itself as an oppressive unit that perpetuates normative gender roles and sexuality. *Rolling the R's* (Linmark 1995) is a powerful account of patriarchal violence and sexual abuse that husbands and fathers use to maintain their dominant positions and enforce normative behavior in several Hawaiian families during the 1970s. In many queer narratives, however, writers depict relations between children and parents erotically. Works such as Allan deSouza's "Re-Placing Angels" (1995, 185-193) and Linmark's *Railing the R's* may shock and repel some readers with their graphic depictions of sons watching their fathers masturbate or of adolescent boys having sex with men old enough to be their fathers, but they are also remarkable for their honest and heartfelt portrayals of children growing into the sexual maturity of adulthood. Lesbian writers in particular have been imaginative and passionate in celebrating connections to an Asian culture through erotic matrilineal bonds. Thelma Seto's poem "My Grandmother's Third Eye" commemorates a Japanese grandmother who prays with orgasmic intensity each morning at her altar to ancestors: "Eros ran through her / like sweat, / honoring her / with hallucinations" (1996, 222). In Mei Ng's short story "This Early," a Chinese American lesbian falls in love with a heterosexual white woman and places her photograph next to a picture of her own mother: "The picture of you is by my bed. Next to the one of my mother. The one where she's sixteen and her face is smooth and white as the inside of a bowl" (1995, 219). In her novel *Eating Chinese Food Naked* (1998), Ng portrays a young Chinese American woman's return to her childhood home and her intense, erotic love for her mother, whom she longs to take away from a husband who does not satisfy her sexually or romantically.

Asian American gay and lesbian writers address the difficulties of living in the closet and of coming out, and they frequently describe feelings of sexual invisibility as an effect of communication problems with parents and relatives. They yearn for alternative familial and communal environments in which they are free to be themselves and have the opportunity to bond with other lesbians and gays. The protagonist of Norman Wong's "Number One Chinese Son" (1993) is a closeted Chinese American high school student in Hawaii. His sexual fantasies about his white gym teacher imply a desire for father figures that is complicated by his own father's poverty and inability to send him to college in the mainland. He strives to be free of his father's adherence to traditional patriarchal customs, knowing that "he would someday eventually live a life that would collide with all of his father's dreams and Chinese ways" (1993, 131). Queer writers redefine family life by depicting networks of friends in homes, jobs, and community organizations as alternative families. In her introduction to *The Very Inside,* Lim-Hing (1994a) explains that she wanted to create a book that affirms the vibrant communities of API lesbians and bisexual women. Writings in the anthology, like Susan Y. E Chen's "Slowly but Surely, My Search for Family Acceptance and Community Continues" (1994), attest to the alternative familial experiences of lesbians and gays in their bonds of friendship and love.

While androcentric cultural nationalist writers like Frank *Chin's Aiiieeeee!* group have referred to popular images of cross-dressing Asian men as an "offense to white manhood" (F. Chin 1972,60), recent queer writers tend to take a politically empowering, counternormative approach to transsexuality and transvestitism. Cross-dressing Asian men and women appear in queer writings as complex human beings. If they occupy roles as agents of subversion who parody and transgress normative gender and sexuality, they do so sympathetically, exhibiting a wide range of human emotions. We do not, for example, find out until the end of Jana Monji's "Kim" (1995) that the Vietnamese immigrant with whom the narrator shares an apartment is really a man. At the end of the story, he fights off two white men who beat and then try to rape the Asian American female narrator. The Asian American "butch dykes" in Villanueva's stories wear men's pants, jam their fists in their pockets, and spit, swagger, and swear; they show off facial scars and wounds from gang fights as badges of masculine honor. With her "hair slicked back into a DA" and a "black V-neck bad boy sweater" stylishly adorning her body, the Filipino butch in Villanueva's "In the Shadows of Love" intimidates any man who might challenge her. Dressed to kill, she asserts that she is ready "to protect [her] girl, ready to fight for [her] butchness" (1995, 12). The straight-A Filipino student in *Rolling the R's* (Linmark 1995), who shows up in school in flamboyant Farrah Fawcett drag, is a trickster challenger of institutional repression, specifically of the "model minority" stereotype. In Larissa Lai's *When Fox Is a Thousand* (1995), which interweaves Chinese legends and contemporary Asian Canadian life, cross-dressing is but one of many Ovidian transformations that the characters undergo. Hwang's *M. Butterfly* (1988b), perhaps the best-known Asian American work about transvestism, according to Hwang, is "a deconstructivist *Madama Butterfly*" that criticizes the Orientalist's imperialistic view of a submissive and exotic East (1988a, 86). Indeed, through the politically symbolic import of transvestism, M. *Butterfly* critiques almost every Orientalist stereotype of Asian gender and sexuality, and it has spawned a virtual explosion of criticism, ranging from outright condemnation of its "fulfillment of white male homosexual fantasy" (F. Chin et al. 1991, xiii) to rigorous analysis of its subversive "antiessentialist" gender politics (Lye 1995, 260).

The kinds of mainstream stereotypes that Hwang challenges render the gender and sexuality of Asian Americans ambiguous and transgressive. Nowhere is this more obvious than in popular depictions of Asian Americans of mixed backgrounds. Mixed-blood, half-breed, half-caste, hapa, mongrel, mestizo, hybrid, Eurasian, Amerasian, and Asiari-descent multiracial: the sheer number of monikers used to identify Asian Americans of mixed racial backgrounds implies that there is something indeterminate — indeed, something queer — about them. Queer writings that address the gender and sexuality of mixed-race Asians often identify and critique the political zones of "ambiguous" heterogeneity and hybridity that mixed-race Asians occupy.[1] In a special issue of *Amemsia Journal* on mixed-race Asians, Russell Leong notes that when students and staff in the journal's main office were shown a photo of two "Asian-descent multiracial men" wearing tank tops and standing with one man's arm around the other, their questions and comments focused on the men's sexual orientation and class background, not their racial identity (1997, v). Indeed, the eroticism of ambiguous racial and ethnic identities, and the transgressiveness of such eroticism, is a notable theme in queer writings that depict mixed-race Asians. Quentin Lee's short story "Illegitimate Intimacy," for instance, portrays a gay Asian American named Daniel who falls in love with a closeted and emotionally unavailable "half White/Chinese" bisexual man (1993, 24). In one provocative scene, Daniel observes his lover's attempt to hide an erection as they sunbathe on a nude beach and regards the whiteness of his lover's penis as "cute" (23). Throughout the story, Caucasian physical features in a Chinese American man are the objects of Daniel's erotic fixation, which is further complicated by his inability to have a committed relationship with a man who is bisexual. Thus the story's title seems to refer to the lover's "indeterminate" racial *and* sexual identities.

Asian American critics have argued that the cultural heterogeneity of mixed-race Asians challenges us to rethink and decenter notions of fixed identities. In arguing for a politics of identity that denaturalizes racial, gender, class, and sexual categories, Dana Takagi considers the example of a "biracial child of a Japanese American and an African American who thinks of herself as 'black' and 'feminist'" (1996, 32). Queer narratives by and about mixed-race Asians bespeak critics' attempts to uphold a politics of identity that does not privilege one category of identity

---

1 By "mixed-race Asians" we mean people of multiple racial backgrounds who describe themselves as part Asian in their work.

over another.[1] Writings such as Ami R. Mattison's "I Am a Story" angrily assert the mixed-race queer's refusal to let others define her and her ability to reappropriate degrading epithets and construct her own empowering antiessentialist, multiform self. "I know the destructive power of words," she says, but "I know their constructive power, as well" (1994, 15). Similarly, Juliana Pegues/Pei Lu Fung, who describes herself as a "hapa middle-class dyke" (Pegues 1994, 461), interrogates people who say she is more "feminine," "white," and "heterosexual" when she wears a dress and makeup (32). She also criticizes America's historical racialization of blood in racist laws that prohibited miscegenation and denied generations of nonwhite people their humanity. Queer writings by nonwhite mixed-race Asians and by multiethnic Asians from outside the U.S. mainland further underscore an evolving multiculturalism within an Asian American identity that is growing increasingly global.

Diasporic studies, one of the most exciting critical methodologies to emerge in the field, takes into account the political-economic phenomena of transnational capital, immigration, and labor in its approach to understanding formations of the Asian American subject. Within Asian American literary and queer studies, scholars are debating a methodological shift away from a politics of cultural nationalism to a politics of transnational culturalism. Eng, for instance, suggests that "if earlier Asian American cultural nationalist projects (like that of the *Aiiieeeee!* group) were built on the political strategy of claiming home and nation-state through the domestic and the heterosexual, a new political project of thinking about these concepts in Asian American studies today would seem to center around queerness and diaspora — its rethinkings of home and nation-state across multiple identity formations and numerous locations 'out here' and 'over there' " (1997,43). To uphold diaspora, then, as a function of queerness in Asian American literature is to argue against cultural nationalism's narrow definition of the ideal Asian American as "male, heterosexual, working-class, American-born, and English-speaking" (34).

Recent analyses that link queerness with diaspora highlight the complex entwinement of Asian and Asian American (queer) subject formations in a postcolonial and postmodern global context.[2] Queer fiction and poetry have been especially adept at complicating constructions of the gender and sexuality of transnational Asian Americans. Russell Leong's "Phoenix Eyes"

---

1 Claudine Chiawei O'Hearn, the daughter of an Irish American father and a Chinese American mother, explains that racially indeterminate facial features have allowed her a certain flexibility within mainstream culture, where national/ethnic identity is identified by physical attributes: "It always amazed me what I could get away with ... Being mixed inspired and gave me license to test new characters, but it also cast me as a foreigner in every setting" (1998, ix). Sec also Lori Tsang's (1998) anecdotal essay about growing up in the United States as the child of Chinese and Jamaican parents.

2 "See, e.g., Bascara 1998; Chi 1998; Chiang 1998b; Puar 1998.

(1996c), suffused by an elegiac diasporic sensibility, portrays an international gay sex trade from the viewpoint of an American-born Chinese. The narrator of Eulalio Yerro Ibarra's "Potato Eater" is a gay Asian American immigrant who spent his high school and college years in the Philippines. Because of his sexual preference for white men, friends call him "Amboy, an American boy, afflicted with colonial mentality" (1995, 314). The imperialist American ideals of white masculine aesthetics are enforced in the narrator's mind through the violent (hetero) sexual interactions of American military men in the Philippines and Filipina women. Norman Wong's *Cultural Revolution* (1994) criticizes a gay white traveler's sexual involvement with a young Chinese American, Michael, who is visiting his father's ancestral Chinese village. Michael calls his white American lover a "rice queen" and, later, accuses him of trying to colonize Chinese men sexually. Likewise, Justin Chin's poem "Bangkok" (1997, 31) satirizes wealthy gay American men who search for sexual partners in magazines that advertise Asian boys as a type of global sexual capital, and Lawrence Chua's *Gold by the Inch* (1998) addresses commercialized transnational sexual desire in its portrayal of a young, middle-class Asian American man's visit to his native "home" in Thailand. The story's criticism of widespread sexual tourism and careless urban overdevelopment is complicated by the protagonist's love for a poor Thai man who works as a prostitute in a Bangkok brothel.

Many recent Asian American queer diasporic writings stress the importance of Asian cultural practices both inside and outside U.S. borders and address the ways norms from specific Asian cultures inform constructions of Asian American gender and sexuality. The emphasis on what Eng calls "a nexus of social differences and concerns" (1997, 41) is particularly evident in narratives of the experiences of children and their families outside the U.S. mainland or in various Asian lands. A notable issue in many queer writings about Asian Americans growing up in Hawaii, for example, is the "othering" of speakers of Pidgin English. In these narratives, a child's awareness of communicating in Pidgin (a "rudimentary bastard" of Standard English) underscores the ways hierarchies of and conflicts between languages construct subaltern — that is, "foreign," aberrant, and "queer" — identities. In Linmark's *Rolling the R's* (1995) and Donna T. Tanigawa's "Pau Trying Fo' Be Like One Haole Dyke" (1993), queer children speak Pidgin defiantly and challenge their schoolteachers' attempts to make them write Standard English. In doing so, they not only resist a heteronormative silencing of their voices but also express pride in a marginalized Hawaiian heritage.

Gay and lesbian South Asian and Vietnamese Americans have been especially proficient at providing autobiographical accounts of growing up gay in their respective Asian homelands.

Their writings are an important contribution to the emerging field of diasporic Asian American narratives. Shyam Selvadurai's popular *Funny Boy* (1994) begins with Selvadurai's poignant and hilarious portrayal of getting into trouble with his parents because of his insistence on cross-dressing and playing with girls in a game called "bride-bride." The book's title refers to a scene in which Selvadurai overhears his father blaming his mother for letting him wear women's clothes and thus turning out "funny" (17) — an interpellative moment when Selvadurai, as a child in Sri Lanka, begins to understand his own queerness. In X C. Huo's *A Thousand Wings* (1998), two Southeast Asian men fall in love with each other as one tells the other about his life in Laos during the Vietnam War. His tale of escape from war-ravaged Southeast Asia and his eventual immigration to the United States brings together memory, love, and self-reinvention in a narrative that underscores hybrid states of being and desire. Queer political activists Svati Shah (1994) and V. K. Aruna (1994) write about cultural hybridiry and South Asian lesbian identity, celebrating the singularity of their multiethnic backgrounds.

III

On the verge of a new millennium, literary scholars must take gender and sexuality into account in their studies of Asian American literature. In this article, we have argued that specific gender and sexuality themes in this literature cannot be understood apart from Asian American history and that any understanding of Asian American history would be incomplete without in-depth analysis of the central roles that gender and sexuality play in sociohistorical productions of Asian American identity in every period. Modern conceptions of gender and sexuality in America would not be intelligible as we know them today without the presence of Asians during the past 150 years. Attempts to develop a comprehensive understanding of the roles that gender and sexuality play in the creation of American national identity must include historicized critical analyses of Asian American gender and sexuality. Moreover, any theoretical understanding of the effects of the global travel of American models of gender and sexuality will have to take into account the ways their specifically Asian American versions both contribute to and contest the increasing Americanization of global culture.

Ethnic Studies Department (Wong)

English Department (Santa Ana)

University of California, Berkeley

References

Adhikary, Qirone. 1993. "The Marriage of Minnoo Mashi." In *Our Feet Walk the Sky: Women of the South Asian Diaspora,* ed. Women of South Asian Descent Collective, 175-190. San Francisco: Aunt Lute.

Aguilar-San Juan, Karin. 1993. "Landmarks in Literature by Asian American Lesbians." *Signs: Journal of Women in Culture and Society* 19(4):936-43.

Alexander, Meena. 1991. *Nampally Road.* San Francisco: Mercury House.

——. 1996. *The Shock of Arrival: Reflections on Postcolonial Experience.* Boston: South End.

Anu. 1993. "Silence of Home." In C. Chin 1993, 90-92.

——. 1994. "Who Am I?" In Lim-Hing 1994b, 19-21.

Aruna, V. K. 1994. "Putih." In Lim-Hing 1994b, 52 63.

Asian Women United of California, ed. 1989. *Making Waves: An Anthology of Writings by and about Asian American Women.* Boston: Beacon.

Au, Chi-Wai. 1993. "We Pass Each One." In C. Chin 1993, 21.

Bacho, Peter. 1991. *Cebu.* Seattle: University of Washington Press.

——. 1997. *"Dark Blue Suit" and Other Stories.* Seattle: University of Washington Press.

Badami, Anita Rau. 1996. *Tamarind Mem.* Toronto: Viking.

Bascara, Victor. 1998. "'A Vaudeville against Coconut Trees': Colonialism, Contradiction, and Coming Out in Michael Magnaye's *White Christmas.*" In Eng and Hom 1998b, 95-114.

Bow, Leslie. 1993. "For Every Gesture of Loyalty, There Doesn't Have to Be a Betrayal': Feminism and Cultural Nationalism in Asian American Women's Literature." Ph.D. dissertation, University of California, Santa Cruz.

Bulosan, Carlos. 1973. *American Is in the Heart.* Seattle: University of Washington Press.

——. 1979a. "The Romance of Magno Rubio." *Amerasia Journal* 6(l):33-50.

——. 1979b. "Sometimes It's Not Funny." *Amerasia Journal* 6(l):51-56.

——. 1983a. "As Long as the Grass Shall Grow." In Bulosan 1983b, 45-52.

——. 1983b. *If You Want to Know What We Are*: A Carlos Bulosan Reader, ed. E. San Juan, Jr. Minneapolis: West End.

Campomanes, Oscar V. 1992. "Filipinos in the United States and Their Literature of Exile. " In Lim and Ling 1992, 49-78.

Cao, Lan. 1997. *Monkey Bridge.* New York: Penguin.

Cha, Theresa Hak Kyung. (1982) 1994. *Dictee.* New York: Tanam.

Chan, Jachison. 1993. "Sexual Ambiguity: Representation of Asian Men in American Popular Culture." Ph.D. dissertation, University of California, Santa Barbara.

Chan, Jeffery Paul. 1974a. "The Chinese in Haifa." In *Aiiieeeee! An Anthology of Asian American Writers*, ed. Frank Chin et ai. 71-92. New York: Mentor.

——. 1974b. "Jackrabbit." In *Yardbird Reader* Vol. 3, 217-238. Berkeley, Calif.: Yardbird Publishing Cooperative.

Chan, Sucheng. 1991. "The Exclusion of Chinese Women." In her *Entry Denied: Exclusion and the Chinese*

Community in America, 1882–1943, 94-146. Philadelphia: Temple University Press.

———. 1996. "Asian American Historiography." *Pacific Historical Review* 65(113): 363-399.

Chang, Juliana. 1995. "Word, Flesh, Materiality, Violence, and Asian American Poetics." Ph.D. dissertation, Berkeley: University of California.

Chang, Leonard. 1996. *The Fruit 'n Food.* Seattle: Black Heron.

Chao, Patricia. *Monkey King.* 1997. New York: HarperCollins.

Chen, Susan Y. F. 1994. "Slowly but Surely, My Search for Family Acceptance and Community Continues." In Lim-Hing 1994b, 79-84.

Cheong, Fiona. 1991. *The Scent of the Gods.* New York: Norton.

Cheung, King-Kok. 1990. "The Woman Warrior versus the Chinaman Pacific: Must a Chinese American Critic Choose between Feminism and Heroism?" In *Conflicts in Feminism,* ed. Marianne Hirsch and Evelyn Fox Keller, 234-251. New York: Routledge.

———. 1993. *Articulate Silences: Hisaye Yamamoto, Maxine Hong Kingston, Joy Kogaiva.* Ithaca, N.Y.: Cornell University Press.

———. 1997a. *An Interethnic Companion to Asian American Literature.* Cambridge: Cambridge University Press.

———. 1997b. "Reviewing Asian American Literary Studies." In Cheung 1997a, 1-36.

———. 1998. "Of Man and Man: Reconstructing Chinese American Masculinity." In *Other Sisterhoods: Literary Theory and U.S. Women of Color,* ed. Sandra Kumamoto Stanley, 173-199. Urbana: University of Illinois Press.

Chi, Ta-wei. 1998. "Queering Chinese America: Intersection of Ethnicity and Sexuality in Three Literary Texts." M.A. thesis, Tai Bei: Taiwan University.

Chiang, Mark. 1998a. "Transnational Crossings of Asian America: Nationalism and Globalization in Asian American Cultural Studies." Ph.D. dissertation, Berkeley: University of California.

———.1998b. "Coming Out into the Global System: Postmodern Patriarchies and Transnational Sexualities in *The Wedding Banquet."* In Eng and Hom 1998b, 374-397.

Chin, Curtis, ed. 1993. *Witness Aloud: Lesbian, Gay, and Bisexual Asian/Pacific American Writing.* New York: Asian American Writers' Workshop.

Chin, Frank. 1972. "Confessions of a Chinatown Cowboy." *Bulletin of Concerned Asian Scholars* 4(3):58-70.

———. 1976. "The Only Real Day." In Gee et al. 1976, 510-524.

———. 1981. *"The Chickencoop Chinaman"; and "The Tear of the Dragon ": Two Plays.* Seattle: University of Washington Press.

———. 1988a. *"The Chinaman Pacific"& "Frisco R.R. Co": Short Stories.* Minneapolis: Coffee House Press.

———. 1988b. "A Chinese Lady Dies." In F. Chin 1988a, 109-131.

———. 1991. *Donald Duhk.* Minneapolis: Coffee House Press.

Chin, Frank, and Jeffery Paul Chan. 1972. "Racist Love." In *Seeing through Shuck,* ed. Richard Kostelanetz, 65-79. New York: Ballantine Books.

Chin, Frank, Jeffery Paul Chan, Lawson Fusao Inada, and Shawn Hsu Wong. 1974. Preface to *Aiiiccece! An Anthology of Asian American Writers,* ed. Frank Chin et al., xi-xxii. New York: Mentor.

——. 1991. *"Aiiieeeee!* Revisited: Preface to the Mentor Edition." In *Aiiieeeee! An Anthology of Asian American Writers,* ed. Frank Chin et al., xxiii-xli. New York: Mentor.

Chin, Justin. 1997. *Bite Hard.* San Francisco: Manic D Press.

——. 1999. *Mongrel: Essays, Diatribes, and Franks.* New York: St. Martin's.

Chiu, Monica. 1996. "Illness and Self-Representation in Asian American Literature by Women." Ph.D. dissertation, Atlanta: Emory University.

Cho, Song, ed. 1998. *Rice: Explorations into Gay Asian Culture and Politics.* Toronto: Queer Press.

Choe, Margaret Mihee. 1993. "Chamwe at the Club." In C. Chin 1993, 1-3.

Chong, Denise. 1994. *The Concubine's Children.* New York: Penguin.

Chu, Louis. (1961) 1979. *Eat a Bowl of Tea.* Seattle: University of Washington Press.

Chua, Lawrence. 1998. *Gold by the Inch.* New York: Grove.

Chua, Siong-Huat. 1993. "Traditional Medicine." In C. Chin 1993, 17-19.

Chuang Hua [pseud.]. (1968) 1986. *Crossings.* Boston: Northeastern University Press.

Chung, C., A. Kim, and A. K. Lemeshewsky, eds. 1987. *Between the Lines: An Anthology by Pacific/Asian Lesbians of Santa Cruz, California.* Santa Cruz: Dancing Bird.

Cobb, Nora. 1988. "Food as an Expression of Cultural Identity in Jade Snow Wong and Songs for Jadina." *Hawaii Review* 12(1): 12-16.

deSouza, Allan. 1995. "Re-Placing Angels." In Kudaka 1995, 185-193.

Divakaruni, Chitra. 1995. *Arranged Marriage.* New York: Anchor/Doubleday.

Eng, David. 1995. "Managing Masculinity: Race and Psychoanalysis in Asian American Literature." Ph.D. dissertation, Berkeley: University of California.

——. 1997. "Out Here and Over There: Queerness and Diaspora in Asian American Studies." *Social Text* 52/53, 15(3,4):31-52.

Eng, David, and Candace L. Fujikane. 1995. "Asian American Gay and Lesbian Literature." In *The Gay and Lesbian Literary Heritage: A Reader's Companion to the Writers and Their Works, from Antiquity to the Present,* ed. Claude J. Summers, 60-63. New York: Holt.

Eng, David L., and Alice Y. Hom, eds. 1998a. "Notes on a Queer Asian America." Introduction to Eng and Hom 1998b, 1-21.

——. 1998b. Q& A: *Queer in Asian America.* Philadelphia: Temple University Press.

Engelhardt, Tom. 1976. "Ambush at Kamikaze Pass." In Gee 1976, 270-279.

Espiritu, Yen Le. 1997. *Asian American Women and Men: Labor, Laws, and Love.* Thousand Oaks, Calif.: Sage.

Fenkl, Heinz Insu. 1996. *Memories of My Ghost Brother.* New York: Dutton.

Fung, Richard. 1991a. "Center the Margins." *In Moving the Image: Independent Asian Pacific American Media Arts,* ed. Russell Leong, 62-67. Los Angeles: UCLA Asian American Studies Center and Visual Communications.

——. 1991b. "Looking for My Penis: The Eroticized Asian in Gay Video Porn." In *How Do I Look? Queer Film and Video,* ed. Bad Object-Choice, 145-160. Seatde: Bay Press.

Galang, M. Evelina. 1996. *Her Wild American Self.* Minneapolis: Coffee House Press.

Gee, Emma, ed. 1976. *Counterpoint: Perspectives on Asian America.* Los Angeles: Asian American Srudies Center, Los Angeles: University of California.

Ghymn, Esther Mikyung. 1995. *Images of Asian American Women by Asian American Women Writers.* New York: Peter Lang.

Goldman, Anne. 1992. "1 Yam What I Yam: Cooking, Culture, and Colonialism." In De/*Colonizing the Subject: The Politics of Gender in Women's Autobiography,* ed. Sidonie Smith and Julia Watson, 169-95. Minneapolis: University of Minnesota Press.

Goto, L. T. 1995. "Asian Penis: The Long and Short of It." In Kudaka 1995, 177-184.

Hagedorn, Jessica. 1990. *Dogeaters.* New York: Penguin.

——, ed. 1993. *Charlie Chan Is Dead: An Anthology of Asian American Fiction.* New York: Penguin.

Hamamoto, Darrell Y. 1994. *Monitored Peril: Asian Americans and the Politics of TV Representation.* Minneapolis: University of Minnesota Press.

Hattori, Tomo. 1998a. "China Man Autoeroticism and the Remains of Asian America." *Novel: A Forum on Fiction* 31 (2):215-236.

——. 1998b. "Psycholinguistic Orientalism in Criticism of *The Woman Warrior* and *Obasan.*" In *Other Sisterhoods: Literary Theory and U.S. Women of Color,* ed. Sandra Kumamoto Stanley, 119-138. Urbana: University of Illinois Press.

Hayslip, Le Ly (with Jay Wurts). 1989. *When Heaven and Earth Changed Place: A Vietnamese Woman's Journey from War to Peace.* New York: Doubleday.

Hom, Alice Y., and Ming-Yuen S. Ma. 1993. "Premature Gestures: A Speculative Dialogue on Asian Pacific Islander Lesbian and Gay Writing." *Journal of Homosexuality* 26(2, 3):21-51.

Hom, Marlon K., comp. and trans. 1987. *Songs of Gold Mountain: Cantonese Rhymes from San Francisco Chinatown.* Berkeley: University of California Press.

Hoo, Maurice L. 1993. "Speech Impediments." In C. Chin 1993, 107-112.

Houston, Jeanne Wakatsuki, and James D. Houston. 1973. *Farewell to Manzanar.* Boston: Houghton Mifflin.

Hsiao, Ruth Y. 1992. "Facing the Incurable: Patriarchy in *Eat a Bowl of Tea.*" In Lim and Ling 1992, 151-162,

Huo, T. C. 1998. *A Thousand Wings.* New York: Dutton.

Hwang, David Henry. 1988a. "Author's Notes." In Hwang 1988b, 85-87.

——. 1988b. *M. Butterfly.* New York: Dramatists Flay Service.

Ibarra, Eulalio Yerro. "Potato Eater." In Kudaka 1995, 314-325.

Jen, Gish. 1996. *Mona in the Promised Land.* New York: Knopf.

Kadohata, Cynthia. 1989. *The Floating World.* New York: Viking.

Kafka, Phillipa. 1997. (*Un*)*doing the Missionary Position: Gender Asymmetry in Contemporary Asian American Women's Writing.* Westport, Conn.: Greenwood.

Kamani, Ginu. 1995. *Junglee Girl.* San Francisco: Aunt Lute.

Kang, Laura Hyun Yi. 1995. "Compositional Subjects: Enfiguring Asian/American Women." Ph.D. dissertation,

Santa Cruz: University of California.

Kang, Younghill. (1937) 1997. *East Goes West.* New York: Kaya.

Keller, Nora Okja. 1997. *Comfort Woman.* New York: Viking.

Kikumura, Akemi. 1981. *Through Harsh Winters: The Life of a Japanese Immigrant Woman* Novato, Calif.: Chandler & Sharp.

Kim, Daniel Y. 1998, "The Strange Love of Frank Chin." In Eng and Hom 1998b, 270-303.

Kim, Elaine H. 1982. *Asian American Literature: An Introduction to the Writings and Their Social Context.* Philadelphia: Temple University Press.

——. 1990a. "A Critique of *Strangers from a Different Shore.*" *Amerasia Journal* 16(2): 101-111.

——. 1990b. "'Such Opposite Creatures': Men and Women in Asian American Literature." *Michigan Quarterly* 29(1):68 93.

——. 1992. Foreword to Lim and Ling 1992, xi-xvii.

——. 1996. " 'Bad Women': Asian American Visual Artists Hanh Thi Pham, Hung Liu, and Yong Soon Min." *Feminist Studies* 22(3):573-602.

Kim, Elaine H., and Chungmoo Choi, eds. 1998. *Dangerous Women: Gender and Korean Nationalism.* New York: Roudedge.

Kim, Elaine H., and Lisa Lowe, eds. 1997. "New Formations, New Questions: Asian American Studies," special issue of *positions: cast asia cultures critique,* vol. 5, no. 2.

Kim, Elaine H., Lilia V. Villanueva, and Asian Women United of California, eds. 1997. *Making More Waves: New Writing by Asian American Women.* Boston: Beacon.

Kim, Patti. 1997. *A Cab Called Reliable.* New York: St. Martin's.

Kim, Ronyoung. 1987. *Clay Walls.* Sag Harbor, N.Y.: Permanent Press.

Kingston, Maxine Hong. 1976. *The Woman Warrior: Memoirs of a Girlhood among Ghosts.* New York: Knopf.

——. 1981. *China Men.* New York: Ballantine.

——. 1989. *Tripmaster Monkey: His Fake Book.* New York: Knopf.

Kogawa, Joy. 1982. *Obasan.* Boston: David R. Godine.

Kondo, Dorinne. 1997. *About Face: Performing Race in Fashion and Theater.* New York: Roudedge.

Koshy, Susan. 1994. "The Geography of Female Subjectivity: Ethnicity, Gender, and Diaspora." *Diaspora* 3(1): 69-84.

Kudaka, Geraldine. 1979. *Numerous Avalanches at the Point of Intersection.* Greenfield Center, N.Y.: Greenfield Review.

——, ed. 1995. *On a Bed of Rice: An Asian American Erotic Feast.* New York: Anchor/Doubleday.

Kwong, Dan. 1995. "The Dodo Vaccine." In Kudaka 1995, 431-437.

Lakh ana, Peou. 1994. "Who Am I?" In Lim-Hing 1994b, 40-41.

Lai, Larissa. 1995. *When Fox Is a Thousand.* Vancouver: Press Gang.

Lau, Evelyn. 1989. *Runaway: Diary of a Street Kid.* Toronto: HarperCollins.

——. 1993. *Fresh Girls and Other Stories.* Toronto: HarperPerennial.

Law-Yone, Wendy. 1983. *The Coffin Tree.* New York: Knopf.

——. 1993. *Irawaddy Tango*. New York: Knopf.

Lee, Chang-Rae. 1995. *Native Speaker. New* York: Riverhead.

Lee, Chin-Yang. 1957. *The Flower Drum Song*. New York: Farrar.

Lee, Gus. 1991. *China Boy*. New York: Dutton.

——. 1994. *Honor and Duty*. New York: Knopf.

Lee, Jeeyeun. 1993. "Chickenshit." In C. Chin 1993, 42-44.

Lee, Mary Paik. 1990. *Quiet Odyssey: A Pioneer Korean Woman in America,* ed. and introduction by Sucheng Chan. Seattle: University of Washington Press.

Lee, Quentin. 1993. "Illegitimate Intimacy." In C. Chin 1993, 22-28.

Lee, Rachel. 1995a. "The Americas of Asian American Literature: Nationalism, Gender, and Sexuality in Bulosan's *America Is in the Heart*, Jen's *Typical American*, and Hagedorn's *Dogeaters*." Ph.D. dissertation, Los Angeles: University of California.

——. 1995b. "Claiming Land, Claiming Voice, Claiming Canon: Institutionalized Challenges in Kingston's *China Men* and *The Woman Warrior*." In *Reviewing Asian America: Locating Diversity*, ed. Wendy L. Ng et al,, 147-159. Pullman: Washington State University Press.

Lee, Robert G. 1999. *Orientals: Asian Americans in Popular Culture*. Philadelphia: Temple University Press.

Lee, Sky. 1990. *Disappearing Moon Cafe*. Vancouver: Douglas & McIntyre.

——. 1994. *Bellydancer*. Vancouver: Press Gang.

Leong, Monfoon. 1975. "New Year for Fong Wing." In his *Number One Son.* 3-16. San Francisco: East/West.

Leong, Russell. 1979. "Writings of Carlos Bulosan," special issue of *Amerasia Journal,* vol. 6, no. 1.

——. 1995a. "Unfurling Pleasure, Embracing Race." Foreword to Kudaka 1995, xi-xxx.

——. 1995b. "A Yin and Her Man." In Kudaka 1995, 338-344.

——, ed. 1996a, *Asian American Sexualities: Dimensions of the Gay and Lesbian Experience*. New York: Routledge.

——. 1996b. "Home Bodies and the Body Politic." Introduction to R. Leong 1996a, 1-18.

——. 1996c. "Phoenix Eves." In *Best American Gay Fiction,* ed. Brian Bouldrey, 128-147. Boston: Little Brown.

——. 1997. "Mediating Multiracial Zones through Text and Image." *Amerasia Journal* 23(1): v-vi.

Li, David Leiwei. 1992. "Filiative and Affiliative Textualization in Chinese American Literature." In *Understanding Others: Cultural and Cross-Cultural Studies and the Teaching of Literature,* ed, Joseph Trimmer, 177-200. Urbana, Ⅲ.: National Council of Teachers of English.

——. 1998. *Imagining the Nation: Asian American Literature and Cultural Consent*. Stanford, Calif.: Stanford University Press.

Lim, Paul Stephen. 1977. *Conpersonas: A Recreation in Two Acts*. New York: Samuel French.

——. 1985a. *Homerica: A Trilogy on Sexual Literature*. Louisville, Ky.: Aran.

——. 1985b. *Woe Man: A Recreation in Two Acts*. Louisville, Ky. Aran.

——. 1989. *Figures in Clay: A Threnody in Six Scenes and a Coda*. Louisville, Ky.Aran.

Lim, Shirley Geok-lin. 1991. *Approaches to Teaching Kingston's "The Woman Warrior."* New York: Modern Language Association of America.

——. 1994. "Semiotics, Experience, and the Material Self: An Inquiry into the Subject of the Contemporary Asian American Woman Writer." In her *Writing S. E./Asia in English: Against the Grain, Focus on Asian English-language Literature,* 3-39. London: Skoob.

——. 1996. *Among the White Moon Faces: An Asian-American Memoir of Homelands.* New York: Feminist Press,

——. 1997. "Immigration and Diaspora." In Cheung 1997a, 289-311.

Lim, Shirley Geok-lin, and Amy Ling, eds. 1992. *Reading the Literatures of Asian America.* Philadelphia: Temple University Press.

Lim, Shirley Geok-lin, and Mayumi Tsutakawa, eds. 1989. *The Forbidden Stitch: An Asian American Women's Anthology.* Corvallis, Ore.: Calyx.

Lim-Hing, Sharon. 1993 "I Was Looking for You, I Was Looking Good." In C. Chin 1993, 51-58.

——. 1994a. Introduction to Lim-Hing 1994b, i-vi.

——, ed. 1994b. *The Very Inside: An Anthology of Writing by Gay, Leshian and Pacific Islander Lesbian and Bisexual Women.* Toronto: Sister Vision.

Lin, Timothy. 1995. "The Size of It." In Kudaka 1995, 175-176.

Lin, Yutang. 1937. *My Country and My People.* New York: Reynal & Hitchcock.

——. 1948. *Chinatown Family.* New' York: John Day.

Ling, Amy. 1990a. *Between Worlds: Women Writers of Chinese Ancestry.* New York: Pergamon.

——. 1990b. "Chinese American Women Writers: The Tradition behind Maxine Hong Kingston." In *Redefining American Literary History,* ed. A. LaVonne Brown Ruoff and Jerry W. Ward, Jr., 219-236. New York: Modern Language Association of America.

Ling, Jinqi. 1995. "Race, Power, and Cultural Politics in John Okada's *No-No Boy.*" *American Literature* 67(2):359-381.

——. 1997. "Identity Crisis and Gender Politics: Reappropriating Asian American Masculinity." In Cheung 1997a, 312-337.

——. 1998. *Narrating Nationalisms: Ideology and Form in Asian American Literature.* New York: Oxford University Press.

Linmark, R. Zamora. 1995. *Rolling the R's.* New York: Kaya.

Liu, Catherine. 1997. *Oriental Girls Desire Romance.* New York: Kaya.

Louie, David Wong. 1991. *Pangs of Love.* New York: Knopf.

Lowe, Lisa. 1991. "Heterogeneity, Hybridity, Multiplicity: Marking Asian American Differences." *Diaspora* 1 (1):24-44.

——. 1996. *Immigrant Acts: On Asian American Cultural Politics.* Durham, N.C.: Duke University Press.

Lowe, Pardee. 1943. *Father and Glorious Descendant.* Boston: Little, Brown.

Luibheid, Eithne. 1998. "Racialized Immigrant Women's Sexualities: The Construction of Wives, Prostitutes, and Lesbians through U.S. Immigration." Ph.D. dissertation, Berkeley: University of California.

Lye, Colleen. 1995. "*M. Butterfly* and the Rhetoric of Antiessentialism: Minority Discourse in an International Frame." In *The Ethnic Canon: Histories, Institutions, and Interventions,* ed. David Paiumbo-Liu, 260-290.

Minneapolis: University of Minnesota Press.

Manalansan, Martin F. 1993. "Your Cio-Cio San." In C. Chin 1993, 11-12.

Mara, Rachna. 1991. *Of Customs and Excise.* Toronto: Second Story.

Marchetti, Gina. 1993. *Romance and the "Yellow Peril": Race, Sex, and Discursive Strategies in Hollywood Fiction.* Berkeley and Los Angeles: University of California Press.

Mattison, Ami R. 1994. "I Am a Story." In Lim-Hing 1994b, 12-15.

McCunn, Ruthanne Lum. 1981. *Thousand Pieces of Gold.* San Francisco: Design Enterprises.

Monji, Jana. 1995. "Kim." In Kudaka 1995, 208-216.

Mootoo, Shani. 1993. "Out on Main Street." *Out on Main Street and Other Stories,* 45-57. Vancouver: Press Gang.

———. 1996. *Cereus Blooms at Night,* New York: Grove.

Moraga, Cherríe, and Gloria Anzaldúa, eds. 1981. *This Bridge Called My Back: Writings by Radical Women of Color.* Watertown, Mass.: Persephone.

Mori, Toshio. 1979. *The Chauvinist and Other Stories.* Los Angeles: Asian American Studies Center, University of California, Los Angeles.

———. (1938) 1979. "Operator, Operator!" In Mori 1979, 51-56.

Moy, James S. 1993. *Marginal Sights: Staging the Chinese in America.* Iowa City: University of Iowa Press.

Mukherjee, Bharati. 1989. *Jasmine.* New York: Ballantine.

Mura, David. 1991. *Turning Japanese: Memoirs of a Sansei.* New York: Atlantic Monthly.

———. 1996. *Where the Body Meets Memory: An Odyssey of Race, Sexuality, and Identity.* New York: Anchor/Doubleday.

Murayama, Milton. (1975) 1988. *All I Asking for Is My Body.* Honolulu: University of Hawaii Press.

———. 1994. *Five Tears on a Rock.* Honolulu: University of Hawaii Press.

———. 1998. *Plantation Boy.* Honolulu: University of Hawaii Press.

Ng, Fae Myenne. 1993. *Bone.* New York: Hyperion.

Ng, Mei. 1995. "This Early." In *Tasting Life Twice: Literary Lesbian Fiction by New American Writers*, ed. E. J. Levy. New York: Avon.

———. 1998. *Eating Chinese Food Naked.* New York: Scribner.

Nguyen, Viet Thanh. 1997. "Writing the Body Politic: Asian American Subjects and the American Nation." Ph.D. dissertation, Berkeley: University of California.

Nieh, Hualing. (1981) 1998. *Mulberry and Peach: Two Women of China.* New York: Feminist Press.

Nunez, Sigrid. 1995. *A Feather on the Breath of God.* New York: HarperCollins.

O'Hearn, Claudine Chiawei. 1998. Introduction to *Half and Half: Writers on Growing Up Biracial and Bicultural.* ed. Claudine Chiawei O'Hearn, vii-xiv. New York: Pantheon.

Okada, John. 1957. *No-No Boy.* Seattle: University of Washington Press.

Okihiro, Gary Y. 1994. "Recentering Women." In his *Margins and Mainstream: Asians in American History and Culture,* 64-92. Seattle: University of Washington Press.

Okimoto, Daniel I. 1971. *American in Disguise.* New York: John Weatherhill.

Okita, Dwight. 1993. "Notes tor a Poem on Being Asian American." In C. Chin 1993, 45-46.

Okubo, Mine. (1946) 1983. *Citizen 13660*. Seattle: University of Washington Press.

Omi, Michael, and Dana Takagi, eds. 1995. "Thinking Theory in Asian American Studies," special issue of *Amerasia Journal* vol. 21, nos. 1, 2.

Pak, Gary. 1998. *A Ricepaper Airplane*. Honolulu: University of Hawaii Press in association with UCLA Asian American Studies Center, Los Angeles.

Palumbo-Liu, David. 1999. *Asian/American: Historical Crossings of a Racial Frontier*. Stanford, Calif.: Stanford University Press.

Pegues, Juliana [Pei Lu Fung]. 1994. "White Rice: Searching for Identity." In Lim-Hing 1994b, 25-36.

Puar, Jasbir K. 1998. "Transnational Sexualities: South Asian(Trans)nation(alism)s and Queer Diasporas." In Eng and Hom 1998b, 405-422.

Rafael, Vicente L. 1993. "White Love: Surveillance and Nationalist Resistance in the U.S. Colonization of the Philippines." In *Cultures of United States Imperialism,* ed. Amy Kaplan and Donald E. Peas, 185-218. Durham, N.C.: Duke University Press.

———. 1995. "Colonial Domesticity: White Women and United States Rule in the Philippines." *American Literature* 67(4):639-666.

Ratti, Rakesh. 1993. *A Lotus of Another Color: An Unfolding of the South Asian Gay and Lesbian Expedience.* Boston: Alyson.

Santa Ana, Jeffrey J. 1998. "Envisioning a Masculine Postcolonial Motherland: José Rizal's Feminization of the Colonized Philippines." Paper presented at the annual convention of the Association for Asian American Studies, Honolulu, Hawaii, June 27.

Santos, Bienvenido N. (1955) 1979. *Scent of Apples: A Collection of Stories.* Seattle: University of Washington Press.

Sasaki, Ruth A. 1991. *The Loom and Other Stories.* St. Paul, Minn.: Graywolf.

Selvadurai, Shyam. 1994. *Funny Boy: A Novel.* New York: William Morrow.

Seto, Thelma. 1996. "My Grandmother's Third Eye." In R. Lyong 1996a, 221-222.

Shah, Sonia, ed. 1997. *Dragon Ladies: Asian American Feminists Breathe Fire.* Boston: South End.

Shall, Svati, 1994. "The Polite Question." In Lim-Hing 1994b, 5-6.

Shigekuni, Julie. 1995. *A Bridge between Us.* New York: Anchor/Doubleday.

So, Christine. 1997. "America Reimagined: Narratives of Nation in Asian American Literature." Ph.D. dissertation, New York: Columbia University.

Som, Indigo Chih-Lien. 1993. "Just Once before I Die I Want Someone to Make Love to Me in Cantonese." In C. Chin 1993, 5.

Sone, Monica. (1953) 1979. *Nisei Daughter.* Seattle: University of Washington Press.

Song, Min. 1998. "The Unknowable and Sui Sin Far: The Epistemological Limits of 'Oriental' Sexuality." In Eng and Hom 1998b, 304—322.

Su, Karen. 1994. "Jade Snow Wong's Badge of Distinction in the 1990s." *Critical Mass: A Journal of Asian*

American Cultural Criticism 2(1):3-52.

——. 1998. " 'Just Translating': The Politics of Translation and Ethnography in Chinese American Women's Writing." Ph.D. dissertation, Berkeley: University of California.

Sugimoto, Etsu Inagaki. 1925. *A Daughter of the Samurai*. New York: Doubleday Page.

Sui Sin Far [Edith Maude Eaton]. 1912. *Mrs. Spring Fragrance*. Chicago: A. C. McClurg.

——. 1995. *"Mrs. Spring Fragrance" and Other Stories*. Ed. Amy Ling and Annette White-Parks. Urbana: University of Illinois Press.

Suleri, Sara. 1989. *Meatless Days*. Chicago: University of Chicago Press.

Tajima, Renee. 1989. "Lotus Blossoms Don't Bleed: Images of Asian Women." In Asian Women United of California 1989, 308-317.

Takagi, Dana Y. 1996. "Maiden Voyage: Excursion into Sexuality and Identity Politics in Asian America." In R. Leong 1996a, 21-36.

Tan, Amy. 1989. *The Joy Luck Club*. New York: Putnam.

——. 1991. *The Kitchen God's Wife*. New York: Putnam.

Tan, Joel B. 1995. "Night Sweats." In Kudaka 1995,402-411.

——, ed. 1998. *Queer PAPI Porn: Gay Asian Erotica*. San Francisco: Cleis.

Tanigawa, Donna T. 1993. "Pau Trying Fo' Be Like One Haole Dyke." In C. Chin 1993, 96-98.

Thom a, Pamela S. 1996. "Asian American Women Writers: Theorizing Transnationalism." Ph.D. dissertation, Berkeley: University of California.

Ting, Jennifer P. 1995. "Bachelor Society: Deviant Heterosexuality and Asian American Historiography." In *Privileging Positions: The Sites of Asian American Studies,* ed. Gary Y. Okihiro et al., 271-279. Pullman: Washington State University Press.

——. 1998. "The Power of Sexuality." *Journal of Asian American Studies* l(l):65-82.

Tsang, Lori. 1998. "Postcards from 'Home.'" In *Half and Half: Writers on Growing Up Biracial and Bicultural,* ed. Claudine Chiawei O'Hearn, 197-215. New York: Pantheon.

Tsiang, H. T. 1937. *And China Has Hands*. New York: Robert Speller.

Tsui, Kitty. 1983. *The Words of a Woman Who Breathes Fire*. San Francisco: Spinsters Ink.

——. 1995. "Gloriously." In Kudaka 1995, 171-172.

Uchida, Yoshiko. 1982. *Desen Exile: The Uprooting of a Japanese American Family*. Seattle: University of Washington Press.

——. 1987. *Picture Bride*. Flagstaff, Ariz.: Northland.

Uyemoto, Holly. 1995. *Go*. New York: Plume.

Vannareth, L. 1993. "Akino's Journal." In C. Chin 1993, 78-87.

Villanueva, Chea. 1991. *The Chinagirls*. N.p.: Lezzies on the Move Productions.

——. 1995. *"Jessie's Song"and Other Stories*. New York: Masquerade Books.

——. 1997. *Bullet Proof Batches*. New York: Masquerade Books.

White-Parks, Annette. 1995. *Sui Sin Far/Edith Maude Eaton: A Literary Biography*. Urbana: University of Illinois Press.

Wong, Eugene Franklin. 1978. *On Visual Media Racism: Asians in the American Motion Pictures.* New York: Arno.

Wong, Hsu Tzi. 1995. "Mangoes." In Kudaka 1995, 149-155.

Wong, Jade Snow. (1945) 1989. *Fifth Chinese Daughter.* Seattle: University of Washington Press.

Wong, Norman. 1993. "Number One Chinese Son." In C. Chin 1993, 123-131.

———. 1994. *Cultural Revolution.* New York: Persea.

Wong, Sau-ling C. 1991. "The Politics and Poetics of Folksong Reading: Literary Portrayals of Life under Exclusion" In *Entry Denied: Exclusion and the Chinese Community in America, 1882–1943,* ed. Sucheng Chan, 246-67. Philadelphia: Temple University Press.

———. 1992. "Ethnicizing Gender: An Exploration of Sexuality as Sign in Chinese Immigrant Literature." In Lim and Ling 1992, 111-129.

———. 1993a. *Reading Asian American Literature: From Necessity to Extravagance.* Princeton, N.J.: Princeton University Press.

———. 1993b. "Subverting Desire: Reading the Body in the 1991 Asian Pacific Islander Men's Calendar." *Critical Mass: A Journal of Asian American Cultural Criticism* 1 (1):63-74.

———. 1995a. "Chinese/Asian American Men in the 1990s: Displacement, Impersonation, Paternity, and Extinction in David Wong Louie's *Pangs of Love.*" In *Privileging Positions: The Sites of Asian American Studies,* ed. Gary Y. Okihiro et al., 181-191. Pullman: Washington State University Press.

———. 1995b. "'Sugar Sisterhood': Situating the Amy Tan Phenomenon." In *The Ethnic Canon: Histories, Institutions, and Interventions,* ed. David Palumbo-Liu, 174-210. Minneapolis: University of Minnesota Press.

———. 1998. *Maxine Hong Kingston's "The Woman Warrior": A Casebook.* New York: Oxford University Press.

———. In press. "The Stakes of Border-Crossing: Hualing Nieh's *Mulberry and Peach* in Sinocentric, Asian American, and Feminist Critical Practices." In *Disciplining Asia: Theorizing Studies in the Asian Diaspora,* ed. Kandice Chuh and Karen Shimakawa. Durham, N.C.: Duke University Press.

Wong, Shawn Hsu. (1979) 1991. *Homebase.* New York: Plume.

———. 1995. *American Knees.* New York: Simon & Schuster.

Wong, Su-ling [pseud.], with E. H. Cressy. 1952. *Daughter of Confucius: A Personal History.* New York: Farrar Straus.

Woo, Merle. 1981. "Letter to Ma." In Moraga and Anzaldua 1981, 140-147.

Yamada, Mitsuye. 1981. "Asian Pacific American Women and Feminism." In Moraga and Anzaldúa 1981. 71-75. Watertown, Mass.: Persephone.

Yamamoto, Hisaye. 1979. Introduction to Mori 1979, 1-14.

———. 1988. *"Seventeen Syllables" and Other Stories.* Latham, N.Y.: Kitchen Table: Women of Color.

Yamamoto, Traise. 1999. *Masking Selves, Making Subjects: Japanese American Women, Identity, and the Body.* Berkeley and Los Angeles: University of California Press.

Yamanaka, Lois-Ann. 1993. *Saturday Night at the Pahala Theatre.* Honolulu: Bamboo Ridge.

———. 1996. *Wild Meat and the Bully Burgers.* New York: Farrar Straus Giroux.

——. 1997. *Blu's Hanging.* New York: Farrar Straus Giroux, Yamauchi, Wakako. 1990. "And the Soul Shall Dance." In *Between Worlds: Contentporaty Asian-American Plays,* ed. Misha Berson, 127-174. New York: Theatre Communications Group.

——. 1994. *Songs My Mother Taught Me: Stories, Plays, and Memoir.* New York: Feminist Press.

Yew, Chay. 1997. *"Porcelain" and "A Language of Their Own": Two Plays.* New York: Grove.

Yogi, Stan. 1989. "Legacies Revealed: Uncovering Buried Plots in the Stories of Hisaye Yamamoto." *Studies in American Fiction* 17(2): 169-181.

——. 1997. "Japanese American Literature." In Cheung 1997a, 125-155.

Yong, Tzc-Hei. 1994. "New Mexico APL." In Lim-Hing 1994b, 7-11.

Yung, Judy. 1986. *Chinese Women of America.* Seattle: University of Washington Press.

6

Racial Form
种族形式

Colleen Lye

评论家简介

　　赖柯灵（Colleen Lye），美国哥伦比亚大学英语系博士，现为美国加利福尼亚大学伯克利分校英语系副教授。研究领域包括太平洋地区文学、20世纪和21世纪美国文学、美国亚裔文学、太平洋地区文学、文学批判理论、文化研究、叙事小说等。专著有《美国的亚洲：种族形式与美国文学，1893—1945》（*America's Asia: Racial Form and American Literature, 1893–1945*, 2005），荣获美国亚裔研究协会文化研究图书奖一等奖。曾合编特刊多部，包括《金融化与文化产业》（*Financialization and the Culture Industry,* 2014）；《外围现实主义》（*Peripheral Realisms,* 2012）；《人文学科和公立大学的危机》（*The Humanities and the Crisis of the Public University*，2011）；《迫在眉睫：为加州的公共教育而斗争》（*Against the Day: The Struggle for Public Education in California*, 2011），荣获美国现代语言协会学术期刊编辑委员会2011年度最佳特刊奖；《亚洲的形式》（*Forms of Asia*, 2007）。

文章简介

　　进入新千年，美国亚裔文学批评出现了"新形式主义"转向，力主将美学与形式分析作为美国亚裔文学的主要研究范式，以矫正长期以来以社会政治为核心的文化唯物主义研究方法。本文首先论证这种矫正无法解决美国亚裔文学的理论建构问题。作者认为美国亚裔文学批评的落脚点应该是对美国亚裔主体形成的历史性做出学理阐释。未能实现这一目标的主要原因在于批评界长期将"种族"作为文学与社会的构成要素，却忽视了种族作为一种形式表征的属性。文章通过阐释雷蒙德·威廉斯"形式即社会历史关系"的历史唯物主义观点，论证了将种族作为"形式"而非"构成"的做法有利于弥合美学与社会政治的对立，从而对美国亚裔的主体历史性做出理论构建。简言之，文章认为包括美国亚裔文学研究在内的族裔文学研究所需要的，不应仅是美学形式主义，而是将族裔作为形式的历史形式主义。

文章出处：*Representations*, vol. 104, no. 1, 2008: pp. 92-101.

Racial Form

Colleen Lye

If there is evidence of a "new formalism" afoot in the discipline of English, or at least rhetorical reference to one, this much might at first also be said of ethnic studies. In the latter case, however, the significance of this development within a field that was from its very inception interdisciplinary means that the call to attend more carefully to matters of literary form can never quite shake off the heteronomy of the aesthetic. The more we open our minds to this truth the better, as what it promises to reveal is the continuing historical potential of the ethnic text to demand a critical practice adequate to the contradictory and peculiar nature of literature as a kind of social fact. In the following discussion, my examples will be drawn from Asian American studies, which I will use to make broader claims about ethnic studies, though ultimately the justification for this use of the Asian American derives from my sense not of its representativeness within ethnic studies but of its especial precariousness.[1]

The appearance of three anthologies in recent years might be taken to signal the "new formalist" direction of Asian American literary criticism: Zhou Xiaojing and Samina Najmi's *Form and Transformation in Asian American Literature* (2005), Keith Lawrence and Floyd Cheung's *Recovered Legacies: Authority and Identity in Early Asian American Literature* (2005), and Rocío G. Davis and Sue-Im Lee's *Literary Gestures: The Aesthetic in Asian American Writing* (2006). *Form and Transformation* would foreground the "formal aspects of literature as an integral part of ideology," "shifting away from a thematically oriented approach" that has proceeded in terms of "fixed cultural boundaries and hierarchies of race and gender."[2] *Literary Gestures* positions "issues of literary aesthetics and formal analysis" at the center of its practice of Asian American literary studies in order to "counterbalance the prevailing dominance of sociological and cultural materialist approaches in Asian American literary criticism."[3] *Recovered Legacies* is geared toward the historical recovery and revaluation of early Asian American literary texts, but its editors too recognize that "to the extent that we have closely and carefully delineated the texts we write about, we have indeed adhered to what might be termed, in the broadest sense, a 'formalist' approach."[4] Lawrence and Cheung go on to add:

> Careful analysis of our volume will see that it is also grounded in a variety of approaches —
> New Historical, feminist, neo-Marxist, neo-Freudian, postcolonial, ethnohistorical — that balance

and contextualize "close reading" (by affording them immediacy and cultural currency) without deemphasizing or displacing the literary analysis (or the corresponding primary texts). We remain convinced that such an approach eschews unwarranted prescriptiveness and encourages significant dialogue with the texts we engage. (8)

The convergence between *Literary Gestures'* recovery of the aesthetic as a "missing category of analysis" (5) and *Recovered Legacies'* recovery of the "authority and identity" of earlier texts from the tyranny of a "presentist trend in existing scholarship" (2) suggests that the turn to form is fundamentally less a reaction against historicism than against instrumental reading. For all three anthologies, a tradition of criticism dominated by political prescriptiveness is held to account for a constricted imagination of Asian American literature's potential power. "What are the possibilities for differences within Asian America to become more than a form of resistance to assimilation? In what way and to what extent can difference become transformative agency?" (9) Zhou asks. "Asian American agency resides in negotiation with, not separation from, dominant ideologies and literary tradition" (13). In quest of a "materialist and formalist" literary criticism, Lee likewise asks: "How would an analysis alert to the way a particular Asian American work 'talks' to other works within that genre, within literary history, within the canon, affect the overall balance of analysis? How would an analysis attuned to the significance of literary genealogy interact with the discernment of material forces at work?" (7). Lawrence and Cheung also agree that the assumption of a "rigidly uniform 'America' existing in juxtaposition with — or opposition to — the ethnic body in question" elides the complexities of "the historical or aesthetic heart of the text in question" (11, 13).

Note the formulation "the historical or aesthetic." I take it to mean not the interchangeability of historical and aesthetic questions, but their joint elision, symptomatic of a relationship between the underdevelopment of both formalist and historicist approaches to the Asian American text. In this regard, the expressed formalist desires of the present corroborate the thenminority view of Jinqi Ling — whose 1998 critical realist reading of Asian American cultural nationalism might still be regarded as our only example of a formally self-reflexive Asian American literary history — that the prevailing discussion of Asian American literary pasts in the 1990s was both ahistorical and formally naive.[5] Ling's particular target was Lisa Lowe's hypothesis of the "heterogeneity, hybridity, multiplicity" of Asian American literature, whose 1991 critique of the essentialism of cultural nationalist discourse and counter-articulation of a coalitional, postnationalist view of Asian American identity is usually thought to have exerted a pluralizing influence on the field and initiated an Asian American cultural studies.[6] Set against today's hunger for the freedoms of form, Lowe's theorization of Asian American identity looks to be more and more of a continuation with a preceding tradition of its political predetermination. In retrospect, the true historical significance of Lowe's intervention may well be that it marked not the beginning of the heteroge-nization of Asian American identity but one of the last compelling occasions of its conceptual salvage. Lowe's conservation of Asian American identity was waged by politicizing its definition, proposing that it be viewed as a matter more of affiliation than filiation. Evidence for this proposal was marshaled by thematizing a deconstructive reading of literary texts as the reflection of the necessarily anti-essentialist essence of Asian American identity. It is precisely against the political instrumentalization of the literary text that today's new formalist (or more appropriately, formalist, since there is no "old formalism" in the field) movements understandably protest. Politically instrumental reading, they suspect, has contributed to dualistic framings of the ethnic text and the American text, and the continuing polarization of the "ethnic" and the "aesthetic"; it has overlooked the critical potential of literary interpretation to discover for the ethnic text more transformative kinds of agency.

In the scrupulous deferral of the political, however, we might observe that the Asian Americanness of the ethnic literary examples studied by the three anthologies has now receded to the status of a presupposition. Even "strategic essentialism" is no longer explicitly evoked, as it once was throughout the 1990s, to justify the use of the pan-ethnic label. Lawrence and Cheung's introduction to *Recovered Legacies* quickly dispenses with the issue of textual selection by pragmatically designating Asian Americanness as a matter of authorial descent: "For more than a century, immigrants from various Asian countries and their descendants have made America their home. Throughout this time, writers whom we could call Asian American have expressed their joys, lamented their losses, crafted new forms, and imagined new worlds in their poetry, stories, novels, and plays" (1, italics mine).

Following Lawrence and Cheung, we shall certainly be glad for "richer, broader, and...more accurate readings" (16). In the long run, though, Asian American literary studies will likely need to discover more theoretical purpose for itself than the appreciation of the "dignity of... writers and the genuine merit of what they wrote" (16). In the current context of Asian American identity's contradictory academic reproduction — contradictory in that the theoretical insistence on its impossibility is coupled with the pressure of its curricular and programmatic expansion — the openly catachrestic quality of the Asian American presents a problematic that cannot be permanently deferred.[7] Ideally, it would constitute an aspect of our literary theorization. The anthological format — wherein individual essays tend to study a single author or single ethnic literature — is a fitting vehicle for the scholarly representation of Asian American identity's current default additive status (as something that exists only as the sum of various ethnic parts), which is why academic publishing in the field is richer in the genre of the anthology than the monograph. This holding pattern can serve for only so long to substitute for a wholesale renovation of the grounds for the field's integrity. To the extent that the twenty-first-century Asian American figures the racial instance where the associated links between cultural marginalization and economic disempowerment are the most blatantly attenuated, Asian American studies in particular affords the opportunity for rematerializing ethnic studies' conceptualization of race and ethnicity.

Zhou rightly asks that we situate Asian American literary texts in more of an intertextual relation to other American traditions, in order to gain a better understanding of how Asian American writers have appropriated and transformed established literary conventions and genres (rather than having merely resisted or subverted them). But a less dualistic approach to the ethnic text promises more than just a fuller integration of the American literary canon and the terms of its discussion. It may allow us more systematically to explore questions such as, What has been its role in the historical construction of race and ethnicity? How has the Asian American text interacted with other texts in the racialization of the Asian American? How does that interaction require that we reconceive what is an Asian American text? What is the difference and relationship between literature and other kinds of discourses, institutions, and material forces in effecting this process? I am suggesting that we put form to work in theorizing what is and has been Asian American literature, and this perforce means engaging even more deeply in interdisciplinary inquiry and research.

Because there can be no such thing as an Asian American aesthetic form, a formalistic formalism is unlikely to offer a means for positing Asian American identity. A historical formalism, however, may generate the kinds of questions that will lead to some persuasive conceptualizations and narratives of it. Though there is no such thing as Asian American aesthetic form, the twentieth century brought into historical being Asiatic racial form across a variety of registers and, in consequence, Asian American social movements. By the late twentieth century, the Asian American became an institutionalized (academic and governmental) sociological category, though we are still uncertain as to what it means to talk about an Asian American subject. If literature is a privileged medium for the documentation of subjectivity, literary criticism's significant contribution to Asian American studies may lie in its ability to theorize the historicity of the Asian American subject, to ask, What is its historical status? What are the subject's temporal and spatial locations? What are its determinate conditions of existence, the varieties of its social effects, the range of its political interests? Investigating the historicity of the Asian American subject will require, as a first step, disaggregating the Asian American subject from any one of the customary textual categories from which it is so often adduced: author, narrator, character, thematic subject matter, and, less often, reception and interpretive community. We might conceive the Asian American subject as the product of the articulation of the links between two or more of these textual categories. Variation in the modes of articulation between these links discloses its historicity. The significance of this historicity can be gauged by placing Asian American subject-formation in relationship to other developments, be they economic, political, sociological, intellectual, or cultural — and whether they belong under the recognizable heading of "Asian American history" or other kinds of history.

As it now stands, theorization of the Asian American subject has largely fallen between the cracks of an Asian American cultural studies whose political conservation of the Asian American has logically required that it be construed as a "subjectless discourse" and an Asian American literary studies whose sense of multicultural responsibility loosely tethers it to a filiative notion of the ethnic author — who is Chinese, Japanese, Korean, Filipino, South Asian, Vietnamese, and so on — but not Asian American.[8] How might Asian American cultural studies' more far-reaching sense of political purpose and Asian American literary studies' emerging investment in discovering "the critical power of the aesthetic" (*Literary Gestures*, 4) be joined? The future of Asian American studies may well depend on it, as it is not clear that Asian American studies, whose epistemological object is constitutively interdisciplinary, can do without a self-renewing sense of the political.

In the absence of a historical account of Asian American subject formation, a focus on form may provide an initial bridge between the notion of race as a representation and the notion of race as constitutive of literary and other social formations. The typical divide between work conducted under the sign of the study of American Orientalism and work conducted under the sign of the study of Asian American literature is, in the end, a reflection of a reification of race whose objective and subjective dimensions remain split off from each other so long as we continue to use race to delineate in advance archives of racial representation from archives of ethnic self-expression.[9] In the interest of putting into practice a fully social (and nonessentialist) consciousness of race, we might describe race as the construction that emerges out of our theorization of the historically shifting relationship between these archives; for this reason, we cannot treat it as an *a priori* determinant of their boundaries. The more than usually obvious impossibility of a filiative notion of the Asian American should help to militate against the impulse to naturalize an Asian American "race."

Conceptualizing race as form can help mediate the usual divde between the aesthetic and the social, which is especially severe in discussions of ethnic literature. To comprehend this, it may be useful to remind ourselves of Raymond Williams's *Marxism and Literature,* whose account of form is thoroughly social and historically active. His historical materialist conceptualization of literature responds to the impasse between traditional formalism and sociological criticism, as can be seen in his meditation on the question of "stance":

> If we are to attempt to understand writing as historical practice in the social material process, we have to look again, beyond traditional generic theory, at the whole question of determination. Modern formalist theory, beginning at the level of modes of formal composition, returned these to questions of stance, which it could then interpret only in terms of permanent variables. This led straight to idealism: archetypal dispositions of the human mind or condition. Sociological theory, on the other hand, beginning at the level of subject-matter, derived formal composition and stance from this level alone: at times convincingly, for the choice of subject-matter includes real determinants, but still in general insufficiently, for what has finally to be recognized is that stance, especially, is a social relationship.[10]

For Williams, form too is a social relationship. The problem of form, Williams writes, is the problem of the relations between social modes and individual projects, the problem of these relations as necessarily variable, and the problem of the description of these variable relations within specifiable material practices. The problem of form for him is distinctly not, as it was for traditional formalists, a question of isolating the art object as a thing in itself, "to be examined only in its own terms and through its own 'means' or 'devices': an attempt founded on the hypothesis of a specifically distinguishable 'poetic language'" (152).

Williams's critique of a base/superstructure theory of culture equally distances his historical materialism from a mechanical materialism. In the transition from Marx to Marxism, Williams argues, the relational sense of Marx's original arguments was often hardened into "relatively enclosed categories" and "relatively enclosed areas of activity" (78). Despite the fact that the force of Marx's original arguments was directed against the separation of areas of thought and activity, this relational emphasis, "including not only complexity but recognition of the ways in which some connections are lost to consciousness," came to be displaced by abstract categories of "superstructure" and "base" (79), which were then related temporally or causally. Interestingly, Williams criticizes Althusser for having overemphasized the complexity and autonomy of the superstructure when it is the base that requires more complexification. The superstructure is more obviously varied and variable, while the base has "by extension and habit come to be considered virtually as an 'object'," or a "particular and reductive version of 'material' existence" (81). To know the base as a process instead "complicates the object-reflection model which had appeared so powerful" (96). Williams thus wrests a genuine historical materialism that at core sees "the material life process as human activity" from mechanical tendencies to see "the world as objects and excluding activity" (96).

Williams's materialist formalist approach to literature seeks to distinguish between aesthetic intentions, means, and effects and other kinds of intentions, means, and effects — *and* to sustain that distinction "through the inevitable extension [of the aesthetic] to an indissoluble social material process" (152). This dialectical project is ambitious indeed. Very few critics had actually managed to execute it in a concrete practice of research, reading, and argumentation before the aspiration lost its currency in the face of deconstruction's critique of totalization. At the present time, varieties of (negative) dialectics and formalisms both seem to be making a comeback, and in this context Williams's 1977 intervention against traditional ideology critique mandated by his fierce literary investments holds new relevance for a contemporary generation of literary critics who are trying to negotiate their own sense of a double commitment to history and form in light of all that has come before.

For the ethnic studies critic, the orientation toward the problem of form modeled by Williams helps to clarify what might be productive about approaching race as form rather than as formation. Since the publication of *Racial Formation in the United States* (1986), Michael Omi and Howard Winant's concept of racial formation as a "sociohistorical process by which racial categories are created, inhabited, transformed, and destroyed" has been the most influential way in which ethnic studies scholars have come to think of race as a historically constructed entity.[11] Nevertheless, as I have argued elsewhere, Omi and Winant's historicization of race was incomplete because of an overconcern to show the irreducibility of race to class analysis, leading them circularly to describe race to be the result of racism ("In Dialogue," 2 – 3). Borrowing Williams's language to describe traditional formalism's reification of aesthetic autonomy, we might say that the examination of race in its own terms and through its own "means" or "devices" results in the description of race as a thing in itself, as autonomous from material social processes.

What if our point of departure were not a straw paradigm that embarrasses questions of determination and forecloses possibilities of change? For Williams, the fallacy of the base/superstructure paradigm was its caricature version of a materialist concept of determination (whose root sense was "a setting of pressures and limits" rather than "causing") and its fixing of social relations in motion as abstract, inert categories; the base/superstructure paradigm was already the reification of the relational meaning, and therefore necessary historicity, of the concept of class. Beginning from the base/superstructure paradigm for a materialist theory of race, we end up pitting "race" against "class," creating a war of abstractions and a deadlock of preferred causalities. Oriented by Williams's materialist approach to form, the problem of race might instead be reformulated as a question of the relationship between language (which consists not of signs, but "notations of actual productive relationships" [170]) and other material processes — between race understood as representation and race as an agency of literary and other social formations. What are the historical conditions and force of the minority subject's affects is a question yet to be much explored. Here too, Williams may afford a point of departure for historicizing the insights yielded by psychoanalytic explorations of the subjective experience of racial melancholia.[12] In Williams, structures of feeling are a medium of the social that is neither institutional nor formalized; their exploration yields potential access to the "true social present" (132). This hypothesis has a special relevance to art and literature, "where the true social content is in a significant number of cases of this present and affective kind, which cannot without loss be reduced to belief systems, institutions, or explicit general relationships, though it may include all these as lived and experienced" (133). This is perhaps why Williams suggests that the study of forms can serve as a specific "point of entry to certain kinds of formations" (138) and that understanding emergent culture "depends crucially on finding new forms or adaptations of form" (126).

In the absence of a historical account of the Asian American subject, race construed as form rather than as formation may help us keep in focus how race is an active social relation rather than a transhistorical abstraction — which is after all what Omi and Winant had originally intended by drawing on Gramsci to elaborate their view of the United States as governed by the shifting arrangements of racial hegemony. But this is only to the extent that we grasp that the formalist desires of Asian American literary criticism today are also deeply at heart historicist desires. The risk of form is that we may find out that institutional justification for Asian American studies relies in the last instance on the *raison* of identity, and that in doing away with our last essentialism, that is, our strategic essentialism, we will also do away with Asian American studies. The gamble is that it opens the future of Asian American studies to wider intellectual reaches and more radical political prospects.

Notes

1. This essay represents a further elaboration of the concerns set forth in my introduction to *Forms* of *Asia*, a special issue of *Representations*. See Lye, "Introduction: In Dialogue with Asian American Studies," in Colleen Lye and Christopher Bush, eds., *Representations* 99 (Summer 2007): 1 – 12.

2. Zhou Xiaojing, "Introduction: Critical Theories and Methodologies in Asian American Literary Studies," in Zhou Xiaojing and Samina Najmi, eds., *Form and Transformation in Asian American Literature* (Seattle, 2005), 15, 17, 16.

3. Sue-Im Lee, "Introduction: The Aesthetic in Asian American Literary Discourse," in Rocío G. Davis and Sue-Im Lee, eds., *Literary Gestures: The Aesthetic in Asian American Writing* (Philadelphia, 2006), 1.

4. Keith Lawrence and Floyd Cheung, introduction to Keith Lawrence and Floyd Cheung, eds., *Recovered Legacies: Authority and Identity in Early Asian American Literature* (Philadelphia, 2005), 8.

5. See Jinqi Ling, *Narrating Nationalisms: Ideology and Form in Asian American Literature* (Oxford, 1998). For an account of Ling's inter vention within 1990s Asian American cultural studies and the shortages of Asian American literary history, see Colleen Lye, "Form and History in Asian American Literary Studies," *American Literary History* 20, no. 3 (Fall 2008): 548 – 555.

6. Lisa Lowe, "Heterogeneity, Hybridity, Multiplicity: Marking Asian American Differences," *Diaspora* 1, no. 1 (1991): 24 – 44.

7. So far, this deferral has resulted in an impasse between a nationally constrained sense of what is political and a sense of transnational inevitability that is more or less academic. It has also allowed observers outside the field to question the intellectual and political integrity of Asian American program-building, though few may be as willing to be as provocatively skeptical as Walter Benn Michaels, who has described Asian American studies as a "kind of blackface, a performance that produces the image of racialized oppression alongside the reality of economic success." See Michaels, "Why Identity Politics Distracts Us from Economic Inequalities," *Chronicle of Higher Education* 53, no. 17, December 15, 2006, B10.

8. This is what Susan Koshy meant over a decade ago by referring to the fictionality of the textual coalition that is "Asian American literature." See Susan Koshy, "The Fiction of Asian American Literature," *Yale Journal of Criticism* 9 (1996): 316 – 346. For the Asian American

as a "subjectless discourse," see Kandice Chuh, *Imagine Otherwise: On Asian Americanist Critique* (Durham, NC, 2003). Chuh explains her use of this term in the following way: "It serves as the ethical grounds for the political practice of what I would describe as a strategic *anti*-essentialism — as, in other words, the common ethos underwriting the coherency of the field. If we accept a priori that Asian American studies is subjectless, then rather than looking to complete the category 'Asian American,' to actualize it by such methods as enumerating various components of differences (gender, class, sexuality, religion, and so on), we are positioned to critique the effects of the various configurations of power and knowledge through which the term comes to have meaning. Thinking in terms of subjectlessness does not occlude the possibility of political action. Rather, it augurs a redefinition of the political, an investigation into what 'justice' might mean and what (whose) 'justice' is being pursued" (10 – 11). Chuh's equation of the "Asian American" with "deconstruction" — the term "Asian American," she writes, "deconstructs itself, is itself deconstruction" (8) — can be understood as a logical extension of Lowe's project to define the Asian American as an identity-in-difference.

9. David Palumbo-Liu is one of the few Asian American critics to have organized his study in a way that crosses this divide. See *Asian/American: Historical Crossings of a Racial Frontier* (Stanford, 1999). My own study of the making of Asiatic racial form has suggested the agency of John Steinbeck and Pearl Buck in the historical emergence of Asian American character; but though it may have complicated and expanded the range of what we think of as Orientalism, by restricting itself to the study of American authors of European descent my work bracketed the difficult question of the historical interaction between the evidentiary status of Orientalist representation and ethnic self-expression. See Colleen Lye, *America's Asia: Racial Form and American Literature, 1893–1945* (Princeton, 2005).

10. Raymond Williams, *Marxism and Literature* (Oxford, 1977), 184 – 185.

11. Michael Omi and Howard Winant, *Racial Formation in the United States*, 2nd ed. (New York, 1994), 55.

12. Some of the most original and generative theoretical work in Asian American Studies has been undertaken by psychoanalytic critics. See Anne Anlin Cheng, *The Melancholy of Race* (Oxford, 2000).

7

Asian American Literature and the Resistances of Theory
美国亚裔文学与理论的对抗

Christopher Lee

评论家简介

　　李明皓（Christopher Lee），美国布朗大学博士，现为加拿大英属哥伦比亚大学温哥华校区英语系副教授，加拿大亚裔及亚裔移民研究项目负责人，《亚裔离散视觉文化与美洲杂志》的加拿大地区编辑。研究领域包括美国文学、亚裔离散研究、加拿大文学、文化研究、后殖民文学、文学理论、战争与后冲突性研究等。专著有《身份的相似性：美国亚裔文学中的审美中介》（*The Semblance of Identity: Aesthetic Mediation in Asian American Literature*, 2012），荣获 2014 年美国亚裔研究学会文学批评图书奖。合编有《追溯足迹：对当代诗学和文化政治的反思 —— 以纪念三木罗伊》（*Tracing the Lines: Reflections on Contemporary Poetics and Cultural Politics in Honour of Roy Miki*, 2012）。除本书收录的论文，其他代表性论文包括《翻译写作》，收于《剑桥亚裔美国文学指南》（"The Writing of Translation," *The Cambridge Companion to Asian American Literature*, 2015）一书；《流动性与隐喻：对亚裔 / 离散中（非）人的理论化》，发表于期刊《边缘：全球亚洲研究》（"Mobility and Metaphor: Theorizing the (In) human in Asian/Diaspora," *Verge: Studies in Global Asias*, 2015）。

文章简介

在美国亚裔研究之中，理论与实践、政治与美学的矛盾自建制之初就一直存在。近二三十年，随着美国亚裔文学的学科化，以及亚裔内部多元异质性的增强，这些矛盾变得更为凸显。本文要探讨的是在这样的背景之下如何看待美国亚裔文学理论的作用与意义。文章认为，美国亚裔文学研究面临的关键理论问题已不是方法论的选择，即在社会历史研究方法与文学本体研究方法之间的选择，而是阐明理论研究本身的指涉性问题。文章分析了为何难以将美国亚裔文学理论化，然后重点阐释了将理论置于美学（美国亚裔文学）、学术（美国亚裔文学研究）和政治（美国亚裔行动主义）的间际空间中运作的合理性。作者认为美国亚裔文学在不断发展、演变，甚至在不断颠覆自身原有的理论基础，不能以支配性的概念和框架进行理论建构；文章以实例分析论证了美国亚裔文学文本本身具有去除"美国亚裔"范畴的性质，文本以语言和叙事承担起了重构与解构阐释空间的功能，文本就是理论的一种形式。

文章出处：*MFS: Modern Fiction Studies*, vol. 56, no.1, 2010, pp. 19–39.

Asian American Literature
and the Resistances of Theory

Christopher Lee

In 1974, the newly established Department of Ethnic Studies at the University of California, Berkeley, submitted "A Proposal for the Establishment of the College of Third World Studies" to the university's Provost. In its proposed structure for a major in Asian American Studies, the committee recommended that students concentrate on one of three areas in addition to taking a set of core courses: community studies, social sciences, or humanities. While the first two concentrations are clearly designed to contribute "to the body of direct experimental knowledge of the conditions in the Asian American community" (A18) and promote "service to the Asian American people" (A17), the humanities concentration is marked by a noticeable lack of content and cohesion. Only two courses, one on Asian American literature and a creative writing workshop, are listed in the proposal, and this lack of structure is reflected in its provisional tone:

> That Asian students be encouraged to venture into the humanities is obvious; what form self-expression will take in the context of the Asian American experience and Asian American Studies is yet to be seen. It is certain that the student with a concentration in the humanities will be given the freedom to explore Asian American and Third World literature, art and dance, and creative writing. At the same time, however, the same amount of rigor and depth of understanding of the Asian American experience expected of the major in the other two areas of concentration will be asked of the student in the humanities.

The proposal goes on to clarify the role of the arts in Asian American Studies: "Of particular importance will be the student's responses to the question of the flow and interchange between life and art. This last point is of considerable importance since it will help to give the individual the clarity of vision necessary in delineating between what is truly an Asian American assertion and what is a replica of what exists, clothed in Oriental paraphernalia" (A21).

Even while the proposal embraces the arts as a means of actualizing the emancipatory goals of Asian American Studies, it seems unsure of what constitutes suitable artistic content and identifies the humanities as an area in which courses and methodologies remain to be developed. In charting future directions for research and teaching, it suggests that barriers between the study and production of culture need to be broken down, a task that resonates with their desire to integrate theory and practice. Moreover, the proposal argues that art and literature must not be "only for the purposes of glorifying the individual writers or artist" but rather must "serve the broader needs of our people." To this end, it insists that the humanities must be driven by political commitment in order to oppose the colonial legacies that have "denied the right [of Third World Peoples] to express themselves in creative ways" (A26). In short, it is only by entrenching the humanities within a larger political project that it can acquire the "clarity of vision" needed to dismantle Orientalist and racist misrepresentations.

Reading this report some thirty-five years later, one cannot help but notice the contrast between its tentative engagement with the humanities and the current status of the humanities within Asian American Studies. Asian American cultural criticism, of which a large portion is concerned in some way or another with literary expression, has flourished in the last two decades and constitutes one of the largest components of an interdisciplinary field. New scholarship on the humanities is being produced at a healthy rate, while courses in Asian American literature are regularly offered at many universities and colleges, which in turn affects the training and hiring of new faculty with expertise in literary and cultural studies. These developments have reconfigured the relationship between the humanities and the social sciences, producing an ongoing tension between methodologies that emphasize theoretical speculation and textual analysis on the one hand and empirical analysis on the other.

Yet the issues raised by the 1974 Berkeley proposal continue to be relevant for Asian American literary studies today. After all, students and scholars of Asian American literature continue to debate questions such as: what is the relationship between aesthetics and politics and, in the case of Asian American Studies, between its intellectual and activist projects? What kinds of knowledge do literary texts provide and what kinds of commitment are required to mobilize culture in the service of an anticolonial, antiracist emancipatory project? By probing the relationship between literary culture and Asian American Studies as a politically committed knowledge project, these questions also frame the conditions under which theory has operated in the field from its inception until now. As Glenn Omatsu explains, the activist-scholars who founded the field in the 1960s and 1970s "reclaimed a heritage of struggle" (168) and forged new ties among scholars, students, and traditionally marginalized communities in a manner that harmonized politics with intellectual work, so that "Theory [became] a material force when it [was] grasped by the masses" (171). But while the organic integration of theory and praxis continues to function as something of a normative goal, the work of theorizing Asian American literature can no longer be contained by a specific political project, not the least because its current institutional circumstances are no longer those that circumscribed its founding. My point is not to lament institutionalization as the abandonment of politics, but rather to ask what is the role and meaning of theory in this pluralistic context.

Instead of offering a detailed account of how the field has engaged with various schools of theory — psychoanalysis, poststructuralism, Marxism and neo-or post-Marxism, feminism, queer theory, postcolonial, and globalization theory and so on — my point of departure is Donald C. Goellnicht's 1997 essay "Blurring Boundaries: Asian American Literature as Theory." Here, Goellnicht insists on the need to read "Asian American texts as theoretically informed and informing rather than as transparently referential human documents over which we place a grid of sophisticated Euro-American theory in order to extract meaning" (340). Goellnicht draws our attention to the political implications of literary and cultural studies in the North American academy, a context in which the demand for referential knowledge from writings by minority authors is part of an imperialist legacy that implicates ethnography, the humanistic disciplines, and the social sciences. For Goellnicht, the task of theory is to interrupt these assumptions in order to "expose the workings of ideology, to uncover the matrices of established power relations, and to challenge traditional canons and official histories" (351).

Goellnicht insists that we pay attention to the theoretical labor performed by Asian American literary texts in order to interrogate the ethnocentrism that pervades much of what gets recognized as theory. In this regard, he cites Barbara Christian's famous declaration, "people of color have always theorized — but in forms quite different from the Western form of abstract logic...often in narrative forms, in the stories we create, in riddles and proverbs, in the play with language" (qtd. in Goellnicht 342). In her widely read essay "The Race for Theory," Christian disparages how the hegemony of high theory has diminished scholarly attention on creative expression, a situation that she considers both an aesthetic as well as political error. Goellnicht draws on this point in order to emphasize the theoretical value of generic and stylistic experimentation on the part of Asian American writers. By reading Asian American literature as theory, he writes, we can "acknowledge that Asian American theory is indigenous to the literature, and so it must take account of the Asian American literary tradition rather than being a tool of domination that polices and mines literary texts" (342).

While I agree with Goellnicht's account of the cultural politics of theory, this essay departs from his assertion of an alternative Asian American literary/theoretical tradition. My point is not that he is a cultural essentialist — to the contrary, he carefully foregrounds the heterogeneity of Asian American culture throughout his essay — but to my mind, it is precisely the fact that such a tradition is fraught with contradiction, instability, and uncertainty that enables theory to intervene in the first place. Not only is Asian American a fairly recent invention, but also its fast changing demographics has constantly undermined its currency and historical stability. For these reasons, I focus on how theory operates at the disjunctures among the aesthetic (Asian American literature), the academic (Asian American literary studies), and the political (Asian American activism). Although Asian American Studies was founded with the admirable goal of integrating these three currents, this goal has become increasingly elusive.

In this regard, I borrow the following formulation from Robyn Wiegman, who writes in the course of a discussion on feminism in the academy, feminism is not reducible to its political function as a heuristic for making women exist in time, nor is its past fully comprehensible as the founding prehistory of our political or psychic present. This is partly because feminism's historical, theoretical, political, and epistemological dimensions do not operate together in the same sphere of articulation and hence do not cohere as a singular (or even collectivized) discourse, a knowable set of commitments, a historical origin, or an agenda of political acts and obligations — no matter how desperate we are for feminism to offer us the means to manage the incommensurable and the inexplicable, to overturn pain and indifference, to move us beyond the agony of our own unknowing, and thereby to provide us with some words that we can learn once and securely for all. (164)

For Wiegman, incongruencies among the various desires that animate Women's Studies — and, for the purposes of the present discussion, Asian American Studies — produce a sense of profound anxiety, even agony. I suggest that it is precisely under such conditions that theory operates or, as it were, takes place. This position is, of course, by no means a politically innocent one to inhabit, and therein lies the difficulty of theorizing Asian American literature today.

In her influential 1996 essay "The Fiction of Asian American Literature," Susan Koshy makes a forceful call for "more substantial theoretical investigation of the premises and assumptions underlying our constructions of commonality and difference" (469). This task, she explains, is different from attempts to recover, build, and substantiate a literary canon through pluralist gestures of inclusion and expansion. Instead of bringing about a sense of coherence, such acts are merely "strategic deferrals" that end up demonstrating the impossibility of bringing heterogeneous cultural formations under the rubric Asian American (467). By refusing to think through their own assumptions, critics unwittingly perpetuate definitional practices that privilege the history and experience of certain Asian sub-groups (especially Chinese and Japanese Americans) or suppress existing contradictions in favor of the political fantasy of a pan-Asian future. Koshy argues that these tendencies underscore the failure of the field to come to terms with the demographic realities of Asian America in the age of globalization.

Koshy's argument has lost none of its urgency over the years. After all, new literary texts continue to challenge the parameters of Asian American literature by including transnational content, using languages other than English, depicting mixed race subjects, and deploying a wide range of formal strategies. To be sure, the difficulty of theorizing Asian American literature does not imply a lack of theory in the field. To the contrary, scholars and critics have theorized Asian American culture in relation to a wide range of topics including race, globalization, immigration, subjectivity, the nationstate, gender, and sexuality. Not only have they deployed a diverse arsenal of approaches, but also their interventions have reconfigured the theoretical discourses that they have drawn on. But while the intellectual diversity of Asian American literary studies has grown substantially since Koshy's essay, the central problem of theorizing Asian American literature continues to challenge those who work in the field. As Colleen Lye has recently written:

> Today it is all too easy to agree that we should dispense with a restrictive definition of Asian American literary belonging...What is much more difficult to agree on is where to draw the line between Asian American literature and Asian Anglophone literature, or for that matter Asian literature in any language at all. If in the early days the legitimation of "Asian American literature" had to confront a skepticism that there might be too few justifying texts, today the field's integrity is perhaps even more challenged by the vertigo of too many possibilities. ("Introduction" 3)

If Asian American literature seems to be flourishing, why is theorizing it so difficult? What, to ask a more basic question, does it mean to theorize Asian American literature in the first place?

For both Koshy and Lye, theorization involves, among other things, defining an object that resists definition by virtue of its internal inconsistencies and constantly shifting content. However, the understandings of theory put forth in their respective essays turn out to be quite different in orientation and practice. For Koshy, theorizing Asian American literature is, first and foremost, a matter of grasping the socio-economic as well as demographic shifts that have occurred since the invention of Asian American identity in the 1960s and 1970s. She writes:

> Asian American literary production takes place within and participates in this transformed political and cultural landscape. Asian American Studies is, however, only just beginning to undertake a theoretical investigation of these changes...Although substantial historical scholarship has been produced, the field has been weak in theoretical work, especially when compared to Chicano, Native American, and African American Studies. The lack of significant theoretical work

has affected its development and its capacity to address the stratifications and differences that constitute its distinctness within ethnic studies. (468)

While Lye also addresses the relationship between theory and history, she focuses primarily on the problem of form. In her book *America's Asia*, she undertakes a brilliant study of how popular stereotypes such as the model minority and the yellow peril have historically worked together to constitute what she calls the "Asiatic racial form" (5). Asiatic racial form is not a matter of misrepresentation that can be corrected once the "truth" about actual Asian Americans is recovered. Rather, it enables "the unrepresentable to be visualized" so that "the unseen power of social abstraction" can be made apprehensible (7). More recently, she has argued that a focus on form enables us to understand "race as a construction that emerges out of our theorization of the historically shifting relationship between these archives; for this reason, we cannot treat it as an *a priori* determinant of their boundaries" ("Racial Form" 96). Borrowing from the work of Raymond Williams, Lye conceives race as a "social relationship" through which we make sense of constantly shifting social conditions (97). Race, then, does not exist in and of itself: it is "an active social relation rather than a transhistorical abstraction" that enables us to grasp and represent material conditions and processes in ways that produce socially engaged knowledge (99). While the contrast that I draw here — between Koshy's theorization of history and Lye's focus on form — is admittedly schematic, this distinction is instructive for delineating different directions for theory in Asian American literary studies.[1] Let me illustrate this distinction by considering two foundational scholarly accounts of Asian American literature. In the "Preface" to her ground-breaking *Asian American Literature: An Introduction to the Writings and Their Social Context*, Elaine Kim locates the meaning of Asian American literature in its social contexts in order to "emphasize how the literature elucidates the social history of Asians in the United States," an approach that gives less attention to the "formal literary merit of Asian American literature" (xv).

If Kim's *Asian American Literature* was written at a moment when the pressing task was to assert the existence of Asian American literature as such, Sau-ling Wong's *Reading Asian American Literature: From Necessity to Extravagance* positions itself as a response to the rise of Asian American literary studies as a field in its own right. Wong begins by explicating the relationship between literary studies and the academic, activist, and cultural formations that have formed around the term Asian American:

> Students of Asian American literature tend to be united by a desire to ensure that voices of Asian Americans are heard and to make known the richness and complexity of Asian American writing.

> Just as the Asian American ethnic group is a political coalition, Asian American literature may be thought of as an emergent and evolving textual coalition, whose interests it is the business of a professional coalition of Asian American critics to promote. (9)[2]

Explicitly modeling literary studies on pan-ethnic coalition building, Wong draws on the ability of Asian America to function as, in Stephen Sumida's words, "a deliberate conjoining of obviously disparate 'Asian' groups" (805).

While reading *Asian American Literature* is deeply engaged with social history, its theoretical project is primarily self-referential insofar as it is concerned with Asian American as a self-conscious formation that organizes the histories and experiences of disparate ethnic groups and subjects into a coherent narrative. Wong is careful to note that there is no singular Asian American history, but goes on to argue that Asian American literary criticism, when understood in light of a textual coalition, is itself a form of community building that "feeds back into history to further realize what has hitherto been tentative and unstable" (9). Whereas Kim offers a contextual approach that mobilizes literature in order to acquire knowledge about Asians in the US, Wong offers a detailed account of Asian American as a self-conscious cultural category. The fact that their respective studies have quite different points of departure not only reflects the different institutional contexts in which they appeared, but it also delineates different understandings of how theory might operate in Asian American literary studies.

What this brief comparison foregrounds are different understandings of theory and referentiality. In other words, the proper referents of Asian American literary theory remain undecided. Should it, again to be schematic, refer to the external socio-historical conditions in which Asian American literature is produced, circulated, read, and interpreted, or should it refer primarily to the terms through which the field constructs itself as a coherent project? While the practical answer is that it should do both, the tension between these two approaches cannot be easily resolved by merely adopting a generous eclecticism. Moreover, the crucial methodological choice facing Asian American literary studies is not between formal readings on the one hand and socio-historical ones on the other, between aesthetics and politics as it were. At this moment the choice of an apolitical formalism is something of a straw dummy when it comes to the study of Asian American literature. With the emergence of a critical mass of scholarship on Asian American literature and culture, historically situated interpretations of texts have undeniably been the dominant mode of reading. Moreover, the rise of ethnic studies, New Historicism, postcolonial studies, feminism, globalization studies, and other related fields has done much to dismantle the notion that knowledge can be ahistorical and apolitical. Thus, even though a number of recent works have been extensively engaged with form and aesthetics, critics invested in these questions are careful to emphasize the compatibility of their arguments with the historical and political commitments of the field.[3]

In recent criticism, Kandice Chuh's *Imagine Otherwise* standsout as an especially rigorous attempt to integrate the critique of referentiality with the political commitments of Asian American Studies. Chuh argues that efforts to adjust, pluralize, or expand the meaning of Asian America end up reinscribing a "normative subject." Such attempts, she writes, "cannot but end in a dead end, where one either is or is not found to be a 'real' Asian American, whether a particular representation is or is not found to be 'authentic'" (21). As an antidote, she calls for Asian American Studies to reinvent itself into a *"subjectless discourse"* (9) consisting of *"collaborative antagonisms"* (28) that keep "contingency, irresolution, and nonequivalence in the foreground" (8). Functioning not as a positivist identity but as a term of criticism, "'Asian American' makes no claim to verisimilitude and instead anchors investigation of the ways that the U.S. nation employs racialization as a technology of power" (84).

The crux of Chuh's intervention lies in her attempts to dismantle the referential assumptions attached to Asian American identity in order to retain its analytical and critical possibilities. As she explains, such referential claims stem from the tendency to endow identitarian categories with fixed meanings. She notes that "within the institutionalized setting of Asian American Studies," the overprivileging of activism "effectively enables a return of referentiality, a reification of the idea of Asian American culture as transcending historical circumstance" (24). Delineating the limitations of referentiality, *Imagine Otherwise* offers alternative ways to understand how Asian American might function as a term of critique:

> "Asian American" is/names racism and resistance, citizenship and its denial, subjectivity and subjection — at once the becoming and undoing — and, as such, is a designation for the (*im*)possible of justice, where "justice" refers to a state as yet unexperienced and unrepresentable…an endless project of searching out the knowledge and material apparatuses that extinguish some (Other) life ways and that hoard economic and social opportunities only for some. (8)

Here, Chuh deploys ideas drawn from deconstruction to conceive Asian American as a paradoxical category that foregrounds the limits of identity politics and gestures to histories of racism and injustice. In doing so, she invests it with a dimension of futurity that calls forth a justice unknowable in the present.

For the purposes of the present discussion, however, I want to emphasize how Chuh's radical gesture is also, to borrow Lye's description, a matter of conservation.[4] It is radical because it recognizes the consequences of the critique of referentiality and departs from an organic vision of Asian American Studies as an integrated political and academic project. Nevertheless, *Imagine Otherwise* conserves the critical impulses of that vision by placing the critique of referentiality within the same tradition that gave rise to ethnic studies. In short, *Imagine Otherwise* remains consciously located within the intellectual traditions of Asian American Studies, a location that accounts for its self-referential orientation. In the concluding paragraph of "The Fiction of Asian American Literature," Koshy describes a similar predicament:

> The tension between the need for political identity and the need to represent the conflicted and heterogeneous formation we call "Asian American." These needs are antagonistic to each other only if we work from the assumption that there is a "real" Asian American identity to which our vocabulary and procedures can be adequated. Hence the pluralist computation that the sum of the parts will give us the whole. I would contend that "Asian American" offers us a rubric that we cannot not use. But our usage of the term should rehearse the catachrestic status of the formation. (491)

But while I agree that there is a strong case for retaining the term "Asian American" given what has been historically achieved through its deployment, the increasing heterogeneity of Asian America not only undermines its coherence, but also suggests the possibility of imagining alternative social formations and identity categories to take its place.

The problem with blanket refusals of referentiality, then, is that they posit a rigid opposition between referentiality, understood as a reifying operation, on the one hand and a completely open-ended notion of critique on the other. Faced with such polarized choices, it is not surprising that pragmatic arguments for maintaining the category Asian American — including the much-deployed notion of strategic essentialism — have been deployed with remarkable frequency even though they are bound to collapse due to their logical shortcomings. While the refusal of referentiality is a necessary step toward dismantling the ethnographic and essentialist assumptions that have underscored identity politics, it does not adequately address the ways in which Asian American cannot be thought of merely as a category of critique. As Iyko Day writes, "We must acknowledge that there are real-life referents of the term 'Asian American,' which include its hard-won role as a state-recognized minority category for civil rights monitoring and its more negative existence in U.S. society as an undifferentiated 'foreign' population subject to racial hostilities" (73).

With these points in mind, I want to revisit the fraught status of referentiality as a symptom of what theory has tried to accomplish in Asian American Studies — namely the dismantling of referentiality in favor of politically engaged critique — by turning to Paul de Man's famous 1982 essay "The Resistance to Theory." There, he responds to the theory wars that were engulfing Anglo-American literature departments at the time by offering a strikingly original account of theory's limitations. According to de Man, theory "can be said to come into being when the approach to literary texts is no longer based on non-linguistic, that is to say historical or aesthetic, considerations or, to put it somewhat less crudely, when the object of discussion is no longer the meaning or the value but the modalities of production and of reception of meaning and of value prior to their establishment" (7). De Man thus aligns theory with modes of reading that are attentive to the ambiguity of signification by refusing to foreclose the openness of a text.

Throughout the essay, de Man develops this argument by distinguishing between aesthetic, historical, and grammatical reading practices — which all take referentiality more or less for granted — and what he calls the rhetorical, which "operates on the level of the signifier and contains no responsible pronouncement on the nature of the world — despite its powerful potential to create the opposite illusion" (10). By bracketing the mimetic capabilities of language, de Man draws our attention to the materiality of the signifier, which, he cautions, should not be confused with "the materiality of what it signifies." Indeed, he defines ideology precisely as "the confusion of linguistic with natural reality, of reference with phenomenalism." This is not, as misreadings of de Man frequently charge, to assert a nihilist position with regards to linguistic meaning, but rather to recognize how the analysis of indeterminacy is "a powerful and indispensable tool in the unmasking of ideological aberrations." As de Man writes, "Those who reproach literary theory for being oblivious to social and historical (that is to say ideological) reality are merely stating their fear at having their own ideological mystifications exposed by the tool they are trying to discredit" (11).

De Man's reproach has wide-reaching implications for Asian American Studies, not the least because it challenges the field's constant demand for social and historical meaning, a demand that, in his terms, is ideological insofar as it forecloses the undecidability of language. In this sense, he defines the resistance to theory as "a resistance to the use of language about language.... a resistance to language itself or to the possibility that language contains factors or functions that cannot be reduced to intuition" (12 – 13); in other words, "the resistance to theory is in fact a resistance to reading, a resistance that is perhaps at its most effective, in contemporary studies, in the methodologies of reading that call themselves theories of reading but nevertheless avoid the function they claim as their object" (15).

At the end of his essay, de Man arrives at his surprising conclusion that what ultimately resists theory is not those who remain attached to other modes of (not) reading, but rather theory itself: "To the extent that they are theory...rhetorical readings, like the other kinds, still avoid and resist the reading they advocate. Nothing can overcome the resistance to theory since theory *is* itself this resistance. The loftier the aims and the better the methods of literary theory, the less possible it becomes" (19). Theory resists theory because it always comes to us in finite forms that circulate as knowledge (consider, for example, how poststructuralist terms such as "difference" or "ambiguity" have, through their repeated use, become tropes in their own right and have acquired a measure of critical power). Theory itself cannot avoid imposing forms of closure that appear to offer a definitive reading or interpretation of a text.

De Man's account of resistance challenges the desire on the part of Asian American Studies to place limits on the work of theory so as not to displace its underlying socio-historical framework, as well as the political commitments that circumscribe its reading practices.[5] Frequently heard injunctions to historicize our scholarship, reaffirm our political commitments, or place Asian American identity under erasure through some form of strategic essentialism are all operations that resist theory, however necessary and useful they are in and of themselves. They resist theory because they foreclose the openness of language by imposing an interpretive horizon, even though they arguably define what it means to read as an Asian Americanist.

Acting on similar concerns as de Man, Chuh puts forth a new definition of Asian American as "an endless project of searching out the knowledge and material apparatuses" in the name of a justice to come. Chuh writes, "'Asian American,' because it is a term in difference from itself — at once making a claim of achieved subjectivity and referring to the impossibility of that achievement — deconstructs itself, is itself deconstruction" (8) — which is to say that Asian American is theory as the ongoing act of critique. But in light of de Man's description of resistance, we also need to rewrite this claim as follows: Asian American is also the resistance to theory because whenever we engage its material manifestations, its finiteness always involves the foreclosure of its own theoretical labor. This resistance is inherent in any project that coheres around the term Asian American and in the intellectual and political work that has been enabled by its invention and circulation. This process becomes manifest whenever texts are read for explicit purposes, no matter how admirable and urgent those purposes may be. If Asian American is the resistance to theory, then theory itself is the impossible horizon of Asian American Studies, what the field cannot allow if it is to maintain any semblance of coherence. Thus to read as an

Asian Americanist is, to some degree, to misread. And herein lies the agonistic relationship between Asian American literature and theory, for, as de Man writes, "literary theory is not in danger of going under; it cannot help but flourish, and the more it is resisted, the more it flourishes since the language it speaks is the language of self-resistance" (19–20).

While the critique of referentiality has been indispensable for dismantling Orientalist discourses and exposing the ways in which signification is socially determined under conditions of domination, de Man's provocative analysis seems to invite criticism and suspicion on the grounds that it is a depoliticizing gesture that paralyzes rather than empowers. But to say that theory cannot be reduced to the political does not mean that it is simply apolitical; it does, however, mean that theory exceeds and disrupts the political commitments that critics bring to their work. Coming to terms with theory requires us to take seriously what Paul Bové, in a discussion of Area Studies, describes as the need to "abandon existing fields and boundaries."[6] As Bové explains:

> This is no soft call for interdisciplinarity…Nor is it merely to alter the forms of existing fields such as area studies…Rather it is a call to adopt abandonment as a critical practice, a call to give up the already known as a sacred value effectively working like Stone's scruple, to rub raw the daring trespasser or anarchist. Can there be a more frightening cry to the human scientist than to abandon the field? Does this not imply cowardice, a giving up and running away? Nor does it mean something trivial like leaving the field and training in another. It means, rather, taking seriously abandoning the organization of knowledge into fields as such and making an effort to hollow out any given field for the knowledge it provides. (305 – 306)

In order to give a sense of what a politics of abandonment might look like, I conclude with a brief reading of a literary text that unravels Asian American literary culture through what we might call the intrusion of theory.

I should note right away that my reading of Nam Le's critically acclaimed collection of stories, *The Boat*, is a conscious misreading because it is not at all clear that *The Boat* can or should be read as an Asian American text. The simple (and simplistic) reason is biographical: Le was born in Vietnam and grew up in Australia after his family arrived as refugees. Le continues to identify himself as Asian Australian, even though he obtained his MFA at the Iowa Writers' Workshop and has continued to live in the US (he is currently fiction editor at *Harvard Review*). To be sure, there are many Asian American writers who migrated to the US as adults, but labeling Le an Asian American writer still seems odd, if not inappropriate.

I am less concerned, however, with matters of biography than with what it means to read *The*

Boat as Asian American literature.[7] *The Boat* includes seven stories, each with a different cast of characters in different places and times. The stories are, by and large, unrelated to what we would call Asian America, with the exception of the first and last stories, which deal with the Vietnamese refugee diaspora. While the concluding title story recounts the harrowing experiences of a young woman fleeing postwar Vietnam by boat, the first story, entitled "Love and Honour and Pity and Pride and Compassion and Sacrifice" is a remarkable meditation on the meaning of "ethnic" writing and the categories through which we read Asian America; for the purposes of this essay, I will focus on "Love and Honour."

The words in the story's title derive from William Faulkner's speech on receiving the Nobel Prize for Literature in 1950. In that address, Faulkner offers this list of keywords as what constitutes the universal content of literature. But for the protagonist of the story, whose name and life are clearly based on Le himself, it is precisely the distance between himself and the universal that plagues his life as a writer by virtue of his racial and ethnic identity. The story is set in Iowa City, where Nam is pursuing his MFA and experiencing an extended bout of writer's block a few days before a looming deadline. When his father arrives from Australia for a short visit, we learn about their strained relationship as Nam reflects on his father's distant and at times violent personality. We learn that his father survived the My Lai massacre as a teenager but saw his family and friends killed by American soldiers. Later conscripted into the South Vietnamese army, he was sent to reeducation camps after the fall of Saigon and eventually came to Australia with his family as a refugee.

While these details account for the drama of the story, Le frames "Love and Honour" as a metacritique of the cultural politics of ethnic American writing. Early in the story, Nam tells a friend about his creative struggles and his friend replies, "'Writer's block?…How can you have writer's block? Just write a story about Vietnam'" (7). As the scene unfolds, Nam reflects on the predicament of being a professional "Asian" writer:

> We had come from a party following a reading by the workshop's most recent success, a Chinese woman trying to immigrate to America who had written a book of short stories about Chinese characters in stages of immigration to America. The stories were subtle and good. The gossip was that she'd been offered a substantial, six-figure contract for a two-book deal. … "It's hot," a writing instructor told me at a bar. "Ethnic literature's hot. And important too." (7 – 8)

But even as Nam is categorized in this manner by patronizing teachers and agents, his (presumably white) friends resent the privileges supposedly acquired by ethnic writers and proceed to demonstrate their resentment by dismissing the aesthetic value of ethnic writings: they tell him, "I'm sick of ethnic lit...It's full of descriptions of exotic food....You can't tell if the language is spare because the author intended it that way, or because he didn't have the vocab....The characters are always flat, generic. As long as a Chinese writer writes about *Chinese*, or a Peruvian writer writes about *Peruvians*, or a Russian writer about *Russians*" (8). At the end of the scene, Nam's friend says, "I know I'm a bad person for saying this...but that's why I don't mind your work, Nam. Because you could just write about Vietnamese boat people all the time.... You could totally exploit the Vietnamese thing. But instead, you choose to write about lesbian vampires and Colombian assassins, and Hiroshima orphans — and New York painters with hemorrhoids" (9).[8]

What Le depicts here, with a good dose of self-deprecating humor, is what Rey Chow has described as "coercive mimeticism," "a process (identitarian, existential, cultural, or textual) in which those who are marginal to mainstream Western culture are expected...to resemble and replicate the very banal preconceptions that have been appended to them, a process in which they are expected to objectify themselves in accordance with the already seen and thus to authenticate the familiar imagings of them as ethnics" (107). Even when Nam is praised for not conforming to his own stereotype, such comments retain a racist logic by positing mainstream writing as, by definition, incompatible with ethnic writing. Le offers a sharp critique of the cultural politics of minority writing in the US; insofar as he gestures to the many Asian American writers who have been educated at the Iowa Writers' Workshop, he suggests that such forms of racism can be found in some of the most respected institutions of American literary culture.

What I have sketched here is a reading of "Love and Honour" as a social commentary anchored on the real-life experiences of the author himself. But this structure unravels as Le rewrites these familiar themes by consciously staging precisely what he appears to mock. When Nam recalls his childhood in Australia, he describes the exotic Vietnamese foods eaten at gatherings with family friends. As he recounts his relationship with his father, we are provided with flashbacks to his father's childhood and the traumatic event that serves as an explanation for his troubled family life, as well as an unflinching indictment of war crimes committed by the US military in Vietnam. "Love and Honour" offers an intergenerational narrative of diasporic migration and, as such, reproduces one of the most conventional narrative structures in Asian American literature. (To add another touch of cliché, Nam has a white girlfriend and refuses to tell his father about her.)

Nam finally overcomes his writer's block by doing exactly what he initially refuses to do: "I had two and a half days left. I would write the ethnic story of my Vietnamese father. It was a good story. It was a fucking *great* story. I fed in a sheet of blank paper. At the top of the page, I typed 'ETHNIC STORY' in capital letters" (17). In the process of writing transparently ethnic literature, Nam and his father tentatively start to reconcile as the latter shares his life story in detail for the first time to help his son correct the "mistakes" in his "Ethnic Story." In light of its autobiographical background, "Love and Honour" seems to exemplify what it otherwise disavows; as the book jacket of the Australian edition tells us, "In 1979, Nam Le's family left Vietnam for Australia, an experience that inspires the first and last stories in *The Boat.*"

But while we are exposed to fragments of Nam's father's story throughout, the entire story is never fully revealed. In other words, while we are made aware of the materials that would potentially constitute an ethnic story, we are never treated to a coherent narrative that they would presumably constitute, even though Nam writes a new version after talking with his father. In a surprising denouement, he catches his father burning the only copy of the story for reasons that are not entirely spelled out. This event raises crucial questions not only about the revised story, but also about the status of the ethnic story as such. After all, his father agrees to recount his life with great reluctance and tells him that his story is "not something you'll be able to write" (25). But while Nam misunderstands these words as an expression of doubt over his abilities as writer, they carry a deeper meaning in the context of the text by casting doubt on the very possibility of writing an ethnic story into existence. This uncertainty stems from the slippages of referentiality between narrative and experience, between different levels of social life and the stories that purport to represent them. Thus even though Nam was named by his father "after the homeland he had given up" (20), he realizes that his ability to embody his namesake is by no means secure; at one point, he wonders "how there could ever be any correspondence" between him and his father, a relationship of referentiality that would authorize him to write his ethnic family story (22).

What makes "Love and Honour" particularly poignant is its carefully shaped emotional arc. Just before he sees his father destroying the manuscript of his story, Nam is optimistic about its success: My father "would read it, with his book-learned English, and he would recognise himself in a new way. He would recognise me. He would see how powerful was his experience, how valuable his suffering — how I had made it speak for more than itself. He would be pleased with me" (29). Just as the text writes into existence an exemplary ethnic text, it also destroys it — with devastating personal consequences. What Le stages, then, is the destruction of an originary narrative that would hold the interpretive key for the story as a whole. We are left with only the structures of allegorical interpretation without a solid sense of their content.

"Love and Honour" reveals what I would call the tropological nature of the ethnic story and its constituting elements. By this, I mean that narrative materials usually understood in the context of an underlying metanarrative, a commonly understood truth that corresponds with what we call Asian American identity, end up acquiring a materiality of their own through slippages of meanings and misinterpretations. Le stages this process in a scene in which Nam's father is talking to a homeless man about his son:

> 'I read his [earlier] story,' my father went on in his lilting English, 'about Vietnamese boatpeople.'…'We are Vietnamese boatpeople.'
> We stood there for a long time, the three of us, watching the flames. When I lifted my eyes it was dark.
> 'Do you have any money on you?' my father asked me in Vietnamese.
> 'Welcome to America,' the man said through his beard. (12)

Even as the father insists on a mimetic relationship between the content of one of Nam's stories and his biographical background, the invocation of a specific category — Vietnamese boatpeople — results in a curious and multiply ironic moment as the homeless man, who never hears Nam's Australian accent, misrecognizes two visitors from Australia as new immigrants to the US.

This misrecognition tellingly illustrates how *The Boat* explores the discursive limits of terms such as ethnic and Asian American/Australian. After opening with a story that destabilizes their meanings, the next story seems to mark a complete break from the last: "Cartagena" chronicles the story of a hired killer in a Colombian slum while other stories feature non-Asian characters who live in New York and Australia. Two of the other stories set in Asia — in contemporary Iran and 1945 Japan, respectively — offer a marked departure, in both tone and content, from the cultural politics of representation that subtend "Love and Honour." In "Halflead Bay," a coming-of-age story featuring a group of (white) Australian teenagers, references to Asians appear intermittently and only in passing; for example, the protagonist observes that some of the new Asian immigrants are "okay" (119), and his nemesis is rumored to have been involved in the local murder of a "Chinese poacher" (123, 142). Details such as these indicate the text's awareness of the multicultural demographics of contemporary Australia, but insofar as they remain largely superfluous details, they do not possess the sociofhistorical depth and meaning that we usually assume as critics and readers of Asian American literature, let alone articulate an antiracist politics. It is not until the final story that we return to a topic that seems more conventionally Asian American, even though the story does not depict the arrival of Vietnamese refugees in the US.

Read together, the stories in *The Boat* demonstrate a range of referential depth when it comes to aspects of Asian identity ranging from intense engagement with the cultural politics of ethnic writing in "Love and Honour" to the reduction of Asia into incidental details in "Halflead Bay" to its complete invisibility in other stories. In this context, Le cannot be accused of erasing or ignoring Asia, but nor does his writing fit into the critical expectations of Asian American literary studies. Is it possible, then, to read *The Boat* as an Asian American text? Or is this question itself limiting insofar as it seems to invite a clear-cut, yes-or-no answer? Even if we confine the discussion to the opening story, the answer is complex because of its paradoxical resonance with Asian American literary culture. Reading "Love and Honour" as Asian American literature would not require us to resort to analogy or similarity; we would not, as is often done with diasporic Asian writing from outside the US, be appropriating the text on the basis of its being close enough to Asian American experiences and therefore subsumable under the category of Asian American culture. To the contrary, "Love and Honour" is about the US. Its relationship to Asian American writing, while not seamless, seems closer than similarity.

Does it matter that Le (and Nam for that matter) is Australian? This may seem to be the issue at the heart of my (mis)reading, but it is the wrong question. The issue at stake here is not whether *The Boat* counts as Asian American literature, if by this we mean that its content sufficiently refers to the realities and experiences that we can categorize as Asian American. Such readings, however construed, are at their basis realist and ethnographic, for they assume that the representation of actually existing socio-historical conditions is the primary function of fiction. But given what I have described as the tropological character of race and Asian-ness in *The Boat*, a realist approach inevitably misses the point because it assumes a referential depth that the text denies. The real question is what does it mean to read Le's writing from the conscious position of an Asian Americanist? What does it mean to read a text whose identity is ambiguous by referencing the intellectual and political traditions of Asian American Studies? This question is not about comparing and contrasting, about what aspects of the text are American and what are Australian. It is about how the very notion of Asian American literature serves as a way of retaining social meaning even when language can no longer guarantee us access to the social, the historical, indeed the real.

Once we recognize these questions, Asian American literary studies ceases to be the site in which our reading practices intersect neatly with our political desires. It ceases to be a reliable analytical framework that enables us to grasp the realities of racialization, except by revealing the limits of our attempts to understand those conditions; instead, its provisional meanings derive from changing discursive contexts. Although it continues to evoke histories of racism and resistance, its meanings cannot be contained or resolved within those terms. It is precisely in this sense that *The Boat* performs the labor of theory by drawing our attention to the workings of language and narrative and articulating a liminal space in which it is possible to imagine the emptying out of Asian America as a meaningful category and, consequently, its abandonment. Being open to such possibilities is not the same as actively calling for such ends. It is, rather, to conceive the project of critique in its most literal, and therefore unsettlingly radical, sense. Theory is what makes us confront these apocalyptic possibilities by challenging our deepest political and intellectual commitments. It is, finally, what elicits and breaks down our resistances even as it resists itself.

Notes

I am grateful to the editors of this issue for their incisive feedback and encouragement. I especially thank Paul Lai for the generative and generous conversations that helped animate my thinking and writing, as well as Wenche Ommundsen and Wei Chi Poon for their generous assistance.

1. To be sure, neither critic restricts herself to only one of these two approaches: Koshy is interested in theorizing the social in abstract terms that take seriously the consequences of representation, while Lye's examination of form is always part of a rigorous examination of history.

2. Wong clarifies that by "Asian American" critics, she is referring to Asian Americanists rather than critics who identify ethnically or racially as Asian American.

3. Recent texts that call for increased attention to questions of literary form include collections edited by Davis and Lee, and Zhou and Najmi. For a review of these texts, see Lye's "Racial Form."

4. For more on this notion of conservation, see Lye's "Racial Form."

5. For various versions of these arguments, see the special issue of the journal *Amerasia* on "Thinking Theory in Asian American Studies," in particular the essays by Keith Osajima and Gordon H. Chang.

6. The fact that Bové is writing here about Area Studies (and Chinese Studies in particular) is especially suggestive for the present discussion given the traditionally antagonistic relationship between Area Studies and ethnic studies. Although this conflict has lessened considerably since the founding of Asian American Studies, there is no doubt that the political valences of the two fields remain rather different. While this is not the occasion to

explore these differences, I would suggest that, at least in regards to Asian American Studies, abandoning the field may well be even more agonizing because it involves (potentially) abandoning a set of deeply held political investments that the term Asian American has come to articulate, however imperfectly.

7. For a critique of biographical criticism in Asian American literary studies, see Hattori.

8. With the exception of lesbian vampires, these themes are taken up in subsequent stories in *The Boat*. In this sense, Le is foreshadowing the diverse content of this collection as well as the ways in which it consciously tries to write outside the confines of ethnic writing.

Works Cited

Bové, Paul. "Afterword. The Possibilities of Abandonment." *Modern Chinese Literary and Cultural Studies in the Age of Theory: Reimagining a Field*. Ed. Rey Chow. Durham: Duke UP, 2000. 301–315.

Chang, Gordon H. "History and Postmodernism." *Amerasia* 21:1&2 (1995): 89–93.

Chow, Rey. *The Protestant Ethnic and the Spirit of Capitalism*. New York: Columbia UP, 2002.

Chuh, Kandice. *Imagine Otherwise: On Asian Americanist Critique*. Durham: Duke UP, 2003.

Davis, Rocío G. and Sue-Im Lee, eds. *Literary Gestures: The Aesthetic Asian American Writing*. Philadelphia: Temple UP, 2006.

Day, Iyko. "Lost in Transnation: Uncovering Canada in Asian America." *Amerasia* 33.2 (2007): 67–86.

de Man, Paul. "The Resistance to Theory." *The Resistance to Theory*. Ed. Wlad Godzich. Minneapolis: U of Minnesota P, 1986. 21–26.

Department of Ethnic Studies. "A Proposal for the Establishment of the College of Third World Studies." University of California, Berkeley. 10 Sept. 1974.

Goellnicht, Donald. "Blurring Boundaries: Asian American Literature as Theory." *An Interethnic Companion to Asian American Literature*. Ed. King-kok Cheung. New York: Cambridge UP, 1997. 338–365.

Hattori, Tomo. "China Man Autoeroticism and the Remains of Asian America." *Novel* 31.2 (1998): 215–236.

Kim, Elaine H. *Asian American Literature: An Introduction to the Writings and Their Social Context*. Philadelphia: Temple UP, 1982.

Koshy, Susan. "The Fiction of Asian American Literature." *Asian American Studies: A Reader. Ed.* Jean Yu-wen and Min Song. New Brunswick: Rutgers UP, 2000. 467–496.

Le, Nam. *The Boat*. Camberwell: Penguin, 2008.

Lye, Colleen. *America's Asia: Racial Form and American Literature, 1893 –1945*. Princeton: Princeton UP, 2005.

——. "Introduction: In Dialogue with Asian American Studies." *Representations* 99.1 (2007): 1–12.

——. "Racial Form." *Representations* 104.1 (2008): 92–101.

Omatsu, Glenn. "The 'Four Prisons' and the Movements of Liberation: Asian American Activism from the 1960s to the 1990s." *Asian American Studies: A Reader*. Eds. Jean Yu-wen Shen Wu and Min Song. New Brunswick: Rutgers UP, 2000. 164–198.

Osajima, Keith. "Postmodern Possibilities: Theoretical and Political Directions for Asian American Studies." *Amerasia* 21:1&2 (1995): 79–87.

Sumida, Stephen H. "Centers without Margins: Responses to Centrism in Asian American Literature." *American Literature* 66 (1994): 803–815.

Wiegman, Robyn. "On Being in Time with Feminism." *MLQ: Modern Language Quarterly* 65.1 (2004): 161–176.

Wong, Sau-ling Cynthia. *Reading Asian American Literature: From Necessity to Extravagance*. Princeton: Princeton UP, 1993.

Zhou, Xiaojing and Samina Najmi. *Form and Transformation in Asian American Literature*. Seattle: U of Washington P, 2005.

8

Asian Amcrican Poetry in the First Decade of the 2000s
新千年第一个十年的美国亚裔诗歌

Timothy Yu

评论家简介

余·蒂莫西（Timothy Yu），美国斯坦福大学英美文学博士，现为美国威斯康星大学麦迪逊分校英语系和美国亚裔研究中心的副教授。研究领域包括美国现当代文学、当代诗歌、美国亚裔文学与文化、先锋性研究、美国文学中的种族研究、离散研究等。专著有《种族与先锋：1965 年以来实验性的美国亚裔诗歌》（*Race and the Avant-Garde: Experimental and Asian American Poetry Since 1965*，2009），荣获 2009 年美国亚裔研究协会文学研究图书奖；除本书收录的论文，其他代表性论文有《东方城市与后现代未来：裸体午餐、银翼杀手与神经漫游者》，发表于《美国多种族文学》（"Oriental Cities, Postmodern Futures: Naked Lunch, Blade Runner, and Neuromancer," *MELUS*, 2008）;《语言诗歌与美国亚裔诗歌的形式与身份》，发表于《当代文学》（"Form and Identity in Language Poetry and Asian American Poetry," *Contemporary Literature*, 2000）等。

文章简介

　　美国亚裔诗歌创作经过几代人的努力，在新千年呈现出蓬勃发展的态势：重要诗人的创作不断涌现而且新人辈出；但相对于美国亚裔文学其他体裁的研究，美国亚裔诗歌研究一直处于边缘地带。评论家余·蒂莫西撰写此文的目的就在于呈现美国亚裔诗歌在美国亚裔文学及美国文学中正在崛起的态势，从而引起学界对美国亚裔诗歌研究的更多关注。文章通过分析诗歌创作的社会、历史、文学背景，深入评析自 20 世纪 80 年代以来美国亚裔诗歌创作中重要诗人的创作特色；同时通过讨论近十年内重要新兴诗人的创作，对亚裔诗歌在新千年的创作特点及发展趋势做出展望。文章一方面在历史维度上总结美国亚裔诗歌代表诗人在不同时期的创作特征，体现亚裔诗歌的传统流变；另一方面在参照美国亚裔族群内部人口结构不断变化的社会背景下，介绍来自亚裔不同族群的新诗人与新的创作手法，展现出亚裔诗歌内部多元种族、多元语言与多元文化的特征。本文以钩沉历史、评析当下、预估未来的论证层次全面而深入地展现了美国亚裔诗歌发展的全貌，为美国亚裔诗歌研究提供了重要参考。

文章出处：*Contemporary Literature,* vol. 52, no.4, 2011, pp. 818-851.

Asian American Poetry in the First Decade of the 2000s

Timothy Yu

At the start of the twenty-first century, Asian American poetry finds itself in a curious position. From one perspective, it is a mature and well-established literature that has produced several generations' worth of major writers since the 1970s, from Lawson Fusao Inada to Li-Young Lee, from Janice Mirikitani to Myung Mi Kim. Over the past two decades, Asian American poets have been widely anthologized, published by small and mainstream presses alike, and recognized with major awards. Younger Asian American writers continue to thrive, form new communities, and push the boundaries set by their predecessors. But from another perspective, Asian American poetry continues to be marginal. Even among readers and critics of Asian American literature, poetry still receives far less attention than novels or prose memoirs. The first book-length studies of the field are only now beginning to be published. Journals, presses, and institutions devoted to Asian American poetry — with a few notable exceptions — have been ephemeral. Even as the ranks of Asian American poets become more numerous and more diverse, there seems to be increasingly less agreement about what the category of "Asian American poetry" might mean (any poetry by an Asian American? poetry with recognizably Asian American content?), with some readers suggesting that the label may be growing less coherent and relevant as time goes on. My goal in this essay will be to confront these questions about the place of Asian American poetry by surveying its development in the first decade of the twenty-first century. While an exhaustive account of Asian American poetic production in the past ten years is not possible here (the sheer quantity of material is itself a sign of Asian American poetry's vitality), I do hope to identify some major authors and trends that situate twenty-first-century Asian American poetry with regard to its history and its literary and social context, and that may provide some guide to where it may go in the future.

I begin by examining the ongoing careers of four major poets who established their reputations in the 1980s and 1990s: Li-Young Lee, John Yau, Mei-mei Berssenbrugge, and Myung Mi Kim. All have continued to publish actively and even reach new heights of prominence in the first decade of the 2000s, and each represents a particular tendency or strain within Asian American poetry at the turn of the century. It is Kim's work, however, that may have been the most influential in setting the direction of Asian American poetry of the past decade. That direction, I suggest, combines the engagement with history and politics that has traditionally characterized Asian American poetry with a burrowing into language, exploring both its limits and its creative potential in poetic styles influenced by experimental modes within American poetry. The result is a poetry that is not always explicitly marked by Asian American sites or subjects, but that clearly emerges from the context of race and ethnicity within which the Asian American author is situated. I move to a discussion of three distinctive Asian American poets who have emerged in the last decade: Linh Dinh, Barbara Jane Reyes, and Cathy Park Hong. These writers' multilingual and multicultural sensibilities problematize the position of the Asian American writer but also create reading positions that can be seen as analogies of Asian American subjectivity. This work is part of several larger trends within Asian American poetry — trends that echo and vary larger trends within contemporary American poetry: language-centered experimentation; formalism and postconfessional lyric; and the sampling and remixing of popular culture. These aesthetic trends unfold against a backdrop of rapid demographic change in the Asian American population, with a particular emergence of South and Southeast Asian American poets; the growth of new genres of Asian American poetry; and a changing institutional context for Asian American writers. Finally, I will examine the long-delayed emergence of a significant critical discourse around Asian American poetry in the past decade, with the publication of the first book-length studies of Asian American poetry and increased academic attention to the topic.

To understand where Asian American poetry found itself at the close of the twentieth century, it's helpful to review the development of Asian American poetry over the preceding three decades.[1] The Asian American movement of the late 1960s and 1970s brought to prominence poets like Lawson Fusao Inada and Janice Mirikitani, whose direct engagement with politics and history resonated with the era's political activism. The 1980s saw a turn away from political polemic toward autobiographical lyrics and more introspective, skeptical modes, marked by the main-stream successes of poets like Cathy Song, Marilyn Chin, David Mura, and Li-Young Lee and culminating in Garrett Hongo's 1993 anthology *The Open Boat: Poems from Asian America*. Existing alongside this lyric tendency, but receiving relatively little attention from readers until the 1990s, was a more experimental strain focused on fragmentation, linguistic exploration,

---

1 This narrative of Asian American poetry since the 1970s is developed in more detail in my *Race and the Avant-Garde: Experimental and Asian American Poetry since 1965.*

and cultural hybridity, epitomized by the work of writers like Theresa Hak Kyung Cha, John Yau, Mei-mei Berssenbrugge, and Myung Mi Kim. By the end of the 1990s, these latter writers appeared to be in ascendance, particularly among academic readers, who found their poems amenable to current theoretical and critical models. The claim by Brian Kim Stefans in his 2002 essay "Remote Parsee: An Alternative Grammar of Asian North American Poetry" that Yau and Berssenbrugge were "the two most visible writers of Asian descent in the States" (45) might have sounded a bit grand at the time, but his sense of their centrality has been confirmed by their increasing prominence over the course of the past decade.

This trend toward a greater mainstreaming of more "experimental" modes reflects larger developments within American poetry during the 1990s. In the wake of the debates around the rise of language poetry in the 1980s, "experimental" became a term applied to an increasingly wide range of poetic practices that diverged from the first-person, postconfessional lyric by foregrounding, to varying degrees, poetic form. This shift away from the first-person lyric mode posed a particularly complex challenge for Asian American poetics, which had moved from using politics and history as its ground in the 1970s to using the autobiographical speaker as the locus of Asian American identification. If experimental writing techniques disrupted the unity or centrality of that subject position, what then would remain to mark the work as Asian American?

That last question might well be asked of some of the recent poetry of Li-Young Lee, who came to prominence with his 1986 book *Rose* and his 1990 collection *The City in Which I Love You*, and who has continued to be one of the most widely read, discussed, and anthologized Asian American poets. Lee's work would seem to fall squarely into the paradigm of the autobiographical lyric mode; his writing dwells consistently, even obsessively, on his own experience and family history, particularly on the figure of his father. In Lee's most powerful poems, personal experience resonates deeply with issues of race and history, as in "Persimmons," from *Rose*, when a remembered corrective from a white teacher about pronunciation opens up into memories of the speaker's father and into an erotically charged scene of teaching between the speaker and his wife. In "The Cleaving," from *The City in Which I Love You*, a visit to a Chinatown butcher shop sparks a wide-ranging meditation on race, immigration, sexuality, and mortality.

The decade that elapsed between *The City in Which I Love You* and Lee's next collection, *Book of My Nights* (2001), saw a shift in Lee's work toward greater abstraction, linked to a deepening engagement with spiritual and existential themes. There are still many poems of the father, but the details of personal history that marked Lee's earlier collection are sparser, the tone of introspection and prayerful meditation stronger, the theme of mortality more prominent. In "Night Mirror," the poet addresses himself, seeking to soothe existential fears:

> Li-Young, don't feel lonely
> when you look up
> into great night ....
> ....
> And don't be afraid
> when, eyes closed, you look inside you
> and find night ...

(19)

The poem's sensuousness is not that of remembered fruit or the lover's skin, but the metaphorical "unequaled perfume of your dying" (20).

The title of Lee's most recent book, *Behind My Eyes* (2008), would seem to reinforce this introspective turn in his work. But *Behind My Eyes* also marks a striking departure for Lee; instead of focusing on fathers and sons, many of these poems place the speaker in dialogue with a female interlocutor. There's a renewed emphasis on the speaker's relationship with his wife, as in the wryly titled "Virtues of the Boring Husband," although there is less of the eroticism that characterizes Lee's earlier work. Although explicitly Asian American themes had largely disappeared from *Book of My Nights*, they return here in two poems, "Self-Help for Fellow Refugees" and "Immigrant Blues," that display a combination of tender humor and sharp irony reminiscent of Marilyn Chin's work. "Self-Help" suggests that "it's probably best to dress in plain clothes / when you arrive in the United States,/and try not to talk too loud" (16), while "Immigrant Blues" satirizes scholarship by imagining an "old story" called "Survival Strategies/and the Melancholy of Racial Assimilation" (28).

But the overall thrust of *Behind My Eyes* is toward a broader spirituality. The book contains more detailed biblical imagery than any of Lee's previous collections, extending Lee's engagement with the Judeo-Christian God. At times Lee achieves a minimalism that echoes the work of a poet like Robert Creeley: "She opens her eyes/and I see.... Do you love me? she asks/I love you, / she answers" (101). Perhaps it is premature to talk of a "late" phase in Lee's career, but *Behind My Eyes* has precisely such an elegiac, even ascetic tone, as if it were pulling away from the earthy and worldly preoccupations with body, race, and history of Lee's earlier work toward a more austere realm.

Austerity of a vastly different kind is evident in the ongoing oeuvre of Mei-mei Berssenbrugge, who seems less a minimalist than a maximalist, known for her long lines requiring landscape-style printing to accommodate them. But Berssenbrugge's long lines are not the sprawling catalogs of a Whitman or a Ginsberg. Instead, her diction tends toward philosophical abstraction, creating a self-reflexive discourse that explores the workings of description, metaphor, and consciousness itself. Berssenbrugge's interest in abstraction can be linked to her deep engagement with the visual arts, most evident in her collaborations with artists such as Kiki Smith and Richard Tuttle.

Berssenbrugge's abstraction might make her seem remote from the political and historical concerns of much Asian American writing, but in fact Berssenbrugge was closely associated with the Asian American movement of the 1970s. Through the 1980s and 1990s, Berssenbrugge maintained a small but devoted critical following, particularly for her exploration of emotion and her formal experimentation. Although poems like "Tan Tien" and "Chinese Space" approached Chineseness through architectural metaphors, critics more frequently engaged with poems like "Empathy" and "The Four Year Old Girl," with their meticulous examinations of the language of thought and affect ("This state of confusion is never made comprehensible by being given a plot" [49]) or of science and medicine ("She's inspired to change the genotype, because the cell's memory outlives the cell" [83]). Perhaps for this reason, Berssenbrugge was read more frequently as an experimental writer than an Asian American one, and she did not receive significant attention from Asian Americanist critics until the later 1990s.

In 2006, the publication of a volume of selected poems, the wittily titled *I Love Artists*, provided an opportunity for a reevaluation of Berssenbrugge's career. Her poems of the past decade make up the last third of the volume, and they mark a notable change in her style — a shift from a poetry of lines to one of sentences. In these recent poems, sentences do not spill over lines but are separated from one another by a break, making the poem feel less dense, its tone more casual. The voice of the poems seems more personal, with a more liberal use of the first person and more conversational diction: "I'm so pleased to be friends with Maryanne, though I don't understand how she has time for me, with her many friends" (110). Perhaps as a result, we see a reassertion of the ethnically marked themes of some of her earlier work, particularly in a poem like "Nest," which reflects on the speaker's "mother tongue, Chinese" (112). Language learning, and the loss of the "mother tongue," is a frequent theme in Asian American poetry, but in her typical style, Berssenbrugge turns the mother tongue into a physical space, as her speaker describes being "inserted into it" and "filling it with intentions" (112), then leaving it as one would move from one house to another: "Change of mother tongue between us activates an immunity, margin where dwelling and travel are not distinct" (113). And over the past decade,

Asian Americanist critics have taken up Berssenbrugge's work, becoming the dominant voices in discussions of her poetry.

A third major poet who has continued to publish actively over the past decade is John Yau, who published his first collection in 1976 and has enjoyed a prolific career as a poet and art critic. Through much of his early career, Yau was read primarily in avant-garde circles, as a protégé of John Ashbery, but by the 1990s had become widely read and discussed by Asian Americanist critics, who were compelled by his remixes of Hollywood cliché s and Asian stereotypes, his skepticism toward autobiography, and the surprising lyricism within his surrealist verve. Since 2000, Yau has published no fewer than five collections; the folding of his longtime publisher, Black Sparrow Press, may ironically have led to even greater prominence for Yau, as his work was picked up by Penguin Poets, which published *Borrowed Love Poems* (2002) and *Paradiso Diaspora* (2006). Yau's most significant point of contact with younger writers may be his facility with the materials of popular culture, particularly in its most apparently degraded or commodified forms (the monster movie, the Charlie Chan film); the recombinatory power of these massculture tropes serves as a model for Yau's formal experiments with collage, repetition and variation, and hybridization.

The very title *Borrowed Love Poems* suggests that the derivative status of popular culture is also characteristic of lyric poetry itself. After all, the love poems of Petrarch and Shakespeare treat the tropes of love poetry as inherited clichés; centuries later, Yau suggests, any poem's material can only be "borrowed," as the poet-lover follows "the claw marks of those/who preceded us across this burning floor" (131). But the fact that *Borrowed Love Poems* contains some of the most compelling lyrics of Yau's career suggests that this skepticism toward originality is no barrier to creativity, subjectivity, or expression — indeed, repetition may be the ground from which subjectivity emerges.

The ability of Hollywood continually to reanimate seemingly dead tropes is Yau's model here — and no genre shows that ability more vividly than the monster movie, which figures centrally in *Borrowed Love Poems*. "I was a poet in the house of Frankenstein," Yau declares in the title of one poem; assembled out of reclaimed parts to be given life, the Frankensteinian monster provides an ideal image for Yau's poetic method. And here, remarkably enough, Yau is able to claim a place for the Asian American that is not marginal, but culturally central. Yau's interest in actors like Peter Lorre and Boris Karloff — who played both monstrous figures (Lorre as a serial killer in *M*, Karloff as Frankenstein's monster) and Asians (Lorre as the Charlie Chan — like detective Mr. Moto, Karloff as Fu Manchu and as the detective Mr. Wong) — taps into the way the figure of the Asian possesses a distinctive cultural mutability, capable of being inhabited by white actors like Lorre and Karloff and perilously (but powerfully) close to the hybrid figure of the monster.

The poems in *Borrowed Love Poems* that focus on Karloff and Lorre (an extension of the Lorre poems found in Yau's 1996 collection *Forbidden Entries*) do not speak for a subjectivity that lurks "behind" these actors' roles. Instead, Yau's poems blur the line between actor and role; movies, in the title of another one of Yau's poems, become "a form of reincarnation," in which an actor like Karloff experiences "being Chinese on more than one occasion" (31). By giving these personae substance — as Karloff remarks, "I tried to tell them that my real name was Mr. Wong" (34) — Yau diverges from traditional critiques of yellowface acting, which call attention to the gap between the white actor and a "real" Asian body. Instead, Yau uses the Asian on film as a figure for the constructedness of all subjectivity, echoing a line from his early poem "Toy Trucks and Fried Rice": "His father also told him that Indians were the only true Americans and everyone else was a fake" (*Radiant Silhouette* 69). Yau is thus skeptical of claims for Asian American identity that are grounded in autobiography; but rather than transcending race, Yau's work places it front and center, remixing Asian signifiers as a means of creating new speaking positions.

Although the career of Myung Mi Kim has been the shortest of the poets I have discussed thus far — her first book, *Under Flag*, appeared in 1991 — she has had perhaps the most significant influence on the work of younger Asian American writers, blending techniques drawn from Language writing with Asian American writing's historical concerns with migration, imperialism, war, and politics. Kim's body of work is grounded in her experience as a Korean immigrant, but her writing is not conventionally autobiographical; instead, Kim follows the example of another Korean American writer, Theresa Hak Kyung Cha, in making language itself the site of her poetry's drama. Early poems such as "Into Such Assembly" approach migration and citizenship through scenes of language learning, asking, "Who is mother tongue, who is father country?" (*Under Flag* 29). Kim's emphasis on the materiality of language resonates with the concerns of the Language writers, with whom she has been loosely identified; her use of the fragment and the page as a visual space is reminiscent of the work of Susan Howe, and Kim now teaches in the Poetics Program at SUNY-Buffalo, as Howe once did.

In her work of the past decade, collected in *Commons* (2002) and *Penury* (2009), Kim has sharpened and broadened her political critiques in response to an evolving landscape of global capitalism, disaster, terror, and violence. We might imagine that the title *Commons* evokes the possibility of a shared space represented by language, but the text portrays language as a site of constant struggle for domination and survival. Images of dissection — of pigs, dogs, human bodies — recur throughout the book and are horrifically echoed in an account of a young girl at Hiroshima whose "insides had imploded" (50). The desire to know and describe the "insides" of things may well be an instrumental and destructive one, part of the "organizing myth of comprehensive knowledge" (44) that can be turned to the ends of power: "The fundamental tenet of all military geography is that every feature of the visible world possesses actual or potential military significance" (32).

Against such instrumentalist views of language, Kim seeks an alternate mapping that dwells on the materiality and opacity of words and objects, following idiosyncratic rather than systematic links: "Those which are of foreign origin. Those which are of forgotten sources" (4). In contrast to the invasive language of dissection, Kim offers the language of agriculture and building, seeking to "Gently, gently level the ground" (7). The aim is not simply offering an alternative narrative or analysis, but "Speaking and placing the speaking," remaining attentive to the location and context of any act of speech. It's because of this awareness of location that Kim's writing does not ascend into pure abstraction or lose its moorings in Asian American discourse. Korean characters and phonemes appear throughout the book, and the poem "Siege Document" offers two competing transliterations of a Korean text — all disruptions of the unquestioned monolingualism of American literature that register the location of Kim's poetic critique.

Penury, Kim's most recent book, is even more pointed in its critique of a post–9/11 world, aimed with a new directness at a world constructed "for the good of the very few and the suffering of a great many" (46). In this new work, Kim seems increasingly willing to speak in a broader, more public idiom, placing her poetry in a present-day context of "increased chatter," filled with phrases like "border security operation," "scorched earth tactics," and "bunker buster bomb." Kim takes this bureaucratized language of violence head-on, declaring that a "sameness of language" produces a "sameness of sentiment and thought" (27). The central section of the book, a poem "*for six multilingual voices*," suggests the possibility of breaking up this sameness through an interplay of different voices and languages, a structure that allows historical experiences to be heard without forcing them into a predetermined narrative or framework. The "level ground" imagined in *Commons* reappears in the later sections of *Penury*, which use nature imagery, "tastes of granite and the rapids" (91), to suggest the creative possibilities of linguistic border-crossing. The collection's final poem imagines a "recitation of acacias," as if poetry could call nature into being; Kim's scrupulous placing of speaking leads to a speaking of place, a new terrain emerging from a fractured language.

The ongoing work of poets like Lee, Berssenbrugge, Yau, and Kim brings a number of major themes within Asian American poetry forward into the twenty-first century. In Lee (and, to a lesser degree, Berssenbrugge), we can see the continuing influence of the postconfessional autobiographical mode, but we also see a desire to make the first person speak within a broader context — of spirituality, philosophy, or politics. Yau provides a counterweight to the autobiographical mode, adopting personae that highlight the constructed nature of subjectivity; his work also reminds us that popular culture continues to be a major terrain of cultural and political struggle for Asian Americans. Finally, Kim's incisive investigations of language are framed by efforts to place those investigations within political, social, and cultural contexts.

How, if at all, have newer Asian American poets followed these trends? This question brings me to the work of Asian American writers who have emerged since 2000. Many continue to engage with issues and themes similar to those of their predecessors, but they also bring distinctive new voices and perspectives that reflect both the changing demographics of Asian America and shifting aesthetic trends within American poetry more broadly.

One of the most distinctive voices to emerge over the past decade is that of Linh Dinh, a Vietnamese American writer whose prolific output has included five books of poetry and two books of short stories since 2000. Linh Dinh came to the U.S. from Vietnam in 1975 ("Linh Dinh"). His first book of poems, *All Around What Empties Out* (2003), registers the experiences of war and migration, but in oblique and unexpected ways: a speaker apostrophizes his bed as "the leaky boat on the South China Sea fleeing / Ho Chi Minh City" (2), and the poem "O Hanoi" narrates the speaker's history through a series of implausible locations: "We lived in the old quarters, on Potato Street, / Then Coffin Street, then Clown Street, / Then Teleprompter Street" (6). But traumatic experience is much more likely to erupt in decontextualized images of violence:

"Oh great," she yells, "a fox hole!" and jumps right in. And just in time, too, because a shell immediately explodes a few feet away....She is bunched up like a mummy, but not too uncomfortable, a woman in the flush of youth squatting in a ready-made fox hole.

("The Fox Hole" 16)

I think "vesicle" is the most beautiful word in the English language. He was lying face down, his shirt burnt off, back steaming. I myself was bleeding. There was a harvest of vesicles on his back. His body wept. "Yaw" may be the ugliest. Don't say, "The bullet yawed inside the body." Say, "The bullet danced inside the body."

("The Most Beautiful Word" 17)

But perhaps the most distinctive element of Linh Dinh's work is his Rabelaisian obsession with the grotesque human body, its organs, orifices, and emissions. The cover of *All Around What Empties Out* features the outline of a toilet seat; a speaker addresses a bed as "sentimental sponge" and "Witness to all my horrors, my Valdez spills" (2); the poem "All Around What Empties Out" is an ode to the speaker 's perineum (10); and "Motate" begins with a "General emission from all orifices" (5). Linh Dinh's visceral, discomfiting diction gives his work a shocking immediacy even as it courts disgust.

It's not just Linh Dinh's content but his tone that seizes the reader's attention, from the phatic expressions in *All Around What Empties Out* ("Whoaaaa!!! Get away from me!!!"; "Arrrghhh!!!"; "Waaa!!!!!"; "Ha ha ha!!!!" [21]) to the Internetsourced language of his most recent book, *Some Kind of Cheese Orgy* ("SEAN AVERY IS / NOW AN EVEN BIGGER DICK. Who's got the bigger / Dick? Chris Brown or Neyo? My senator is a bigger / Dick than your senator. How can I get a bigger dick / (Naturally)?" [35]). Linh Dinh's sampling of materials from popular culture may echo Yau, but his collages of online material and his harnessing of crude, offensive, in-your-face discourse make his work even more strongly reminiscent of Flarf, a movement with which he has sometimes been loosely associated. Flarf, which has gained significant attention and notoriety over the past decade, collages language generated from Google searches to create poems that consciously court "bad taste" or use degraded, offensive, or unpoetic language.[1] Linh Dinh's work is not Flarf in the strictest sense — he often seems to be imitating rather than actually quoting online discourse, and such poems make up only part of his oeuvre — but he very much partakes of the irreverent, provocative sensibility of Flarf.

If Linh Dinh's work engages Asian American politics, it does so in ways that poets of earlier generations might well not recognize. There are no political polemics or pieties in his work; indeed, it's difficult to identify any stable political position within Linh Dinh's work at all. He is instead a satirist, at times possessed by a gleeful misanthropy:

> Because of the chemical phthalate in plastic, dicks
> Are shrinking — tell me all about it — sperm counts
> Are way down, but not low enough, unfortunately,
> To slow down this full-throttle-ahead fuck boat,
> About to burn, capsize and sink.

(Jam Alerts 57)

---

1 A full discussion of Flarf is beyond the scope of this essay; its best-known practitioners include K. Silem Mohammad, Michael Magee, Katie Degentesh, Gary Sullivan, Drew Gardner, and Nada Gordon. For an account of the history of the movement, see Sullivan.

At the same time, Linh Dinh is not a borrower of personae like Yau; the plain diction and visceral immediacy of his voice are consistent and immediately recognizable throughout his work. Rather than arranging and mixing cultural references in controlled fashion, as Yau does, Linh Dinh seems (in the spirit of Flarf) to amplify them, drawing on their raw power.

Perhaps what marks Linh Dinh most of all as a twenty-firstcentury American poet is that his deepest obsession is not with the body, or with popular culture, but with language itself, as evidenced in *Some Kind of Cheese Orgy*. In a surprising echo of Myung Mi Kim's engagements with Korean, Linh Dinh includes several poems in the later part of the book that "translate" or "explain" various Vietnamese words and concepts — with withering irony:

Cú't means shit. Vietnamese already see turds often, so they don't need to be reminded, no voided victual after every other word. *Ngu nhu cú't* means stupid as shit. *Mày chẳng biết cái đéo gì* means You don't know fuck, as opposed to You don't know shit.

(95)

These "translations" hover uneasily between patient explanation and an assault on the reader. Linh Dinh, like Berssenbrugge and Kim, registers the violently fractured and unequal terrain crossed by any act of translation, even as translation is an explosively creative act:

Translation, like jazz, is a form of revenge.

Translation, like jazz, is a tool of imperialism.

Translation, like jazz, is an improvised explosive device.

(98)

The linking of translation to jazz offers a surprising resonance with another pioneer of Asian American poetry, Lawson Fusao Inada, whose love of jazz has long shaped the forms of his poetry, marking a point of contact with American culture through an African American vernacular form. But the effect of these acts of translation differs sharply from that seen in the work of a writer like Kim. If Kim's use of language is centripetal, trying to pull back commodified and bureaucratized uses of languages into a local, human context, Linh Dinh's language is centrifugal, exploding outward to implicate the reader wherever that reader might be: "That's no mirror, dude, that's a translation" (97).

If twenty-first-century Asian American writing like Linh Dinh's seems to explode the idea of any fixed location for Asian American poetry, that may be because the context of Asian American writing has become increasingly multicultural and multiethnic. If it was ever possible to think of Asian American identity as monolithic or indivisible, existing in isolation from other groups, the new century, with its new migration patterns, shifting coalitions, and global cities, has made such essentialist thinking about Asian Americanness unimaginable. These complex contexts are hardly new — the Asian American movement of the 1970s took place against the backdrop of a multiracial struggle for civil rights and global critiques of imperialism — but twenty-first-century Asian American poets increasingly recognize a multicultural America as the new normal, even as they map the fissures, conflicts, and inequalities that characterize this diverse social landscape.

The urban spaces of California, long seen as epicenters of the Asian American community, provide a window into the multiracial America of the twenty-first century; recent poetry suggests to us what those spaces look like when viewed from an Asian American perspective and navigated by an Asian American body. Barbara Jane Reyes's *Poeta en San Francisco,* winner of the 2005 James Laughlin Award from the Academy of American Poets and one of the more widely discussed books of the past decade, provides a kaleidoscopic, multilingual portrait of urban life in San Francisco, shot through with the sharp critical perspective of a Filipina American writer. The collection's title, echoing Federico García Lorca's *Poeta en Nueva York*, places it in a transnational tradition of urban portraiture and critique while calling attention to the very different context that lies behind Reyes's work: the history of Spanish colonization that links the Americas and Asia, and the history of American imperialism that conditions the Filipina poet's presence in San Francisco.

The first section of *Poeta en San Francisco* is a vivid and visceral evocation of the experience of walking through San Francisco's streets — but this *flâneuse* is all too aware of the charged terrain she traverses. The section's title, "orient," ironically "orients" us to the city by showing how San Francisco is haunted by "the Orient" — at least from the perspective of the "oriental" body that traverses it:

> en esta ciudad, where homeless 'nam vets
> wave old glory and pots for spare change;
> she grows weary of the daily routine:
>
> fuckinjapgobacktochina!
> allthemfuckingooknamessoundthesame!
>
> and especially:
> iwasstationedatsubicbay.

(21)

The Filipina American walking through the streets of San Francisco experiences racist language as a physical assault, each shouted line becoming a single, attacking object. But the final line, with its reference to the Subic Bay U.S. naval base in the Philippines, opens up this racist encounter to reveal its historical, global context: this white-Asian confrontation does not take place in a vacuum, but in a history of war and imperialism that implicates both the white Vietnam veteran and the Filipina American passerby.

The colonial history that structures daily encounters on the streets of San Francisco is embedded in language itself, Reyes suggests in the book's second section, "dis ● orient." Reyes widens the critical frame around such urban encounters in part by challenging the centrality of English. *Poeta en San Francisco*, of course, already signals a bilingual space of Spanish and English; the opening poems of "dis ● orient" add Tagalog to this mix, represented through the precolonial Baybayin script. By evoking this terrain of linguistic difference, Reyes links the colonial impulse to linguistic and literary projects of "exploration," ironically quoting the slogan of Ezra Pound: "(nū, nyū) / adj. // *as in, make it*" (43). Throughout the twentieth century, where writers found the "new" was often through appropriations of other cultures: "what pound appropriation of the ancient oriental" (43). Reyes's inclusion of Baybayin both alludes to this appropriation and disrupts it, thematizing the white, male writer-explorer's desire for the "foreign" while refusing to translate the Tagalog script, making it a site of resistance to the monolingual Anglophone reader. Reyes's assertion of the interface between language, race, and the body — "what avant garde experiment carves her lover's flesh" (43) — resonates with the twenty-first-century Asian American writing of Myung Mi Kim and Linh Dinh, positing language itself as a possible site of intervention into the physical violence of racism and imperialism.

The book's final section, "re ● orient," returns to a newly opened-up urban space, in which the female speaker seems newly capable of replying to the binaries that define her: "today i am through with your surface acts of / contrition, i am through witnessing your mimicry / of prescribed other, your fervor for the part" (83). Reyes turns the tables on the white "explorer" by sardonically diagnosing the "Asiaphile," from the "non-Asian male who prefers Asian women" to the "white western male with a pathological, sexual obsession with Asians and their cultures" (84). And Tagalog retains a central place, with entire poems offered in untranslated Tagalog and English-language poems given Tagalog titles. This is a reimagined urban and linguistic landscape, reclaimed and reconstructed by the female poet: "one day she will build a temple from detritus, dust of your crumbling empires' edicts;…she will melt down your weapons, forge her own gods, and adorn her own body….it is for no glory, no father, no doctrine" (94).

Part of the power of *Poeta en San Francisco* comes from its insistence on the integrity of the different languages that underlie Filipina/o American history. Cathy Park Hong's *Dance Dance Revolution,* in contrast, uses linguistic hybridization as a metaphor for Asian American experience. Much of the book is written in an invented dialect that is the lingua franca of "the Desert," a Las Vegas-like city-state filled with "state-of-the-art hotels modeled after the world's greatest cities" (20). This dialect is described as "an amalgam of some three hundred languages" that still employs "the inner structures of English grammar" (19); the result is a creole that draws from Caribbean and Shakespearean English, echoing the dialect poems of Claude McKay, John Berryman's *Dream Songs,* and Hawaiian pidgin, with a little Spanish and Latin thrown in:

> …I's born en first day o unrest …
> Huzza de students who fightim plisboi patos!
> En gangrene smoke, youngins t'rew butane Colas,
> chanted poor ole cantanka Rhee to step down…he did!
> Chased out en a perma holiday,
> Hawaii him Elba …
>
> (41; ellipses in orig.)

The book's main speaker is a Desert tour guide, a woman from South Korea who is described as a leader of the 1980 Kwangju uprising against the rule of Chun Doo-hwan. The poems written in the guide's voice are framed by commentary in Standard English by "the Historian," a young Korean American woman researching the Kwangju revolt.

Hong's alternate-reality premise (the events of the book are said to take place in 2016) provides an ingenious means of exploring Asian Americans' complexly mediated relationship with their history. The text provides a compact narration of the events of the Kwangju uprising and the context of Korean history that surrounds it, but it provides access to those events only at a remove, through the filter of a hybridized language. In contrast to Reyes, whose use of Tagalog suggests the possibility of a more direct access to Filipino culture, Hong's invented dialect dramatizes the many layers through which the Korean American narrator must struggle to grasp Korean history. The guide is a "double migrant" who is "Ceded from Koryo, ceded from /Merikka" (26), occupying a liminal space. She comes from a collaborationist family (her grandfather is described as having collaborated with the Japanese, while her father ensures his own survival by becoming a tool of the U.S. army), and the Desert itself is a space riven by economic and political conflict.

But the brilliance of Hong's conceit emerges in the power and creativity of the guide's language. While the Historian's narration appears in a restrained Standard English that struggles for self-awareness, the guide's lively, freewheeling speech forces our attention to the texture of language, refuting any conception of linguistic transparency. Without engaging an Asian language directly, Hong creates a sense of linguistic foreignness that powerfully allegorizes the Asian American perspective on language, from the accented speech of the immigrant to the alienated relationship of American-born Asians to their parents' language.[1] We might say that the invented dialect of *Dance Dance Revolution* forces the reader into an Asian American reading position, in which the reader approaches her "native" language from an angle, guided by a distinctive history.

Reyes's and Hong's foregrounding of language as the terrain of Asian American identity points toward a strain of language-centered experimentation within Asian American poetry, one whose prominence has only increased over the past decade. Again, Myung Mi Kim, strongly influenced by Language writing, is perhaps the most prominent exponent of this experimental mode, but she is certainly not alone.

The poet Tan Lin has produced some of the boldest, and at times most enigmatic, innovative work within Asian American writing. His first collection, *Lotion Bullwhip Giraffe*, was published by the avant-garde Sun & Moon Press in 1996. Since 2000, he has published *BlipSoak 01* (2003) and *Seven Controlled Vocabularies and Obituary 2004, The Joy of Cooking* (2010), among other works. As Brian Kim Stefans notes in "Streaming Poetry," over the past decade, Lin has eschewed the "linguistic difficulty" of the avant-garde in favor of an aesthetic of "boredom" or "relax-ation," establishing in his work "a tone of disinterest while never failing to follow the course of his own mind." "The beautiful book," Lin writes in the preface to *BlipSoak 01*, "should not be read but merely looked at … Poems should be uninteresting and non-metaphorical enough to be listened to in passing or while 'thinking of something else'" (11, 13). This pursuit of the uninteresting has led Lin, like a number of other writers, to the use of found language, from instruction manuals to indexes to cookbooks — "ambient" language that surrounds us constantly but that we take in only at a glance or in passing. In an interview 3. with the Poetry Foundation's *Harriet* blog, Lin describes *Seven Controlled Vocabularies* as a "bibliographic 'collection' whose general subject is reading and its objects," in which text and image are "captured/reproduced in

---

1 Hong's invented dialect might be seen as a form of what Evelyn Nien-Ming Ch'ien calls "weird English," a rule-bending use of language that "revives the aesthetic experimental potential of English" by "see[ing] through the eyes of foreign speakers and hear[ing] through their transcriptions of English a different way of reproducing meaning" (6 – 7).

numerous ways, with…scanning, digital photography of printed book pages, retyping of printed matter, reading and re-reading, bibliographic citation, footnoting, indexing, and self-plagiarism of earlier sources." But rather than the jagged collages characteristic of Linh Dinh's work, Lin's work obscures sources to create an apparently seamless surface, presenting its images and text as objects to be looked at.

Lin's work makes contact with Asian American writing in its awareness of the ways seemingly neutral systems of classification can structure and be structured by race, nation, and culture. The cover of the Wesleyan edition of *Seven Controlled Vocabularies* contains what appears to be a Library of Congress classification for the book — text that is usually hidden in small print alongside a book's copyright information and rarely noticed by readers. The first subject heading given for the book is "China — poetry." In what sense should *Seven Controlled Vocabularies* be classified under "China — poetry"? Lin doesn't answer that question but does include an anecdote in which the narrator describes buying "his first Chinese cookbook" (perhaps *How to Eat and Cook in Chinese*, cited a few pages later) but never using it because "the recipes did not seem at all Chinese … The language was arch, old-fashioned, colonial and depressing … The language of true Chinese is very spare and very very thin, just like a recipe or a very fine novel" (114). When the narrator repeats a piece of wisdom from the cookbook — "cornstarch is the glue that holds all Chinese food together" — to his mother,

> she just laughed and laughed and said:
>
> That is very true
>
> OR:
>
> That is a load of nonsense (hoo sha ba dao)
>
> (114)

In an interview with *BOMB* magazine, Lin remarks on the "extreme relevance" of the cookbook — in particular, *The Joy of Cooking* — to him as he "grew up Chinese American in SE Ohio." *The Joy of Cooking* "was a culinary Bible of things that are eaten in America," but it was also a system of classification in which "The noun 'Chinese' is followed by seven adjectives: celery, chestnuts, dressing, egg rolls, meatballs, rice (fried), and sauce (sweet-sour)." If the cookbook is a model for Lin's work, then a book like *Seven Controlled Vocabularies* creates a system within which the Asian American can be placed and located, or within which the Asian American reader can locate himself, vis-à-vis the other seemingly arbitrary categories that make up culture.

Repetition and recombination, techniques used throughout Lin's work, are also put to powerful use by the Filipino American poet Paolo Javier, author of several poetry collections and the current poet laureate of Queens, New York (following the Korean American poet Ishle Yi Park, who held the position from 2004 to 2007). Javier 's *60 lv bo(e)mbs* (2005) has its roots in a series of homophonic translations from the work of Pablo Neruda. As Javier remarks in an interview with Eileen Tabios, he "fished out discrete words & phrases from Neruda's Spanish in 'Veinte Poemas De Amor,' then re-combined/configured these." The result is a framework that provides recurring phrases, patterns, and characters ("Alma," "Paolo," "Villa" — an evocation of the Filipino poet José Garcia Villa) but that remains open to an unconstrained and unexpected range of language. Like Reyes, Javier juxtaposes English, Spanish, and Tagalog, in order to, as he puts it in the Tabios interview, "confront my Pilipino past of Spanish & American imperialism" and "complicate my lingual reality of living & writing as an immigrant poet in the U.S." Like Yau's *Borrowed Love Poems, 60 lv bo(e)mbs* retains from Neruda the structure of the love poem but fills it with fragments that evoke Hollywood culture, U.S. imperialism, and Asian American history, placing the political at the core of the erotic:

> Crescendo Subic Destitute Alma
> Il Duce in the highest hassle warp speed sever my Alma
> Hosannas sickest the tone of gearing up against the Taliban into Alma
> Abeyance bilang zoom bus inebriated emailing my Alma

(27)

Far from letting linguistic experimentation draw him away from the Asian American literary tradition, Javier signals his deep engagement with that tradition through an imagined dialogue with José Garcia Villa. Javier's linguistic pyrotechnics are at times reminiscent of Villa's, but he responds to Villa's haughty aesthetic purity ("Bah! They're all centaurs...Why does the East continue to mingle?" [72 – 73]) with a fierce argument for engagement: "I will vent against the lynching horde with an initial canto" (72).

While poets like Lin and Javier have pursued Asian American poetics in this more experimental vein, formalist and postconfessional tendencies are also strongly present in Asian American writing. Perhaps the most accomplished of Asian American formalists is the Kashmiri American poet Agha Shahid Ali, who died in 2001; his collected poems, *The Veiled Suite*, appeared in 2009. Ali may be best known as a master of the ghazal, a form that, as Ali notes, "can be traced back to seventh-century Arabia" and reached its canonical form in Persian poetry of the eleventh century (325); the opening couplet sets out a rhyme scheme and refrain that are then repeated in the second line of each subsequent couplet, as in these lines from the opening of "For You":

> Did we run out of things or just a name for you?
> Above us the sun doubles its acclaim for you.
>
> Negative sun or negative shade pulled from the ground…
> and the image brought in one ornate frame for you.
>
> At my every word they cry, "Who the hell are you?"
> What would you reply if they thus sent Fame to you?
>
> (327; ellipsis in orig.)

Ali's work is richly and complexly allusive. The ghazal "Of It All" includes references to T. S. Eliot, James Wright, Danilo Kis, mathematics, and cosmology, framed through the phrase "[the] Arabic of it all" (329). "Tonight," one of Ali's best-known ghazals, quotes Emily Dickinson's mention of "Fabrics of Cashmere" — a layered allusion to Ali's own Kashmiri heritage — while also referencing Laurence Hope's "Kashmiri Song" and the biblical confrontation between Elijah and Jezebel (374).[1] But a particular feature of the ghazal — the poet's reference to himself in the final couplet ("Poetic Form: Ghazal") — gives Ali's tissues of citation a charged intimacy: "And I, Shahid, only am escaped to tell thee — / God sobs in my arms. Call me Ishmael tonight" (375). Ali's layering of allusion within an Arabic form adapted to English generates powerful Asian American lyrics that are both culturally grounded and exhilaratingly capacious.

Like Ali, Srikanth Reddy uses literary allusion and traditional form to structure his work, but Reddy eschews mere reverence for tradition in favor of a flexibility and a playfulness that open up a self-conscious, critical space. *Facts for Visitors* (2004), Reddy's debut collection, is partly structured around Dante's *Inferno*, employing a loose terza rima in poems named for the various circles of hell. But the circles are presented out of order (the ninth circle followed by the third), and the poems' contents display only a tenuous connection to Dante's theology. Reddy employs an equally free hand with two poetic forms, the villanelle and the sonnet; his villanelles are reminiscent of Elizabeth Bishop's, varying the repeated lines to push the poem's narrative forward, while his "sonnet" has fourteen lines but strips the form down to its bare bones: "I was cold. / You wove me a mantle of smoke. / I was thirsty. / You sent me a cloud in a crate" (55). Reddy's inventive, cryptic imagery allows him to construct a shifting series of personae, loosely linked through an insistent intensity of language. Some poems touch lightly on Reddy's Indian heritage — the "lorries," "bullock carts," and "untouchable girl" of "Thieves' Market" (23), the

---

1 For a fuller discussion of these references, see the annotated version of "Tonight" on the website of the Poetry Foundation.

"blue-skinned Rama" of "Monsoon Eclogue" (37) — but they do so at a stylized, even ironic distance (the speaker of "Thieves' Market" is a man in a bear suit). Reddy evokes instead a subject wandering through language and tradition, engaging with the literary past of the West but at a critical remove from it. That subject is most wittily evoked in "Fundamentals of Esperanto," in which the speaker shares the dream of a universal language represented by Esperanto but sees that dream "corrupted / by upstart languages such as Interlingua, / Klingon, Java & various cryptophasic tongues" (45). The speaker 's only hope is "to write / the Esperanto epic" in an effort to "freeze the mutating patois" (45). This quixotic task is, ironically, characterized by a mutability in which "Every line of the work / is a first & a last line" (45), and the epic ultimately becomes a solitary journey in which the hero "sits on a rock & watches his friends / fly one by one out of the song, / then turns back to the journey they all began" (46).

Kimiko Hahn, like Ali, uses a non-Western form to structure her 2006 collection *The Narrow Road to the Interior*, borrowing the Japanese form of the zuihitsu, a fragmentary, diaristic style epitomized by *The Pillow Book* of Sei Shonagon. While Ali's use of the ghazal imposes a strict discipline on his work, Hahn's use of the more open-ended zuihitsu allows her to work in an accessible postconfessional mode. She catalogs "things that make me cry instantly" and "things that are full of pleasure" (125-26), muses on being "a mother separated from two daughters three nights a week," imagines an Asian American literature final ("Cock-sucker, motherfucker. Thief. Wetback. Colonial pig. Explain" [90]), and depicts the aftermath of the attacks on the World Trade Center.

A witty riff on the Asian American postconfessional mode can be found in Ken Chen's *Juvenilia* (2010), the first book by an Asian American author to win the Yale Younger Poets Prize since Cathy Song's *Picture Bride* in 1983. The opening poem of the collection depicts the speaker 's father and mother debating his future but adds an unexpected character, the Chinese poet Wang Wei, "restrained beside me by backseat-belt and streetlight / world" (3). Chinese poetry is referenced throughout the text as a lens through which the Chinese American speaker's life can be seen; the book's final section intersperses allusions to the life and work of the poet Li Yu throughout an account of a visit between the speaker and his mother. The result is an Asian American family history that is held at an ironic distance, as in "Dramatic Monologue against the Self": "We find ourselves bored by creative nonfiction, autobiography, and memoir, which forsake the personality of thought for the impersonality of narrative. We sit in the essay as in a room of normal talk, free from aesthetics, until we are only selves, struggling to unhide the strangeness of our souls!" (19).

A final tendency evident in recent Asian American poetry — and, indeed, in contemporary American poetry more broadly — is an ongoing sampling and remixing of the materials of popular culture. Both Yau and Linh Dinh, in rather different ways, have mapped out how such engagements with popular culture might unfold within Asian American poetry — Yau with a pointed focus on Hollywood images of Asians, Linh Dinh with a much more freewheeling sampling using methods reminiscent of Flarf. Nick Carbó's *Secret Asian Man* (2000) expands beyond and critiques American popular culture by taking as his protagonist Ang Tunay na Lalaki, a "bare-chested muscled Filipino male character" from Filipino TV commercials whom Carbó reimagines in New York, relegated to sidekick roles and studying poetry with a writer named Nick Carbó. Sueyeun Juliette Lee's *That Gorgeous Feeling* (2009) is a riotous challenge to the perceived absence of Asian American icons in popular culture, featuring odes to unexpected "heroes" like Margaret Cho, Daniel Dae Kim, Congressman Mike Honda, and even a U.S. senator: "Daniel Inouye, oh no you don't!" (43). Monica Youn's *Ignatz*, a finalist for the 2010 National Book Award, takes Krazy Kat and Ignatz Mouse, the main characters of George Herriman's *Krazy Kat* comics, as the subjects of a fractured sequence of love lyrics.

Beyond the complex aesthetic currents swirling through Asian American poetry of the 2000s, another major force that has changed the terrain of twenty-first-century Asian American poetics is the ongoing demographic change within Asian America. Since the 1970s, when "Asian American literature" referred primarily to the writing of Chinese and Japanese Americans, the scope of Asian American writing has expanded to incorporate the work of newer immigrant groups that have grown rapidly in the wake of post — 1965 changes in U.S. immigration policies and patterns.

South Asian American poets have achieved particular prominence over the past decade. While poets such as Vijay Seshadri, Meena Alexander, and Chitra Banerjee Divakaruni achieved prominence in the 1990s, the first decade of the 2000s saw an explosion of South Asian American poets writing in a dizzying array of styles. *Indivisible*, the first anthology of South Asian American poetry, appeared in 2010; edited by Neelanjana Banerjee, Summi Kaipa, and Pireeni Sundaralingam, the volume demonstrates the diversity of this new poetic community with selections from forty-nine poets. In addition to Ali and Reddy, significant South Asian American poets who have emerged in the past decade include Bhanu Kapil, a cross-genre writer whose 2009 book *Humanimal: A Project for Future Children* is a work of experimental prose based on the story of two girls found living with wolves in India in 1920. Prageeta Sharma's wry, self-deprecating speaker in *Infamous Landscapes* (2007) characterizes herself as "a juvenile high on Marxism, / a false and reconstructed / humanist" (1), a rebel who "punched out breakfast teachers with lunch money" (4), and a "fool" who wants to be "informing and alluring and adaptable," as well as "a tropical / American for you to hold back" (13). Aimee Nezhukumatathil's three collections develop a lively, attentive, sensuous voice that ranges across her Indian and Filipino heritage, the travails of childhood and motherhood, and the curiosities of the natural world.

Filipino American poets such as Al Robles and Luis Cabalquinto came to prominence during the Asian American movement, but the past decade has seen Filipino American writers take leading roles in Asian American poetry. In addition to Reyes, Javier, Carbó , and Nezhukumatathil, other significant figures include Eugene Gloria, whose first collection, *Drivers at the Short-Time Motel* (2000), was selected for the National Poetry Series and won an Asian American Literary Award, and whose second collection, *Hoodlum Birds* (2006), is suffused with a reflective lyricism; Patrick Rosal, whose two collections feature powerful rhythms, masculine swagger, and sensual diction; and the prolific poet, editor, publisher, and blogger Eileen Tabios, whose more than twenty collections range over a vast aesthetic and cultural terrain.

As Southeast Asian American communities have become an increasingly central part of Asian America, poets from those communities are gaining new attention. Linh Dinh may be the best-known Vietnamese American poet; other notable authors include Truong Tran, whose unpunctuated prose poems in *Dust and Conscience* (2002) self-consciously navigate autobiography and politics; Hoa Nguyen, whose *Hecate Lochia* (2009) adapts the everydayness of New York school poet Bernadette Mayer to the scene of contemporary politics and Asian cultural influences; and Mộng-Lan, whose staggering of lines across the page and archetypal imagery is reminiscent of the early work of Janice Mirikitani.

Hmong and Laotian American writers are among the newest poetic communities to emerge on the literary scene. *Bamboo among the Oaks* (2002), edited by Mai Neng Moua, is the first anthology of Hmong American writing in English, featuring numerous poets. Hmong American poet Pos Moua's chapbook *Where the Torches Are Burning* (2002) shows the striking influence of his teacher, Gary Snyder, in poems of history and cultural adaptation. Bryan Thao Worra, a Laotian American writer, has published several collections of poetry, establishing a powerful voice that ranges authoritatively from the history of Laos to contemporary science fiction.

The Tibetan American poet Tsering Wangmo Dhompa has published two collections, *Rules of the House* (2002) and *In the Absent Everyday* (2005). Her even-toned poems are at times reminiscent of Berssenbrugge's in their abstraction and objectivity. Her first collection emphasizes family and cultural history, while her second explores perception and affect in the present.

Many of the writers already discussed are of mixed race, or hapa, including Yau (three-quarters Chinese and one-quarter white), Berssenbrugge (of Chinese and Dutch descent), Hahn (of Japanese and German descent), and Nezhukumatathil (of Indian and Filipino descent). Other mixed-race Asian American poets include Jenny Boully, who is part Thai, and whose book *The Body: An Essay* (2002) consists of a series of footnotes to an absent text, and Ronaldo V. Wilson, an African American and Filipino American writer whose *Poems of the Black Object* (2009) moves from intensely focused verse to lively prose to encompass racial objectification, family history, and queer sexuality.

Pacifc Islanders are often overlooked in discussions of Asian American culture; the poetry of Craig Santos Perez, a native Chamorro from Guam now living in California, has given Pacific Islander writing a new voice within Asian American literary discourse. Perez's two collections, installments of a larger work titled *From Unincorporated Territory* (2008, 2010), form a magisterial collage of Chamorro, Pacific, and American history and culture, employing multiple languages, excerpted and crossed-out historical text, and graphical variation to map a Pacific terrain marked by U.S. imperialism but also resistant to it.

While this article has focused on poetry published in conventional print collections, Asian American poets have also worked actively in genres that go beyond the printed page. Asian American poets have been a vital part of the spoken word scene since the 1990s, and over the past decade spoken word artists such as Beau Sia, Ishle Yi Park, Bao Phi, and Kelly Zen-Yie Tsai have reached Asian American audiences and large national audiences alike. A full discussion of Asian American spoken word is beyond the scope of this essay, but Bao Phi's article "A Decade of Asian Am Spoken Word" provides a useful overview of some of the major artists and recordings of the 2000s. In the burgeoning field of digital and electronic poetry, Brian Kim Stefans has emerged as a major creator and critic, a pioneer in the use of Flash animation in online poetic texts. His poem "The Dreamlife of Letters," an animated indexing of a text by Rachel Blau DuPlessis, has been highly influential.

One of the biggest challenges to the flourishing of Asian American poetry has been the relative paucity of institutions designed to support Asian American writers. Although the 1970s saw an upwelling of Asian American magazines and journals, most were ephemeral and few survived the decade. In the 1980s and 1990s, acceptance by mainstream poetry institutions, in the form of prizes and publication by trade and academic presses, seemed vital to many authors precisely because an infrastructure for Asian American poetry did not exist.

The most robust Asian American literary institution has been the Asian American Writers' Workshop (AAWW), founded in 1991 in New York City. In addition to literary programs and workshops for Asian American writers, AAWW, beginning in 1992, published *The Asian Pacific American Journal*, which for a time was the only Asian American literary journal, but issues have ceased appearing in recent years.[1] Kaya Press, founded in 1994, has published a number of works of innovative poetry, including Walter K. Lew's 1995 anthology Premonitions and, more recently, Shailja Patel's *Migritude* (2010) and Lisa Chen's *Mouth* (2007). Tinfish Books, a Hawaii-based press founded by the poet Susan M. Schultz, has published a number of Asian American and Pacific Islander writers, including Perez, Reyes, Linh Dinh, and Yunte Huang. *Interlope*, a journal of innovative Asian American writing edited by Summi Kaipa, appeared in 1998 but ended publication in 2003.

Several new Asian American literary journals have emerged in the past few years. *Kartika Review*, founded in 2007, is an online journal of Asian American literature, while *Lantern Review*, founded in 2010, is an online journal devoted to Asian American poetry. *The Asian American Literary Review*, a print journal that first appeared in 2010, includes a range of poetry, fiction, and criticism. Other kinds of literary spaces have also begun to open up for Asian American poets. Kundiman, an organization dedicated to supporting Asian American poetry, has since 2004 organized an annual summer retreat for Asian American poets, allowing younger poets to work with more established Asian American writers. Modeled on Cave Canem, an African American poets' community, Kundiman is led by the poets Sarah Gambito, Joseph O. Legaspi, Vikas Menon, Jennifer Chang, and Oliver de la Paz and is now based at Fordham University in New York.

From the perspective of the academy, perhaps the most significant development in the critical discourse around Asian American poetry is that such a discourse has finally come into being. For most of the history of Asian American literary studies, the field has been dominated by discussion of narrative memoir and fiction. The first monograph on Asian American poetry did not appear until 2006. Before that time, only a few articles had attempted to give a comprehensive view of the field, including Shirley Lim's "Reconstructing Asian-American Poetry: A Case for Ethnopoetics" (1987), George Uba's "Versions of Identity in Post-Activist Asian American

---

1 In a comment on Facebook, AAWW executive director Ken Chen reports that the AAWW plans to revive The *Asian Pacific American Journal* as an online publication in the near future.

Poetry" (1992), and Juliana Chang's "Reading Asian American Poetry" (1996). The 2001 *Resource Guide to Asian American Literature* published by the Modern Language Association included two articles, by Uba and Sunn Shelley Wong, on Asian American poetry, but no poet received the single-author treatment given to works of fiction and drama in the rest of the collection.

The monographs on Asian American poetry that have finally begun to appear in the past five years have often sought to locate Asian American poetry within the larger context of modern American literature. Josephine Nock-Hee Park's *Apparitions of Asia: Modernist Form and Asian American Poetics* (2008) argues that Asian American poets such as Lawson Fusao Inada, Theresa Hak Kyung Cha, and Myung Mi Kim are "heirs to an avant-garde shot through with Orientalism" (95), extending the modernist poetics of Ezra Pound and Gary Snyder but also critiquing those writers' appropriations of Asian sources. Steven G. Yao's Foreign *Accents: Chinese American Verse from Exclusion to Postethnicity* (2010), which focuses exclusively on Chinese American poets, also sees Pound as a crucial forerunner for Asian American writing, arguing that Pound's *Cathay* establishes "a veritable grammar *for the very idea* of Chinese emotion in English" (55). Yao offers a taxonomy of the varied ways poets such as Li-Young Lee, Marilyn Chin, and John Yau re-stage encounters between Chinese and American culture, from "mimicry" to "mutation."

Yunte Huang's *Transpacific Imaginations: History, Literature, Counterpoetics* (2008) widens the modernist context for Asian American poetry by reaching back into the nineteenth century, seeing the work of the Angel Island poets, Inada, and Cha as part of an American literature of transpacific exchange that extends back to Herman Melville and Henry Adams. Finally, my own *Race and the Avant-Garde: Experimental and Asian American Poetry since 1965* (2009) focuses on the contemporary context, reading Asian American poetry as an avant-garde that emerges alongside, and at times in tension with, other contemporary poetic avant-gardes such as Language writing.

———————

Asian American poetry of the first decade of the century displays a dizzying diversity, and this essay only scratches its surface, seeking to describe an object that is still very much in the process of formation. I have argued that Asian American poetry of the past decade can be characterized by its incisive investigations of contemporary language, through techniques ranging from postconfessional skepticism about the autobiographical "I" to the challenging of the centrality of English through multilingual writing. Yet Asian American poetry also maintains a deep continuity with the Asian American literary tradition, not merely through its treatment of Asian American themes but likewise through its attempts to imagine an Asian American reading position through linguistic estrangement, political and historical contextualization, and critique of the narratives of imperialism and mass culture. The need to imagine an Asian American reading position is in part a response to the ever-increasing diversity of Asian America, giving Asian American poetry a crucial role to play in articulating the perspectives and angles of critique that Asian Americans might share. The long-awaited emergence of a critical discourse about Asian American poetry suggests that far from fading into incoherence or irrelevance, the conversation sparked by Asian American poetry is just beginning.

University of Wisconsin–Madison

Works Cited

Ali, Agha Shahid. "Tonight." *Poetry Foundation.* Web. 10 Apr. 2011.

——. *The Veiled Suite: The Collected Poems.* New York: Norton, 2009.

Banerjee, Neelanjana, Summi Kaipa, and Pireeni Sundaralingam, eds. *Indivisible: An Anthology of Contemporary South Asian American Poetry.* Fayetteville: U of Arkansas P, 2010.

Berssenbrugge, Mei-mei. *I Love Artists: New and Selected Poems.* Berkeley: U of California P, 2006.

Boully, Jenny. *The Body: An Essay.* Athens, OH: Essay, 2007.

Carbó, Nick. *Secret Asian Man.* Chicago: Tia Chucha, 2000.

Chang, Juliana. "Reading Asian American Poetry." *MELUS* 21.1 (1996): 81–98.

Chen, Ken. Comment. *Facebook.* 11 Apr. 2011. Web. 11 Apr. 2011.

——. *Juvenilia.* New Haven, CT: Yale UP, 2010.

Chen, Lisa. *Mouth.* New York: Kaya, 2007.

Ch'ien, Evelyn Nien-Ming. *Weird English.* Cambridge, MA: Harvard UP, 2004.

Dinh, Linh. *All Around What Empties Out.* Honolulu, HI: Subpress, 2003.

——. *Jam Alerts.* Tuscon, AZ: Chax, 2007.

——. *Some Kind of Cheese Orgy.* Tuscon, AZ: Chax, 2009.

Gloria, Eugene. *Drivers at the Short-Time Motel.* New York: Penguin, 2000.

——. *Hoodlum Birds.* New York: Penguin, 2006.

Hahn, Kimiko. *The Narrow Road to the Interior.* New York: Norton, 2006.

Hong, Cathy Park. *Dance Dance Revolution.* New York: Norton, 2007.

Hongo, Garrett, ed. *The Open Boat: Poems from Asian America.* New York: Anchor, 1993.

Huang, Yunte. *Transpacific Imaginations: History, Literature, Counterpoetics.* Cambridge, MA: Harvard UP, 2008.

Javier, Paolo. *60 lv bo(e)mbs.* Oakland, CA: O Books, 2005.

——. "Interview with Barbara Jane Reyes and Paolo Javier by Eileen Tabios." *e-x-c-h-a-n-g-e-v-a-l-u-e-s* (blog), by Tom Beckett, 20 Sept. 2005. Web. 10 Apr. 2011.

Kapil, Bhanu. *Humanimal: A Project for Future Children.* Berkeley, CA: Kelsey Street, 2009.

Kim, Myung Mi. *Commons.* Berkeley: U of California P, 2002.

——. *Penury.* Richmond, CA: Omnidawn, 2009.

——. *Under Flag.* Berkeley, CA: Kelsey Street, 1991.

Lee, Li-Young. *Behind My Eyes.* New York: Norton, 2008.

——. *Book of My Nights.* Rochester, NY: BOA, 2001.

——. *The City in Which I Love You.* Rochester, NY: BOA, 1990.

——. *Rose.* Rochester, NY: BOA, 1986.

Lee, Sueyeun Juliette. *That Gorgeous Feeling.* Atlanta, GA: Coconut, 2008.

Lew, Walter K., ed. *Premonitions: The Kaya Anthology of New Asian* North American Poetry. New York: Kaya, 1995.

Lim, Shirley. "Reconstructing Asian-American Poetry: A Case for Ethnopoetics." *MELUS* 14.2 (1987): 51–63.

Lin, Tan. *BlipSoak01.* Berkeley, CA: Atelos, 2003.

——. "The *BOMB* Intervw Unedited 7000." Interview. Conducted by Katherine Elaine Sanders. *Tanlin.* Tumblr. Web. 9 Apr. 2011.

——. *Lotion Bullwhip Giraffe.* Los Angeles: Sun & Moon, 1996.

——. "Poetics of Distribution, Metadata as Poesis: Tan Lin's 7CV @ EDIT: Processing Network Publishing." Interview. Conducted by Christopher W. Alexander et al. *Harriet.* Chicago: Poetry Foundation, 17 Apr. 2010. Web. 9 Apr. 2011.

——. *Seven Controlled Vocabularies and Obituary 2004, The Joy of Cooking: Airport Novel Musical Poem Painting Film Photo Hallucination Landscape.* Middletown, CT: Wesleyan UP, 2010.

"Linh Dinh." *Wikivietlit.* Viet Nam Literature Project. Web. 3 Apr. 2011.

Moua, Mai Neng, ed. *Bamboo among the Oaks: Contemporary Writing by Hmong Americans.* St. Paul: Minnesota Historical Society, 2002.

Moua, Pos. *Where the Torches Are Burning.* Davis, CA: Swan Scythe, 2001.

Nezhukumatathil, Aimee. *At the Drive-In Volcano.* North Adams, MA: Tupelo, 2007.

——. *Lucky Fish.* North Adams, MA: Tupelo, 2011.

——. *Miracle Fruit.* North Adams, MA: Tupelo, 2003.

Nguyen, Hoa. *Hecate Lochia.* Prague: Hot Whiskey, 2009.

Patel, Shailja. *Migritude.* New York: Kaya, 2010.

Park, Josephine Nock-Hee. *Apparitions of Asia: Modernist Form and Asian American Poetics.* New York: Oxford UP, 2008.

Perez, Craig Santos. *from unincorporated territory [hacha].* Kaneohe, HI: Tinfish, 2008.

——. *from unincorporated territory [saina].* Richmond, CA: Omnidawn, 2010.

Phi, Bao. "A Decade of Asian Am Spoken Word — A Personal History (and My Favorite Asian Am Recordings of the Decade)." *Star Tribune* 4 Jan. 2010. Web. 10 Apr. 2011.

"Poetic Form: Ghazal." *Poets.org.* Academy of American Poets. Web. 10 Apr. 2011.

Reddy, Srikanth. *Facts for Visitors.* Berkeley: U of California P, 2004.

Reyes, Barbara Jane. *Poeta en San Francisco.* Kaneohe, HI: Tinfish, 2005.

Sharma, Prageeta. *Infamous Landscapes.* Albany, NY: Fence, 2007.

Song, Cathy. *Picture Bride.* New Haven, CT: Yale UP, 1983.

Stefans, Brian Kim. "The Dreamlife of Letters." *arras.net.* Web. 11 Apr. 2011.

——. "Remote Parsee: An Alternative Grammar of Asian North American Poetry." *Telling It Slant: Avant-Garde Poetics of the 1990s.* Ed. Mark Wallace and Steven Marks. Tuscaloosa: U of Alabama P, 2002. 43 – 75.

——. "Streaming Poetry." Rev. of Tan Lin, *BlipSoak01. Boston Review* 29.5 (2004). Web. 9 Apr. 2011.

Sullivan, Gary. "Flarf: From Glory Days to Glory Hole." *Brooklyn Rail Feb.* 2009. Web. 3 Apr. 2011.

Truong Tran. *Dust and Conscience.* Berkeley, CA: Apogee, 2002.

Tsering Wangmo Dhompa. *In the Absent Everyday.* Berkeley, CA: Apogee, 2005.

——. *Rules of the House.* Berkeley, CA: Apogee, 2002.

Uba, George. "Coordinates of Asian American Poetry: A Survey of the History and a Guide to Teaching." *A Resource Guide to Asian American Literature.* Ed. Sau-ling Cynthia Wong and Stephen H. Sumida. New York: Modern Language Association, 2001. 309 – 31.

——. "Versions of Identity in Post-Activist Asian American Poetry." *Reading the Literatures of Asian America.* Ed. Shirley Geok-lin Lim and Amy Ling. Philadelphia: Temple UP, 1992. 33 – 48.

Wilson, Ronaldo V. *Poems of the Black Object.* New York: Futurepoem, 2009.

Wong, Sunn Shelley. "Sizing Up Asian American Poetry." *A Resource Guide to Asian American Literature.* Ed. Sau-ling Cynthia Wong and Stephen H. Sum-ida. New York: Modern Language Association, 2001. 309–331.

Worra, Bryan Thao. *Barrow.* Cedar Rapids, IA: Sam's Dot, 2009.

——. *On the Other Side of the Eye.* Cedar Rapids, IA: Sam's Dot, 2007.

Yao, Steven G. *Foreign Accents: Chinese American Verse from Exclusion to Postethnicity.* New York: Oxford UP, 2010.

Yau, John. *Borrowed Love Poems.* New York: Penguin, 2002.

——. *Forbidden Entries.* Santa Rosa, CA: Black Sparrow, 1996.

——. *Paradiso Diaspora.* New York: Penguin, 2006.

——. *Radiant Silhouette: Selected Writing, 1974–1988.* Santa Rosa, CA: Black Sparrow, 1989.

Youn, Monica. *Ignatz.* New York: Four Way, 2010.

Yu, Timothy. *Race and the Avant-Garde: Experimental and Asian American Poetry since 1965.* Stanford, CA: Stanford UP, 2009.

9

(In Lieu of An) Introduction: The Asian American Subject between Liberalism and Neoliberalism

替代性导言：介于自由主义与新自由主义之间的美国亚裔主体

David Leiwei Li

评论家简介

李磊伟（David Leiwei Li），美国得克萨斯大学奥斯汀分校英语系博士，现为美国俄勒冈大学英语系教授。研究领域包括：20世纪文学与文化、北美与东亚的地缘政治、尤其关注在晚期资本时代，种族／族裔、现代性、以及全球化对（跨）国家主义想象以及个人主体性的构建的影响。专著有《中国电影中的经济、情感和伦理：全球化的速度》（*Economy, Emotion, and Ethics in Chinese Cinema: Globalization on Speed*, 2016）、《全球化与人文》（*Globalization and the Humanities*, 2004）、《想象这个国家：美国亚裔文学和文化认同》（*Imagining the Nation: Asian American Literature and Cultural Consent*, 2000）。编著有《美国亚裔文学》（*Asian American Literature*, 2012）。除本书收录的论文，其他代表性论文包括：《论归属与习得的美国性：偶然的亚洲与同化的非逻辑性》，发表于《当代文学》（"On Ascriptive and Acquisitional Americanness: The Accidental Asian and the Illogic of Assimilation," *Contemporary Literature*, 2004）；《美国亚裔批评的现状与主体：心理分析、跨国话语与民主理想》，发表于《美国文学史》（"The State and Subject of Asian American Criticism: Psychoanalysis, Transnational Discourse, and Democratic Ideals," *American Literary*

History, 2003）等。

文章简介

  本文是李磊伟教授为其主编的四卷本《美国亚裔文学》（*Asian American Literature*，2012）所作的导言部分。文章指出"美国亚裔"(Asian American) 这一称谓的出现恰逢美国由自由主义向新自由主义转化之际；1965 年移民法案颁布后，美国对于亚裔的官方承认与接纳的过程恰与美国"治理术"的巨变、自由民主制的不断瓦解以及世界政经形势的变化同时发生，因而研究新自由主义的基本构成及其全球化是揭示美国亚裔主体构成的必要手段，反之亦然。在新自由主义精神指导下，实现市场理性与个人责任的最佳化是最重要的，文章就此指出美国亚裔被冠以的"模范族裔"标签实质上是服务于新自由主义"文化工程"的策略性口号，进而使亚裔脱离自身被压迫的历史，抵消其政治诉求。在此前提之下，文章阐释了为何美国亚裔主体在冒现之时起就处于集体表现需求与个体表现需求的矛盾之中。而自 20 世纪 70 年代至本世纪的前十年，美国亚裔文学批评范式的转换正是对这一矛盾的焦虑性回应，并与新自由主义的兴起紧密相关。文章通过批判亚裔文学批评中过分强调差异性，主张"去主体性"的观点，进一步论证了美国亚裔主体的含混性是自由主义与新自由主义矛盾性的体现的观点。文章最后系统介绍了《美国亚裔文学》的编写原则与主体框架。

文章出处：Li, David Leiwei. *Asian American Literature.* vol.1, London & New York: Routledge, 2012, pp. 1–29.

(In Lieu of An) Introduction: The Asian American Subject between Liberalism and Neoliberalism

David Leiwei Li

To be Asian American is to be in need of perpetual arrivals. The publication of *Asian American Literature* marks yet another significant arrival of a minor subject in the academic American grain. While "strangers from a different shore" have entered the sanctuary of canonical formation and scholarly conservation, this movement from the "margins [to] the mainstreams" of the multicultural marketplace occasions both cautious celebration and critical reflection (Takaki 1989; Okihiro 1994). For it has always been the historical arrivals of the Asian stateside, be they physical or social, actual or symbolic, upon which the definitions of and debates about U.S. democracy rest.

1.

One cannot but recall the foundational moments of the "immigrant acts" (Lowe 1996):

> [F]rom debates on the Fourteenth Amendment through the 1882 Chinese Exclusion Act, the "Gentleman's Agreement" of 1908 barring Japanese Immigration, the Immigration Act of 1917 creating the "Asiatic barred zone" that extended racial exclusion to exclusion by region, the Immigration Act of 1924 denying admission for permanent residence to persons racially ineligible for citizenship, the Tydings-McDuffie Act of 1934 stripping Filipinos of their noncitizen American national status, to the Japanese Internment during World War Ⅱ.

to see in the denial of Asian arrival and detention of the arrived the deferral of an American liberal democratic promise (Li 1998: 3). One cannot but consider the fact that the 1965 Immigration Reform Act's *de jure* inclusion and recognition of "(the) Asian America(n)" — as the permissible formal subject Primarily intelligible in the image of "the model minority" — also coincided with the seismic shift in the "governmentality" of the United States as well as in the political economy of the world.[1] Like no other constituency of the American citizenry perhaps, the categorical emergence of "(the) Asian America(n)" comes to crystallize the troubling transition of the U.S. from the regime of liberalism to the regime of neoliberalism.

My usage of "liberalism" begins with the term's definition by Raymond Williams:

"Liberalism" is a doctrine based on individualist theories of man and society and is thus in fundamental conflict not only with socialist but with most strictly social theories. The further observation, that "liberalism" is the highest form of thought developed within bourgeois society and in terms of capitalism, is also relevant, for when "liberal" is not being used as a loose swear-word, it is to this mixture of liberating and limiting ideas that it is intended to refer. "Liberalism" is then a doctrine of certain necessary kinds of freedom but also, and essentially, a doctrine of possessive individualism.

(1983: 181)

Williams' summary of "liberalism" in C. B. Macpherson's classic phrase of "possessive individualism" points not only to the concept's European political and philosophical origins in Locke, Hobbes, and Rousseau, but also opens up a triangular field of concerns about state, capital, and citizen/labor in the doctrine's American materialization. A universal democratic theory of bourgeois subjectivity and society, this highest form of liberal thought was realized for the longest stretch of U.S. history in the form of a lowest common denominator, i.e. its partial and particular embodiment in the Euro-American citizenry. As the enslavement of African Americans constituted an absolute monopoly of value and essential refusal of access for the black subject to alienate his or her labor through the market in exchange for the putative liberty such acts of self-possession nominally entail, so did the disqualification of native American enfranchisement (Li 1998: 207, f3) and the exclusion of Asian American citizenship — the 1882 Chinese Exclusion Act being the legislative solution to the labor and capital conflict in California, a class struggle deflected and resolved by the state through the racialization of labor and rights (Saxton 1971).

In spite of its idealistic premise and universalistic claims, the real life of liberalism has been, in the view of Charles W. Mills, "predominantly a racial liberalism" or "white liberalism" (2008: 1381-2). Since the onset of capitalist modernity, this actually existing liberalism has manifested itself both as internationally and intranationally Janus-faced. As a language of freedom against a feudal monarchical order in favor of the voluntary wage laborer and the citizen of representative government, racial liberalism legitimated colonial and imperial domination "by articulating the superiority of Euro-Atlantic political cultures over those subjugated by them" (Brown 1995: 137-38).[2] As the language of a racially exclusive American democracy, "white liberalism" "originally restricted full personhood to whites and relegated non whites to an inferior category, so that its schedule of rights and prescription for justice were all color-coded" (Mills 2008: 1382). The actually existing liberalism of the U.S. thus laid the material foundation of what Omi and Winant regard as *Racial Formation* (1994), what Mills calls *The Racial Contract* (1997), what David

Theo Goldberg delineates as *The Racial State* (2002), culminating in its American historical translation into what George Lipsitz has cogently characterized as *The Possessive Investment in Whiteness* (1998).

It is important to remark that the afore-cited critiques of the actually existing liberalism in the U.S. neither advocate liberalism's abolition nor the advancement of an alternative communist modernity against which capitalist liberal democracy is historically and ideologically defined. Instead, they argue for a deracialization of the apparently raceless liberal democracy so that the benefits of its social contract — as achieved since the New Deal's correction of market excess and especially the tangible social goods accrued after the end of World War II — are extended to American citizens regardless of race, gender, and sexuality. In other words, the demands made by racial and gender minorities, of which the newly constituted Asian American is a significant part, are aimed at achieving a more inclusive form and practice of postwar liberalism. For this liberalism is "Keynesian" in substance in that state "dampen[s] business cycles" and "ensure[s] reasonably full employment" in order to obtain a "'class compromise' between capital and labor" and to guarantee "domestic peace" "economic growth" and "the welfare of its citizens" (Harvey 2005: 10). A political and economic organization often informed by social contract theory and not infrequently supported by a strong sense of EuroAmerican national identity, the *modus operandi* of this prevailing governmental reason and political practice is known as "embedded liberalism" (ibid.: 11-12).[3] Though evidently racially discriminatory, this liberalism strives to maintain a triangular equilibrium among state, capital, and citizen/labor interests, to constrain wayward market processes in a regulatory environment of the geopolitically bounded nation-state, and succeeds in bringing in a period of American economic prosperity and global hegemony between the end of World War II and the beginning of the 1970s.

Asian American arrival as the subject of American democracy and literary representation owes as much to the antinomianism of the counter-cultural, civil rights, and anti-war movements stateside, and decolonization worldwide, as it does to embedded liberalism's earlier accommodation of ethnic democratic agitation and aspirations. Had it not been for postwar school desegregation, the removal of restrictive laws in citizenship that culminated in the 1965 Immigration Reform Act, there would not have been the social access afforded U.S.-born Asians and the acceptance into the U.S. of professional and entrepreneurial immigrants from Asia, two requisite objective conditions that have made possible the advent of an Asian American middle class and its subsequent struggle for subjective embodiment within American democracy. It is competence in English literacy and command of dominant cultural capital, be it scientific, technological, or entrepreneurial know-how, of this particular class that have enabled the formal incorporation of the Asian American constituency into the U.S. nation as a newly registered subject of liberal democracy, of the capitalist market, as well as a nascent ethnic subject of national literature. However, this moment and state of incorporation — when the Asians of historical legislative exclusions are beginning to be symbolically aggregated into the American nation and embodied in the white liberalism characteristic of the postwar welfare state — are simultaneously the moment when American liberal democracy is being disaggregated and disembedded, when the caretaking welfare state is under assault for the advancement of transnational production and financialization of capital, and when the validity of social contract theory is yielding to the authority of rational choice theory. In this light, we can contend with considerable confidence that not only are the subjectivation of (the) Asian America(n) subject to the neoliberalization of liberalism but the very processes of Asian American self-definition are also pivotally informative of the transition and transformation of liberalism to neoliberalism. Without an adequate understanding of Asian American subject formation, our apprehension of neoliberalism's fundamental constitution and its globalization is woefully incomplete.[4]

2.

Three examples may illuminate how neoliberalism reconfigures the state, the individual, and the market in and through the emergent Asian American subject. "At a time when Americans are awash in worry over the plight of racial minorities, one such minority, the nation's 300,000 Chinese-Americans," read a 1966 article in *U. S. News and World Report,* "is winning wealth and respect by dint of its own hard work." "At a time when it is being proposed that hundreds of billions be spent to uplift Negroes and other minorities," it continued, "the nation's 300,000 Chinese-Americans are moving ahead on their own — with no help from anyone else" (qtd in Tachiki *et al.* 1971: 6). This bootstrapping narrative unprecedentedly casting Asian Americans in the indiscriminate role of Euro-American Horatio Algers signaled an imminent exhaustion of liberalism. It reached its apex in Ronald Reagan's 1984 speech when he touted Asian American preservation of "the sacred worth of human life, community spirit, [and] fiscal responsibility," going so far as to say that "we need your values, your hard work" in "our political system" (qtd in Takaki 1989: 475). Reagan's newspeak was complemented three years later by the sister act of Thatcher in her infamous claim that "there is no such thing as society. There are individual men and women, and there are families" (qtd in Harvey 2005: 23).

As these instances amply illustrate, the dominant discursive figuration of the Asian American subject concurs and coincides with a dominant Anglo-American cultural rejection of postwar Keynesian legacies. Touted as a self-possessive individual subject of liberal theoretical success yet independent of liberal institutional support, the freshly minted Asian American "model minority" has turned out to be the figurative front of "the Reagan/Thatcher Revolution" to undo the effects of the interventionist social state, "to re-establish the conditions for capital accumulation and to restore the power of economic elites" (Harvey 2005: 19). More crucially, the Asian American "model minority" has also become central to neoliberalism as a "cultural project," "a mode of governance encompassing but not limited to the state, and one which produces subjects, forms of citizenship and behavior, and a new organization of the social," whose ultimate "object," as the Iron Lady has it, "is to change the soul" (Brown 2003: 1; Thatcher qtd in Harvey 2005: 23).

Key to this soul transforming production of the neoliberal subject, of which the Asian American is suddenly supposed to be exemplary, is the dismissal of state rule and provision, the disentanglement of national society and its citizen subject, the intensified privatization of social reproduction, and last but not the least, the drastic deregulation and disembedding of capital from its national and social moorings. If embedded liberalism still rests on the belief of social contract, representative government, and constitutional citizenry, if it still "signifies an order in which the state exists to secure the freedom of individuals on a formally egalitarian basis," neoliberalism "indexes state success according to its ability to sustain and foster the market and ties state legitimacy to such success" (Brown 2003: 2,4). In this neoliberal sphere, both the state and the individual subject are simultaneously enfolded and animated by a reigning economic rationality: not only is "the human being configured exhaustively as *homo oeconomicus*," but state "sovereignty" is also limited to "guaranteeing economic activity," "state practices" submitted to "a generalized calculation of cost and benefit," and "state policies" aimed exclusively at producing "prudent subjects" through a shared "calculus of utility" against "the grid of scarcity, supply, and demand" (ibid.: 3-5). Contrary to the classical liberalism of Adam Smith, for whom the market remains an instrument of the state, wealth an indicator of national strength, and capital subordinate to social goods, the neoliberalism of Hayek and Friedman has radically reduced the social to the economic and equated free society with the free market.[5] The "modest ethical gap between economy and polity" that seems to sustain the integrity of a liberal democratic society and insulates its subjects from "the ghastliness of life exhaustively ordered by the market" is rapidly closing (ibid.: 7).

In the neoliberal vision of the world, what matters is the optimal realization of market rationality and individual accountability. Thus, the apparent ascent of the Asian American model minority subject was justified in the glaring absence of reference to structural removal of discriminatory laws at a time when the embedded form of liberalism was on its last legs. Instead, values of hard work, fiscal responsibility, transcendental self-reliance, and individual self-possession were singled out for their perfect fit, in the phrase of "the great communicator," to "our political system," a system of capitalist liberal democracy being drastically eviscerated as he spoke. The dominant discourse of Asian American "model minority" therefore serves as a rudimentary neoliberal pretext. This pretext functions as a discursive draft to wipe out the narrative potential of American liberal democracy while it simultaneously serves as a representational excuse from the liberal commitment to egalitarianism. In conceiving the Asian American subject as one who succeeds through self-reliance alone, the neoliberal discourse is not just setting up Asian Americans against African Americans, but is also promulgating a myth of individual mobility without the need of society. It disavows, on the one hand, the legacy of embedded liberalism that has made possible the postwar Euro-American story of "upward mobility and the common good" (Robbins 2007). On the other hand, it normalizes the entrepreneurial subject of radical individualism who is theoretically free to make choices and stands by the consequences, regardless of the given historical conditions and capabilities of his choosing (Peters 1999: 6-7). Neoliberalism thus disengages Asian American emergence from both the history of systemic liberal exclusion and the opening of its inclusion in order to displace the demands made by racial and gender minorities on the waning welfare state.[6]

3.

In the 1970s the Asian American articulation of self as the emerging ethnic subject rejected outright the model minority discourse I've just described as formative of neoliberalist rationalizations. As first generation Anglophone Asian Americans of U.S. college education, the editorial collectives of *Roots* (Tachiki *et al.* 1971) and *Aiiieeeee!* (Chin *et al.* 1974/1983) both confronted with valor the challenge of nascent neoliberal value determinism and took on the burden of representation with a vengeance. The problem of Asian American identity, as Chin *et al.* intuited before the publication of Edward Said's titular tome, is such that *Orientalism* displaced the Asian stateside onto Asia and into the past, making them the actual subject of taxation without representation. Thus, in a gesture reminiscent both of *No-No Boy* (1957/1976), John Okada's novel of the Internment, and *Black Fire* (1968), Leroi Jones and Larry Neal's (1968) signature anthology of the "Black Aesthetic Movement," *Aiiieeeee!* debunked ancestral Asia and white America only to embed the emergent Asian American on native American grounds, claiming at once the geopolitical space and history of U.S. democracy as constitutive of Asian American subjectivity (Vol. I: Chapter 1).[7]

This vehement and vociferous grandstanding of collective identity against Asian American "alienation" and "abjection" is nothing short of revolutionary (Vol. I: Chapter 8). In conceiving the space of Asian American subjectivity as correspondent and integral to the social and temporal terrains of the U.S., *Aiiieeeee!* insists that there can be no citizen/subject without the nation-state.[8] Not only does this insistence respond actively to Asian Exclusion and the historical preclusion of rights justified by racial and regional origins, its coupling of the subject with the state relies on both racial and national signifiers to reinstate the proper role of Asian Americans within U.S. democracy. Insistent on the inalienable bonds between the state and the citizen/subject, symbolic nation and actual peoplehood, this representational recuperation comes to enable an Asian American political address to the state and its cultural recognition within the nation. As an excluded subject of liberal democracy, the Asian American demands redress for the historical states of injury. As an expressive subject of literature and art, the Asian American seeks voice and visibility in the U.S. cultural imaginary. The subjectivation of Asian Americans thereby corresponds, on the one hand, to an ethnic American aspiration for upward class mobility in and through the liberal state, while on the other hand, to a conscious colored coalition in national culture and the American literary canon (Vol. I: Chapters 3, 11, 12, 13; Goldberg 2008; Li 1990). This two-pronged ethnic nationalization sets the premise of what is loosely known as "multiculturalism," lays the foundation of Asian American Studies and its constitution of the Asian American subject, and enacts accordingly an identity politics typical of the prescribed practices in "embedded liberalism."[9]

But to nationalize "panethnically" an Asian American subject out of historical erasure for the mobilization of an aggregate identity politics entails tremendous representational challenges (Espiritu 1992). First is the implicit conflation of laws and letters in the practice of ethnic nationalism, with its attendant logic of inclusion and exclusion. Percy Bysshe Shelley regardless, neither are poets literal "legislators of the world," nor does literary persuasion operate with the binding efficacy of the law. The discursive bonds between legal and literary representations do not their substitutes make. Second is the constitutive inability of the Asian American subject to transcend its historical condition of representation, the condition of such compulsory "minority metonymical collectivity" that a singular feature or partial reference of one is inevitably called upon to stand for the whole, the "I" for the "we" (Li 1998: 65, 174–183).[10] To a great extent, the coalitional necessity of group articulation at the advent of the Asian American subject certainly exacerbates this compulsory collectivity. Always already symbolic of its ethnicity, the emergent Asian American subject appears fixed in racial significance, condemned to the reduction of group characteristics, and precluded from the process of self-possessive individualization requisite of liberal subject formations.

It is not that Euro-Americans are without race or group significations: the construction of their racial identity has so merged with the construction of an American national identity and the particulars of a European culture has claimed such American centrality and continuity that race has practically disappeared into nation and the normative white subject has appeared as absolutely autonomous. As a result, a Euro-American -speaking subject seems to have become an identity without identity.[11] S/he can comfortably assume both universality and particularity in representation, taking for granted not only his or her own unquestionable common humanity but also prized individuality. S/he is thus released from the involuntary bond to a race and nation delimited collectivity upon which the emergence of the Asian American subject seems to depend. Essentially disengaged from the necessity of justifying democratic rights through the cataloguing of cultural competencies, the normative white subject is able to take for granted his or her subjective inclusion within the nation, endowed with resources in embedded liberalism while at the same time able to fashion himself or herself self-possessively as an authentic liberal subject.

With this comparative understanding, we return to the moment of Asian American subjective inauguration only to find ourselves at a point of analytic quandary. For to become the citizen/ subject, the emergent Asian American has to address the nation/state collectively in the sense of a panethnicity, but to achieve democratic authenticity the subject so being constituted will also have to individualize, for the ideal liberal subject is nothing short of being the owner of himself owing little to others. This predicament very much indexes *Aiiieeeee!'s* mixed legacy. To tap into the representational power of the collective, the editors distinguish Asians stateside from Asians in Asia, biology from culture, and race from rights, making possible the American subject of Asian descent whose political disenfranchisement and cultural illegitimacy have until then been justified by its presumed racial essence. Unfortunately, however, *Aiiieeeee!* also acts out two other impulses: the negation of a dominant racial essentialism that consolidates Asian psycho-social passivity and its resolute replacement by the editors' own positive inventory of an assertive and individualistic "Asian American sensibility." In place of a model minority radalization of diligence, discipline, and docility come rebelliousness, belligerence, and defiance. In its last resort to an Asian American interiority and its analogous aesthetic expression, *Aiiieeeee!* seems to have inadvertently reverted phenotype into personality type, race into culture, when elective characteristics begin to substantiate, validate, and idealize an ethnic subjectivity presumed to be common and coherent. Ironies abound not only in the appearance of a resultant "racial individualism" but also its indefensible exclusivity, be it through the requisites of American nativity or masculinity.

Aiiieeeee!'s shortcoming seems attributable both to the editorial obsession with masculine aggression and to the over-determination of different representational conditions. Staking out the geopolitical boundary and history of the U.S. as the proper terrain of Asian American subjectivity would have been quite sufficient and successful had the editors simply retained this emphasis. This is because liberalism *in theory* does not require a substantive subject nor does democracy tolerate *in theory* a hierarchical ordering of subjects through aristocratic entitlement in genealogy and gender. Theoretically speaking then, as far as citizenship is assured, the liberal subject is presumed to be the sole proprietor of one's own capacity to labor and meaning making. For quintessentially the liberal subject is a self-possessive individual whose relationship to society is as tangential as his or her relationship to the market is fundamental. Finally, as Macpherson instructs us, the ideal liberal subject is independent from the will of others, or as I shall put it, s/he is essentially extricable from any representational relations except those willingly entered into according to self-interests (1962: 263–264).[12] *Aiiieeeee!*'s ill success at liberal representation not only indicates an editorial failure but also the unavailability to them of the more fluid representational assumptions and associations characteristic of liberalism. So far as the claim to both universality and particularity and the capacity to exercise both individual sovereignty and flexible attachment to society remain the privileged domain of the normative white subject, the Asian American subject shall remain fixed in metonymical collectivity.

Because of the duality in liberalism and its correspondent condition of representational unevenness, the evolution of Asian American literary history has been punctuated with controversies and contestations. The critique of *Aiiieeeee!*'s and *The Woman Warrior*'s (Kingston 1976) perceived partiality and prejudice (Vol. I: Chapter 4; Vol. II: Chapter 30), and for that matter, the debates over Lois-Ann Yamanaka's *Blu's Hanging* (1998; Vol. I: Chapter 16; Vol. II: Chapter 45), or the more recent ruckus over Amy Chua's *The Battle Hymns of the Tiger Mother* (2011) mark the continual negotiation of Asian American subjectivity under the categorical pressure of representativeness, and of the concept of representation in general.[13] To a great degree, the scholarly shifts of emphases between the 1970s and 2010s from that of identity to difference (Vol. I: Chapter 5), politics to aesthetics (Vol. I: Chapter 19), and ethnic nationalism to cosmopolitan transnationalism (Vol. I: Chapters 6, 7, 9, 15, 17, 18) also respond to the conflicting representational needs of social solidarity and individual sovereignty. There is in this period an overall migration of critical preoccupation from the racialized subject of exclusion and disenfranchisement to the "compositional subject" of agency and hybridity, from anger to autonomy, "grievance to grief" (Kang 2000; Cheng 2002).[14] I shall not reiterate this chapter of subjective evolution through the overlapping phases of "ethnic nationalism" "feminism" and "heteroglossia" since this formulation has admittedly achieved "a rough consensus" in Asian American literary scholarship (Sohn, Lai, and Goellnicht 2010). I only want to call the reader's attention to the reprint of this chapter (Vol. I: Chapter 8), to Volume I in general where the divergent constructions of Asian American subjectivity are substantially sampled, and to the set as a whole where interpretations of an authorial galaxy reveal such a complex scope of Asian American subject formation as never before so singularly showcased.

What I do wish to accomplish is to pick up the theoretical threads at the turn of the millennium, when Asian American subjectivity experienced a dramatic inward as well as outward turn through psychoanalytical and transnational discourses (Li 2003), when an increasingly sophisticated treatment of Asian American texts promised alliances dialectically positioned on the "horizon of difference" (Lowe 1996: 83). Enriching and energizing in and by itself, the decisive swing of critical pendulum towards the end of "difference" also betrays a representational anxiety of institutionalized critics caught between the mainstream academy and their putative ethnic constituency, when changes in the nature of the nation-state as an institution of modernity and political representation have necessitated changes in the university and the humanities, both of which have historically functioned as the state's ideological apparatus (Readings 1996). Besides its apparent ongoing struggle against collective representational strictures, the proposal of difference seems to have moved beyond a pluralizing and individualizing critical impulse: the complication of Asian American subjectivity through an inclusive consideration of gender, sexuality, and native/immigrant birth has morphed into a fundamental questioning both of subjectivity as such and the necessity of political and aesthetic representations. When a poststructural suspicion of the subject is coupled with the privatization and celebration of irreducible individual difference, the idea and ideal of social solidarity and democratic equality rapidly lose their emotional and ethical appeals. With the benefit of historical hindsight, I think the turn in the American academy towards poststructural difference, Asian American or otherwise, is not utterly unrelated to the neoliberal efforts to unhinge the terms of social contract, to release the state from its monopoly of ethical authority and caring responsibility, and to urge instead the individual to marshal his or her own destinies through the "free" market. With the diminishing influence of democratic states, the waning of embedded liberalism, and the rising empire of neoliberal corporate power, where do we place the subject whose individual "I" must, as we used to believe with conviction, complete its passage through the collective "we"?[15]

4.

One way to answer this question is to call for the subject's demise, to transform its materiality into pure epistemology, and to "embrac[e]," as Kandice Chuh does in *Imagine Otherwise*, "the undecidability and insubstantiality of "Asian American" [*sic*] (2003: 113–114).[16] According to Chuh, "the centrality of citizenship and subjectivity to the politics of modernity" is truly *passé* in our era of postmodernity (ibid.: 10). "In spite of claims about the death of the Subject heralded by postmodernism," she complains, "the idea and importance of a consummate subjectivity remain unabashedly vital":

> But a subject is always also an epistemological object ... Recognition of the subject as epistemological object cautions against failing endlessly to put into question both "Asian American" as subject/object of Asian Americanist discourse and of US nationalist ideology, and Asian American studies as the subject/object of dominant paradigms of the US university.
>
> (ibid.: 9-10)

Contrary to King-kok Cheung's critical caution many years ago that the subject has to be born before its death becomes viable (1993: 23), Chuh wishes to *Imagine Otherwise*. Equating "Asian Americanist discourse" with "U.S. nationalist ideology" "Asian American studies" with "dominant paradigms of the U.S. university," she wants to move us beyond the materiality of both the nation-state and the university so as to "conceiv[e] Asian American studies as a subjectless discourse" (2003: 9). Chuh's proposal of "subjectlessness" confronts both the "political activist narrative" that has its "rootedness in the socio-political movements of the 1960s and 1970s" and a "multiculturalism" that retains "a liberal conception of subjectivity" (ibid.: 5, 6). "Subjectlessness" is for her an affirmative response to the "transnationalism" of the 1980s and 1990s that "recognizes contemporary flows of capital and information," and that "find[s] national borders irrelevant and 'patriotic' loyalties displaced from nation-states to differently configured collectivities" (ibid.: 3). Finally, Chuh deploys "subjectlessness as a conceptual tool, [and] as a strategic *anti*-essentialism, to manufacture 'Asian American' situationally" (ibid.: 10).

"Subjectlessness" is surely a loaded assertion, but it reminds me of a fictive situation in the "Legend of Sleepy Hollow," which, as you may recall, involves a headless horseman as the subject of the story and a round object that turns out to be a harmless pumpkin. Risking being hopelessly essentialist, I would like to know if the subjectless Asian American is also headless, skinless, living in a sleepy hollow immune from the everyday effects of both transnational geopolitics and racial dynamics stateside. I wonder if "subjectlessness" is merely a harmless pumpkin, a playful "deconstructive attitude that keeps contingency, irresolution, and nonequivalence in the foreground" (ibid.: 8). This query effectively leads us to the actual situations of Vincent Chin and Wen Ho Lee at a time when transnational/neoliberal capitalism of the sort that has inspired Chuh's theoretical speculation is disembedding the postwar liberal state, outsourcing industrial production while expanding U.S. military presence around the world. Are "national borders irrelevant and 'patriotic' loyalties displaced," or do they continue to be racialized and manifest themselves in and through not Asian Americans of mere epistemology but embodied subjects of flesh and blood (ibid: 3)? Have Vincent Chin, a Chinese American engineer mistaken for a Japanese and consequently clubbed to death by laid-off white autoworkers in the 1982 Detroit, and Wen Ho Lee, the Chinese American scientist at Los Alamos Lab indicted in 1999 by a Federal Grand Jury as a spy for China, had the chance to evoke the "contingency, irresolution, and nonequivalence" defense? Asian American metonymic collectivity persists despite transnational flow of image and information and Chuh's strident claims of "strategic anti-essentialism" (ibid.: 10).

But "anti-essentialist historicism," writes Žižek in his cogent critique of a tendency with which Chuh seems adamantly aligned, "has a strange ahistorical flavor: once we fully accept and practice the radical contingency of our identities, all authentic historical tension somehow evaporates in the endless performative games of an eternal present" (2009: 22). It is small wonder then that Chuh should "call for reflexivity in discourse and politics," and envision Asian American Studies "as a formation of the critical landscape configured by a (poststructural) problematization of referentiality" and meaning (2003: 4, 5). This is certainly unsurprising, because "radical anti-essentialists have to deploy all their hermeneutical-deconstructive skills to detect hidden traces of 'essentialism' in what appears to be a postmodern 'risk society' of contingencies," remarks Žižek (2009: 22). "[W]ere they to admit that we already live in an 'anti-essentialist' society, they would have to confront the true difficult question of the historical character of today's predominant radical historicism itself," he resumes, "i.e. confront the topic of this historicism as the ideological form of 'postmodern' global capitalism" (ibid.: 22).

Remarkably, Chuh's subjectless discursive reflexivity does hinge on a particular reference to Lois Ann Yamanaka's *Blu's Hanging* (1997), the novel which bookends the theoretical treatise of *Imagine Otherwise*. In her last chapter, Chuh reads the novel to further her agenda of "(dis) owning America" and secure her claims of "subjectless Asian Americanist critique" (Vol. I: Chapter 16).[17] Extensive excursions into postcolonial theory and Hawaiian history precede her reading. For the first part, a summary of such seminal scholars as Sharpe and Cherniavsky convinces Chuh to wisely consider "the U.S. as a neocolonial power" (ibid.: 119–122). This recognition, however, is not to reintroduce "the model of 'internal colonization' in the 1960s and 1970s to harness the language of decolonization," she hastens to add (ibid.: 122). Rather, Chuh wants to "map 'denaturalization' and 'denationalization' onto Asian American studies as a tactical orientation" that "encourages the deconstruction of U.S. nationness itself, its seemingly inevitable status as nation" (ibid.: 123). Since "living in the U.S. means inhabiting 'the house race built'," and since insistence on "national belongingness does not solve injustice," Chuh holds it "imperative to disarticulate 'nation' from 'home'" (ibid.: 124–125).

With this confusing rendition of postcolonial discernment, Chuh goes on to the second detour where she reiterates the U.S. annexation of Hawaii and engages Haunani-Kay Trask's significant work on settler society and Hawaiian sovereignty (Vol. I: Chapter 14). Curiously enough, her attention to Trask's indigenous nationalist struggle for homeland and its conflict with an immigrant localism driven by ethnic nationalism should result in Chuh's emphatic disassociation of home from place, similar to her disarticulation of nation from home. "[A]s demanded by modernity," Chuh states, "ownership of territory legitimates nations, and nationalisms, even if unintentionally (as in cultural nationalism), can lead to territorialization in ways that can resemble colonialism" (2003: 138). For this reason, "the home Asian American studies pursues," she concludes, "cannot be conceived as a desire *for* place" (ibid.: 139;original italics).

After dwelling on a U.S. imperialism that frames the contestation between indigenous and ethnic nationalisms yet blithely dismissing the role of the state and the struggle for place, Chuh comes to trivialize the intra-ethnic controversy over a Japanese American writer's alleged stereotyping of a Filipino American character. The representational flare-up over *Bin's Hanging* seems to her yet another instance of misguided "liberal multiculturalism" that "consolida[es] an essentialist understanding of racialized identities" (ibid.: 142).[18] To eschew such essentialism, she wants to complicate the question raised by the award controversy — "Is *Blu's Hanging* racist or not?" — "by revising it to ask, what, in addition to race and racism, is the novel about?" (ibid.).

For Chuh, the miserable malfunction of the novel's principal family "illuminate[s] the need for Asian American studies to revisit the implications of working with nation as its presumptive basis and parameters" (ibid.: 145).

Before we examine Chuh's execution of her confounding thesis, let us recall the basic elements of the novel. Set on the island of Moloka'i in Ronald Reagan's United States, *Blu's Hanging* features the Ogata family in total disarray, mother Ella deceased, father Bertram drunk, leaving Ivah, the oldest of the children, at the tender age of 13, to shoulder the familial responsibility of a surrogate parent, taking care of her 8-year-old brother Blu who overeats, and her 4-year-old sister Maisie who turns mute, as the aftermath of their mother's passing. Narrated in poetic pigeon English and filtered through the first person adolescent consciousness of the eldest daughter, the novel rounds out a picture of a near-Darwinian universe of primitive nature where animal abusers abound and sexual predators prowl, and where Ivah, alone in her fierce resolve, struggles to rope her family together for the sake of collective survival without having herself suffocated as a result. With the construction of this scenario, Yamanaka has clearly taken on a classic conflict in the classic genre, for the rise of the English novel as is well known not only shapes the bourgeois subject of nascent liberalism but also contemplates on the formation of a society in which individual desires and social goods may achieve optimal equilibrium.

Chuh appears not entirely unaware of Ivah's inner tension, forced upon her by the inevitable choice of saving herself alone or sustaining her family. Instead of focusing on the protagonist's deep dilemma, upon which the novel accumulates most of its emotional power and accentuates its ethical indictment, Chuh considers the failure of the Ogata family to be "the failures of the heteronormative family as a construct" and offers her reading of "a nonheteronormative family as the mechanism for potential salvation" (ibid.: 142,144). That family of Chuh's reference consists of Miss Ito, Maisie's caring teacher, and Big Sis, the older cousin of the children from Honolulu, who is doing a teacher's practicum on Moloka'i and who rooms with Miss Ito for the duration of her training. At this moment of the narrative upon which all of Chuh's critical assertions seem to hinge, Big Sis and Miss Ito are visiting the Ogata house to volunteer their support of Blu and Maisie in Ivah's anticipated absence from home: they hope such assurances would free Ivah of her guilt so she can leave her family carefree to attend Mid-Pac, a prep-school on Oahu. When the possibility of Ivah's possible departure begins to sink in, "Maisie wants to cry," prompting Big Sis to "change the topic" by teasing Miss Ito about her admirers (Yamanaka 1997: 198-99). "Though not explicitly erotic," Chuh writes, this scene of banter "implies an eroticized pleasure between Big Sis and Miss Ito as shared intimate smiles and the familiarity of cohabitation are recounted" (2003: 143).

With this line of interpretation as her premise, which is not persuasively established by her own citation of the novel (Yamanaka 1997: 199), Chuh makes two additional claims of equally dubious textual bearing: the first is Big Sis and Miss Ito's presence as the children's only source of "happiness" and the second is their exclusive ability to "mitigate the harsh circumstances of the Ogata children" (2003: 144). She then proceeds with a series of theoretical declarations that I now quote at length:

> By closing with a nonheteronormative family that functions as the mechanism for potential salvation, the novel interrogates the presumptive value of normatively wrought conceptions of family and home as places and spaces of safety and innocence. Home and family, metaphors for national belongingness, are reconstituted in *Blu's Hanging* as processes that occur in negotiation with but in difference from heteronormativity... [T]his newly formed family that augurs a hopeful future ... is "queer" in the sense that the term ... designate[s] an alternative to the naturalized, heteronormative, masculinist social and political configurations installed by the U.S. hegemonic nationalism. In this sense, Yamanaka articulates what might be conceived as a transnational sensibility. Transnational here names a space that eludes conscription by the national imaginary, and one in which practices of subjectivity that cannot be represented within a national symbolic economy might find legibility [*sic*][19]... The novel and debates about it ... illuminate the need for Asian American studies to revisit the implications of working with nation as its presumptive basis and parameters.

> (ibid.: 144–145)

For starters, *Blu's Hanging* does not "close" with the scene of what Chuh characterizes as "eroticized pleasure" that constitutes a new family in the "mitigation of [the children's] harsh circumstances" (ibid.: 143). In fact, Big Sis and Miss Ito's promise of assistance aside, the scene in question only ushers in another sixty pages of the narrative in which Yamanaka intensifies the crisis of the Ogata family with Ivah's conflicting thoughts over her younger siblings' precarious condition. By eschewing a due consideration of this last one-fifth of the novel, with which Yamanaka grounds her original treatment of the dysfunctional family in the disappearance of the welfare state, and armed with a hypothetical homoerotic family as her fictional if not fictive foundation, Chuh is able to proceed quite wistfully with her own critical contrivances. In her pronouncements, the old Ogata home and family exemplify the national, which is in essence "naturalized, heteronormative, masculinist," — therefore bad, and therefore in need of dismissal (ibid.: 144). The "newly formed family," on the other hand, is "queer," and therefore, "transnational" and, necessarily good. Although neither Yamanaka fleshes it out in the novel proper, nor does Chuh herself elaborate on it, the model family of Chuh's pure projection has nevertheless become her presumptive if not altogether presumptuous ground to unsettle the parameters of the nation-state in Asian American studies *and* to "disown America."

Besides the rather suspect use of textual evidences, the theoretical reason here seems to have suffered from comparable leaps of faith. Readers familiar with *Blu's Hanging* cannot fail to note that Yamanaka's central concern with the family and the nation is expressly a concern with subjectivity and sociality whose significance at the level of the novel, simply put, is not sexual. Yamanaka never implies, as Chuh clearly does, that the homosexual form of sociality is essentially more egalitarian and caring than the heterosexual one. Nor can we discern anywhere from the text Yamanaka's attempt at recuperating queer sexuality into the same formation of heteronormative marriage and children of the sort that Chuh's interpretation has imposed upon Big Sis and Miss Ito as a putative lesbian couple, with their supposed incorporation of the Ogata kids.[20] This is not to say that Yamanaka's narration of subjectivity and sociality is insensitive to the role of gender and sexuality, for they indeed haunt Ivah's narrative consciousness and the political unconscious undergirding her emotional turmoil and ethical quandary:

> Be a veterinarian, a taxidermist, a zoologist.
> *You like her come all mute again?*
> . . .
> The best sekihan I ever ate. I was twelve the last time the red rice stuck to my teeth.
> *Who going cook for the two of them?*
> Who comes first in your life?
> *Family always come first.*
> Should I stay?
> I want to go.
> *You betta live with what you choose.*
> Mama, teach me bow to be Ivah too.
> . . .
> Smoke hangs on the still night. Mama's a cloud shape that moves into the form of a mother, a shape that funnels as it forms. I've seen this with my eyes open and clear.
>> "Go, Ivah," my Mama says, "Save yourself."
>> (Yamanaka 1997: 243–245, original emphases)

Yamanaka's deployment of free indirect speech triangulates the voices of the father, mother, and the narrator Ivah in dialogical tension and crystallizes what is truly at stake in the novel. Ivah's aspiration is typically modern liberal democratic: she wants to leave home to attend Mid-Pac, getting a foothold in the upward modern trajectory of personal and professional development by first accessing available dominant cultural capital. Bertram's italicized scolding assumes the voice of a patriarch not only in the name of familial integrity but also a taken-for-granted gender division of caring responsibilities. Finally, the spectral resonance of Ella, the sacrificial mother coming from the dead with all her caring credentials and ethical authority, releases Ivah from her inherited obligations by urging her daughter, as though on a mid-air plane about to crash, to "put on the oxygen mask" for herself first. "'Mama,' Blu yells into the night. 'Heaven is not here,'" because there in the ideal society, we believe in both the realization of individual potentials and the thriving of families and communities (ibid.: 260). The fact that Yamanaka has throughout kept the unnerving choice of either saving yourself or your family in relentless suspension — never resorting to the thematic closure Chuh forces upon the text in her formulaic celebration of "variegated freedoms" of "differences"   speaks volumes about the novelist's conviction in the power of literature to indict injustice and imagine equitable commons (Chuh 2003: 145).

Yamanaka's targets are allusive but not at all elusive as though lost in the fun house discursive deferrals. For the author of *Blu's Hanging*, the failure of the Ogata family is symptomatic of the failure of the post-civil rights U.S. as a liberal democracy, a territorially bound nation-state promised to its citizenry as a haven from the foes of actually existing communism of the Eastern bloc and the creative destruction internal to its own system of capitalism. Let us recall briefly the expansion of industrial capitalism along with the evolution of the family form and individual subjectivity.[21] With the enclosure movement and the removal of the productive force from the household, the historical advent of capitalism has irrecoverably altered the traditional or natural family, its localized economy, as well as its reproductive functions. Because capital's extraction of human labor from the family is driven by the profit motive and has little consideration for the filial cycle of reproduction, the state, as a political institution of affiliation, has to step in to impede the cannibalism of capitalism. It has to assume the nurturing functions of reproductive sustenance that accumulation for its own sake has left behind and the unclear family alone can no longer maintain, thus securing the state's own *raison d'être*. This bio-political as well as geopolitical arrangement that tries to stabilize the triangular interests of labor/citizen, the nation-state, and a territorially circumscribed capitalism is, as I borrow from David Harvey earlier, a kind of "embedded liberalism," whose "welfare institutions, however imperfectly they have delivered on their promises," argues Bruce Robbins in his recent literary history of the welfare state, "offer the version of common good within which most of the upward mobility genre makes the most sense" (Robbins 2007: xiv).[22]

I would not characterize *Blu's Hanging* as a novel from the era of embedded liberalism, for the obvious reason that it is firmly situated in the Reaganite States of de-regulated, de-territorialized, and therefore dis-embedded capitalism. However, I shall not hesitate to consider Yamanaka's as a work of "spectral liberalism" in that it seizes the residual tensions of a vanishing liberalism in the neoliberal social setting. As such, the novel performs the cultural work to reassess the contemporary viability of an upward mobile fiction through the characters' complex negotiations of individual and familial interests. With her eyes on Moloka'i, Yamanaka scans the island's wasteland of material impoverishment, psychological injury, and social impasse, in order to summon up the liberal democratic ghost that global capitalism of the historical present seems to have exorcized. What haunts the fictional landscape of *Blu's Hanging* is understandably not the spaceship of "flexible citizens" in Aihwa Ong's critical coinage, consisting of "mobile managers, technocrats, and professionals seeking to both circumvent *and* benefit from different nation-state regimes by selecting different sites for investments, work, and family relocation" (1999: 112).[23] Instead, Ivah, Blu, and Maisie, the children who have to work in order to eat, and, Bertram, their ineffectual father who has to take on multiple deadbeat jobs to keep the family from drowning, are specters of the kind of American citizens in the neoliberal era — who are literally stripped of the most rudimentary capacities of choice, utterly grounded in their given location, unattended and unseen by both capital and state — precisely when individual choice is the mantra of reigning ideologies and the cornerstone of policies. Deserted by the symbolic ship of the liberal democratic nation, they are stranded on the tropical island very much like the "stateless people" in Hannah Arendt's original description, living in what Giorgio Agamben has later aptly termed as "states of exception."

As Etienne Balibar writes appreciatively, the author of *Origins of Totalitarianism* (1951) not only provides us with a singular history that connects "anti-Semitism, colonialism and imperialism with the genealogy of the racial state as a state of exception," but she also "reverses the traditional relation between human rights and political rights (the rights of man and the rights of the citizen)" (2008: 1637). This reversal, Balibar reasons, paves way for Arendt's "insistence on the situation of the stateless people, who lose their human rights, practically their human condition, when they are deprived of their legal status as national citizens" (ibid.). The value of Arendt's insistence on citizenship exposes the insufficiency of a humanism that merely reflects on "the indivisibility of the species" "from an ideal point of view, from which the common element of human beings is their origin and destination but not actual social or political structures" (ibid.: 1638). For Arendt, such a transcendental view of the humankind has little political or social significance until "such a common element or an element of ideal community [is] imagined as a moral goal underlying the construction of particular communities" (ibid.). For this reason, she "puts the right to have rights at the core of her conception of polity," and I shall add, she puts the rightful subject of the state at the core of her conception of the human (ibid.: 1637).[24]

Balibar's insightful take on Arendt's liberal conception of rights throws new light, first, on the status of the Asian American subject as it has been imagined at different historical junctures, and, second, on the ideal state and subject that *Blu's Hanging* intends to invoke. To reiterate a point from the beginning of this chapter, liberalism is notoriously a racial liberalism and thus helplessly Janus-faced. As subjects of historical legislative exclusion, the Asian immigrants embodied the states of exception to the liberal racial state of the U.S. and its constitution of national citizenry. The inaugural moment of Asian American formal incorporation into the national community on the heel of the 1960s' immigration reform, civil rights and anti-war movements, on the other hand, was followed by a neoliberal representation of the state and the subject. In the neoliberal regime of representation, rights are no longer conceived as goods guaranteed by the state but something the individual has to earn through his/her engagement with the market. The post-civil rights deracialization of U.S. democracy, if such transformation has indeed been more than superficial, is driven by a more substantial disaggregation of liberal democracy and the general dissolution of social welfare for American citizens regardless of race. The demands of racial and gender minorities to access the benefits of an embedded liberalism historically enjoyed by the majority are met with a war on welfare in the state's alignment with global capital and its withdrawal of commitment to the multiracial American citizenry.[25]

Yamanaka has taken full narrative account of the neoliberal revolutionary impact by her figuration of the succor-less Ogata family as almost "stateless people." Although not excluded from it *de jure,* the Ogata family has *de facto* eluded the civil order of basic security and sustenance. With her fictional lens zoomed on their abjection, Yamanaka avoids the pitfalls of privatizing narrative cause and effect and resolutely refuses intimations of any personal solution. Contrary to Thatcher's neoliberal slogan that dismisses the role of national society, exhorting individual and familial salvation while gutting structural support, and contrary to Chuh's similar suggestion of salvation through a privatized form of homoerotic sociality, Yamanaka dares to imagine otherwise. For the Asian American novelist, the failure of the Ogata family is not the failure of either Ivah or Bertram as individuals, nor the failure of the unclear form of sociality evolved under the historical needs of capitalist development. Instead, it is the failure of neoliberal capitalism, which, by obscuring its own absolute dependency on human labor, has externalized all the indispensable costs of bio-socio-reproduction from health care to education. It is also the failure of the neoliberal state, which — instead of checking capitalism's ruthless exploitation of nature, of both the living species and their environment — has complied with its short-term profit motive at the expense of the labor/citizen's enduring value and the planet's ecological health. In foregrounding the dilapidation of the Ogata family and the abhorring statelessness of the Moloka'i community, Yamanaka does not celebrate "the death of the subject" nor does she advocate the nirvana of "subjectlessness." Attuned to Arendt's insistence on the human entitlement to rights, Yamanaka has instead mercilessly condemned the neoliberal abandonment of the people for the sake of profit and willfully conjured up the representational specter of liberal democracy so that the rights of the citizen can be restored and the story of upward democratic mobility revived.[26]

The emergence of the Asian American subject is a product of transnational nationalism, caught between third world decolonization abroad and civil rights movements stateside. It is a paradoxical birth because the discursive emergence of Asian America also marks the retreat of the subject from social movements/legislative politics of the state and its entry into the academy in the form of textual politics and canon debates. Questions of political representation as a result are considerably transfigured into questions of literary and aesthetic representation. While Asian America owes its initial rise to the residual power of the U.S. in its unfulfilled liberal democratic promises, the transformation of the U.S. into a neoliberal post-nation-state has meant that the nation's historical covenant with the people is broken and its nefarious new nuptial with late capital has begun. Interestingly this reformation of state allegiance seems to coincide with the gradual institutionalization of both Asian American literature and Asian American academic critics, a twin development that at once signals the respectability of a hitherto little studied body of texts and the respectable rise of the Asian American professional managerial class in the form of tenure track professors, who, as we well know, swear their allegiance and owe their survival primarily to the ivory tower. The poststructural and postnational turn in Asian American criticism, cryptically informed by Michel Foucault's grievance against the French welfare state and his belief in "the technology of the self" has to be understood in two related contexts.[27] It has to be apprehended, first, in the context of how the subject of historical liberalism is dissolved on a global scale to make way for the thinkability and ascendancy of neoliberalism. Second, it has to be grasped in the social processes of Asian American embourgeoisization in the academy. The theoretical problematization of (collective) identity politics and of the (common) subject, appears integral to the individualization and privatization of the Asian American critic as a self-interested and self-possessive subject; the appropriation of poststructuralism in Asian American criticism without due attention to textual and historical specificity seems in this regard little other than a quick act of legitimating one's intellectual labor in trendy discourses of distinction.

To historicize: the so-called demise of "grand narratives" literally follows the actual death of "great societies," and the "deconstructive attitude" that Chuh adopts for her academic analysis cannot be divorced from the logic of finance capital, whose most spectacular non-referentiality and deferred effects, is the "derivatives." While Chuh sounds ecstatic that "subjectlessness" designates "the *(im)possibility of justice*, where 'justice' refers to a state as yet unexperienced and unrepresentable" (2003: 8; original emphasis), we can claim with epistemological certainty and ethical sobriety that justice cannot possibly be derived from the operations of either Madoff or the market. In view of this reasoning, we are ready to reassess Chuh's conclusion:

> As I have attempted to suggest through this book's arguments, the political may be seen to be animated by difference, not identity ... To address, account for, and accommodate difference, we must remember that there is no common subject of Asian American Studies; there are only infinite differences that we discursively cohere into epistemological objects.

> (ibid.: 147)

> Permanently fluctuating and irregular, justice cannot be conceived within a politics of heterogeneity as a fixed goal but emerges rather as an orientation, as a commitment to an indefatigable and illimitable interrogation of myriad relations of power and how they give, shape, and sometimes take life. When difference meets itself in the shape of deconstructed identity, the complex personhood of every self and other rises to the surface. If "Asian American" could name such a space and Asian American studies could sustain it, we would make, I think, an important move toward imagining otherness otherwise, in ways that immediately accord agency, complexity, and contradiction.

> (ibid.: 150)

As much as I am appreciative of the poetic indeterminancy of Chuh's utopianism and sympathetic to her suggestion that justice is a measure of historical evolution and expansion, I strongly disagree with her claims for the future of Asian American cultural politics. When Chuh proposes to have "difference meet itself," the tautology she deploys essentially reinstates "difference" as a thing in itself rather than a deconstructive signifier for "relationship," discursive and social. Despite her vehement disavowal of the subject, then, her "politics of heterogeneity" practically becomes a new form of identity politics: the only difference is that Chuh is advocating an identity politics not of the democratic commons but of radical individual alterity. In her euphoria about the infinity of difference, the "political" has become purely discursive if not forever deferred, and the "justice" that is supposed to emerge from it has become, in her own words, "a state as yet unexperienced and unrepresentable" (ibid.: 8). We recall here Arendt's distaste for the transcendental conception of rights and justice without the imagination of actual political communities, and we should count ourselves fortunate that Chuh has at least rendered her alternative agenda for Asian American Studies in the subjunctive mood.

Regardless of Chuh's mystification, however, the concept of justice was in fact at the heart of two clearly delineated ideological oppositions in the 1970s, when the Asian American subject began to emerge and when liberalism and neoliberalism came to loggerheads. *Theory of Justice* (1972) by John Rawls is the liberal representative. Central to Rawls is his famous "difference principle" that justifies inequalities in the distribution of scarce goods (power, money, access to education and healthcare) *as long as* such inequalities serve to enhance the advantage of the least favored groups in society. Based on this principle, and a set of other principles of social contract that logically constitute his argument of "justice as fairness," Rawls concludes that justice, for it to materialize, will entail such arrangements by social and economic institutions that are aimed to benefit maximally the worst-off. In this liberal regime of justice, individual and group differences, be they natural or artificial, are accounted for by the provision of the greatest equal opportunity for all. While Rawls conceives of rights and justice as fundamental concerns of society, of national community, and thus of the liberal democratic state, Fredrich Hayek considers the whole idea of "social justice" "a mirage" and the consignment of agency to society a mistake (Hayek 1976). Typical of the latter-day anti-statist, anti-government, and anti-regulatory discourse of hegemonic neoliberalism that he has helped to hatch, Hayek touts the free market as the level playing field for the attainment of liberty. Equality yields to the tyranny of an alleged market efficiency, whose mechanisms Hayek erroneously believes are able to deliver scarce resources to where they bring the mightiest return, so that even in an admittedly unequal system of distribution, the rewards shall trickle down and the poor would be better off.[28]

Since the birth of the Asian American subject, a deregulated and disembedded capitalism — in its ever more unfettered and reckless exploitation of difference in labor markets and stock exchanges, in its indefatigable and illimitable push for commodification of all differences that do not yet conform to the logic of cash-nexus — has been changing the subject and altering the soul, as Thatcher once promised. Neoliberal capitalism is producing its own desirabie subjects, who, apparently oblivious to the growth of the greatest economic and social inequality that our nation has seen, would delight in the non-referentiality of the social, the unrepresentability of the political, and the heterogeneity of individual agency and choice in the "promotion of a culture where difference is perceived as a variation in style and opinion" (Willis 1991: 374). What we urgently need — for Asian American Studies in specific and humanistic and social scientific inquiries of an ideal subject and an ideal society in general — is neither the celebration of private difference nor the suspension of justice in endless theoretical hubris but the active cultivation of democratic commons. In the predominance of the global market and the glaring absence of global democratic governance, such commons will have to be reconstituted from the flawed and fragile formation of national democracies.[29]

I wish to conclude my musing on the subject of "(the) Asian America(n)" by joining Wendy Brown in her mourning of American liberal democracy. While liberalism is riddled with "hypocrisy" and its historical humanistic subject has been hopelessly "bourgeois, white, masculinist, and heterosexual," "given the other historical possibilities" and the current historical deprivation of its meaning, liberalism is also that which, to quote Brown's strategic use of Spivak, we "cannot not want" (Brown 2003: 11). Instead of a "subjectless discourse" that condemns liberalism by bypassing its legacy and ignoring its own dependency on it, this double negative betrays an ambivalence of attachment to and disavowal of liberalism. The contradictory constitution of the Asian American subject is very much an expression of this ambivalence, an ambivalence that acknowledges our "mix of love and hostility to [liberalism]" so that a diligent as well as intelligent ethical counter-vision to the neoliberal world order can be imagined (ibid.: 13).

5.

The organizational principles of *Asian American Literature* reflect both the theoretical orientations I have so far outlined and the actual abundance of scholarship available for assemblage at this point. While the editorial decision is solely mine, limited by an individual's inevitable partial command and particular take on an academic field at large, the content selected here has been significantly predetermined by the collective wisdom of my colleagues, who, with their prodigious publication in distinguished scholarly books and journals, have together identified the literary merit of an existing Asian American oeuvre and made possible this substantive sampling of Asian American criticism. It is this communal critical judgment, individually expressed in the various interpretive and theoretical writings and fruitfully accumulated over the past four decades, that has shaped the contours of Asian American literature of which I hope to have brought into sharper focus. No worthy work, however marginal to my idiosyncratic preferences in aesthetics and politics, is not given its due consideration. Any negligence of significant authors who should have received critical treatment here will have to be attributed entirely to my own ignorance. Students and scholars of Asian American literature should therefore consider this set of Asian American criticism a vital first-stop research and pedagogical resource from which to embark on further explorations.

Besides a shared scholarly recognition of aesthetic merit as the guiding spirit, the selection of representative works in *Asian American Literature* are premised both on the particularity of authorship, consisting of the writer's ethnic descent, citizenship and/or residency status, and the specificity of the author's subject of reference. National Book Award winner Ha Jin would not have earned a chapter, had he continued to publish his fiction and poetry exclusively on China (Vol. II: Chapter 28). Though set primarily in Manila, Jessica Hagedom's *Dogeaters* has gained a single entry, however, for the novel's systematic evocation of U.S. colonialism in the Philippines (Vol. II: Chapter 26). Robert Olen Butler, the Pulitzer Prize-winning author of *A Good Scent from a Strange Mountain* featuring an ensemble cast of Vietnamese immigrants, is not included, because of his non-Asian American origin. Nor shall one find in this set an extensive examination of the critically acclaimed novelist of *Obasan* (1981), Joy Kogawa, for the simple fact that she is Japanese Canadian. While there are critical anthologies that group Asian American texts under the rubric of Asian North American literature or Asian Pacific American literature, suggestions of a Pacific Rim or a transnational Asian American literary formation that combine Asian and Asian American texts by foregrounding works of authorial racial affinity beyond geopolitical sovereignty, and renewed attention to works by Caucasian Americans portraying Asians or Asian Americans that both contributes to and is constitutive of the dominant epistemology of the Asian in Anglophone discourse (Vol. I: Chapter 19), these have not been the critical criteria with which this Routledge reference set abide by. Importance has been selectively placed both on the creativity of the Asian American writing subject and on his or her imagination of the real or ideal United States.

Foregrounding the racial and national dimensions of Asian American imagination is not to delimit the scope of imagination as such, but to center a way of seeing, reading, knowing, and feeling in its embodied and embedded complexities. The definitional parameter circumscribed by racial and national particularity is meant to couple literary production with democratic participation so that the representation of the Asian American is intimately tied to the imagination of the *res publica*. Such a formation wrestles with the historical duality of liberalism in the States' exclusive assignment of rights and liberties, combats the de-realization of race in the neoliberal dissolution of social contract, and enables the materialization of the Asian American subject not as aliens nor abstractions but democratic equivalence in the United States. In this manner, the "Asian America(n)" of our categorical understanding effectively opens up a more materially grounded, historically astute, and ethically aware critical inquiry of transnational imaginaries, diasporic movements, and interethnic formations (Vol. I: Chapter 15) that neither resorts to the cosmopolitan kitsch of "hybridity" that never quite transcends its original biological associations, nor enacts an American imperial unconscious that eagerly enfolds Asia into the globalization of Asian American studies.[30] I regret, however, *Asian American Literature*'s emphases on race and nation matters have not significantly helped inclusion of works that are embedded in and engendered from the soil of America yet rendered in Asian languages. Although linguistic transplantation in Chinese and Japanese language poetry is examined in two separate chapters (Vol III: Chapters 50 and 51), the set as whole has not provided an adequate picture of a multilingual Asian American corpus.[31] This shortcoming at once betrays the fact that the construction and dissemination of the Asian American canon remain an officially Anglophone pedagogical and scholarly enterprise and reveal the critical need to archive, translate, present and to preserve the linguistic diversity of Asian American literary production.

Asian American Literature is organized by genre into four volumes. Volume I ("Literary History: Criticism and Theory") showcases in approximate chronological order the foundational work that defines the parameters of Asian American literature in its various stages of evolution. The subsequent three volumes follow a general alphabetic arrangement based on the last name of the chosen author. Volume II ("Prose") brings together the best interpretive work and practical criticism on key works of Asian American fiction and non-fiction. Volume III ("Poetry") assembles the essential scholarship on Asian American verse, while the final volume in the set ("Drama and Performance") highlights significant research on theatrical texts, performance, and "cyberrace." Readers are encouraged to consult with both the table of contents and the extensive index to take full advantage of this set's wealth of scholarly material and rich cross-reference.

Notes

1. The term, "governmentality," is from Foucault, which refers to the rationality of government or governmental reason that has implications for the conduct of both the state and the individual subject. See in particular, *The Foucault Effect: Studies in Governmentality* edited

by Graham Burchell, Colin Gordon, and Peter Miller (Chicago: U of Chicago P, 1991) and Nikolas Rose's *Powers of Freedom: Redefining Political Thought* (Cambridge: Cambridge UP, 1999).

2. On liberalism's historical translation, see a helpful critique of "historicism" in Dipesh Chakrabarty (2000: 2–23).

3. The period of embedded liberalism is also known as a period of "Fordism" or welfare capitalism (Harvey 1990).

4. Like liberalism, its historical antecedent, neoliberalism has both national and transnational dimensions. While generally regarded as the globalization of the Anglo-American form of market capitalism and its restructuring of the state, labor/citizen, and capital relationship worldwide, my emphasis in the subsequent analysis of neoliberalism is on its manifestation stateside through the construction of Asian American subject. See Harvey's brief history of neoliberalism (2005), and Foucault (2008).

5. Here, my readings of classical liberalism draw from Arrighi (2007: 43–44), and of neoliberalism from Brown (2003: 5) and Michael Peters (1996).

6. Goldberg notes when "state bureaucracies grew into major employers of historically excluded groups" in the wake of civil rights and anti-colonial movements, "a commanding sector of the electorate" began to view "the state, if not as black, certainly as tending to promote and service the interests of racially minoritized citizens" (2008: 1712–1713). As I shall elaborate in Section 4, the post-racial discourse that seems to coincide with the anti-statist and anti-government discourse is part and parcel of the neoliberal programmatic dissolution of the liberal social contract.

7. From this point on, I shall use in-text parenthesis to indicate the volume and chapter number of the piece that I refer to in *Asian American Literature*.

8. The latter is essentially the argument of Etienne Balibar, "Subjection and Subjectivation" (1994: 1–15).

9. Two points of clarification are in order: (a) "Multiculturalism" can be "conservative" or "critical" and mean different things to different people. For the most part, it has become a euphemism for "racial diversity" within the U.S. While I reject the equation of "race" and "culture" implicit in the term, "multiculturalism" does seem to register cultural pluralism and the diverse demography of American democracy. In this regard, multiculturalism appears to have ethnic nationalism at its core in ways that "postcolonialism" does not in the context of the United States. (b) To follow Lipsitz, we can appropriately call "embedded liberalism" an

abstract form of "identity politics" from which "white people [have historically] profit[ed]" (1998: vii-xx).

10. The infamous Bush TV commercial against Dukakis should sufficiently illustrate this representational divergence between the normative and the minority subjects in the American imaginary. The visceral effectiveness of Willie Horton's mug shot lies in its incitation of a racist cultural unconscious that equates blackness with felony. Horton's image evokes collective fear, but a substitute picture of Ted Bundy, however, would never remotely suggest white criminality en masse. This is because the Euro-American Bundy can, in the entrenched representational scheme of things, be detached from any undesirable group associations, but the Afro-American Horton simply cannot. Ted Bundy is always and already individualized and de-racialized, while Willie Horton, forever the racial subject, only achieves the effect of group signification in the seconds of his televisual fame as black urban threat.

11. The literature on "whiteness" is too vast to list here. For its particular manifestation in cultural representation, see the scintillating analysis by Toni Morrison (1992).

12. When market relations and rationalities override the subject's relationship to society, the liberal subject practically becomes the neoliberal one.

13. For a reading of Hanna Pitkin's "concept of representation" in the context of Asian American literary production and reception, see Li (1998: 174–184). Maxine Hong Kingston, *The Woman Warrior: Memoirs of a Girlhood Among Ghosts* (1976); Amy Chua, *The Battle Hymns of the Tiger Mother* (2011).

14. See Ann Anlin Cheng (2000) and Laura Kang (2002).

15. For an illuminating reflection on the humanist inquiry of race and representation in Asian American Studies, see Susan Koshy, James Lee, and Viet Nguyen from a Shu-mei Shih coordinated forum in *PMLA* 123. 5 (2008): 1540–1564.

16. The scholarly significance of *Imagine Otherwise* can be partially gauged in its book reviews. See Yoonmee Chang who notes that the book is the "winner of the American Studies Association 2004 Lora Romeo First Book Publication Prize" (858; *American Literature* 77.4 (2005): 858-61), and Nhi Lieu who writes about the book's inspirational impact on "a new generation of cultural studies scholars" (496; *American Quarterly* 60.2 (2008): 491–496). Because the study is indicative of a popular yet disturbing trend in Asian American criticism, I shall engage its terms with the care of critical consideration its daring claims deserve.

17. My discussion of Chuh's work draws primarily from the last chapter and the conclusion of her book (2003: 112-51), both of which are included in full, as Chapter 16 of Volume I. Page

references are to the original text.

18. See Fujikane and Okamura, Special Issue of *Amerasia* 26.2 (2000); and Fujikane (2000): 158–194.

19. "Transnational" as an adjective cannot be properly used as the subject of a sentence, which has to be a noun (except perhaps in a subjectless discourse).

20. The heated debates on the desirability of gay marriage and gay family, for instance, evidence a clear queer difference on biological and social reproduction.

21. See Zaretsky (1976).

22. See also Paul Bové's helpful review assay, "The Novel, the State, and the Professions: On Reading Bruce Robbins" (2010).

23. For Aihwa Ong, " 'flexible citizenship' refers to the cultural logics of capitalist accumulation, travel and displacement that induce subjects to respond fluidly and opportunistically to changing political economic conditions" (1999: 6). As such, the "flexible citizen" is a class-specific subject with abundant capital at his disposal for his self-interested manipulation of state and market mechanisms. Neither stateless nor subjectless, he is appropriately the entrepreneurial subject of global capitalism.

24. My addition is derived from Hannah Arendt, *The Human Condition* (1958/1989: 7–21).

25. While the neoliberal dismantling of liberal democracy affects U.S. citizens negatively regardless of race, the apparently "raceless" policies that redistributes national wealth upwards toward the super-rich tend to have a stronger harmful impact on people of color.

26. Although the controversy over *Blu's Hanging* seems an intraethnic feud, in which the Filipino American community charges a Japanese American author with alleged racial stereotyping, the argument against Yamanaka in effect expresses a conviction in democratic representation which the author of the novel unambiguously shares. In the conflation of literary and political representations, the desire for the benefits of embedded liberalism from an economically disadvantaged ethnic group was, however, racially displaced onto another more advantaged ethnic group, revealing ever so poignantly both the consequences of the neoliberal redistribution of national wealth and the enduring Hawaiian colonial legacy of divide and conquer. Hurt and outrage at different personal and communal levels aside, the novel has served an important public function in foregrounding the issue of poverty and exposing the seed of inequality inherent in the neoliberal revolution.

27. See Brook Thomas on the use of continental theory without due attention to national historical specificities (2003: 148–149), and Paul Bové's caution against "how cultural studies

absorption of the academic humanities plays havoc with the value and importance of historical evidence" (2003: 278).

28. Of great interest is Pierre Bourdieu, *Acts of Resistance: Against the Tyranny of the Market* (1998).

29. See Peter Singer (2002).

30. For the last point, see Kuan-Hsing Chen's especially cogent critique of a certain kind of "programmatic move to forge a disciplinary space *between,* intended to *cross* or *disrupt* the boundaries of Asian and Asian American Studies" (Vol. I: Chapter 15).

31. Readers interested in learning about the Sino-phone component of Asian American literature may start with Chapters 5 and 6 of Xiao-Huang Yin's *Chinese American Literature since the 1850s* (2000: 157–228).

Works cited

Agamben, Giorgio. *Homo Sacer: Sovereign Power and Bare Life.* Trans. Daniel Heller-Roazen. Stanford, CA: Stanford UP, 1998.

Arendt, Hannah. *The Human Condition.* Chicago, U of Chicago P, 1958/1989.

Arrighi, Giovanni. *Adam Smith in Beijing: Lineages of the Twentieth-First Century,* London: Verso, 2007.

Balibar, Etienne. "Racism Revisited: Sources, Relevance, and Aporias of a Modern Concept." *PMLA* 123.5 (October 2008): 1630-39.

—— "Subjection and Subjectivation." *Supposing the Subject.* Ed. Joan Copjec. New York: Verso, 1994: 1-15.

Bourdieu, Pierre. *Acts of Resistance: Against the Tyranny of the Market.* Trans. Richard Rice. New York: The New Press, 1998.

Bové, Paul "Afterword: Can We Judge the Humanities by Their Future as a Course of Study?" In *Globalization and the Humanities,* ed. David Leiwei Li. Hong Kong: Hong Kong UP, 2003: 273-284.

—— "The Novel, the State, and the Professions: On Reading Bruce Robbins." *Comparative Literature* 62.2 (Spring 2010): 179-88.

Brown, Wendy. *States of Injury: Power and Freedom in Late Modernity.* Princeton: Princeton UP, 1995.

——. "Neo-liberalism and the End of Liberal Democracy." *Theory and Event* 7.1 (2003).

Burchell, Graham, Gordon, Colin, and Miller, Peter. *The Foucault Effect: Studies in Governmentality.* Chicago: U of Chicago P, 1991.

Chakrabarty, Dipesh. *Provincializing Europe: Postcolonial Thought and Historical Difference.* Princeton: Princeton UP, 2000.

Cheng, Ann Anlin. *The Melancholy of Race: Psychoanalysis, Assimilation, and Hidden Grief.* New York: Oxford UP, 2000.

Cheung, King-kok. *Articulate Silences: Hisaye Yamamoto, Maxine Hong Kingston, Joy Kogawa.* Ithaca, NY:

Cornell UP, 1993.

Chin, Frank, Jeffrey Paul Chan, Lawson Fusao Inanda, and Shawn Wong. eds. *Aiiieeeee!: An Anthology of Chinese and Japanese American Literature*. Washington D.C.: Howard Up, 1974/1983.

Chua, Amy. *The Battle Hymns of the Tiger Mother*. New York: Penguin, 2011.

Chuh, Kandice. *Imagine Otherwise: On Asian Americanist Critique. Durham,* NC: Duke UP, 2003.

Espiritu, Yen Le. *Asian American Panethnicity: Bridging Institutions and Identities*. Philadelphia, PA: Temple UP, 1992.

Foucault, Michel. *The Birth of Biopolitics: Lectures at the Collége de France*. Ed. Michel Senellart. Trans. Graham Burchell. New York: Palgrave Macmillan. 2008.

Fujikane, Candace. "Sweeping Racism Under the Rug of 'Censorship': The Controversy Over *Blu's Hanging,*" *Amerasia* 26.2 (2000): 158-94.

Fujikane, Candace and Jonathan Okamura, eds. *Whose Vision? Asian Settler Colonialism in Hawai'i*. Special Issue of *Amerasia* 26.2 (2000).

Goldberg, David Theo. *The Racial State*. Malden, MA: Blackwell, 2002,

——. "Racisms without Racism." *PMLA* 123.5 (October 2008): 1712–1716.

Harvey, David. *The Condition of Postmodernity: An Enquiry into the Origins of Social Change*. Cambridge: Blackwell Publishers, 1990.

——. *A Brief History of Neoliberalism*. New York: Oxford UP, 2005.

Hayek, Fredrick, *The Mirage of Social Justice*. Chicago: University of Chicago Press, 1976.

Jones, Leroy, and Larry Neal, eds. *Black Fire: An Anthology of Afro-American Writing*. New York: William Morrow, 1968.

Kang, Laura. *Compositional Subjects: Enfiguring Asian American Women,* Durham: Duke UP, 2002.

Kingston, Maxine Hong. *The Woman Warrior: Memoirs of a Girlhood Among Ghosts,* New York: Vintage Books, 1976.

Li, David Leiwei. "*China Men:* Maxine Hong Kingston and the American Canon," *American Literary History*. 2.3 (Fall 1990): 482-502.

——. *Imagining the Nation: Asian American Literature and Cultural Consent*. Stanford, CA: Stanford UP, 1998.

——. "The State and Subject of Asian American Criticism: Psychoanalysis, Transnational Discourse, and Democratic Ideals." *American Literary History* 15.3 (Fall 2003): 603–624.

Lipsitz, George. *The Possessive Investment in Whiteness: How White People Profit from Identity Politics*. Philadelphia: Temple UP, 1998.

Lowe, Lisa. *Immigrant Acts: On Asian American Cultural Politics*. Durham: Duke UP, 1996.

Macpherson, C. B. *The Political Theory of Possessive Individualism: Hobbes to Locke*. Oxford: Oxford UP, 1962.

Mills, Charles. *The Racial Contract*. Ithaca, NY: Cornell UP; 1997.

——. "Racial Liberalism." *PMLA* 123.5 (October 2008): 1380–1417.

Morrison, Toni. *Playing in the Dark: Whiteness and the Literary Imagination*. Cambridge, MA: Harvard UP, 1992.

Okada, John. *No-No Boy*. Seattle: U of Washington P, 1957/1976.

Okihiro, Gary. *Margins and Mainstreams: Asians in American History and Culture*. Seattle: U of Washington P, 1994.

Ong, Aihwa, *Flexible Citizenship: The Cultural Logics of Transnationality*. Durham, NC: Duke UP, 1999.

Omi, Michael, and Howard Winant. *Racial Formation in the United States: From the 1960s to the 1990s*. 2nd ed. New York: Routledge, 1994.

Peters, Michael. "Neoliberalism." *Encyclopedia of Philosophy of Education*. London: Routledge, 1999. *(www. vusst. hr/ENCYCLOPEDI/Aineoliberalism,him)*.

Rawls, John. *Theory of Justice*. Rev. ed. Cambridge, MA: Harvard UP, 1992.

Readings, Bill. *The University in Ruins*. Cambridge, MA: Harvard UP, 1996.

Robbins, Bruce. *Upward Mobility and the Common Good: Towards a Literary History of the Welfare State*. Princeton: Princeton UP, 2007.

Rose, Nikolas. *Powers of Freedom; Redefining Political Thought*. Cambridge: Cambridge UP, 1999.

Saxton, Alexander. *The Indispensable Enemy. Labor and the Anti-Chinese Movement in California*. Berkeley, U of California P, 1971.

Singer, Peter. *One World: The Ethics of Globalization*. New Haven, CT: Yale UP, 2002.

Sohn, Stephen Hong, Pani Lai, and Donald Goellnicht eds. "Theorizing Asian American Fiction," a Special Issue of *Modern Fiction Studies* 56.1 (Spring 2010).

Tachiki, Amt, et al., eds. *Roots: An Asian American Reader*. Los Angeles: Asian American Studies Center, UCLA. 1971.

Takaki, Ronald. *Strangers from a Different Shore: A History of Asian Americans*. Boston: Little Brown, 1989.

Thomas, Brook. "The Nation-State Matters: Comparing Multiculturalism(s) in an Age of Globalization." In *Globalization and the Humanities,* ed. David Leiwei Li. Hong Kong: Hong Kong UP, 2003: 135-158.

Williams, Raymond. *Keywords: A Vocabulary of Culture and Society* (Revised Edition). New York: Oxford UP, 1983.

Willis, Susan. *A Primer for Daily Life*. New York: Routledge, 1991.

Yamanaka, Lois Ann. *Biu's Hanging*. New York: Avon, 1997.

Yin Xiao-Huang. *Chinese American Literature since the 1850s*. Urbana and Chicago: University of Illinois Press, 2000.

Zaretsky, Eli. *Capitalism, Family, and Personal Life*. New York: Harper & Row, 1976.

Žižek, Slavoj. *First as Tragedy, Then as Farce*. New York: Verso, 2009.

10

Asian American Autobiography/Memoir
美国亚裔自传 / 回忆录

Traise Yamamoto

评论家简介

　　山本特莱西（Traise Yamamoto），美国华盛顿大学英语系博士，现为美国加利福尼亚大学河滨分校英语系副教授。研究领域包括美国亚裔文学和文化、诗歌、种族和性别理论、自传研究以及英美现代主义。专著有《掩饰自己，塑造主体：日裔美国女性、身份及身体》（*Masking Selves, Making Subjects: Japanese American Women, Identity, and the Body*, 1999）。其论文发表于《性别与阶级》（*Gender and Class*）、《亲密批判：自传体文学批评》（*The Intimate Critique: Autobiographical Literary Criticism*）、《符号：文化与社会中的女性杂志》（*Signs: Journal of Women in Culture and Society*）等期刊；代表论文《对阿尔西亚·康纳的道歉：个人回忆与公开回忆录的伦理》，收于《肤色之下：女孩如何在美国体验种族区别》（"An Apology to Althea Connor: Private Memory and the Ethics of Public Memoir," *Under Her Skin: How Girls Experience Race in America*, 2004）一书。

文章简介

　　自传曾经是美国亚裔文学最广泛使用的文学体裁之一，也曾引起过巨大争议。美国亚裔自传的创作和发展与美国的社会历史紧密相关，受到了诸如美国与亚洲国家关系、移民政策、重大历史事件、出版市场等多种因素的影响。文章依照历史分期呈现了美国亚裔自传各阶段的创作特征，同时将具有范式革新意义或曾引起争议的重要作品放在亚裔自传史的框架下重新解读。文章解析了早期与中期美国亚裔自传对个体经历、族群历史以及个人与族群关系的表现方式，同时也包含对原创与出版修改、事实与虚构、反叙事等自传研究本身等重要问题的探讨。除此之外，文章还分析了 20 世纪后期美国亚裔自传创作的两个主要方面：一是以东南亚裔作家为主要代表创作的、突显极端暴力与创伤的见证者叙事；二是文学回忆录，包括回归叙事以及在后殖民与跨国流动性背景下书写自我的回忆录。最后文章指出，美国亚裔自传创作在新世纪进入了蓬勃发展的时期，以更加多样的风格书写个体，体现个体、族群与世界的关系，诠释了在现实与历史的张力间亚裔美国人复杂的主体性。

文章出处：Lee, Rachel C., editor. *The Routledge Companion to Asian American and Pacific Islander Literature.* London & New York: Routledge, 2014, pp. 379-391.

Asian American Autobiography/Memoir

Traise Yamamoto

Introduction

Autobiography is at once one of the most widely used genres in Asian American literature and the most controversial. In a 1985 essay, "This is Not an Autobiography," writer Frank Chin declared that the form is a "peculiarly Christian literary weapon" that has "destroyed knowledge of Chinaman history and culture" (1985. 109). Chin's objections to the form rest primarily upon two functions of classic Christian autobiography, from which he sees a straight line of descent to the present day: conversion and confession. Conversion, according to Chin, powers what he asserts is an Asian American autobiographical tradition that tells "the same Cinderella story of rescue from the perverse, the unnatural, and cruel Chinese" (1985: 110). Confession is the mode through which this storytelling is enacted. While much of what follows in Chin's essay is pocked by misogyny, homophobia, and reductive masculinism, Chin's contention that "My life is not one of my market commodities" (1985: 123) might be read as responding to some of the earliest examples of Asian American autobiographical writing. At the same time, reading the body of Asian American autobiography in agonistic relationship to Chin's statement productively highlights the many ways in which these texts self-consciously resist and radically destabilize the notion of a discrete self whose singular "life" is commodifiable or reducible to dominant stereotypes of Asian Americans as exotic foreigners. An examination of the range and variety of Asian American autobiography and memoir puts this group of texts in productive conversation with some of the most important issues in autobiography studies.

While there has been discussion in autobiography studies about the distinctions between "autobiography" and "memoir" — much of it centered around a narrative that attempts to relay the events of a lifetime versus one that is more temporally particular and focused around a singular event or thematic — this chapter will largely collapse the two meanings in order to examine issues of self versus group representation and commodification or destabilization of the self, as well as some of the contentions and controversies that have attended some of the most significant publications in the field. Additionally, the terms "life writing," "oral narrative," and "personal writing" are also referenced by this generally capacious definition of autobiography.

Early Asian American autobiography: late nineteenth century to 1940s

Popular misconceptions and stereotypes and their resultant market forces, U.S. relations with Asia, and immigration histories have significantly shaped the publishing history of Asian American autobiography, and this is particularly true in its early formation. From the late nineteenth century through approximately 1940, texts such as Yan Phou Lee's *When I Was a Boy in China* (1887), Etsu Sugimoto's *A Daughter of the Samurai* (1925), New Il-Han's *When I Was a Boy in Korea* (1928), and Younghill Kang's *The Grass Roof* (1931) largely confirmed dominant cultural notions of Asian foreignness and exotic customs that stand in sharp contrast to Western modernity and U.S. American cultural practices. These early texts tended to be written by Asian-born authors of the upper class, who were often well-educated and English-speaking. While there had already been significant Asian immigration to the United States by the 1920s, particularly from Japan, China, Korea, and South Asia, most immigrants were poorly educated, working class, and far too busy trying to eke out a living to learn fluent English or write books. Thus, early self-representations of Asians in the United States are atypical and do not reflect the lives or experiences of the vast majority of Asian immigrants. But as Elaine Kim has argued with her term "ambassadors of goodwill" (1982: 24), the primary purpose for these authors was to write narratives that would introduce and humanize what was then referred to as "The Far East" or "The Orient" to a white North American audience. As such, these texts tend to be less autobiographical than ethnographic. To this extent, many of these early narratives do, as Chin argues, commodify Asian identity in that they are largely addressed to a curious non-Asian audience and generally progress along a teleological arc that implicitly privileges the West.

However, even in this early period, the autobiographical writings of Edith Maud and Winnifred Eaton, who wrote under the pen names Sui Sin Far and Onoto Watanna, respectively, suggest another direction Asian American life narratives would take. In "Leaves from the Mental Portfolio of an Eurasian" (1909) and "Sui Sin Far, the Half Chinese Writer, Tells of Her Career" (1912), Edith Eaton depicts the difficulties of being a mixed-raced woman during a period of overt anti-Asian racism. Though some critics have noted the "muted Orientalism" (Ferens 2002: 2) in Eaton's work, she generally avoids the auto-Orientalism of most of her contemporaries, opting instead to represent the doubled effects of racism and sexism in her life. Her sister Winnifred, who purposefully adopted a Japanese pseudonym due to the anti-Chinese sentiment of the time, is often criticized for acceding all too readily to Orientalist stereotypes in her fictional and semi-autobiographical work; however, Annette White-Parks has argued that Winnifred Eaton's work contains a muted critique of racialized and gendered identities. The Eaton sisters thus exemplify two strains in Asian American autobiographical writing: one that is overtly critical of the construction of Asians and Asian Americans, and one that requires a resistant reading that makes legible a buried or coded critique that resists dominant narratives and interrogates the incommensurabilities of identity formation.

Beginning in the 1940s, something of a sea change occurs in Asian American autobiography, largely the result of two factors: by this time, there was a significantpopulation of English-speaking, U.S.-born Asian Americans whose primary connection to Asia was through their immigrant parents. The second major event was World War II and the internment of Japanese Americans. Miné Okubo's *Citizen 13660* (1946) inaugurated a number of autobiographical narratives that reach into the present, among them Monica Sone's *Nisei Daughter* (1953), Jeanne Wakatsuki Houston's *Farewell to Manzanar* (1973), Yoshiko Uchida's *Desert Exile: The Uprooting of a Japanese-American Family* (1982), Gene Oishi's *In Search of Hiroshi* (1988), Minoru Kiyota's *Beyond Loyalty: The Story of a Kibei* (1997), Toyo Suyemoto's *I Call to Remembrance* (2007), and Kimi Cunningham Grant's *Silver Like Dust: One Family's Story of America's Japanese Internment* (2012). A notable tendency among these narratives, particularly the earlier ones, is to avoid the intimately personal that is often associated with a general understanding of "autobiography." Overall, these narratives serve to bring to light a collective experience, of which the particular author is a paradigmatic case. Internment narratives also require a flexible understanding of autobiography, as in recent years, in response to the aging Issei and Nisei populations, organizations such as the Densho Project have been collecting oral histories that focus on personal accounts of the war years.

We might refer to such autobiography projects as "witness narratives," texts whose main purpose is to historically document Asian American experiences of immigration, war, displacement, social marginalization, and economic hardship that have been fundamentally shaped by U.S. policy, laws, and international relations. Two notable narratives that depict the life of Asian immigrant women — Akemi Kikumura's *Through Harsh Winters: The Life of a Japanese Immigrant Woman* (1981) and Mary Paik Lee's *Quiet Odyssey: A Pioneer Korean Woman in America* (1990) — recount the personal struggles each faced in the early years of the twentieth century, but these narratives also serve as an invaluable source of information about a generation whose experiences were rarely recorded autobiographically. Both texts also highlight issues of authorship and representation. *Through Harsh Winters* is the story of the pseudonymous "Michiko Tanaka," who was Kikumura's mother. The text is transcribed and edited from oral interviews the attributed author conducted with "Michiko." Moreover, the original interviews were conducted in Japanese and were subsequently translated into English before being edited for cohesiveness and chronology. Thus, this is a highly mediated narrative that makes a key contribution to our understanding of autobiographical self-representation. *Quiet Odyssey: A Pioneer Korean Woman in America* by Mary Paik Lee offers another variation. Lee had written a 65-page typescript in English that came to the attention of Sucheng Chan, a professor at the University of California, Santa Cruz. Chan interviewed Lee, edited the typescript, and wrote an extensive introduction contextualizing the period about which Lee wrote. While authorship of Quiet Odyssey is fully credited to Lee, hers is also a mediated narrative that pushes us to recognize the extent to which all autobiographical narratives are mediated, albeit to different degrees.

The 1946 publication of *America is in the Heart* by Carlos Bulosan offers yet another issue in autobiography studies, one that becomes highly important for texts published in and after the 1970s. Like many of the autobiographies published earlier in the century, Bulosan functioned as something of a cultural ambassador and addressed himself to a white American audience, and he was urged by his publisher to write from a personal point of view to increase the book's market appeal (Kim 1982: 48). However, Bulosan's purpose was not to present Filipinos through the lens of bestselling orientalist fantasies, but rather was linked to his desire to improve the social and economic conditions Filipinos faced in the United States. In order to do this, Bulosan wrote what we might call a fictionalized autobiography — not because he simply "made up" events, but because he actively sought to heighten parts of his narrative for greater impact. Moreover, many of the events in the book did not happen to Bulosan himself; rather, he aggregates events that represent the Filipino experience in the United States. Thus, the line between personal and group experience is blurred for the purpose of representing the realities of racism, exclusion, and exploitation for the thousands of Filipinos who had come to the United States with dreams for the future.

While variety and variation mark autobiographical narratives in this period, it is nevertheless possible to offer some generalizations that provide a productive context for later narratives: there is a desire on the part of the writer to narrate experiences that have not hitherto been represented, sometimes to offer an insider's view of "oriental" culture for public consumption; sometimes to provide an ambassadorial narrative to bridge the divide between "East" and "West"; and sometimes to depict or document a collective experience of oppression and hardship, often with the objective of influencing the behavior of the dominant culture in relation to Asians and

Asian Americans. Additionally, these early autobiographical writings evoke a number of issues central to thinking about autobiography as a genre: personal and group identities, authorship and mediated narratives, the meaning of and relationship between "fact" and "fiction," and the necessity of reading for muted or counter-narratives.

1950/1976: Jade Snow Wong and Maxine Hong Kingston

The publication in 1950 of Jade Snow Wong's *Fifth Chinese Daughter* is arguably one of the most important junctures in Asian American autobiography, serving as something of a flashpoint for many of the issues above. Written in the third person, Wong's original preface claims that she wanted only "to evaluate personal experiences" (1950: xiii). However, in her introduction to the 1989 edition, she says she "wrote with the purpose of creating better understanding of the Chinese culture on the part of Americans" (Wong 1989: vii). These two statements position *Fifth Chinese Daughter* both as what Kim refers to as a "cultural ambassador" text and as an Asian American autobiography that is an explicitly personal narrative; that is, it is a text that seeks to both represent a community and Wong's individual struggles. However, the latter are generally resolved through actions and values attributable to "Chinese values," which largely confirm an American liberalism that tolerates difference that can be easily absorbed into dominant values, and which privilege individual effort and upward mobility. Shortly after the book's publication, the U.S. State Department sent Wong on a four-month speaking tour of various Asian countries, where she and her book were presented as proof of American democratic, non-racist ideals and the attainability of "the American Dream." While much of the narrative details Jade Snow's struggle to negotiate between Chinese and American cultural systems, it also includes several sections devoted to Chinese festivals, food, and ritual. Frank Chin and others have criticized Wong for pandering to a white American audience and turning Chinese American culture into a stereotypical, commodified spectacle (Chin 1991: 8) and for a seemingly uncritical acceptance of dominant discourse. However, it is also possible to read a muted narrative, often signaled by moments of frustration, that point to the ways in which Wong's text registers the ruptures between trying to negotiate between dominant culture racial hierarchies on the one hand, and familial patriarchal hierarchies on the other.

Feminist critics have been particularly attentive to issues of gender in *Fifth Chinese Daughter.* Sau-ling Wong notes that it details how "growing up Chinese American meant vastly different things for the male child than for the female" (Wong 1997: 46). While Jade Snow's frustration with her status as female is often clear in her text, it is also possible to read these occurrences in conjunction with and as an analogue for her feelings about racial inequality. That is, we might be attentive to telling contradictions and disruptions in Wong's narrative which point to issues that are unresolvable within the liberal humanist framework that pervades the text. While such a reading does not wholly recuperate *Fifth Chinese Daughter* From its generally accommodationist orientation and liberal multiculturalist stance, it recognizes how Wong's narrative both registers and performs the difficulty of being both Chinese American and female during a time when the available discourse of racialized gender was wholly inadequate to nonexistent.

In many ways, Maxine Hong Kingston's *The Woman Warrior: Memoirs of a Girlhood Among Ghosts* (1976) is the inheritor of many of the criticisms lodged against *Fifth Chinese Daughter* by Frank Chin and others. Kingston sees *The Woman Warrior* as the descendant of a literary tradition inaugurated by *Fifth Chinese Daughter.* She has said that Wong's book was "the only Chinese American author she read before writing her own book" and considers Wong as "the Mother of Chinese American Literature" (Ling 1990: 120). Chin's contention that Wong falsifies Chinese culture and demonizes Chinese men is intensified with *The Woman Warrior*, which he identifies as "fake" (Chin 1991: 9) because it is "not consistent with Chinese fairy tales and childhood literature" (8) and fails to cleave to a "pure heroic tradition" (30). Autobiography, which Chin refers to as the "traditional tool of Christian conversion" (11), is always suspect because it is always already a falsification of authentic, true Chinese culture. It is salient to note that Kingston herself never offered her text as an autobiography; rather, in the tradition of the publishing industry relative to Asian American writing, her editor and publisher decided to label it as nonfiction, a decision reflected in the published book's subtitle.

The importance of Kingston's text, irrespective of its generic categorization, lies precisely in the ways in which it confounds categorization, interrogates truth and ethnic authenticity, complicates the construction of the raced and gendered self, self-reflexively questions narrative representation, and highlights women's relationship to language, storytelling, and authorship. As Sau-ling Wong notes, "Every issue raised by *The Woman Warrior* touches a nerve and exposes a fundamental tension in the Chinese American experience that cannot be resolved through debate" (Wong 1997: 50). Kingston's text has been read through any number of critical frameworks. Feminist critics both within and outside of the field of Asian American literary studies have recognized that *The Woman Warrior* stages "confrontations with the fictions of self-representation and with the autobiographical possibilities embedded in cultural fictions, specifically as they interpenetrate one another in the autobiography a woman would write" (Smith 1987: 151). Kingston's narrative opens up the possibilities for female self-representation through its refusal of easy categorization and linear narrative, as well as in its use of pastiche, interruption and fragmentation. Other critics ascribe Kingston's narrative strategy less to issues of gender and more to a postmodern sensibility and style that refuse a master narrative of selfhood (Yalom 1991: 3). Still others read the text as emblematizing the many, sometimes contradictory, vectors of identity and identification for Asian Americans, taking their cue from Kingston's own words:

> Chinese-Americans, when you try to understand what things in you are Chinese, how do you separate what is peculiar to childhood, to poverty, insanities, one family, your mother who marked your growing with stories, from what is Chinese? What is Chinese tradition and what is the movies?
>
> (Kingston 1976: 5 – 6)

Kingston's inquiry indexes the conflicts represented in a text that repeatedly stages and performs the ground of its own questioning. The narrative's refusal to represent a discreet Chinese American subject, fully determinable or determining, both invites and requires a flexibly wide range of theoretical approaches. The richness and variety of the critical work generated by *The Woman Warrior* suggests not only multiple possible textual readings but the multiple possibilities, trajectories, and intersections that become legible through being attentive to the performative aspects of autobiographical writing.

1980s–1990s: *Dictee*

This period witnesses a proliferation of autobiographies and life writing, representing the range of approaches, sub-genres and concerns of the earlier period, but also expanding in new directions. Some of these approaches are the result of the increasing interest in women's lives and voices, the influence of academic feminism, the ascendancy of literary multiculturalism, and the growing popularity of autobiography and memoir generally.

Additionally, two crucial historical events help account for the bourgeoning of Asian American autobiographical texts in this period. One is the Immigration and Naturalization Act of 1965, which abolished the national origins quota system that had favored northern and western European countries and severely restricted Asian immigration. The 1965 Act resulted in a surge of emigration from Asian countries, significantly increasing the Asian population in the United States. By the 1980s, many of those who immigrated as children were coming of age. A corollary result of the 1965 Act was that transnational identification increasingly begins to characterize Asian America.

Second, the formal end of the U.S. war in Vietnam in 1975 resulted in a large number of immigrants from Southeast Asia. A second major wave of emigration from Vietnam began in 1977 and extended well into the 1980s. While pre-1965 Asian America was primarily comprised of Chinese, Japanese, Koreans, Filipinos, and South Asians, post-1965 Asian populations in the United States reflected significantly increased emigration from Vietnam, Cambodia, and Laos.

These changes are reflected in the autobiographical literature that begins appearing in the early 1980s, most notably with the publication of Theresa Hak-Kyung Cha's *Dictee* (1982). Like *The Woman Warrior*, Cha's text is difficult to categorize, the narrative itself performing the disjunctions and ruptures of identity wrought by war, displacement and colonization, but also by memory and language. Generally categorized as literary fiction, *Dictee* is often included in discussions of autobiography, though it nowhere explicitly positions itself as such. Because it narrates the stories of the author's mother, Hung Soon Huo, as well as of Cha herself, *Dictee* appeals to scholars of autobiography. However, it is clear that Cha refuses the notion of a privatized, bounded, and seamless self, as she also focuses on the stories of mythological figures Demeter and Persephone, French national heroine Joan of Arc, and Korean revolutionary Yu Guan Soon, who was tortured and killed by the Japanese at the age of sixteen. By refusing the usual conventions of autobiography, as autobiography theorists Julia Watson and Sidonie Smith have noted in relation to the discursive practices of marginalized women, Cha is able to "constitute an 'I' that becomes a place of creative and, by implication, political intervention" (Cha 1992: xix). *Dictee* thus offers a model of identity that is constructed polyphonically through the mythic and the historic, the familial and the national, and the individual and collective. Yet far from suggesting that identity is simply the aggregated result of plural forces, Cha insists on the ways in which identity, either as woman, immigrant, or Korean national exceeds these narratives and is never fully attainable or stable, as suggested by her claim that "our destination is fixed on the perpetual motion of search. Fixed in its perpetual exile" (Cha 1995: 81).

Similarly, language also places the subject in a position of perpetual search and perpetual exile. As the title, frontispiece, and first few pages attest, dictation and translation are key tropes for the ways in which language is always mediated and mediating, whether exemplified by the disjunctions between dictation and notation, the coercive relationship of language to the movements of the body (Cha 1995: 3 – 5), or the deployment of narratives that erase particular histories in the interests of the State. Nevertheless, it is through language and storytelling that one counters suppressed and invisibilized histories: one must "extract each fragment by each fragment from the word from the image another word another image the reply that will not repeat history into oblivion" (Cha 1995: 33). While Cha's focus on female figures and issues of gender have drawn much commentary from feminist theorists, and her deployment of pastiche, memory and fragmented narratives have attracted poststructuralist critics, both have often done so, as Elaine Kim writes, "without considering the importance of her Korean American identity to the text. *Dictee* is a subversive book about a specific set of excluded experiences" (Kim 1997: 175). The difficulty and rich density of Cha's text can often tempt critics to ignore a Korean American analytic framework, and this serves as something of an analogy for the disappearances of history that *Dictee* strives to narrate into memory.

Several of the autobiographies and memoirs that appear over the next two decades also seek to narrate into history that which cannot be forgotten or erased. Although it is difficult to account for all the types of autobiographies and memoirs published in this period, this discussion will focus on two general categories: witness narratives that differ from earlier such work in terms of the extreme violence or trauma out of which they are written; and literary memoirs that tend to center around issues of gendered identity, home, transnational identifications, and/or postcoloniality.

Southeast Asian autobiography

One of the most significant developments in Asian American autobiography is the number of Southeast Asian autobiographies, memoirs, and life narratives that begin to appear in the mid-1980s. It is significant that the earliest Vietnamese American autobiographies — Truong Nhu Tang's *Vietcong Memoir: An Inside Account of The Vietnam War and Its Aftermath* (1985), Bui Diem's *In the Jaws of History* (1987), and Nguyen Thi Thu-Lam's *Fallen Leaves: Memoirs of a Vietnamese Woman from 1940–1975* (1989), and Le Ly Hayslip's *When Heaven and Earth Changed Places: A Vietnamese Woman's Journey from War to Peace* (1989) — are all by authors of the refugee/immigrant generation and written with English-fluent collaborators. Mediation in these cases occurs through American English, the language of the country that significantly contributed to the harrowing circumstances these narratives detail. But this vexed mediation also attests to the strength of these authors' desire to represent an experience that would otherwise be threatened with slipping into silence and invisibility. In 1994, the first Vietnamese American autobiographies written without collaborators were published: Jade Ngoc Quang Huynh's *South Wind Changing* and Nguyen Qui Duc's *Where the Ashes Are: The Odyssey of a Vietnamese Family*. The latter text is particularly interesting from an autobiography studies perspective because Nguyen's narrative incorporates his father's autobiographical writing and poems. That the story of the self is the story of family, nation, and the past is also evident in what might be considered the most atypical of the texts under discussion here, Andrew X. Pham's *Catfish and*

Mandala: A Two-Wheeled Voyage Through the Landscape and Memory of Vietnam (1999).

Like Vietnamese American autobiographical writing, Cambodian American autobiography is also motivated by the need to witness and document histories of war and displacement, but it is more overtly linked to the tradition of survival narratives. The earliest published autobiography is *Cambodian Witness: The Autobiography of Someth May* (1986), which recounts May's family life before and during the rule of the Khmer Rouge (1975 – 9). In 2000, two publications received widespread notice: *When Broken Glass Floats: Growing Up Under the Khmer Rouge,* by Chanrithy Him, and *First They Killed My Father: A Daughter of Cambodia Remembers*, by Loung Ung. These two texts, as Rocio G. Davis has argued, "must be analyzed in the context of what has been called 'literature of trauma'" (Davis 2007: 75), given the extreme nature of the terror and brutality inflicted by the Khmer Rouge that both authors experienced as children. Trauma theory highlights the ways in which language in these narratives is at once inadequate to the experience of suffering and the only vehicle through which the traumatized subject can fulfill "the need to tell and retell the story of the traumatic experience, to make it 'real' both to the victim and the community" (Tal 1996: 17, quoted in Davis 2007: 75). Also published in 2000, *Music Through the Dark: A Tale of Survival in Cambodia* recounts the experiences of Daran Kravanh, but is credited to Bree Lafreniere. This text revisits and complicates issues of authorial mediation, by noting "although it is written in Daran's voice, it is not a translation, an oral history, or an autobiography. Rather, it is a literary account of a personal experience told by one person and written by another with all the interpretations of such a transfer" (frontispiece note).

In addition to Kao Kalia Yang's *The Latehomecomer: A Hmong Family Memoir* (2008) — to date the only Hmong American autobiography — the texts discussed above highlight issues of language, narrative, and documentation through histories of colonialism, war, displacement, and violent upheaval.

Literary memoirs

Perhaps inspired by the success of Kingston's *The Woman Warrior,* several literary autobiographies, written either by academics or writers in other genres, take up questions of identity. The most widely known texts tend to fall roughly into two categories: narratives of "return" and memoirs that examine the self in the context of postcolonial rupture or transnational mobility. Curiously, the first group of texts are primarily written by Japanese Americans: David Mura's *Turning Japanese: Memoirs of a Sansei* (1991), Lydia Minatoya's *Talking to High Monks in the Snow: An Asian American Odyssey* (1992), Kyoko Mori's *Dream of Water* (1996), and Garrett Hongo's

Volcano: A Memoir of Hawai'i (1995). Characterizing these as narratives of return is somewhat problematic, given that before the recounted events, neither Mura nor Minatoya had previously been to Japan. However, both authors discuss the ways in which they had grown up disinclined to identify with their Japanese heritage, and their journeys to Japan connect them to a familial past that helps them claim a Japanese American identity. In *Dream of Water and Volcano*, Mori and Hongo recount their returns to Japan and Hawai'i, respectively, each to come to terms with a childhood past in ways that enable them to move forward in their adult lives. That all four memoirs are primarily personal narratives, unlike earlier internment narratives or the narratives of witness in Vietnamese and Cambodian American autobiography, indexes the significance of historical context and temporal distance from events of ethnic group upheaval and the exigencies of documenting those events. While there can be no firm line between historical and personal past, these narratives demonstrate something of a shift from privileging the documentation of historical events and social forces out of which a collective identity is formed — and of which the author is a paradigmatic example — to understanding the effects of those larger forces within the context of the personal.

In contrast to the memoirs above, Sara Suleri's *Meatless Days* (1989) is the first in a group of autobiographical narratives written by Asian Americans who identify transnationally, often within a postcolonial context: Meena Alexander's *Fault Lines: A Memoir* (1993) and *The Shock of Arrival: Reflections on Postcolonial Experience* (1996), Li-Young Lee's *The Winged Seed: A Remembrance* (1995), and Shirley Geok-lin Lim's *Among the White Moon Faces: An Asian-American Memoir of Homelands* (1996). Born and raised in Asia, shaped by geopolitics and by what Alexander calls the "central theme" of "migrancy" (1996: 1), these writers self-consciously foreground the contradictions and necessary fictions of identity as they are shaped, constrained, and grounded in place. These narratives self-consciously construct identity as multiple, rather than unitary. For these multilingual writers who primarily publish their work in English, language is a contestatory site and central issue with which they grapple. Alexander writes: "There is a violence in the very language, American English, that we have to face, even as we work to make it ours, decolonize it so that it will express the truth of bodies beaten and banned" (Alexander 1993: 199). At the same time, Lim recounts the ways in which, as girl growing up in British-colonized Malaya, literature written in English was both a tool of social control and the means through which she could imagine a different life. Through what Alexander calls "fault lines," these writers foreground issues of gender, home, nation, and inter-permeability of the public and private.

Twenty-first century: the memoir boom

In the past decade, autobiography and memoir have become extremely popular and Autobiography Studies has firmly established itself as an academic discipline. Accordingly, a plethora of Asian American life writing has appeared, most of it intended for a general audience. Many of these texts, particularly collections of personal writing by non-professional writers, represent increasingly specific groups within Asian America: *Yell-Oh Girls! Emerging Voices Explore Culture, Identity, and Growing Up Asian American* (young women aged between fourteen and twenty-one years old; Nam 2001)*, Asian American X: An Intersection of 21st Century Asian American Voices* (Gen Xers; Han and Hsu 2004), and *Once They Hear My Name: Korean Adoptees and Their Journeys Toward Identity* (Lee et al. 2008). While this trend may well represent an opportunity for new voices to be heard and for particularities of identity to be recognized, one might also ask whether the atomization of identity reduces it, as per Frank Chin's objection, to a commodity. Single-authored memoirs tend to focus on seemingly anomalous or very specific personal situations that may or may not foreground issues discussed throughout this chapter. At least three books have been published that focus on Asian American girls growing up in the Midwest: Linda Furiya's *Bento Box in the Heartland: My Japanese Girlhood in Whitebread America* (2006), Mary-Lee Chai's *Hapa Girl*: *A Memoir* (2007), and Bich Minh Nguyen's *Stealing Buddha's Dinner: A Memoir* (2007). Memoirs that are largely geared toward the dynamics of family or relationships include Kim Sunee's *Trail of Crumbs: Hunger, Love, and the Search for Home* (2008), Lac Su's *I Love Yous Are for White People: A Memoir* (2009), Rahna Reiko Rizzuto's *Hiroshima in the Morning* (2010), and Amy Chua's *Battle Hymn of the Tiger Mother* (2011). Widely varying in style and complexity, some contemporary memoirs retreat into the realm of the private; others retain a sense of the continual negotiation between self, community, and world, between present realities and past histories in a way that opens up rather than closes down the complex possibilities of Asian American subjectivity.

Bibliography

Alexander, M. (1993) *Fault Lines: A Memoir*, New York: Feminist Press.

Alexander, M. (1996) *The Shock of Arrival: Reflections on Postcolonial Experience*, Boston: South End Press.

Bui, D., with Chanoff, D. (1987) *In the Jaws of History*, Boston: Houghton Miffin Company.

Bulosan, C. (1946) *America is in the Heart,* Seattle: University of Washington Press, 1973.

Cha, T. (1982) *Dictee*, Berkeley: Third Woman Press, 1995.

Chai, M.-L. (2007) *Hapa Girl: A Memoir*, Philadelphia: Temple University Press.

Chan, J.P., Chin, F., Inada, L.F. and Wong, S. (eds.) (1991) *The Big Aiiieeeee! An Anthology of Chinese American and Japanese American Literature*, New York: Meridian.

Cheung, K.-K. (ed.) (1997) *An Interethnic Companion to Asian American Literature*, Cambridge: Cambridge University Press.

Chin, F. (1985) "This is Not an Autobiography," *Genre*, xviii(2): 109 – 130.

Chin, F. (1991) "Come All Ye Asian American Writers of the Real and the Fake," in J.P. Chan, F. Chin, L.F. Inada and S. Wong (eds.) *The Big Aiiieeeee! An Anthology of Chinese American and Japanese American Literature*, New York: Meridian, 1 – 92.

Chua, A. (2011) *Battle Hymn of the Tiger Mother,* New York: Penguin.

Davis, R.G. (2007) *Begin Here: Reading Asian North American Autobiographies of Childhood*, Honolulu: University of Hawai'i Press.

Far, S.S. (Edith Maud Eaton) (1909) "Leaves from the Mental Portfolio of an Eurasian," in J.P. Chan et al. (eds.) (1991) *The Big Aiiieeeee! An Anthology of Chinese American and Japanese American Literature,* New York: Meridian, 111 – 122.

Far, S.S. (1912) "Sui Sin Far, the Half Chinese Writer, Tells of Her Career," in A. Ling and A. White-Parks (eds.) (1995) Mrs. *Spring Fragrance and Other Writings,* Urbana: University of Illinois Press, 288 – 296.

Ferens, D. (2002) *Edith and Winnifred Eaton: Chinatown Missions and Japanese Romances*, Urbana: University of Illinois Press.

Furiya, L. (2006) *Bento Box in the Heartland: My Japanese Girlhood in Whitebread America*, Emeryville: Seal Press.

Grant, K.C. (2012) *Silver Like Dust: One Family's Story of America's Japanese Internment*, New York: Pegasus Books.

Han, A. and Hsu, J. (eds.) (2004) *Asian American X: An Intersection of 21st Century Asian American Voices*, Ann Arbor: University of Michigan Press.

Hayslip, L., with Wurts, J. (1989) *When Heaven and Earth Changed Places: A Vietnamese Woman's Journey from War to Peace*, New York: Doubleday.

Him, C. (2000) *When Broken Glass Floats: Growing Up Under the Khmer Rouge,* New York: Norton.

Hongo, G. (1995) *Volcano: A Memoir of Hawai'i*, New York: Alfred A. Knopf.

Houston, J. (1973) *Farewell to Manzanar*, New York: Bantam Books.

Huynh, J.Q H. (1994) *South Wind Changing*, Saint Paul: Graywolf Press.

Kang, Y. (1931) *The Grass Roof*, New York: Charles Scribner's Sons.

Kikumura, A. (1981) *Through Harsh Winters: The Life of a Japanese Immigrant Woman*, Novato: Chandler and Sharp.

Kim, E.H. (1982) *Asian American Literature: An Introduction to The Writings and Their Context, Philadelphia:* Temple University Press.

Kim, E.H. (1997) "Korean American Literature," in K.K. Cheung (ed.) *An Interethnic Companion to Asian*

American Literature, Cambridge: Cambridge University Press, 156–91.

Kingston, M.H. (1976) *The Woman Warrior: Memoirs of a Girlhood Among Ghosts*, New York: Pantheon.

Kiyota, M. (1997) *Beyond Loyalty: The Story of a Kibei, trans. L. Keenan, Honolulu:* University of Hawai'i Press.

Lafreniere, B. (2000) *Music Through the Dark*: *A Tale of Survival in Cambodia*, Honolulu: University of Hawai'i Press.

Lee, E., Lammert, M. and Hess, M. (2008) *Once They Hear My Name: Korean Adoptees and Their Journeys Toward Identity,* Silver Spring: Tamarisk Books.

Lee, L.-Y. (1995) *The Winged Seed: A Remembrance*, New York: Simon & Schuster.

Lee, M.P. (1990) *Quiet Odyssey*: *A Pioneer Korean Woman in America*, edited by S. Chan, Seattle: University of Washington Press.

Lee, Y.P. (1887) *When I Was a Boy in China,* Boston: D. Lothrop Co.

Lim, S. (ed.) (1991) *Approaches to Teaching Kingston's The Woman Warrior*, New York: Modern Language Association of America.

Lim, S. (1996) *Among the White Moon Faces: An Asian-American Memoir of Homelands*, New York: Feminist Press.

Ling, A. (1990) *Between Worlds: Women Writers of Chinese Ancestry*, New York: Teachers College Press.

Ling, A. and White-Parks, A. (eds.) (1995) *Mrs. Spring Fragrance and Other Writings,* Urbana: University of Illinois Press.

May, S., with Fenton, J. (ed.) (1986) *Cambodian Witness: The Autobiography of Someth May*, London: Faber & Faber.

Minatoya, L. (1992) *Talking to High Monks in the Snow: An Asian American Odyssey*, New York: HarperCollins.

Mori, K. (1996) *Dream of Water*, New York: Ballantine.

Mura, D. (1991) *Turning Japanese: Memoirs of a Sansei,* New York: Atlantic Monthly Press.

Nam, V. (ed.) (2001) Y*ell-Oh Girls! Emerging Voices Explore Culture, Identity, and Growing Up Asian American,* New York: HarperCollins/Quill.

New, I.-H. (1928) *When I Was a Boy in Korea*, Boston: Lothrop, Lee & Shepard Co.

Nguyen, B. (2007) *Stealing Buddha's Dinner: A Memoir*, New York: Viking.

Nguyen, Q.D. (1994) *Where the Ashes Are, Reading*, MA: Addison-Wesley.

Nguyen, T.-L.T., with Kreisler, E. and Christenson, S. (1989) *Fallen Leaves: Memoirs of a Vietnamese Woman from* 1940 –1975, New Haven: Yale University Southeast Asia Studies.

Oishi, G. (1988) *In Search of Hiroshi*, Rutland: Charles E. Tuttle Company.

Okubo, M. (1946) *Citizen 13660*, Seattle: University of Washington Press, 1983.

Pham, A.X. (1999) *Catfish and Mandala: A Two-Wheeled Journey Through the Landscape and Memory of Vietnam*, New York: Farrar, Straus and Giroux.

Rizzuto, R. (2010) *Hiroshima in the Morning*, New York: Feminist Press.

Smith, S. (1987) *A Poetics of Women's Autobiography: Marginality and the Fictions of Self-Repre-sentation*, Bloomington: Indiana University Press.

Sone, M. (1953) *Nisei Daughter*, Seattle: University of Washington Press, 1979.

Su, L. (2009) *I Love Yous Are for White People*: *A Memoir*, New York: HarperCollins. Sugimoto, E. (1925) A *Daughter of the Samurai*, New York: Doubleday Page & Co.

Suleri, S. (1989) *Meatless Days,* Chicago: University of Chicago Press.

Sunee, K. (2008) *Trail of Crumbs: Hunger, Love, and the Search for Home,* New York: Grand Central Publishing.

Suyemoto, T. (2007) *I Call to Remembrance: Toyo Suyemoto's Years of Internment*, edited by S.B. Richardson, New Jersey: Rutgers University Press.

Truong, N.T., with Chanoff, D. and Doan, V.T. (1985) *Vietcong Memoir: An Inside Account of The Vietnam War and Its Aftermath,* New York: Harcourt Brace Jovanovich.

Uchida, Y. (1982) *Desert Exile: The Uprooting of a Japanese-American Family*, Seattle: University of Washington Press, 1984.

Ung, L. (2000) *First They Killed My Father: A Daughter of Cambodia Remembers*, New York: Harper Collins.

Watson, J. and Smith, S. (1992) *De/Colonizing the Subject: The Politics of Gender in Women's Autobiography,* Minneapolis: University of Minnesota Press.

Wong, J.S. (1950) *Fifth Chinese Daughter*, Seattle: University of Washington Press, 1989.

Wong, S.-L. (1997) "Chinese American Literature," in K.-K. Cheung (ed.) *An Interethnic Companion to Asian American Literature,* Cambridge: Cambridge University Press, 39–61.

Yalom, M. (1991) "The Woman Warrior as Postmodern Autobiography," in S. Lim (ed.) *Approaches to Teaching Kingston's The Woman Warrior*, New York: Modern Language Association of America, 108–115.

Yang, K.K. (2008) *The Latehomecomer: A Hmong Family Memoir,* Minneapolis: Coffee House Press.

11

Contemporary Asian American Drama
当代美国亚裔戏剧

Esther Kim Lee

评论家简介

李·艾斯特·金（Esther Kim Lee），美国俄亥俄州立大学戏剧史、文学与批评专业博士，现任美国马里兰大学帕克分校艺术与人文学院戏剧系副教授，同时担任全球移徙研究中心和美国亚裔研究计划研究员。研究领域包括戏剧历史、美国亚裔戏剧、亚洲离散戏剧、韩裔离散戏剧、戏剧理论和批评、表演理论全球化与戏剧等。专著有《亚裔美国戏剧史》（*A History of Asian American Theatre*，2006），曾荣获 2007 年度高等教育戏剧协会杰出图书奖;《黄哲伦戏剧》（*The Theatre of David Henry Hwang*，2015）。编著有《来自美洲韩裔离散者的七部当代戏剧》（*Seven Contemporary Plays from the Korean Diaspora in the Americas,* 2012）。

文章简介

经过五十年的发展，美国亚裔戏剧从几近空白逐渐发展成为美国戏剧及文学中的一个重要部分。评论家李·艾斯特·金撰写这篇文章，试图对各个历史阶段的美国亚裔戏剧从主题、形式和影响三个方面进行梳理，整体呈现美国亚裔戏剧的发展脉络。文章依据美国亚裔戏剧创作的历史和社会背景，将其划分为初始、上升、繁荣三个阶段，总结各阶段特征，并对未来发展做出展望。结合亚裔生活创作的历史背景，本文论证了亚裔戏剧在表现种族矛盾、文化冲突、族裔经历与情感等方面发挥着重要而独特的作用。当前，亚裔戏剧创作逐渐超越族裔主题，更加着重挖掘战争、艺术、死亡、全球化等人类普遍关注的议题，更加强调形式上的创新与对社会问题的深入思考。本文是全面了解美国亚裔戏剧发展历程的重要参考文献。

文章出处：Srikanth, Rajini., and Min Hyoung Song, editors. *The Cambridge History of Asian American Literature.* New York: Cambridge UP, 2016, pp. 406-421.

Contemporary Asian American Drama

Esther Kim Lee

Introduction: The First Wave

In 1968, the East West Players in Los Angeles held its first playwriting competition to encourage Asian Americans to write for theater. Founded in 1965, the East West Players originally aimed to promote the careers of Asian American actors, but it became clear that without original plays by and about Asian Americans the company would not last.[1] In the 1960s, playwriting was not perceived as a possible profession for Asian American writers, and Asian American plays were virtually nonexistent. Plays, by definition, need to be produced and staged, and playwrights must work within an infrastructure and industry of theater. The East West Players' playwriting competition lasted three years during which playwrights such as Momoko Iko and Frank Chin made their debut in theater. In 1973, Frank Chin led the founding of the Asian American Theatre Workshop (later renamed Asian American Theatre Company) in San Francisco with the explicit agenda to create and produce Asian American plays. Although Chin left the company in a few years, his influence as a playwright has been lasting in Asian American theater. His two published plays, *Chickencoop Chinaman* (1972) and *The Year of the Dragon* (1974), are considered foundational in Asian American drama, and the Asian American Theatre Company has continued to support new Asian American playwrights.[2]

Frank Chin belongs to the first wave Asian American playwrights who pioneered Asian American drama. Also in the first wave are Jon Shirota, Momoko Iko, Dom Magwili, Wakako Yamauchi, Karen Tei Yamashita, Perry Miyake, Bill Shinkai, Paul Stephen Lim, Jeffery Paul Chan, Garrett Hongo, and Edward Sakamoto. These writers used the genre of drama to imagine new narratives about both the general history and the individual stories of Asian Americans. Many of their plays deal with important Asian American historical moments such as the internment of Japanese American during World War II and the creation of Chinatowns. Autobiography and realism were the dominant modes of dramatizing their stories and characters. Wakako Yamuchi, for instance, wrote in her play *The Music Lessons* (1977) about her childhood in a Japanese American farming family during the Great Depression in California's Imperial Valley. The first-wave playwrights included in their plays details of their personal experience with racism, displacement, and what Karen Shimakawa calls "national abjection."[3] The influence of the first-wave playwrights on contemporary Asian American drama has been substantial and enduring. Themes of history, autobiography, assimilation, and racism usually associated with first-wave playwrights would continue to be dramatized and investigated by second and third-wave playwrights.

Going Mainstream: The Second Wave

In 1986, David Henry Hwang's play Rich Relations premiered at the Second Stage Theatre in New York City. By then, Hwang had written three plays — *FOB* (1979), *The Dance and the Railroad* (1981), and *Family Devotions* (1983) — all of which were received well and advanced Hwang's career as an Asian American playwright. The three plays have been described by Hwang as his Chinese American Trilogy, and they deal directly with issues of assimilation, identity, and racial politics. *Rich Relations* was Hwang's first attempt to write characters not defined by their race or ethnicity. The play is about his family's preoccupation with money and religion, and it is considered the most autobiographical of Hwang's oeuvre. However, the cast of the premiere was all white, and the play was staged as a story about an affluent WASP family in Los Angeles. The play was not received well by critics and audiences, and Hwang has called the play his first "flop." Soon after the failure of the play, Hwang went on to write *M. Butterfly* and win the Tony Award for Best Play in 1988. However, he has described *Rich Relations*, his least successful work, as the play he had to write.

Hwang's imperative to write the play raises a number of questions that affected second-wave Asian American playwrights. By *second wave*, I refer to Asian American playwrights who began their playwriting careers in the late 1970s and the 1980s. The wave indicates a particular generation in terms of the age of the writers, but it also marks a unique approach to playwriting. In general, the second-wave playwrights faced a new set of questions that had not affected the first wave. Does an Asian American play have to feature Asian American characters? Why do white male playwrights get to write about any topic while women and minority writers are expected to write only about their personal experience? What happens when race is erased out of what is otherwise an autobiographical story? What requirements are imposed on minority playwrights, and for whom should they write? Since the 1980s, these questions stemmed from American theater's tendency to use the rhetoric of multiculturalism to pigeonhole minority and women writers. At the time, it was difficult for playwrights of color to have their plays produced at main-stream venues, which include Broadway, Off-Broadway, and regional theaters. The only way their plays could be staged was through multicultural programming, and Asian American playwrights slowly found opportunities to write for a wider audience, albeit in a limited way.

The question of what the word *wider* means in the phrase "wider audience" was a central question that vexed second-wave Asian American playwrights. For Velina Hasu Houston, "wider" and "whiter" were synonymous.[4] Despite being advised by her teacher to write for a "wider" audience, Houston chose to write about her own specific experience of growing up with a Japanese mother and an American father of African American and Native American ancestry in Junction City, Kansas, at a segregated army base for multiracial families. Her play *Tea* is based on interviews she conducted with her mother and other Japanese wives of American GIs at the base. In the play, four friends gather to have tea and to commemorate a mutual friend who committed suicide. During their conversation, they share stories of suffering, joy, and hopes of living as Japanese women in the United States. Houston initially had difficulty finding interest in her plays at both Asian American theater and African American play companies. Within the construct of multicultural theater, her plays were not Asian American enough and not African American enough.[5] Houston was, instead, welcomed by companies that promoted feminist and women issues, and *Tea* has become one of the most revived Asian American plays for both Asian American and "wider" audiences.

The Japanese American playwright Philip Kan Gotanda has described his playwriting process as a negotiation between the specific and the universal. He has stated in an interview, "I come from a specific place as a Japanese-American, but I want to make sure audiences can meet me halfway. When you want to reach a lot of people, your work should be inclusive enough for everyone to find its center."[6] For Gotanda, his central place is the Japanese American experience that has been haunted by the trauma of the internment camps and the subsequent silence of the community. A Sansei growing up in Stockton, California, Gotanda had questions about the camps, but he found the Nisei generation unable and unwilling to disclose the past. All of his plays dramatize characters whose subconscious minds continue to be affected by the unspeakable experience of racism and disenfranchisement exemplified most prominently by the internment of Japanese Americans.

In Gotanda's play *The Wind Cries Mary* (2004), the protagonist, Mary, finds herself unable to adapt to the fast changing culture of the 1960s. A daughter of an affluent Japanese American businessman, she vowed to become "American." She declares in the first scene, "I *am* American, goddamnit!"[7] She is married to a white man and rejects anything Japanese, but her desperate attempt to assimilate backfires when her former Japanese American lover emerges as a leader of the Asian American movement. The play ends tragically for both Mary and the lover. Gotanda's plays require audiences to confront the complex history of race and power in the United States while celebrating the tenacity of the human spirit. At its core, Gotanda's plays are about how characters live (or fail to live) with life's bitterness — whether it is the internment camp, the death of a child, or the betrayal of a lover. Gotanda's portrayal of broken and bitter characters is always sympathetic and nuanced. They may be quintessentially Japanese American characters with the deep trauma of the internment camps, but they are also familiar characters that represent the contemporary American experience.

Writing for a "wider audience" in theater has often meant writing plays featuring white male protagonists, and Asian American playwrights have had to ask whether they could write such a play and what that play would be like. Gotanda's answer to that question can be found in *Under the Rainbow* (2005), which includes two one-act plays, *Natalie Wood Is Dead* and *White Manifesto and Other Perfumed Tales of Self-Entitlement, or, Got Rice?* A white male character appears in the first piece as an imaginary person who lives in the minds of the Japanese American women, the main characters of the play. In the second piece, the white male is the protagonist who spews out his sexist and racist views of Asian women. By complementing the two plays, Gotanda has the female characters and the white male characters mirroring each other to reveal the complexities of their relationship.

David Henry Hwang's play *M. Butterfly* (1998) is the most famous Asian American play and Hwang's most commercially successful play. It should be underscored that the play features a white male protagonist. Loosely based on a true story, the play takes place in China during the 1960s at the height of the Vietnam War. Gallimard, the protagonist, is a French diplomat who has a long-term romantic relationship with a Chinese opera singer, Song, whom he believes to be a woman. The opera singer turns out to be a man and a spy working for the Chinese Communist Party. Song deceives Gallimard by playing the role of the perfect "Butterfly" or the submissive "Oriental" woman dramatized in Puccini's opera *Madame Butterfly*. Hwang's *M. Butterfly* explores the intersections of race, gender, and imperialism, and dramatizes the East-West relationship through the two main characters.

For David Henry Hwang, the dramatic form of a play is as important as the story it tells. He has experimented extensively with how the form of the stage should be used to represent the world of the play. For his Chinese Trilogy, for instance, he emulates the style and form of Maxine Hong Kingston's *Woman Warrior*, Frank Chin's *Gee Pop!*, and Sam Shepard's plays. From the three writers, Hwang has borrowed the style of magic realism in which mythic characters coexist with realistic characters in the diegetic world of the play. While he has looked to other writers for new forms of playwriting, Hwang has, in turn, been recognized for creating his own form of Chinese American theater. Early in his career, he worked with the actor John Lone, who is a professionally trained Chinese opera performer. Lone taught Hwang about Chinese theater, and the collaboration between the two has deeply affected Hwang's development as a playwright. Many of Hwang's plays feature Chinese opera as both a form and a theme: in *FOB* (1979), Grace and Steve who embody the mythic figures Fa Mulan and Gwan Gung, respectively, battle each other in Cantonese opera style, and in *Kung Fu* (2014), a biographical play based on Bruce Lee, Chinese opera is used to represent Lee's troubled relationship with his father. Hwang's style of Chinese American theater incorporates the physicality of Chinese opera with American realism.

The vast majority of plays by second-wave Asian American playwrights do not borrow from traditional Asian theater, and the wave is partly defined by the writers' ability to use a wide range of dramatic styles and forms. Such range can be observed in the plays produced and published in the 1990s, during which six collections of Asian American plays were published.[8] Additionally, plays by Philip Kan Gotanda and David Henry Hwang were published both individually and as collections during the decade.[9] There are a number of reasons for the sudden surge in publications of Asian American plays during the 1990s. For one, the international popularity of David Henry Hwang's *M. Butterfly* generated interest in other Asian American plays, and Asian American theater companies such as the East West Players and Pan Asian Repertory Theatre grew noticeably both in size and in the range of plays they produced. Moreover, mainstream theaters increasingly included Asian American plays during their seasons. Indeed, the plays published during the 1990s accurately represent the creative output of second-wave Asian American playwrights.

Two of the six anthologies published during the 1990s are devoted to plays by women writers: Roberta Uno's *Unbroken Thread* and Velina Hasu Houston's *Politics of Life*. Both anthologies feature plays written by first-wave and second-wave playwrights. Uno and Houston have been instrumental in supporting Asian American women playwrights, who have been overshadowed by the success of male playwrights such as Hwang and Gotanda. In 1993, Uno established the Roberta Uno Asian American Women Playwrights Scripts Collection, 1924 – 2002, which is archived at the University of Massachusetts, Amherst. The collection includes original scripts, many of which have not been produced or published. The plays featured in the anthologies dramatize topics that are significant to the construction of both womanhood and Asian Americanness. For instance, Jeannie Barroga's *Walls* (1989), which is included in Uno's anthology, is about Maya Lin's design of the Vietnam Veterans Memorial in Washington, D.C. Barroga explores Lin's position as a Chinese American architect caught in the controversy over her design. As an Asian American woman, Lin is not considered by the veterans to be qualified to represent their experience of the war. Barroga uses the metaphor of walls to dramatize how Americans are divided through racism, sexism, and politics. On a macrolevel, the play is about the lasting social impact of the Vietnam War, and on a microlevel, the play dramatizes the details of individual lives and relationships.

Genny Lim's *Paper Angels* (1978) also dramatizes an actual historical moment while exploring the toll it has on individuals. Set in 1915, the play is about Chinese detainees on Angel Island off the coast of San Francisco. Based on Lim's research of the poems carved on the walls of the detention center, the play showcases archetypal characters from Chinese immigration history. Lum is an ambitious young Chinese man eager to pursue his American dream while Chin Gung is an "old timer" who is only too familiar with racism in the United States. Together, the characters in the play portray the hopes and disappointments of Chinese immigrants and what they had to endure to arrive in the United States. The play shows what Roberta Uno calls "the impressionistic sensibility" of the playwright in dramatizing the history of Angel Island.[10] The structure of the play is similar to that of Barroga's *Walls* in that the scenes move between time and space fluidly.

History continued to be an important topic for Asian American playwrights throughout the 1980s and 1990s, but, unlike the first-wave writers, the second-wave writers wrote about historical moments they had not directly experienced. As exemplified by Genny Lim and Jeannie Barroga, Asian American playwrights increasingly wrote about nonautobiographical yet personally relevant topics. Elizabeth Wong's play *China Doll* (1996), for instance, is about the Chinese American actress Anna May Wong and the stereotypes of Asian women that have been pervasive throughout the twentieth century. Elizabeth Wong comments on such stereotypes by using Anna May Wong as an emblematic figure who succeeded in her career despite racism in the American film industry.

Whereas first-wave playwrights began playwriting without formal training in the craft, the majority of second-wave playwrights had opportunities to work with playwriting teachers and to develop their plays in workshops sponsored by theater companies. Such opportunities meant that the playwrights could revise their drafts during many phases of the scripts' develop-ment. Such detailed fine-tuning has also led the playwrights to focus more on the tone and the mood of the play. Gotanda articulates this approach in his description of his play *Ballad of Yachiyo*: "All pieces try to say something, do something, leave the audience with something. This one for me was dif-ferent. It wasn't about politics, the tyranny of our cultural mores, the tragic death of my blood relation, or even about constructing the perfect play, though all were important considerations. Rather this one for me was all about tone."[11] The creation of tone and mood on stage is accomplished by many production elements, including setting, lighting, costume, music, and sound. For playwrights, the use of silence and movement also function as indispensable tools for creating emotional affects for the audience. Indeed, what is not said by a character is often more important than what he or she says out loud.

During the 1980s and 1990s, solo performance emerged as a major genre of Asian American drama. Solo performances are often written and performed by the individual performer, and it is rare to see them revived or reenacted by another performer. However, the written scripts of the solo performances have been included in published anthologies, and they have been a major influence on the development of contemporary Asian American drama. In *Asian American Drama* edited by Brian Nelson, Amy Hill's *Tokyo Bound* and Denise Uyehara's *Hiro* are included. Both pieces are solo performances that describe the performer's experience autobiographically. In a typical solo performance piece, the performer narrates her story in first-person voice and often embodies other characters for dramatic effect. Most solo performances are about self-discovery and negotiation with the outside world. Some of the major Asian American solo performers include Dan Kwong, Denise Uyehara, Sandra Tsign Loh, lê thi diem thúy, Shishir Kurup, and Brenda Wong Aoki. Dan Kwong, who is perhaps the most well-known Asian American solo performer, always writes and performs stories that are autobiographical. For example, he has performed stories about growing up as a Japanese-Chinese-American with a Nisei mother and a Chinese American father. In *Secrets of Samurai Centerfield* (1989), he uses dance and storytelling to explore what it means to be an American of multiethnic and multicultural heritage. In the piece, the samurai sword and the baseball bat converge as a new metaphor for his life in the United States.

Multimedia performance was also instrumental in the development of Asian American drama in the 1980s and 1990s. In particular, Ping Chong and Jessica Hagedorn led prolific careers by creating numerous multimedia works that included projection, film, dance, music, art installation, and performance art. While language and dialogues are less significant in multimedia pieces than in straight plays, many of them have been published in script format. Notably, the first anthology of Asian American drama, *Between Worlds: Contemporary Asian-American Drama* (1990) edited by Misha Berson features Ping Chong's *Nuit Blanche: A Select View of Earthlings* and Jessica Hagedorn's *Tenement Lover: no palmtrees/in new york city*. Both are highly visual multimedia works, and the scripts do not do justice to the actual performance. However, the fact that they have been published as part of Asian American drama underscores the need to examine them as both poetry and dramatic literature.

Version 3.0: The Third Wave

Version 3.0: Contemporary Asian American Plays is the title of Chay Yew's edited anthology published in 2011.[12] In his foreword to the anthology, David Henry Hwang declares that third-wave playwrights "have expanded the world of Asian American theatre." He continues, "My generation, so close to the birth of Asian America, sometimes saw it as the key to the riddle of our identity: I am Asian American, therefore I am. Third wave writers, who grew up taking the idea for granted, regard ethnicity as simply one piece in a much more complicated mosaic of identity."[13] Hwang's statement accurately describes the general characteristics of third-wave Asian American playwrights. As defined by Hwang and Yew, the third-wave writers are of a younger generation, and they did not directly experience the emergence of Asian American identity in the 1960s and 1970s. Some of them grew up learning about the Asian American movement and immigration history while others had no contact with an Asian American community.

Starting in the late 1990s, third-wave playwrights began to debut in theater in large numbers. Playwrights such as Sung Rno, Diana Son, Ralph Peña, Han Ong, Alice Tuan, Prince Gomovilla, Chay Yew, Julia Cho, and Lloyd Suh have had their plays produced at both Asian American and mainstream venues. Their plays have been published as both individual plays and in anthologies. One significant trend during the time was the increase in the diversity of ethnicity among Asian American playwrights. First-wave and second-wave playwrights were mostly Chinese and Japanese Americans, but more writers of different ethnic backgrounds began to write for theater. Moreover, some playwrights also worked as directors and producers of ethnic-specific theater companies and workshops. Ralph Peña, who is Filipino American, cofounded the Ma-Yi Theater Company in New York City in 1989 with the purpose of promoting plays by Filipino Americans. He has been the artistic director and, in 1998, expanded the company's mission to include all Asian American plays. Its Ma-Yi Writers Lab, which was founded in 2004 by Sung Rno, has had great success in providing opportunities for emerging Asian American writers, and it has been the country's largest residency program for Asian American playwrights.

Ralph Peña's *Flipzoids* (1996) was a defining production for Ma-Yi Theater Company, and it exemplifies the approach and style of third-wave playwrights.[14] The play is about the Filipino American experience, and Peña uses three characters to dramatize what he saw as the immigrant experience of Filipinos in the United States. The title is a wordplay of "flip," which is derogatory term to label Filipino Americans, and "schizoid," a term to describe those with personality disorder. In the play, Aying is the mother of Vangie, who emigrated from the Philippines to the United States to work as a nurse. While Aying longs to "touch" her homeland, Vangie does everything in her power to assimilate as an American. Aying spends her days on a beach of Southern California where she meets Redford, a confused young man who talks to strangers in public bathrooms. Aying and Redford form a bond as he learns about their ancestral home and as she is kept company during her dying days. Redford is characterized as gay, which worsens his confused state of existence. The way Peña approaches issues of Filipino American identity is not didactic or overly political; rather, he juxtaposes many different representations of home and belonging. On the surface, the play is about Filipino Americans and their diaspora history, but on a deeper level, it is about sin and salvation. By sharing stories of the Philippines and remembering home, Aying saves Redford from his dangerous way of living, and Redford helps Aying perform the ritual of purification before her life comes to an end.

For third-wave writers, issues of ethnic and racial identities converge with existential questions of the human condition. The questions of "who am I" and "why am I here" may be answered in terms of immigration history and hyphenated identities, but they are also addressed as broader philosophical questions. The increase in globalization and transnationalism has also contributed to the expanded application of ethnic identities in exploring the human condition. In their plays, the diasporic condition of displacement and lost identity is the primary human condition of the late twentieth century and the early twenty-first century.

Cleveland Raining (1995) by the Korean American playwright Sung Rno best illustrates the diasporic condition frequently dramatized by third-wave Asian American playwrights. Rno wrote the play while he was a student of Paula Vogel at Brown University's creative writing program. It premiered at the East West Players in 1995 and was considered by many as one of the best representations of the third wave at the company. The play is set in the Midwest, which is not common in Asian American drama. Described by Rno as surreal tragicomedy, *Cleveland Raining* is about Jimmy "Rodin" Kim and Mari Kim who are siblings living in a countryside in Ohio. Their parents have left without explanation, but Mari is convinced that she could find her father if she drove endlessly on the interstate highway. Jimmy believes that the great flood is coming and prepares to escape the disaster on the Volkswagen bug, which he converts into an ark with the help of Mick, a white Ohioan mechanic. He tells Mick that the car engine should run on "emotional loss." Jimmy sleeps in the car and eats kimchi and drinks beer while waiting for rain. The play ends with Mari discovering in the backyard a painting by her mother, who was a painter. Jimmy puts the painting in the car engine, which then "roars to life, glowing with a surreal and bright light."[15]

Rno describes the setting as "fluid, ephemeral, barely real," and the only real object onstage is the Volkswagen. Similar descriptions of setting can be found in other plays by third-wave playwrights. The stage is used not as a metaphorical mirror to reflect reality, but rather it is a space to explore embodiment and presence of Asian Americans. Put in another way, the stage functions as a laboratory for both the performers and spectators to investigate the conditions of being humans and Asian Americans.

Instead of using realism as a dramatic style to represent a sense of authenticity or "real" Asian American experience, the third-wave writers have preferred nonrealistic forms to explore their characters and stories. In their plays, what is real or unreal do not get distinguished, and time does not move linearly. In Alice Tuan's *Last of the Suns* (1994), the grandfather character, Yeh Yeh, sees and hears characters from both Chinese mythology and his past. While one can guess that the Yeh Yeh's mind is overrun by his failing memory, Tuan does not make an explicit distinction between the figments of his mind and what actually happens onstage. In fact, Tuan deliberately integrates the two worlds to enhance the dramatic conflict. Similarly, Sunil Kuruvilla's *Rice Boy* (2000) dramatizes two different worlds to coexist onstage. He describes the setting in detail to underscore the importance of such coexistence: "1975, Canada and India, both places exist on stage simultaneously, with scene shifts indicated quickly by light and sound (not by set changes). At times, the sounds of the countries mix — we hear the Nut Seller's sad call in India blend with the winter gusts of Canada."[16] In the play, the physical simultaneity of different scenes is central in depicting the diasporic experience of the main characters. The play is about Tommy, a twelve-year-old boy who grew up in a city in Ontario, Canada, with his father who could never fully adapt to the new country. Tommy's mother drowned ten years earlier when they were still in their native India. The play interweaves Tommy's memories of his recent trip to India and his efforts to find a "normal" Canadian family that might adopt him. In particular, he remembers his seventeen-year-old cousin Tina, who is paraplegic and spends her days making *kolam*, intricate and decorative patterns made on the floor with rice flour. Tommy's memories coexist with the bleak and cold reality of his life in Canada as he contemplates where he belongs and what he should do with his life.

Nonconventional use of language is another significant feature of third-wave playwrights. In Chay Yew's *A Language of Their Own* (1996), the characters, Oscar and Ming, are defined by how they speak English. They speak through a series of monologues and dialogues, and their conversations transcend time. The script can be interpreted as a collective stream of consciousness of the two Asian gay lovers who are caught in a fraught relationship. Oscar is HIV-positive and breaks up with Ming, and both struggle with being Asian and gay. They often speak directly to the audience, and how they speak to each other is as important as what they say. In the play, dialogues weave in and out of present and past moments, and words are more important than action. It is through language and poetry that Yew creates the intimate world of love, betrayal, and human connection.

In Han Ong's *Swoony Planet* (1997), characters speak in short sentences and phrases that often overlap with each other's lines. The lines in the play are written in verse form with minimal explanation of what the characters are thinking. This means that the intention of the characters must be interpreted by the actor and the director with detailed attention to the beat and flow of language. What is said becomes verbal choreography of thoughts that are not always continuous or logical. In one of the stage directions, Ong has two characters — Artie and a man he imagines to be his father — speak while moving their bodies in a choreographed manner. Ong writes, "Each line they speak is punctuated by an arm being fitted into a sleeve, leg into pants, buttons being buttoned, etc. — gestural, like dance."[17] In the subsequent dialogue, rhythm and tone capture the nuance of the interaction between the two characters. The man is not the father Artie is seeking, and the ill-fitting clothing that results from the "dance" symbolizes the mismatch.

The plays by third-wave Asian American playwrights reflect the overall trend in contemporary American drama, which emphasizes experimentation in form and social issues in content. Many American plays since the 1990s have been about politics of race, gender, and sexuality. This trend has made it imperative for Asian American playwrights to add their voice to the debates of American culture. Moreover, with the controversy surrounding the musical *Miss Saigon* in the early 1990s, casting once again became a central issue in theater, and Asian American playwrights responded by writing plays that could function as a vehicle for Asian American actors.[18] Some, like the Korean American playwright Diana Son, wrote plays with characters that could be played by actors of any racial background. Her play, *Stop Kiss* (1998), is about two women — Callie and Sara — who fall in love, but when they kiss for the first time on a street in New York City, one of them gets assaulted by a bystander. The sequence of the scenes is structured in a way that the story is told in reverse: the play begins with the assaulted woman in a hospital and ends with the first kiss. Although Son did not write the characters with racial specificity, she has insisted on casting them with minority actors. In the premiere at the Public Theatre in New York City, the role of Sara was played by the Korean Canadian actress Sandra Oh, and a male character was played by Kevin Carroll, an African American actor.

In an interview, Son asks rhetorically, "Was *Stop Kiss* the Asian American play of the season at the Public Theater? Is it an Asian American play because I wrote it? Is it an Asian American play because Sandra Oh was in it? The dominant theme of the play was sexuality, sexual identity and committing and not ethnic identity. So I don't know or care if it fulfills that Asian slot. I would think that they chose to produce *Stop Kiss* because it was a good play."[19] She has resisted being labeled Asian American or Korean American and has insisted in writing about anyone and anything. Son's view of the labels is the same as the one held by David Henry Hwang and others in the 1980, but the mainstream success of her plays that are not about Asian American topics epitomizes a significant shift in Asian American theater. She expresses this sense of liberation when she comments that previous generation of Asian American playwrights needed to say, "We are here," but her generation is saying, "We are weird."[20]

While New York City has been a central location for third-wave playwrights, other cities such as Los Angeles, Chicago, and the Twin Cities of Minneapolis and St. Paul have been major sites for new Asian American plays. Additionally, the geographical locales of the plays' settings vary noticeably. The Korean American playwright Julia Cho, for instance, was born in Los Angeles and spent part of her childhood in Arizona, and the West Coast and the Southwest desert function prominently as settings and themes in her plays. In Cho's *BFE* (2005), a teenaged Korean American girl living in a suburb of the Southwest desert feels isolated and ugly, and she tries desperately to fit in. In Lloyd Suh's *American Hwangap* (2009), Texas is the setting for a dysfunctional family with a father who imagines himself to be a hero in a western movie.[21]

Plays published in *Asian American Plays for a New Generation* edited by Josephine Lee, Donald Eitel, and Rick Shiomi represent plays developed and produced in the Twin Cities, which Josephine Lee describes as a "hospitable home for new theatrical writing and production."[22] In her introduction to the anthology, Lee articulates the critical significance of examining Asian American drama in a wider geographical landscape. She writes, "Moving away from a bicoastal Asian America suggests more broadly how Asian American experience never has had a real center. Instead, it is a mass of changing relationships among often quite disparate individuals and groups, whose sense of self, community, and home must be renegotiated time and again."[23] Moreover, the Twin Cities has a large Korean adoptee population, and the anthology features *Walleye Kid: The Musical*, which is about the adoptees' experience in the American Midwest.

The Next Wave: Into the Twenty-First Century

In the twenty-first century, Asian American playwrights have increasingly found inspiration in popular culture, avant-garde performance, social media, and the effects of globalization. The Vietnamese-American playwright Qui Nguyen describes himself as a "playwright, screenwriter, and geek," and he cofounded Vampire Cowboys, a theater company in New York City. He calls the company "geek theatre," and, according to its website, it is "the only professional theatre organization to be officially sponsored by NY Comic Con."[24] His play *The Inexplicable Redemption of Agent G* (2012) is a meta-theatrical comedy about a character named playwright who is kidnapped by his main character to finish the story he has been avoiding for ten years. The play features David Henry Hwang as a character, and Nguyen and Ma-Yi Theater Company produced three YouTube video episodes to promote the play. In the videos, Hwang makes a cameo appearance as a famous yet disgruntled playwright.[25]

The Internet and social media have become an essential tool for Asian American playwrights to advertise and share their plays. In the case of Young Jean Lee, she has used social media to write her play. She would, for example, solicit ideas and examples on her Facebook page and include them in her new play. A Korean American, Young Jean Lee is a playwright and director who has recently emerged as one of the most exciting American theater artists of her generation. She is recognized as an experimental playwright who has written about various topics in ways that many consider subversive and avant-garde. Charles Isherwood of *The New York Times* has called her "hands down, the most adventurous downtown playwright of her generation."[26] Lee, however, did not emerge from Asian American theater. Rather, she founded her own theater company, Young Jean Lee's Theater Company, and has created works that defy convention and expectations of contemporary theater. *Songs of Dragons Flying to Heaven* (2006) is Lee's only play about Asian American identity, and it is a deconstructive parody of identity plays. She deliberately makes the play fail at the end by sabotaging it with two boring white characters.[27]

The future of Asian American drama will include more writers like Qui Nguyen and Young Jean Lee. It will also see a growing number of playwrights with multiracial identity. Playwrights such as Naomi Iizuka and Rajiv Joseph are award-winning writers with parents of Asian and non-Asian descent. While they do not identify themselves singularly as Asian American, their plays have dramatized issues of identity, race, and cultural belonging. For instance, Naomi Iizuka's *36 Views* (2003) is about Orientalism and cultural authenticity, and Rajiv Joseph's Pulitzer Prize — nominated *Bengal Tiger at the Bagdad Zoo* (2009) is about the U.S. involvement in the Middle

East. Joseph's *The North Pool* (2011) addresses the experiences of an Arab American student in an American high school. Almost fifty years have passed since the first playwriting competition sponsored by the East West Players. In those years, Asian American drama grew from virtually nonexistent to becoming established as a major part of American theater and literature. In the beginning decades of the twenty-first century, Asian American playwrights continue to explore both familiar and new issues of Asian American identity and history. At the same time, a number of them have written about topics that have nothing to do with Asian America. Asian American plays can be seen in multiple cities in the country, and the range of genres, styles, and topics varies as widely as the growing diversity of Asian Americans. Whether a fourth wave has to be defined is yet to be seen, but the first-, second-, and third-wave playwrights continue to write and to exert their influence on American theater.

Notes

1. For a detailed history of the East West Players, see Yuko Kurahashi, *Asian American Culture on Stage: The History of the East West Players* (London: Routledge, 1999).

2. For a study on Chin's plays, see Josephine Lee, *Performing Asian America: Race and Ethnicity on the Contemporary Stage* (Philadelphia: Temple University Press, 1997).

3. Karen Shimakawa, *National Abjection: The Asian American Body Onstage* (Durham, NC: Duke University Press, 2002).

4. Velina Hasu Houston, "Introduction," in *The Politics of Life: Four Plays by Asian American Women*, ed. Velina Hasu Houston (Philadelphia: Temple University Press, 1993), 2.

5. For details of Houston's early career, see Esther Kim Lee, *A History of Asian American Theatre* (Cambridge: Cambridge University Press, 2006), 146 – 154.

6. Misha Berson, "Role Model on a Role: Philip Kan Gotanda's Work Grabs Mainstream Attention and Inspires *Younger Artists,"* *Seattle Times* (October 10, 1996): D₁.

7. Philip Kan Gotanda, *The Wind Cries Mary in No More Cherry Blossoms: Sisters Matsumoto and Other Plays* (Seattle: University of Washington Press, 2005), 96.

8. The six anthologies are Misha Berson, ed., *Between Worlds: Contemporary Asian-American Plays* (New York: Theatre Communications Group, 1990); Roberto Uno, ed., *Unbroken Thread: An Anthology of Plays by Asian American Women* (Amherst: University of Massachusetts Press, 1993), Velina Hasu Houston, ed., *The Politics of Life and But Still, Like Air, I'll Rise* (Philadelphia: Temple University Press, 1997); Brian Nelson, ed., *Asian American Drama: Nine Plays from the Multiethnic Landscape* (New York: Applause, 1997); Alvin Eng, ed.,

Tokens? The NYC Asian American Experience on Stage (Philadelphia: Temple University Press, 1999).

9. Philip Kan Gotanda, *Fish Head Soup and Other Plays* (Seattle: University of Washington Press, 1996) and David Henry Hwang, *FOB and Other Plays* (New York: Plume, 1990). For a more complete list, see the bibliography of Esther Kim Lee's *A History of Asian American Theatre*.

10 Uno, *Unbroken Thread, 14.*

11. Philip Kan Gotanda, *Ballad of Yachiyo* (New York City: Theatre Communications Group, 1997), 5.

12. Born in Singapore, Yew was the director of the Asian Theatre Workshop from ten years (1995 – 2005) at the Mark Taper Forum in Los Angeles. He has been a prolific playwright and recognized for his directing and producing. In 2011, he became the Artistic Director of Victory Gardens Theater in Chicago, which was the first time an Asian American was appointed the leader of a mainstream theater company.

13. David Henry Hwang, "Foreword," in *Version 3.0: Contemporary Asian American Plays,* ed. Chay Yew (New York City: Theatre Communications Group, 2011), xi.

14. *Flipzoids* is published in Alvin Eng, *Tokens? and Savage Stage: Plays by Ma-Yi Theater Company,* ed. Joi Barrios-Leblanc (New York: Ma-Yi Theater Company, 2007).

15. Sung Rno, *Cleveland Raining*, in Houston, *But Still, Like Air, I'll Rise,* 260.

16. Sunil Kuruvilla, *Rice Boy, in Yew, Version* 3.0, 469. A Canadian of East Indian descent, Kuruvilla wrote the play as an MFA playwriting student at Yale School of Drama. *Rice Boy* is one of the most produced South Asian American plays in the United States and Canada.

17. Han Ong, *Swoony Planet, in Yew, Version 3.0*, 214.

18. Asian American actors protested the casting of a white actor in yellow-face makeup in the role of a Eurasian character. For details of the controversy, see chapter 7 of Esther Kim Lee's *A History of Asian American Theatre.*

19. Alvin Eng, *Tokens?*, 439.

20. Ibid., 415. Diana Son has indeed broaden her writing opportunities in and out of theater, and she has also worked as a television producer and writer on shows such as "The West Wing," "Law and Order: Criminal Intent," and "Blue Bloods."

21. Lloyd Suh's American Hwangapis published in *Seven Contemporary Plays from the Korean Diaspora*, ed. Esther Kim Lee (Durham, NC: Duke University Press, 2012).

22. Josephine Lee, Donald Eitel, and Rick Shiomi, eds., *Asian American Plays for a New*

Generation: Plays for a New Generation (Philadelphia: Temple University Press, 2011), 5.

23. Ibid., 5 – 6.

24. Online resource: http://quinguyen.com/bio.html (accessed August 14, 2014).

25. Online resource: https://www.youtube.com/watch?v=ImsCxXB2HQ8 (accessed August 14, 2014).

26. Charles Isherwood, "Beneath Pink Parasols, Identity in Stark Form," *The New York Times* (January 16, 2012). Online resource: http://theater.nytimes.com/2012/01/17/ theater/reviews/ young-jean-lees-untitled-feminist-show-review.html (accessed July 14, 2012),

27. For studies on Young Jean Lee's play, see Karen Shimakawa, "Young Jean Lee's Ugly Feelings about Race and Gender," *Women & Performance: A Journal of Feminist Theory* 17.1 (March 2007): 89 – 102 and Esther Kim Lee, "Asian American Women Playwrights and the Dilemma of the Identity Play: Staging Heterotopic Subjectivities," in *Contemporary Women Playwrights: Into the Twenty-First Century,* ed. Penny Farfan and Lesley Ferris (New York: Palgrave Macmillan, 2013).

12

Asian American Short Fiction and the Contingencies of Form, 1930s–1960s
20 世纪 30—60 年代美国亚裔短篇小说及其形式的可能性

Jinqi Ling

评论家简介

凌津奇（Jinqi Ling），美国华盛顿州立大学美国研究方向博士，现任美国加利福尼亚大学洛杉矶分校英语系教授及美国亚裔研究系主任。研究领域包括美国亚裔小说、文学分期、体裁研究、批评理论（主要涉及历史化美学、现实主义与现代主义 / 后现代主义交叉性）等。专著有《叙述民族主义：美国亚裔文学中的意识形态与形式》（*Narrating Nationalisms: Ideology and Form in Asian American Literature*, 1998）；《越过子午线：山下凯伦跨国小说的历史与虚构》（*Across Meridians: History and Figuration in Karen Tei Yamashita's Transnational Novels*, 2012）。除本书收录的论文，其他代表性论文有《身份危机与性别政治：重新审视美国亚裔的男性气质》，收于《种族间美国亚裔文学指南》一书（"Identity Crisis and Gender Politics: Reappropriating Asian American Masculinity," *An Interethnic Companion to Asian American Literature*, 1996）等。

文章简介

　　凌津奇教授在文章开篇指出19世纪30—60年代是美国亚裔文学发展的重要历史时期，它见证了美国亚裔长篇小说的早期发展与美国亚裔短篇小说创作的显著增长。文章重点分析了部分重要的美国亚裔作家在此期间选择短篇小说而非长篇小说作为创作体裁的原因。为了回答这一问题，文章首先通过对比长篇小说与短篇小说在传统文学理念中的体裁特征，指出短篇小说创作不仅彰显形式的技巧性与内容的现代性，同时承载着表现现实性与历史性的功能。接着文章主要从主题角度分析了四位重要的美国亚裔作家在这一历史时期的短篇小说创作特点，证明这一时期美国亚裔作家短篇小说创作繁荣发展的事实以及短篇小说的创作是如何满足这些作家在那个特定时期的个人、历史及社会环境需要的。文章最后以理论的视角与对比的方法阐释了短篇小说在以打破时间连贯性来建构意义方面比长篇小说有更大的优势。

文章出处：Srikanth, Rajini., and Min Hyoung Song, editors. *The Cambridge History of Asian American Literature.* New York: Cambridge UP, 2016, pp. 187-202.

Asian American Short Fiction and the Contingencies of Form, 1930s–1960s

Jinqi Ling

The period spanning the 1930s to the 1960s is pivotal to Asian American literary history in that it witnessed both the early development of the Asian American novel and a phenomenal growth of Asian American short fiction.[1] In making this observation, I do not suggest that these overlapping formations were coeval with each other, or that they fit comfortably into the familiar confines of periodization in American literary history. Rather, my entwining an examination of Asian American short fiction with that of the Asian American novel facilitates a more sophisticated understanding of the former than what a purely content-based analysis permits. Such a comparative approach demands a consideration of the formal differences between these two basic modes of Asian American narrative, as well as the personal, historical, and circumstantial factors that led important Asian American writers to choose the short-fiction form over the novel as a preferred instrument for representing their experiences in this period.[2]

To illustrate the argument, which is necessarily retrospectively constructed, this chapter performs a two-pronged mission. First, I contextually examine the works of two groups of Asian American writers whose practice in short-fiction writing contributed to the genre's prominence: those by Toshio Mori (1910–1980) and Hisaye Yamamoto (1921–2011), on the one hand, and those by Bienvenido Santos (1911–1996) and Carlos Bulosan (1913–1956), on the other[3] — a survey that teases out major themes and motifs of selected texts, especially relative to the authors' positions toward tensions leading to internment (for the first pair) or ruptures within immigrant communities occasioned by generational conflict, national identity, and race, gender, and class differences. Second, I theorize the relationship between the novel and short fiction as different formal responses to modernity, with an assessment of the realist origin and premises of the novel vis-à-vis the temporally more modulated — and referentially less predictable — tendency in short fiction. I argue that these four Asian American writers turned to the brevity of the short-fiction form in this period because the form is uniquely suited for examining disjunctive modes of temporality, as well as for legitimizing small-scale disruption of the patterns of continuity closely associated with the novel form.

Preliminaries

Most will agree that the novel, with its implicit or explicit attempt to offer exhaustive transcriptions of the world, stands in contrast to short fiction, a generic species that aims at aphoristic brevity, metaphorical ellipsis, and implied significance. Writers often turn to the novel's narrativized duration, as well as its emphasis on a symbolic unity between language/mind and world/nature, to represent diachronic shifts of time and indulge an allegorical cast of imagination. Writers of short fiction, by contrast, seem prone to the synchronic, ambiguous, and ironic investments that the latter form invites — a mode of representation especially open to modern sensibilities of discontinuity, contingency, and fragmentation. Furthermore, short fiction, by dint of its compactness both in form and content, makes the process of storytelling more technical.[4] Hence, Edgar Alan Poe celebrates the importance of craft in the form and regards the short tale as belonging to "the loftiest region of art," while Cary Saul Morson considers short genres in general "a banquet of delicious morels" strewn with particular worldviews, philosophical premises, speculative scenarios, and witticism.[5] These formal traits of short fiction determine that its content — even when designed to be social and political — often manifests itself as intense personal dramas that point, more than does the novel, to "the strangeness and ambiguity of life" or "absurdity in all its undisguised and unadorned nakedness."[6] Such a formally dictated orientation in short fiction may occasionally be used to affirm ahistorical arguments about the universality of all literatures. By contrast, I assume here that the meaning of a work of short fiction is historically specific: it bears the burden — as Edward Said argues — of the "worldly" occasions and empirical realities from which a literary text emerges, which also constitute textual and circumstantial constraints on its interpretations.[7]

The Asian American short fiction under examination, as a type of peripheral literary production, must be understood as both formally and historically contingent. Basic questions to ask include: Why did Asian American writers choose short fiction rather than the novel when both seemed available to them in the era? What did the writing of Asian American short fiction entail, not only as an act of self-representation but also a form of intellectual and even physical labor in the historical context in which it was composed?

The writers' life experiences are telling. In the early 1930s Mori decided to become a writer at the age of twenty-two while working as a full-time nurseryman, and, to realize his dream, scheduled a rigorous after-hour writing practice that typically lasted till daybreak.[8] Yamamoto began her writing career by first getting involved in the launching of a camp newspaper in

Poston, Arizona, where she was interned and, in the immediate postwar years, by contributing to the English sections of Japanese-language newspapers, as a housewife and mother of several children.[9] After immigrating to the United States in 1930, Bulosan became a unionized itinerant laborer in the Pacific West and acquired his creative competence from mining public libraries, while practicing left-wing journalism for workers publications.[10] With the exception of Santos — who received formal training in creative writing in the United States as a *pensionado* sponsored by the Philippine government[11] — none of the writers mentioned fits the category of the professional writer. And none — with Santos included — had their stories published in book form in the United States before the mid-1970s, when Asian American literature finally made its successful claim on the cultural establishment.

As the foregoing discussion makes clear, these Asian American writers' turn to short fiction in the period was not simply a matter of formal choice, although the short-fiction form, given the range of affective and temporal possibilities it manages to localize, did contribute to thematizing the uncertainty and open-endedness of Asians' experiences, either as labor immigrants or as members of a socially marginalized ethnic minority. Rather, these writers opted for short fiction mainly because the latter is unorthodox in its formula, flexible in its topical range, and innovatively eclectic in its construction of artistic visions. Compared with the novel, short fiction appealed to Asian American writers especially in a pragmatic sense: the writing of this type of narrative did not require guaranteed time, regular financial support, or the availability of professional audiences. As such, short fiction presented itself as a far more accessible aesthetic platform for experimenting with ways of realizing these writers' expressive dreams. The latter fact shows that whatever readership Asian American writers had in mind when they started their short-fiction projects, they were keenly aware that America's publishing industry and book trade operated in affirmation of the existing social, cultural, racial, and gender stratifications. Retrospectively, what these writers achieved in the period is not so much getting their individual talents recognized as contributing to the public dissemination of knowledge about Asians' suffering from discrimination, their struggles, and their daily aspirations, when such knowledge was conspicuously absent in the American popular imagination.

Nisei Views: Life before and beyond the Camp

Mori and Yamamoto participated in this process of ethnic cultural codification through portrayals of Japanese immigrant life from Nisei perspectives — portrayals set largely outside the traumatic experience of internment, despite the fact that both writers were interned and occasionally wrote about the camp. The primary focus of Mori's literary project was the prewar community; while Yamamoto straddled both the pre-and postwar Japanese American worlds cohabited by Issei and Nisei from a woman-centered and interethnic perspective. The representational priority that both writers give to prewar Japanese American life is rich in its historical implications: (1) it allows readers a rare access to the internal dynamics of the ethnic community in the era, about which there is a dearth of literary attention, and (2) it fosters an understanding of the internment not as an isolated event but as the cumulative result of prior histories, tendencies, practices, and attitudes, both within and outside the United States. Commenting on Mori's short-fiction productions along this line, Yamamoto observed that Mori's descriptions of Japanese America of the 1930s were filled with concerns about "the awkward Nisei situation" when "the storm clouds gathered," as if in anticipation of the concentration camps of 1942–5.[12] What Yamamoto refers to are the pressures felt by the American-born Japanese, both of Mori's and of her own genera-tions, from the "disapproving" attitude that the world took toward Japan's expansionist behaviors during the interwar years, a situation that exacerbated the already prevalent racial prejudices against the Japanese living in the United States.

Mori's story "1936" (1936) implicitly addresses such a concern. Concentrating on a single day's activities, the narrator is seized by an intense desire to know the white people, the minds of his own generation, the concerns of Issei, and the culture of Japan. Such an urge to know culminates in the narrator's musings about "the bizarreness" of a scene of seeming racial harmony that he observes in a barbershop, whose customers include, besides himself, a Mexican, a Spaniard, and an Italian. "If one tiny barber shop could have four nationalities at one time," he reflects, "I could believe the vastness and the goodness of America's project. This is the place, the earth where the brothers and the races meet, mingle and share, and the most probable part of the earth to seek peace and goodwill through relations with the rest of the world."[13]

Worries about misunderstandings that would divide Issei and Nisei from the rest of American society implicitly inform "The Eggs of the World" (1949), another story that Mori evidently wrote in the 1930s. Central to the plot of the story is an Issei alcoholic, who roams about with warnings against the danger of living within the shells of eggs, much to the confusion and disgust of others. The eggshell is a metaphor that Mori used to problematize the early immigrants' tendency to band together in Japanese enclaves. As if insinuating the violence that would eventually befall the ethnic community during the war, the drunkard predicts that an egg that remains unbroken from the inside would eventually be smashed from without in the form of "rape" or "assault."[14] But the speaker's appeal for racial integration goes unheeded because people do not know when he is sober and when he is drunk.

Mori implies that Issei and Nisei carry on their day-to-day activities under such an atmosphere with resilience and sobering practicality. "The Chessmen" (1941) describes the cutthroat competition between two nurserymen — an elderly Issei and a Nisei hired on a temporary basis during a prewar economic slump. The tension originates from the nursery owner's plan to lay off the less experienced temporary help, a possibility that the latter seeks to prevent through his youthful aggression. Mori presents the physical and mental struggle between the two as a duel between two "strangers" meeting "face to face with fear" on a "lonely road," with the younger Nisei emerging as the ultimate winner of the contest (102–3). The theme of Issei's decline in workplace is also at stake in Mori's "Operator, Operator!" (1938). Its central character is an elderly gardener several months into debt on his rent because nobody wants to hire him. As a last resort, he uses the only coins left in his pocket to pay for a job advertisement in a local newspaper, hoping that an employer would respond. The story shifts between the man's recollections of his youthful days, his anxious waiting in the apartment room for a call, and his dread about being asked to leave by his landlady.

Such are the socioeconomic conditions facing several of Mori's male characters memorable for their tenacious quests for spiritual or artistic fulfillment. "The Seventh Street Philosopher" (1949), for example, features a middle-aged launderer obsessed with delivering public speeches on Buddhist traditions, utterly oblivious to his amateurish grasp of the topic, apathy among his audiences, and the irony of his narcissism. "Japanese Hamlet" (1939) describes an Issei's determination to become "the ranking Shakespeare actor" by spending all his time reciting lines from the English master's complete works, to the derision and annoyance of his friends, but the nodding approval of the story's narrator who sees merits in his "simple persistence" (40–1). "The Distant Call of the Deer" (1937) focuses on an Issei's strange habit of conducting a nightly exercise of playing a piece of Japanese music. The practice disturbs the neighbors' sleep, scares dogs and cats, and infuriates his wife, but it becomes solidified after he wins, at the age of fifty-three, the third prize from a community-sponsored music contest.

"The Chauvinist" (1935) is perhaps the most speculative of Mori's stories about prewar Japanese immigrant life. The title of this story is ironic: it refers to what is opposite to traditional understandings of male superiority, that is, an Issei man's humorous acceptance of his sudden loss of hearing and subsequent confinement to the role of cooking for his socially active wife and fastidious children. Sustaining the man's positive attitude is a "new philosophy" that he invents for the occasion: he sees his hearing impediment as a higher "calling" that demands his display of "humbleness," "dignity," and "silent endurance" in the face of his misfortunes. From this perspective, his deafness and his relegation to the kitchen both become metaphors: as a "handicapped" male immigrant rendered socially relevant only for food preparation, his best hope is "cooking up the greatest taste of life" — by "scraping for crumbs" (17–18, 20–4).

A number of Yamamoto's most effective stories, though all written and published in the immediate postwar decades, are similarly vectored in the preinternment years, against a background of economic hardship and the embryonic formation of a Japanese American community bustling with agricultural activities. "Life among the Oil Fields" (1979), for example, uses an eight-year-old Nisei girl's perspective for a nonfictional account of her experience with the Roaring Twenties, an era marked, on the one hand, by the Volstead Act, Al Capone, flaming youth, and Black Thursday and, on the other, by the narrator's linguistic struggle at an American elementary school, her family's itineration across impoverished multiracial farming communities, her participation in agricultural labor and ethnic food preparation, and, above all, her witnessing of an arrogant white couple's perpetration, without reprisal, of a hit-and-run accident in an oil-field neighborhood that almost kills her younger brother. The white couple's careless treatment of human life is described in the story as a shameless repetition of Scott and Zelda's lifestyle,[15] the enigmatic couple of the Jazz Age.

Yamamoto's "Yoneko's Earthquake" (1951) is a work widely celebrated for its multiple layers of meaning and rich symbolism. On the surface, the story is about the young Nisei girl Yoneko's experience of having her religious faith dashed, as well as her subsequent loss of psychological balance, both triggered by an earthquake that disrupts the routine of her parents' tomato farm and leaves her father permanently incapacitated for outdoor work. Underlying this manifest story are the reshuffled class and racial dynamics on the farm that result from the father's displacement as a patriarchal figure, a development that in turn contributes to the demystification of Yoneko's secular construction of Marpo — a hired Filipino hand with colorful personality and multiple talents — as the ultimate bearer of "the word of God" (47). What puzzles Yoneko before the earthquake is that Marpo always appears "shy," "meek," and deferential in the presence of her parents (49). The earthquake and its aftermath both muddle and clarify Yoneko's thoughts: these events not only allow Marpo to replace her father symbolically as the mainstay of the family and have an affair with a mother increasingly unhappy about her loveless marriage, but also subsequently lead to Marpo's dismissal from the farm. The parallel developments generated by the earthquake — socially, emotionally, and psychologically — thus contribute to Yoneko's growing maturity as a "free thinker," in the wake of what she considers a devastating "desertion" by Marpo — her beloved God figure (46, 55).

"Seventeen Syllables" (1949) is another of Yamamoto stories well-known for its verbal economy and dramatic overtones. In contrast to Mori's depiction of how Issei males are tolerated — either grudgingly or with good humor — for their impractical investments of time and energy, this story offers a critique of the flat denial of Issei women's artistic pursuits, in this case of Tome Hayashi's humiliating experience with her husband, who, angered by her taking extra time to receive the presenter of the prize she has won in a haiku poetry contest, burns the trophy in front of their children. The gender bias that Yamamoto exposes in traditional definitions of who can serve as the creative agents in a fledging ethnic community points to a range of attendant problems. The value of Tome's physical labor — her "ample share of picking tomatoes out in the sweltering fields and boxing them" in the packing shed, as well as her performance of the wifely/ motherly duties of cooking, washing, cleaning, and housekeeping (9) — rarely figures in her husband's calculation of what constitutes daily work. Further complicating the matter is Tome's perception of her artistic impulse as being stifled by her arranged marriage. Hence, she asks her American-born daughter Rosie not to marry in the future. Despite "the familiar glib agreement" with which Rosie concedes to the mother's request, she daringly embarks on a relationship with Jesus Carrasco, the son of the Mexican family hired for the tomato harvest. Tome's recognition of the growing cultural gap between herself and Rosie is registered, at the end of the story, in her hesitation to embrace her daughter, who sheds frustrated tears about being torn between her own individual pursuits and her mother's expectations.

Short Fiction from the Filipino Diaspora

Santos and Bulosan contributed to the development of Asian American short fiction in rather different ways: not only did they depart from the U.S.-centered perspectives of Mori and Yamamoto, thereby showing the relevance of alternative histories to Asian American literary imaginations, but they differed from each other in their respective investments as well. Santos wrote compassionately about his "grief" over the pain of his less-fortunate compatriots,[16] while Bulosan interpreted the wider implications of such pain from the perspective of an organic intellectual. The two writers' social inclinations explain the different modalities of the Filipino immigrant life each emphasized: Santos took a keen interest in exploring manong's existential dilemmas through a sophisticated literary lens, whereas Bulosan historicized such dilemmas from a prolabor and critically international perspective.

"Scent of Apples" (1948) is paradigmatic of Santos's fictional construction of the predicament facing Filipino immigrants. It describes the ironic life of Celestino Fabia, who has been away from his home country for more than twenty years and subsists, as the story begins, on an isolated country farm in the Midwest with his American wife and their biracial son. Drama unfolds when Fabia invites the first-person narrator to dinner at his home; the latter is a Filipino scholar appointed by the government-in-exile during the war to give a speech at a women's college in the area. The story does not explicitly state the purpose of Fabia's invitation, except through a mention of his asking the narrator a question about the current state of Filipino women toward the end of the lecture. The women that Fabia has in mind are long-haired, appropriately dressed, modest, and faithful — qualities emblemized in a framed picture that he keeps at his home, which shows the faded figure of a woman in Philippine dress, with her once "young and good" face "blurred."[17] Read as Fabia's discourse on domesticity, the parallel between the ideal Filipino women he nostalgically remembers and the anonymous Filipino woman he has framed in a picture underscores the class implications of his marriage of convenience. His wife is plain, humble, and weather-beaten, exactly the same way he is — poor and aging — with the exception of their racial difference. Fabia's inviting the narrator to his home thus acquires satiric implications: he hopes to change his wife's impression of him through his association with the narrator, whom he considers a "cleaner looking," "first-class" Filipino (24). Fabia's futile attempt to gain respectability in such a way is what Santos criticizes through the metaphor of the scent of apples: the permeating smell of the overripe fruit suggests the state of Fabia's Americanization, whose condition consists of nothing but lonely winters, dying trees, a rundown homestead, and the spiritual decay of clinging to unexamined attitudes from his past.

"The Day the Dancers Came" (1955) strikes a similar note. It tells of the different attitudes taken by two manong bachelors — Filemon Acayan and Antonio Bataller — toward the visit of a dance troupe from the Philippines. The former sees the dancers' coming as an occasion to renew his ties with the home country, while the latter, bedridden with a disease that has ironically turned his skin completely white, is indifferent to the event. Santos begins the story with a snow scene that highlights brightness — an uplifting moment — amidst the overwhelming gloom of the city, a scene during which Fil goes jubilantly to meet the dancers in a hotel and then records the sound effects of their performance in a theater. But the dancers ignore Fil, who, back in his apartment, inadvertently erases the content of his recording by pressing a wrong button. As Fil's nostalgic dream turns sour, the snow stops falling; the snow-covered ground becomes slushy in the sun; and Tony's diseased white skin turns cancerous and deadly.

Santos's satiric portrayals of the Filipino immigrant condition in the pre-1965 era find perhaps their most poignant expression in "The Door" (1948), a story about the enigmatic function of an apartment door in a building rented by all-male Filipino immigrants. Behind the door live Delfin, a young Filipino, and his wife Mildred, a white woman with two little girls from a previous marriage. Central to the story is a tacit agreement between the couple that, when outside, Delfin not enter the apartment if the door appears closed until he sees a visitor leave. It happens that the first-person narrator of the story, Ambo, who is an elderly friend of Delfin's, is asked by Mildred to fix the blinkers in her apartment on a Christmas Eve. While Ambo works inside, one of the little girls bolts the door by mistake, inadvertently treating Ambo as one of Mildred's customers. Focusing on the stunned shock on Delfin's face at the sight of Ambo's coming out of the door, the story ends with the moral question that Delfin has avoided facing: the nature of the compromise by which he deals with his loneliness by accepting Mildred's prostitution — presumably as a way of supporting her children — so long as the identities of her visitors remain unknown to him.

Compared with Santos's subtly wrought tales, Bulosan's short fictions are self-consciously historical in scope and explicitly partisan in their attempt to inventory images, memories, and moments, with a preference for sublimating his portrayals of misery and suffering onto a socially symbolic terrain.[18] A good example is "The Story of a Letter" (1946), which tells of an impoverished Filipino father's futile attempt to get a letter written in English — sent home by his oldest son from the United States — translated into the native language. The father's frustration is associated with a series of misfortunes: the village priest, whom he initially approaches for assistance, unexpectedly dies from overeating; the second son, whom he sends to study in the city, goes to America rather than return to help; a newly built country school, to which he sends the narrator — his youngest son — for education, turns out to offer courses only in Spanish; and the narrator, who ends up in the United States to study, finally sends the translated letter to him from a hospital bed. Ironically, the father has died several years before. Even more ironic is the content of the letter that is ultimately returned to the narrator at his American address: his oldest brother confesses to feeling "sad" and "sentimental" upon his arrival in America — a familiar story that takes almost eighteen years to be told, without ever reaching its designated audience.[19]

"Life and Death of a Filipino in America" recalls the first-person narrator's five encounters with death: (1) as a small boy, he witnesses his mother's violent death during childbirth; (2) at the age of ten, he watches his father decapitate the family's carabao out of rage; (3) during his passage to America, he observes a compatriot's being knifed to death; (4) in Seattle, he watches a talented Filipino roommate die from starvation; and (5) in California, he is present at a Filipino union advocate's brutal murder by a white mob. What Bulosan offers through such a heavy emphasis on the loss of lives is not only an indictment of arbitrary power but also a critique of the brutalizing results of colonial impositions and forced exile.

In light of the two stories examined in the preceding text, "Homecoming" seems most suggestive of Bulosan's strategy for working through the contradictions that threaten to paralyze Filipinos in diaspora: their homeland's continuing subjugation to the United States, and the systemic racism that leaves little space for the struggling immigrants except for the rhetorical promises of American democracy. The story tells of Mariano's return to the Philippines after twelve years of absence by focusing on his activities that span only one evening. Central to these activities is Mariano's homebound walk from the bus depot, which is punctuated by memories of his childhood affections for his mother and of his American doctor's chilling diagnosis of his terminal lung disease, by his excitement about finally reaching home and his fear of having to disclose to the loved ones that he is returning to die. The reunion that follows offers no solace. From his mother's "deadening solemnity," his first younger sister's muffled cry, and his second younger sister's bitter revelation of the family's economic despair, Mariano realizes that they "suffered the same terrors of poverty, the same humiliations of defeat, that he had suffered in America" (95). With both the horror of recognition and anger at the forces that have reduced his family to such hopelessness, he decides to leave. The home to which Mariano returns proves no less alienating than the America that "had crushed his spirit" (93). Home then becomes the starting point of Mariano's renewed exile, as well as Bulosan's emblem for his ongoing search for answers to the Filipino condition — other than that offered by his protagonist's physical demise.

On the basis of this examination of selected works of four Asian American writers, I wish to suggest that the short-fiction form employed by these writers is highly effective for organizing experiences in ways both unique to a limited period of time and distinct in the temporal series from which they each spoke. The brevity and semiautonomy of this form seem especially appropriate for the writers' examination of the still points of social and cultural turmoil in which they located their characters, as well as for their demonstration of the varied functions — hence the mimetic illusions of coherence — of an everyday that is shot through with contradictions. To a certain degree, the internal heterology of the short stories discussed in this chapter might best be understood as the product of the authors' attempts to represent the ruptures of Asian American history in literary form: Mori's witty and affectionate exploration of the paradox of generational tensions through manipulations of narrative distancing, Yamamoto's staging of dramatic conflicts or transgression through the whisper of poetic insinuation, Santos's provocative hesitations and skillful dancing between storytelling (*fabula*) and representation (*sjuzet*) of the immigrant plight, and Bulosan's synthetic collage of analogous moments or situations that can be grasped only through structures of feeling embedded in alternative time frames.

These fictional techniques are profoundly political in that the vicissitude of tastes on the American literary market and its conditional opening to Asian American voices are rarely free of ideological presumptions, as evidenced in William Saroyan's supportive but somewhat condescending assessment of Mori's first published short story from *Coast* magazine in 1939. He saw Mori's writing as blemished by its occasional lapses in grammar and syntax, despite his simultaneous recognition of Mori's promise as "a natural born writer."[20] What frustrated Saroyan at the time, one may argue, was a cultural mission that Asian American writers aimed to accomplish through the short-fiction form: to diversify, enrich, and transform the way English had been used in American literature through innovative injections of historically concrete and ethnically specific grammatical indices, points of view, tonality, and cultural idioms.

Rethinking the Novel through Short Fiction

This chapter concludes with a theoretical perspective on how short fiction *legitimizes* small-scale disruption of the patterns of continuity closely associated with the novel form, by engaging with major positions about the latter's realist premises and actual functions. The novel — as the dominant narrative form in Euro-American literatures since the mid-nineteenth century — is generally understood as an extended prose with structured plots, fictional settings and characters, diverse points of view, and, in some, sequential development with a clear beginning and ending. One complicating factor in entering discussion in this way is that the novel went through a decline after World War II;[21] it gave way to the concept of "prose fiction," which was subsequently displaced by the idea of "narrative." In this context, the category of "novel" continued to be used, as scholars working on periodization generally agree, specifically as a mode of realism, a genre that Franco Moretti aptly describes as "the symbolic form" of "modernity."[22] Prose fiction, by contrast, is more associated with the ascendency of structuralism since the 1950s, and it treats the novel as but one of its designated formal variants.[23]

Narrative is a category most favored by boundary-breaking poststructuralists and postmodernists, who see the metonymical and the metaphorical as cohabiting all linguistic utterances, hence making no rigid distinction between literary and nonliterary discourses.[24] Sophisticated assessments of the realist novel may still be found in the early writings of Lukács, whose enduring contributions include seeing the novel as having a deceptively complete form but inherently incomplete content — an "inner problematic" that results from the increasing separation, as well as abstraction, of art from its life-sustaining networks or environments under forces of capital's reification.[25] The realist novel's structural internalization of the conflicting values of modernity thus makes it an artifact of irresolvable tensions, all repressed under the finished novel form as a kind of textual — and, correspondingly, interpretive — effect of ideological "containment."[26]

Such an understanding of the European realist novel is useful for discussing similar Asian American narrative forms. For example, Yoon Sun Lee observes that the realist novel often renders Asians' presence in capitalist modernity simultaneously invisible and conspicuous through its form, which at once hides the social consequences of Asians' racialization and affirms their stereotypically rendered designation as a cultural other. Focusing on the iterative routine of the modern Asian American everyday, Lee argues that Asian American writers' novelistic investment in the trivial, the repetitive, and the predictable is emblematic of the effects of Asians' insertion into and struggle against Western modernity, while it also affirms the rigor and ongoing relevance of Lukács's critical realist paradigm.[27] Based on my examination of selected Asian American short fictions, I wish to delineate a different line of argument — beyond Lee's dialectical syncretism premised on the assumption that Asians' experience of racialization in the West both emblemizes and contributes to the singular effect of modernity, the primal rhythm of realism constituted by steady repetition,[28] and Lukács's uncompromising vision of totality — with two cautionary comments. First, the realist novel's tendency to confine its portrayal to the everyday is not unique to Asian American literary representations. This is so mainly because the novel form requires "a constant elusion of historical turning points and breaks" in its content, so that the coherent "unfolding" of the subjective individuality (or the "equilibrium" of the ego) essential to the novel form can be maintained.[29]

The deliberate avoidance of temporal ruptures in the realist novel through its fusion of content with form centering on the everyday, as scholars have observed, is premised on a past-oriented historical vision, one that is shaped more by the organic ideals of Romanticism than by the crisis-ridden Benjaminian sense of the present.[30] Second, patterns of repetitive similarity deducible from the novel are not necessarily innate to the latter's realist bent, but rather often determined by particular ways of seeing or reading.[31] For example, the frequent mention of "demons" or "ghosts" and the radical rewriting of Chinese folklore in Maxine Hong Kingston's memoirs *The Woman Warrior* (1976) strike only those with little knowledge about the Chinese language and culture as symptoms of free-wheeling postmodernism;[32] they appear starkly realist to readers privy to the Cantonese vernacular and its Chinese American redeployment, whether these readers agree to Kingston's strategy for cultural appropriation or not. As such, the reality in a realist novel is always relative because readers have different degrees of familiarity with and access to its contexts, use different modes of interpretation, and occupy different cognitive domains of the novel's shifting horizon of expectations. Understood in this way, the repetitive everyday events described in the Asian American realist novel should also be seen as inherently varied in scale and irregular in duration as a result of their association with multiple temporalities that condition reading experiences, as well as the unsteady pulses produced by different forms and degrees of Asians' participation in modernity, the resultant disjunctions and upheavals always lurking beneath the given textual symptoms.

If the internal heteroglossia of the realist novel is often masked by its culturally conservative form and by naïve readers' failure to recognize the form's structural tensions, then short fiction works to expose both the dangers of "traditional" modes of constructing meaning through the novel form and the problematic of single modes of reading premised on essentialist conceptions of temporality. More important, it legitimizes a rhetorical means of representing reality without the routine drive for narrative completion, resolution, and coherence. In refusing to let readers be soothed by the apparent referential certainties of the realist novel, the short-fiction form thus becomes a more logical choice for dealing with the "random or aleatory event as the debris of temporality" both within and outside modernity.[33] Iteration of the quotidian in the Asian American novel contributes to renewal of critical realism only when readers are willing to pluralize the cognitive lens used for examining the everyday and to transform the narrow classical rendering of the quotidian in ways beyond the ken of Lukács's epic imagination. The short-fiction form, as a realized miniature of signifying contingency, is structurally subversive to the developmental time of modernity, a possibility that remains abstract under the formal constraints of the realist novel.[34]

Notes

1. I want to thank Alexander Hammond, Lane Hirabayashi, Mark Seltzer, Min Hyoung Song, and Rajini Srikanth for reading and commenting on draft versions of this essay, and E. San Juan for sharing insights about Carlo Bulosan's short stories.

2. Amy Ling and Annette White-Parks designate Sui Sin Far's 1912 *Ms. Spring Fragrance* as the inaugurating publication of Asian American short fiction. See Amy Ling and Annette White-Parks, "Introduction," in Sui Sin Far (Edith Eaton), *Ms. Spring Fragrance and Other Writings*,

ed. Amy Ling and Annette White-Parks (Urbana: University of Illinois Press, 1995), 5 – 6. Susan Koshy traces the first Asian American novel to Onoto Watanna's 1904 *A Japanese Nightingale*. See Susan Koshy, "The Rise of the Asian American Novel," in *Cambridge History of the American Novel*, ed. Leonard Cassuto (Cambridge: Cambridge University Press, 2011), 1050 – 2. I consider the literary environments between the 1930s and the 1960s more conducive to Asian American experimentations with both narrative forms.

3. Most of the writers examined in this chapter were also practitioners of the novel. E.g., Mori authored *Woman from Hiroshima* (1978) and completed several novel-length manuscripts. Santos published five novels and four nonfictions in the Philippines, while Bulosan's *America Is in the Heart* (1946) and *The Cry and the Dedication* (1995) are Asian American novelistic classics. In addition, the writers surveyed were not the only Asian American artists who produced short fictions in the era. E.g., Milton Murayama had "I'll Crack Your Head Kotsun" published in 1959, a story that later became part of his novel *All I Asking for Is My Body* (1975). Wakako Yamauchi composed her story "And the Soul Shall Dance" during the 1960s, which was subsequently included in *Aiiieeeee!* (1974).

4. This observation seems also true of the realist novels of Flaubert and Henry James — both claimed by the modernist canon — versus the realist works of Balzac and Charles Dickens.

5. Edgar Alan Poe, Review of *Twice-Told Tales*, by Nathaniel Hawthorne, *Graham's Magazine* 20 (May 1842): 299; Gary Saul Morson, *The Long and Short of It: From Aphorism to Novel* (Stanford, CA: Stanford University Press, 2012), 6, 14.

6. Georg Lukàcs, *The Theory of the Novel*, trans. Anna Bostock (1920 Cambridge, MA: MIT Press, 1971), 51.

7. Edward W. Said, *World, Text, and Context* (Cambridge, MA: Harvard University Press, 1983), 35.

8. Hisaye Yamamoto, "Introduction," in Toshio Mori, *The Chauvinist and Other Stories* (Los Angeles: Asian American Studies Center, UCLA, 1979), 7.

9. Charles L. Crow, "A MELUS Interview: Hisaye Yamamoto," *MELUS* 14.1 (1987): 73 – 77.

10. E. San Juan Jr., "Introduction," in Calose Bulosan, *On Becoming Filipino: Selected Writings of Carlos Bulosan*, edited by E. San Juan, Jr. (Philadelphia: Temple University Press, 1995), 6 – 7.

11. Santos studied with I. A. Richards at Harvard, took classes with Whit Burnett, Editor of *Story* magazine, at Columbia, and won a Guggenheim Award while he participated in the University of Iowa Writers Workshop. See Bienvenido N. Santos, *Memory's Fictions: A Personal History* (Quezon City, Philippines: New Day Publishers, 1993), 100, 186.

12. Yamamoto, "Introduction," 4, 6.

13. Mori, *The Chauvinist*, 25, 29. Further references in parentheses in the text.

14. Toshio Mori, *Yokohama, California* (Seattle: University of Washington Press, 1985), 117. Further references in parentheses in the text.

15. Hisaye Yamamoto, *Seventeen Syllables and Other Stories* (Latham, NY: Kitchen Table: Women of Color Press, 1988), 95. Further references in parentheses in the text.

16. *Santos, Memory's Fictions*, 154 – 155.

17. Bienvenido N. Santos, *Scent of Apples and Other Stories* (Seattle: University of Washington Press, 1979), 23, 27. Further references in parentheses in the text.

18. Of the three Bulosan stories examined, only "The Story of a Letter" was published. The rest had remained in typescript in the University of Washington archives until San Juan found them and had them published in *On Becoming Filipino*. All these stories, suggests San Juan, were written from 1944 to 1947.

19. Bulosan, *On Becoming Filipino*, 65. Further references in parentheses in the text.

20. Yamamoto, "Introduction," 1.

21. The novel's decline as a creative practice in the postwar decades coincided with a growing interest in its theorization. This is the context in which Lukács's *The Theory of the Novel* was introduced to American readers.

22. Franco Moretti, "From the Way of the World: The Bildungsroman in European Literature," in *Theory of the Novel: A Historical Approach*, ed. Michael McKeon (Baltimore, MD: Johns Hopkins University Press, 2000), 555.

23. Wayne Booth, *The Rhetoric of Fiction* (Chicago: University of Chicago Press, 1961), 271–374; Northrop Frye, *The Anatomy of Criticism: Four Essays* (Princeton, NJ: Princeton University Press, 1957), 33 – 67.

24. Roland Barthes, *The Rustle of Language*, trans. Richard Howard (Oxford: Basil Blackwell, 1986), 141 – 8; Jonathan Culler, *The Pursuit of Signs: Semiotics, Literature, Deconstruction* (Ithaca, NY: Cornell University Press, 1981), 188 – 209.

25. Lukács, *The Theory of the Novel*, 47, 71 – 74.

26. Fredric Jameson, *The Political Unconscious: Narrative as a Socially Symbolic Act* (Ithaca, NY: Cornell University Press, 1981), 52 – 53.

27. Yoon Sun Lee, *Modern Minority: Asian American Literature and Everyday Life* (Oxford: Oxford University Press, 2012), 3 – 15.

28. Whether repetition contributes to realism is a complex issue, which points, on the one hand, to

the traditions represented by Aristotle, Homer, Cervantes, and Rousseau, and, on the other, to those maintained by Kierkegaard, Nietzsche, Heidegger, Derrida, and de Man. Short of a full hearing of such histories, it seems sufficient to say that interpretations of how repetition relates to realism rest on different understandings of the nature of temporality. Notably, the first group of thinkers presumes a somewhat causal connection between repetition and realism, while the second typically evokes traditional views of mimesis to argue for the opposite.

29 See Moretti, "From the Way of the World," 561 – 562. Moretti's thesis apparently draws from what Lukács calls the "biological form" of the realist novel — the Bildungsroman — which both embodies and promises a fulfillment of the subjective aspect of totality. See Lukács, *The Theory of the Novel*, 74, 77. Jameson reworks this Lukácsian argument, through Freud, into a question of subject formation on the part of the novel's readers; see Jameson, *The Political Unconscious*, 151– 184.

30. Peter Bürger, *Theory of the Avant-Garde*, trans. Michael Shaw (Minneapolis: University of Minnesota Press, 1984), 84 – 86; Said, *World, Text, and Context*, 230 – 242.

31. Gérard Genette, *Narrative Discourse: An Essay in Method*, trans. Jane E. Lewin (Ithaca, NY: Cornell University Press, 1980), 127; Tzvetan Todorov, "Reading as Construction," trans. Marilyn A. August, in *The Reader in the Text: Essays on Audience and Interpretation*, ed. Susan R. Suleiman and Inge Crosman (Princeton, NJ: Princeton University Press, 1980), 67 – 68.

32. See Michael M. J. Fischer, "Ethnicity and the Post-Modern Arts of Memory," in *Writing Culture: The Poetics and Politics of Ethnography*, ed. James Clifford and George E. Marcus (Berkeley: University of California Press, 1986), 208 – 209.

33. Dominick LaCapra, *History, Politics, and the Novel* (Ithaca, NY: Cornell University Press, 1987), 137.

34. The critical potential of the realist novel can be brought into play only through historicization, a readerly procedure geared toward demystifying the referential certainty that appears given, and to identifying — as the short-fiction form accustoms them to seeing — the imperfectly joined ideological seams in the novel's formal surface, as entry points for getting for getting as its repressed content.

13

Popular Genres and New Media
畅销体裁与新媒体

Betsy Huang

评论家简介

　　黄贝茜 (Betsy Huang)，美国罗切斯特大学博士，现为美国克拉克大学英语系副教授。主要研究领域为体裁理论、文化理论、批判种族研究以及 20、21 世纪美国多族裔文学与文化的交叉性，族裔文学和科幻小说之间的密切关系等。她的研究尤其关注文学与文化产品如何参与少数族裔、公民以及人类的文化与法律建构。专著有《当代美国亚裔小说中的体裁之争》(*Contesting Genres in Contemporary Asian American Fiction*, 2010); 合编有《技术东方主义：在推测性小说、历史和媒体中想象亚洲》(*Techno-Orientalism: Imagining Asia in Speculative Fiction, History, and Media*, 2015);《高等教育与社会背景中的多样性与包含性：国际与跨学科方法论 》(*Diversity and Inclusion in Higher Education and Societal Contexts: International and Interdisciplinary Approaches*, 2018) 等。

文章简介

　　近十几年，畅销小说与新媒体逐渐成为美国亚裔作家新兴的创作场域。亚裔作家开始折桂科幻与奇幻小说的大奖，犯罪小说与鸡仔言情小说销量稳健增长，基于电子传媒的新媒体创作活力四射。美国亚裔作家在畅销文学与新媒体的创作中，在主题、形式、体裁、传播手段等方面不断突破，成为美国亚裔文学版图中一个活跃与多元的板块。本文一方面详细介绍亚裔文学在言情小说、鸡仔文学、犯罪与侦探小说、科幻小说、新媒体等大众体裁中的新兴发展，另一方面旨在分析在不被主流创作平等对待、可能受制于亚裔主导文本限定主题的情况下，新兴创作如何利用自身体裁写作的优势，以更加多元、微妙的方式颠覆主流社会对亚裔族群普遍持有的刻板印象，破除种族主义观念、性别歧视，超越娱乐性，转变为社会批判的平台。

文章出处：Parikh, Crystal., and Daniel Y.Kim, editors. *The Cambridge Companion to Asian American Literature.* New York: Cambridge UP, 2015, pp. 142-154.

Popular Genres and New Media

Betsy Huang

The Perils and Possibilities of Popular Genres

The new millennium has been a banner time for Asian American writers of popular genres. In the past decade, we have witnessed new Asian American writers win top awards in science fiction and fantasy, enjoy healthy sales in crime fiction and "chick lit" romance, and create viral new-media productions in the digital sphere. Indeed, popular fiction and new media are the new playgrounds for Asian American writers, offering vast, devoted fan bases (for broad audience reach), nonrealist narrative toolboxes (for formal as well as social and ideological "thought" experiments), and readily accessible digital creative and publishing apparatuses (for immediate distribution). The exponential growth and variety of literary and new-media productions among Asian Americans in this period testify to the way that popular genres have inspired the field to go where it has not gone before.

Despite the contemporaneity of both bodies of literature's emergence and development into legible literary institutions over the course of the twentieth century, the odds were somewhat stacked against their cross-pollination. The popular genres' rather inglorious histories of racist and sexist representations as well as exclusionary practices against writers of color proved uninviting for Asian American writers. And until recently, Asian American writers made few forays into romance, crime fiction, and science fiction because of these genres' historically disreputable status among mainstream and academic literary establishments. Because Asian American literature's legibility and legitimacy in the U.S. literary and cultural consciousness are hard earned, writing genre fiction, commonly perceived as lowbrow and derivative, would appear misguided or even irresponsible. Recounting his experience as a budding science fiction writer during his undergraduate years at Brown University, acclaimed science fiction writer Ted Chiang recalls the instructor's discouraging words in the first creative writing class he ever took: those who intend to write "genre fiction" will not find a place for them in the course.[1] The instructor's dismissal not only exemplifies what science fiction scholar Marleen S. Barr calls the pervasive "textism" that genre has had to endure from the academy and the mainstream literati but also

*The author would like to thank Jennifer Ho and Sue Kim for their keen editorial feedback.

reveals the reputational stakes for those who wish to write it.[2]

The Asian Americanist canon has also been built largely on a set of social and ideological themes that have become its dominant scripts: migration and diaspora; assimilation and citizenship; racism and discrimination; ethnic authenticity and familial loyalties; and the model minority myth. Crucial as these political and aesthetic imperatives are in establishing an Asian American literary tradition, they have nonetheless unwittingly circumscribed thematic and formal choices in the process. Forays into unfamiliar genres, modes, or themes might be perceived as "extravagant" pursuits, to loosely borrow Sau-ling Wong's term.[3]

Romance and Chick Lit

While the romance genre and its most well-known publisher, Harlequin, have been around for quite some time, Asian American writers made their entrance most consequentially in its adjacent genre, "chick lit." Jeff Yang describes the genesis of chick lit as a recent, explosive, and potentially short-lived commercial phenomenon in which publishers, cashing in on the success of Helen Fielding's *Bridget Jones's Diary* (1996) and Melissa Bank's *The Girls' Guide to Hunting and Fishing* (2001), produced "hundreds of candy-colored clones."[4] In the decade following *Bridget Jones's,* the chick lit market grew 7 percent per year, reaching about $140 million in sales by 2005.[5] Despite its commercial success, chick lit has been maligned for all the predictable reasons, including the genre's "shallow" preoccupations with brand names, gossip, romantic and sexual pursuits, professional climbing, unabashed promotion of bad behaviors encouraged by dominant neoliberal values, excess consumerism, individualism, and forms of entrenched misogyny. As Felicia Salinas-Moniz points out, critics "perceive the genre as Working against the tenets of feminism and at the expense of 'serious' women's literary fiction."[6] Asian American chick lit, then, would seem a compromise of the antisexist, antiracist work of trailblazers like Sui Sin Far, Hisaye Yamamoto, and Maxine Hong Kingston.

But, as Pamela Butler and Jigna Desai point out in their study of South Asian American chick lit, "we might ask whether subgenres of chick lit written by and about women of color in the U.S. ... illuminate relations of power in the U.S., or address multiple social and economic formations?"[7] Warning against roundly dismissing the entire genre in one homogenizing gesture (which assumes that all texts reproduce the same formula), Butler and Desai pose the more interesting question of "why issues such as immigration and race ('Bollywood' and 'black' chick lit), labor ('nanny lit'), and consumption ('shopping lit') are such popular topics in contemporary women's genre fiction,"[8] The diversification of chick lit's authorship, themes, and subjects made it possible to tell women's stories from multiple class and ethnic positions, bringing new insights into what traditional (white) bourgeois values mean to women positioned differently in the social strata. Read from these critical angles, the works reveal the disciplinary power such values and the institutions that enforce them have on women's lives.

It was, in fact, the commercial publishers during the nineties' chick-lit fad who saw writers of color as the best way to introduce interesting — and, problematically, exotic — variations to a clichéd genre. As Neelanjana Banerjee explains, "Throw identity issues, Asiaphiles and arranged marriages into the picture, and it seems like Asian Americans and chick lit are a match made by the highest paid matchmaker in Edison, NJ."[9] At the height of the fad, titles such as Caroline Hwang's *In Full Bloom* (2003), Kim Wong Keltner's *The Dim Sum of All Things* (2004) and *Buddha Baby* (2005), Sonia Singh's *Bollywood Confidential* (2005), and Blossom Kan and Michelle Yu's *China Dolls* (2007) sold well, and the writers landed multiple book contracts, securing what seemed like longevity in the genre. Interest in Asian American chick lit, however, leveled after the first boom decade, and few new writers have joined the ranks. Today, the genre still faces the diversity issue, both in authorship and in range of theme and plot; as Stephanie Harzewski points out, "Despite blurbs claiming to address 'universal female dilemmas' and the struggles of the 'everywoman,' a characteristic chick lit novel features a first-person narrative of a white, middle or upper middle class woman engaged in a seriocomic romantic quest or dating spree."[10]

In spite of their low numbers, Asian American women writers' contributions are substantial in both formal range and market visibility. There are the orthodox romance writers such as Jade Lee who faithfully produce Harlequin-like stories. Aforementioned writers like Keltner, and Yu and Kan, continue to deploy all the conventional elements of chick lit with both earnest and ironic relish. Other writers compel the publishing industry to invent new genre categories; Marjorie Liu's *Dirk and Steele* series, for instance, forged the new genre of "paranormal romance" that blends romance with detective fiction. As for market visibility, romance and chick lit — particularly the latter — have been extremely effective instruments for Asian American writers to reach a broader audience.

But Yang's 2007 feature story also raises the question of whether the chick-lit label produces a reputational disadvantage. Harvard student Kaavya Viswanathan's plagiarism scandal surrounding her debut title, *How Opal Mehta Got Kissed, Got Wild and Got a Life* (2006) doesn't help the cause, as it is taken as evidence of the genre's boilerplate storylines that facilitated her ruse. Problematic, too, are the Orientalist titles, which include *Ftdl Blossom*, *The Dim Sum of All Things*, and *China Dolls*, just to name a few. These may be tongue-in-cheek titles, but they require a knowing audience who reads these as consciously ironic. But because popular genres are also fan cultures, and because no fandom operates monolithically (one only needs to go to any fansite for a cult text and see the diversity of views shared), the assumption that there would not be divergent receptions of texts is elitist and critically myopic. As Butler and Desai remind us, "like formulations that recognize Asian American chick lit's well-heeled literary (magical realist) counterparts, such as Chitra Divakaruni's *Mistress of Spices* and Karen Tei Yamashita's *Tropic of Orange*, as offering significant political visions, we see the possibility that popular genres might make their own significant interventions and critiques."[12] And the more nuanced chick lit texts do engage, however modestly, in what Jennifer Ho calls "social justice lite."[13] The question that remains is how romance and chick lit will adapt to an increasingly nonheteronormative cultural lexicon in domestic, romantic, labor, and consumer economies.

Crime and Detective Fiction

By dint of the breadth of their distribution and consumption, popular genres are potent instruments for disseminating and enshrining stereotypes. Crime fiction in particular has a long Orientalist history that gave us some of the most pernicious Asian stereotypes, many of which still persist today. The genre and its related forms — mystery, detective fiction, the police procedural, the court drama, the spy novel, the fugitive tale, and the hard-boiled and noir modes[14]— drew heavily from the proliferation of "yellow peril" fiction, such as Sax Rohmer's *Fu Manchu* series (1912–1913), that dramatized Western fears of Asian hordes in the late nineteenth and early twentieth centuries.[15] But the genre did not confine Orientalist characterizations to villainy. Earl Derr Biggers put the Asian on the right side of the law in his Charlie Chan mysteries, the first in the genre to feature a Chinese American in the role of a detective and thus as a figure who upholds rather than breaks the law. While this opened representational possibilities for Asians in popular culture, Chan's intelligence, deferent demeanor, and linguistic quirks ("broken English" and Yoda-like syntax) did their share of damage in creating enduring Orientalist stereotypes today. As Charles J. Rzeplca notes, Chan has become the "very model of a complacent 'model minority,' personifying the status assigned Asian American citizens by the dominant culture in its attempt to delegitimize, by contrast, the angry militancy of the African American and Latino equal rights movements of the 1960s."[16]

Asia and Asians thus populated the genre as polarized metonymies of uncontainable foreign evil and domesticated model minority long before Asian Americans entered as writers. But the genre has evolved and grown significantly in recent decades; as Tarik Abdel-Monem points out, "Modern writers have brought new perspectives on race, justice, and social inequalities to contemporary crime stories, infusing the crime narrative with critical race, feminist, post-colonial, gay/lesbian, and other perspectives.... Crime fiction has thus become more and more a platform for social commentary as well as entertainment."[17] In the new millennium, a score of Asian American writers is also expanding the genre as they write against its Orientalist vocabulary.

It took a filmmaker rather than a writer to initiate a revision of crime fiction's Orientalist history. Wayne Wang's 1982 film, *Chan Is Missing*, is the first major Asian American cultural production that lambastes the genre's Orientalist typologies and typographies by reviving and debunking them in tongue-in-cheek fashion. Wang upends the "positive" stereotype of Charlie Chan by making the titular Chan an illusory fugitive who consistently eludes the pursuit of searching eyes and overturning the history of sinister Chinatown by depicting it as a tight-knit and culturally rich community. The film opened the genre to Asian American writers as a platform for critiquing not only the genre's racist history but also the flaws of the U.S. legal system. It engendered a new class of Asian American detective fiction: Dale Furutani's Ken Tanaka series (1996's *Death in Little Tokyo* and 1997's *The Toyotomi Blades*), Leonard Chang's Allen Choice series (2001–2004), Naomi Hirahara's Mas Arai mysteries (2004–) and the new Ellie Rush series (2014–), Henry Chang's Jack Yu series (2006–2011), and Ed Lin's Robert Chow series (2007–). These writers enter the genre as creators rather than the creation, taking the reins of representational authority as they introduce more nuanced dramatizations of social themes around race, ethnic culture, gender, and class.

Informed by a different sociohistorical consciousness and much more attuned to identity politics in conceptions of crime and justice, the Asian American detectives decode clues and observe settings with a different cultural vocabulary and forensic logic. Hirahara's Mas Arai, for example, is an aging Japanese American sleuth whose investigative lenses are informed by the histories of state-sponsored racism and the old wounds of the Japanese American internment. Chang's Allen Choice, whose last name is deliberately Anglicized from the Korean "Choi," reflects Chang's examination of ethnic affiliations and colorblind or postracial ideals as forms of entrapment or mobility. Ed Lin's Officer Chow must constantly negotiate issues of credibility and loyalty as he interacts with the Chinatown residents, with whom he identifies and sympathizes, and the police force assigned to protect (and investigate) them, for whom he works.

Asian American writers also recuperate "ethnic enclaves" or ethnically diverse urban geographies from their paradigmatic typecasting as dangerous, seedy crime scenes. In the hard-boiled and noir modes, such locales have been used time and again as Chandlcresque "mean streets" — a term Raymond Chandler used as a shorthand for the realistic — that is, unromantic — "tough neighborhood" settings his detectives must explain and contain.[18] Chinatowns have become the quintessential "mean streets" to the point where the invocation of the word "Chinatown" insinuates inscrutable people and inexplicable crimes. Dashiell Hammett's short story "Dead Yellow Women" (1925) in the Continental Op series, for instance, describes San Francisco's Chinatown as a place where "Chinese passed up and down the alley, scuffling in American shoes that can never fit them."[19] The Op declares at the end of the story, after he has solved the case but not the mystery of Chinatown: "I don't mind admitting that I've stopped eating in Chinese restaurants, and that if I never have to visit Chinatown again it'll be soon enough."[20]

Chinatown as the site of moral degeneracy was forever sealed in crime fiction lore by Roman Polanski's detective Jake Gittes in the film *Chinatown* (1974), who describes Chinatown as a place where "you can't always tell what's going on there," and who, failing to solve the case because it involved a crime too taboo for him to have considered, is told by his associate in the film's most indelible' line, "Forget it, Jake, it's Chinatown."[21] Writing consciously against this deeply ingrained Orientalist legacy, Ed Lin and Henry Chang feature detectives who are also members of the very community they serve and protect, dissolving the conventional adversarial relationship between the detective and the crime scene. Naomi Hirahara's detectives also have positive, vested relationships with the neighborhoods they serve; Hirahara, whose fiction is set primarily in Los Angeles, explains, "I don't look at L. A. as an archetype, a holder of genre, but as a nexus of people with very different histories but similar aspirations."[22]

The impact of the mixing of Asian American literature and crime fiction is, of course, bidirectional. Some Asian American writers who do not identify themselves as writers of crime fiction *per se* borrow amply from the crime fiction toolbox. Don Lee's novel *Country of Origin* (2004), for instance, dramatizes questions of national belonging and loyalties as a transnational mystery, which lends itself to interrogating meanings of national and racial identities in diasporic and international contexts. Susan Choi's *American Woman* (2003), a fictionalized account of Patricia Hearst's years on the run with fellow Symbionese Liberation Army member Wendy Yoshimura, blends the roman a clef with the fugitive narrative to comment on the chilling inequities of the American justice system and the susceptibility of minorities to criminalization.

In her next novel, *Person of Interest* (2008), a fictionalized account of the espionage case against Los Alamos scientist Wen Ho Lee, Choi writes both within and against the grain of Grisham-esque legal thriller by dismantling rather than building a solid case against the suspect *from the suspect's perspective.* Whether they write within or beyond the generic parameters, Asian American writers regularly reject postracial claims by uncovering the "racial clues" of systemic racism and sexism still pervasive in the laws of genre and society.

Science Fiction

Like crime fiction, science fiction (or SF, the favored acronym of genre insiders) has its own sad Orientalist history to tell. The genre, which Philip K. Dick describes as a speculative space for "crying doom," has historically imagined Asia and Asians as part of the "doom" in Western conceptions of the future.[23] Early SF traded in Orientalist figurations akin to those in crime fiction, from Alex Raymond's Ming the Merciless in the *Flash Gordon* series and *Star Trek*'s Khan Noonien Singh as future reincarnations of Fu Manchu to Daoism and other forms of Eastern mysticism in the postwar SF of Philip K. Dick and Ursula K. Le Guin to the iterations of techno-Orientalism in the cyberpunk SF of *Blade Runner,* William Gibson, and Neal Stephenson. And as a corollary of the rhetoric of the "rise of Asia" in the age of global neoliberalism, figurations of the Asian threat take the form of a rival empire that has dethroned the West as the new world order (see, for instance, Philip K. Dick's *The Man in the High Castle* [1962], Maureen McHugh's *China Mountain Zhang* [1992], Kim Stanley Robinson's *The Years of Rice and Salt* [2002], and Gary Shteyngart's *Super Sad True Love Story* [2010]).

In spite of its yellow peril legacies, the genre affords Asian American writers unique narrative tools for destabilizing the generic and social imperatives that have governed both SF and Asian American literary production, Robert Scholes notes that SF gives the writer license to dispense with the imperatives of verisimilitude and realism, precisely because the genre's *raison d'etre* is founded on an emphasis of the not-real, of fab ulation.[24] Fabulation in science fiction is usually triggered by a *novum*, a term coined by Darko Suvin in *Metamorphoses of Science Fiction* as the "new thing" that does not yet exist in our world,[25] the main formal device that distinguishes a work of science fiction from "realistic" fiction and enacts the process of defamiliarization that Suvin elsewhere calls "cognitive estrangement."[26] Writers of color saw such capacities as a means to imagine or record their own realities and futures on their own terms; as Walter Mosley succinctly puts in his anthemic essay, "Black to the Future," "We make up, then make real."[27]

Drawn to this "make up, make real" process, Asian American SF writers introduced themes of immigration, assimilation, and otherness from an Asian American perspective into the genre. Laurence Yep, one of the earliest Asian American SF writers, thematized his experiences as a cultural outsider via classic SF tropes: "in science fiction and fantasy, children leave the everyday world and go to a strange place where they have to learn a new language and new customs. Science fiction and fantasy were about adapting, and that was something I did every day."[28] Ken Liu and Charles Yu, two of the most prolific new SF writers today, have contributed more finely tuned and complex representations of Asian histories and Asian American experiences to the genre. But not all Asian American science fiction writers address the master themes of Asian American literature; many address a broader range of social themes, historical events, ideological struggles, and philosophical meditations through elegant fables and allegories woven with the toots of SF, as Adam Roberts points out, SF in recent decades has "demonstrated remarkable sensitivities on the subjects of gender and racial diversity and contact, offering a space in which complex representations of the other can critically deconstruct the naturalized norms of the dominant culture."[29] Alice Sola Kim's "Beautiful White Bodies" (2009) is a plague narrative about a "beauty" epidemic infecting young women that leaves indeterminable effects in its wake, E. Lily Yu's "The Cartographer Wasps and the Anarchist Bees" (2011) captures the cyclical nature of colonization and rebellion. Charles Yu's short story "Standard Loneliness Package" (2010) comments on the implications of technologizing a foreign workforce in the outsourcing industry. Ken Liu's Nebula-winning "The Paper Menagerie" (2011) features animated origami animals that literalize a young boy's process of reanimating memories of his deceased mother. Greg Pak's anthology film *Robot Stories* (2003) comprises four parables about the technologizing of Asians in particular and humans in general that proffers a profound critique of techno-Orientalist visions. And Ted Chiang, one of the most award-decorated SF writers today, thoughtfully explores the implications of new technologies — broadly defined to include life-changing apparatuses from artificial intelligence to religion — on our pasts and futures.

Many Asian American writers who would not identify as card-carrying members of SF write "slipstream" fiction by drawing on SF devices and tropes to write what N. Katherine Hayles and Nicholas Gessler call "mixed reality."[30] Slipstream is defined by Bruce Sterling as the kind of fantastic, surreal, speculative writing that "set[s] its face against consensus reality;"[31] it has since broadened to include fiction that straddles multiple modes and subgenres-social realism, magical realism, folklore, allegory, fantasy, dystopian fiction, the plague narrative, alternate history, and more. The speculative and fantastical elements in the work of Karen Tei Yamashita, Chang-rae

Lee, Cynthia Kadohata, and Ruth Ozeki, for instance, constitute slipstream qualities that push the generic envelopes of Asian American literature and SF.

New Media

If genre fiction in the popular print culture has been slow to grant access to Asian Americans, popular new media has been quick in enabling it. "New media," a new term that gained purchase in the 1990s, is defined by Wendy Hui Kyong Chun as the use of media — largely but not exclusively digital — that exemplify or encourage "fluid, individualized connectivity" and stress interactivity and wide, fast, direct distribution.[32] It comprises a network of locales in the digital world that radically expands the way we live and narrate our lives by putting at our fingertips tools that allow us to create, appropriate, remix, mash up, and immediately disseminate our cultural productions. Such tools include but are not limited to video-hosting services like Vimeo and YouTube, social networking services like My Space and Facebook, community-based content-sharing networks and microblogging platforms like Buzz Net and Tumblr, all of which facilitate content production and immediate distribution and access; and video games, more specifically massively multiplayer online role-playing games (MMORPGs), which allow players to participate in the writing of new storylines with every gameplay. Interactivity and sharing are the governing principles and practices of new media; as Vin Crosbie usefully explains, new media stresses the model of "many-to-many" in the control of content, which distinguishes it from the "one-to-one" (interpersonal) or "one-to-many" (mass) models of traditional media.[33] Publications of new texts in old media occur at a glacial pace compared to those in new media; for instance, responses to or parodic sendups of a text or event that used to take days, months, or even years (depending on how far back in time you go) to publish in old media are now "posted" — the new term for "published" — with dizzying rates of immediacy. The transnational geography of new media has also made national boundaries either highly porous or nonexistent; new media products travel across cultures and "go viral" via global networks in a matter of hours and days.

What this means for Asian Americans is that the barriers of accessibility in old media — institutional mechanisms such as acquisitions and market analysis in mass and trade publishing, peer review in academia, and greenlighting in film production — are sidestepped in the creative, editorial, and distribution processes in new media. Nor does new media concern itself with textism. Rather, it revels in the popular, and its users understand that the tools of new media are effective precisely because it enables visibility through popularization. Those who have had to suffer lack of message and image control in old media now find numerous platforms for publishing on their own terms.

Asian Americans have indeed taken full advantage of new media, making their presence known most substantially on YouTube. Comics Kevin Wu (a.k.a. Kevjumba), Ryan Higa, and Christine Gambito, Wong Fu Productions' director/writer/producer Philip Wang, and many other producers of digital shorts each boast millions of views and almost the same number of subscribers.[34] Ryan Wong extols the cultural import of these new media artists: "Banal as it might seem, in today's media-dominated America, faces-on-screens are an essential tool of staking a claim in the conversations — cultural and political — that shape this society."[35] Jennifer Im of *Clothes Encounters* and Michelle Phan's videos of cosmetics tips interspersed with lifestyle advice provide what can be seen as videologging (or vlogging) versions of chick lit. Blogger and news aggregator Phil Yu of *Angry Asian Man* has been the go-to source for millions of followers since its launch in 2001, New creative content as well as mash ups of responses to the news, art, literature, and music, in both earnest or satirical modes, appear every day on Tumblr and Buzz Feed by Asian Americans who are plugged in and hyperattuned to the latest by and about Asian Americans in the digital world.

Lest I paint too utopian a portrait of new media as an exceptionally creative and liberatory space, I should point out that its interactivity and "viral," replicating power present some familiar perils for Asian Americans, too. Not every new media production is "new"; rather, much of it isn't. Video games are perhaps the most problematic sites of ongoing racist, sexist, and Orientalist representations despite the fact that Asians and Asian Americans comprise a large part of the industry's demographic; Lisa Nakamura has written extensively on the ways in which racial and gender stereotypes are replicated in alarming fashion in cyberspace and in MMORPGs.[36] The problem is ultimately authorship. As is the case in genre fiction, authors hold most representational power, and integration of Asian American identities and histories remains minimal or stereotypical in the gameplay as long as Asian Americans are not among the ranks of the developers and writers. Interactivity coupled with the ease with which one can create avatars and alter egos, too, can enable problematic identity performances and cooptations that replicate abuses of race, gender, and class in the offline world.

Describing her research on Internet chat communities, Nakamura observes that users who were "adopting personae other than their own online as often as not participated in stereotyped notions of gender and race. Rather than 'honoring diversity,' their performances online used race and gender as amusing prostheses which could be donned and shed without 'real life' consequences."[37] And finally, idealized visions of Asian Americans as "digital natives" with limitless entitlements to new media fail to account for the wide swaths of the U.S. population who do not have access to the digital world and hence have neither production nor consumer power in a world increasingly governed by a growing class of technocrats.[38] Thus, new media may paradoxically exacerbate the invisibility of a nondigitized Asian American underclass as we migrate into the digital world.

Conclusion; or, a Progress Report

Popular genres and new media are technologies. As such, we analyze and prognosticate their implications as we have with every new form of technology that has radically affected our lives. As much as popular genres are fraught with representational perils, they also offer prodigious creative and critical possibilities. Each is governed by a dominant aesthetic and a community of readers that the writer can adopt, adapt, and change. Asian American writers of popular fiction and producers of new media achieve, in form and in theme, what Chiang calls the "conceptual breakthrough story," in which "the characters discover something about the nature of the universe which radically expands their understanding of the world."[39] The traffic among Asian American literature, popular genres, and new media, then, is both necessary and extravagant. It has radically expanded each site of production and will undoubtedly continue to be transformative for all.

Notes

1. Ted Chiang, email message to the author.
2. In her essay for her edited special issue of *PMLA* on science fiction, "Textism — an Emancipation Proclamation," *PMLA* 119.3 (May 2004), Marleen Barr describes "textism " as "a discriminatory evaluation system in which all literature relegated to a so-called subliterary genre, regardless of its individual merits, is automatically defined as inferior, separate, and unequal" (429 – 430).
3. In the introduction to *Heading Asian American Literature: From Necessity to Extravagance* (Princeton, NJ: Princeton University Press, 1993), Wong delineates her deliberately constructed binarism of "necessity" and "extravagance" as "two contrasting modes of existence and operation, one contained, survival-driven and conservation-minded, the other attracted to freedom, excess, emotional expressiveness, and autotelisn" (13).
4. Jeff Yang, "Asian Pop/Bridget Jung's Diary," *SF Gate,* Feb. 13, 2007, Web.

5. Ibid.

6. Felicia Salinas-Moniz, "Teaching Resources — Chick Lit," *Feminist Teacher* 22.1 (2011), 84.

7. Pamela Butler and Jigna Desai, "Manolos, Marriage, and Mantras: Chick Lit Criticism and Transnational Feminism," *Meridians: Feminism, Race, Transnationalism* 8.2 (2008), 4.

8. Ibid.

9. Neelanjana Banerjee, "Can I Get a Purse with That? A Foray into the World of Asian American Chick Lit," *Hyphen Magazine* (Fall 2005). Web.

10. Stephanie Harzewski, *Chick Lit and Postfeminism* (University of Virginia Press, 2011), 29.

11. Yang, "Asian Pop."

12. Butler and Desai, "Manolos," 27.

13. Jennifer Ho, email to the author.

14. For in-depth discussions of all of the subgenres and related forms, see *The Cambridge Companion to Crime Fiction*, ed., Martin Priestman, and John Scaggs, *Crime Fiction: The New Critical Idiom* (Routledge, 2005).

15. For full detailed histories and analyses of "yellow peril" fiction, see Urmila Scshagiri's "Modernity's (Yellow) Perils: Dr. Fu-Manchu and the English Race Paranoia," *Cultural Critique* 62 (2006), 162-194 and John Tchen and Dylan Yeats's *Yellow Peril! An Archive of Anti-Asian Fear* (London: Verso, 2014).

16. Charles J. Rzepka, "Race, Region, Rule: Genre and the Case of Charlie Chan," *PMLA* 122.5 (October 2007), 1464.

17. Tarik Abdel-Monem, "Images of Interracialism in Contemporary American Crime Fiction," *American Studies* 51. 3/4 (Fall/Winter 2010), 131.

18. Raymond Chandler, "The Simple Art of Murder" in *The Simple Art of Murder* (1950; reissue, New York: Vintage, 1988).

19. Dashiell Hammett, "Dead Yellow Women," in *The Continental Op*, ed., Steven Marcus (New York: Vintage, 1975), 208.

20. Ibid., 249.

21. *Chinatown*, DVD, directed by Roman Polanski (1974; Paramount, 1999).

22. David L. Ulin, "Naomi Hirahara on her new mystery series ... and the new L.A.," *The Los Angeles Times*, April 14, 2014, Web.

23. Philip K. Dick, "Pessimism in Science Fiction," in *The Shifting Realities of Philip K. Dick: Selected Literary and Philosophical Writings* (New York: Pantheon Books, 1995), 54.

24. Robert Scholes, "The Roots of Science Fiction," in *Science Fiction: A Collection of Critical*

Essays, ed., Mark Rose (Englewood Cliffs, NJ: Prentice-Hall, 1976), 47-48.

25. Darko Suvin, *Metamorphoses of Science Fiction: On the Poetics and History of a Literary Genre* (New Haven, CT: Yale University Press, 1979).

26. Darko Suvin, "On the Poetics of the Science Fiction Genre," in *Science Fiction: A Collection of Critical Essays*, eel., Mark Rose (Englewood Cliffs, NJ: Prentice-Hall, 1976), 57.

27. Walter Mosley, "Black to the Future," in *Dark Matter: A Century of Speculative Fiction from the African Diaspora*, ed., Sheree Renee Thomas (New York: Warner Books, 2000), 405.

28. Laurence Yep, "Laurence Yep Interview," *Scholastic.com*, n.d., Web, April 25, 2014.

29. Adam Roberts, *Science Fiction: The New Critical Idiom* (New York: Routledge, 2000), J8.

30. Katherine Hayles and Nicholas Gessler, "The Slipstream of Mixed Reality: Unstable Ontologies and Semiotic Markers in *The Thirteenth Floor, Dark City,* and *Mulholland Drive,*" *PMLA* 119.3 (May 2004), 482-499.

31. Bruce Sterling, "Slipstream," *Catscan* 5, n.d., Web.

32. Wendy Hui Kyong Chun, "Introduction: Did Somebody Say New Media?" in *New Media, Old Media: A History and Theory Reader*, ed., Wendy Hui Kyong Chun and Thomas Keenan (New York: Routledge, 2006), I.

33. Vin Crosbie, "What is New Media?" (1998; https://www.academia.edu/1054828/ What_is_ new_media).

34. For more information on Asian American online digital producers and artists, see Alan Van, "NMR Exclusive: Uploaded — Asian Americans in New Media," *New Media Rock Stars*, April 20, 2012; and Christine Bacarcza-Balance, "How It Feels to Be Viral Me: Affective Labor and Asian American YouTube Performance," *Women's Studies Quarterly* 40.1/2 (Spring/ Summer 2012), 138 – 152.

35. Ryan Wong, "A Billion Hits and Counting: Asian Americans and YouTube," *Hyperallergic: Sensitive to Arts & Its Discontents*, July 18, 2012, Web.

36. For a comprehensive analysis, consult Lisa Nakamura's *Cybertypes: Race, Ethnicity, and Identity on the Internet* (New York: Routledge, 2002), and Thien-bao Thuc Phi's essay, "Game Over: Asian Americans and Video Game Representation," *TWC*, 2 (2009).

37. Lisa Nakamura, "Cybertyping and the Work of Race in the Age of Digital Reproduction," in *New Media, Old Media: A History and Theory Reader*, ed., Wendy Hui Kyong Chun and Thomas Keenan (New York: Routledge, 2006), 323.

38. The term "digital native" and its counterpart "digital immigrant" are coined by Marc Prensky to describe members of the digital generation ("native") and members of the older generation

migrating from a traditional or analog media world into the digital. Marc Prensky, "Digital Natives, Digital Immigrants," *On the Horizon* 9.5 (2001).

39. "Interview with Ted Chiang," interviewed by Betsy Huang, *Asian American Literary Review*, May 24, 2013, Web.

14

Pacific Rim and Asian American Literature
环太平洋与美国亚裔文学

Viet Thanh Nguyen

评论家简介

阮越清（Viet Thanh Nguyen），美国文学评论家，小说家，美国加利福尼亚大学伯克利分校英语系博士，现为南加州大学英语系、美国研究与种族系，以及比较文学系教授。作为文学评论家及学者，长期担任《洛杉矶时报》《纽约时报》等报刊的评论员，其研究领域涉及美国研究、美国族裔研究等。专著有《种族和抵抗：美国亚裔的文学与政治》（*Race and Resistance: Literature and Politics in Asian America*, 2002）；非小说类书籍《从未消逝：越南与战争记忆》，（*Nothing Ever Dies: Vietnam and the Memory of War*, 2016），此书入围美国国家图书奖非小说类奖与美国国家书评奖非小说类奖终选名单。合编有《跨太平洋研究：构筑新兴领域》（*Transpacific Studies: Framing an Emerging Field*, 2014）。在《美国现代语言学协会》（*PMLA*）、《美国文学史》（*American Literary History*）、《东亚文化批评》（*east asia cultures critique*）等期刊上发表多篇论文。作为小说家，著作有长篇小说《同情者》（*The Sympathizer*, 2015），此书获 2016 年普利策小说奖；以及短篇小说集《难民》（*The Refugees*, 2017）等作品。

文章简介

　　当今美国亚裔文学作品的创作数量急剧增长，内容与种类更为丰富多元。亚裔作家也相继斩获重要的文学大奖。美国亚裔文学已经成为美国族裔文学中重要的一员。在这样的背景下，文学评论家阮越清将美国亚裔文学创作中一直所宣扬的"宣称美国"（claiming America）的政治诉求放在全球化的时代背景中，对照 9·11 后美国的国际形象，重新审视其内涵、实质及其局限性。与此同时，阮越清全面分析了随美国亚裔文学一并兴起的"环太平洋文学"的概念。文章解读了何为"环太平洋"，"环太平洋文学"的书写指向是什么，并举例说明美国亚裔作家中"环太平洋"写作的代表作家。文章重点在于说明"环太平洋文学"概念的提出有助于揭示美国亚裔文学概念的局限性，同时建立亚裔文学内部新的分类与关联。然而，但其自身也存在着诸多局限性。阮越清认为，由于两个概念内涵所指不同，所以环太平洋文学不能取代美国亚裔文学，但是可以将其作为参照与互补的对象。所以环太平洋文学范式有助于美国亚裔文学创作冲破边缘与主流的二元对立，跨越国界。

文章出处：Goyal, Yogita., editor. *The Cambridge Companion to Transnational American Literature*. Cambridge: Cambridge UP, 2017, pp. 190-202.

Pacific Rim and Asian American Literature

Viet Thanh Nguyen

Literature, like humanity, yearns to be free. Yet labels and categories persist and serve a function, creating and closing off possibilities. So it is that "Asian American literature" arose in the 1970s, proclaimed by those who began to call themselves Asian Americans in the 1960s. These young radicals saw that their freedom was restricted by a long history of racism and the ramifications of a war in Southeast Asia that was being fought by fellow Americans. These Americans could not distinguish between Asians over there in Southeast Asia and Americans of Asian descent over here in the United States, where some had lived for generations. For Asian Americans to name themselves as such was thus a rebuke to the American perception that they were forever foreigners, or, at best, honorary whites, their status always transitory or ambivalent. Creating an utterly new category thus opened a realm of possibility that Asian Americans are still exploring today, guided by the idea that writer Maxine Hong Kingston helped to pioneer: the necessity, for Asian Americans, of "claiming America."[1]

Besides Kingston, many other authors who can be classified as Asian American have forcefully asserted this claim to America. Sometimes the literature placed its stake in America explicitly through plot and story, but it always did so implicitly through simply existing, written in English. Throughout the 1970s and 1980s, and even into the 1990s, the appearance of a book by an Asian American author writing in English was an occasion for celebration by Asian American readers. The most momentous was, of course, Amy Tan's best-selling *The Joy Luck Club* (1989), which for many readers remains the only Asian American book they have heard of, much less read. Even until the present, the influence of *The Joy Luck Club* remains felt in publishing circles, where new Asian American writers, particularly women, are often expected by readers and publishers to write mother-daughter stories or tales of woe in Asia. The paucity in numbers of Asian American books and authors meant that the category of Asian American literature itself was emergent and struggling and hence something to be advocated for and defended by its practitioners, critics, and audience. But by the new millennium, it would be difficult even for the most passionate or professional readers of Asian American literature to keep up with the rate of literary production, as dozens of memoirs, novels, short story collections, and poetry collections poured forth each year. The demographic consequences of the 1965 Immigration Law, which ended racially exclusionary policies directed at Asian immigrants, had been realized. The law created the "children of 1965," as literary critic Min Hyoung Song calls the generation descended from those immigrants who came subsequent to 1965.[2] The effects of the law were immediate and long-term: 135,844 Asian immigrants came in the 1950s; 358,563 came in the 1960s; and in 2013 alone, 389,301 Asian immigrants arrived.[3] The children of these immigrants went to college in large numbers: their percentages in public universities like UC Berkeley (40 percent)[4] and UCLA (33.5 percent),[5] and in private universities like Harvard (21.1 percent),[6] Yale (20 percent),[7] and Princeton (22 percent),[8] far outstrip their portion of the US population (5.6 percent in 2010).[9] Some percentage of these college students became writers. These writers found opportunity in an era born from the new social movements of the 1960s, which pushed American culture toward an embrace of multicul-turalism and diversity. By 2001, then, Asian American literature had arrived as an increasingly respectable ethnic subset of American literature, its writers publishing best sellers and gaining wide literary acclaim, including winning the most prestigious prizes in the land. Fiction writer Jhumpa Lahiri and poet Vijay Seshadri, for example, won the Pulitzer Prize in 2000 and 2014, respectively, and Ha Jin won the National Book Award in 1999, as well as two PEN/Faulkner awards.

But while the work of claiming America remains an important one for Asian American writers in a time when racism has hardly dissipated, 9/11 and its consequences would trouble that claim. What exactly were Asian American writers claiming? Belonging and citizenship, yes, but did those come free from those aspects of American culture that troubled some, namely excessive consumption and heedless capitalism, not to mention the desire for global domination and the regular use of American military force? The latent nationalism that underlay the claim to America would become. harder to deny after 9/11, when what it meant to be American was thrown into relief against America's Mideast wars. But these wars only made much more visible, and visceral, what had been evident since the very first Asians came to American shores with the Spanish galleons, which was that the plight of Asian Americans could never actually be separated from what happened outside American borders. Perhaps in the future, looking back retrospectively, the period of claiming America for Asian Americans will appear to be a necessary but limited stage in understanding the place of Asian Americans in American and global society. Claiming America, while it does not preclude claiming the world, does discourage it, adopting almost inevitably the American tendency toward national insularity and American exceptionalism, the belief that America was the greatest country of all. Such a belief prevents Asian Americans from seeing how their fates are tied to global currents.

Parallel to the rise of Asian America came the idea of the "Pacific Rim," which began in the 1960s as a way of harnessing some of these global currents for the good of capitalism.[10] Even as Asian Americans were organizing themselves, the engineers of global capital in Japan and the United States — the twin powers of the post-World War II Pacific — were thinking of how the Pacific Rim might serve as a more capacious concept than the nation-state for understanding and promoting the flow of capital. The Pacific Rim included more than just those two countries, but also the emerging capitalist states of Asia, the redoubts of Australia and New Zealand, as well as all of North America and much of Latin America. Of course, capital, as well as its goods and agents, were not the only things moving along the Pacific Rim or through the Pacific Ocean. There were also the people who worked for capital or who were exploited by it, and the militaries deployed to secure the Pacific or struggle over it. Those who celebrated the Pacific Rim tended to overlook problematic figures like laborers or soldiers whose presence implied that the flow of capital across the Pacific was maintained by cheap labor or armed force. Still, the very notion of a Pacific Rim that transcended nations allowed for the possibility of imagining movements, affiliations, and imaginations that crossed borders. So far as we believe the category of a Pacific Rim literature is useful, it is because it allows us to address how people and culture are not easily contained in national categories like American or its subsidiary, Asian American.

Even turning to Kingston, it is easy to see that "Asian American literature" is a useful lens that only focuses on the American dimension of her work. The opening page of *The Woman Warrior* (1976) acknowledges how Chinese men were leaving China destined not only for the United States, but elsewhere:

> In 1924, just a few days after our village celebrated seventeen hurry-up weddings — to make sure that every young man who went "out on the road" would responsibly come home — your father and his brothers and your grandfather and his brothers and your aunt's new husband sailed for America, the Gold Mountain. It was your grandfather's last trip. Those lucky enough to get contracts waved goodbye from the decks. They fed and guarded the stowaways and helped them off in Cuba, New York, Bali, Hawaii. "We'll meet in California next year," they said, All of them sent money home.[11]

Kingston's *China Men* (1980) makes even more explicit how the Chinese American experience in the United States needs to be understood in the context of how Chinese migrants traveled all over the Americas, and sometimes ended up in the United States after stops elsewhere. Once a concept like the Pacific Rim is used to pry open the Asian American category, it becomes easier to see how even the American dimension of the Asian American experience is obfuscated. When the term "Asian American" is used in the United States, for example, it means the experiences of Asians in the United States. It does not mean the experiences of Asians in Canada, or Mexico, or any points further south in the Americas, despite the significant numbers of Asian migrants to many countries in the Americas. "Claiming America" for Asian Americans in the United States is thus even more so a claim to the American empire of the United States, and a reinforcement of the claim the United States has made on all of the Americas as its sphere of influence. From one vantage point on the Pacific Rim, Asian American literature, for all that it often records the negative dimensions of migration and assimilation into the United States, also participates in the celebration of the United States as the most exceptional country of the Americas, the only country most people outside of the Americas think of when they hear "America." An event like the Japanese American internment becomes remembered only for the suffering inflicted on Japanese residents of the United States, erasing how Japanese in Latin America were deported to internment camps in the United States, and how Japanese Canadians were deported to the interior of Canada to do forced labor. Joy Kogawa's *Obasan* (1981) connects this experience to the bombing of Hiroshima and Nagasaki, a Canadian trauma and a Japanese trauma that are simultaneous effects of a Pacific war. These events all happen on what will be called the Pacific Rim.

The writing of Karen Tei Yamashita might be classified as the kind of Pacific Rim literature that serves to expose the history of the capitalist and militarized exploitation of the Pacific Rim by powerful countries, particularly the United States and Japan. While her novels *Through the Arc of the Rainforest* (1990) and *Brazil-Maru* (1993) looked at Japanese immigrants who came to Brazil seeking work, *Circle K Cycles* (2001) dealt with their Japanese-Brazilian descendants who went to Japan searching for economic opportunity. Japan of the 1990s was in need of cheap, unskilled labor, but was also fearful of the cultural differences that migrant labor would bring, The government turned to the Japanese Brazilians in hopes that they could fulfill the country's labor needs with minimal disturbance to Japanese culture, given their Japanese heritage. As it turned out, however, the Japanese Brazilians were too Brazilian for the Japanese, symbolized, for example, in the ways that they had difficulty absorbing basic Japanese attitudes toward things like waste. "Which days, at what time, where, and how must we dispose of our trash?" one character anxiously wonders. "I listen to the answers conscientiously. I want to be a good neighbor."[12] The Japanese are punctilious about everything, including their waste, which must be sorted into four trash groups, and would never use secondhand goods. But the Japanese Brazilians "hardly have to buy anything upon arriving in Japan," as plenty of hand-me-downs from other sojourners are to be found.[13] These differing attitudes toward waste and commodities represent economic and cultural attitudes toward wealth, commodities, and lifestyles across the Pacific — a staple of Yamashita's writing.

From a pan-American perspective, though, her work is also Asian American literature, except that it concerns the relationship between Japan, or Asia, and Latin America. Still, her work pushes well beyond the American borders of Asian American literature, whether those borders are in the north or the south. Yamashita is most concerned with the circulation of people who are forced to move by the demands of capitalism, and ultimately with capitalism itself. One of her best-known works, *Tropic of Orange* (1997), takes as one of its subjects the impact of the North American Free Trade Agreement. The novel's political vision reaches its climax in a surreal wrestling match between El Gran Mojado (The Gigantic Wetback) and SUPERNAFTA, characters modeled on lucha libre wrestlers. El Gran Mojado triumphs, and "*everyone gasped as the great SUPER NAFTA imploded.*"[14] The novel itself straddles the United States and Mexico, examining an ensemble cast who represent different races, genders, nationalities and economic strata, caught up in not only NAFTA but also the Japanese American internment, undocumented immigration, racial tensions, and natural disasters. The novel is pan-American but also a cultural product of the Pacific Rim, with NAFTA as one manifestation of the efforts of nation-states to build trade agreements that cross borders, even as they also attempt to block people from moving freely across borders.

Yamashita's writing, while always taking into account the Asian presence in the Americas, often overflows these racial and geographic boundaries. This is evident in her most ambitious novel, *I Hotel* (2010). During the 1970s, the *I Hotel*, inhabited by aging Filipino and Chinese workers, became the site of an important civil rights struggle as community activists sought to defend the workers from eviction. The construction of an Asian American movement depended partially on the idea that Filipinos and Chinese were both Asian, which, at the time, was not necessarily a given for Filipinos. Yamashita connects this fight to defend workers and build a panethnic coalition to the history of the Vietnam War, the antiwar movement that had preceded it, and the journey some of these activists undertook to China. The novel affirms how the Asian American movement was always what critics would now call transnational, or would then, in the 1960s, call international. The I of *I Hotel* itself stood for International, and becomes a sign of how the hotel's poor workers were emblematic of the global pressures and currents that had brought so many to the United States.

A novel like Ruth Ozeki's *A Tale for the Time Being* (2013) makes literal this idea that currents connect continents. In the novel, a writer named Ruth finds the diary of a Japanese girl washed up on the shore near her Vancouver home, drifting along with the flotsam and jetsam from a Japan recently devastated by a tsunami. The impetus for the novel is thus the ecological and environmental, of which the Pacific Ocean is the most massive embodiment. But the term "Pacific Rim," at least in its most common deployment, avoids the ecological and the environmental by foregrounding instead economic potential. Cultural possibilities come second, and the ecological and environmental are barely mentioned at all by advocates for a capitalist Pacific Rim. For Pacific Rim advocates, whose most contemporary manifestation is embodied in the supporters of the Trans-pacific Partnership, there is the sense that the possibilities of economic and cultural transformation in the Pacific Rim are contemporary, a part of something called globalization.[15] But Ozeki's novel and its gesture toward the forces of the ocean imply that the Pacific parr of the Pacific Rim has been a global force for much longer than the fashionable term "globalization." Furthermore, the impact of globalization on the Pacific's ecosystem will continue far into the future. Even in the short period of human history, the Pacific has long been the site for ships, boats, and people to cross through and over, not to mention live in. Commerce and trade, war and exploration, conducted by Asians, Europeans, and Pacific Islanders, flourished for centuries before the contemporary moment, even before the age of European imperialism. The Pacific Rim is then a belated term, one of several, that arise to help scholars and others make sense of the movements of people, goods, cultures, and ideas across man-made boundaries.[16]

What terms such as "Pacific Rim" allow scholars to do is figure out new ways of classification. A person, a culture, or a text looks different when being called Asian American versus Pacific Rim, or transnational, international, diasporic, or cosmopolitan, which are all influential terms in contemporary academic scholarship. A person, a culture, or a text can be grouped with others in novel ways, depending on the term being used. The utility of Asian American literature is that it allowed for a grouping of people and texts that had heretofore not been grouped, and as a result had suffered in isolation as being anomalous in the landscape of American culture. Authors such as Sui Sin Far (*Mrs. Spring Fragrance*, 1912) at the turn of the nineteenth century, or Younghill Kang (*East Goes West*, 1937) in the 1920s, or Carlos Bulosan (*America Is in the Hearty,* 1946) in the 1940s, or John Okada (*No-No Boy*, 1957) in the 1950s, who when looked at alone were exceptional figures from small ethnic populations, could then, in retrospect, be part of a larger literary and political movement that had greater force in numbers. But every system of classification also excludes and limits, and the drawback of Asian American literature is that it discourages the possibility of seeing Asian American authors as having other alignments, while encouraging Asian Americans to see themselves as Americans. But seeing themselves as international might provoke Asian Americans into adopting the radical vision of Yamashita, where international stands for border-crossing movements of resistance and revolution.

The place of Asian Americans on the Pacific Rim, and the Pacific Rim itself, has unpredictable political possibilities. In the case of Pacific Rim literature, for example, its existence is tied to the idea of the Pacific Rim as part of a "United States Global Imaginary," as Christopher Connery puts it. Likewise, scholar Rob Wilson made the case for doing cultural studies within APEC at the time, when APEC, an economic alliance of Asian Pacific countries, was at the forefront of the news. Now, with the Transpacific Partnership being debated by many countries as they ponder signing on to the vast trade agreement, the term "Transpacific" is appearing in more and more articles and books dealing with literature and culture. Much as the theorist Slavoj Žižek describes "multiculturalism" as the cultural logic of multinational capitalism, these terms are also the cultural logic of phases in the global organization of the economy. They are made possible by changes in the global economy and the concomitant movements of people, culture, and ideas, and they potentially become sites of critique and resistance to those changes. Asian American as a term serves similar functions.

For Asian American studies, "Asian American" is not simply a demographic category, but the name for a population that is premised on resistance to oppression and injustice.[17] But another way to understand Asian American as a category is in regards to how markers of cultural diversity also facilitate the growth of capital (a point also made in related ways by Inderpal Grewal about feminism's vulnerability to neoliberal exploitation and Rey Chow in regards to ethnic difference as commodity in the academy). Just as one is encouraged by financial advisers to diversify one's investments, all forms of human diversity are vulnerable to investment and exploitation in capitalism. After all, corporations and the military are also interested in diversity, not just civil rights groups and universities. So it is that "Asian American" can also name a population that is another marketing category or a lifestyle, while Asian American people can be as interested in participating in capitalism as they are in social justice struggles. In that sense, Asian American and Pacific Rim as names could be seen as domestic and international mirrors of each other, describing how capitalism categorizes populations on different scales of the local and global.

Nevertheless, because "Asian American" also did arise from a history of political mobilization and resistance, it has a different valence than does Pacific Rim, which was never a term claimed by people seeking to defend themselves. Asian American retains a politically charged, if unresolved, meaning, whereas Pacific Rim still implies something more capitalist and commercial, a cosmopolitanism of the jet-set class rather than what Paul Gilroy calls the vulgar cosmopolitanism of the classes forced to migrate.[18] A novel like Kevin Kwan's *Crazy Rich Asians* (2014) is about the jet-set class, embodied in the Asians of the title, who traverse the Pacific between Singapore and New York at will. They might be called Asian American, given their ability to live and shop in the United States, but Pacific Rim is better. They are the flexible citizens described by anthropologist Aihwa Ong, swearing loyalty not to country but to capital and cash. They are the elite Asians of many countries who send their children to the United States or other foreign countries of the west to study and to earn degrees that will guarantee their career advancement in Asia. They buy property in the west, speak English in addition to an Asian language, and live lives in multiple countries, the parents sometimes in one while the children are in another. Not surprisingly, while scholarly movements have been built around Asian American literature or transnational or diasporic studies, there has been less interest in Pacific Rim literature. Scholars of these fields tend to adopt a more critical stance toward capitalism, and look for literature that would be similarly critical. A Pacific Rim literature that simply reflects the capitalist bias of the Pacific Rim itself does not lend itself to such critical appropriation.

Another issue undermining the attractiveness of Pacific Rim as an organizing motif for literary studies is what it generally overlooks — the actual Pacific itself, meaning not just the ocean but also the islands in it and the peoples who live on those islands. To the extent that some of those islands are owned, more or less, by the United States, they are also potentially the concern of Asian American literature. A literary movement exists in the Pacific Islands, seeking to prove what the scholar Epeli Hau'ofa argued for in this influential essay, "Our Sea of Islands," which is that the Pacific is not empty.[19] Even when it is recognized by Europeans, Americans, and Asians to have inhabitants, these people are thought to be residents of small, inconsequential places. Hau'ofa argues for an epistemology of the Pacific — what he calls Oceania — that arises from the islands and their inhabitants, who he presents as people with rich, complex histories and cultures. They are not simply local or indigenous, but are the inheritors of navigators and explorers who traveled between islands in their own cosmopolitan adventures. The literature of their descendants fits neither into Pacific Rim nor Asian American literature, even if it is sometimes overshadowed by those literatures. Take, for example, the case of "Hawaiian" literature, which is often not written by native Hawaiians even if it is called such. In the United States, one of the best-known "Hawaiian" writers — not including James Michener — is Lois Ann Yamanaka, who would be described by the residents of Hawai as a "local" rather than a "Hawaiian" because she is of

Japanese descent. What Americans call "Hawaiian" literature is often comprised of the writings of settlers, whether they are white or Asian or some other group. But as the native sovereignty movement argues, settlers are settlers, regardless of their racial descent.

Foregrounding the Pacific, rather than the rim around it, is the closest equivalent to the insurgent tradition in Asian American literature. Even examining the literature of Asian settlers, like Yamanaka, throws Asian American literature into question, for Yamanaka and other Asians in Hawai'i do not necessarily see themselves as Asian Americans, but as local. Asian Americans from the continental United States are put in their place as part of an American imperium in relation to locals who occupy an ambivalent place in the American nation. Locals identify with a peripheral state that is a colonized outpost of the United States and a forward military base in the American effort to dominate the Pacific. Locals are both colonized subjects and also participants in settler occupation over indigenous people and the projection of American power throughout Asia and the Pacific. But the writings of indigenous peoples in the Pacific, by their very existence, dispute the idea that the Pacific is simply an empty region whose fate is to be decided by others.

Besides Epeli Hau'ofa, writers such as Albert Wendt and Sia Figiel of Samoa have become notable in Pacific literature and elsewhere. Wendt's *Leaves of the Banyan Tree* (1979) examines three generations of West Samoans grappling with family drama and the impact of being colonized by New Zealand, while Figiel's *Where We Once Belonged* (1996) looks closely at the life of a young girl in her village as she struggles with coming of age. These novels insist on the importance of indigenous life as something not to be passed over, either figuratively or literally in a passenger jet. Like Asian American literature is "minor" literature, while Asian Americans are a minority in the United States, Pacific Islanders — a majority their own lands — are minor on a global scale. But being minor does not mean being inconsequential, as Hau'ofa insists. Being minor instead means being able to critique — even feeling that one is called on to critique — the major, the powerful, the dominant.[20]

Can Pacific Rim literature carry out such a task, or is it consigned to supporting, implicitly or explicitly, the capitalist and militarist energies of the nations bordering the Pacific? The answer lies with the writers who might call themselves Pacific Rim writers, and the activists and critics who would read their work or mobilize movements and identifications along the Pacific Rim. Pacific Rim literature allows those writers who do not fit easily into any national or racial classification to find another kind of home with like-minded anomalies. What would emerge as ways of classifying writers, instead of nation, race, or region, would be thematic, experiential, linguistic, or historical issues.

Take war as one example of how to reorganize literature around theme, experience, and history. The history of the Pacific Rim and its development into its current status as a horizon of economic growth is made possible by war and occupation. In the twentieth century, the United States fought Japan during World War II over control of the Pacific. After the United States defeated Japan, it brought the conquered country into a postwar alliance that allowed the loser to become a rebuilt American ally. Twentieth-century wars and conflicts waged after World War II in the Pacific are a part of this American campaign to establish hegemony in the region, from the Korean War to the Vietnam War, and from the suppression of communism in Indonesia to the similar campaign in the Philippines. Under Pacific Rim literature, writers could be taken out of their national traditions or racial groupings and be put into alliance and conversation with each other around this theme of war. Authors with seemingly no connection to each other could be placed in new relationships. Tim O'Brien (*The Things They Carried*, 1990) writes about the Vietnam War from the American perspective and could be put in conversation with Vietnamese war writers Bao Ninh (*The Sorrow of War*, 1990) and Duong Thu Huong (*Novel without a Name*, 1996).

The connections between different authors who write about war in the Pacific and its corollaries of power, violence, and abuse are manifold. This list could stretch to Yusef Komunyaaka (*Dien Cai Dau*, 1988), Ahn Junghyo (*White Badge*, 1989), Suk-young Kim (*Shadow of Arms*, 1994), Le Ly Hayslip (*When Heaven and Earth Changed Places*, 1989), Maxine Hong Kingston (*The Fifth Book of Peace*, 2003), Vaddey Ratner (*The Shadow of the Banyan*, 2012), Anne Fadiman (*The Spirit Catches You and You Fall Down*, 1997), and many more. These authors talk about black American soldiers, Korean soldiers and contractors, and Vietnamese peasants in the Vietnam War, as well as the consequences of the war with the antiwar and peace movements in the United States, the Khmer Rouge genocide in Cambodia, and the struggles of Hmong refugees in California. Jessica Hagedorn's *Dogeaters* (1990), set in a martial law Philippines supported by an America eager for a staging base in the Pacific that could help with the Vietnam War, could also be included.

These events from the 1960s to the 1990s occur as the corporate and governmental imagination of the Pacific Rim is taking shape, and connect the events of one seemingly isolated war to several countries and populations. This list of authors and connections is far from exhaustive, but they gesture at how a Pacific Rim literature oriented around war and its effects produces a very different constellation, or web, of writers, events, and populations than what might be found under Asian American literature. While Pacific Rim literature may not have the same constituency of readers that Asian American literature has, the potential for critics and writers to selfconsciously fashion such a literature exists. Pacific Rim literature does not displace or replace Asian American literature, but exists as a supplement, a complement, a partner in dialogue and contrast. The two literatures mutually show the limitations of the other.

Asian American literature fulfills a needed political and cultural function within the borders of the United States, articulating the cultures of an extremely diverse racial minority. The literature is the outcome of decades of political struggle and organizing, and is important not only because it speaks about the population it is named after. Asian American literature also plays a role in the wider fight for greater justice and equality for all American populations. And it has earned an audience, both from within and outside Asian America. But its once radical political spirit has been domesticated to some extent, blunted by its own success and that of some Asian American populations. It also finds itself on territory that is increasingly defined by not only national consciousness but also transnational sensibility, one where being Asian American — with its implicit investment in an American national identity — may seem too local or parochial.

The concerns that have motivated Asian Americans around race, economy, war, inequality, and injustice seem now to be difficult to separate from global contexts. Here a Pacific Rim framework encourages Asian Americans to make common cause with others outside national borders, although that common cause might be to advance capitalism as much as to contest it. A Pacific Rim framework also allows Asian American literature to signify differently, and to allow Asian American writers to attempt an escape from the ethnic ghetto that most minority writers fear. The typical dilemma for minority writers in the American context is to feel that they are offered a choice between identifying as a minority or siding with whiteness. But rather than seeing this as their only choice, or believing that their work is only about Asian Americans, Asian American writers can find a larger horizon on the Pacific Rim. This horizon is already one that states, corporations, and militaries are seeking to control. Contesting this control is one important reason for Asian American writers — at least those who are committed to the widest possible definition of justice — to see themselves as part of a Pacific Rim.

Notes

1. In *China Men*, one of the Chinese immigrants is described as "coming to claim the Gold Mountain, his own country" (52). Contextually, the Gold Mountain refers to America. See Peter Grier's interview with Maxine Hong Kingston, "Chinese Roots in America," in *Christian Science Monitor*, 23 September1965, pp. 14–16.

2. Min Hyoung Song, *The Children of 1965: On Writing, and Not Writing, as an Asian American.* Durham, NC: Duke University Press, 2013.

3. United States. Department of Homeland Security. *Yearbook of Immigration Statistics: 2013.* Washington, DC: DHS, Office of Immigration Statistics, 2014.

4. "Diversity Snapshot." Berkeley Diversity. Fall 2013. <http://diversity.berkeley .edu/sites/default/files/Diversity-Snapshot-web-FINAL. pdf>. Accessed 1st February 2016.

5. "Quick Facts about UCLA." UCLA Undergraduate Admission, Fall 2014. <www.admissions.ucla.edu/campusprofile.htm>. Accessed 1 February 2016.

6. "Harvard Admitted Students Profile." Harvard College Admissions and Financial Aid, 2015. <https://college.harvard.edu/admissions/admissions-statistics>.Accessed 1st February 2016.

7. "Yale Facts and Statistics." Office of Institutional Research, 2015. <http://oir yale. edu/sites/default/files/factsheet_2014-15_o.pdf>. Accessed 1st February 2016.

8 "Admission Statistics." Princeton University Undergraduate Admission, 2015. <https://admission.princeton.edu/applyingforadmission/admission-statistic>. Accessed 1st February 2016.

9. "The Asian Population: 2010." United States Census Bureau, 2011. <www.census .gov/prod/cen2010/briefs/c2010br-II.pdf>. Accessed 1 February 2016.

10. See Arif Dirlik, ed., *What Is in a Kim? Critical Perspectives on the Pacific Region Idea* (New York: Rowman & Littlefield, 1998), an invaluable collection of essays that historicize the meaning of the Pacific Rim.

11. Maxine Hong Kingston, *The Woman Warrior: Memoirs of a Girlhood Among Ghosts* (New York: Knopf, 1976), 3.

12. Karen Tei Yamashita, *Circle K Cycles* (Minneapolis, MN: Coffee House Press, 2001), 28.

13. Ibid., 30.

14. Ibid., 264.

15. See the essays in *The Trans-Pacific Partnership: A Quest for a Twenty-first-Century Trade Agreement*, Deborah K. Elms, C. L. Lim, and Patrick Low, eds. (New York: Cambridge University Press, 2012).

16. For an overview of those terms, culminating in the transpacific, see *Transpacific Studies: Framing an Emerging Field*, Janet Hoskins and Viet Thanh Nguyen, eds. (Honolulu: University of Hawai'i Press, 2014).

17. I elaborate on this point in *Race and Resistance: Literature and Politics in Asian America* (New York: Oxford University Press, 2002).

18. Paul Gilroy, *Postcolonial Melancholia* (New York: Columbia University Press, 2006), 67.

19. Epeli Hau'ofa, "Our Sea of Islands," *The Contemporary Pacific* 6.1 (1994): 147-61.

20. For more on the theory of minor literature, see Gilles Deleuze and Félix Guattari, "What Is a Minor Literature?" *Mississippi Review* 11.3 (1983): 13-33.

15
20 世纪兴起的亚裔美国文学

吴 冰

评论家简介

吴冰，毕业于北京大学西语系，曾任北京外国语大学英语系教授，博士生导师；全国美国文学研究会理事，北京外国语大学英语学院华裔美国文学研究中心主任。研究领域包括美国小说、亚裔美国文学、英语文体学、英语写作和口译等。出版专著《亚裔美国文学导读》（2012）；《美国全国图书奖获奖小说评论集》（2001）；《华裔美国作家研究》（2009）。合编有《20 世纪外国文学史》（2004）；《美国文学名著精选上、下册》（1994）；《杰克·伦敦研究》（1988）。代表性论文有《20 世纪兴起的亚裔美国文学》（2001），发表于《英美文学研究论丛》；《从异国情调、忠实反映到批判、创造——试论中国文化在不同历史时期的华裔美国文学中的反映》（2001），发表于《国外文学》等。

文章简介

文章发表于 2001 年，是吴冰教授站在世纪之初的视角，对 20 世纪兴起的美国亚裔文学的回顾与评析。文章主要涉及五位文学评论界公认的重要美国亚裔作家，即菲裔作家卡洛斯·布洛桑（Carlos Bulosan）、日裔作家约翰·冈田（John Okada）、华裔作家朱路易（Louis Chu）、汤亭亭（Maxine Hong Kingston）、赵健秀（Frank Chin）。文章全面介绍了每位作家的身世和创作背景，以及代表作品的主要内容及其反响；重点剖析作品的主题思想、写作手法，揭示作家的独特之处以及作品在美国亚裔文学史上的重要地位。本文对读者了解这些重要作家以及美国亚裔文学在 20 世纪的创作特点具有重要参考价值。

文章出处：《英美文学研究论丛》，2001 年第 00 期，第 172-195 页。

20世纪兴起的亚裔美国文学

·吴　冰·

从广义上讲，亚裔美国文学包括所有具有亚洲人血统的美国公民用英文或其他亚洲文字所写的作品；从狭义上讲，常指具有美国国籍的亚洲人后裔用英文所写的关于亚裔美国人在美经历的作品。本文所讨论的是狭义的亚裔美国文学，主要涉及 5 位评论界公认的重要亚裔作家，即菲裔作家卡洛斯·布洛桑（Carlos Bulosan 1913 — 1956）、日裔作家约翰·冈田（John Okada, 1923 — 1971）、华裔作家朱路易（Louis Chu, 1915 — 1970）、汤亭亭（Maxine Hong Kingston, 1940 — ）、赵健秀（Frank Chin, 1940 — ）。

尽管亚洲人早在 19 世纪中期就到了美国，亚裔美国文学的兴起却几乎是一个世纪以后的事情。非白人、非英裔、非基督徒的弱势群体作家要在美国发表作品向来不容易；再加上美国读者对亚洲文化和亚洲人知之甚少，亚裔作家的作品更难被人接受。此外，除了巨大的文化差异，亚洲各国和美国之间的政治、军事、外交、经济关系也极大地影响着亚裔作家的处境和他们的作品在美国出版发行。20 世纪后半叶，亚裔美国文学随着美国多元文化的发展而繁荣起来，亚裔美国作家的作品被收入多种美国文学选集，新编的美国文学史中也开始有了专章讨论亚裔美国文学。[1]

亚裔作家，尤其是早期的作家或作家早期的作品大多带有自传成分，其中很重要的原因是出版商认定亚裔作家的作品以自传销路最好。如菲裔作家卡洛斯·布洛桑的杰作《美国在心中》（*America Is in the Heart*, 1946）和汤亭亭的《女勇士》（*The Woman Warrior*, 1975）都有自传的成分。

在美国的亚洲人中，菲律宾人的地位较特殊。1898 年美国从西班牙手中夺得菲律宾这块管辖地后，允许菲律宾人自由出入美国，名义上他们算美国国民，但没有公民权。在西班牙殖民主义者长达三百年的统治下，菲律宾人与其他亚洲人不同，其早就接触到欧洲文化，和西方人的关系也较密切。后来他们的世界观又受到上千名赴菲律宾的美国教师的影响 —— 许多菲律宾人在美国人开办的学校中接受教育，他们在校园里向星条旗敬礼，看着教室里挂着的华盛顿、林肯画像，学习《独立宣言》，读着美国是"自由人和勇敢者的故乡"的英文课本。20 世纪初期成千上万的菲律宾青年先到了夏威夷，继而在 20 年代又到了美国本土。美国当局相继采取排斥华人、日本人、朝鲜人和印度人入境的政策后，菲律宾人填补了劳动力的不足，截至 1930 年，在美国本土的菲律宾人已达 4.5 万余人。在国内受到的美式教育使菲律宾人对美国抱有很多幻想，布洛桑在一封信中说："西方人从小受到的教育就是把东方人或有色人种看成下等人，但是最具有讽刺意味的是菲律宾人所受的教育却是把美国人看作是和我们平等的人。"[2]因此美国种族歧视的现实使他们格外失望。由于菲律宾人多为农业季节工，流动性大，因此难以建立自己的聚居区。他们大多会说英语，就业的机会比其他亚洲人要多，同时他们还能和美国妇女交往。西班牙文化赋予许多菲律宾青年某种浪漫的气质，加上他们在休息日衣着潇洒、出手大方，颇受白人女孩的青睐，因而更招致白人男子对他们的憎恨，尤其是在加州，布洛桑说在那里"作为菲律宾人就等于是罪犯"，警察可以毫无理由地殴打、枪击他们。正因为接受了美国的自由、民主理想，他们奋起抗争，有学生参加的工会不但领导农工们罢工，还办刊物。布洛桑参与了工会活动，在1934至1938年间他协助建立"美国罐头食品和加工包装工人联合会"（UCAPAWA）并在工会领导人克里斯·门萨尔瓦斯的鼓励下为工会办的报纸写文章。所有这些在他的书中都有体现。1952年在门萨尔瓦斯安排下，他做了UCAPAWA年鉴的编辑，并以此为生一直到4年后他去世。

《美国在心中》分四大部分。第一部分写主人公"我"在菲律宾的童年生活。后面三部分分别描写了菲律宾人在美国的处境和经历，青年学生和工人在追求真理、提高民族和阶级意识的过程中所走得艰难、曲折的道路以及"我"自学成才的过程。美国当局残酷逮捕、枪杀工会领导人，火烧农工住所和工会机关所在地，白人妇女利用和工会领导人同居破坏工会斗争等等。菲律宾人所受的压迫最深重，日本农场主、华人的赌场都参与对他们的剥削；他们的反抗也最英勇、激烈，因为他们受到过"美国理想"的熏陶，所以他们深信"美国在为自由而牺牲的人们心中"。对作者和许许多多菲律宾人来说，"美国"两个字代表着所有外国移民追求的自由、民主的理想。作者宣称"我们大家，从第一批来的亚当们到最后来的菲律宾人，不论是本地生人还是外国人，不论是受过教育者还是文盲——我们就是美国！"《美国在心中》反映了千万菲律宾人于20世纪三十至四十年代之间在美国受歧视和迫害的集体经历以及他们的英勇斗争史，也表达了他们追求自由的强烈愿望。和许多亚裔作家一样，布洛桑渴望在美国的各民族、各种族能平等、和睦相处；他认为凡是在美国这块土地上流血、流汗、辛勤劳动的人都有权称自己为美国人！

1960年前，第二代在美国出生的华裔作家的作品中唯一得以在大出版社发表的只有黄玉雪（Jade Snow Wong）的《华女阿五》（*Fifth Chinese Daughter*，1945）和刘裔昌（Pardee Lowe）的《父亲和光宗耀祖的后代》（*Father and Glorious Descendent*，1943）两部自传。当时的社会背景是——美国把中国看作盟友，华人地位之高是前所未有的。但最能反映美国华人早期社会状况的当数朱路易的《吃碗茶》（*Eat a Bowl of Tea*，1961）。小说的功绩在于其第一次真实地描写了由美国排华政策造成的、持续了近百年的畸形"单身汉"社会及其在第二次世界大战后的解体。

故事发生在1948年处于变化前夕的纽约唐人街。王华基和李江是十几岁时同乘一条轮船来美的广东新会同乡。王曾以开餐馆为生，1923年回国结婚,待妻子怀孕后又回到美国,此时他在唐人街地下室经营一家麻将馆。李江来美后开过洗衣店，1928 年回国成亲，返美后不久就听说自己得了个女儿。1938 年他正想回国，不料发生了日本侵华战争，后来蒋介石垮台，他又对回老家顾虑重重，于是只得滞留纽约。王华基的独子宾来 17 岁来美后，父亲怕儿子会在自己开的麻将馆里染上赌博恶习，请求王氏家族的头号人物王竹庭把宾来安排到康州他开的餐馆里做跑堂，没想到宾来不久就被店里比他年长的伙计钱源带到纽约嫖娼。第二次世界大战期间，宾来入伍随军到中国香港、印度等地，每到一处，无不拈花惹草。战后，24 岁的宾来已到结婚年龄，正巧李江的妻子多次来信让他为 18 岁的女儿美爱物色一个"金山客"丈夫，于是两个老朋友谈起了儿女婚事，为此王华基决定让宾来回国相亲。年轻的"金山客"回新会后，上门提亲的人很多，最后宾来还是相中了美爱。他们比老一辈幸运的是可以双双返回美国。宾来过去的荒唐行为终于导致他新婚后不久就失去了性功能，美爱不满足没有性爱的婚姻，于是无正当职业的阿桑乘虚而入，最后竟使美爱怀孕，搞得唐人街满城风雨。王华基气不过割了阿桑的左耳，被阿桑告到了美国警方。最终还是王竹庭出面，依靠王氏宗亲会的势力和他曾任多年全美平安堂会长的关系，迫使无家族宗亲会做后盾的阿桑撤回诉讼并离开纽约 5 年之内不得返回。王华基和李江也因丢了"面子"而在纽约待不住了。宾来和美爱则远走旧金山这座华人在美最早落脚的城市。摆脱了家长的控制，宾来终于在中草药和妻子的帮助下成了一个名副其实的男人。华人"单身汉"社会也象征性地结束了。

亚裔评论家一致肯定《吃碗茶》在华裔，乃至亚裔美国文学中的里程碑作用。朱路易与过去的华裔作家的不同之处在于他既不回避华人"单身汉"社会，也不粉饰中国传统文化中的糟粕，并且在文字上力图再现纽约唐人街华人的语言。读者看到的是一个被迫封闭、由老年男子统治的父权制社会和形形色色的华人"单身汉"单调、寂寞的生活。

《吃碗茶》比较集中地反映了中国的封建家长制，这一制度下个人与集体的关系，对妇女的蔑视，视婚姻为"传宗接代"的手段，以及"面子"对华人的重要性。封建家长制不仅表现在父母和子女的关系上，也表现在家族和个人的关系上。父母，尤其是父亲，要求子女言听计从，工作和婚姻大事全由他们做主。这不仅扼杀了年轻人的自由意志，也增加了他们的依赖性，限制了他们的发展。早期海外华人由于和子女长期分离，造成彼此陌生、感情疏远。父亲不能尽到教育的责任，也不会关心子女，当然更谈不上思想交流。宾来到美国后很少和父亲见面，即使见面也无话可说；美爱则是到美国后才第一次见到父亲，而李江是听到女儿和阿桑的丑闻后，才第一次踏进女儿的家门。海外华人的宗亲会也是由"家长"统治的，从王竹庭在王华基父子的家事中起的作用可以看出个人的命运在相当大程度上掌握在家族首脑人物手中，他的素质也决定着家族的成败、兴衰。宗亲会帮助同姓，为维护小集团的利益一致对外。在以集体为重的制度下，个人的地位紧密地和他与他人的关系连在一起，宾来在唐人街是以"王华基的儿子"而为人所知的。美爱出事后，王华基首先想到的是儿子给他丢了"面子",而不是怎样去帮助儿子解决家庭问题。王氏会馆为了维护所有姓王的人的"面子",以强欺弱,私了了一桩告到美国警察局的公案。由于华人极为重视"面子",公众舆论和流言蜚语往往能左右华人的思想和言行,起着其他社会不能起的作用。

美国长期禁止华人妇女入境的政策造成了男女比例严重失调,助长了唐人街诸多的婚外情。由于缺乏正常的家庭生活,昔日人们嫖、赌的不良习气也变得更加严重。业余闲来无事的男人们沦为过去他们所不齿的长舌妇,理发店、咖啡馆成了他们议论、传播各种绯闻和小道消息的场所。华文报纸刊登的寻妻启示、某人妻子的外遇,甚至王华基的儿媳来美快一年了还没有"大肚子"以及后来美爱怀孕,都是"单身汉"们议论的话题。他们最后的结论总是"如今的女人不可信赖"。他们看不惯他们称之为"竹心"的、在美国出生的第二代华人,尤其鄙视"竹心"姑娘们着装不检点、追求安逸、贪图享受、未婚先孕等等。在年长的华人男子心目中,妇女应该像他们留在老家的妻子那样,对丈夫年轻时的放荡和婚后长年不归毫无怨言;她们不应该有性的要求,而应该忠贞不渝,既完成传宗接代的任务,又为丈夫几十年如一日地侍奉公婆。由于女人的价值在于"传宗接代",美爱怀孕后,她和宾来都松了一口气,过去从不上门的王华基也开始提着食物和补品去探望儿媳了。

唐人街的华人信奉"男大当婚""女大当嫁",把婚姻看作年轻人应尽的"义务"。封建包办婚姻不需要以爱情为基础,宾来和美爱相亲后,双方最急于通过媒人了解的是女方是否哑巴,男方是否四肢健全。结婚既然是为了"传宗接代",婚宴上客人们祝酒时自然会表示"希望来年此时再举杯"的庆贺。

《吃碗茶》除了描绘华人的相亲、婚宴、打麻将、看中医等习俗外,还反映了中国的茶文化。书中多次提到茶的功能:首先,宾来虽然先找西医,但最后还是中医的药茶治好了他的病;李江到康州去了解他相中的女婿时,不知情的宾来特地给他送上一壶茉莉花茶以便得到更多小费;宾来和美爱是在新会的茶馆里相亲的;在婚宴上,新娘又给来宾敬茶表示谢意;阿桑到美爱家是以喝茶为借口才得以留下并最后达到勾引美爱的目的。或许作者将书取名《吃碗茶》是想表明代表中国传统文化的"茶"具有积极和消极两个方面,华人要在美国生存,应该"取其精华,去其糟粕"。让华人全盘否定中国固有的文化,显然是不可能的,但顽固坚持也不可取,最好的办法是立足于祖国优秀的文化传统,同时学习西方文化中顺应历史潮流的因素。

从写作技巧上看,朱路易描述华人的传统习俗是服从故事的需要而不是为了迎合美国读者的趣味。同时他采用了唐人街华人生动的语言,如阿桑交了"桃花"运,宾来戴了"绿帽子",以及"男女授受不亲","一回生、二回熟","肥水不流外人田","文章是自己的好,老婆是人家的好"等等。书中的理发师借用店里正在放送的粤剧唱片《金瓶梅》试探宾来的反应,但他错误地把金瓶梅当作人名,且仅指潘金莲一个人。

应该指出，如果朱路易想表明妇女的到来终于结束了近百年的华人"单身汉"社会，他选择的美爱绝不是一个称职的妇女代表。她肤浅、爱虚荣，没有自强、自立的精神。而自强、自立的华裔女性还必须在汤亭亭等女作家的书中去寻找。

日裔作家约翰·冈田虽和黄玉雪是同代人，但由于日本在第二次世界大战中成了美国的故人，他震撼人心的《不—不仔》(No-No Boy) 于 1957 年才出版。尽管战争已结束了十余年，这部描写第二次世界大战期间在美日本人所受到的不公平待遇和悲惨遭遇的小说仍然受到冷落。1971 年，此书被华裔作家陈耀光在旧金山书店"重新发现"，当赵健秀去西雅图寻找在那里出生、成长的冈田时，他不幸刚刚在默默无闻中死去，终年 47 岁。如今《不—不仔》已成为亚裔美国文学的"经典"，1974 年出版的《哎咿！》[3] 就是献给约翰·冈田和朱路易的。

约翰·冈田的《不—不仔》讲的是二世 (nisei，即第二代) 日裔青年一郎第二次世界大战后的经历。第二次世界大战期间，美国当局强行集中日裔美国人的做法致使他们原有的社区完全瓦解。他们被迫变卖家庭农场和商店，搬迁到远离城镇的沙漠地区的集中营里。临行前，他们烧毁了和服、日记、日文书籍、亲友信件、相片、唱片等一切会被当作他们和日本保持联系的物品。集中营里分配给各户的拥挤、狭小的"公寓"迫使家庭成员各奔东西去寻找生存的空间，昔日正常的家庭生活一去不复返了。即使战后集中营关闭后，大部分日本人也未能重新获得他们过去的家园和享有的财产，只好流落四方成为挣工资的劳动者。在集中营里所有的日本人中，"一世" (yisei，即第一代移民)，尤其是平均年龄为 55 岁的"一世"男子受打击最大。他们被剥夺了养家活口的谋生手段，非但不能保护妻小，连自己也要靠政府施舍度日。更悲惨的是，他们过去在家庭和社区里至高无上的权威丧失殆尽，地位一落千丈，成为不可信赖的人。"二世"则因为算美国公民，会说英语，在集中营里头一次找到了符合他们所学专业的工作。两代人原有的代沟和隔阂因此被人为地加深了。1944 年集中营当局为区分"忠诚"与"不忠诚"的日本人，要求日裔美国人填写"放行许可证申请书"，其中两个关键问题是：第一、你是否愿意加入美国军队？第二、你是否愿意宣誓背弃日本、效忠美国？填表引起了人们极大的思想混乱与不安。大家担心家里有人会获准离开，而另一些人将被留下，有的人还可能被送到其他集中营去。许多"一世"因害怕家庭成员永远分离，强迫子女填写和自己同样的回答。没有获准成为美国公民的"一世"处于进退两难的境地，他们担心填写"愿意"宣誓背弃日本、效忠美国后会落得个无国籍的下场；况且回答"愿意"背弃日本很可能使当局认为他们过去一直在从事破坏活动。对许多"一世"来说，忠于日本并不排斥忠于美国，而宣誓"背弃"日本则意味着他们从来就不是日本人。第二次世界大战严酷的现实也加剧了"二世"人格的分裂。黄皮肤的亚裔本来就不可能被白人当作"完完全全的美国人"；他们既不完全是美国人，也不完全是日本人、中国人、菲律宾人……如果不发生第二次世界大战，美国社会或许还能够允许日裔青年作为边缘人存在。但战争迫使他们必须做出"非此即彼"的困难、痛苦抉择：是参军还是入集中营？是忠于他的祖国美国，还是忠于父母的祖国日本？日本是父母的祖国，但又代表军国主义和法西斯；美国虽代表美好生活和民主的理想，但他们亲身经历的又是种族歧视的严酷现实。

一郎的母亲因美国一再拒绝接纳她和丈夫成为公民而更加忠于日本，她始终不相信日本会战败。为了母亲，一郎拒绝参军因而被判坐牢两年，出狱后他满腹怨恨，不知这一切该归罪于谁。有时他怪罪母亲，有时又认为有"比她更重要的原因"。美国当局先把日本人从西海岸搞到集中营来证明他们不是可信赖的美国人，然后又要他们作为美国人参军，一郎认为这"毫无道理"，尽管如此，许多人还是参军了，但他没有。因此他出狱后常常自责，认为自己在关键时刻犯了"错误"。为此，日本人恨他，认为他给日裔美国人脸上抹黑。为他感到羞愧的弟弟大郎甚至把他骗到街角让伙伴们把他揍了一顿。为表白自己对美国的忠诚，洗刷哥哥给家庭带来的污点，大郎不听家人劝告，不等中学毕业就积极要求参军。一郎的好友健次在战争中变成了残疾人，一条腿被截肢，只剩下 11 英寸。战后他虽然得到"山姆大叔"嘉奖他的一辆小汽车，但因病情不断恶化，需要一次次住院，将剩下的残腿一点点截去，最后终于在开刀时死去。

可以看出健次是作者最喜爱的正面人物。他虽是第二次世界大战中的英雄，但和其他加入美军作战的日本人不同，他并没有对"不一不仔"们采取趾高气扬或仇视的态度，而是真心想帮助一郎卸下自责的沉重包袱，勇敢地面对现实，重新开始生活。他是个勤于思索的青年，因此他不快活，因为他愤恨每天都能见到的种族歧视现象——公共汽车上一个黑头发、大鼻子的妇女，自己还不大会讲英语，但在一个黑人坐在她旁边的座位上时，立即起身走开；一个可爱的华人女孩，只因为和白人男友一起参加中学的舞会，就马上变得高傲，在其他华人和日本女孩面前装腔作势；在意大利餐馆里，一个自以为比中国人强的日本人带来一个犹太朋友，但没有侍者前去为他们服务，最后老板出来说这不是日本人来的地方，叫他滚回日本去；一个被人误认为白人的黑人为他的同类所恨；年轻的日本人恨不大年轻的、却比自己更带日本味的日本人，而不大年轻的日本人又仇恨老年日本人，因为老人是纯粹的日本人。健次渴望到一个只有人们（people）而不分日本人、德国人的地方去。因为他在战争中打死过德国人，他再也不愿这样干了。作者热切希望有一天人们不再因为是同宗、同姓、同一种族才互相亲近、互相帮助。

值得一提的是此书出版后并没有受到日裔美国人的欢迎，其中原因可能很复杂：或许是日裔美国人不愿回忆这段伤心的历史；也可能因为作者把最终自杀的母亲塑造成一个坚定站在日本帝国主义一边的死硬分子、敌对国的象征，一个令儿子反感、不通人情的干瘪老妇人。尽管冈田本人在第二次世界大战中曾加入美军参战，与主人公大郎的经历完全不同，却能把"不一不仔"痛苦、怨恨、自责的矛盾心理描写得淋漓尽致、感人肺腑，这点应该充分肯定。但作者的立足点不够高。虽然他也指出美国当局对与日裔美国人身份相同的德裔和意大利裔美国人采取截然不同的政策，但他更多的是反映日本人的自责。主人公大郎可以怪罪母亲，认为是她害得自己成了背叛美国的罪人，可以责备自己当初做出了错误的选择；但作者冈田却应该能够看清造成悲剧的罪魁祸首是美国当局采取的种族歧视政策，而个人的"错误"完全是源于国家的错误政策。

华裔第二代女作家汤亭亭和赵健秀同为 20 世纪六七十年代美国弱势族裔民权意识增长中涌现出来的作家。她毕业于加州伯克利大学，是华裔作家中较早成名且名气最大的。汤亭亭通过写作来揭露不公[4]，她创造性地利用中国传统文化，既批判其中的糟粕，也抨击美国社会的种族、性别歧视。她的《女勇士》获 1976 年美国全国图书评论界非小说类最佳作品奖，《中国佬》(China Men, 1980) 获 1981 年美国全国图书奖非小说类最佳作品奖，1989 年发表的第一部长篇小说《孙行者》(Tripmaster Monkey)[5] 获该年美国笔会小说奖。

《女勇士》和《中国佬》可以算是姐妹篇，分别描写华人妇女和华人男子在美的经历。《女勇士》的副标题是"一个生活在群鬼中间的女孩的童年回忆"(Memories of a Girlhood among Ghosts)，全书包括"无名女子"、"白虎山学道"、"乡村医生"、"西宫门外"和"羌笛野曲"五部分，[6] 其中第一、三、四部分讲述"我"的姑姑、母亲和姨母的故事。"白虎山学道"一章中"我"的故事是以中国读者熟悉的花木兰和岳飞的传说为基础的；"羌笛野曲"则是借用蔡文姬的故事。《女勇士》中虽然也有反映华人饮食、婚姻习俗的内容，但最引人注目的是作者创造性地反映、利用中华文化。可以说《女勇士》是华裔美国文学发展的一个新的里程碑。

汤亭亭是通过改变中国文化中的历史故事、神话传说、文学名著等来表达自己的思想的，《女勇士》中"白虎山学道"这一章就是一个例子。白虎是中国古代神话中的西方之神，汤亭亭在这里可能暗示她讲述的故事发生在西方。她借用了花木兰的故事，又"嫁接"了经她改编了的岳母刺字传说。汤亭亭的女勇士和我们中国人熟知的那个爱国、忠君、尽孝的花木兰有许多不同之处。首先，替父从军的花木兰未婚，只有一个年幼的弟弟；而女勇士"我"不但有丈夫，有一个被征去当兵的弟弟，还有一个在战役间出生的儿子。其次，花木兰是和远离家乡的外部敌人作战，而"我"的敌人在国内。离家前，父母在"我"背上刺了"报仇"、"誓言和名字"以及说不尽的"怨愤"。他们甚至刻上了他们自己的姓名和住址。"我"领导的子弟兵进京后杀了"皇帝"(50)，回乡后，"我"又杀了地方官报仇，因为那恶霸把女孩子比做"米里的蛆"，说"宁养呆鹅，不养女娃"，同时他还夺走了"我"的弟弟和"我"的"童年"。"我"解放了被恶霸关押的小脚妇女后回到婆家，安心地过着一个普通妇女种地、持家、育子的生活（ 51 — 54 ）。

由此可以看出汤亭亭的"女勇士"是当代的华裔美国花木兰，她反对歧视、压迫妇女，反对剥削和种族歧视，反对征兵作战。所有这些无不受作者本人经历的影响。汤亭亭家族中的男性长辈大多重男轻女，在家乡做教书先生的父亲到美国后曾不得不靠开洗衣店为生，因此孩子们童年的课余时间，除了上华人学校，都是在店里打工度过的。她的母亲是个有文化、有独立意识的坚强女性，常给孩子们讲故事，花木兰的故事就是其中之一。汤亭亭上大学前后，正值越南战争期间，国内民权运动、妇女解放运动轰轰烈烈，这些在《女勇士》中都有反映。作者在书中说，母亲生怕她的"美国"儿女们忘了祖国和家乡，不断在儿女耳边念叨"广东省，新会村"，并告诉他们"顺着我们来的路走，你们就能找到我们的房子。别忘了。只要提你们父亲的名字，村里人谁都能指得出我们的房子来"（88 — 89）。因此，女勇士的父母会把自己的姓名和住址刺在女儿背上。《中国佬》告诉我们，汤亭亭的弟弟被征兵到越南去打仗，她也曾不止一次说过，让她焦虑的是从越战归来的美国士兵受到战争的心理创伤后，再也不能回到昔日的生活中去，而花木兰却能做到。[7]

汤亭亭的《中国佬》讲的是家族中的几代男人，包括"我"的曾祖父、祖父、父亲、弟弟和堂、表兄弟等人的故事。与《女勇士》不同的是，《中国佬》一书中的某一华人男子，如"我"的曾祖父、祖父、父亲等，往往代表了某个历史时期的一群华人，甚至一代华人。因此，更确切地说，这是一部华裔男子在美国排华政策迫害下的血泪史、奋斗史。在家族故事中，汤亭亭提到中国的科举考试、私塾的体罚、华人的结婚、抓周儿等习俗。和朱路易不同的是，这些也都经过作者的"加工"，如她在讲科举考试时加入了我们熟知的头悬梁、锥刺股等故事。在家族故事前后，汤亭亭穿插了一些寓意深刻的短小章节，创造性地借用中、外神话传说或名著片段来表达自己的思想，如《镜花缘》中女儿国的故事、希腊神话中迈达斯（Midas）的故事、鲁滨逊的故事、关于屈原以及粽子的传说等等。汤亭亭在书的开篇《论发现》一章中，不仅改变了武则天在位的年代，而且把在《镜花缘》的女儿国中受屈辱，被缠足、穿耳、毒打、倒吊而后被国王逼迫成亲的林之洋改成了唐敖。她还增加了唐敖的手足被扣上枷锁，双唇被缝合，以及被迫洗涤自己的裹脚布等情节。最后汤亭亭写到据一些学者讲，女儿国在北美。作者无疑是一方面揭露、批判了旧中国歧视、压迫妇女的现象，同时用暗喻的手法表明华人男子在美国受屈辱、被奴役、被迫保持沉默的处境。由于华工在建成横贯美国大陆的铁路后就被排挤出工业领域，不得不从事洗衣这项过去完全由家中妇女承担的工作，华人男子在美国实际上已被迫"女性化"了。汤亭亭改变有关武则天年代的细节，意在拉开虚构与历史的距离，让读者明白这不是历史，而是艺术的创作。

《女勇士》出版后深受读者欢迎，被赞扬书的内容"像中国织锦缎一样绚丽多彩"，文字"像瓷器般细腻""抒情诗般优美"等等。汤亭亭本人却认为美国读者大多曲解了《女勇士》，把一本集家史、历史、回忆、神话传说和奇想为一体的著作当成了真正意义上的"自传""回忆录"，中了出版商为了招来读者而设下的圈套。另一方面，《女勇士》在一些中国通和相当多的华裔和华人读者中引起的反响却截然不同。他们批评作者完全不懂中国历史和文化,误导了无知的读者;说她写这样一本书是为了取悦白人读者,满足他们追求异国情调的好奇心。赵健秀甚至认为汤亭亭在书中有意夸大父权制度下中国妇女受压迫的现象,歪曲中国历史传说,而其"种族主义"的恶果在于进一步加深了人们固有的概念:即中国传统社会更加歧视妇女,因而和西方文明相比处于劣势。他批判汤亭亭说,在华人男子备受白人蔑视的情况下,揭发、批评华人男子对妇女的态度的做法无异于助纣为虐。赵健秀和一些人还指出,美国社会把华裔美国人视为文化上的"他者",汤亭亭以"自传"形式出版《女勇士》,正好以"内部"知情人的身份为这一观点提供了论据。

汤亭亭在《女勇士》和《中国佬》中采取了现代拼贴艺术手法(collage),集家史、历史、回忆、华人习俗,以及中、外文学名著和神话传说(在《中国佬》中还有一节专述美国的排华法案)于一体,这些再经过她的新奇构想,组成了极其丰富多彩的画面。这种技巧使用得好时,会具有很强的震撼力。实际上,一些当代美国作家,如巴思(John Barth)在《吐火女怪喀迈拉》(Chimera)中也是创造性地利用希腊和阿拉伯神话故事。这是作家在叙述方法上的创新,优秀的作家总是能够使读者明白创新要达到的目的。[8] 汤亭亭在谈到汉学家批评她歪曲中国神话时说:"他们不明白神话必须变化,如果没有用处就会被遗忘。把神话带到大洋彼岸的人们成了美国人,同样,神话也成了美国神话。我写的神话是新的、美国的神话。"[9] 作者的这番话应该是我们理解、欣赏华裔美国文学的一把钥匙。的确,老一代作家黄玉雪把自己看作生在美国的华人(Americanborn Chinese),[10] 而汤亭亭从来就视自己为华裔美国人(Chinese American)。她在《中国佬》一书中表达的中心思想就是华裔美国人有权把美国称为自己的国家,她把用铁路将美国的南方与北方、东部与西部连接起来的"中国佬"誉为"连接、建设美国的先辈",[11] 就是要向全世界宣布她的先辈对美国的重大贡献以及被美国当局有意埋没的一段可歌可泣的历史。

赵健秀出生在加州,母亲是唐人街的第四代华人,因此他一向以第五代华裔美国人自居。他的外祖父曾任南太平洋铁路公司的客车乘务员,这对他日后选择职业和创作题材都有影响。[12] 同时赵健秀在华人办的中文学校读过书,对中国传统文化也有些了解。

赵健秀 1972 年发表的《鸡笼里的中国佬》(The Chickencoop Chinaman)是第一部在纽约上演的亚裔作家的剧作。在这一评论界对其褒贬不一的剧本里,赵健秀的文艺思想和日后作品的主题已略见端倪。该剧的主人公华裔青年谭林因拍摄某黑人拳击冠军成长的传记片去匹兹堡采访了一位据冠军说是他的父亲兼教练的老人。到匹兹堡后他找到儿时好友日裔美国青年谦次。谦次儿时有"黑日本"的外号,因为他和谭林为抗拒白人语言文化,在言谈举止上有意模仿黑人。谦次陪同谭林找到老黑人后,发现老人竟不是冠军的父亲。黑人拳击冠军撒了谎,他们一直被他编造的关于自己以及"父亲"的故事所蒙骗。少年时期崇拜的偶像竟这样被打碎,谭林不禁悲愤交集,喝得酩酊大醉回到谦次的寓所。

在《鸡笼里的中国佬》中读者可以看到赵健秀利用西方文学中的"寻父"和"寻求自我"的模式来表现亚裔美国文学的主题。谭林拒绝承认、接受自己的父亲，他说"中国佬都是糟糕的父亲"。[13] 他和白人妻子离了婚并希望他的两个孩子能忘掉他，他自嘲地告诉别人说，他给孩子留了"一份礼物"，"他们有了个新的、有抱负的、成功的、能挣大钱的、优越的白人爸爸"（27）。作者可能想利用谭林"寻父"的失败来表现多种含义。赵健秀在剧本开头就通过谭林之口尖锐地点出"中国佬是制造出来的，而不是生出来的"，他是"一个奇迹的合成物"。主流文化用它塑造的丧失男子气概的刻板中国佬形象使人们，包括华人，接受"白人优越"的观点，从而使华人鄙视、摈斥自我以至拒绝接受自己的父亲。

谭林是个"愤怒的"华裔美国青年，性格中充满矛盾。他一方面受到白人主流思想的腐蚀，对自己的华裔身份产生自憎，另一方面又表露出强烈的反抗情绪。谭林（Tam Lum）与剧中另一华裔美国人汤姆（Tom）的名字只有一个字母的差别，汤姆使人联想到赵健秀多次提及并批判的"黄色汤姆叔叔"式的人物。剧中的汤姆是个完全按照白人价值观改造自己的华人。他自以为高明地对谭林说他也曾经不喜欢自己的华人身份，但华人被人欺凌的情况已成为"历史"，今天华人有"好职业、高工资"，而且"美国人骄傲地说我们往大学里输送的子弟比其他任何种族都多。我们被接受了。"（59）但同时他又来请求借住在谦次公寓的莉和他复婚。莉有华人血统，她皮肤白皙，染了头发就可以冒充白人。谭林一针见血地指出汤姆在为白人做宣传，汤姆如此渴望得到白人的"接受"，竟然到了看不出莉的华人血统，甚至"创造"出了她这样一个白人来接受自己！

谭林的不幸还在于他自称是个语言上的"孤儿"。赵健秀一方面表现了谭林的语言天才：他会说一口地道的黑人英语，能流利地使用美国南方《圣经》地带的布道语体，甚至能惟妙惟肖地模仿著名的白人盲女——耳聋的海伦·凯勒发音困难、含混不清的语言，另一方面又揭示谭林除了知道"风吹""落雨""今日热""今日冷"几个粤语词外，并不会说中国话，他不具有能够表现"自我"的语言。赵健秀等指出亚裔美国人自我感觉比黑人情况好，但黑人却创造了自己的美国文化。美国语言、时装、音乐、文学……道德、政治都深受黑人文化的影响，而亚裔美国人的"名声"却是白人文化造就的。赵健秀等还指出语言是文化和人们感性（sensibility），包括男子汉气派（style of manhood）的媒介。制止人的语言无异于砍去他的文化和感性。任何文化中的人都要为自己说话。没有自己语言的人不能称其为人。白人文化一直在利用语言的专政来压制亚裔美国文化，并将其排斥在美国主流意识之外。[14] 由此可以看出作者把谭林写成语言"孤儿"，让他讲黑人英语带有深刻的寓意。

1973 年，赵健秀在旧金山创办亚裔美国人戏剧讲习班，其目的是"为亚裔剧作家提供实验场所，而不是为黄脸戏子提供向好莱坞谄媚邀售的橱窗"。[15] 讲习班在启发、提高亚裔美国人的独立意识上影响深远。1974 年，他和陈耀光（Jeffery Paul Chan）、劳森·稻田

（Lawson Fusao Inada）和徐忠雄（Shawn Hsu Wong）所合编的亚裔美国作家文选《哎咿！》（Aiiieeeee!）可以说是第一次发出了亚裔作家震撼人心的呐喊,被《党派评论》杂志（Partisan Review）称作"亚裔美国文艺复兴的宣言"。[16] 有的评论家认为《哎咿!》的前言和引言在亚裔美国文学史上的地位犹如爱默生宣告美国文学已脱离英国文学而独立的《论美国学者》,它们可以说是亚裔美国人"思想和语言的独立宣言"。[17] 以赵健秀为第一署名人的编者们在前言中对书名解释说:"广为推销美国白人文化的人把黄种人描绘成在受伤、悲哀、愤怒、惊讶或骂人时悲号、尖叫、呼喊'哎——咿'的人,亚裔美国人长期以来一直被忽视并被迫不能参与创造美国文化,……'哎——咿'不仅仅是悲号、尖叫、呼喊。这是我们 50 年来的声音。"引言指出尽管亚裔美国人已有 140 年的历史,但在美国出生的华裔、日裔、菲裔作家出版的小说和诗集不足 10 部。而实际上亚裔美国人从 19 世纪以来就在认真地写作,并有好作品。第二次世界大战时期国际风云的变幻使 20 年代后期蓬勃发展的日裔美国文学受到压制,同时,华裔美国文学突然得到重视而流行,当局通过宣传"忠诚的少数族裔"来打击日裔美国人。此前白人主流文化通过大众媒体推销他们创造的"刻板模式亚裔美国人",其中最有名的是傅满洲（Fu Manchu）[18] 和陈查理（Charlie Chan）[19],其结果造成了包括华裔在内的亚裔美国人的自我鄙视、自我摈弃、分裂解体。前言清楚地表明亚裔美国人既不是半个亚洲人、半个美国人,也不能要他们选择或做亚洲人,或做美国人,他们有自己独特的文化。赵健秀因此被不少人推崇为亚裔美国文学的"奠基人"。[20] 前言在推崇朱路易等个别作家的同时,严厉地批评容闳、林语堂、刘裔昌、黄玉雪等有一定声望的华人前辈、华裔作家接受白人至上的观点、迎合白人的猎奇心理,谴责他们发展了陈查理模式的华裔美国人,批评他们为得到白人的接受,有意识地用白人赋予华人的忠诚、顺从、消极、守法的好人形象来规范自己的行为。

在 1991 年扩编的《大哎咿!》（The Big Aiiieeeee!）里,赵健秀在 92 页题为《真真假假的亚裔美国作家们,大家一起来》（Come All Ye Asian American Writers of the Real and the Fake）的序文中将华裔作家分成真假两派。他批判的对象包括七八十年代涌现出来的女作家汤亭亭、谭恩美和以其剧本《蝴蝶君》（M. Butterfly）获得 1988 年托尼奖的新秀黄哲伦（David Henry Hwang）等 10 余人,认为他们作品中的中国和华裔美国人是"白人种族主义想象的产物,不符合事实,不是中国文化,不是中国文学,也不是华裔美国文学。"他斥责汤亭亭、谭恩美、黄哲伦在标榜创新、"贡献"的名义下伪造广为人知的亚洲文学和传说,并引用了中文的《木兰诗二首》及其译文 [21] 为证。他武断地说"迄今为止,在华人中,只有基督徒写自传,[22] 批判黄玉雪和汤亭亭的"自传体"作品丑化了华人男子,是基督教文化的产物。他否认首批抵美的华人和日本人为无意定居的旅居者（sojourers）,并以帮会（tongs）的存在为证;否认中国和日本文化是厌恶妇女的（misogynistic）,否认亚洲文化是反个人独特个性的（anti-individualistic）。赵健秀在文中"引证"了《孙子兵法》

《三国演义》《西游记》，并选了六幅《水浒传》连环画来表现中国传统文化中的英雄形象。他把帮会的组织和刘、关、张的桃园三结义联系起来，说旧金山的中华会馆（the Chung Wah Wooey Goon）[23] 正是按照桃园三结义和梁山好汉结拜兄弟的模式建立的。[24] 赵健秀把《水浒传》看作是《三国演义》的续编，后者探讨了报私仇的道德观念（the ethic of private revenge），前者则表现了大众报仇反对腐败官府的道德观念（the ethic of popular revenge against the corrupt state），或"天命"（the mandate of heaven）[25]；而《西游记》的"齐天大圣"又表达、发扬了《水浒传》中的一百零八将的精神。[26] 赵健秀把孔子看作史学家、战略家、武士，因此认为他和孙子有了共同点。他认为中华文明的传统是信仰"人人皆生为战士。我们生来就是为维护个人的完整人格（personal integrity）而战。一切艺术皆武术。写作即战斗"，《孙子兵法》正是培育了"生活即战争"的精神。[27]

比较赵健秀在两本选集中的观点后我们可以看出他的思想变化。在《哎咿！》中他指出华裔文化的独特性，以此衡量汤亭亭创造性地利用中国传统文化正是一个"独特性"的好范例。但在《大哎咿！》中他重点批判的就是汤亭亭，提出华裔作家绝对不应让作品中的中国传统文化变形。为此他大量引用《三国演义》《水浒》《西游记》以及孙子、司马迁等等，以表现自己的正统中国古典文学学识，同时以华人英雄形象来对抗华裔女作家和白人作家对华人男子的丑化。实际上，华裔美国文学的确有其异于中国文学的独特性，但它又割不断与中国文化千丝万缕的联系。提倡华裔美国作家的绝对独立或绝对继承既不可取也不可能。由于自幼生长的环境和所受的教育，华裔作家对中国文化的理解和继承是独特的，赵健秀在《大哎咿！》中的长文本身就是一个很典型的例子。

1991 年赵健秀的上述思想大都在他的第一部长篇小说《唐老亚》（*Donald Duk*）中体现出来。极为有趣的是，在文艺创作上他竟然也和自己所批判的汤亭亭一样，创造性地利用中国传统文化——他借助一个 11 岁男孩在春节期间对自己华人身份的态度大转变将美国种族歧视的现实、早期华工在美修建铁路的历史和中国古典文学、唐人街的华人习俗结合起来。赵健秀在《唐老亚》中表现的创新和汤亭亭 16 年前发表的《女勇士》相比，思路更清楚，但书中完全没有对中国传统文化糟粕的批判，他要宣扬的是中华男儿的英雄主义气概。

旧金山唐人街上的唐纳德·杜（Donald Duk）因为和家喻户晓的卡通明星唐老鸭（Donald Duck）谐音，同学们总拿他的名字开玩笑。唐老亚不但恨自己的名字，也怨恨自己的中国血统。他就读的私立学校灌输的是白人优越论，在中国待过一年且会说"国语"的历史教师用儒家的"天命"思想来解释华人为何"被动""不能维护自己的权利"。老师引用自己伯克利大学历史老师的著作说"胆怯、内向"的华人对具有"好胜心和强烈竞争意识"的美国人"束手无策"。唐老亚对中国一无所知，自认为是"美国人"。令他心烦的是春节又来了，别人老是问他有关华人干的"古怪"事情、吃的"古怪"东西等"愚蠢"

问题。唐老亚不喜欢唐人街，可他住在这里，爸爸在唐人街经营餐馆。春节期间，同名的伯父——粤剧大师兼剧团老板——来旧金山演出，唐纳德的白人好友、比他对华人"更感兴趣"的阿诺德·阿扎里亚也要求在他家小住，共同参与春节庆祝活动，包括在元宵节夜晚点燃捻了放飞爸爸、妈妈和双生的姐姐几年来利用业余时间制作的 108 盏飞机烟花灯。由于好奇，唐纳德在年前偷偷放飞了其中一架，不料被伯父发现。伯父告诉孩子这 108 盏灯代表《水浒》故事中罗宾汉式的英雄，他烧掉的正是其中的李逵。伯父还说唐纳德原本也和李逵一样姓李，[28] 他四代以前的李姓先人是最早来美参加建造中央太平洋铁路的华工之一，他当年差不多就是唐纳德现在这个岁数。唐纳德记得庆祝铁路竣工的老照片里并没有华人，伯父让他看爸爸旧书里的相片，指着上面的华工说："你看我们来建造铁路时多么年轻。"伯父要孩子向父亲坦白，并保证补做一架飞机。

唐纳德回到房间后不禁做起梦来。过去他常做噩梦，都是关于华人的，但他并不理解。这次他梦见 12 岁的他和同胞们一起修建铁路。他不但看到了自己的先辈们在荒漠中艰苦奋战的情景以及华工和爱尔兰工人的较量，还在现场见到身着戏装、手持青龙偃月刀的关公。醒来后，唐纳德和阿诺德一起去图书馆查找有关资料，他对图书管理员解释说："我们修建了铁路。我们最好也读一读铁路方面的书。"此时他已经认同了他的华人身份。唐纳德发现事实竟和他梦中所见完全吻合。此后他连续梦见华工在关姓领班带领下创造了 10 小时铺路 10 英里 1 200 英尺的世界纪录，还有雷鸣电闪中关公骑着赤兔马，领着 108 将前来喝彩助威的壮观场面。但是根据他查到的资料，书中只列了为华工搬卸铁轨的 8 个爱尔兰工人的姓名。创造历史的是 1 200 名华工，可连他们领班的名字都未载入史册！唐纳德感到这"不公平"，爸爸回答说"历史是战争，不是游戏！……你应该自己保存历史，不然历史就会永远丢失。这就是天命。"爸爸对"天命"的解释与老师不同:孔子的"天命"是警告皇帝的，"权力会腐蚀人。把王孙、诸侯引上邪道，使老实百姓造反，腐败的王朝必将灭亡。王国兴起又衰败。国家来了又去。这就是天命。"[29] 这次唐纳德"是真正仔细听着"爸爸讲"天命"了。

对中国文化产生了兴趣并有了民族自豪感的唐纳德回到了学校，当老师重谈华人"被动""没有竞争意识"的老调时，他终于能够以"我们"曾为抗争拖欠工资、为要求华人做领班而罢工并取得胜利和"我们"创造了铺轨的世界纪录等真实历史驳斥老师的谬论，阿诺德也拿出一堆书来为此做证。

小说的结尾颇有寓意。唐纳德一家在元宵节把 108 架飞机都送上了天，在唐纳德亲手放飞了他自己补做的"李逵号"时，发现父亲在机体上画上了在美国人人皆知的唐老鸭。爸爸曾经说过做美国人并不一定需要放弃做华人。他以新移民为例——他们仍然说着原来的语言，同时也在学英语；他们没有"放弃"而是在"增加"，这就使他们比任何在美国出生的人都强。赵健秀在书中批判了对白人的盲目仇视。爸爸告诉唐纳德，华人的朋友是"战争中的盟友"。唐纳德和阿诺德的友谊正说明白人并不都是种族主义者。在新的一年里唐纳德将满 12 岁。按照中国的说法，华人孩子在 12 岁就告别了童年。小唐纳德恰恰在新的一年到来时有了一个认识上的飞跃。

比较《鸡笼里的中国佬》和《唐老亚》两部作品的结尾就会发现 12 岁的唐纳德在民族意识和对自己的华裔身份的认识上都比 20 岁的谭林要成熟得多，而赵健秀在创作上成功地运用超现实主义的时空换位手法将早年华工建造铁路的历史同中国古典文学和传说结合起来，不但恢复了美国这段铁路史原来的面貌，还表现了一个深刻主题。不仅如此，他还力图再现唐人街华人的生动语言，在描写华人过节、唱戏等习俗时，内容充实，笔墨适中。应该说这是赵健秀在创作生涯上迈出的新的、可喜的一步。1994 年他写了《甘卡丁公路》，该小说通过一个家族故事来阐述华裔美国人的集体命运。[30]

在亚裔作家中，赵健秀的独特之处在于他公开宣称"写作即战斗"，"生活即战争"。这位剑拔弩张的作家，其立论往往失之偏颇，打击的常常不是敌人而是本该团结的战友。好在在艺术创作上他并没有完全按照自己的观点行事，在提高亚裔美国人的独立意识上，赵健秀功不可没。

亚裔美国文学作品不仅描写亚裔美国人为实现自己的美国梦所付出的代价，他们作为"边缘人"的思想混乱和人格分裂，以及两种不同文化在他们身上的冲突，也从不同侧面反映了他们对开发、建设美国所做的巨大牺牲和杰出贡献。不容忽视的是 —— 正是后来这些不断涌入的新移民坚持、继承了早期美国移民追求自由、民主、平等的理想，他们的行动和业绩也有力地证明了亚裔美国人同样有权称自己为美利坚合众国的主人。

注释：

1. 《希思美国文学选集》(1990) 收入了汤亭亭的《女勇士》中"白虎山学道"一章，《哥伦比亚版美国文学史》(1988) 中有单独一章论述亚裔美国文学。

2. 见 Elaine H. Kim 著 *Asian American Literature*, Temple University Press, 第 49 页。

3. 赵健秀等四位亚裔作家合编的一部亚裔美国文学选集，详见本文赵健秀部分。

4. 她在《女勇士》中有"报导即报仇"一说，见 *The Woman Warrior*, Vintage Books, 1977 年版第 63 页，以后引用本书时均用括号内页码表示出处。

5. 《孙行者》讲的是华裔美国青年剧作家威特曼·阿辛的故事。据说作者讲过"赵健秀是威特曼的'一个灵感'"。详见康士林所写《七十二变说原形一〈猴行者：他的伪书〉中的文化属性》一文，单德兴、何文敬主编《文化属性与华裔美国文学》1994 年版第 62 页。《孙行者》已译成中文，由漓江出版社出版。

6. 文中章节的译文均选自李剑波、陆承毅所译《女勇士》一书，漓江出版社 1998 年版。

7. 1994 年来华访问期间，汤亭亭对北京外国语大学英语系的师生说，花木兰的故事对她启发很大，因为花木兰能够在战争结束后脱下战袍，立即回去过战前的生活。

8. 应该承认，汤亭亭的"创新"并不都是成功的，有时不免使读者感到扑朔迷离，分不清事实与虚构，当然也分不清错误与创造；如《中国佬》中将包括在《十三经》中的《五经》分两项列为科举考试内容，有关屈原的传说部分有明显的改变，不知作者目的何在。

9. 见 Shirley Geok-lin Lim 编 *Approaches to Teaching Kingston's The Woman Warrior*, The Modern Language Association of America, 1991 年版第 24 页。

10. 见 Jade Snow Wong 著 *Fifth Chinese Daughter*，University of Washington Press，1989 年版第 109 页。

11. 原文为 the binding and building ancestors，见 *China Men*, Alfred A. Knopf, Inc. 1980 年版第 146 页。

12. 赵健秀在西大平洋铁路公司做过小职员，在南太平洋铁路公司做过司闸。见 Dorothy Ritsuko McDonald 为 *Chickencoop Chinaman and The Year of the Dragon* 一书所写的"引言"，University of Washington Press，1981 年版第 xi 页。

13. 同上书，第 23 页。

14. 赵健秀、陈耀光（Jeffery Paul Chan）、劳森·稻田（Lawson Fusao Inada）和徐忠雄（Shawn Hsu Wong）合编的亚裔美国作家文选《哎咿！》(*Aiiieeeee!*)，Anchor Books, 1975 年版第 7—8 页，第 35—36 页。

15. 见俞宁《是"奠基人"还是"邪教主"——试评华裔美国作家赵健秀创作道路的是非曲折》一文，《外国文学》2000 年第 4 期。

16. 见 Mentor 出版社 1991 年出版的该书简装本封面。

17. 见 Dorothy Ritsuko McDonald 为 *Chickencoop Chinaman and The Year of the Dragon* 一书所写的"引言"，University of Washington Press, 1981 年版第 xix 页。

18. Fu Manchu, 英国作家 Arthur Sarsfield Wade（笔名 Sax Rohmer, 1883—1959）笔下的华人形象，这个具有西方科学知识的魔鬼化身，为达到个人目的，可以不择手段、甚至牺牲亲人。

19. Charlie Chan, 夏威夷的华人侦探，是美国作家 Earl Derr Biggers 在 1925 (*The House without a Kay*) 至 1932 年间所写的 6 部小说中的主人公。由于在 48 部好莱坞影片中出现（见 Elaine Kim 著 *Asian American Literature*, Temple UP, 1982, 第 18 页），这个被作者称为"可亲""维护法律与秩序"的陈查理，迈着女式碎步、说着洋泾浜英语、引用孔子名言，他的名气比作者要大得多。

20. 见俞宁《是"奠基人"还是"邪教主"——试评华裔美国作家赵健秀创作道路的是非曲折》一文，《外国文学》2000 年第 4 期。

21. 见 *The Big Aiiieeeee!* Meridian, 1991，第 4—6 页，赵健秀引用的 "原文" 把《木兰辞》一分为二，成 "诗二首"，译文也有值得商榷之处。

22. 同上书，第 11 页。

23. 即 the Chinese Consolidated Benevolent Association，以 the Chinese Six Companies 闻名。见 *The Big Aiiieeeee!* 第 25 页。

24. 同上书，第 25，41 页。

25. 赵健秀认为这两种观念正是孔子的基本思想，同上，第 34— 35 页。

26. 同上书，第 39 页。

27. 不知何故，赵健秀在孙子的拼音 Sun Tzu 后又加上 the Grandson?

28. 当年华人常有持他姓人的有效证件进入美国的，故有 "paper" 某某一说，作者在书中说或许最早来美的唐纳德·杜的祖先是个 "paper Du"，即持姓杜者证件进入美国的。见 Frank Chin 著 *Donald Duk*，Coffee House Press，1991 年版第 132 页。

29. 同上书，第 125 页。

30. 详见李有成的《陈查理的幽灵：〈甘卡丁公路〉中的再现问题》一文，何文敬、单德兴主编《再现政治与华裔美国文学》1996 年版，第 161—183 页。

（北京外国语大学英语系）

16

绪论:《他者与亚美文学》及其脉络化意义

单德兴

评论家简介

单德兴，台湾大学外文研究所博士（比较文学），现任"中央研究院"欧美研究所特聘研究员、岭南大学翻译系兼任人文学特聘教授。研究领域包括美国文学史、亚美文学、比较文学、文化研究、翻译研究等。专著有《萨依德在台湾》（2011）、《翻译与脉络》（2009）、《越界与创新：亚美文学与文化研究》（2008）、《反动与重演：美国文学史与文化批评》（2001）、《铭刻与再现：华裔美国文学与文化论集》（2000）等。出版访谈集《却顾所来径：当代名家访谈录》（2014）、《与智者为伍：亚美文学与文化名家访谈录》（2009）、《对话与交流：当代中外作家、批评家访谈录》（2001）。译著有《权力、政治与文化：萨依德访谈集》（*Power, Politics, and Culture: Interviews with Edward W. Said*, 2006）;《格理弗游记》学术译注版（*Gulliver's Travels*, 2004）;《文学心路：英美名家访谈录》（*Writers at Work*, 1998）;《美国梦的挑战：在美国的华人》（*The Challenge of the American Dream: The Chinese in the United States*, 1997）;《知识分子论》（*Representations of the Intellectual*, 1997）;《近代美国理论：建制·压抑·抗拒》（*The Ideological Imperative: Repression and Resistance in Recent American Theory*, 1995）等。

文章简介

　　本文是单德兴教授为其所主编的《他者与亚美文学》一书所作的绪论。文章回顾了美国亚裔文学研究（文章称之为"亚美文学研究"）在台湾地区的建制及发展脉络。全文以宏观与微观相结合的视角，介绍了华美、亚美以及亚英文学研究在台湾地区的发展历程和取得的丰硕成果，尤其详述了包括组织学术会议、建立国际学术联盟、编著专书专刊、培养年轻学者等多种带动研究与交流的学科发展策略。与此同时，文章深入探讨了有关他者的议题，介绍了《他者与亚美文学》一书的内容与特色。单德兴教授对亚美文学研究的意义与价值，以及在学术全球化的背景下，如何实现本地特色与全球视野相结合的学科发展等重要问题给予了深刻反思。

文章出处：单德兴编：《他者与亚美文学》，台北："中央研究院"欧美研究所，第 vii-xxxv 页。

绪论:
《他者与亚美文学》及其脉络化意义[1]

单德兴

一、研究欧美（文学），所为何事？

《他者与亚美文学》于此时此地出版，自有其主客观因素。本绪论拟兼由宏观与微观的角度，从亚美文学研究在台湾的建制化的脉络，以及此书的内容与特色，回顾并反思其可能具有的意义，并提供未来发展的参考。

在台湾从事欧美研究，或较狭义地说，从事英美／亚美文学研究，究竟所为何事？如何善用利基（niche），发挥创意，贡献于国内外学界，一方面与国际接轨，促进交流，另一方面引领国内研究方向，提振学术风气，甚至进而联结学院与社群？[2] 这是许多台湾学者念兹在兹的课题。对于负有引领与提倡学术研究之任务的"中央研究院"而言，更是责无旁贷。

就建制史来说，不容讳言，"中央研究院"欧美研究所的前身 —— 1972 年于中美人文社会科学合作委员会之下成立的美国研究中心，1974 年改制为"中央研究院"美国文化研究所 —— 是冷战时期的产物，旨在对于影响台湾深远的美国进行多方位的研究，"文化"二字则标明相关研究系由文化的角度切入，以免被视为官方智库，因此既不违背"中央研究院"的学术属性，也符合当时欧美主流的美国研究取向。后来为了推展我国的欧洲研究而扩大领域，于 1991 年易名为"欧美研究所"，即使不复强调"文化"二字，但基本的学术取向并未改变，除了个人研究之外，也根据实际需要成立几个集体的重点研究计划，包括文化研究重点研究计划在内，进行多方位的个人与集体研究，前后四十年来已成为我国与华人世界独具特色的多学门之欧美研究建制。[3]

在学术全球化的情况下，许多学术建制都面临类似的处境，一方面要面对全球竞争的态势，另一方面也不能忽略在地的关怀，如何在两者之间取得平衡，既不因国际化而漠视在地的议题，也不因在地的关切而囿限国际的视野，甚至陷入画地自限的困局，就成为必须严肃以待的挑战。换言之，如何在两者之间协调出可行之道，既能随时掌握国际学术思

---

1 本文承蒙李有成、冯品佳、李秀娟、张锦忠、王智明等人提供意见与数据，谨此致谢。
2 如周英雄在担任国科会外文学门召集人时便强调，我国的外文学门学者要建立自己学术的"niche"，"花点精力做些我们比较能胜任的工作"（7）。他进一步指出："其实，研究愈是具本土特色，往国外投稿，命中率往往愈高。也就是说，找niche，谈方法、角度不妨尽量求本土化，可是讲论文的发表与学术的沟通，我们的眼光也不妨放宽一点"（7-8）。
3 有关欧美研究所的历史，参阅由欧美研究所所史编纂委员会主编、魏良才主笔的《孜孜走过四十年：欧美研究所的历史与展望，1972—2012》。

潮，也能善用在地的资源与发言位置，于国际竞争中凸显在地的优势，发挥全球在地化（glocalization）的特色。这种情形对于在台湾从事涉外研究的学者，特别是欧美研究的学者，尤其显著。

二、华美／亚美／亚英文学研究在台湾

由于欧美研究所的历史与属性，文学同仁都出身于英美文学，而且学术背景之养成集中于经典文学。以笔者为例，在学生时代读的几乎全是英美主流文学作品，唯一的弱势族裔文本就是 1970 年代中期在朱炎老师的"美国现代小说专题研究"课堂上读到的非裔美国作家艾利森的《隐形人》（Ralph Ellison, *Invisible Man*, 1952）。当时距离 1960 年代美国如火如荼的民权运动已有若干年，由社会运动唤起的族裔觉醒已逐渐传播开来，因为秉持开放多元的原则与族裔正义的要求，沛然莫之能御，但距离反映于英美学术建制则还有一段时间上的落差。以亚美文学为例，相关的社会与文化运动滥觞于 1960 年代末，直到 1982 年金惠经出版《亚美文学及其社会脉络》（Elaine H. Kim, *Asian American Literature: An Introduction to the Writings and Their Social Context*），才有这个领域的第一本专著，同时也树立了亚美文学研究的里程碑。六年后艾理特主编的《哥伦比亚版美利坚合众国文学史》（Emory Elliott, *Columbia Literary History of the United States*, 1988）收入金惠经的〈亚美文学〉（"Asian American Literature"）专章，亚美文学才算正式纳入主流的美国文史。

亚美研究（Asian American Studies）内容多元，为跨学科的族裔研究领域，并且重视与亚裔社群的互动。传播到台湾之后，由于学科的特色与在地的条件，转而以文学研究为主，参与者绝大多数为研究英美文学出身的学者。[1] 台湾在 1980 年代已出现若干相关的中、英文学术论文与译介，其中刘绍铭的两本中文译介《唐人街的小说世界》（1981）与《渺渺唐山》（1983）发挥了相当的引介之功，[2] 而林茂竹于 1987 年以 *Identity and Chinese-American Experience: A Study of Chinatown American Literature since World War II*（《属性与华裔美国经验：第二次世界大战以来的唐人街美国文学研究》）取得美国明尼苏达大学（University of Minnesota）博士学位，他也是第一位以华美文学研究取得博士学位返台的学者。与美国相较，华美／亚美文学研究在台湾的发展除了时间上的落差之外，数量也望尘莫及，其在台湾的迅速发展与建制化，必须等到 20 世纪 90 年代初期，而且与欧美研究所密切相关。以下拟从学术建制史的角度来看待这个现象，并将本论文集置于此一脉络中

1　冷战时期台湾为美国围堵政策的一环，各方面与美国关系密切。赵绮娜在《美国政府在台湾的教育与文化交流活动（一九五一至一九七〇）》一文中指出，美国在台湾致力于推动美国研究，但"除了美国文学之外，在台湾的发展始终不如美国官员所预期那样蓬勃"（123）。而台湾的外文学界，尤其是英美文学界，由于语文之便，接触之广，在不少领域，如女性主义、后现代主义、后殖民论述、弱势论述等，往往得风气之先。据笔者从美国、日本、韩国、中国大陆以及欧洲等地的学者得知，亚美研究传播到美国境外，以文学研究为主，是相当普遍的现象。

2　参阅刘绍铭接受笔者的访谈，《寂寞翻译事：刘绍铭访谈录》，页285-287。

申论。

首先必须指出的是，本所对于族裔议题的重视绝非始于 1990 年代，而是在创所之初便已显现，并且不限于文学学门。本所出版的下列专书便涉及族裔与跨文化的议题：历史学者孙同勋的《历史学家与废奴运动》（Tung-hsun Sun, *Historians and the Abolition Movement*, 1976），教育学者范承源的《旧金山华文学校与家庭整合和文化认同之关系》（Chen-yung Fan, *The Chinese Language School of San Francisco in Relation to Family Integration and Cultural Identity*, 1981），文学学者余玉照的《赛珍珠小说之跨文化证释》（Yüh-chao Yü, *Pearl S. Bucks Fiction: A Cross-Cultural Interpretation*, 1981）以及田维新的《史诺普斯家族与犹克纳帕陶法郡》（Morris Wei-hsin Tien, *The Snopes Family and the Yoknapatawpha County*, 1982）。其他如朱炎老师有关福克纳（William Faulkner）的研究涉及黑白种族问题，[1]李有成于 20 世纪 70 年代后期对于犹太裔美国作家贝娄（Saul Bellow）的研究以及 20 世纪 80 年代中期起对于非裔美国自传、文学批评与文化评论的研究。因此，华裔美国文学之研究可说是此一传统的延续与拓展。

再者，为了加强与国际学界的合作，美国文化研究所于 1989 年曾与来访的加州大学洛杉矶校区（University of California, Los Angeles）亚美研究学者成露茜（Lucie Cheng）举行座谈会，并于 1989 年 5 月 26 日的人文组座谈会中决议，关于本组与成露茜教授之合作研究计划："讨论结果认为以'华人文学'为研究主题较妥。并拟以公开征选之方式延聘研究'华人文学'之学者进入本组，参与研究。"此一合作研究计划，除了社经组的郭实渝前往该校进行研究，并出版《由台湾前往美国的"小留学生"问题之研究》（1992）之外并无其他较具体的成果。

20 世纪 90 年代初，李有成与笔者分别结束在美国的傅尔布莱特博士后研究（Fulbright post-doctoral research）返所，曾于《美国研究》刊登过非裔与华裔美国文学比较研究的何文敬于 1992 年初加入本所，文学同仁便积极思索开拓此一研究领域。[2]为了因应英美学术

1　如《美国文学评论集》（1976）收录的九篇论文中，有四篇讨论福克纳：《美的丧失与复活——福克纳的痴人狂喧》、《黑色十字架——福克纳八月之光中黑人的意象》、《福克纳黑人意象的雏形》与《白神之死》。二十二年后根据前书增订出版的《海明威·福克纳·厄卜代克：美国小说阐论》（1998）的《前言》提到，他在台大外文研究所开过"美国文学中的黑人意象"等专题研究（1）。该书收录二十篇论文，其中"福克纳篇"收录五篇论文（包括前书四篇论文），三篇比先前更凸显黑人意象：《黑色的十字架：福克纳〈八月之光〉中的黑人意象》、《福克纳黑人意象的离形》与新添的《福克纳小说中的黑人意象》。《福克纳黑人意象的离形》与《白神之死》二文在刊登于《中外文学》之前，先以英文刊登于美国文化研究 所出版的《美国研究》（*American Studies*）季刊，标题为"The Embryonic Image of Faulkner's Negro: Sartoris"与"Death of a White God: Absalom, Absalom！。

2　李有成1988至1989年在杜克大学（Duke University）钻研法兰克福学派、西方马克思主义与后现代主义，并有系统地阅读后殖民主义与非裔美国文学理论和批评。笔者1989至1990年在加州大学尔湾校区英文暨比较文学系（Department of English and Comparative Literature, University of California, Irvine）研究访问期间，曾于1990年春季班在该系兼任教师，讲授中西叙事文学比较研究，在课堂上曾讲解汤亭亭（Maxine Hong Kingston）的成名作《女勇士》（*The Woman Warrior*），带入中国文学与比较文学的观点，学生反应热烈。何文敬（Wen-ching Ho）的论文为"In Search of a Female Self: Toni Morrison's *The Bluest Eye* and Maxine Hong Kingston's *The Woman Warrior*"（《追求女性的自我：童妮·墨莉生的〈黑与白〉和汤亭亭的〈女战士〉》）'*American Studies*（《美国研究》）17·3（Sept. 1987）：1-44。

思潮，强化国际竞争力，提升在国内外学界的可见度，善用我国的学术利基，便决定在本所以往的美国文学研究的基础上，推动华裔美国文学研究，除了个人投入研究之外，并以召开研讨会的方式来建立学术社群。

就推动学术与召开会议的策略而言，大致分为两阶段。第一阶段可称为"培元固本"，目标在于提倡风气，培养年轻学者与研究生的兴趣，使华美文学研究在我国生根，因此先从国内研讨会开始，以中文为会议语言，邀请相关学者宣读论文（首次研讨会并举行座谈会）。为了加强与国外学者的联系，并且邀请具有代表性的华裔美国学者与会，宣读论文。此阶段总共举行三次研讨会：第一次的主题为"文化属性与华裔美国文学"（Cultural Identity and Chinese American Literature, 1993），邀请加州大学洛杉矶校区的张敬珏（King-Kok Cheung）与会；第二次的主题为"再现政治与华裔美国文学"（Politics of Representation and Chinese American Literature, 1995），邀请威斯康星大学麦迪逊校区（University of Wisconsin-Madison）的林英敏（Amy Ling）以及著名华美作家汤亭亭与会；第三次的主题为"创造传统与华裔美国文学"（Invention of Tradition and Chinese American Literature, 1997），邀请加州大学柏克莱校区（University of California, Berkeley）的黄秀玲（Sau-ling Cynthia Wong）与会。

为了配合首次会议的进行，笔者事先与张敬珏进行英文书面访谈，将其中译发表于当年二月号的《中外文学》月刊，[1] 为会议暖身，并在会前1993年2月25日于《自立早报》副刊发表《华裔美国文学在台湾》一文，说明此次会议的意义，如今看来其中的论点大多依然成立，如除了"就文学的角度来讨论"之外，"其实华裔美国文学可以置于不同的脉络（如美国华人社会、美国华人移民史、海外华人研究、弱势论述、后殖民论述等）而建构出不同的意义"。文中也特别提到以中文作为会议语言，"这种行为本身就具有相当的意义，而且也是使学术研究本土化的具体实践"。这种以中文论文让学术扎根本土的做法，早见于外文学界前辈学者朱立民老师与颜元叔老师的大力提倡，而在美国文学研究上执行最有力的就是朱炎老师，不但迭有著作，而且不少重要的论文都分别以中英文出版。[2]

前两次会议论文经审查后由笔者与何文敬合编，附上编者的绪论，笔者与张敬珏和汤亭亭的访谈录，以及台湾地区华裔美国文学研究的书目提要，由欧美研究所出版论文集《文化属性与华裔美国文学》（1994）与《再现政治与华裔美国文学》（1996）。由于是华文世界头两本以华裔美国文学为主题的学术书籍，开风气之先，为相关学者多所引用，发

---

1 除了发表中译版，英文原版刊登于《淡江评论》："An Interview with King-Kok Cheung," *Tamkang Review* 24.1（Autumn 1993）: 1-20，运用中英双语的推动方式以利于本土与国际的接轨。

2 1972年台大文学院院长朱立民老师与台大外文系主任颜元叔老师联手创立的《中外文学》，就是台湾学界推动外国文学研究扎根中文世界的最佳例证，四十多年来于华文文学与文化界影响深远。朱炎老师的英文论文大都刊登于《美国研究》，中文论文大都刊登于《中外文学》，先结集出版为《美国文学评论集》，后来增订为《海明威·福克纳·厄卜代克》。有关朱炎老师的学术综合评述，参阅何敬《探道索艺，"情系文心"：朱炎教授的美国文学研究》。

挥了相当的影响。尔后台湾的学术风气偏向于期刊论文,因此第三次的会议论文经审查后纳入《欧美研究》季刊的"创造传统与华裔美国文学"专题(2002),并由笔者撰写绪论。

由于这三次会议是华文世界率先以华美文学为主题的研讨会,因此会议颇受瞩目,报名人员参加踊跃,讨论热烈,会后并出版论文集与期刊专题,几年间便使得华美文学研究成为外文学门的热门领域,出现了不少学术论文,许多研究生也以此撰写学位论文,以致相关研究顺利在台湾生根与成长。[1] 此外,由于会议论文具有一定的质量,会场讨论热烈,令在场的华裔美国学者与作家印象深刻,透过他们的口碑,如预期般地为台湾的华美文学研究打造出更大的发展空间。

第二阶段可称为"拓外惠中",也就是在先前打下的基础上,借由举行国际会议,以英文为会议语言,提供交流平台,让国内外学者相互切磋,并阔彼此的视野,并提升本所在国际上的可见度。另一个重大的变革就是会议主题的拓展,为了配合本所的属性、同仁的兴趣以及国内的研究与教学环境,将原先的华美文学扩展到亚美文学与亚英文学(Asian British literature),先后召开了下列的国际研讨会,这种亚美文学与亚英文学兼筹并顾的取向,即使今日在国际上依然颇为罕见:

1999 "Remapping Chinese America: An International Conference on Chinese American Literature"(重绘华美图志:华裔美国文学国际研讨会);

2003 "Negotiating the Past: An International Conference on Asian British and Asian American Literatures"(与过去协商:亚裔英美文学国际研讨会);

2008 "In the Shadows of Empires: The Second International Conference on Asian British and Asian American Literatures"(在帝国的阴影下:第二届亚裔英美文学国际研讨会);

2011 "War Memories: The Third International Conference on Asian British and Asian American Literatures"(战争记忆:第三届亚裔英美文学国际研讨会)。[2]

由以上回顾可看出欧美研究所二十多年来对于相关领域的投入与发展策略。至于亚美文学,尤其是华美文学,在台湾的发展,冯品佳的近作提供了自 1981 年至 2012 年的数据。

---

[1] 有关2000年之前台湾出版的华裔美国文学研究之中英文学术论文与学位论文,参阅笔者编撰的《台湾地区华裔美国文学研究书目提要》。此书因提要附录于1994年出版的《文化属性与华裔美国文学》(195–208),其增订版附录于1996年出版的《再现政治与华裔美国文学》(223–243)与2000年笔者出版的《铭刻与再现:华裔美国文学与文化论集》(365–387),三本书里的中文论文分别为16篇、31篇、37篇,英文论文分别为17篇、21篇、28篇,学位论文分别为6篇、11篇、20篇,数量之增加明显可见。

[2] 欧美研究所将于今(2015)年12月18、19日举办 "Re-visioning Activism: The Fourth International Conference on Asian British and Asian American Literatures"(重观行动主义:第四届亚裔英美文学国际研讨会),回应当前的关切,将触角伸展到另一个议题。

表一：台湾的亚美文学期刊与博硕士论文（1981–2012）[11]

中文期刊论文		博士论文		硕士论文	
华美文学	其他亚裔	华美文学	其他亚裔	华美文学	其他亚裔
156	53	8	2	104	20
209		10		124	

表二：台湾的亚美文学研究成果

	其他亚裔	华美文学	比例（其他亚裔 / 其他亚裔 + 华裔文学）
1980 年代	0	9	0%
1990 年代	13	80	14%
2000-2012 年	62	179	26%
合计	75	268	22%

　　从表一可看出中文期刊论文以及博、硕士论文中的华美文学与其他亚美文学的统计数字。表二则以十年为单位，显示华美文学与其他亚美文学的资料与比例，可看出一方面华美文学研究在数量上急速增加，另一方面其他亚美文学的比例由 20 世纪 50 年代挂零，尔后逐渐攀升，见证了国内学者在亚美文学研究上逐渐趋于多元的可喜现象。这些资料证明"利基"之说绝非一厢情愿的想法，而是的确有其根据与效应，值得再接再厉，继续发挥。[2]

三、台湾学界的发展与反思

　　台湾的亚美文学研究在二十年间累积了丰硕的成果，成为外文学界的显学，在华文学界与国际学术社群享有相当的知名度，但相关学者不以此自满，一直抱持着高度自省的态度，不仅从自己的发言位置来了解在此地从事此一研究的意义，也试图从学科的流传与国际的版图加以定位与评估，作为进一步发展的参考。[3] 相较于外文学门其他领域，亚美文学研究很可能是最自我反思的领域，相关讨论屡见不鲜，例如笔者的《华裔美国文学

1　此二表分别来自 Pin-chia Feng（冯品佳），"East Asian Approaches to Asian American Literary Studies: The Cases of Japan, Taiwan, and South Korea", 55 页 265和266，由笔者中译。

2　就笔者实际观察，此现象并不限于台湾，如韩国学者着重于韩美文学研究，日本学者着重于日美文学研究，中国大陆学者更是偏重于华美文学研究……

3　笔者强调台湾的华美/亚美文学研究者的双语言与双文化背景，并将此特殊发言位置描述为"既处于二者（中、美两个文化霸权）的交集之下，也与二者各有距离。这种既相交又逾越的位置，创造出第三空间，不断摆荡并游离于两个中心及其边缘"（单，《铭》26）。

的定位 —— 一个台湾学者的观察》(1999)、"Positioning Chinese American Literature — A Perspective from Taiwan"(2000)《冒现的文学/研究:"台湾"的亚美文学研究 —— 兼论美国原住民文学研究》(2001)、张锦忠的《检视华裔美国文学在台湾的建制化(1981—2001)》(2001)、王智明的《亚美研究在台湾》(2004)、笔者的《从边缘到交集:探寻美国华文文学的位置》(2005)、冯品佳的《世界英文文学的在地化:新兴英文文学与美国弱势族裔文学研究在台湾》(2006)、笔者的《台湾的华裔美国文学研究:回顾与展望》(2006)、王智明的 "Thinking and Feeling Asian America in Taiwan"(2007)、笔者的 "Branching Out: Chinese American Literary Studies in Taiwan"(2007)、张锦忠的 "The Institutionalization of Asian American Literary Studies in Taiwan: A Diasporic Sinophone Malaysian Perspective"(2012)、李秀娟的《"欧美"与"我们"之间:从亚美研究看美 —— 亚的距离与传会》(2014)、冯品佳的 "East Asian Approaches to Asian American Literary Studies: The Cases of Japan, Taiwan, and South Korea"(2014)等。这些后设批评也见于学位论文,如清华大学外文研究所吴贞仪(Wu Chen-yi)的硕士论文 "利基想象的政治:殖民性的问题与台湾的亚美文学研究(1981-2010)"("Politics of Niche Imagination: The Question of Coloniality and Asian American Literary Studies in Taiwan, 1981—2010", 2013,王智明指导),该论文附录吴贞仪与笔者的访谈,经修订后出版为《亚美文学研究在台湾:单德兴教授访谈录》(2013)。

相关期刊专号、专题或专辑也见于张琼惠与张锦忠为《中外文学》编辑的 "亚美文学专号"(2001),笔者为《欧美研究》编辑的 "创造传统与华裔美国文学专题"(2002)以及为《中外文学》编辑的 "美国华文文学专题"(2005),李秀娟为《中外文学》编辑的 "亚美的多元地方想象专题"(2006),王智明为《亚际文化研究》(Inter-Asia Cultural Studies)编辑的 "亚美研究在亚洲"(Asian American Studies in Asia)专辑(2012),张琼惠为《同心圆》(Concentric)编辑的 "幽灵亚美"(Phantom Asian America)专辑(2013)等。这些期刊与后设批评证明了相关学者对此领域的持续关切与反思。

此外,王智明分别于 2010 年在欧美研究所举办 "亚美研究在亚洲:国际工作坊"(Asian American Studies in Asia: An International Workshop),2012 年举办 "我们的'欧美'":文本、理论、问题、学术研讨会(Our Euro-America: Texts, Theories, and Problematics),顾名思义便可看出这两个国际工作坊与研讨会的焦点在于欧美/亚美研究中的亚洲视野与在地观点。再者,冯品佳担任国科会文学二(外文学门)召集人时,建请人文处积极推动亚美文学研究与国际策略联盟。自 2013 年起,接连三年分别于 "中央研究院" 欧美研究所、清华大学与台湾师范大学举行亚美研究暑期研习营(Summer Institute in Asian American Studies),为国际上此一领域的创举,在国科会/科技部大力支持下,由冯品佳、傅士珍、李秀娟、王智明、柏逸嘉(Guy Beauregard)等人筹划,逐年针对亚洲、帝国、人权等不同议题 —— "Asian American Studies Through Asia: Fields, Formations, Futures"(2013),

"Empire Reconsidered"（2014）与 "The Subject（s）of Human Rights"（2015）—— 邀请学有专精的美国与亚洲学者担任主讲人，为数十位国际学员进行三天的密集演讲、讨论与交流。主讲人与学员多能体认在亚洲 / 台湾从事亚美文学研究，确实有异于美国及亚洲其他地方之处，对于彼此的在地关怀也有第一手的了解。此项活动三年来颇受主讲人与国际学员的肯定，至今（2015）年完成其阶段性任务。

与亚洲学者的策略联盟也日益加强，近三年来分别于韩国光州的全南大学举办 "当前东亚的亚美研究"（Current Asian American Studies in East Asia）研讨会（2013，由韩国学者李所姬〔So-Hee Lee〕筹办），于日本东京的明治大学举办 "亚美文学与亚洲：公民权、历史、记忆、外交"（Asian American Literature and Asia: Citizenship, History, Memory, Diplomacy）研讨会（2014，由日本学者佐藤〔Gayle Sato〕筹办），于台湾的高雄师范大学举办 "亚 / 美文学与亚洲：教学、历史、记忆"（Asian/American Literature and Asia: Pedagogy, History, Memories）研讨会（2015，由我国学者李翠玉筹办），都吸引不少亚洲学者参加，除了一般亚美文学的议题之外，特别强调从亚际的角度来探讨亚美文学研究，以及亚洲不同国家相关研究的异同，其成因、过程与效应，以收攻错之效。

同时我国学者也积极向欧美国际迈进，以此领域最具代表性的两个学会为例，每届在美国举行的亚美研究学会（Association for Asian American Studies〔AAAS〕）年会以及在欧洲举行的欧美多族裔研究学会（The Society for Multi-Ethnic Studies: Europe and the Americas〔MESEA〕）双年会，台湾学者不但无会不与，而且人数经常为亚洲之冠，以坚强的学术实力和积极主动的参与，和国外学者建立起紧密的关系，若干学者且进入这两个学会的委员会，实际参与组织运作。

总之，借由稳扎稳打的策略与多年持续的努力，台湾学者逐渐累积出在此一领域的学术实力与可见度，而欧美研究所在其中扮演的角色在国内外有目共睹。因此，本所国外咨询委员、美国研究学会（American Studies Association）前会长费雪金（Shelley Fisher Fishkin）在 2015 年致本所的咨询委员报告中指出："全球对于亚美研究的兴趣与日俱增，从这个立场来看，将亚洲观点带入其对话，是‘中央研究院’特别值得扮演的角色"（"From the standpoint of a growing interest globally in Asian American Studies, bringing Asian perspectives into that conversation is a particularly valuable role for Academia Sinica to play."[2]）。此一观察与肯定正是欧美研究所文学同仁自 1990 年代以来努力的目标，此后也将在已有的基础上，与国内外的学者及年轻学子继续努力。

四、他者论述，论述他者

2013 年举办的 "他者与亚美文学" 研讨会距离本所初次举办华美文学研讨会整整二十年，距离上次以中文举办的华美文学会议也有十六年之久。在这些年之间，国内外的美国研究与亚美文学研究出现了若干重大的转变。首先,就美国而言,美国研究学会与亚美研究学会近年来摆脱本土独大的心态,将视野扩及世界各地,强调"国际转向"(international turn),而在亚美研究方面尤其重视"亚洲转向"(Asian turn),主动加强与亚洲学者的联系与交流,并重视双语言与双文化的能力。其次,亚洲各国学者有感于对美国学界熟悉的程度往往远超过对亚洲邻国的认识,因而逐渐重视亚际的关系,形成正式或非正式的策略联盟,一方面从各自的立足点出发,寻求发挥自己的特色,另一方面共同向美国主流学界进军,强化彼此的互动,甚至在美国的学术组织中扮演一定的角色,提供亚洲的观点,使其胸襟更为开阔,视野更为多元,运作更为灵活,影响更为扩大,以达到互惠的目标。

再就华文世界而言,亚美文学研究以台湾与中国大陆为主,尤其由于语言与文化的缘故,更集中于华美文学。台湾这些年来由于积极提倡,出现了不少学术论文、学位论文、专书与翻译,成为外文学界的显学,不仅在数量上超过其他的美国族裔文学(包括起步较早的非裔美国文学),在声势上往往也超过主流的白人文学,晚近则更为多元,扩及日裔、韩裔、菲裔、南亚裔美国文学等,在相关背景的掌握与理论的运用上更为熟练。因此中国大陆学者多次在公开与私人场合坦言,其华美与亚美文学研究大致始于21世纪初,落后台湾整整十年,起步时借镜台湾学术之处甚多,尤以前述《文化属性与华裔美国文学》与《再现政治与华裔美国文学》二书最为显著。然而大陆学界人多势众,投入大量资源(包括国家型研究计划),相关学术活动众多,再加上大学与民间出版社的支持,论著与翻译的数量众多。反观台湾,由于研究人口相对较少,学术把关严谨,加上出版社的市场考量,相关出版品在数量上已被超越。面对海峡两岸的学术竞争,台湾必须精益求精,扩大视野,慎选议题,掌握学术品量,力求精实,以期维持一定的特色与优势。置于上述脉络中,2013年9月欧美研究所举办的"他者与亚美文学"研讨会的意义更为明显。

古往今来,"识己"("Know thyself")以及自他之间的关系都是个人与团体的重要课题,而自我的认知往往来自与他者的对照、对比,甚至对立而来。其实,自我与他者或异己之间的关系并非固定不变,而是具有相当的流变性。以许倬云的《我者与他者:中国历史上的内外分际》为例,自史前时代讨论到当代,上下数千年。该书〈引言〉指出:"所谓'中——外'关系,若从日常语言的含意看,当是一个国家或一个文化系统,在面临'他者'时'自——他'之间的互动。……不论是作为政治性的共同体,抑或文化性的综合体,'中国'是不断变化的系统,不断发展的秩序,这一个出现于东亚的'中国',有其自己发展与舒卷的过程,也因此不断有不同的'他者'界定其'自身'"(26)。在《周代封建的天下》一章中,他引用汤恩比(Arnold Toynbee)有关"内在的普罗"(the Internal Proletariat)与"外在的普罗"(the External Proletariat)之说,表示这两个相对于"当权的少数"(the Dominant Minority)的他者,"与诸侯国内的'他者',及华夏世界之外的'他者',颇可互相比较。无论内外的他者,都衬托了'我人'的内部凝聚"(43)。此书固然是由群体的角度探讨，但对于该群体内的个体之自我认知，以及自他与内外关系的厘清与流变，颇有值得参考之处。

他者的议题不仅源远流长，更有强烈的现实意义，可谓自古已有，于今尤烈。晚近由于全球化的缘故，不同地区之间各种资源的流动更是频繁，人流、金流、物流、信息流等达到史无前例的高峰，各种固有的疆界频频遭到挑战与跨越，不同族群与团体之间的接触益形频繁，摩擦、冲突、甚至流血事件时有所闻，有识之士纷纷对此表示关切，并提供自己的观察与省思。李有成在《他者》一书的〈绪论〉中便指出："早在一九八〇与九〇年代，克莉丝蒂娃（Julia Kristeva）就一再析论陌生人的角色；德希达（Jacques Derrida）也反复讨论如何待客，如何悦纳异己；列维纳斯（Emmanuel Lévinas）则以伦理学为其哲学重心，畅论自我对他者的责任；哈贝玛斯（Jürgen Habermas）更主张要包容他者。这些论述或思想之出现并非偶然，其背后应该有相当实际的现实基础与伦理关怀"（15）。

有关他者的议题，在亚美研究萌生时便居于重要的地位，尔后屡见不鲜，晚近的研究可以刘大伟（David Palumbo-Liu）的"他者递送系统"（the system of the deliverance of others）之说为代表。如陈淑卿在本书收录的论文中指出："他者递送系统是现成的、经过制码的论述、结构与体制，当此系统将他者呈现在吾人面前时，同时通过对沟通语言及行为的制约，将他者的他者性去除，使其合于社会需求（Palumbo-Liu 10）"（174）。值得一提的是，由此引申出的"内部他者"（the inside other）与"外部他者"（the outside other）之说，与前述汤恩比和许倬云的论点颇有相通之处，可见此一现象由来已久，中外皆然。

有鉴于这个议题的重要性，此次会议特地以"他者与亚美文学"为主题。首先，不论就历史或现实而言，相对于白人，亚裔在美国的处境有如非我族类的他者，富裕承平时尚可能相安无事，但主流社会出现问题时，亚裔经常就沦为代罪羔羊，最明显的就是1882年的《排华法案》（*Chinese Exclusion Act*），是美国历史上唯一针对单一族裔而通过的排除法案，以及第二次世界大战时，美国政府将日裔美国人强行迁徙，集中安置（Japanese American internment），这些固然都成为亚美人士的集体创伤与记忆，也是美国历史上令人羞愧的事件。而亚美文学的产生，相对于美国主流文学、其他族裔文学，甚至相当多元的亚美文学内部，也往往处于他者的地位。因此，这次会议的征稿启事对于亚美文学有如下的描述："相对于强势的英美主流文学与文化，亚美文学往往是以他者（the other）的姿态出现。而相对于美国其他弱势族裔，彼此之间也时常以他者相看待。再就亚美文学内部而言，也存在着不同的历史脉络、文化政治与权力关系。"

其次，相对于美国的亚美研究者，亚洲的亚美研究者具有不同的文化资本与发言位置，多少有如他者。再者，亚洲学者之间由于各自不同的历史、国族与文化背景，往往也成为彼此眼中的他者，必须透过英文的中介才能彼此沟通。这正是征稿启事中所指出的："当亚美文学跨出了美国，而到达其他地区，尤其是亚洲时，其处境与关系更形复杂。不同亚洲国家的学者对于亚美文学时时抱持不同的想象,除了以一般亚洲的角度来观察亚美文学之外,更常是从自己的国族、文化、文学、历史、政治、地缘等背景来观察并反思亚美文学。"当选择以中文为会议语言、以华文世界的学者与读者为对象时,进一步出现了征稿启事中所提到的值得思索的议题:"具有中英双语能力的学者在面对亚美文学时,其发言位置如何?有何利基?如何将其置于英语语系文学与华文世界?"

五、他者与亚美文学

这次会议以"他者与亚美文学"为主题,一方面与先前的"文化属性""再现政治""创造传统"等议题有一脉相承之处,因为自他之关系与认定涉及文化属性与认同,其再现涉及彼此之间的权力关系与阶序,而再现的起始、过程与结果往往又涉及传统之承袭、转化与创新。另一方面,此会议有意扩及新的议题,如征稿启事就建议了十多项议题:"亚美文学与他者,亚美文学作为他者,亚美文学与美国主流文学的关系,亚美文学中的主流社会形象,亚美文学与其他美国弱势族裔文学的关系,亚美文学中所呈现的弱势族裔,亚美文学与英语语系文学的关系,亚美文学与华文文学的关系,亚美文学与亚洲文学的关系,跨太平洋之后的亚美文学,美国作为他者,亚洲作为他者,作为他者的华裔/日裔/菲裔/韩裔……"。

主办单位安排本所李有成特聘研究员发表主题演讲,并特邀周英雄教授主持。李有成于2012年出版《他者》一书,颇受华文学界瞩目,甚至被国家文官学院选为每月一书,除了应邀到国家文官学院针对我国文官演讲,并远赴偏乡为基层公务人员演讲相关议题,结合了学术研究与公众事务参与。周英雄教授是我国英美文学与比较文学的资深学者,曾数度担任本所咨询委员,更是李有成大学时代的英文老师与文学启蒙师。在场人士包括了国内外学者与研究生,出现"四代同堂"的盛况。由于使用中文讨论,与会者更能畅所欲言,会场气氛热烈,每个场次的讨论都欲罢不能,延续到茶叙与用餐时间。为了发挥更广泛的影响力,论文修订稿依本所标准作业程序送交《欧美研究》季刊编辑委员会,经审查后结集出版。

本书总共收录六篇论文,每篇论文各有其关怀与特色,因为议题多元,内容繁复,所以依照被讨论的作家的生年顺序排列。冯品佳的《阅读罗丽塔之外:伊朗裔美国移民女性回忆录书写》,探讨的是21世纪出版的三部伊朗裔美国女性移民的回忆录:卡夏华兹(Fatemeh Keshavarz)的《茉莉与星辰:在德黑兰不只阅读'罗丽塔'》(*Jasmine and Stars: Reading More Than Lolita in Tehran*, 2007)、芮琪琳的《波斯女孩》(Nahid Rachlin, *Persian Girls: A Memoir*, 2006)以及纳菲西的《我所缄默的事》(Azar Nafisi, *Things I've Been Silent About*, 2008)。这些书在纳菲西畅销的第一本回忆录《在德黑兰读罗丽塔》(*Reading*

Lolita in Tehran, 2003）之后相继出版，反映了西方世界对于伊朗裔美国女性回忆录的浓厚兴趣。[1] 如果说《茉莉与星辰》（其副标题明言《在德黑兰不只阅读'罗丽塔'》）是直接响应并辩驳《在德黑兰读罗丽塔》，那么资深小说家芮琪琳的自述《波斯女孩》则属间接委婉的回应，而《我所缄默的事》则借由提供前一本《在德黑兰读罗丽塔》中未叙之事，补充先前的生命书写，并回应外界的质疑。早期华美女作家也多有自述之作，甚至因此遭到华美男作家的批评（最明显的例子就是汤婷婷与赵健秀〔Frank Chin〕之争，已成为华美/亚美文学的历史公案）。相较于华美女作家所承受的双重压抑（族裔与性别），伊朗裔美国女作家更承受了三重压抑（族裔、性别与宗教）。冯文首先爬梳了有关伊朗裔美国文学以及女性生命书写的论述，接着逐一解读三部作品，讨论"族裔身份与再现政治"（1,3）的议题（与先前两次"文化属性"与"再现政治"的会议主题若合符节），进而探究"自我东方化"（self-orientalization）的争议。此文的开创性贡献在于将亚美文学研究的视野拓展到西亚的伊朗，因为"作为亚裔美国研究学者，我们没有理由画地自限于太平洋地区，应该正视及重视中亚与西亚地区族裔在亚美研究中的地位"（2），此呼吁值得我们严肃以待。

　　笔者与陈重仁的论文不约而同探讨哈金（Ha Jin）有关华美离散社群（Chinese American diasporic community）的小说。哈金先前以非母语写作中国相关的作品，屡获美国的代表性文学奖项，成为华美作家中的异数（anomaly）。近年来他将笔锋转向美国华人离散社群，先后写出了长篇小说《自由生活》（*A Free Life*, 2007）与短篇小说集《落地》（*A Good Fall*, 2009）。笔者的《他者·诗作·自由：解读哈金的〈自由生活〉》从离散与他者的角度切入，结合相关论述（包括哈金本人的评论集《在他乡写作》〔*The Writer as Migrant*, 2008〕）以及笔者与哈金的访谈，指出《自由生活》以巴斯特纳克的《齐瓦哥医生》（Boris Pasternak, *Dr, Zhivago*，1957）为互文（intertext），将坚持写作理想的男主角武男（Nan Wu），呈现为相对于故国、美国与物质主义的多重他者，具有一定程度的自传色彩，有如"一位以英文写作之离散华人诗人的画像（'A portrait of the poet as a diasporic Chinese writing in English'）"（44）。全书大半描述武男的外在遭遇与心路历程，书末附加的武男的诗话与诗作是哈金个人小说中的首创，为先前的叙事呈现具体的结果。论文之末分析这些诗作的意义，它们与叙事的相互呼应，并且置于哈金的创作与论述脉络中，呈现了武男（以及哈金）作为"在他乡以非母语写作的他者"（40），其中涉及的忠诚、家园、美国梦及其不满等议题，以及如何在诗歌写作（文学创作）中获得自由，进入"文字花环编织的家园"（64），以期在康拉德（Joseph Conrad）和纳博科夫（Vladimir Nabokov）树

1　《在德黑兰读罗丽塔》原书出版次年，台湾便出版了朱孟勋的中译本（台北：时报文化，2004），并于七年后出版同是由朱孟勋中译的《我所缄默的事》（台北：时报文化，2011）。至于《茉莉与星辰》与《波斯女孩》在台湾则未见中译本上市。

立的非母语之英文文学传统中发挥特色，翻转出新意，为英文增添活力。

陈重仁的《"美国给我的最好的东西"：〈落地〉的离散记忆与创造性乡愁》，在旁征博引、广泛讨论多位学者有关离散、记忆、乡愁等论述之后，拈出"创造性乡愁"（"creative nostalgia"）一词，强调其所具有的开放性、积极性、批判性、建设性，并以此解读《落地》中所呈现的纽约新华埠法拉盛（Flushing）的华人众生相。陈文透过绵密的理论铺陈与细致的文本分析，解读哈金的短篇小说集如何依循乔埃斯的《都柏林人》（James Joyce, *Dubliners* 1914）以及安德森的《小城畸人》（Sherwood Anderson, *Winesburg, Ohio,* 1919）的写作传统，刻画出聚居于法拉盛的华人离散故事。故事中的主人翁都来自中国，背景分歧，能力不一，职业迥异，之所以远赴异乡，是因为美国这块机会之地（the Land of Opportunity）、应许之地（the Promised Land）提供了新契机、新名字、新身份、甚至新面孔，亦即〈美人〉中的女主人翁吉娜（Gina）所说的，"美国给我的最好的东西"。然而这些"最好的东西"并非凭空而来，也不是没有代价，因为在将他乡打造成家园的过程中，往往是对记忆与乡愁的压抑与转化，推挤于故土与新乡之间的华人难逃"双向他者的宿命"（75）。其中的成功者往往过着兢兢业业、谨小慎微的日子（如〈英语教授〉中申请终身教职审查的唐陆生），失败者的命运则更为悲惨，难容于新土，却又不愿或无法回归故乡（如〈耻辱〉中的南京大学美国学教授孟富华）。透过哈金这位"离散作家中介游离的特殊角度"（75，79），《落地》呈现了法拉盛华人社群的移民梦或梦魇，其所具现的"离散记忆与创造性乡愁"（75），提供了美国梦的另类视角与版本。

吴慧娟的《亚/美文学的他者：李昌来的〈悬空〉》以郊区叙事文体（suburban narrative）的角度切入，探讨韩美作家李昌来的长篇小说《悬空》（Chang-rae Lee, *Aloft*, 2004）。此文首先讨论郊区叙事文体，说明其特色，将《悬空》纳入此一文学传统中，并试图就题材与内容来扩大亚美文学的范畴。吴文指出，"郊区叙事作为小说的次文类，所捕捉和描述的正是在第二次世界大战后，兴起于美国郊区的小区开发和生活形态……一方面见证了美国战后的经济发展以及社会阶层流动，另一方面将白人中产阶级塑造成一个特殊的"族裔"群体，生产与复制了美国文化想象中的中产阶级家庭。……郊区地理景观中的房子和以家庭为中心的生活方式成了美国梦的表征"（129-130）。然而，李昌来挪用这种以白人中产阶级家庭为主轴的次文类来撰写第三部长篇小说，以非亚裔美国人为主角，一方面进入并"颠覆这个由白人作家，如刘易斯（Sinclair Lewis）、厄普代克（John Updike）、契弗（John Cheever），以及叶慈（Richard Yates）所建立的文类传统"（131），另一方面也面对了个人身为亚美作家的"转变与创新"127以及亚美文学的界定。全文将《悬空》置于郊区叙事的文学传统与文化脉络中，探讨此一主题与主角皆异于一般认知的亚美文学作品，视其为"越界的文本"（"transgressive text"）（128n），解析其作为"亚/美文学的他者"（123）的处境，以及可能带来的省思。

陈淑卿的《经济、生命与情感：王瀚〈风水行骗〉中的亚美他者与族裔扮演》从美国新自由主义（neoliberalism）与多元文化主义（multiculturalism）的角度切入，尤其着重于柔性族裔治理，指向一种以市场逻辑与理性选择来形塑或界定他者"（174），并将菲美作家王瀚的《风水行骗》（Han Ong, *Fixer Chao*, 2002）置于此脉络中加以探讨。文中引用了亚美批评家刘大伟的"他者递送系统"与维多利亚文学专家嘉乐格（Catherine Gallagher）的"生命经济情节"（bioeconomic plots）与"体感经济情节"（somaeconomic plots）等观念，并"以经济人的观点来讨论内部他者，从经济主体的角度来析论外部他者"（173n）。小说中的主人翁包灵华（William Narciso Paulinha）原为纽约底层的菲美男同志，具有"族裔、阶级及性取向各面向的多重他者身份"（180），却借由扮演华裔风水大师打入大都会的上流社会，甚至成为许多人的心灵上师，成功跨越了内部他者 / 外部他者以及他者 / 主流中心的分野，最后事迹败露，逃往加州，再次改名换姓，重新形塑自我。陈文技巧地结合理论的铺陈与文本的分析，解读《风水行骗》所凸显的美国社会里外部他者 / 内部他者 / 主流中心之间错综复杂的关系与逾越的可能，展现美国族裔之多元性以及亚美族裔之异质性，借以呈现"基进他者性"（radical otherness）的可能与限制。

李翠玉的《〈难言之隐〉：临界、创伤书写与亚美哥德志异叙事》探讨的是 1.5 代越南裔美国作家莫妮卡·张的第二部长篇小说《难言之隐》（Monique Truong, *Bitter in the Mouth*, 2010），借由被领养的主人翁琳达·汉莫力克（Linda Hammerick）为舅公哈珀（Harper）奔丧之旅，逐渐揭露 1.5 代越裔美国人的成长与处境。全文首先由哀悼（mourning）与创伤书写（trauma writing）的角度切入，指出此小说〔所探触的核心即是越战世代无以名之却如魔随形之创伤经验〕（205），而哀悼与创伤固然具有负面的作用，但也具有正面的意义。李文继而以临界（liminality）的观点来诠释女主角的处境，指出此书"有成长小说（*bildungsroman*）的外观"（210），而身为孤女的琳达则处于一个"转折空间；此一空间的特性是开放、模糊、流离、游移不定、介于其中（in-between）的文化混杂经验，诸如离散现象、战争遗孤或难民漂洋过海等均属于临界之状态"（210），无怪乎她有苦难言（即其英文书名）。文中援引黄福顺（Andrew Hock Soon Ng）有关哥德志异美学（Gothic aesthetics）与亚美文学的论述，指出"哥德志异传统所涵盖之主题，如压抑、离奇、悬疑、诡异、创伤、恐惧、人格分裂、暴力或鬼魂，无一不是后殖民文学或亚美文学念兹在兹，设譬取喻，抒情论理的母题"，而琳达的"自我东方化 / 鬼魅化"也强化了她的"东方化、边缘化的'脆弱主体'（vulnerable subject）位置"（219），以致沦为鬼魅般的他者。尽管如此，女主角依然能从美国早期移民英国孤女弗吉尼亚（VirginiaDare）的传说以及黑奴诗人荷登（George Moses Horton）的生平故事得到力量，"以伤痛的身体铭刻历史的沉郁，却以昂首之姿立誓驱向未来"（222），并具现了骆里山（LisaLowe）所指出的亚、非、欧、美四大洲之亲密联系（the intimacies of the four continents）。

这六篇论文从不同的角度出发，选择不同的文本，各自探讨与表述，呈现出丰饶多元的面貌，然而彼此之间也有相通之处。作为会议主题的"他者"自然是焦点之所在，因而出现了他者／她者（冯品佳）、多重他者（单德兴）、双向他者（陈重仁）、鬼魅他者（李翠玉）、亚／美文学的他者（吴慧娟）、甚至内部他者／外部他者（陈淑卿）等不同诠释与解读。这些不同类型的亚裔他者基本上都是相对于美国主流白人社会，不同的亚裔之间往往也互为他者，然而彼此之间的界线并非铁板一块，无法撼动或逾越，这点尤见于王瀚的《风水行骗》。

其次，这些亚裔角色之所以成为他者，都与各自的族裔离散经验密切相关，因此"离散"一词反复出现于多篇论文中（冯文与单文中更出现高达二三十次），成为"他者"之外的另一个重要议题。[1] 诸篇论文在各自的族裔与文本脉络下讨论不同的离散经验，其中笔者与陈重仁的论文花了相当篇幅探讨离散论述，作为各自立论的张本，而冯品佳对于伊朗裔美国文学的历史铺陈与文献探讨，更可增加读者对于这个冒现中的新领域及其离散经验的认识，拓展现今学界的视野。

这些不同的亚裔人士之所以离散到美国，有些出于自愿，有些则为环境所迫，以致成为他者，其实他们都怀抱着一定程度的美国梦，期盼能在这块机会之地、应许之地展开新生。如拒斥高压、封闭的伊朗的三位女作家，各自透过回忆录书写，期盼达到言论自由、宗教解放与性别平等；哈金笔下的华裔离散者希望得到政治解放、创作自由、经济自足、社会地位与安全感，甚至把新身份与新面孔视为"美国给我的最好的东西"；《风水行骗》中的菲裔主人翁原处于纽约大都会底层，却借由扮演华裔风水大师，由原先的亚裔他者摇身一变，成为出入于白人上层社会的名流，宛如新纪元运动的上师，靠着扮演另一个亚美他者而名利双收；《难言之隐》中的女主角原为越战孤儿，在寄养家庭中成长，就读耶鲁大学，后来在律师事务所工作。由这些人物看来，他们在相当程度上都达到了原先抱持的美国梦。

然而为了取得这些成就，这些亚裔移民付出了不少代价，最起码的就是离乡背井，成为异地的他者，某种程度的舍弃历史、遗忘过去在所难免，但乡愁也不可能全然抹杀，至于如何协商故土与新乡，甚至化他乡为家圈，都涉及对于忠诚与家园的重新认知。至于原先怀抱的美国梦若未能达到，便成为引诱他们陷入眼前困境的原因。另一方面，即使达到物质层面的满足，也可能会如哈金的《自由生活》中的武男般发现，不仅在一夕之间受到严重威胁（没有健康保险的妻子罹患重病），而且长久牺牲了自己的理想，于是幡然悔悟，另觅他途，以期安身立命；或如王瀚的《风水行骗》中的包灵华，一时靠着假冒而名利双收，但事迹败露后就得逃往异地。又如李昌来的《悬空》中以郊区住宅与中产家庭为代表

---

1 顺带一提的是，主题演讲者李有成在《他者》之后出版的专书即是《离散》，其论述有一脉相承之处。

的美国梦，也会因为家族成员投资失误而动摇，暴露出原先不曾察觉的脆弱。换言之，美国梦固然有吸引人之处，提供了起始的诱因，但能否达成，或者达成之后察觉其本质的脆弱，发现自己内心深处还有更殷切的期盼与更高超的理想，不愿自我设限于物质层面。至于未能达到起码目标的移民，这些美国梦则沦为挥之不去的梦魇，必须以离乡背井与格格不入作为代价，不知此生能否寻得安顿。因此，陈重仁与李翠玉引用佛洛伊德的哀悼／忧郁之说加以解析，李翠玉并进一步运用创伤论述，探讨透过书写达到疗愈的可能。

与美国梦相关的还有成功的亚裔移民可能成为美国主流社会眼中的模范少数族裔或模范弱势族裔（model minority）。然而这个表面上的良好评价其实是刻板印象，在以主流价值肯定他们的同时，也把他们定位为永远的他者，并使他们对立于其他成就较差的弱势族裔，甚至对立于自己族裔中未能达到此标准的成员，对于彼此都形成额外的压力。而在面对主流价值时，不论作家或笔下的人物都有可能落入自我东方化的陷阱，或遭到类似的质疑，怀疑他们以凸显自己的东方族裔特色来迎合主流社会之所好。冯品佳、陈淑卿与李翠玉的论文都触及这个议题，而哈金的作品有时也难免遭到类似的质疑，这些显然又涉及主流／他者之分，甚至内部他者／外部他者之别，个中关系错综复杂，有待仔细寻思。

六、继往与开来

从以上概述可知此论文集的大要以及反复出现的议题：他者、离散、乡愁、美国梦（魇）、创伤、疗愈、模范少数／弱势族裔、自我东方化……此外，与本所先前召开的华美／亚美／亚英会议相较，可看出其间的"亲密联系"与歧异之处。首先就世代而言，六位作者中既有筹划和参与第一届华裔美国文学会议的笔者，多次参加相关会议的资深学者（冯品佳与陈淑卿），青壮辈的学者（李翠玉与陈重仁），以及曾在先前会议中担任观察员、这次会议时仍是博士候选人、现任教于国立大学的新秀（吴慧娟），是名副其实的老中壮青学者的世代大结合。相较于1990年代的华美文学会议中多为同世代或年龄层相近的作者群，可以看出亚美文学研究在台湾经过二十多年的努力耕耘，不仅后继有人，而且蔚然成风，令人期待未来更精彩丰硕的成果。

六篇论文的内容更呈现了亚美文学的多元异质，除了两篇华裔美国文学的论文之外，其他四篇分别探讨了韩裔、菲裔、越裔、甚至伊朗裔美国文学（会场宣读的论文尚包括了印度裔与东南亚裔），在选材方面由早年独沽一味于华美文学（《文化属性与华裔美国文学》收录的七篇论文中，高达四篇集中于汤亭亭一人），到如今的众声喧哗，而且讨论的几乎都是近十年的文本，其间的差别不可以道里计。这一方面因为创作者的族裔背景更为多元，另一方面因为研究者的胸襟更为开阔，触角更为敏锐，反应更为迅速，才会有此繁花异果的现象。此外，近年来亚美文学的论述在国内外学界的努力耕耘下已蔚为大观，可资援引的理论与观念更形丰富,而研究者在理论的抉择上也与时俱进,在阐发上各擅胜场,为后来者打造出更宽阔的研究、教学与论述空间。

笔者于 2006 年的《台湾的华裔美国文学研究:回顾与展望》一文中曾表示,"国内学界若有意在此研究领域再创新猷,宜审慎考量以下诸项",并提出六项呼吁:(一)视野和主题的广化,(二)历史的深化与研究的脉络化,(三)理论的细致化与对反化,(四)手法的多样化与跨学门化,(五)目标的国际化与研究的全球化,(六)思维与发展的跨语文化(343-46)。这些观察也适用于台湾的亚美文学研究。由台湾近年来的亚美文学研究与国际学术交流来评断,第一、三、四、五、六项已有了长足的进步,第二项虽有进展,但仍存在着相当的成长空间。尽管如此,我们绝无自满之意,因为置于台湾的英美文学、外文学门、文学研究,甚至人文学的脉络下,台湾的亚美文学研究虽在群策群力下奠定了良好的基础,但依然不到而立之年,来日方长,未来发展不可限量。

身为台湾的文学学者、人文主义者与双语知识分子,之所以会多年投入亚美文学研究,除了个人的兴趣与选择之外,还涉及对族裔意识的警醒、对弱势团体的关切、对公理正义的寻思,以及对学术的关怀与介入。套用李有成的说法,对于他者以及亚美文学的探索,"在一个仍然充满偏见、愚昧、仇恨的世界里,这不仅是学术问题,也是伦理责任的问题"(23)。希望借由《他者与亚美文学》的出版,能对相关议题提出兼具国际与在地观点的探讨与论述。此书只是为台湾的亚美文学研究添加一小块砖,未来的宏伟殿堂仍待有志者永续经营。

引用书目

"中央研究院"欧美研究所"他者与亚美文学"学术研讨会征稿启事。2013 年 1 月 23 日。

中研院美文所人文组第三次座谈会会议记录。1989 年 5 月 26 日。

朱炎。《美国文学评论集》。台北:联经,1976。

——。《海明威·福克纳·厄卜代克:美国小说阐论》。台北:九歌,1998。

《孜孜走过四十年:欧美研究所的历史与展望,1972—2012》。"中央研究院"欧美研究所所史编纂委员会,魏良才主笔。台北:"中央研究院"欧美研究所,2012。

李有成。《他者》。台北:允晨文化,2012。

李翠玉。《〈难言之隐〉:临界、创伤书写与亚美哥德志异叙事》。《他者与亚美文学》,201-226。

何文敬。《探道索艺,"情系文心":朱炎教授的美国文学研究》。《在文学研究与文化研究之间:朱炎教授七秩寿庆论文集》。李有成、王安琪编。台北:书林,2006。349-377。

——、单德兴编。《再现政治与华裔美国文学》。台北:"中央研究院"欧美研究所,1994。

吴慧娟。《亚/美文学的他者:李昌来的〈悬空〉》。《他者与亚美文学》,123-163。

周英雄。《漫谈外文学门的生态》。《人文与社会科学简讯》2.3(1999 年 11 月):7-8。

陈重仁。《"美国给我的最好的东西":〈落地〉的离散记忆与创造性乡愁》。《他者与亚美文学》,75-121。

陈淑卿。《经济、生命与情感：王瀚〈风水行骗〉中的亚美他者与族裔扮演》。《他者与亚美文学》，165-99。

许倬云。《我者与他者：中国历史上的内外分际》。台北：时报文化，2009。

冯品佳。《阅读罗丽塔之外：伊朗裔美国移民女性回忆录书写》。《他者与亚美文学》，1-37。

单德兴。《他者·诗作·自由：解读哈金的〈自由生活〉》。《他者与亚美文学》，39-74。

——。《寂寞翻译事：刘绍铭访谈录》。《却顾所来径：当代名家访谈录》。台北：允晨文化，2014。269-306。

——。《越界与创新：亚美文学与文化研究》。台北：允晨文化，2008。

——。《铭刻与再现：华裔美国文学与文化论集》。台北：麦田，2000。

——。《华裔美国文学在台湾》。《自立早报》，1993 年 2 月 25 日，14 版。

——《台湾的华裔美国文学研究：回顾与展望》。《在文学研究与文化研究之间：朱炎教授七秩寿庆论文集》。李有成、王安琪编。台北：书林，2006。331-48。

—— 编。《他者与亚美文学》。台北："中央研究院"欧美研究所，2015。

—— 何文敬编。《文化属性与华裔美国文学》。台北："中央研究院"欧美研究所，1996。

赵绮娜。《美国政府在台湾的教育与文化交流活动（一九五一至一九七〇）》。《欧美研究》31.1（2001 年 3 月）：79-127。

Feng, Pin-chia（冯品佳）, "East Asian Approaches to Asian American Literary Studies: The Cases of Japan, Taiwan, and South Korea." *The Routledge Companion to Asian American and Pacific Islander Literature*. Ed. Rachel C. Lee. London and New York: Routledge, 2014. 257-267.

Fishkin, Shelley Fisher. "The Advisory Committee Report on the Institute of European and American Studies, Academia sinica." 9 June 2015. 4pp.

ACKNOWLEDGEMENTS

Temple University Press gives permission to reprint Elaine H. Kim, "Preface" *Asian American Literature: An Introduction to the Writings and Their Social Context.* Philadelphia: Temple UP, 1982, pp. xi-xix.© 1982 by Temple University. All rights reserved.

Taylor &Francis (Routledge) gives permission to reprint King-Kok Cheung, "The Woman Warrior versus the Chinaman Pacific: Must a Chinese American Critic Choose between Feminism and Heroism?" *Conflicts in Feminism*, edited by Marianne Hirsch and Evelyn Fox Keller. New York: Routledge, 1990, pp. 234-251. © 1990 by Taylor and Francis Books USA.

Lisa Lowe, "Heterogeneity, Hybridity, Multiplicity: Marking Asian American Differences."The essay first appeared in *Diaspora: A Journal of Transnational Studies*, vol 1, no. 1, 1991, pp. 24-43. (DOI: 10.1353/dsp.1991.0014). Reprinted with permission from University of Toronto Press (https://utpjournals.press).

Johns Hopkins University Press gives permission to reprint Susan Koshy, "The Fiction of Asian American Literature." *The Yale Journal of Criticism*, vol. 9, no. 2, 1996, pp. 315-342.© 1996 Yale University and The Johns Hopkins University Press.

University of Chicago Press gives permission to reprint Sau-ling Cynthia Wong, Jeffrey J. Santa Ana, "Gender and Sexuality in Asian American Literature." *Signs: Journal of Women in Culture and Society*, 25 Jan.1999, pp.171-226.

Taylor &Francis (Routledge) gives permission to reprint David Leiwei Li," (In Lieu of An) Introduction:TheAsian American Subject between Liberalism and Neoliberalism"*Asian American Literature.* vol. 1, London & New York: Routledge, 2012, pp. 1-29.© 2012 by Taylor &Francis Books UK.

University of California Press gives permission to reprint Colleen Lye," Racial Form" *Representations*, vol. 104, no. 1, 2008, pp.92-101.

图书在版编目（CIP）数据

美国亚裔文学评论集：英文 / 郭英剑，赵明珠，冯元元主编 . —北京：中国人民大学出版社，2018.9

（美国亚裔文学研究丛书）

ISBN 978-7-300-26116-4

Ⅰ . ①美… Ⅱ . ①郭… ②赵… ③冯… Ⅲ . ①文学评论 – 美国 – 文集 – 英文 Ⅳ . ① I712. 06-53

中国版本图书馆 CIP 数据核字（2018）第 187704 号

美国亚裔文学研究丛书

美国亚裔文学评论集

总主编 郭英剑

主 编 郭英剑 赵明珠 冯元元

Meiguo Yayi Wenxue Pinglunji

出版发行	中国人民大学出版社				
社 址	北京中关村大街 31 号		**邮政编码**	100080	
电 话	010-62511242（总编室）		010-62511770（质管部）		
	010-82501766（邮购部）		010-62514148（门市部）		
	010-62515195（发行公司）		010-62515275（盗版举报）		
网 址	http://www.crup.com.cn				
	http://www.ttrnet.com（人大教研网）				
经 销	新华书店				
印 刷	北京东君印刷有限公司				
规 格	185 mm × 230 mm 16 开本		**版 次**	2018 年 9 月第 1 版	
印 张	25		**印 次**	2018 年 9 月第 1 次印刷	
字 数	500 000		**定 价**	65.00 元	

中国人民大学出版社外语出版分社读者信息反馈表

尊敬的读者：

感谢您购买和使用中国人民大学出版社外语出版分社的 ＿＿＿＿＿＿＿＿ 一书，我们希望通过这张小小的反馈卡来获得您更多的建议和意见，以改进我们的工作，加强我们双方的沟通和联系。我们期待着能为更多的读者提供更多的好书。

请您填妥下表后，寄回或传真回复我们，对您的支持我们不胜感激！

1. 您是从何种途径得知本书的：
   □书店　　　　□网上　　　　□报纸杂志　　　　　□朋友推荐
2. 您为什么决定购买本书：
   □工作需要　　□学习参考　　□对本书主题感兴趣　　□随便翻翻
3. 您对本书内容的评价是：
   □很好　　　　□好　　　　□一般　　　　□差　　　　□很差
4. 您在阅读本书的过程中有没有发现明显的专业及编校错误，如果有，它们是：

   ＿＿＿＿＿＿＿＿＿＿＿＿＿＿＿＿＿＿＿＿＿＿＿＿＿＿＿＿＿＿＿＿＿＿＿＿

   ＿＿＿＿＿＿＿＿＿＿＿＿＿＿＿＿＿＿＿＿＿＿＿＿＿＿＿＿＿＿＿＿＿＿＿＿

5. 您对哪些专业的图书信息比较感兴趣：

   ＿＿＿＿＿＿＿＿＿＿＿＿＿＿＿＿＿＿＿＿＿＿＿＿＿＿＿＿＿＿＿＿＿＿＿＿

   ＿＿＿＿＿＿＿＿＿＿＿＿＿＿＿＿＿＿＿＿＿＿＿＿＿＿＿＿＿＿＿＿＿＿＿＿

6. 如果方便，请提供您的个人信息，以便于我们和您联系（您的个人资料我们将严格保密）：
   您供职的单位：＿＿＿＿＿＿＿＿＿＿＿＿＿＿＿＿＿＿＿＿＿＿＿＿＿＿＿＿
   您教授的课程（教师填写）：＿＿＿＿＿＿＿＿＿＿＿＿＿＿＿＿＿＿＿＿＿＿
   您的通信地址：＿＿＿＿＿＿＿＿＿＿＿＿＿＿＿＿＿＿＿＿＿＿＿＿＿＿＿＿
   您的电子邮箱：＿＿＿＿＿＿＿＿＿＿＿＿＿＿＿＿＿＿＿＿＿＿＿＿＿＿＿＿

请联系我们：贾乐凯　黄　婷　程子殊　鞠方安

电话：010-62515580，62512737，62513265，62515576

传真：010-62514961

E-mail：jialk@crup.com.cn　　huangt@crup.com.cn　　chengzsh@crup.com.cn
　　　　jufa@crup.com.cn

通信地址：北京市海淀区中关村大街甲 59 号文化大厦 15 层　　邮编：100872
中国人民大学出版社外语出版分社